Dancing Through the Cosmos

RACHEL KORMAN

CITIOFBOOKS, INC.
3736 Eubank NE Suite A1
Albuquerque, NM 87111-3579
www.citiofbooks.com
Hotline: 1 (877) 389-2759
Fax: 1 (505) 930-7244

Ordering Information:
Quantity sales. Special discounts are available on quantity purchases by corporations, associations, and others. For details, contact the publisher at the address above.

Printed in the United States of America.
ISBN-13:   Paperback   979-8-89391-893-9
                eBook   979-8-89391-894-6
                Hardback   979-8-89391-895-3

Library of Congress Control Number: 2025917866

PROLOGUE

A sequel to *We Will Always Have The Stars*. A story about heartbreak and betrayal that remains to be timeless. Isabella Foster is stuck in between two different worlds. Her mother's world in the light and her father's world in the darkness. She's been wandering from place to place. Looking for her purpose. Trying to find her meaning within a cruel and heartless world. Learning that she only belongs in the world of darkness with her father. The struggle to survive when she knows that her existence is a lie. How there was never any meaning to why her father died. This is a journey that Isabella finds herself on. A journey that will lead her to look for an answer to the mystery. Why did her father kill himself?

Table of Contents

Chapter One
(Winter 1959 – New York, New York)

Isabella sat on the couch with her fifteen-year-old cousin Sasha as they whispered secrets to each other. They whispered about boys that they knew from school. The television played a Christmas cartoon in the background that her thirteen-year-old cousin Nina watched with Uncle Stan who sat on the other couch. Uncle Stan's boyfriend Thomas Weiss and her mum Abby sat on the loveseat while they talked to each other with a glass of wine in their hands. Once she pulled away from her conversation with Sasha, she looked at the television until her ten-year-old cousin Ivan and her seventeen-year-old cousin Anastasia's boyfriend Damien Kostov walked through the front door after they spent the day outside in the snow. As soon as she looked over at them, Nina turned away from the television when she told them to take off their snow boots at the door. The boys laughed at his sister as they took off their boots at the door before Ivan took a seat on a couch next to Isabella and Sasha as Damien walked into the kitchen. Sasha handed Ivan a blanket from the couch that he grabbed from her. She leaned her head onto Sasha's shoulder before she fell asleep with her arms wrapped around her legs. Sasha nudged her side where she moved her head off of her shoulder as she opened her eyes to see that they were alone in the living room. Once she got up from the couch, she followed Sasha into the kitchen where everyone sat at the table. Her mother and her mum got up from the table as they kissed her on her cheeks before she took a seat at the table. Her mother's hand was on her leg and her mum's arm was around her shoulder while she ate what Aunt Valeria made of them. After everyone was done eating dinner, her mum put away the leftovers as her mother and Aunt Valeria got glasses of wine for the adults and cups of hot chocolate for the children that they carried into the living room. She grabbed a cup of hot chocolate from them as her other cousins did the same except for Anastasia who grabbed a glass of wine for herself and Damien who was helping Uncle Sam clean the dishes When she took a seat on the couch next to her mother, her mum took a seat on the other side of the couch with two glasses of wine in her hands for them. As she sipped on her cup of hot chocolate, everyone sat down in the living room with the radio playing Christmas music in the background as they had soft conversations with each other. She listened to the radio with her mother and her mum's arms around her. Sasha and Anastasia sat on the loveseat as they read the books that they opened from their parents. Nina and Ivan sat on the floor as they played a game of marbles that they were obsessed with. Uncle Sam and Aunt Valeria sat on the other couch with their arms around each other as they had a soft conversation with each other. Damien left after they ate dinner to go home since he had to work early in the morning. Damien had his real estate license. Uncle Stan and his boyfriend Thomas left after dinner to go to their hotel room since they were flying back to Los Angeles in the morning. Once the sun went down in the sky, Uncle Sam told her cousins that they were leaving for their house before Sasha pulled her into a tight hug with her face hidden in her chest before she told Isabella that she would call her in the morning. As soon as Sasha let go of her, she hugged her cousins, her aunt, and her uncle goodnight before they left to go to their house for the night. She helped her mum collect the cups in the living room as she brought them into the kitchen. Once she finished cleaning the cups in the sink, she grabbed a slice of apple pie from the refrigerator that Aunt Valeria made before she walked into the living room where her mother and her mum were wrapped up together in a blanket on the couch. As soon as they looked up at her, she made a pouty face at them before her mother opened up the blanket to let her into it. Once she placed her plate on the coffee table, they wrapped the blanket around them with the wood stove burning on the other side of the room.

When she was comfortable in the blanket, she leaned her head on her mother's shoulder with her arm around her as her mother kissed her on top of her head when she asked Isabella, "Did you have a good day, baby girl?"

She nodded her head at her when she responded to her mother with a smile on her face, "I did. It was everything that I dreamed it would be. I love you, mom. I love you, mum. Thank you for my presents."

As her mother and her mum kissed each of her cheeks, she pretended to squeeze away from them even though she loved the constant attention they gave her. She hid her face into her mum's chest as her mother ran her fingers through her hair when her mother said to Isabella with a smile on her face, "I don't care how old you are. You will never outgrow our hugs and kisses. We will always love you no matter what, baby girl. Abby? Can you believe that our girl is graduating from high school in a few months? I remember the day that she was born like it was yesterday."

She took her head out of her mum's chest before she pulled her mother into a hug with her head hidden into her mother's chest where her mum's arms wrapped around her. Once she let go of her mother, the anxiety slowly crept into her bones when she asked them with a frown on her face, "Mum? Mom? Do you remember what I told you when I turned thirteen?"

Her mother gave her mum a look that she knew too well. She knew where this conversation was going since they had it over a dozen times in the last two years. As her mother wrapped her arms around her, her mum grabbed onto her hands when she said to her daughter in a firm voice, "You know our stance on this honey. If you're expecting it to be different since the last time that you brought it up, then it is the same. We don't want you to get involved in an industry that might try to hurt you. How much do you really want this honey? Tell us why you want it."

Isabella said to them with anger laced in her voice, "You know why I want this, mum. That's all I've wanted to do since I turned thirteen was become an actress and work in Hollywood. I want to be on television where millions of people watch me. Would it make you feel better if I did modeling instead? Sasha wants to be a model. Anastasia got her into fashion magazines, and she's obsessed with it. Would you be mad at me if I did modeling and acting?"

Her mother gave her mum another look that was different from the other look when her mother responded to her daughter with her holding onto her hands, "We would never be upset with you for anything, baby girl. Soon enough you're going to be an adult. You can make those decisions for yourself. We will support you no matter what you decide to do with your life. Whether that is being an actress or a model. Tell us something. Do you only want to do it because Sasha is doing it? That isn't a reason to do anything. I don't want you to do anything unless you feel it in your soul like you're meant to do it. Take it from us, baby girl. We know how much work it takes to fulfill dreams that we never thought were possible."

She placed her face into her mother's chest when she said to them muffled into her shirt, "Yes, mom. You guys put your hearts and souls into your book publishing company. I know that I can do anything that I set my mind to because you guys taught me that. I want to be an actress more than anything in the world. When I watch movies, I imagine myself there on the screen. I know that I can do it. It's better if I would do it with Sasha. We can keep each other accountable and safe from the world. Modeling is more of Sasha's dream, but I understand why she has it. The feeling that you must feel when the whole world wants something that you made possible. That feeling is worth anything in the world. You understand that feeling, mom. Don't you?"

Her mother told her with her arms tightly wrapped around her, "I'm not completely opposed to this. I have to talk to your mum about it before I tell you anything. Don't get ahead of yourself, baby girl. This isn't a yes."

She pulled her mother into a hug as her mum gave her mother a look of confusion that told her that they would talk about it later. Once she let go of her mother, she got off of the couch before she jumped up and down on the floor in excitement in front of the television when she shouted at them with a smile on her face, "Thank you, mom! You won't be disappointed in me! I'm going to make you and mum proud of me! I have to tell Sasha! Can I call Sasha before I go to bed tonight?"

Her mother softly sighed when she said to her with her hands holding onto her mum's hands, "You can call Sasha, baby girl. You can only talk to her for a few minutes before bedtime. I expect to see your bedroom light out by ten. Do I make myself clear?" She nodded her head at her mother as she hugged them before she went into her bedroom to tell Sasha about what happened with her parents. She heard a knock on her bedroom door, and she fell asleep for the rest of the night.

Chapter Two
(Spring 1959 – New York, New York)

Her mother and her mum walked into her bedroom to greet her for her high school graduation. Her parents pulled her into a tight hug until they let go of her when she whined that she had to go to the bathroom. Isabella got dressed into her white dress for the ceremony before she was treated with a special breakfast of waffles and berries. Aunt Valeria walked into the house with her cousins Anastasia and Sasha following behind her. Isabella and Sasha sat in the living room as Aunt Valeria did her hair and Anastasia did Sasha's hair. While they were preparing for the ceremony, her mother and her mum decorated the house for the party that afternoon. Uncle Sam and her cousins Nina and Ivan told them that they would meet them at the high school. Uncle Stan and his boyfriend Thomas were staying at a hotel, and they would meet them there. After Aunt Valeria finished doing her hair, she helped her parent's set up the house for the party before they left for the high school where the family waited for them. Isabella hugged her parent's goodbye before Isabella and Sasha joined their classmates in the gymnasium where they took their places in the line of students. When it was time for the ceremony to begin, she grabbed onto Sasha's hand as they walked outside to the football field where the ceremony was taking place before she took a seat on a folding chair next to Sasha. They called her name first as she quickly squeezed Sasha's hand before she walked onto the stage where the principal handed her a diploma with her name on it with her family cheering for her in the crowd. After they took a picture of her with her diploma in her hands, she walked to her seat where she gently squeezed Sasha's hand before she took a seat next to her cousin. When it was Sasha's turn to go on the stage, she hugged her before she cheered as loud as she could for her cousin until Sasha took a seat next to Isabella. As soon as the principal said congratulations to everyone, she smiled at Sasha before they threw their caps up in the air with smiles on their faces. Once they grabbed their hats off of the ground, Sasha pulled her into a tight hug with her face hidden in her chest as Isabella grabbed onto her hand before they walked to the bleachers where their family waited for them. When they got to the bleachers, she pulled her cousin Anastasia into a tight hug with her boyfriend Damien pulling her into a side hug before she pulled her cousin Nina and her cousin Ivan into a tight hug with her face hidden in Ivan's chest. Once she let go of them, Uncle Stan and Thomas pulled her into a tight hug. Before she could let go of them, Aunt Valeria pulled her into a tight hug before Uncle Sam pulled her into a tight hug with her face hidden in his chest. He kissed her on the top of her when he told her that he was proud of her. Once she let go of him, her mum pulled her into a tight hug with her face hidden into her chest when she told her that she was proud of her and that she loved her. Once she let go of her mum, her mother pulled her into a tight hug as she melted in her mother's arms like it was only placed that she belonged in the world. When her mother let go of her daughter, she wiped away tears that fell down her face as Isabella grabbed onto Sasha's hand before she followed her family into the parking lot. After they got into three cars, her mum drove to her house where everyone was about to arrive to their party from not only her family, but friends from school, friends that they made through the modeling agency, and people that they knew from their church over the years.

After their conversation on Boxing Day a few weeks later, her mother picked them up from school before she took Isabella and Sasha to a modeling agency. Her mother told Uncle Sam and Aunt Valeria about it before she told them. She was shocked that they were able to keep it a secret from them for as long as they did. Once they were signed to the modeling agency, they worked on their portfolios that they used to get their first jobs a few weeks later. In their last few months of school, her mum took them to events on the weekends and her mother took them to events on the weekdays after school. After she received her first paycheck from modeling, she stuffed it into her piggy bank under the bed where she had the money that she saved for when she would move to Los Angeles. She didn't know that she was going to like modeling as much as she did until her third photoshoot where she got to wear a gown that made her feel more beautiful than she felt in her life. That was the moment that made her think that she could keep doing this. When she expressed this feeling to her parents, she could tell that they were excited for her that she found the ambition that they found for themselves in their lives. Her goal after graduating from high school was for her to move to Los Angeles to become an actress. Her parents hadn't denied her the ability to become an actress, but they didn't make any mention of it since Boxing Day. Even though she figured out that a non-answer meant that it wasn't good, she held out hope that they would change their minds when she proved to them that she could handle working as a model. Modeling was a stepping stone to her getting closer to achieving her goals of working in Hollywood. During the long hours of photo shoots with Sasha, they talked to each other about what they wanted their lives to look like after they graduated from high school. These fantasies were about them becoming actresses and meeting the dream boy that would have their epic romance like it was on the television.

Whether or not they believed that it was going to happen, she learned from her mother that life never worked out in the ways that they expected it to. She knew that when her mother told her this that she was referring to her father. Not like he meant anything to her because he was never in her life. Her father died when she was eight years old. She only saw him in a courtroom. She heard stories from Uncle Sam, Uncle Stan, and Uncle Nathan about her father that her mother didn't like sharing with her. It wasn't that her mother wasn't open about her struggles with her father, but it was hard for her mother to talk about it without getting emotional. She hated it when her mother cried in front of her. It was easier for her to hear about her father from other people. She could tell that her father was a funny person that was a serious child much like herself. She was told by her family that she looked like her father and that she couldn't unsee it after she saw pictures of him.

She knew that her father struggled with addiction problems, and he made a lot of mistakes along the way with her mother and Uncle Stan. Despite all these things, she could tell that her mother loved him, and she would always love him no matter what. When she was thirteen years old, she asked her mother how her father died, and she didn't know about it. Her mother told her the truth about what happened to him. Her father's addiction was what killed him. Her mother gave her the suicide note to read where she learned more about her parents than she could imagine. Her mother kept her father's suicide note for all of those years to later to give to her when she was old enough to understand it. She didn't know that her mother had another brother besides Uncle Sam. She also didn't know that her mother was molested by her older brother and that her father knew about it for years before she knew about it. She always knew that something horrible happened between her parents that changed everything. She never knew what it was though until she read her father's suicide note. It was like everything made sense to her for the first time in her life. She had a completely new understanding of her mother after that. After she read her father's suicide note, she thought about everything she did that was like her father. She couldn't change that she looked like her father, but she stopped herself from getting involved in the drinking that Sasha was doing with their friends from school on the weekends. She tried to stop herself from saying things that he would say to her mother because she didn't want to upset her. Little things that she subconsciously did her entire life that she didn't question until that moment. When her mother noticed this shift in her behavior, her mother sat her down in her bedroom when she told her that she didn't have to do this to protect her. She was over what happened with him. She could take care of herself. She hugged her mother for a while before she fell asleep in her arms for the rest of that night. Every now and then they would have conversations about her father where they were honest with each other that brought them closer together.

Once they got back to the house, she floated around the room with Sasha by her side while she talked to everyone in the room that came up to her that congratulated her on graduating from high school. By the end of the night, she felt completely exhausted from the social interaction as people made their way out of the house. When it was only her family left in the house, she helped her parents clean up the house as her other family left to go back home for the rest of the night. She hugged Sasha a few times as they promised each other that they would call each other in the morning before Sasha left to go home with her parents and her siblings. Uncle Stan and Thomas left to go back to their hotel where they would meet them for brunch tomorrow morning before they went back to Los Angeles. Once they cleaned up the house, she went into her bedroom to change into her nightgown before they cuddled on the couch with the television playing a re-run of her favorite show in the background. After they watched television in silence for a while, her mother turned down the volume before she grabbed two wrapped gifts from behind the couch. She grabbed onto them when she asked them with excitement laced in her voice, "What's in these, mom? Can I open them?"

Her mother wrapped her arms around her when she said to her daughter, "You can, baby girl. Open the smaller one. Don't look at it until I tell you."

As soon as she looked away from her mother, she opened the smaller box as she peeled the paper back from the cardboard box before she opened the box to see a piece of folded paper. Once her mother nodded her head in approval for her to take it out of the box, she grabbed the folded paper out of the box. She couldn't contain the scream that came out of her mouth when she read what the paper said on it. She instantly dropped the piece of paper on her lap as she pulled her mother into a tight hug with her face hidden into her chest where she shouted at her mother, "Thank you, mom! I can't believe that I'm going to be an actress! How long have you known about this?"

Once she took her face out of her chest, her mother looked at her as she wrapped her arms around her when she responded to her with a smirk on her face, "We've known for over a month. Your uncle and your aunt knew too. We were waiting to tell you until you guys graduated from high school. Since you're still under eighteen years old, we needed to sign the agreement on your behalf. It shouldn't interfere with your modeling contract either. So, that's a good thing for you. Open the gift, baby girl."

She grabbed the other gift from her lap as she peeled off the paper from the cardboard box before she opened the box to see a set of keys with a keychain that spelled Hollywood on it. Before she asked her mother what it was, she let out another sudden scream as she threw the keys on the floor when she asked them, "Am I moving to Los Angeles, mom?"

As soon as her mother got up from the couch, she pulled her into her tight hug with her letting out soft sobs into her chest as her mum also wrapped her arms around her. Isabella took her head out of her mother's chest as she pulled her mum into a tight hug before she grabbed the keys off of the floor with her taking a seat on the couch. After her parents took a seat on the couch next to her, her mother wrapped her arms around her as her mum grabbed onto her hands when her mum said to her daughter with a smile on her face, "We've been talking about this for a while, but we feel that you have proven that are capable of taking care of yourself. If this is what you want to do with your life, then who are we to stop you from fulfilling your dreams? We have been looking for houses in Los Angeles for a few months since the modeling agency told us how they wanted to sign you in California too. Uncle Stan told us about the house down the street from him that was put on the market, and we bought it that day. We have some ground rules for you living in California."

Her mother nodded her head at her when she responded to her daughter in a serious voice, "Yes, we do, Abby. Since we can't be with you in California, we made an agreement with Uncle Stan and Thomas that they would report to us every week if you guys get into trouble. You aren't living there alone, baby girl. Sasha is going to live with you. We hired cleaners for the house and a personal chef to make meals for you. We are going to come in unannounced every so often, but most of the time it's going to be you and Sasha at the house. Do we have any reason not to trust you, baby girl?"

She shook her head at them with a frown on her face when she promised them with a smile on her face, "There's no reason not to trust me. We will be on our best behavior. I promise."

Once her mother gave her mum a look that was in agreement, she looked at her with a smile on her face when she said to Isabella, "That's great to hear, baby girl. I knew that we could trust you. One more surprise. We lied to you about going to brunch tomorrow morning. We are going to Los Angeles to look at the house with Uncle Stan and Thomas. Don't worry. Sasha and Nina are coming with us. I asked Uncle Sam and Aunt Valeria a few weeks ago if they could come with us. Your mum already packed our bags for us this afternoon. We are leaving for the airport tomorrow morning at eight am, so you need to be up by six am. Do I make myself clear?"

She nodded her head as she pulled her mother into a tight hug as her mum wrapped her arms around them before she pulled away from them when she asked them with an innocent smile on her face, "Can I call Sasha before I go to bed, mom? It won't be long. I'll go to bed after I talk to her."

Her mum grabbed onto her hands when she said to her, "You can honey. Make it short. We will be listening on the other phone. We want your light to be out in your bedroom in twenty minutes. We have an early morning tomorrow. I don't want to hear you complaining that you're tired the entire plane ride." Once she hugged her parents' goodnight, they kissed her on the cheek before she walked into her bedroom where she called to tell Sasha about their graduation presents which she already knew about since her parents gave her the same thing. When she was done talking to Sasha, she turned out her bedroom light as her mother knocked on her door to make sure that she knew that they were getting up at six am tomorrow before she fell asleep for the night.

CHAPTER THREE
(SUMMER 1959 – LOS ANGELES, CALIFORNIA)

After they graduated from high school, Isabella and Sasha prepared to move to Los Angeles as they packed up their belongings into a few bags. Since they had so many bags, her mother decided to drive to California in a road trip across the country with her family except for Anastasia who stayed in New York to run the hair salon while they weren't in New York. Anastasia offered to stay back home since it was her anniversary with Damien. Uncle Sam left the toy factory in the hands of his most trusted employees before they embarked on the journey to California. They took Uncle Sam's car since it was the biggest and the most trustworthy before Isabella, her mother, her mum, Uncle Sam, Aunt Valeria, Sasha, Nina, and Ivan left for their long road trip. After almost two weeks on the road, they stopped numerous times in different states where they saw a variety of new places and new landmarks before they got to Los Angeles where Uncle Stan and Thomas lived. They greeted them with hugs and a homecooked meal that they were craving after all the fast food that they ate on the road. Once they got to the new house, Isabella and Sasha ran around the house as they figured out what rooms that they would sleep in. That was hard to do since there were five bedrooms to choose from in the house. They chose to sleep in one of the suites together while they left the other four bedrooms untouched for when guests visited them. Not only did the house have five bedrooms in it, but it had two living rooms, a large dining room, a large kitchen that they never used, and a pool and hot tub on the Hollywood hills. Once everyone got their room assignments figured out, their parents helped them unpack their belongings as Nina and Ivan entertained them with games in the pool. When it was time to say goodbye to their family, it was emotional for them because they never lived anywhere without their parents before in their lives. As she said goodbye to her parents, she fell apart in her parent's arms before they told her that they loved her, and they would always be there for her. Before their family left them alone for the first time, Uncle Sam told them that they could have his car where they thanked him for it before their family got on the plane to go back to New York. Isabella and Sasha retreated into the suite for a few weeks in sadness that they weren't with their families anymore. By the third week of them moping around the house, Uncle Stan and Thomas came over to the house to show them around Los Angeles as they dragged them out of the house for fun. That was when Isabella fell in love with Los Angeles. She never wanted to lose that feeling again. Once they were pulled out of their sadness, Sasha suggested that they start looking for modeling and acting jobs in the city. She agreed with Sasha about it because they needed to make money. Despite them easily getting modeling jobs in New York, they struggled to get jobs in Los Angeles since it was more competitive here than back home. Since they realized that getting acting jobs was close to impossible for them, she told Sasha that they should focus on getting modeling jobs since the acting jobs would come to them later. Less than a week later they got a modeling job with a big clothing brand. That was the beginning of more modeling jobs to come for them. After a few weeks of working as models in Los Angeles, they developed a new routine to their daily schedule. Since most photoshoots started early in the morning, they went to bed super early during the week, and they were at photoshoots most of the day until late in the evening. When they got home from the photoshoots, she fell asleep as soon as she got home while Sasha stayed up late on the phone with her family. She got up early in the morning while they allowed the cleaners to clean the house while they hung outside by the pool and hot tub with Uncle Stan and Thomas until they would go out to eat at a new restaurant that one of Thomas' clients recommended to him in their personal training session. Uncle

Stan dropped them off at the house before Sasha invited their model friends over the house where they drank cocktails and played games. There were many weekends that their model friends were at their house sleeping in the guest rooms until they left on Monday. On the rare occasion that their parents came to visit them, they told their model friends that they couldn't come over that weekend because their parents were in town.

Chapter Four
(Fall 1959 – Los Angeles, California)

She received her first acting job through Chloe, who was their closest friend from modeling, who told her about a movie that was casting for young girls in Los Angeles. They had to audition for it regardless of what it was about. It could be their big break in Hollywood. On the morning of the audition, she called her mother while she had a panic attack when she told her that she couldn't do it before her mother told her that she would regret it if she didn't do it. Once she calmed herself down, she told her mother that she was right before she went to the audition with Sasha. She did her best in it. It completely surprised her when she got a phone call from the producer of *The Hearts Ambition* that she got the lead role in the movie where Sasha got one of the supporting roles in the movie. Even though she felt horrible that Sasha didn't get a significant role in the movie, Sasha told her that she was happy for her, and she was going to be wonderful in the lead role. When she called her parents to tell them about it, they told her that they were happy for her and that they were proud of her. As soon as she started production on *The Hearts Ambition*, she stopped modeling until she would finish the movie within the next year. On her first day on set, she met the cast and the director of the movie before she was fitted for clothing and her makeup was professionally done for the shoot. She spent any free moment that she had memorizing lines for the movie. She had to change a lot about her appearance for the role. She got her hair cut to her shoulders that made her mother cry when she saw it for the first time. She sat outside by the pool most days to work on her tan lines. When they started filming the movie, Isabella spent more hours on set than Sasha who was modeling in her free time. For the first time in her life, she felt alone since she was no longer doing the same thing as her best friend. When she was on set, she isolated herself from the cast. She only talked to them when she was about to do a scene with them. When she wasn't on set filming *The Hearts Ambition*, she was home alone in the house since Sasha went out to clubs on weekends with her model friends. It wasn't like Sasha never invited her to go with them. She was so tired when she got home from filming the movie that she didn't have the energy to go out with them.

Usually in the middle of the night, Sasha made her way into their suite to fall asleep next to her where she would sleep in until the early afternoon. Despite her growing concerns that she had about Sasha, she wasn't going to say anything to their parents about it since she didn't want to rat her out to them. She told Thomas her concerns that she had about Sasha's drinking and partying. She made him promise her that he wouldn't tell Uncle Stan about it since he would definitely tell her mother about it. Even though Thomas wasn't comfortable keeping it from his boyfriend, he promised her that he would keep it to himself for now until she found the courage to tell her mother about it. She didn't find it in enough time.

In the middle of filming her movie, she was told by the director that the hospital called to tell her that her cousin Sasha was admitted in the hospital for alcohol poisoning. She called her parent's and Sasha's parents from the studio to tell them about Sasha being in the hospital. They told her that they would be in Los Angeles by the end of the day. When she got to the hospital, Uncle Stan and Thomas waited for her in the lobby before they walked into Sasha's hospital room. She cried into Uncle Stan's chest when she saw her best friend in the hospital bed. For the rest of the night, she slept in the lobby with her head laying on one of the chairs while Uncle Stan and Thomas sat on other two chairs in the lobby. In the early morning, her mother gently tapped onto her shoulder before she fell apart in her mother's arms while Sasha was alone with her parents in the hospital room. As she hid her head into her mother's chest, her mum held her hands as she listened to Uncle Sam yelling at Sasha with Aunt Valeria crying as she held onto her daughter. They stayed in the lobby until Uncle Sam stormed out of the hospital to smoke a cigarette outside as her mother followed him outside to talk to him. Her mum kissed her on the check with their hands holding onto each other as they watched her mother and Uncle Sam's heated exchange with each other by the emergency room. They were fighting about Sasha's drinking problem and Uncle Sam was blaming Isabella for the incident. Her mother walked inside of the hospital with Uncle Sam following behind her before her mother grabbed onto her hands as she dragged them into Sasha's hospital room. Aunt Valeria held onto Sasha's hands as she ran her finger through her hair with Sasha staring at her father who screamed at her. Uncle Sam apologized to his daughter as he told her that he loved her before he wrapped his arms around her with Sasha falling apart in her father's arms. Once everyone's emotions calmed down, the doctor came into the room to inform them that Sasha was in the clear and they could discharge her that day. When the doctor left the room, her mother and her mum left the room with Uncle Sam and Aunt Valeria. Isabella took a seat next to her with their hands around each other. After their parents walked into the room, Uncle Sam told Sasha that she would be allowed to stay in Los Angeles if one of them stayed with them. Her mum told them that she would stay with them until Aunt Valeria would stay with them. Once Sasha was discharged from the hospital, they went to the house where her mum put her stuff in one of the bedrooms that they didn't use before their parent's left to go to New York. She didn't miss the way that her mother held onto her when she told her that she loved her. Uncle Sam told them to take care of each other. After Sasha got out of the hospital, she went back to filming her movie and Sasha went back to modeling since her part in the movie was replaced by another person. Her mum stayed with them for a few weeks until Aunt Valeria came with Ivan since he was out of school for fall break. Around the time that Aunt Valeria stayed with them was when they received a phone call from Aunt Sylvia in England saying that she wanted to know if they could come to her seventeen-year-old cousin Audrey's wedding to her cousin Oliver's best friend Teddy Oswald in York around Boxing Day. Once she received the filming schedule from the studio, she told Aunt

Sylvia that they could go to the wedding in England. Her mum made all the plans for their trip to York with her family in the states coming with to the wedding. She was excited to see her family in England for the first time since she went to her father's funeral eight years ago. She knew that so many things had changed since the last time that she was in England. She was an adult with a career of her own. She was no longer that little girl that lost a father that she never had nor was she the person that was defined by her parents anymore. Sometimes she wondered why she was born in this family. A family that was damaged beyond repair. A mother that was broken by a father. A mother that was broken by a daughter.

Chapter Five
(Winter 1960 – York, England)

Once Aunt Valeria and Ivan went back to New York, they were alone at the house for the first time since Sasha's hospitalization. Isabella kept track of Sasha's whereabouts when she was at home, and she came with her to clubs with their model friends. She tagged along with Sasha to make sure that she wasn't drinking too much. She liked having to be accountable to someone that wasn't herself. She made an effort to be more truthful with their parents about what they were doing on the weekends. No one wanted Sasha back into a hospital anytime soon. When it came time for New Years to come, she took a break from filming *The Hearts Ambition* and Sasha took a break from modeling since they were going to England for their cousin Audrey's wedding. On the night before their flight to New York, she packed all their stuff into one suitcase as Sasha told her which outfits that they were going to wear to the wedding and the afterparty. On the morning of their flight to New York, Uncle Stan and Thomas picked them up at their house before they got on a flight to New York. When they landed in New York, her parents were there at the airport to meet them as she spent the night at her house before their flight to England the next morning. When it was time for their flight to England, her aunt and her uncle's family met them at the airport as her mum checked their bags for them before they went on their flight to England. Once their plane landed in London, her twenty-year-old cousin Oliver and his wife Juliet were there to greet them with hugs and kisses on the cheek. This was the first time that they met Oliver's wife since they got married at the courthouse two years ago. After they spent the night at a hotel in London, Oliver and Uncle Sam drove two separate cars to York. Oliver parked the car at Aunt Priscilla and Uncle Nathan's house as Uncle Sam parked the other car at Aunt Sylvia and Uncle James' house. Once she got out of Uncle Sam's car, she was tackled into a tight hug by her eighteen-year-old cousins Audrey and Amelia that she didn't let go of until Aunt Sylvia pulled her into a tight hug with her twelve-year-old cousin Jamie hugging her legs. After she walked into Aunt Sylvia's house, Uncle James pulled her into a tight hug as her fourteen-year-old cousin Sean and her ten-year-old cousin George did the same thing after their father let go of her. As soon as she let go of them, Audrey and Amelia grabbed onto her hands as they dragged her into their bedroom to show her the bridesmaid dress that she was going to wear for the wedding. Once she was in their cousin's bedroom, Audrey pulled the silk dress out of her closet as she got the dress out of the plastic covering that it came with before she revealed that it was the same gown that she wore in the photoshoot in New York that made her fall in love with modeling last year.

After she grabbed the dress from Audrey, she went into the bathroom to try it on before she walked into their bedroom to reveal herself in the dress. Once her cousins gave her the stamp of approval, she walked into the living room as her mother talked to Uncle Sam and Aunt Sylvia on the couch where her mother melted when she saw her in the dress with her aunt and her uncle doing the same thing. After she changed out of her bridesmaid dress, they went over to Aunt Priscilla and Uncle Nathan's house to eat dinner where she sat with her thirteen-year-old cousin Poppy and her eleven-year-old cousin Tommy as her nine-year-old cousin George sat across from them. For the two weeks that they were in England, Isabella and her parents stayed at Aunt Sylvia's house as Sasha's family stayed at Aunt Priscilla's house since they had room in the main house. Uncle Stan and Thomas stayed in the guest house at the back of the Heartley property. She didn't meet Audrey's soon-to-be husband Teddy Oswald until a few days before the wedding where he got the groomsmen together at Aunt Priscilla's house. For the wedding, Audrey had her twin sister Amelia as her maid of honor with Isabella, Sasha, Anastasia, Nina, Juliet, and Poppy as her bridesmaids. Teddy had Oliver as his best man with Sean, Jamie, Damien, Ivan, and Tommy as his groomsmen with George and Alfie as his junior groomsmen. Audrey and Teddy were getting married at Carlton Towers. It was a beautiful Victorian home with gardens attached to it. Since it was the middle of the winter, they were getting married inside of the barn where the after party would be at the house with lots of food and drinks. At the dress rehearsal for the wedding, all the groomsmen and bridesmaids took their places in front of the room as Aunt Sylvia and Uncle James walked Audrey down the aisle with Teddy's parents doing the same thing. Once the dress rehearsal went by without any problems, the children and their parents went home as Isabella went out to the pub with Sasha, Oliver, Teddy, Juliet, Audrey, Amelia, Anastasia, and Damien for a night of drinking through the town. Their parents were aware of them going out to get drunk, but they were old enough to drink in England. They couldn't stop them from going out and having a good time. After they went to the second pub of the night, the boys and the girls ended up separating into two groups on the other side of the pub. Oliver, Teddy, and Damien played pool as Isabella, Sasha, Juliet, Amelia, and Audrey sat at a table while they talked to each other about their lives. This was where she learned some important things about her cousins that she didn't know about them before their night at the pub. She learned that Audrey fell in love with Teddy when she was four years old, but he didn't notice her until they were in secondary school. She learned that Juliet met Oliver through her ex-boyfriend who was his roommate their first year in university. Oliver fell in love with Juliet before she fell in with him.

She learned the most important thing about Amelia when they were alone at the bar as she smoked a cigarette outside of the pub when she told Isabella that she didn't like living in England, and she wanted to do something different with her life. When she asked Amelia what she wanted to do, she told her that she wanted to work in Hollywood as a hair and makeup artist. She told Amelia that she could live with them since they had four bedrooms' open in their house. Even though she was shocked at first by her generous offer, she immediately accepted it when she told her that she would love to live with them in Los Angeles after she told her family about it. When she walked into the pub, she told Sasha about it. Sasha told her that it was great for someone else to live with them. The house was too empty with only them there. She had a similar conversation with Oliver and Juliet at the third pub of the night where Juliet told her that she wanted to be a scriptwriter in Hollywood. Juliet and Oliver couldn't move to California until they graduated from university in a few months where she told them that her house was always open if they wanted to live with them. She didn't bother saying anything to Sasha about it until the next day because she knew that Sasha was wasted despite their best efforts to stop her.

When they got back to Aunt Priscilla's house in the early hours of the morning, she walked into the house with Anastasia, Damien, and Sasha since Oliver went to Juliet's house for the night. Uncle Sam and her mother sat in the living room waiting for them. As soon as they saw their parents, Damien excused himself into his bedroom before Uncle Sam lectured his daughters about the dangers of drinking too much while they looked at him with blank expressions on their faces. Once Uncle Sam was done yelling at them, he stormed into one of the guest bedrooms before Anastasia and Sasha went into their bedrooms for the rest of the night. As soon as her mother looked at her, she rolled her eyes at her mother without saying anything before she stormed out of Aunt Priscilla's house to Aunt Sylvia's house. She ignored the concerned glare of her mum before she went into her bedroom for the rest of the night.

On the morning of the wedding, she was woken up by her younger cousin George jumping up and down on the bed as she wrestled with him until Aunt Sylvia appeared in her bedroom with an apron on with some flour on it. As Aunt Sylvia carried George out of her bedroom, she told Isabella that they needed to leave for Carlton Towers before she was left alone in her bedroom with George holding onto her hand. After they ate a quick breakfast together, they took four cars to the wedding venue where the girls and the boys separated into different rooms to get ready for the wedding. The girls drank champagne as Anastasia, Amelia, and Aunt Valeria helped do everyone's hair and makeup while the boys played cards and drank scotch in crystal glasses. The children were already in the barn where the wedding was taking place with her mum and Uncle Nathan. Audrey looked beautiful in her wedding dress. Isabella left to go to the boy's room to grab Teddy for the first look while Oliver and Amelia tagged along with them before the wedding party to get together for wedding photos. As the photographer took pictures of them, she stood in between her parents with their arms around her with smiles on their faces. When it was time for the ceremony to begin, she kissed her parents on the cheek before she went into the house attached to the barn to find her partner that was walking down the aisle with her. She was assigned by her cousin to walk down the aisle with Sean as they were partnered by Oliver & Amelia, Sasha & Jamie, Anastasia & Damien, Nina & Ivan, Poppy & Tommy, and Juliet & George & Alfie. Once the wedding started, she followed them down the aisle where she fell apart when they read their vows to each other. At the end of the wedding, Isabella and Sasha changed out of their bridesmaids' dresses before they joined the family at the afterparty where they were served a meal as they drank alcohol and danced for the rest of the night. When the party was over, Audrey and Teddy left to go on their honeymoon to the Capri Islands for two weeks. On the morning after the wedding, they left to go back to the states where she struggled to say goodbye to her family. Amelia, Oliver, and Juliet told her that they were taking her up on her offer to move to California with them. That made some of the goodbyes easier on her since she would see them in a short amount of time. On the flight to New York, she fell asleep with her head on her mother's shoulder until she woke up from a nightmare about her father that scared her awake. She stayed awake for the rest of the flight until they landed in New York where she said goodbye to her parents and her uncle's family before Isabella and Sasha got on a flight to California with Uncle Stan and Thomas. When they landed in Los Angeles early the next morning, Uncle Stan dropped them off at their house before Isabella and Sasha went into their suite to sleep for the afternoon. Their friend Chloe showed up at the house with a bottle of Moscato and a mystery bag of pills. For the rest of the weekend, Chloe stayed with them as they drank and took whatever pills that Chloe offered them while they watched television outside by the pool. It was Sasha's idea to bring the television outside by the pool since their high minds thought it was a good idea to have the television by water. For what happened that weekend, she couldn't remember it for the rest of her life, but it was the beginning of what was going to come for them. A pattern of destruction behavior that would follow her for the rest of her life.

CHAPTER SIX
(Spring 1960 – Los Angeles, California)

The pattern of self-destructive behavior was only beginning for her. No one around her noticed that she was engaging in it least of all her parents since they saw less of her since they got back from England. When she engaged in this behavior, she knew that it was wrong, but something inside of her couldn't stop her from doing it. It wasn't like she tried to stop it from happening. She shouldn't like it as much as she did. She knew that this was something that her father did for many years. It terrified her that it wasn't good enough for her to stop her from doing it. She knew how it ended for her father. Every time Chloe showed up at the house with a mystery bag of pills, she wanted to try them to see what would happen if she took them. Sasha wasn't any better about it since she was the one that asked Chloe to bring them over every weekend from her drug dealer. She wrapped up filming her first movie *The Hearts Ambition* a few weeks after she got back from England. They went on their press tour for the movie where she wasn't home for five weeks as she went all across the country with the cast from the movie. She told Thomas in secret to keep an eye on Sasha when she wasn't home. She received a phone call in her hotel room from Sasha when she told her that Amelia was moving into their house. When she got back to Los Angeles from the press tour, she found out that Amelia got there a few days ago. Once she greeted Amelia with a tight hug and a kiss on her cheek, they decided to take Amelia on a tour of the city with Uncle Stan and Thomas where they ended up at a club after they went to their house. After their night at the club, she called a taxi to take them home where Amelia slept in their suite with them. They realized that the guest room that Amelia moved into went completely unused before she moved her stuff into the suite with them later that day. Despite Amelia moving in with them, things didn't change for them. Isabella was in the process of working on a new movie called *Fool's Gold* with the same director from the previous movie as Sasha modeled with the same agency that she used to be signed to. Isabella let go of her modeling contract when her acting career took off for her. Amelia got a job as a hair and makeup artist on *Fool's Gold* based on her recommendation to the producer of the movie. Sasha and Chloe left for Italy for a photoshoot with a clothing brand. Isabella and Amelia decided to have a party at the house with other people from the studio that turned out to be a complete disaster. Someone overdosed on heroin in one of the upstairs bathrooms. An ambulance showed up at the house and the person was taken to the hospital, but not before Uncle Stan told her parents about the incident, the party, and the drinking at nightclubs on the weekends. She was grateful that Thomas didn't tell them about the pills since she really didn't want her parents knowing about that. Her parents were furious with them about it, and they told her that she would have to pay the fine that the police gave her for partying underage as her punishment. Isabella didn't consider that a punishment since it was only money that she lost. After their party went horribly wrong, Sasha and Chloe came home to Los Angeles knowing about the party since Isabella's parents told her parents about it when it first happened a few weeks ago.

It started off as an unremarkable weekend for them. Chloe arrived at their house with another bag of mystery pills in her hand and many bottles of wine in her other hand. The girls spent the entire night in the suite with a few bottles of wine, an empty bag of pills that they took as soon as Chloe walked into the house, and fast food from their favorite restaurant. She was usually the last person awake at night. Sasha and Chloe slept in the bed together and Amelia slept on one of the couches in their bedroom. She should've been sleeping with them. She wandered outside by the pool on one of the pool chairs as she stared up at the stars. She heard the stars talking to her. She knew that it was the drugs doing it to her. As she stared at her reflection in the pool, a thought entered her mind that she couldn't get rid of. She grabbed the outside phone to call a number that she knew by heart. She laid down on the ground with the phone into her ear. Her mother answered the phone in a groggy voice when she frantically asked her, "What's wrong, baby girl? Why are you calling in the middle of the night? Did something happen?"

She let out a shaky breath when she responded to her mother on the verge of tears, "No, I'm not okay, mom. I messed up. You're going to be mad at me if I tell you what happened."

She heard her mother's breath quicken when she said to her daughter a soft voice that almost made her burst into tears, "No, baby girl. I'd never be mad at you. Tell me what happened. I promise you that I won't be upset with you. Please honey. You're scaring me."

She took a deep breath when she confessed to her mother with tears falling down her face, "I've been doing drugs, mom. I should say that we've been doing drugs. I am. Sasha, Amelia, and our friend Chloe who brings them for us. We get high every weekend. Chloe brings us a bag of mystery pills. Chloe brought us something we never took before. It made me feel strange. Like I'm outside of my body. I can hear the stars talking to me. They sound like dad when they talk to me. I'm by the pool. I can't get up without feeling like I'm going to pass out. I almost went swimming tonight until I remembered that one time I almost drowned when I tried to swim when I was high, and Sasha saved me from drowning. If I went swimming right now, I'd drown, and no one would be here to save me. I think about drowning without being high. Do you think that I have a problem, mom? Did I tell you about the nightmares that I have about dad dying? Do you think that I'm doomed to become like dad?"

Her mother softly sighed when she responded to her with concern laced in her voice, "I figured that something was going on with you, baby girl. You've been acting strange since we got back from England. I knew that you would tell us when you were ready to. What have you been taking? Do you know what you've been taking?"

Isabella softly chuckled when she said to her mother with a wide grin on her face, "I have no idea what I've been taking, mom. All that I know is that I like how I feel when I take them. I've never felt this good until I started doing drugs. I don't know what to do about it. What do I do about it, mom?"

Her mother wrecked her brain with the right words to say to her daughter who was high on unknown substances talking about wanting to kill herself. It scared her more that she left her mother completely speechless since her mother always had something to say no matter what happened. Despite how much her own behavior scared her; it terrified her that her mother didn't know what to say to her. Like she broke her mother as soon as she told her everything that she said to her. She never wanted to hurt her mother. She loved her mother more than life itself. She couldn't believe that she hurt her mother like this. She never intended to tell her mother any of these things until her reflection in the pool mocked her. She couldn't stop thinking about throwing herself into the pool to drown. Once her mother found the words to say, she responded to her daughter in a soft voice, "It's going to be okay, baby girl. I promise you. You should go back into the house to sleep off the drugs that you took. We'll be at your house tomorrow to talk about this in person. I don't know what to say to you. I don't want to say anything that might upset you more than you are. Please go to bed honey. I know that you're going to feel better in the morning. Promise me that you're going to go to bed when we hang up the call."

She responded to her mother as her hands shook uncontrollably at her sides from the drugs that she took earlier in the evening, "I promise that I'll go to bed after we hang up the call, mom. I'm not going to throw myself into the pool. I'm not in the mood for drowning tonight. I love you, mom. Thank you for listening to me."

Her mother laughed at her daughter when she responded to her in an amused voice, "You think that you're so funny, don't you? You're too much like your father. What am I going to do with you? I love you too, baby girl. Go to bed. We'll see you tomorrow."

When she hung up the phone on her mother, she got up off of the cement as she put the phone onto the receiver before she made her way into the house where Sasha stood in the kitchen drinking a glass of water. Sasha put the empty glass into the sink when she asked Isabella with a frown on her face, "Are you okay? Where were you hiding? I looked all over the house for you."

She pulled Sasha into a sudden hug where she hid her face into her shoulder when she said to Sasha with a blank expression on her face, "My parents are coming over to the house tomorrow. Can you tell Chloe to leave? I'm upset with her."

Sasha tightened her grip on her arms when she responded to her with a concerned look on her face, "I can do that, Isabella. Why are you upset with Chloe? You were laughing with her all night."

As she pulled out of Sasha's arms, she softly sighed when she responded to Sasha with a wide grin on her face, "Wouldn't you love to know that? I'm going to sleep in a guest bedroom. I need to get a good night of sleep before I have to deal with the consequences of my own actions. Tell Chloe not to come back to the house. I don't want her here. I don't care what you think about it because this is my parent's house, so you can't tell me what to do about it. She can keep her fucking mystery pills to herself from now on. I want absolutely nothing to do with it or her after this. Goodnight, Sasha. Don't expect to see me in the morning. I'm going to brunch with Thomas." She stormed into one of the guest bedrooms. As soon as she walked into one of the guest rooms, she slammed the door behind her before she threw herself face first on the bed as she laid down into one of the pillows with tears running down her face. She passed out on the bed until the next morning where she promised herself she wouldn't do drugs.

Chapter Seven
(Summer 1960 – Los Angeles, California)

Despite her best efforts to stay away from drugs, she found her way back to them like she was always meant to do them. As it turned out, her cutting off her friendship with Chloe didn't stop her from doing drugs. After she talked to her parents about her indulging in pills when they visited her, she took up Amelia's offer to go to a club with some of the people from the studio the next weekend. Since she told Chloe that she couldn't come back to the house, Sasha wasn't speaking to her as she chose to sleep in one of the guest bedrooms instead of sleeping in the suite with them. It wasn't like she had to explain herself to Sasha, but she tried many times until Sasha stormed out of the house for long periods of time without coming home. At the nightclub, they took their usual spots in a private room that they always reserved when they went there. She didn't know how it started, but someone pulled out some powder from their pocket for everyone to snort off the table. Once she did a few lines of the powder off of the table, she felt like she was on top of the world as she danced with Amelia's arms around her until an older man caught her attention from the other side of the bar. She ended up alone with him behind the club with the pulsating music in the background as they made out with each other until Amelia told her that a group of their friends were heading back to their house for the night. Once she was pulled away from the older man by Amelia, she followed them to the taxi before their driver dropped them off at the house where they sniffed powder off of the bathroom counters until the sun came up in the morning.

After the first night that she relapsed from doing drugs, she told Sasha that Chloe could come over to the house again if she brought them more of that powder that she had at the club that she couldn't stop thinking about. This was the beginning of something more dangerous that she was doing to herself. She got a phone call from Oliver that they were moving to Los Angeles in a few weeks. After she hung up the phone on him, she told Sasha and Amelia to hide all the drugs in the house since Oliver and Juliet wouldn't approve of the lifestyle that they were living in secret. When Oliver and Juliet arrived in Los Angeles, they picked them up at the airport as they gave them a tour of the city before they got back to the house with it being clean after they trashed it last night. Isabella paid the cleaning staff extra money to keep them from telling her parents about the parties that they had there on the weekends. Once Oliver and Juliet picked one of the guest bedrooms, they ate dinner that their chef made for them as they played a board game outside by the pool until Oliver and Juliet went to bed for the rest of the night.

As soon as they knew that they were in the clear, she called Chloe to tell her to come over with the products that she asked for the other day. After Chloe showed up to the house, she paid her a large amount of money before she dragged her into the suite where the girls stayed up most of the night getting high until they passed out in the early hours of the morning. Juliet got a job as a writer with a movie studio before they moved to the country and Oliver got a job as a psychologist in Los Angeles as soon as he graduated from university a few months ago. She was off from filming the movie since they were reshooting scenes that she wasn't in. They didn't expect her at the studio. On the first morning with Oliver living with them, he waited until everyone left for work when he dropped the newest bombshell of information on her that she wasn't expecting to hear from him. When Oliver told her that he knew what they were doing in the suite last night, she could've tried to deny it to him, but she knew that it would've been pointless since her cousin studied people for a living. She told him the truth about what they were doing in the suite and what they did in the house most nights of the week before he moved in with them. He told her that her mother told him about their habits when she encouraged him to live with them since he could keep an eye on her. Despite her anger that she felt towards her mother, she understood where her mother was coming from. She didn't know what to do about her daughter. Sasha and Amelia weren't open about it with their families. They didn't understand how to deal with it. It didn't scare her that Oliver knew about their bad habits. She knew that her mother and Oliver weren't coming from a place of judgement. At least they cared enough to confront her about it in an attempt to try to stop her. After her emotional conversation with Oliver about her drug use, he left for work, and she went into her bedroom to snort another line of the powder off the counter in the bathroom without a care in the world. When Oliver returned back from work with her high for most of the day, he never said anything to her about it where he acted like it wasn't happening. Despite her biggest fears being that Oliver would try to change her behavior; it became apparent very quickly that he accepted things for the way that they were without uttering another word to her about it. Oliver and Juliet went to clubs with them on the weekends to dance and drink while they went into the bathroom to snort the powder off the sink until they did the same thing as soon as they got home after they were sleeping for the night.

After their first weekend with Oliver and Juliet living with them, they easily found themselves falling into a new routine that they stuck to like a clock. Oliver left for work at the psychiatric hospital as Sasha left to go to her photoshoot of the day with Chloe picking her up before Isabella, Amelia, and Juliet drove together to Hollywood studios where they got home late into the evening at the same time. After they ate dinner together in the kitchen, Oliver and Juliet went into their bedroom for the rest of the night as they spent the rest of the night in the suite doing what would normally be done on a weekend. They went from only getting high on the weekends to them getting high almost every day of the week. She noticed that she was the person that always asked them if they were going to get high after dinner every night. It was almost never the other way around for them. She wrapped up production as the leading actress on *Fools Gold* and she never felt better about herself. After she got back to Los Angeles from the press tour with the cast, she got high when she was at the house by herself as everyone else was at work for the day. This was the beginning of a new pattern of behavior that she kept from her cousins who lived with her. On one of the weekends that they were at the club, Chloe introduced her to her drug dealer who was a middle-aged man wearing an overly expensive suit. After that fateful weekend, she met with him a few times a week to get her own products that her cousins didn't know that she was buying from him. She didn't have to see him to deliver the products that she wanted from him because he came to the house with them. She ordered them from him over the phone in code words that he insisted on her using with him at all times. After everyone left for work that day, he came over to the house with the products that she asked for before she spent the day getting high in her bedroom until her cousins came home from work. After they ate dinner together in the kitchen, they got ready to leave for the club where they met up with some of their friends from work before the taxi dropped them off at the same club that they went to every weekend. She got separated from everyone else at some point in the night when she went to one of the private rooms with someone that flirted with her at the bar. After she got back from a private room with the stranger, she felt worse than when she walked into the room with him. She took something with him that she didn't know what it was since he didn't know it himself. Their dealer gave it to them that night. She took a seat next to Oliver and Juliet in a booth as Sasha and Amelia danced with guys on the dance floor as she felt so dizzy that she couldn't sit up anymore before she laid her head on Oliver's shoulder to rest her eyes. All that she knew was that when she woke up again she wasn't in the same place that she remembered being in when she closed her eyes.

She opened her eyes to see that she laid down on her back with her head on Oliver's lap as everyone around her stared at her with terrified looks on their faces. She was about to ask them about it before she threw herself off of Oliver's lap where she puked on the floor with Sasha holding her hair as Oliver caught her before she fell down on the floor. Once she was done puking out everything that she left in her body, she was guided back onto Oliver's lap as Sasha and Amelia grabbed onto her hands with looks of terror on their faces. When she asked them where Juliet was, Oliver told her that she was outside waiting for the ambulance as it suddenly clicked in her mind what happened to her. She knew that the mystery guy that she slept with gave her something that made her overdose. Even though she pleaded with them not to take her to the hospital, Juliet came into the club with paramedics following behind her. As soon as the paramedics walked into the room, Sasha and Amelia helped her sit up from Oliver's lap before the paramedics helped her onto the stretcher as they asked her questions that she didn't have the ability to answer. Oliver answered the questions for her to the best of his ability until they asked her what she took as she shrugged her shoulders at them when she blankly told them, "Honestly what haven't I taken tonight."

With none of their questions being answered, the paramedics took her to the ambulance where Oliver got into the back of the ambulance with her. Amelia, Sasha, and Juliet went to the hospital with Uncle Stan and Thomas who they called after she overdosed. She didn't need to ask them to know that they already told her parents about what happened to her. Uncle Stan's presence instantly confirmed that for her. During the drive to the hospital, Oliver desperately held onto her hand as she went in and out of consciousness with the paramedics having a conversation with each other. Once they pulled up to the hospital, Oliver stayed with her until the nurse wheeled her into a sterile room where she went unconscious again until the next morning when she woke up to the sounds of machines going off behind her. As soon as she opened her eyes, she saw that Sasha was asleep on the chair next to the bed with Oliver and Amelia asleep on the couch on the other side of her hospital room. Once she tried to sit up in the bed, she immediately felt nauseous before she laid back down in the bed in silent defeat. Before she could wake up everyone in the room, Uncle Stan walked into her hospital room when he asked her with a frown on his face, "What happened, Isabella? You almost died last night. Did you know that?"

Her heart dropped into her stomach when she responded to him with tears falling down her face, "I don't know what happened, Uncle Stan. Do my parents know about this?"

Uncle Stan nodded his head at her with a look of concern on his face when he told her with his hands grabbing onto her hands, "Yes, they know about it. They will be here in a few hours when their plane lands. Do you want to tell me what's been going on with you? It might be easier to tell me than your mother about it."

Before she found the strength to respond to him, Sasha suddenly jolted awake on the chair next to her with Oliver and Amelia doing the same thing before all of their attention was on her. Uncle Stan pulled her into a tight hug with her face hidden into his chest with tears falling down her face as he kissed her on the top of her head before he left her alone with her cousins. As soon as Uncle Stan left her hospital room, Sasha pulled her into a tight hug with Oliver and Amelia wrapping their arms around her as she sobbed into Sasha's chest letting out the pain that she felt in the last six months. Sasha and Amelia let go of her where Oliver pulled her into his arms with her face hidden in his chest when she thanked him for saving her life. She knew that Oliver was the one that stuck his fingers down her throat to make her vomit in the club. She heard the doctor thanking him before she passed out. Oliver didn't let go of her until her parents walked into the hospital room looking emotionally and physically exhausted from the events of last night. Once she was alone with her parents, she fell apart in her mother's arms as they wrapped their arms around her with her sobbing into her mother's chest like she was a little girl. It didn't matter to her that she was an adult with a career. She felt like that eight-year-old girl that lost her father all over again. Despite having everything that she always dreamed about having, she never felt more miserable in her life. That was the moment that she knew that something was wrong with her that she couldn't fix. She was like her father. Everything that she hated about him was pointless. She was becoming her father. She slowly pulled her head out of her mother's chest with their arms around her when she confessed to them in a soft voice, "I need help, mom. I can't do it by myself. Every time that I try to stop it, it gets worse than it was before. I'm sorry for scaring you guys. I didn't think that it would get this bad. I want to stop doing drugs. I don't like how I feel when I don't have them. I feel like I'm dying when I can't get them and I'm killing myself by taking them. Please help me, mom. Help me get better, mum. I don't want to be this person. I don't want to be like dad. I don't want to die like dad did. I don't want this to be my life."

She threw herself into her mum's arms as she sobbed into her hands when her mother responded to her with her arms around her as tears fell down their faces, "Baby girl. You're going to be okay. We are going to get you help. You're not going to be like your father. You're a better person than he was. I love you so much, baby girl. No matter what happens I will always love you."

As she took her head out of her mum's chest, her mother kissed her on the top of her head as she ran fingers through her hair when her mum told her with their hands holding onto each other, "Here's what we're going to do honey. After you get discharged from the hospital, you're coming to New York with us, and you are going to stay with us while you go to the best medical treatment center where you're going to get the help that you need to get back to yourself. Have you taken a new job honey?"

She shook her head at her mum with their arms tightly around her when her mum told her with a wide smile on her face, "Thanks for being honest with us honey. We are going to make sure you get all the help you need. I love you so much. You're going to get past this moment. I promise you that things are going to be better again. Your mother and I will be back in a few moments. We need to talk to your doctor about what happened last night. Do you want your cousins back in the room?" They hesitantly let go of her as they left her alone in her hospital room before Oliver walked back into the room with Sasha and Amelia following behind him. In the next few days at the hospital, she learned from her parents what happened at the club. She mixed two dangerous drugs that were lethal that killed people. Whatever that guy gave her in the club wasn't supposed to be mixed with cocaine that she took a lot of earlier in the day. When she took cocaine and this pill at the same time, it caused her heart to stop beating in her chest where Oliver did CPR on her until she was breathing again. He stuck his finger down her throat before she puked on the floor with her passing out many times in the ambulance on the way to the hospital. Oliver saved her life twice that night, so she owed him more than anyone to get better. Once she was discharged from the hospital, she went to New York with her parents where she got the help that needed from a rehab center. She could never touch drugs without her getting addicted to them now. She realized that this was going to be a battle that she was going to deal with for the rest of her life. Just like her father dealt with for his entire life. She didn't want to be like her father. She didn't want to die like her father had died. She didn't want to become her father. She knew that she was a better person than her father was. She knew that things would have to be different for her.

CHAPTER EIGHT
(FALL 1960 – NEW YORK, NEW YORK)

Uncle Sam waited for them as he pulled her into a tight hug with her face hidden in his chest before he drove them to the medical treatment center where she spent the next few days detoxing from the drugs that she had left in her body. For the rest of her stay at the medical treatment center, she attended daily individual therapy in the morning and group therapy in the afternoon with the same psychiatrist named Dr. Keber who she met on the first day of rehab. Dr. Keber was a quiet woman without anything to say, but she was incredible at listening to her as she cried in their sessions in her floral designed office at the hospital. When she first met Dr. Keber, she refused to tell her anything because she didn't think that it was going to make her feel better to complain about her life to a middle-aged woman that she didn't know. It wasn't until the third day of her being at the treatment center where she started telling her anything about herself as Dr. Keber silently took notes the entire time that she talked to her. She cried every time that Dr. Keber brought up her father. She didn't know why she couldn't stop crying when she told Dr. Keber about her father since she never knew him. Dr. Keber mentioned to her that it didn't matter that she never knew her father in life because she knew her father in death. As soon as Dr. Keber said that to her, she instantly fell apart for the rest of the session where she realized something for the first time in her life. She realized that she never had to meet her father to know him because he was always going to be a part of her. Her father was inside of her chest. She could never get rid of that part of him. She told her about everything that she felt towards her father that was built up inside of her chest. She told her that he wasn't a good person. He never bothered being in her life. He was the biggest coward in the world. He loved her mother so much. She felt angry at him for abandoning her like it was nothing to him. She meant absolutely nothing to him. She hated him for leaving them behind in this cruel world. She was angry at her mother for not making him stay with them. She didn't want to forgive him for any of it because he didn't forgive himself for doing it. Not like it would even matter to the world. He would still be dead no matter what she did about it. The thought that always scared her more than anything else in the world was that she only knew her father because she would become him someday. She was doomed to repeat the cycle that her mother worked so hard to break for them.

When Dr. Keber asked her if her father was an addict, she couldn't stop laughing when she told her that wasn't the only thing that her father was. Her father was an addict, a liar, a cheater, a closeted homosexual, a rapist, a felon, a lover, a brother, and a son. Worst of all, he was dead. Something that he never was a father and that was why she resented him so much. That was all that she wanted him to be. She didn't want her father to be anything except her father. It broke her heart that she was never going to have her father. It wasn't like she didn't receive love and support from her mother and her mum. She loved them more than life itself. She owed her life to them, and she was grateful for that. They would never be her father. They weren't Will Heartley. She wanted her mother Ella Foster, her mum Abby Knight, and her father Will Heartley. Her heart would never feel complete without him. When Dr. Keber asked her if she thought that she was an addict, she didn't say anything to her since she didn't know how to answer that question without sounding like a complete hypocrite. She pondered on that question for a while until the next few sessions later where she came up with an answer to it. She told her that she must be an addict if she ended up where she did in life despite her own mind refusing to see herself in that way. She must be an addict because she knew that she couldn't stop herself from doing drugs. She stopped doing drugs when they almost killed her, and she still wanted to do them after that. She realized that she never wanted to stop doing drugs because they killed her. The only reason that she stopped doing drugs was because she was acting like her father, and it was scaring her. If someone would give her cocaine right now, she wouldn't be hesitant to do it despite knowing that it could kill her or that she was acting like her father. She was worried that there was no reason that would stop her from wanting to do drugs exactly like her father had been like when he was alive. Dr. Keber nodded her head at her without saying anything about it. When she got discharged from the medical treatment center, she set up an appointment to meet Dr. Keber at her outpatient office once a week. It felt really odd with her being in New York for the first time in over a year. Despite only a year passing her by, she felt like so much changed within that time period. It was a completely different lifetime ago. Once she was in New York living with her parents, she felt like a little girl who danced around in her parent's living room as she was in a tutu with Sasha dancing next to her. She reconnected with her family in New York as she spent a lot of time with Anastasia, Nina, and Ivan. She also reconnected with some of her friends that she had in high school where many of them were already married with babies on the way. She spent a lot of time with her parents where she did everything that she could with them at the house. She helped her parents with their book publishing company when she needed a distraction when she wasn't at NA meetings or at a session with Dr. Keber. Around the time that Boxing Eve came up, her parents told her that their family in Los Angeles was coming to New York to celebrate the holiday season with them. She was excited to see her cousins again for the first time since she got out of the medical treatment center. There was a part of her that was nervous to see them because she hadn't seen them since her drug overdose a few months ago. As soon as she saw them in the airport, her fears were immediately dissolved into nothing as she fell apart in their arms like nothing bad happened to her. When they got back to her parent's house, they ate dinner together before Sasha and Amelia went to Uncle Sam and Aunt Valeria's house with her cousins. Oliver and Juliet were staying in the guest room at her parent's house as Uncle Stan and Thomas stayed at the hotel that they always stayed at when they visited them in New York. Once her parents went into their bedroom for the rest of the night, she took Oliver and Juliet to her hiding spot-on top of the roof where there was snow on it from the last snowstorm. As she laid down on top of the roof with Oliver and Juliet laying down next to her, she pointed to stars in the sky when she told them about each of the constellations from her memory that she learned from her mother. After they star gazed together for a few hours, Juliet went back into the house to get ready for bed before Oliver wrapped his arm around her as she laid her head down on his chest. As she turned around to face him in the darkness, she nervously picked at her fingers when she told him with his arms tightly around her, "Thank you for saving my life, Oliver. I've told you this, but I want you to know that I meant it."

Oliver tightened his grip on her arms when he responded to her with a frown on his face, "I know that you mean it. I would do it again if I had to. Not that it will happen. I don't want to do it again."

She lightly hit his arm when she responded to him with a smile on her face, "No, it's not going to happen again, Oliver. I promise. Things are better now. I'm better. It was a wakeup call for me. I don't want to be that person. Not at the cost of my life."

Oliver let out a sigh of relief as he grabbed onto her hands when he told her with a wide grin on his face, "You don't know how good it feels to hear you say that. I've been worried sick about you, Isabella. Even before the overdose happened. I was worried about you when your mother told me about it. I knew that it would get to that point where something bad was going to happen to you, but I never imagined that it would be that bad. Do you remember what happened?"

She shook her head at him when she responded to him with tears threatening to fall down her face, "I remember bits and pieces of it, but I don't remember much of anything about it. I can't imagine how horrible it must have been for you. I'm sorry for scary you, Oliver. I've heard from Amelia and Sasha how horrible it was for them. We don't have to talk about it if you don't want to. The only person that I've talked about it to is my psychiatrist and in group therapy at rehab."

Oliver shook his head at her when he firmly told her with a tight grip onto her hands, "No, it's fine, Isabella. We can talk about it. I brought it up, remember? I'm glad that you're talking to a psychiatrist. Is it making you feel better? How do you feel about it? I know how I feel about it because I go to a psychiatrist too."

Her jaw dropped in shock as Oliver laughed at her when he told her with a wide grin on his face, "What? Why are you surprised by that, Isabella? Don't you think that a psychiatrist needs therapy? You can't watch someone that you love almost die and not get impacted by it. Enough about me. I want to know what you've learned in therapy from your fancy psychiatrist. I'll be the judge of if they are any good."

Once Oliver let go of her hands, she couldn't stop laughing into her hands when she told her with tears falling down her face, "I can't imagine it, Oliver. Are you going to therapy? It's almost unbelievable for me in therapy. I love you even though we're losers. My psychiatrist is great. She doesn't do a lot of talking, but she says important things when she does talk to me. It's been a lot of crying in her ugly floral office every week. How has it been for you?"

Oliver sat up on the roof that they were laying on when he responded to her with a frown on his face, "Therapy? It's been great. He doesn't have any ugly floral office like yours does, but he has a lot of dead animals that he killed hanging on the wall. It's been a lot of crying for me. You know that you weren't the person that made me get therapy. I was going to go before you almost died, but it sped up the timeline for me."

She responded to him with her sitting up next to him, "Sure, Oliver. I'm flattered that you think that is true. I'm glad that it got us to go to therapy. If nothing else good came out of that. Do you want to know what I thought about that moment when it happened?"

Oliver wrapped his arms around her when she confessed to him with tears falling down her face, "The first thing that I thought about was what my mother was going to think of me. Her only daughter died the same way that her father did. The second thing that I thought about was my father. He would be disappointed in me for following in his footsteps. I cry a lot about my dad in therapy. It's like I've cried more for him than he did for me. I wonder if I was destined to become him. He was a part of me. Do you think that I'm becoming my father? Tell me the truth, Oliver."

Oliver grabbed onto her hands when he told her with tears falling down his face, "You don't have to be like your father, Isabella. I chose not to be like mine. I promised myself that I never would become the person that my father was. I cry a lot about my father in therapy too and he died when I was a baby. You can't only cry about a father that knew you and loved you. You can also cry about a father who you didn't know. I think that two things can be true at the same time. You can feel the void that your father left inside of you and believe that there was love that existed inside of him for you. He loved you enough to let you go. He knew that you would be better without him in your life. That's all that matters about him. He loved you and your mom enough to let you go. It was the best gift that he could've ever given you, Isabella. You'll see it someday."

She leaned her head on his shoulder when she responded to him with tears falling down her face, "Thanks for making me feel better, Oliver. You must get paid to do this. Should we go back into the house? I'm getting cold now." As Oliver helped her onto her feet, they climbed into her bedroom through the window as they hugged each other before they went to bed for the rest of the night.

CHAPTER NINE
(WINTER 1961 – LOS ANGELES, CALIFORNIA)

After they celebrated Boxing Day with her family, she got a call from the director on the last two movies that she worked on about a movie that he wanted her to be in called *Showgirls*. It was an offer that she couldn't refuse, and her parents knew that she couldn't turn it down. She told the director that she would love to be in the movie. Once they finalized her contact, she prepared to go back to Los Angeles for the first time since her overdose. As she said goodbye to her parents at the airport, she knew that they felt the same way that she did about leaving them. She held onto her composure until she got on the plane with her cousins, Juliet, Uncle Stan, and Thomas where she hid her face into Sasha's shoulder. When their plane landed in Los Angeles, Uncle Stan drove them to the house. As soon as she walked into her house for the first time in months, she froze in front of the door as Oliver placed a comforting hand on her shoulder before he carried the rest of their bags into the house. After she worked up the nerve to walk into her house, she went straight into the suite to fall asleep for the rest of the day despite it being the afternoon. She woke up in the middle of the night as Amelia and Sasha slept on the other side of the bed with Oliver and Juliet sleeping in their bedroom down the hallway. She checked if she had any cocaine in her hiding spots around the house before she went back up to the suite in defeat that her cousins got rid of the drugs in the house while she was living in

New York with her parents. She sat on the balcony of the suite as she smoked Sasha's cigarettes that she found in her purse with no one in the world except the stars in her company. As she stared up at the stars in the sky, she held onto a cigarette in between her fingers as she softly sighed when she whispered to the stars like it was only a secret between them, "How do I do this, dad? How do I live my life like you never existed in the world?"

She softly chuckled with a wide grin on her face when she responded to herself in a soft voice, "Of course no one is going to answer you back, Isabella. He's dead. He can't tell you anything. You know that you did this to me, dad. It's your fault that I'm like this. I can't believe that you made me this way and you left me alone to deal with it by myself. I hate you for doing this to me. I hate you so much, dad. How dare you leave me like this? Did you honestly think that it would be better like this? There was nothing good about it. Instead of two addicts, there's one addict left in the world to struggle. Oh well there's nothing that I can do to change it. You're dead, dad. What can you do to help me? Thanks for making things worse than they were. I hope that you're happy about this. I'm not happy about it. Goodnight, dad. I love you."

She went into the studio to film her new movie *Showgirls*. They were no longer doing drugs or going out to clubs since she couldn't tempt herself into doing drugs. Instead of going out to clubs and getting high, they opted to stay in the house to play board games and they went swimming in the pool. Isabella was the only person that wasn't drinking alcohol. Actually, she wasn't the only person not drinking alcohol. Juliet stopped drinking since she was in the early stages of pregnancy with her first child. When they got back from the holiday season in New York, Juliet found out that she was pregnant. She told them as soon as they got back from work that day before they went to their favorite restaurant in the city to celebrate. She was happy for Oliver and Juliet since they deserved to be parents more than anyone else. Juliet wasn't the only person in the family pregnant. Amelia told her that her cousin Audrey was pregnant with fraternal twins which was ironic because her mother also had twins too. She attended NA meetings for a few days, and she saw a new psychiatrist in Los Angeles. She couldn't see Dr. Keber anymore since she wasn't in New York. Dr.

Keber referred her to an associate office in Los Angeles where she met Dr. Perkin for the first time. She was a middle-aged woman in a bright pink office that she couldn't stand any more than Dr. Keber's floral office. Unlike Dr. Keber's meek and shy personality, Dr. Perkin was very energetic, but she was also compassionate and understanding every time that she talked to her about anything that made her upset. She talked about her father to Dr. Perkin a lot like she did with Dr. Keber. She told her about how Uncle Kenny molested her mother when she was a child. Her grandfather died in the war before she was born. Her grandmother died from a drug overdose when she was two years old. Her father raped Uncle Stan and her mother. She was a byproduct of rape that ruined her mother's life. Her father abused her mother when they were together. Her father did the same thing to Uncle Stan. Her father cheated on her mother with Uncle Stan. Her mum was in an abusive relationship with her ex-husband who died too. The worst thing that she told her was that she had thoughts that scared her. She didn't know how to get rid of them. Like when she called her mother ten months ago. Or the thoughts that she had when she was overdosing in the club four months ago. Or even the thoughts that she got on the balcony on the first night that she was in Los Angeles for the first time in two months. She wasn't trying to do anything to make it happen, but she wouldn't be upset if it ended up happening. She didn't know where the feeling came from, but she couldn't stop thinking about it every morning before she went to bed with the same dreams of death haunting her. Before she did drugs to repress the feeling inside of her. Those feelings came back to her even stronger than they were before drugs entered her life. Dr. Perkin described it as a suicide ideation. Dr. Perkin told her that her brain wanted her to distract her from what she repressed in her childhood. She dealt with things from her childhood. She wasn't ready to deal with it until that very moment.

CHAPTER TEN
(SPRING 1961 – NEW YORK, NEW YORK)

After her first few sessions with Dr. Perkin, she was making a small process towards getting back to herself again. She had those dark thoughts less and less every day. She stopped craving drugs every time that she felt that way towards herself. She had the power to not engage in that lifestyle. She didn't want to be a person that was addicted to drugs her entire life. She had dreams that she wanted to fulfill in her life that she couldn't do if she was doing drugs. She forgot why she moved to Los Angeles. She didn't move to Los Angeles to become a drug addict that hated her life. She moved to Los Angeles because she wanted to be a movie star that other girls could look up to like she did to her movie icons when she was a little girl growing up in New York. While she filmed her movie *Showgirls* in the studio, she enjoyed herself more on this movie than any other movie that she did before. She loved the beautiful outfits that she wore and the designed sets that people worked hard on. She loved the people that she worked with on this movie. They were other girls around the younger age that were getting started in the acting industry where she felt protective over them being older than them. When she was on a filming break from shooting her movie, they packed their bags for a trip to New York for her cousin Nina's high school graduation. On the morning of their flight, they got up in the early hours of the morning where Uncle Stan and Thomas picked them up at their house before they drove them to the airport. When they got to the airport, they got on the plane where she slept with her head on Amelia's shoulder before her parents picked them up from the airport until they took them to her parent's house where they had dinner with the rest of the family. Once everyone was finished eating dinner together, Sasha and Amelia left to go to Uncle Sam's house as Uncle Stan and Thomas went to the hotel for the night before she went up on the roof with Oliver to star gaze. Juliet was asleep on the couch from their long day of traveling as she was exhausted from being pregnant while her parents watched a movie in the living room. They didn't go inside until her mother walked into her bedroom where she told her that it was time to go to bed where Oliver took Juliet into the guest room before she went to bed for the rest of the night.

On the morning of Nina's high school graduation, she woke up to Ivan standing in her bedroom with a wrapped present in his hand that she took from him with a smile on her face. When she opened the gift that Ivan gave her, she placed the silk dress on the bed as she pulled him into a tight hug when she thanked him for the present before she went into the kitchen to eat breakfast. After she got dressed into the silk dress that Ivan gifted her, she went into the living room to help her parents set up for Nina's graduation party after the ceremony was over at the high school. Once Aunt Valeria and Nina left to go to the high school, she opened her presents from her parents before they left to go to the high school where the rest of her family was waiting for them. After they got to the high school, they met up with her family at the bleachers where she congratulated Anastasia and Damien on their engagement as she looked at Anastasia's diamond engagement ring on her left hand. As she took a seat in between Amelia and Sasha, she told Aunt Valeria and Uncle Sam about the movie that she was working on with excitement laced in her voice as they listened to her with smiles on their faces. They stood up clapping as they cheered Nina's name when she walked across the stage before she grabbed her diploma from the principal. After Nina and her classmates threw their hats up in the air, they drove to her parent's house where they ate brunch that was catered by Nina's favorite restaurant. The dessert was an ice cream cake for Nina since she preferred ice cream more than any other dessert. After they ate dessert together in the living room, Uncle Sam and Aunt

Valeria took Ivan back home with them as Juliet stayed home with her parents before they left to go celebrate Nina's graduation and Anastasia & Damien's engagement at a bar downtown that Damien insisted on taking them that his older brother owned. Despite her cousins not willing to go on her behalf, she told them that she would be okay in the bar, and she wasn't going to be tempted to drink when she was there. When they got to Damien's older brother's bar, Damien instantly went to go look for him while everyone except her ordered a drink from the bartender. As they sat together in the back of the bar, she drank a club soda as she talked to her cousins about what was happening in their lives. Nina took sips of something that Sasha ordered for herself to give her a small taste since she promised her parents that she wouldn't get her younger sister drunk tonight. When Damien walked over to them with his older brother following behind him, he gave her a quick look before he pulled his soon-to-be sister-in-law Anastasia into a hug before he disappeared into the crowd. Sasha and Amelia disappeared with some guys that bought them drinks at the bar as Oliver and Damien played pool against Anastasia and Nina with her watching them play with a club soda in her hand. While she watched Oliver score a point against Anastasia who was bitter about it, Damien's older brother caught her eyes from the other side of the room before he made his way towards her.

As soon as he walked up to her, he looked up at her with a smile on his face when he asked her through all the noise in the room, "Do you want to go somewhere quiet?"

She nodded her head at him when she responded to him with a smirk on her face, "I've been waiting for you to ask me that."

She ignored Oliver's concerned glance at her where he guided her through the crowd into his office before he closed the door behind them. When they were alone with each other, he stared at her with a smile on his face when she asked him with her hands on her hips, "Are you going to the wedding? I'd love to see you there. My name is Isabella since you were about to ask me."

As soon as he took a seat at the desk, he told her with a smirk on his face, "That's a beautiful name. My name is Daxton. I'm going to the wedding. Will you be at the wedding, Isabella?"

She hid her red face into her hands when she responded back to him with a wide smile on her face, "I wouldn't miss it. What do you do, Daxton? Besides running this establishment of drunkards in the city."

As Daxton got up from the desk chair, he sat down on top of the messy desk as he looked at her eyes when he told her with his hands in his pocket, "I went to college for business management. I worked at this bar in college until the owner gave it to me when he retired a few years ago. The previous owner of the bar was my father, and he was one that made me go to business school to run the bar. I didn't want to run the family business, but my brother Damien became a real estate agent instead of going to college. This wasn't the dream, you know? The dream is to be a musician, but I can't pursue that until my father dies or we go out of business. Whatever comes first. Now, it's your turn. What do you do? Do you live in New York?"

As she got closer to Daxton with their arms rubbing against each other, she shook her head at him when she responded to him with her hands holding onto his arms, "I don't live in New York anymore. I was born in England until I moved to New York with my mother when I was three years old. I moved to Los Angeles two years ago. My family lives in California and New York, but most of my family still live in England. I'm an actress. I used to do modeling until my acting career took off. My parents run a book publishing company. My mother is an author, so that's why we moved to New York. She wanted to be an author. I wanted to be an actress. Looks like we got what we wanted in life. Why can't you be a musician? You seem so confident about yourself."

As he wrapped his arms around her waist, Daxton told her with a wide grin on his face, "I am confident about myself. You're confident about yourself too. Apparently confidence doesn't mean much of anything, does it? Has anyone told you that your confidence is infectious? I think anyone can be confident if they were around you. Do you want to kiss me, Isabella?"

She pulled him into a desperate kiss until their lips broke apart when they were out of breath. He pulled her into another desperate kiss where he laid her down on the desk with the papers pushed onto the floor. As he laid down on top of her on the desk, Daxton pulled her jacket off of her as she undid his buttons on his top before they suddenly froze when there was a knock on the door before Damien told her that they were leaving the bar if she wanted to come home with them. As soon as she let go of him, Daxton smiled at her as he helped her off of the desk when he told her with him not letting go of her hand, "Looks like our fun got cut short. How much longer are you in New York?"

She pulled him into another desperate kiss until they broke away from each other before she responded to him with a smirk on her face, "I'm here for two weeks until I have to go back to California. Do you want to meet up tomorrow night? I have something that I have to do during the day, but I should be free in the evening."

Daxton smiled at her when he responded to her with his hands holding onto her hands, "Perfect. It's a date. We can meet at my place tomorrow night. I'll give you my address before you leave. I live with my brother. Damien is going to be at Anastasia's house. We should be alone with each other. I'll see you tomorrow. It's been a pleasure meeting you." She pulled her jacket over her shoulders before Daxton opened up the door with a smirk on his face. She walked out of the office with a smile on her face as she met up with her cousins at the front of the bar. She didn't care about the look of concern that Oliver gave her and the looks of curiosity that Sasha and Amelia gave her. Once they got back to her house for the night, Oliver went into the guest bedroom where Juliet was already asleep before Sasha and Amelia followed her into her bedroom where they laid down in her bed. She fell asleep with a smile on her face. She dreamed about the mystery boy that she met at the bar that made her heart skip a beat.

CHAPTER ELEVEN
(SUMMER 1961 – MARINA GRANDE, CAPRI ISLANDS)

On the night after their fateful meeting, Sasha dropped her off at Daxton's apartment building as Sasha and Amelia wished her good luck before they drove to the concert they were going to on the other side of the city. She told her parents that she was going to the concert with Sasha and Amelia. That was true since she originally planned on going to the concert with them until Daxton invited her to his place for the night. She decided that it was better if her parents didn't know what was going with them since she knew that they would disapprove of him without needing to meet him. As soon as she walked into Daxton's apartment, he kissed her with her kissing him back as they made their way into his bedroom where they finished where they left off last night. After they got dressed in their clothes, she followed him into the kitchen where they ate homemade pizza that he made for them before they kissed each other most of the night until Damien came back home from Anastasia's house late into the night. She didn't remember who decided that she was going to spend the night at his place. She woke up early the next morning to get ready to go back to her parent's house. He didn't let her leave his apartment until he kissed her again for a while before she promised him that she would see him a few days before she would go back to Los Angeles with her cousins. On the morning of her flight back to Los Angeles, he met her at the airport where he kissed her in front of her parents and her cousins for the first time as he promised her that he would visit her in a few weeks before she went on the plane with her cousins. Uncle Stan and Thomas went back to Los Angeles the morning after Nina's graduation party since they couldn't miss work. Uncle Stan met them at the airport before he dropped them off of their house. As she filmed *Showgirls* during the day, she spent the evenings with her cousins in the living room playing board games with them until everyone went into their bedrooms where she talked to Daxton for the rest of the night until she passed out on the couch in the living room. They had a phone in the suite that she could've used, but she didn't want to keep her cousins awake even though she knew that they weren't sleeping in there. Chloe came over to the house to hang out with Amelia and Sasha. She kept her distance from her when she was in the house. She could've told them not to let Chloe come to the house, but she knew that it was a losing battle since she couldn't stop them from doing what they wanted to do no matter what she said to them. If they were going to do drugs in her house, then she chose not to be a part of it. As soon as Chloe started coming to the house, she moved all her stuff into the other suite since she didn't want anything to do with what they were doing. When she moved her stuff into the other suite, she forgot that she moved her emergency cocaine slash into this room that no one used for some unknown reason before she flashed it down the toilet in her commitment to be sober. Daxton told her that he was going to visit her since his manager could handle the bar for a few days without him. On the morning that Daxton's plane landed in Los Angeles, she met up with him at the airport where she pulled him into a tight hug as they kissed each other for a while until she took him to the car before she drove him to her house. When they got the house, Oliver and Juliet sat in the living room with their arms around each other as the television played in the background when they briefly greeted Daxton before they turned attention to the television. She decided to give him the whole tour of her house. She ran into Amelia outside by the pool as she tanned on a pool chair. She ran into Chloe and Sasha in the basement where they were working out in the gym. They went into her suite on the other side of the house.

When they were alone in her room, she started the first kiss as Daxton pulled her closer to him with wide grins on their faces before she guided them over to the bed. After they made up for lost time in the bed, they laid under the sheets with her head laying on top of his chest as they draped their arms around each other while he gently ran his fingers through her hair. Their intimate moment was interrupted as Oliver knocked on the door when he asked them if they wanted to go out to lunch with them. She shouted out to Oliver that they would love to go to lunch with them as Daxton shook his head at her before he pulled her into a long kiss where she giggled with him until Oliver knocked on the door to remind them about reservations that he made without asking them. Once she pulled away from Daxton, she went over to her closet to grab a floral dress that she bought with Amelia at their favorite store. After she fixed her hair in the bathroom mirror, she grabbed onto Daxton's hand as they left the house to go to Juliet's favorite restaurant since she had intense pregnancy cravings for months. Daxton stayed with her a few weeks until he had to go back to New York since his manager was going on vacation and he had to work at the bar. Before he left to go back to New York, he promised her that after she was done filming *Showgirls* that they would go on vacation wherever she wanted to go with him, and he would pay for everything. After thinking about where she wanted to go on vacation, she told Daxton on a phone call that she wanted to go to the Capri Islands. When he asked why she wanted to go there, she told him that it was where her father dreamed of going there. Her parents wanted to go there on their honeymoon when they got married to each other. Of course, that never happened, but the dream was alive after all these years. After she finished filming *Showgirls* by the summer, she left with the cast for the press tour around the country where they ended the tour in New York. She visited her parents and her cousins where she got her bridesmaid dress fitted for Anastasia's wedding before Isabella and Daxton got on the flight to the Capri Islands where she slept with her head leaning on his shoulder as he read a book next to her. When their plane landed in the Capri Islands, Daxton picked up a rental car at the airport before he drove them to their hotel that they were staying at that was on the beach where they made up for lost time. Once she changed into her bathing suit, he grabbed his book from earlier before they spent that first day on the beach until they went to a restaurant for dinner.

They spent a lot of time in their hotel room being intimate with each other without any interruptions. They always got interrupted when they were at his apartment by his brother and when they were at her house by her cousins. The other half of the trip they spent time on the beach until they ended up at a restaurant before they went to their hotel room for the rest of the night. On the last night of the trip, they decided to do something different. He took them to a picnic on the beach with the sun setting in the background. As Daxton held onto her hand, she sat down on the blanket next to him as she pulled him into a long kiss when she thanked him for this trip. After they let go of each other, they helped themselves to the food from their favorite seafood restaurant on the island before she grabbed onto his hand where she dragged him into the ocean with her. Even though he tried to fight it, he let her drag him into the cold water as they screamed in shock before they kissed each other with the waves crashing around them. One of the waves was so strong that it tried to knock them down into the sand as she let out a scream where he caught her before she could fall into the sand until she let him drag her to their blanket. As they laid down on the blanket together with the sound of the waves crashing in the background, she laid her head onto his chest as he kissed her forehead when she said to him with a smile on her face, "This was an incredible vacation, baby. Thank you for spoiling me. It was exactly what I needed. A break from the world. A place where I can go so that I can escape. I love you, Daxton."

Daxton kissed her on her lips with a smile on his face when he responded to her, "I love you too, Isabella. I'd do anything for you darling. You know that I would. Can I confess something to you? It seems like time that I tell this."

As her heart dropped into her stomach, she put on a brave face when she nodded her head at him with her desperately grabbing onto his hands. When Daxton looked at her, she tightened her grip on his hands when he revealed to her in a soft voice, "I sold the bar before we left for the Capri Islands. I didn't want to say anything about it until we were home, but my dad already knows about it. I don't care what he says about it. He knew it wasn't what I wanted to do with my life. He shouldn't have been surprised that I decided to sell it. I want to move to California with you. I want to be a musician. I don't want to wait until my father is dead until I do what I love. Following your dreams motivated me to fulfill my dreams. Can I move in with you? Do you have to get permission from the cousins to move in with you?"

She pulled Daxton into a long kiss with him wrapping his arms around her waist. She moved away from him when she told him with a smile on her face, "I own the house, Daxton. I don't give a fuck what the cousins think about it. You can move in with me. When are you thinking about moving in? You can move in as soon as you want."

He grabbed onto her hands when he told her with a smile on his face, "I was thinking after the wedding. I know that Damien doesn't want me to live with him after he gets married to Anastasia. It would be awkward if I did live with him. Imagine that honey. It's better this way, you know, because now we don't have to do travel long distances."

Once she pulled him into another kiss, they pulled away from each other as they stared into each other's eyes when she told him with a smirk on her face, "That's true. You know that I've heard Oliver and Juliet having sex before. I heard them before I left for New York a week ago. The pregnancy hasn't stopped them. That's for sure. I heard Sasha and Chloe having sex a few weeks ago in the suite in the middle of the night. Did you know that they were together? It was news to me that they were."

As Daxton kept a tight grip on her hands, he doubled over in laughter as he tried to stop it when he told her through his breathlessness, "Honey they have been together for a long time. I only met them a few times and I could tell that as soon as I met them. It was pretty obvious that they were sleeping with each other. Isn't Chloe your dealer?"

She hid her face into his chest when she responded to him with a frown on her face, "It was obvious to everyone except for me. That's why Sasha was so upset with me when I tried to kick Chloe out of the house. No, Chloe was my dealer honey. I thought that she was a dealer to Sasha. I guess not. Do you think that Chloe is sleeping with Amelia?"

As soon as Daxton went into another laughing fit, she hid even farther into his chest when she responded to him, "Alright. Either I'm pretty oblivious to everything around me or I'm so unattractive that Chloe doesn't want to have sex with me. It could be both. Why wouldn't Chloe want to have sex with me? I'm attractive."

Daxton placed his hands on her face when he told her with a serious look on his face, "Stop it honey. You're the most attractive person that I know. Why do you want Chloe to have sex with you? Do you even like women?"

That was when they went into a laughing fit together where she shook her head at him when she told him, "I don't like women. I'm pointing out that Chloe doesn't want to have sex with me. I'm not attracted to her. Would you love me any less if I did like women?"

Daxton grabbed onto her hands with a smile on his face when he told her, "It might be a little weird if you liked women and you were with me. I'm glad that you don't want to have sex with the dealer like your cousins do. Do you think Oliver has had sex with Chloe too? I mean, everyone should get to have sex with Chloe. It would only be fair. What? Don't look at me like that, Isabella. We don't know what happens when you aren't home." She lightly smacked him on the arm as he pretended to be in pain from it before he pulled her into a long kiss where he almost took her dress off at the beach before she forced him to take it to the hotel room. After they finished what they started on the beach, she slept with her arms around him for the rest of the night.

Chapter Twelve
(Fall 1961 – New York, New York)

She woke up in the morning to Daxton telling her that they needed to leave for the airport. After he pulled her into a long kiss on the bed, she quickly got dressed into a comfortable outfit before they left the hotel for the airport. When their plane landed in New York, she spent the night at his apartment before they said an emotional goodbye to each other at the airport where she got on a plane all by herself to Los Angeles where Sasha picked her up at the airport. On the drive to the house, she told Sasha that Daxton was moving in with them after the wedding where Sasha nodded her head at her before she caught her up with what happened at the house while she was away. It was a few months that she was preparing to go back to New York for Anastasia and Damien's wedding where she would see Daxton again. As she packed her suitcase for her trip to New York, she listened to music that played on her record player on the other side of the suite until she went into one of the drawers that held her belts inside of it. She saw from the corner of her eye that there was a bag of cocaine from her emergency stash that she hid in this room a year ago. She pretended not to notice it when she placed the bag of cocaine in one of her jacket pockets as she zipped up her suitcase before she placed her suitcase in the corner of her bedroom. On the morning of their flight to New York, she was woken up to the sound of Sasha and Chloe blasting music outside by the pool before she walked out on her balcony when she yelled at them to turn it down where she went back into her bedroom to get more sleep. Once it was time to leave for the airport, she went into the living room with her cousins, a very pregnant Juliet, and Chloe before Uncle Stan and Thomas took them to the airport. Chloe was coming to the wedding because she was Sasha's plus one despite her knowing that it wasn't going to go well when their family found out about their relationship with each other. She had yet to have a conversation with Sasha about her strange arrangement with Chloe because Sasha was ignoring her since she caught them having sex in the other suite. When they got to the airport, she sat next to Amelia on the plane while she read a book that Daxton bought for her on their vacation in the Capri Islands. Once their plane landed in New York, her parents picked them up from the airport with her cousins Nina and Ivan tagging along with them. Her mother's jaw dropped in complete shock when she realized that this was the infamous Chloe that she told her about over a year ago over the phone. When they got to her parent's house, she was greeted by Uncle Sam and Aunt Valeria as they ate dinner together in soft conversation with each other before she told her parent's that she was going to spend the night at Daxton's apartment. She would see them in the morning with Uncle Stan and Thomas who were at the same hotel that they always stayed at in the city.

Even though her parents didn't like it, they knew that she spent more time with Daxton in the last six months than anyone else. They kissed her on the cheek when they told her that they would see her in the morning. She got a ride from Sasha and Chloe to Daxton's apartment since they were staying at a hotel away from her uncle's house for reasons that were obvious to her. Amelia, Juliet, and Oliver were staying at her parent's house since Uncle Sam was in the middle of doing renovations to the first floor of the house, so that they didn't have room to put additional guests. As soon as she walked into Daxton's apartment, he pulled her into a long kiss with her leaning against the door as he ran his arms up and down her torso before they instantly froze in front of the door when Damien walked into the living room with Anastasia following behind him. Once she straightened her jacket back to the way that it was, she pulled herself away from Daxton as she gave Damien and Anastasia a quick hug before she guided Daxton into his bedroom with him closing the door behind them. After they made up for lost time in the bed, she slept with her arms around him for the rest of the night. Anastasia walked into his bedroom when she asked her if she wanted to go out with them that morning to get their nails done. As she pulled herself out of Daxton's arms while she kissed him on the cheek, she got dressed into the outfit that she wore last night before she left the apartment to go brunch with her parents, Uncle Stan, and Thomas at their favorite cafe in the city. She tried her best to ignore the way that her mother looked at her when she saw her at the cafe like she was looking at her father in a mirror. Once she ate brunch with her parents and her uncles, her parents dropped her off at the house as she got dressed into a new outfit from her suitcase where Amelia took a nap in her bed before she left the house with Juliet to get their nails done with Nina and Anastasia at their nail place that they always went to. She got matching nails with them that went with their bridesmaid dresses and their flower bouquets that they were holding for the wedding. Amelia went to the nail salon later in the day with Sasha and Chloe since Chloe insisted on going there without her. Despite her own bitterness that she felt towards Chloe, she bit her cheeks so hard that it started bleeding when Nina told her that before they went to the nail salon. After they left the nail salon, they went shopping together in Time Square where they met up with Amelia, Sasha, and Chloe at a restaurant for dinner. As soon as she saw the smug look on Chloe's face, she balled her hands into a fist so hard that it bled on the palm of her hand before she excused herself to the bathroom to clean off the blood. After she washed the dried blood off of her hand, she opened her jacket pocket to grab a handkerchief before she saw the bag of cocaine that she put into that jacket pocket when she packed for the trip that she hid in her bedroom in Los Angeles. She was staring at the bag of cocaine that she was taunting her into doing lines off of the bathroom sink. She angrily stuffed it back into her pocket before she joined the girls at the table for dinner. Once they ate a delicious meal at the restaurant, she told Amelia to drop her off at Daxton's apartment for the night and to tell her parents that she was too tired to come home tonight. Even though Daxton was surprised to see her, they went straight into his bedroom where she let out the frustration with Chloe onto Daxton in bed before she fell asleep in his arms for the rest of the night. She ended up staying at Daxton's apartment one more night before she brought her suitcase over to his place since she was tired of having to go back and forth to her parent's house to get her stuff. She didn't care to look of disappointment on her parent's faces when their only daughter told them that she didn't want to stay with them anymore during her visits to New York.

On the morning before the wedding, her family from England came to New York for the wedding where she went to the airport with a few of her cousins, her parents, and Uncle Sam to greet them. The Heartley's were the first family from England to get to New York with Uncle Nathan carrying their bags for them with Aunt Priscilla holding onto her ten-year-old cousin Alfie's hand while her fourteen-year-old cousin Poppy held onto her twelve-year-old cousin Tommy's hand where Oliver and Juliet greeted them. As Uncle Nathan pulled her into a tight hug, she closed her eyes as she hid her face into his chest when he looked at her the same way that he used to look at her father all those years ago. It made her want to fall apart all over again, but she held onto her composure until she was alone in Daxton's apartment. She went to the airport that evening with her parents, Amelia, and Uncle Sam where they greeted the Tucker family as their plane landed into New York. As Uncle James carried their bags in his arms, Aunt Sylvia held onto her eleven-year-old cousin George's hand while her fifteen-year-old cousin Sean walked behind her thirteen-year-old cousin Jamie. Amelia hugged her younger brothers as she was pulled into a hug by Aunt Sylvia who looked at her in the same way that Uncle Nathan looked at her earlier in the day. She was about to fall apart until she saw Audrey walking over to them with her three-month-old niece Lena in her arms while Teddy walked behind her with her three-month-old nephew Leo in his arms. After Isabella and Amelia fought over who got to hold their niece and their nephew, her mother dropped off the Tucker's at the same hotel that the Heartley's were staying at with Uncle Stan and Thomas. Her mother paid for them to stay in the hotel since they didn't have room to stay at their houses. She went back to Daxton's apartment where they had a movie night with Damien and Anastasia in their living room until they went into his bedroom for the rest of the night. On the morning of the dress rehearsal for the wedding, she woke up to Daxton shaving his face in the mirror where she helped him shave the rest of his face before they went into the bed for round one with them completing round two in the bathroom not very long after that. After they finished round three in the bed, she got ready to leave the house for the dress rehearsal at the wedding venue where she kissed Daxton with a smirk on her face before she left with Anastasia to go to the wedding venue with the bridesmaids and their parents. Anastasia and Damien were getting married at Castle Terrytown where it was an outdoor wedding with the reception in the meeting hall of the castle. Anastasia chose Nina to be her maid of honor since they were best friends with Sasha, Isabella, Amelia, and Juliet as her bridesmaids. Damien chose Daxton to be his best man since he was his brother with Oliver, Ivan, Teddy, and Sean as his groomsmen. At the wedding rehearsal, she was partnered to walk down the aisle with Ivan with the others being partnered with Nina & Daxton, Oliver & Juliet, Sasha & Teddy, and Amelia & Sean. After everything went by without any problems at the dress rehearsal, the family ate dinner together at the most expensive restaurant in the city that Damien paid for them. She spent the whole day ignoring Sasha and Chloe who rolled her eyes at her when they saw her walk into the room before she went into the bathroom where she snorted one line from the bag of cocaine that she had in her pocket.

On the day of the wedding, she woke up early in the morning as she went into the bathroom to do a line of cocaine off of the sink. She ran to the water to make sure that Daxton couldn't hear her. After she told him that she would see him at the wedding, he rolled back to sleep as she left to go back to Terrytown Castle with Anastasia and the bridesmaids where they got ready for the wedding in a room full of beautiful paintings and glass-stained windows. Aunt Valeria worked on everyone's hair as Amelia did everyone's makeup before Damien saw Anastasia in her wedding dress for the first time. She went with Anastasia, Amelia, and Nina for the first look with Daxton and Damien where she smiled at Daxton with tears falling down her face before it was time to take wedding pictures. They took pictures with the wedding party and pictures of the family before they took their places for the wedding party after everyone took a seat. She held onto Ivan's arm as they walked down the aisle together before she stood in between Nina and Sasha with her hands in a fist behind her back. After Anastasia walked down the aisle with Aunt Valeria and Uncle Sam holding onto her arms, she was pulled to a side hug by Nina when she noticed that there were tears falling down her face. The wedding ceremony was absolutely stunning as she changed into a more comfortable dress for the wedding reception where they ate a delicious meal before she danced in the meeting hall with Daxton's arms around her while her family danced around her. She pulled Daxton away from the meeting hall where they kissed each other on a second-floor balcony that overlooked where Anastasia and Damien got married earlier that day.

While they passionately kissed each other, he was about to unzip her dress when she told him that they couldn't do it here and they had to wait until they got back to his apartment. After Daxton pretended to look hurt by it, he pulled away from her with a smirk on his face when he told her that was going to look for his brother before she walked into one of the bathrooms to snort the rest of the cocaine that she brought with her. Once she walked onto the balcony, she saw that Chloe and Sasha had their arms around each other as they smoked a joint together. As soon as she took a seat on the balcony near them, Chloe looked at her with a scowl on her face before she walked off of the balcony. She hadn't been alone with Sasha since she got back from the Capri Islands. Once she stood next to her on the balcony, she grabbed the joint from Sasha's hands before she inhaled the smoke when she asked her with a frown on her face, "Why have you been ignoring me, Sasha? I'm your best friend. You can't ignore me forever. Are you upset with me?"

As soon as Sasha grabbed the joint out of her hands, she turned around to look at her when she told her with a scowl on her face, "I'm not ignoring you, Isabella. I'm doing things with someone that isn't you. I thought that you didn't notice it since you're so busy with Daxton. It's so gross how clingily you guys are with each other. We get it. You are in love with him. You don't have to rub it in our faces all of the time."

After she took the joint from Sasha's hands, she inhaled the smoke from it when she responded to her with a hand making a fist in her jacket pocket, "I'm not trying to rub it in your face, Sasha. We're happy. What's so wrong with us being happy? I thought that you wouldn't care since you have Chloe to fulfill your every whim."

Sasha's face turned white as she shook her head when she responded to her in complete shock, "How the fuck would you know anything about what Chloe, and I do together? Did Amelia tell you?"

As she took another hit of the joint, she laughed at Sasha when she told her with a wide grin on her face, "Amelia didn't have to tell me anything. Thank you for confirming it for me. Anyone with eyes can tell that you guys are having sex with each other. Why didn't you tell me that you were dating Chloe? Come on. You're my best friend, Sasha. We don't keep secrets from each other."

Once Sasha took a seat on the balcony, she let out a soft sigh as she shook her head to her in defeat when she confessed to her with tears falling down her face, "It wasn't my decision to tell you that, Isabella. I was going to tell you, but you got so busy with Daxton. We have been having casual sex for a while, but we didn't start dating until you were in New York after you went to hospital. I don't know what I was thinking. I didn't realize how hard it was going to be for us to be together. Chloe and I are in an open relationship. We have sex with other people when we aren't in the same place or someone else can join us. I didn't want to tell you because you wouldn't look at me the same way. I'm jealous that you can openly be with Daxton. I would do anything to have that with Chloe. It hurts me that we can't do that unless we are behind closed doors. I want that passionate love that you have with him. I'm jealous of Daxton. I admit it."

She couldn't stop laughing into her hands as she looked at Sasha when she responded to her with a smile on her face, "I knew that you were jealous of Daxton! You want to hear something hilarious? I've been jealous of Chloe. I've been thinking how dare Sasha replace me with Chloe. I'm way better company than Chloe is. Chloe never saw Sasha perform in her first dance recital with a homemade sign made with glitter that was all over my parent's house until we were teenagers. Chloe never helped Sasha after she fell off her bike when we learned to ride without training wheels. We're idiots, Sasha. I love you."

When Sasha got off of the chair, she pulled her into a tight hug where she hid her face into her chest when Sasha told her with a kiss on the top of her head, "I love you too even though we are jealous idiots. I'm sorry that we fought. I don't want to fight with you anymore. Do you know what we should do next?"

As she pulled her head out of Sasha's chest, she nodded her head at her with a smirk on her face when she responded to her, "Let's do it, Sasha. I thought that you would never ask." As she grabbed Sasha's hands, they ran away from the balcony to the meeting hall where the rest of their family were dancing and drinking before they danced together with Daxton laughing at them from the corner of the room. They said goodbye to Anastasia and Damien who were going to Mexico on their honeymoon. She pulled Sasha into a tight hug before Sasha and Chloe went back to the hotel for the night. She went back to Daxton's apartment with him where they finished off where they left off at the wedding before she slept in his arms for the rest of night. She dreamed of the wedding that she wanted to have with Daxton.

Chapter Thirteen
(Winter 1962 – Los Angeles, California)

On the day after the wedding, her family went back to England before she went back to Los Angeles with her cousins, Juliet, Uncle Stan, and Thomas. Daxton was moving in with them after Anastasia and Damien got back from their honeymoon since someone needed to watch their place while they were gone. As Daxton prepared to move in with them, she got a call from someone that she worked with on *Showgirls* that told her that there was a movie called *Flowergirls* that she would be interested in getting involved in. Once she got the part that she auditioned for in *Flowergirls*, she took her cousins out to eat at their favorite restaurant to celebrate her new project. She started filming for *Flowergirls* in the same week that she received the news. It happened to be the same week that Juliet's water broke in the middle of the night before Oliver took them to the hospital where they anxiously waited to hear from them about the baby. When Juliet and Oliver came back from the hospital with her niece Posey, she was obsessed with her. Sasha and Amelia were too. Juliet left her job as a Hollywood writer to become a stay-at-home mother where Oliver took a week off from work before he went back to work at the psychiatric hospital. It was a few weeks after Posey was born that Daxton moved in with them with his belongings in two suitcases and a guitar in a black case. He moved his belongings into the suite that she claimed as her own a while ago where Sasha and Amelia kept the other suite for themselves. While she was away during the day filming her new movie, Daxton got a job as a bartender to make his own money where he was allowed to play music for free on the nights that he was off from work. She went to his performances on the weekends with her cousins and Juliet since Uncle Stan and Thomas offered to babysit Posey for them before they went to a new club that opened up that Amelia's co-worker at the studio ran and owned. Her cousins were aware that she was drinking alcohol again and she smoked weed with them. They didn't know that she was snorting cocaine during the week to get through the day.

Daxton knew that she was getting high behind his back. He started getting high with her when she prepared lines of cocaine for herself. In all the months that they were dating each other, he never once mentioned to her that he did drugs before. She didn't say anything to him about her problems with drugs either. She accepted that it was meant to be since he didn't stop her from getting high. She relapsed from doing drugs on the day of wedding in New York. They were together one night in the club without her cousins since they didn't tell them that they were going out. She ran into her old drug dealer outside of the bathroom where she told him that he was the only person that she was looking for. He gave her his phone number where he gave her a few things to start off with before he visited her at her house in a few days with the products that she wanted from him. She didn't tell Daxton about meeting her dealer at the club until the next night in the bed where she made him promise her that he wouldn't tell her cousins what they were about to get into. Once he promised her that they wouldn't say anything to them, she shared some of the products that she purchased from him at the club last night. This was the beginning of a very dangerous pattern for her. She wasn't living this lie by herself like she did in the past. She was living this lie with her boyfriend. She didn't realize that Daxton was an addict until she brought drugs around him where he suddenly changed right before her eyes. It wasn't like they lost the passion between each other that Sasha was jealous about from them. It was more like the passion changed into something more corrupt than the sweet innocence that they once had together. When Daxton was high, he was a different person than the guy that she fell in love with. He was angry at her for every little thing that she said to him, or she did to him. When they got back from the club after they were high, they got into these screaming matches with each other that always ended up with him storming out of the house and her crying herself to sleep for the rest of the night. Sometimes he would try to grab her before she locked him into their closet until he passed out for the rest of the night. These screaming matches happened when they were the only people home. Oliver and Juliet moved into their own house a month after Posey was born. Chloe moved in with them as soon as Amelia moved into Oliver's old bedroom. Chloe shared the other suite with Sasha since they were out to them after they got back from New York. Sasha hadn't come out to her parents, but she came out to her siblings while they were in New York.

On that particular weekend, everyone was spending the night at her house since they were celebrating Oliver's birthday together with a nice meal and a delicious cake that the chef made for them. After they finished eating dinner together, they went out by the pool to swim as Juliet held onto Posey in the pool. Posey cried as soon as her feet touched the water where Oliver rushed to grab her out of the pool before he brought his daughter on a pool chair. She fell asleep on the pool chair in between Amelia and Oliver. She woke up in the evening where she came inside the house where everyone was in the living room watching a movie on the television. She told them that she would be back down after she changed out of her swimsuit. She walked upstairs to the suite where she saw Daxton laying on the bed staring at her without saying anything to her. When she walked into the closet to put on a t-shirt and a pair of jeans, she grabbed their hidden stash of drugs that her dealer brought for them the other night before she went to do a line of cocaine off of the cabinet before she placed them back into the hiding spot. After she walked into their bedroom, Daxton stared at her refusing to say anything to her looking at the television where she stood in front of him when she asked him with her hands on her hips, "What's wrong baby? You keep staring at me and you're refusing to say anything."

As soon as Daxton got off of their bed, he gave her that same look when he responded to her with a frown on his face, "Wouldn't you love to know that honey? Do I have to spell it out for you? Are you an idiot?"

She shook her head at her when she responded to him with her hands in front of her, "We aren't doing this right now, Daxton. Not when my family is in the living room. We can talk about it in the morning. I don't want to start something with you when you are like this."

Before she could get out of their bedroom, he grabbed onto her body as he pushed her against the wall with her letting out a small groan when he screamed at her with this grip tightening on her arms, "What am I like right now? You don't want to start anything when I'm what? When I'm high? You can say it, Isabella! It's not going to burn you if you say that word! Don't act all fucking innocent in this honey! You started this! If I would have kept the bar, then none of this would be happening to me! I wouldn't be fired from my job! I wouldn't be broke. You did this to me!"

In a complete fit of anger, she pushed him onto the bed when she screamed at him with anger laced in her voice, "Fuck you, Daxton! It's not my fault that you got fired for stealing money from the bar! You didn't have to take their money! It was your decision to do it! I'm so tired of this same argument that we have over and over again! Do you really want to get into this right now? Let's get into this! I never told you to sell the bar, Daxton! You wanted to sell the bar to become a musician! Except all that you do all day is whine and cry about how much you miss the bar! Maybe you should have stayed in New York because you wouldn't be here making me miserable every day of my life! I'm such a fucking idiot for believing you! You're never going to change no matter how much I want you to change for me! You need to get the fuck out of my house! You're not welcome here anymore! Get out of my sight before I make you leave!"

Before he got the chance to respond to her, she heard footsteps running towards their bedroom where Oliver came into the room with Sasha, Amelia, and Chloe behind him when Oliver asked her with a concerned look on his face that she hated more than anything in the world, "What is going on up here? Is he causing you problems, Isabella? Instead of taking your problems out on her, why don't we have a conversation outside?"

As she shook her head at Oliver, Daxton grabbed onto her hands as he pushed her up against the wall when he screamed in front of her face with tears falling down her face, "Oh now here come the waterworks! You're such a good actress! It's convenient that you're crying now that everyone is in the room! How come I'm not welcome here when you let the universal drug dealer in the house! I'm the fucking problem, but you're the one who buys the drugs that we take together! Make it make sense, Isabella! Something isn't adding up here! It's you! Do they know about us doing drugs? I don't think that they do! They looked like they saw a ghost when I said that! Don't follow me!"

She shook her head at him with tears running down her face as they stared at her in shock about what Daxton told them. She refused to look at the disappointment on Oliver's face when Daxton let go of his grip on her arms before Daxton stormed out of the house in rage against her. The front door slammed so loudly behind him that it made her body jump up in the air. As soon as she looked up at her cousins, she shook her head at them as Oliver pulled her into his arms where she let out muffled sobs into his chest with him running his hands down her arms in comfort. Oliver guided her to her bed as she took a seat next to Amelia and Sasha with him maintaining his tight grip on her arms when he asked her with a concerned look on his face, "Is he right? Are you doing drugs, Isabella?"

She nodded her head at him when she confessed to him with tears falling down her face, "Yes, I'm doing drugs. I'm sorry, Oliver. I don't know how it happened. Something changed when I found my hidden stash of cocaine before the wedding in New York. I didn't know that Daxton was an addict. It was a pure coincidence that any of this happened. Are you mad at me?"

As Oliver looked over at Sasha and Amelia who were in shock about everything, he grabbed onto her hands when he responded to her with a serious look on his face, "I'm pissed at you, Isabella. If you wanted to know the truth about how I feel about it. As much as I'm upset with you, I'm more upset with myself for not noticing it. Of course, you've been using drugs. It makes sense why you have been acting secretive since we got back from New York. What have you guys been using? Tell me the truth."

She shook her head at him as she hid her face into her hands in complete embarrassment until Sasha tried to pry her head out of her hands to look her into the eyes. After Sasha took her face out of her hands, she firmly kept her hands on the sides of her face to tell if she was high or not right now. They knew that she wasn't going to tell them the truth if she was high. In an instant, she shook her head at Oliver and Amelia when she said to them with a frown on her face like she wasn't in the room with them, "She's high right now. She's not going to remember having this conversation with us. Neither will Daxton since he was high too. I think that we should talk to her about it when she is sober. Let's go to bed for the night. I think that it's time to go to bed, Isabella. Come on, you can sleep with us, okay."

As Sasha and Amelia helped her off of the bed, Oliver looked at her like she was going to break when he asked them like she wasn't in the room, "Can you handle this for the night, Sasha? I have to take Juliet and Posey back to the house."

Sasha nodded her head at him with a frown on her face when she said to him, "Yeah, we can handle it. Take your family home, Oliver. We'll make sure that she's okay and that asshole can't get back into the house. We'll talk about everything tomorrow." After Oliver pulled Sasha and Amelia into a tight hug, he let go of them to pull her into a desperate hug where she cried into his chest again as he kissed on the top of her head when he told her that he loved her and that it hurt him to see her do this. Once Oliver left the house, Sasha pulled her into a tight hug with Amelia holding onto her shoulders before she went to the other suite where Chloe waited for them on the bed. She cried herself to sleep.

Chapter Fourteen
(Spring 1962 – Los Angeles, California)

She woke up before the sun came up the next morning after the chaos from last night to soft noises of her cousins and Chloe sleeping next to her in the bed. She softly groaned when she remembered what happened last night. Once she managed to get herself out of the bed without waking them up, she walked out onto the balcony with a pack of cigarettes and a lighter in her hands that she stole from Sasha's purse before she took a seat on one of chairs with a blanket around her legs. She smoked the rest of the pack of cigarettes in complete silence until Amelia walked out on the balcony with a concerned look on her face that she despised more than anything in the world. As Amelia took a seat next to her, she grabbed the last cigarette out of the box as she lit it up with her inhaling the smoke from it before she placed the empty box onto the glass table that was between them when she asked her in a soft voice that made her want to cry, "Are you okay?"

She inhaled the smoke from her cigarette when she responded to her with her hands shaking from withdrawal, "Things are a never-ending nightmare, Amelia. I'm in a relationship with a man who is like my father, and I've become the worst version of my mother. I'd have an easier time telling you what wasn't wrong with my life than what was wrong with my life."

After Amelia inhaled the smoke from her cigarette, she placed it in between her fingers when she asked her in a soft voice, "Do you want to stop doing drugs?"

She shook her head at her when she told her with a smirk on her face, "No, I have no interest in not using drugs. Thanks for your concern though, Amelia. It's been noted."

Amelia let out a sarcastic laugh as she put out the end of her cigarette onto the ashtray when she responded to her without any emotion left in her voice, "Fine. Don't come crying to me until you care enough about your life not to throw it anymore. I really hope that you'll care about your life as much as I do someday. I can't stand you when you're like this. Kill yourself or don't kill yourself. I'm done trying to change your mind about it. I'm going to work. Don't expect to see me until tonight. I love you even though you're a complete idiot. Goodbye."

Amelia stormed into the house to the guest bedroom where she moved into after they got back to New York where her body jumped from her slamming the door behind her. Once she was alone on the balcony, she put out the end of the cigarette into the ashtray where she got up from her seat before she walked into her suite with Daxton in a deep sleep on the bed. She wordlessly got into the bed next to him where she wrapped her arms around him before she fell back to sleep in his arms. She didn't care about the hypocrisy of it. It wasn't until a few weeks later that her cousins attempted to have an intervention on her. It was in the living room of her own house where she was ambushed after work. She was surprised to see that Uncle Stan and Thomas sat in the living room. Oliver and Juliet sat on the couch with her four-month-old niece Posey sitting in her lap. Amelia and Sasha, who had her arms around Chloe, sat on the couch on the other side of the living room. It shocked her that her parents weren't there until she reminded herself to thank them later for not telling her parents about it. Despite all her efforts to return back to her suite where Daxton was waiting for her, she was forced to take a seat in between Oliver and Uncle Stan before they read their letters to her off of pieces of paper that came from their pockets. It was fitting that Amelia was the first person to talk because their conversation on the balcony was in the front of her mind. Amelia changed her story to one that sounded too pretty and cute for even her cousin. When she pointed this out to her, Amelia defensively told her that she said it to her because she was angry at her at the time and that she didn't mean it. Isabella bluntly told her that she didn't believe her. Sasha was the next person to talk with Chloe holding on to her hand where she told her own version of a sob story that she wasn't in the mood to hear about. As her body twitched in her spot on the couch, Uncle Stan grabbed onto her hand to calm her down where she failed to shove him off her before she leaned on the couch. She closed her eyes from the room since it was too bright for her. When it was time for Juliet to speak, she recounted the time that she almost died in the club that she was not in the mood to hear about right now. Sasha interrupted Juliet to tell Isabella that she was being an insensitive asshole where she rolled her eyes at them before Juliet finished telling her sob story with her being the only person in the room that wasn't crying. Thomas went next where he told her all the things that she did without doing drugs like it was supposed to motivate her to want to get better. When Uncle Stan talked to her about how she was turning into her father, she couldn't hold it back as she sobbed into her hands before Oliver pulled her into his chest with her sobbing into his arms while Uncle Stan talked about her father. She planned on what she was going to take when she got back to the suite before Oliver pulled away from her before he told her his sob story that he prepared on the folded paper from his pocket. She leaned on the couch with her eyes closed again. She thought about drugs the entire time that he talked to her. She got up from the couch to thank them for their concern, but she was going to be okay. No one in the room believed her. She didn't believe herself when she said it. It didn't stop her from declaring it to them a few more times before she tried to take off to her suite where her drugs were hidden in the closet before Uncle Stan pulled her onto the couch in a fit of anger with her. There were a few moments of silence until she asked them if her parents knew about their intervention before Thomas told her that they knew about it since they were the ones that set it up. She maintained her composure when she told them that she didn't want to go to rehab, and she didn't want to stop doing drugs.

She stormed out of the living room into her suite where she locked the door behind her. Oliver quickly followed her to the bedroom with him pounding on the door as soon as she locked it. Daxton looked over at her with a look of confusion on his face where she laughed with him when she told him about their failed intervention on her before they got high for the rest of the night. After their failed intervention against her, she made a deliberate attempt to ignore her cousins while she was home. That was easy since she hardly left the suite. She only left the house to go to film *Flowergirls* during the day where she hid in her suite with Daxton for the rest of the night. They would get into screaming matches with each other about the littlest things. They fought over drugs before they had makeup sex until they passed out for the night where they would do it again the next day. It was one thing to self-destruct by herself, but it was a whole other thing to self-destruct with someone else. It was fun to self-destruct together since she didn't feel so alone through it. She stopped getting hungry since they were taking so many drugs that they stopped eating all together. She never ran into her cousins since she didn't need to go into the kitchen. She ate on the set if they set out food in her trailer, but she didn't make any efforts to eat when she was at home. She was smoking so many cigarettes that it destroyed what appetite that she had left for food. When they would run out of drugs, which was happening more frequently than usual, her dealer would come to the house in the middle of the night when everyone else was asleep where they would get high outside by the pool until they ended up passing out in the suite for the rest of the night.

She knew that her cousins were having conversations with her parents and Daxton's family about them, but she couldn't find it within herself to give a shit about it. She didn't want to stop it no matter what they said to her. She had no desire to stop doing drugs. She felt like she could do anything when she was high. She could be the person that everyone expected her to be at the studio. She was a wonderful actress when she was high compared to when she was sober. She could be the person that her family expected her to be. A huge disappointment. She could be the person that her father wanted her to become. A complete failure. She thought about her father when she was high. Not only did she dream about him every night, but she thought about him when she was with Daxton as they got high every day. She thought about what he would think of her if he could see her. Would he be disappointed that his only daughter was like him? Or would he be strangely proud of her for completing the circle that her mother worked so hard to close? She liked to think that he would be proud of her in ways that her mother would never understand. He understood her in ways that her mother wouldn't see her. It was like they were one being that existed in the same moment. They were always together when they were apart from each other. Her mother never attempted to talk to her about this. That was something that she wasn't going to complain about. She wouldn't listen to her anyways. She didn't know if her mother tried to call her since she unplugged the phone in her bedroom a few months ago. Her mother realized that it would have all been in vain. The only person that she talked to that she didn't work with at the studio was Daxton who never left their suite since he got fired from his job. Her mother was one of the smartest people that she met in her life. It was naive of her to think that her mother was going to be at her beck and call when she was like this. Her mum was smarter than her mother since she told her cousins to leave her alone until she reached out to them. She told herself that she would never do that.

After she got back from the studio, she picked up food from a restaurant where she went over to her dealer's house to pick up the products that she wanted from him before she went to her house for the rest of the night. She walked through the front door of the house with a bag of takeaway food in her hands and a bag of drugs hidden inside of it. Sasha and Chloe watched a movie together in the living room with their arms around each other where Amelia made popcorn on the stove when she walked into the house. She sprinted into their suite where Daxton laid down on the bed watching television like always.

After they ate the food that she picked up for them, Daxton broke into their products that she purchased for them where she changed into a t-shirt and a pair of Daxton's boxer shorts before she joined him on the fun. They found themselves outside by the pool after everyone in the house was asleep in their bedrooms where they were kissing each other on one of the pool chairs. She pulled away from him for a moment where she did another line of cocaine off the glass table before she pulled him into another long kiss. They didn't break apart from each other until Daxton went into the house to grab another bottle of wine from the wine cellar in the basement. She grabbed the pack of cigarettes off of the glass table where she inhaled the smoke from it after she lit it. As she laid down on the pool chair with the cigarette between her lips, she looked up at the stars when she said to herself with a frown on her face, "I hope that you're happy, dad. I hope that you're proud of yourself that I became you. Things are shit right now, but at least I'm so high all of time that none of it matters. I wonder what it's like to be dead. I bet it's nice to be dead. To be in a place where nothing exists, and nothing matters. That sounds like my life. I'm already dead. We are dancing in the cosmos. I know that you're never going to answer me, but I wanted to say that I'm sorry for telling you that I hated you. I don't hate you. I've never hated you. I was angry at you for leaving me. I didn't understand it until right now. I love you so much that it hurts me. I want to be with you. I can't wait to see you again when I can join you in the stars. Just like you told mom in your suicide note."

She blinked back tears that fell down her face as she inhaled the smoke from her cigarette when she responded to herself with a frown on her face, "I should've expected that much to happen. You aren't going to say anything to me. You're dead and I'm alive despite my best efforts to change that. I inherited your addiction problems, but I got my stubbornness from mom. It's not fair, dad. None of this is fucking fair. Sometimes I think about not existing anymore. I could walk off the mountain and fall to death without a care in the world. I could jump in the deep end of the pool and not try to swim up to the surface. I could snort enough cocaine to make my heart stop beating in my chest. I can't do it though, dad. Do you want to know why I can't follow through with it? I couldn't leave mom alone without us in the world. Not after everything that she did to get us here. I can't rob mom of her only daughter that she put all her hopes and dreams into only for that shatter into absolutely nothing. It might kill her if I did that. If I killed myself and I killed mom at the same time, then we would all be in the stars together. We would be the brightest stars in the sky, dad. Wouldn't that be a beautiful story? A family together in the stars for the rest of time. Nothing will be the same again. No matter what we do to change it, it will never change what happened to us. You're dead and I'm half-way there with you. Someday I'll be there with you. Someday we'll be together again." After Daxton walked outside with a new bottle of wine in his hands, she got up from the pool chair where she wiped tears off of her face before she grabbed onto his hand where he dragged her into their suite. They got rid of the drugs that she bought from the dealer. They passed out in their bed for the rest of the night. She wished that she would never wake up, so that she could spend the rest of her life with him. She woke up the next morning.

Chapter Fifteen
(Summer 1962 – Los Angeles, California)

This same pattern of behavior happened to them over and over again. They started every morning coming down from a high where they immediately did more drugs to never lose that feeling. She left Daxton alone in the suite where he slept most of the day as she was at the studio where she got home to get high with him for the rest of the day. They kept repeating this cycle over and over again without any attempt to stop it until she was finished filming *Flowergirls* where it was time for her press tour with the cast across the country. As she prepared to leave for a five week long trip away from Daxton, she made sure that he was supplied with everything that he needed while she was away from him before she packed her own stuff. She hid it in the pockets of every item of her clothing. When it was time for her to leave on her press tour, she got into a horrible argument with Daxton in the middle of the day when no one was home before she left him to be pissed at her for over five weeks. As soon as she got home from the press tour, she brought an olive branch in the form of drugs for him to not be mad at her before they had a couple of rounds together in the suite where they repeated the cycle all over again. Their secret bubble popped when she was told against her will by Sasha in the kitchen where she went down to get bagels that Anastasia and Nina were coming to visit them. When she asked Sasha why they were coming to visit in a rude tone, Sasha rolled her eyes at her in frustration when she told Isabella that they were coming to see them because they missed seeing them. That didn't sound like a reason to her. Her saying this valid point to Sasha caused her to storm into her suite for the rest of the day. When she told Daxton that his brother Damien was coming to visit them, his face turned white as soon as she said it out loud to him where he told her that Damien couldn't find out about their lifestyle. Isabella wasn't in the mood to tell him that his family already knew that they were doing drugs. She helped him create a lie about what his life looked like for him even though it was the farthest thing from reality. Daxton insisted that they don't do drugs when their family visited them since it would imply that they were trying to hide something from them. They were trying to hide something from them. She was in even less of a mood to explain the irony in that to him. She promised him that they wouldn't do drugs when their family from New York visited them with her fully intending to still do drugs when they were visiting them.

On the morning that their family arrived in Los Angeles, Sasha picked them up from the airport where she was shocked when her mum walked into the house with Anastasia, Damien, Nina, and a male that she assumed was Nina's boyfriend. She didn't know that her mum would show up unannounced like that with her cousins and their partners. She immediately regretted doing three lines of cocaine off her bathroom sink right before her mum walked through the front door. To say that there was tension between them was the understatement of the century. She hadn't had a proper conversation with someone that wasn't Daxton in over five months. Her cousins were playing it off as nothing was going on between them when it was clear that there were a lot of problems going on in the house. Her mum insisted on staying in the guest bedroom right next to their suite. She knew that was unnecessary since they had an open bedroom on the other side of the house. Amelia wasn't using it since she was sleeping in the other suite with Sasha and Chloe for reasons that she didn't care to know about. Damien insisted on them staying in the other guest bedroom that was right next to their suite. She knew that wasn't necessary since there was a bedroom next to the bedroom that Nina and her boyfriend Joseph Sullivan were staying in. She hardly ate anything since she couldn't remember the last time that she ate a meal with someone other than

Daxton on the floor of their bedroom. She tried to hide from them that she did a line of cocaine off of the downstairs bathroom sink in the middle of the meal. Anastasia kept putting her hand on her stomach when she talked to them about the early stages of her pregnancy while Damien couldn't take his eyes off of Daxton. He knew what was going on with them, but he didn't know how to talk about it with him. After that nightmarish experience at dinner, she dragged Daxton into their suite for the rest of the night where he immediately broke his only promise to himself to not do drugs before he did four lines of cocaine off of the bathroom sink that he didn't even offer to share with her. In the middle of the night, there was a knock on their bedroom door when they were high out of their minds on the bed before Daxton suddenly pushed her into the closet with all the lights off in the room before he locked the door behind them. They heard footsteps walk into their bedroom where he pressed his hand over her mouth to keep her from laughing so loudly that they would get caught by Damien who was silently walking around their bedroom. Daxton didn't take his hand off of her mouth until they heard Damien close the door behind him where she pulled him onto the floor before they desperately kissed each other. She told him to check on his brother to see what he wanted from him. Even though Daxton tried to distract her by taking off her shorts, she pushed him off of her when she told him to talk to his brother right now and that she would reward him after he got back to their bedroom later in the night.

After Daxton left to go talk to his brother, she held a box of cigarettes and a lighter in her hands before she went outside by the pool where her mum sat in one of the pool chairs with a glass of wine in her hands. As soon as she took a seat next to her mum, her mum looked up at her with a look that she couldn't stand as she grabbed one of cigarettes out of the box before she lit up with her with her inhaling the smoke from the cigarette. Her mum shook her head when she asked her with a frown on her face, "Since when do you smoke?"

Isabella responded to her with a smirk on her face, "Since when do you care? Why are you here, mum? I'm not trying to be an asshole about it. Never mind. I am trying to be an asshole. Did you come to watch your daughter disappoint you in person? Did you not feel comfortable watching me kill myself from New York? Why did you come, mum?"

Isabella took a drag of her cigarette when her mum responded to her with her hands grabbing onto her free hand, "I've always cared about you. I can't believe that you would say that I don't care about you. Honestly, I don't know why I came here. I guess that I wanted to see it for myself instead of hearing it from other people. I didn't realize that it got this bad. I wanted to know how bad things were. I know that you don't give a shit honey. Maybe that's all I'm asking for you to do. I'm not asking you to be perfect or not make any mistakes in your life. I just want you to give a shit about something that matters. I'm asking you to care about yourself. Is that too much to ask from my daughter?"

She pulled her hand away from her mum when she responded to her with a frown on her face, "Yes, that's too fucking much, mum. You can't expect me to give a shit about myself when my father didn't a shit about me. How am I supposed to care about myself when the one person that was supposed to care never cared about me? I don't know what you guys expect from me. I don't know, mum. Do you want me to not be someone that I'm never going to be? I can pretend to be anyone that you want me to be. I can play any part that you can want me to. I can be the devoted daughter who carries on the family name for you. I can be the daughter that takes over the business after you die. I can be the daughter who dedicates her life to pleasing you. I can be anyone that you want me to be. You just can't expect me to care about it. You shouldn't expect me to play the role that you want me to play for you and make me care about it at the same time."

She lit up another cigarette that she inhaled the smoke from as she blinked back tears that fell down her face when her mum responded to her while she looked her into the eyes, "I don't want you to play a part honey. I'm not asking you to be someone that you aren't. I'm asking you to be who you are. I love you no matter who you decide to be. Okay? I want you to care about the person that you truly are."

As she took another drag of the cigarette, her hand's balled into fists at her sides when she confessed to her mum with tears falling down her face, "What if the person that I am on the inside is my father? What if I'm my father? Would you make me care about it even though it's the most despicable version of myself? I don't think that you would make me care about it if you knew who I was on the inside. I know that you wouldn't, mum. It's always been easier for me to play the part that everyone wants me to be than to let that part of myself out. Do you want to know why I like drugs, mum?"

Her mum grabbed onto her hands when she asked her in a desperate voice, "Why?"

Isabella confessed to her with tears falling down her face, "It makes me feel like I can do anything. I can be the person that people expect me to be. I can do what I'm supposed to do. I feel like I can take a deep breath without wanting to scream. For a moment, I feel like I'm not drowning. Even though that feeling only lasts for a moment, it's worth every consequence in the universe. I don't know how to be a person without drugs anymore, mum. I don't want to be a person without drugs. For my entire life, I've been searching for anything in this world that could fill up the hole inside my heart that my father left open in my chest when he died. The only thing in the world that fills that hole in my heart is drugs. It's not like I've tried to fill it up with other things. I've fucking tried to, mum. Nothing worked until I found them. Drugs made me feel like myself. It makes me feel like I am with dad. All that I've wanted was to be with dad. I can never be with him because he's dead. When I get high, I feel like he's with me. I tell him things that I never got the chance to tell him when he was alive. He never says anything back to me, but I know that he's listening to me. When I look up at the stars, I know that he's with me. I don't care if it's not real. He's real to me. It's the only part of him that is left for me."

Her mum pulled her into her arms where she let out desperate sobs into her mum's chest before her mum tightened her arms around her with her desperately clinging onto her shirt. She pulled her head out of her chest as her mum kissed her on the top of her head when she responded to Isabella with her hands holding onto her face, "I'm sorry honey. I know that you don't want to be like this. It's not your fault what happened to your father. What he did to himself had nothing to do with you. Everything to do with him. It was a decision that he made that impacted your life. I know that you're in pain. I can see that. It hurts me to watch you hurt yourself. You deserve the world. You deserve the most beautiful parts of the world. You are experiencing the ugliest parts of the world. I promise you that you will see how beautiful the world is someday. It's going to make the ugly parts worth it. You don't have to believe me honey. I don't need you to believe it. I only need you to know it." Once her mum let go of her, she hid her face into her chest as she blinked back tears that fell down her face with her mum's tightly arms around her. When she took her head out of her mum's chest, her mum kissed her on the top of her head before her mum left to go to bed for the rest of the night. She put out her cigarette onto the ashtray as she went to their suite where Daxton laid down in their bed watching television before she went into the bathroom to snort a line of cocaine off of the sink. Once she threw herself into the bed, he pulled her into his arms as she hid her face into his chest with his arms around her.

Chapter Sixteen
(Fall 1962 – Los Angeles, California)

After a few weeks of putting up with her unexpected house guests, they left to go to New York despite her knowing that her mum didn't want to leave her alone in a fragile state. When they were alone at the house, their lives went back to the way that things were before their family came to visit them. She lived in the suite with Daxton where they left to go to the other parts of the house when everyone was asleep in the middle of the night or when they went to her dealer's house to get more products a few days in the week. She was co-existing in the same space with her cousins. She hadn't had a conversation with them since their failed intervention with her over six months ago. She hadn't seen Oliver, Juliet, or Posey since that same failed intervention. It wasn't like they were intentionally ignoring her because they kept trying to talk to her every time that she saw them walking around the house. She was the person that was ignoring them. She didn't want to hear the shit that they were going to give her for how she was acting towards them or that she was very heavily addicted to drugs right now. She didn't care to be around them since Amelia told her that she couldn't stand her when she was high all the time. It wasn't like Amelia made any attempts to take that comment back since she was with Chloe and Sasha all of the time. When Sasha and Chloe traveled for their jobs, Amelia stayed over at Oliver's house or Uncle Stan's house since she couldn't stand being around her anymore. She didn't know that Amelia's comment hurt her so much until her twin sister Audrey called the house to ask if her sister was home. In complete bitterness towards Amelia, she told Audrey that her sister didn't live here anymore since she couldn't stand being in her presence. Audrey was immediately taken back from this since things were great between them the last time that they saw each other at Anastasia's wedding. Audrey asked for her new phone number where she gave her Oliver's number before she hung up the phone on her.

It was less than an hour later that she was sitting on a pool chair with a joint in her mouth and a glass of wine on the glass table where Amelia stormed towards her with Oliver following behind her before Amelia threw the joint that she lit out of her mouth into the pool. Her face turned red in anger as she punched Amelia in the face where Amelia held onto her nose with blood pouring down her face before Oliver stepped in between them to separate them from each other. Once they stopped attacking each other, they pushed Oliver off of them where she fished the joint out of the pool as she lit it again with surprising success when Amelia asked her why she told her sister that she didn't live here since she did live there. She told her with a smirk on her face that she didn't have to live there if she was so miserable with her. This caused Amelia to push her down onto the ground where she barely caught herself with her hands before her body hit it. This time Oliver did nothing to stop them from fighting each other since he told her that she deserved to be pushed on the ground for the way that she treated them in the last ten months. As she picked up the joint from the ground, Oliver kicked it into the deep end of the pool with his hands folded in front of him like it was intimidating her when he told her that she didn't need to do anymore either where she rolled her eyes at him before she grabbed her glass wine before she took it into the suite with her. On the next morning, Amelia took her advice as she moved her stuff into Oliver's house with him where Sasha and Chloe were pissed off at her when they got back their trip to Spain that she kicked Amelia out of the house. She told Sasha and Chloe the same thing that she told Amelia that they didn't have to live there if they didn't want to where they took her advice before they moved their stuff into Uncle Stan and Thomas's house down the street the next day. Once they were alone in the house, they moved their drug use into the living room where she fired the chef and the housekeepers that her parent's paid for. After she fired her parent's staff, she got a call from her mother the next morning when she screamed at her for firing the staff where she hung up the phone without saying another word to her. Things were worse than she could imagine in her life. They didn't leave the house anymore for any reason. They didn't bother buying food since they weren't going to eat it, and they didn't have anyone cooking anything for them. They stopped eating all together. Her dealer came to the house instead of her going to him. He came by two times a day with products that she didn't remember asking him for. The pool stopped getting cleaned as well as the house since she fired the staff, so they stopped going outside by the pool. She wasn't paying the bills, so they got their electricity and water shut off which didn't faze them since they weren't bathing anymore. When the power was out in the house, the phones stopped working, which was fine with them because they weren't using them anymore. No one came over to the house except for her dealer. Her family stopped coming all together. She didn't give a shit about that since she didn't want to see them. If she thought that things were bad before for them, then things were about to get worse for them. Since neither of them were working anywhere, they were running out of money faster than they could keep it. She didn't know how it started for them, but Daxton always found a way to get the money for their drugs. She suspected that he was robbing places to get that said money, but she never once asked him where he got it before they spent it on more drugs that they knew that they didn't need to use. She knew things were bad when she stopped sleeping all together. She went over a week without sleeping before she heard her father talk to her on a regular basis. This encouraged her to sleep less and less until she wasn't sleeping at all anymore.

On that fateful day, her dealer brought over a new mixture of drugs that they had never tried before that he told them were going to make things exciting. She didn't know what he meant by that until she felt like she could do anything in the world. It had the completely opposite effect on Daxton where he passed out in their bed, and he wouldn't wake up no matter what she did to get him to wake up. She tried to call someone to help him from her phone until she remembered that they didn't have electricity anymore. She thought about what to do next because she could run over to Uncle Stan's phone or Oliver's phone to call an ambulance for him. Before she could make it out of the house, she passed out in the middle of the living room. The dealer gave her something that was going to kill them together in a fucked-up version of Romeo and Juliet. As soon as she woke up again, her body was strapped down in an ambulance as Oliver stared at her blinking back tears that fell down his face with him tightly holding onto her hand when she asked him with her nauseous, "Oliver? What's going on?"

A paramedic pushed back down on the stretcher as Oliver pushed her hair behind her ear when he told her in the softest voice that heard from him, "You'll be okay. Stay still, Isabella. Don't get up."

She passed out again in the ambulance where she didn't wake up until she was in a sterile hospital room with Oliver sleeping on the chair next to the bed as Sasha and Amelia slept on the couch by the door. As she looked around the room, she laid back down on her bed when she whispered to herself, "Oh fuck me. Did I really do this again?"

She didn't try getting out of the bed since she found that her legs were restrained to the bed. When she tugged on Oliver's arm to wake him up, he suddenly jolted awake as he grabbed onto her hands when he told her, looking like he didn't sleep for a long time, "Thank God you're awake. You've been out for days. They didn't know if you were going to wake up, Isabella."

She nodded her head at him in complete indifference when she asked him in a voice that she didn't recognize, "Where's Daxton?"

Oliver tightened his grip on her hands when he responded to her in a shaky voice, "I didn't want to be the person to tell you this. Daxton died, Isabella. He was dead before the ambulance got there. I'm sorry. I know that you loved him, but we saved you."

She threw herself into his arm where she sobbed into his chest with his arms tightly around her. Sasha and Amelia woke up to her crying on the other side of the room when she responded to him in a broken voice, "He was the love of my life. We were supposed to get married and have a family. What am I going to do, Oliver? I ruined everything. I wish that I could die with him. I wish that they didn't save me. They should have let me die with him. I killed him, Oliver. I killed the love of my life. Please let me die. I don't want to live without him. I love him. What am I going to do?"

Sasha and Amelia wrapped their arms around her as they blinked back tears that fell down their faces. No one knew what to say to each other. Isabella pulled her face out of Oliver's chest as she looked at them for the first time since she woke up when she profusely apologized to them on the verge of a panic attack, "I'm so sorry. I didn't mean for any of this to happen to us. I'm sorry for being an asshole. I don't want you guys to hate me. I love you guys so much. Please don't leave me."

She threw herself into Oliver's arms again where she sobbed into his chest as he tightened his grip on her when he told her in a voice that made her want to cry harder than she already was, "It's okay, Isabella. We never hated you. We were worried about you. I love you. Nothing could make me hate you. It's setting off your monitors. The nurses are in here. Give her something to calm her down."

Once Sasha and Amelia moved away from her, she kept her head hidden in Oliver's chest who was sitting on the bed with her while the nurse put medicine into her iv to calm her down. After the medicine kicked in for her, Oliver and a nurse gently lowered her on the bed before she passed out when everything got dark. When she woke up the next day, her mother sat in the seat next to the bed as her mum slept on the couch before a doctor walked into her room. As soon as the doctor walked into the room, she grabbed onto her mother's hand as her mother and her mum jolted awake at the same time before her mother grabbed onto her hand when she asked the doctor with desperation laced in her voice, "Is my daughter going to be okay, doctor? Is there going to be any permanent damage?"

Once her mum grabbed onto her other hand, the doctor pulled out a folder when he told them with an unreadable expression on his face, "Your daughter is going to be okay, Ms. Foster. She is in the process of detoxing from heroin and cocaine. She had too much in her system when she came into the hospital that we couldn't determine what she overdosed on until we found out through trial and error. Her heart stopped twice in the ambulance before we had to stabilize her in the intensive care unit. It's a miracle that you're alive, Isabella. You're lucky your cousin called an ambulance when he did, or you would have died at home. Are you looking into rehab after this, mom?"

Her mother and her mum tightened their grip onto her hands as her mother told him with a serious look on her face, "We are going to rehab after this. Aren't we, baby girl?"

She nodded her head at her mother before the doctor excused himself out of the room with her parents looking at her like they wanted to say something to her, but they didn't know what to say to her. As she held onto her parent's hands, she looked at them as she blinked back tears that were falling down her face when she asked them, "Did Oliver save my life again? I'm never going to hear the end of this one. He's never going to let me die, is he?"

Her mother chuckled at her daughter when she responded to her with a smirk on her face, "There's our daughter, Abby. The sarcastic little shit is back again. You better be nice to Oliver every moment after this or else I'm going to make you appreciate him. We decided that we are going to make you live with Oliver when you get out of rehab as your punishment. If being around Oliver is what keeps you alive, then you are going to live with him forever. He's a good influence on you." As she pressed her face in her hands in embarrassment, her parents pulled her into a tight hug where she hid her face into her mother's chest until the nurses gave her medicine through her ivs. She tried not to think about her lover Daxton and how she killed him. She wouldn't think about him if could help it.

Chapter Seventeen
(Winter 1963 – New York, New York)

She spent over a week in the hospital detoxing from drugs. When she was in the hospital, her parents and her cousins visited her every day during visiting hours. No one mentioned Daxton to her since she had a panic attack every time that someone said his name. She heard from eavesdropping on her parent's conversation with Uncle Stan and Thomas when they thought that she was sleeping that Daxton's family was in Los Angeles to bring him home. Those words made her cry because she knew what they meant by that. Her family was worried that Daxton's family was going to show up at the hospital. She heard from listening to a conversation with Oliver and Sasha while she was pretending to sleep that Anastasia wasn't letting Damien come to the hospital. She stopped pretending to be asleep when she told them that he would be in the right to yell at her because it was her fault that Daxton was dead. She was bitter with Oliver for saving her life even though she knew that things would be a million times worse if they were planning two funerals instead of one funeral. She stopped herself from pointing this out to them. She realized that they had that conversation with each other when she was unconscious. When the doctor told her that she was ready to leave the hospital, she told her parents that she didn't want to leave the hospital since she didn't know what would happen to her once she was back in the real world. On the morning of her being discharged from hospital, she didn't sleep no matter what medicine that they gave her through her iv to calm her down. As soon as her parents walked in her hospital room with a wheelchair, she stared at them without saying anything to them. She refused to get out of the bed, so they had to carry her over to the wheelchair where she closed her eyes before she ignored them while they pushed her out of the hospital. Since her parents thought that being at her house would upset her, they went over to Uncle Stan and Thomas's house where she slept in one of the guest bedrooms with her parents sleeping with her since she wasn't ready to sleep alone. She had to wait over two weeks until she could go to a medical treatment center since they didn't have any space for her. After three days of her refusing to leave the guest bedroom, her parents laid in bed with her all day as she stared up at the ceiling without saying anything to them. She hadn't said a word to anyone since she left the hospital. She didn't have anything that she wanted to say to them. She hasn't eaten anything since she was in the hospital. That was the part that made her parents the most scared since she lost a lot of weight in the last year from not eating when she was actively addicted to drugs. After five days of her refusing to get out of her bedroom, Uncle Stan came into the room with a bowl of soup that they knew that she wasn't going to eat before he pulled her into his arms where she laid her head in his chest for the rest of the day.

After six days of her refusing to leave her bedroom, she woke up to Uncle Stan and her mother having a hushed conversation on the balcony about Daxton's funeral that was in a few days. She surprised them where she appeared on the balcony when she told them that she wanted to go to Daxton's funeral where her mother nodded her head at her before she pulled her into the house where she spent the rest of the day in her arms. Her mum walked into the bedroom the next morning with a black dress and a jacket from her house when she told her that they were getting ready to get on a plane to New York in two hours before she left her alone in her bedroom. She got on the plane with her parents, Oliver, Sasha, and Amelia. Juliet was staying home with her one-year-old niece Posey and Uncle Stan and Thomas were staying home to clean up her house for her while they were away in New York. It was that afternoon when their plane landed in New York where Uncle Sam met them at the airport. She tried to ignore him before he pulled her into an affectionate hug. She hid her face into his chest as she blinked back tears that fell down her face when he told her that he loved her and that he was glad that she was alive before he let go of her. After she wiped away the tears that were on her face, she grabbed onto her mother's hand before she went to the car to go to her parent's house. On the first night that she was at her parent's house, she couldn't stop thinking about Daxton. She would've cried herself to sleep if she had any tears left to cry in her body. She thought about Daxton every moment since she woke up in the hospital. She never felt someone's absence as much as she felt his absence. It felt worse that she was here without him. It wasn't fair that she was alive, and he was dead. She thought about killing herself a few times before she gave up from trying to do it since she didn't have any energy to do anything. It was the next morning that she slept on her comfort spot on the roof that she didn't remember going to until it came back to her that she tried to jump off of the roof of her parent's house. She ignored the bruises on her arms and legs from throwing herself off of the roof. Her parents were all over her when she walked into the house where she let them clean her up before they determined that she didn't have any broken bones from her fall. She shocked her parents in the best way when she ate breakfast with them because she was hungry for the first time in weeks. As she got dressed in her bedroom for the funeral, she couldn't stand to look at herself in the mirror before she threw a blanket over it. On the drive over to the church, she watched the other cars moving around them as her parents' held hands in the front of the car before she thought about throwing herself in the middle of traffic to kill herself. Before she got close to doing it, her mum pulled the car into the parking lot of the church where she got out of the car with her parents holding onto her hands before they walked into the church together. As soon as she walked into the church, her body froze in the door frame when she saw the closed coffin in the front of the room with pictures of Daxton all over the room. She didn't move until her parents gently guided her over to one of the pews where she was forced to take a seat in front of the church with the rest of her family. When she took a seat in a pew in between her parents, she looked back to the pew behind her to see that Oliver was smiling at her with his arms around Sasha and Amelia who smiled at her. Uncle Sam, Aunt Valeria,

Ivan, Nina, and her fiancé Joseph Sullivan sat in the pew with them holding onto each other's hands. As soon as she looked around the room looking for Anastasia, she saw that Anastasia was in the front of the room with Daxton's family as she shook everyone's hands coming into the church.

Her face turned white when she caught Damien's eyes who was standing next to Anastasia and his parents before she looked down at the floor instead of matching his eye contact. She didn't miss the way that he looked at her with hatred in his eyes that made her want to crawl out of her skin. Her mother wiped away the tears that fell down her face. Anastasia and Damien took a seat in the pew in front of them with his parents sitting next to them before the priest began the funeral with a prayer that she knew that Daxton would've despised more than anything in the world. Once Daxton's parents said their kind words about him, Damien let go of Anastasia's hand as he made his way in front of the room before he said his last words to his brother without looking away from her. She looked down at the floor the entire time that he talked to the room after he made eye contact with her. After Damien took a seat in the pew in front of her, the priest asked if there was anyone else that wanted to say a few words before she wordlessly got up out of her seat to go to the front of the room with her family letting out shocked gasps from what was happening. As she stood up in front of the microphone, she wiped away tears that fell down her face as she cleared her throat when she confessed to the room with her unable to look away from Daxton's closed coffin, "I wasn't planning on saying anything, but I would never forgive myself if I didn't get to say goodbye to him. I'm sorry, Daxton. I'm so sorry that this happened to you. I will spend the rest of my life trying to make it up to you. I let you down, Daxton. I let everyone here down. I let myself down. I have a lot of regrets in my life, but this is one of my biggest regrets. I wish that we never met each other at the bar. If we never met in the bar, then you would still be alive, and we wouldn't be in this mess. I wanted to spend the rest of my life with you. I can't do that anymore. We did that, Daxton. We did this to ourselves. It's my fault what happened to him. I realize that Damien. I knew that the moment that I woke up in the hospital. I can't stop thinking about him. I can't stop thinking about where everything went wrong with us. I can't figure that out for the life of me. Maybe that moment doesn't exist. My dad promised something to my mother and I after he killed himself. He told us that we would always have stars. Even though this lifetime wasn't meant for us, there was a world where we would be together. I'm so sorry, Daxton. I love you so much. We'll always have the stars."

Once she walked back to the pews, her mother pulled her into a desperate hug where she hid her head into her chest with tears falling down her face before her mum wrapped her arms around them. Her parents guided her outside to the cemetery where Daxton got buried where she leaned her head on her mother's shoulder before they lowered his coffin into the ground. Once the priest invited everyone back into the church for some refreshments, she told her parents that she wanted to sit at Daxton's grave on the ground. After a while of her sitting alone at Daxton's grave, Damien took a seat on the ground next to her with his eyes sore from crying all morning like her eyes were before he looked over at her when he told her with a frown on his face, "Your speech was beautiful, Isabella. He would've loved it."

She looked up at him as she blinked back tears that fell down her face when she told him with a frown on her face, "Thanks, Damien. I appreciate hearing that from you. I know that you're angry with me. You have every right to be angry at me. I'm angry at myself too. It's my fault that he is dead."

As soon as he wrapped his arms around her, Damien shook his head at her when he told her with a look of compassion on his face, "I'm not mad at you, Isabella. I was never mad at you. I'm pissed off at the world. My brother was born an addict. I've spent most of my life waiting for this moment. I had nightmares about it when I was a child since the first time that he overdosed when I was nine years old. No one in this world would have stopped him from doing drugs. I know that you know that more than anyone in the world. I love my brother, but he was never going to change for anyone. Not for me. Not for himself. Not even for you. It's been hard watching him do this to himself for all these years. It's almost like a weight has been lifted off of my shoulders since he died. It sounds mean to say that, but you know what I mean."

After she leaned her head on his shoulder, she closed her eyes when she responded to him with a smile on her face, "I get it, Damien. I know what you mean by that. Do you think that there is hope for me? Am I doomed to become him?"

Damien instantly shook his head at her when he told her, "No, there's hope for you, Isabella. There has to be some hope left in this world or else I'm going to lose my mind. You want to do better. He never wanted that. I can see it inside of you. That push to be a better person. Are you going to rehab when you go to California?"

She nodded her head at her when she said to him with a genuine smile on her face, "Yeah, I'm going to rehab a few days after I get home. There was a waitlist, so I have someone with me at all times to make sure that I don't do drugs."

Damien tightened his grip on her arms when he told her with a look of concern on his face, "Good. You need to go. I'm happy that you survived it. We thought that you weren't going to make it. Reach out to me when you're in the city and we can talk about him. Don't be a stranger. We're family." She nodded her head at him as she promised him that she would call him when she was in the city. After she walked into the church, her parents took them to the house before they went back to California. As soon as their plane landed in Los Angeles, Uncle Stan picked them up at the airport where she packed her bags that she was going to take to rehab before her parents drove her to the medical treatment center. She spent the next two months getting back to herself again for the first time in almost over a year.

CHAPTER EIGHTEEN
(SPRING 1963 – NEW YORK, NEW YORK)

She went to sessions with a new therapist named Dr. Taylor who was a younger man with a full head of hair that had the most normal office that she saw from her previous therapists. She attended group therapy where she talked about her father and Daxton at the same time. Her parents visited her once a week where they brought gifts with them every time that they visited her in forms of forbidden food that they didn't serve at the hospital. She shared a room with a girl around her age that had the same problems that she did with drugs where they bonded with each other when they talked about it late into the night. For the first time in a long time, she felt like she did when she was a small child. Like she was that naive girl dancing with Sasha in her parent's living room in tutus. After she spent two months in rehab, she was discharged into the real world where she was more prepared to deal with it. Her parents drove her to her house for the first time since Daxton died. When she walked into her house, it looked different from the last time that she was there. Her parents had every room renovated so much that she didn't recognize it anymore. Her cousins, Uncle Stan, and Thomas were there to greet her in the living room with wide smiles on their faces. Oliver pulled her into a tight hug where she hid her face into his chest with tears falling down their faces until her one-year-old niece Posey ran into her legs. Once she let go of Oliver, she placed Posey on her hip before Juliet pulled her into a tight hug with Posey trying to get down on the floor. After Juliet took Posey out of her arms, she pulled Sasha and Amelia into a tight hug where she didn't let go of them until Amelia kissed her on the cheek that made her hide her face into her hands in embarrassment. She didn't see Chloe at the house, but a quick glance from Sasha showed her that this wasn't the time or place to ask her about it. She was pulled into a tight hug by Uncle Stan where she hid her head into his chest as he kissed her on the top of her head when he told her that he loved her. Thomas pulled her into a tight hug as soon as Uncle Stan let go of her where he did the same thing until Sasha and Amelia dragged her around the house to show her the renovations that were done to the house when she wasn't there. After they ate a delicious meal together, Uncle Stan and Thomas went to their house before Oliver and Juliet, who had Posey asleep in her arms, went to their house. Once her parents went into the suite that she used to sleep in with Daxton, she slept in the other suite with Amelia and Sasha. Her parents stayed with them for over a month before they went back to New York to take care of their book publishing company. She would see them in New York for Nina and Joseph's wedding in a few months. She got back to work since she couldn't stand not being busy.

She started working on her new movie called *Ocean's Eyes* where she played the leading love interest. Amelia worked as a hair and makeup artist on the movie since they knew the same people that got them on the movie. She enjoyed working with Amelia. She forgot how much fun they had together. It was around this time that they had a movie night together in the living room where Sasha told them that she wasn't with Chloe anymore. Sasha broke up with Chloe when she was in the hospital after her overdose. She wanted to ask her why they broke up, but she wrapped her arms around Sasha instead of prying into things that she didn't need to know about. While they were working on *Ocean's Eyes*, Sasha went on trips to Italy, France, and Germany for fashion shows as well as she was in a fashion show in New York. When she wasn't filming *Ocean's Eyes* in the studio, she was going to NA meetings twice a week and she was going to Dr. Taylor's office once a week to talk to him. Even though she stopped going to therapy when she met Daxton, she found herself going back to it after she got out of rehab since she wanted to get better this time. It was hard for her to talk about Daxton to Dr. Taylor without her falling apart. She felt guilty about what happened to him. Even though Damien didn't think that it was her fault, she thought that it was her fault. That was enough for her to believe that it was the truth. She told Dr. Taylor everything that happened with Daxton. She told him about their love story from the beautiful beginning to the tragic ending that broke her heart. She fell in love with Daxton like her mother fell in love with her father. Daxton's death opened up new emotions about her father's death. When she fell in love with Daxton, it was like when her mother fell in love with her father. When she lost Daxton, it was like when her mother lost her father. It was the same tragic story being told all over again. It was the love story of her grandparents Richard and Bertha. It was the love story of her parents Ella and Will. It was the love story of Isabella and Daxton. It was going to be the love story of her children someday. They were stuck living in this cycle where they repeated the same mistakes over and over again regardless of the consequences. The ending was the same no matter what they did to stop it from happening to them. When she told him that she's lived this life, he told her that it was the life that her mother and her grandmother experienced before she was born. He asked her why she fell in love with Daxton where she couldn't give an answer to the question before she told him a bold statement that she never thought would come out of her mouth. She told him that she fell in love with Daxton because he reminded her of her father. A father that she never knew. She had no idea how she knew that Daxton was like him. She never needed to know her father to see him in other people around her. He was always there inside of her. He was in every place that she went in her life. He was in every person that she met in her life. He was every star in the sky. She realized that she didn't need drugs to be with him. She didn't need Daxton to feel like she was with him. He was with her for every step of the way. He was with her even before she was born. They were together in the stars before they were here. They would be together in the stars after they died. They would always be together for the rest of time. As he waited in the sky for her, he watched over her to make sure that she was safe from harm that would come to her. He was with her when she was born, and he would be with her when she died. He was with her when she overdosed at the club. He was with her when she overdosed at home. He would be with her for the rest of time. After she had this startling realization in therapy, she asked Oliver how he knew that she was dying that night of her overdose at the house where she thought that she was completely alone in the world. Oliver told her that he knew that something bad was happening to her because her father told him to save her from herself. Even though she knew that Oliver was the person that saved her in life, her father was the person that saved her in death. For the first time in her life, she didn't feel alone. The void in her heart was never missing. He was there. She lost him and all she needed to do was to find him.

It was the week that she got together with her cousins at Oliver's house. Juliet made a birthday cake for her since they missed her birthday where her family gave her presents before they slept on the couch in a childish sleepover. For the week that she was in Los Angeles, she finished filming for *Ocean's Eyes* for their break before she packed her bags for their trip to New York. On the morning of their flight to New York, Sasha made them crepes to eat in the car before Uncle Stan and Thomas picked them up to take them to the airport. After they were dropped off at the airport, they met up with Oliver, Juliet, and Posey before she slept with her head on Sasha's shoulder for the flight. When their plane landed in New York later that day, her parents picked them up at the airport where they dropped off Uncle Stan and Thomas at the hotel before she ate dinner at her parent's house. Sasha and Amelia went home with Uncle Sam, Valeria, Ivan, and Nina. Damien and Anastasia, who was pregnant, went back to their apartment for the rest of the night. While Oliver and Juliet slept in the guest bedroom, Posey slept in her childhood bedroom that her parents turned into an office in the last year before she slept in her parents' bedroom with them. She didn't mind sleeping in the same bed since she hadn't slept by herself since she got out of rehab, and she didn't want to start sleeping by herself. She was dragged out of the house by Juliet who insisted on them going shopping before they got their bridesmaids dresses altered with her cousins at the dress store. Oliver spent the day golfing with Uncle Sam, Joseph, Damien, and Ivan at the country club while her parents watched Posey during the day while she went shopping in Times Square with Juliet, Aunt Valeria, and Nina. They met up with Anastasia, Sasha, and Amelia to get their dresses altered for the wedding later that day. On the second day in

New York, Audrey and Teddy Oswald were the first group to fly into New York from England with her two-year-old niece Lena and her two-year-old nephew Leo in their arms. Audrey pulled her into a hug over her large stomach. This was what she wanted to tell Amelia about when she called the house. She felt like a complete idiot because it was supposed to be a happy memory. She was about to ask Audrey why she didn't tell her that she was pregnant. She remembered that she wouldn't have cared about it at that time. On the third day in New York, she met up with Damien at a cafe where they caught up with each other for the first time since Daxton's funeral. After they hugged each other, he told her that she looked radiant when she told him with a smile on her face that she hadn't felt this good in a long time. They talked to each other over coffees and baked pastries. She talked to him about her time in rehab, her second chance with therapy, and filming her new movie. He talked to her about the real estate market, his marriage to her cousin, and how they were preparing for parenthood together. They talked about Daxton for a little bit before he left to meet up with a client about a condo that they wanted to buy before she went back to her parent's house for the rest of the day. Her family from England flew into New York for the wedding before she went to the airport with her parents to pick them up. Uncle James, Aunt Sylvia, her fifteen-year-old cousin Jamie, her thirteen-year-old cousin George, her seventeen-year-old cousin Sean, and Sean's girlfriend Polly Turner came on the first plane. Uncle Nathan, Aunt Priscilla, her sixteen-year-old cousin Poppy, her fourteen-year-old cousin Tommy, and her twelve-year-old cousin Alfie came on the second plane. They stayed at the hotel while Audrey and Teddy stayed at Uncle Sam's house.

Nina and Joseph chose to get married in the countryside in Upstate New York. The wedding venue had plenty of room for them to stay at a hotel for a few days since they would be in the middle of nowhere. Nina wanted Anastasia to be her maid of honor since they were best friends with her bridesmaids being Isabella, Sasha, Amelia, and Juliet. Joseph wanted Damien to be his best man with his groomsmen being Oliver, Ivan, Sean, and Teddy. On the morning of the dress rehearsal, she packed her bags before she got into one of the many cars that they were taking to the countryside where she got into a car with her parents, Sasha, Amelia, Oliver, Juliet, and Posey. After they arrived at the venue that afternoon, she moved her stuff into her hotel room that she was sharing with Sasha and Amelia before they prepared for the dress rehearsal with dinner following after it. On the night before the wedding, she went outside to stargaze with Oliver, Amelia, and Sasha. Nina, Ivan, and Jamie ended up joining them later in the night when they heard them laughing from outside their bedroom windows. As she laid down in the grass next to Nina, she looked over at Oliver, Amelia, and Sasha who were running around and chasing each other in the field before Ivan and Jamie laid down next to them in a hushed conversation with each other. Nina whispered into her ear that Ivan and Jamie became best friends last year at Anastasia's wedding and they talked to each other on the phone every night before bed. She told Ivan and Jamie to follow her into the barn where she wanted to show them something before she led them to the barn where they passed lightning bugs that she passed to them back and forth until they flew away from them. She fell asleep in Jamie and Ivan's hotel room with her sleeping on one of the beds with Jamie and Nina sleeping on the other bed with Ivan. On the morning of the wedding, she woke up to Ivan and Jamie jumping around her on the bed where she wrestled with them. Nina dragged her into Aunt Valeria's hotel room to get their hair done and their makeup done by Amelia before she shared stories from the studio. She went with Sasha and Ivan to look at Nina and Joseph seeing each other for the first time before the wedding with not a dry eye in the group. Once it was time for them to walk down the aisle, she grabbed onto Ivan's arm before she joined her cousins in front of the room before Nina walked down the aisle with her parent's arms around her. Sasha wrapped her arms around her when they cried during Nina and Joseph's vows to each other before it was time for the wedding reception. After they ate a delicious meal, she danced for most of the night with Amelia and Sasha's arms around her. Sasha went to the bathroom to calm down Ivan who was taking it hard that his last sister was leaving him. Nina, Sasha, and Jamie could handle it without her. She went outside to get away from the party. Oliver sat on one of the lawn chairs by the barn before she took a seat next to him.

Oliver looked up at her when he asked her with a frown on his face, "Is Ivan going to be okay? He looked really upset about Nina getting married."

She nodded her head at him when she responded to him with a reassuring smile on her face, "Yeah, he'll be okay. His sisters and his best friend are with him. He's going to miss her. It's so sweet."

As soon as she leaned back on the lawn chair, she closed her eyes with the sound of crickets in the background when Oliver asked with concern laced in his voice, "How are you doing, Isabella? I haven't asked you that question in a long time."

She looked up at him when she responded to him with a smirk on her face, "It's been two weeks since you last asked me that question, but I'll tell you again. I'm doing great, Oliver. Thanks for asking me. How are you doing? Can I ask you that question?"

After Oliver rolled his eyes in fake annoyance towards her, he grabbed onto her hands when he responded to her with a smile on his face, "I'm good, Isabella. I'm happy that you're happy. You wouldn't have answered that question honestly this time last year. You would've lied to my face. That's why I'm asking you to see if you're lying to me or not."

She told him with a wide grin on her face, "I would've lied to your face. I wouldn't trust anything I tell you. What's the verdict, Oliver? Am I lying to you?"

Oliver shook his head at her when he told her with a serious look on his face, "You're being honest. I'm testing you. I love you, Isabella. I can't trust you, but I want to trust you. I need more time."

Once she tightened her grip on his hands, she told him with a frown on her face, "I get it. Take all the time that you need, Oliver. I'll be here when you're ready. I broke your trust, and I have to earn it back. Dr. Taylor told me that I need to learn how to trust myself before anyone can trust me."

Oliver let go of her hands when he responded to her with a smile on his face, "I like Dr. Taylor. He gives you good advice. You should listen to him. He sounds like he knows what he's talking about. I'm not trying to be corny here, but I'm happy for you. You've come so far since you went to rehab."

As she hid her face in her hands, Oliver pulled her into a side hug when she responded to him with her face red from embarrassment,

"You're so corny. I love you. Are you this corny with Juliet?"

Oliver gently pushed her away in fake anger before they leaned back on the lawn chairs with smiles on their faces. As soon as she looked up at him, she laughed with her face hidden into her hands before Oliver did the same thing. They didn't stop laughing until Oliver gently nudged her side when he told her with a smirk on his face, "You think that you're funny, don't you? I missed you, Isabella. Things weren't the same when you were gone. You aren't allowed to leave me. Do you know that?"

She told him with a mischievous look on her face, "Is this your way of telling me that I'm not allowed to die? I already know this, Oliver. You wouldn't let me die no matter what I do. What if I move to another country? Are you going to follow me there?"

Oliver responded to her with a serious look on his face, "I'd follow you wherever you go, Isabella. You won't die if I can do anything about it."

As Oliver pulled her into a tight hug, she hid her head in his chest with tears falling down her face before he tightened his grip on them. She wiped away the tears from her face when she told him, "Oliver. Should we go back inside? I think that we're missing the party or something." After he kissed on the top of her head, she grabbed onto his hand as they smiled at each other before she gently pulled him into the barn. She felt like she was on top of the universe.

Chapter Nineteen
(Summer 1963 – Los Angeles, California)

While Nina and Joseph were on their honeymoon in Spain, she went over to their apartment with Damien, Anastasia who was ready to give birth, Sasha, and Ivan to move their stuff in for them. Their apartment was in the same building that Damien and Anastasia lived in before they got married to each other. In the last year, Damien bought the apartment building for himself. On top of being a real estate agent, Damien was a landlord in New York. It was a more profitable business than the real estate market was. Damien told Nina and Joseph that they could live in the apartment building for free since Joseph was in medical school right now. Her family from England went home except for Audrey, Teddy, and their two children to spend extra time with Amelia and Oliver while they were in New York. It was emotional for Ivan and Jamie to say goodbye to each other since they were attached at the hip for the last week. On the night before the wedding, she sat in the barn with Nina, Ivan, and Jamie where they talked about what the boys wanted to do when they graduated from school next year. Ivan and Jamie told them that they wanted to move out of the country after they were done with school where she encouraged them to go anywhere that they wanted to go in the world. When Nina and Joseph returned to New York from their honeymoon, they were surprised to see that they had their stuff in the new apartment while they were out of the country. In the same week that they got back from their honeymoon, Anastasia went into labor at the hair salon where Aunt Valeria closed the business before she took her to the hospital where Damien and Nina were already waiting for them. Isabella and Sasha came to the hospital with Ivan, Uncle Sam, and her parents later in the day closer to when the baby was going to be born. Amelia, Oliver, Juliet, and Posey were on a week-long trip to Cape Cod with Audrey, Teddy, Lena, and Leo as a vacation before they would have to go to England again. After Uncle Sam drove them to the hospital, they heard that Anastasia had the baby an hour prior to them getting there. She waited in the waiting room with her parents as Uncle Sam, Sasha, and Ivan went into the hospital room with Anastasia, Damien, Nina, and Aunt Valeria. When it was their turn to come into the room, she held her newborn niece Alina Kotov where she pulled Anastasia and Damien into tight hugs before she gave Alina to her mother. After they left the hospital, she packed her bags to go back to California once Oliver and Amelia got back from Cape Cod with Audrey and Teddy. On the morning of Amelia and Oliver getting to New York, they met Alina for the first time with Posey being confused about her cousin because she was so small before she got a plane to Los Angeles with Oliver, Amelia, Sasha, Juliet, and Posey. Audrey, Teddy, and their two children got on a plane back to England before Anastasia and Damien went home with their daughter. Uncle Stan and Thomas went back to Los Angeles the day after the wedding.

When their plane landed in Los Angeles, Uncle Stan picked them up from the airport where he dropped Oliver's family at their house after he dropped the girls off at their house. She went back to filming *Ocean's Eyes* at the studio with Amelia in the hair and makeup trailer before Sasha traveled all around the world for her modeling photo shoots. There were rare occurrences that she was alone in the house at night if Sasha was traveling for work or Amelia was out with friends from work at bars. She would go over to Oliver's house for the night, or she would go over to Uncle Stan's house for the night. Despite her being out of rehab for months, she didn't like being in the house alone because she couldn't shake Daxton's absence. She told Dr. Taylor that she didn't like being alone in her house where he asked her what she thought would happen if she was alone at her house at night. She couldn't give him an answer in that session, but she came up with an answer by the next session when she told him that she couldn't be alone in the house because it reminded her of everything that she lost. They knew that she was talking about her father and Daxton, so it didn't need to be clarified to him who she was referring to. She told him that she didn't deserve to be alive. It was a feeling hidden so deep inside of her mind that she never told anyone these thoughts before. She discovered where the seed for her addiction came from. She used drugs to fill a void. Instead of her filling a void, she suppressed the void with things that she knew wouldn't make her deal with it. She didn't want to deal with any of it. She didn't want to deal with her feelings that she held against her father that would never be resolved. She didn't want to deal with the emptiness that came with being alive. She didn't want to deal with the reality that she was alone in the world. She didn't want to admit that she was missing pieces of herself. She was terrified of the world. She was scared that something bad was going to happen to her. The only time in her life when she wasn't scared was when she was doing drugs. She craved that feeling after she found it that first time that she got high. That's what made her addicted to drugs. That feeling of invincibility that she could do anything. That she could become anyone that she needed to be. She craved that feeling more than any other feeling. She could do anything or become anyone without any other consequences. She didn't know what to do without that feeling of invincibility. She felt like a shell of herself without it. She couldn't be who people expected her to be. She couldn't be who she wanted herself to be. That made her relationship with Daxton so addicting. He made her feel like she was invincible when she was with him. He was the only thing besides drugs that made her feel that way about herself. She saw him the same way that she saw drugs. She never thought that could live without him just like she said that she could never live without drugs. Dr. Taylor told her that she was living without them right now. She didn't realize that until he told her that. She told him that she didn't know how she was doing it. She didn't want to imagine a life without them. This led to a much larger conversation that they had about the way that she saw herself compared to the way that her family saw her. He challenged her to look at herself the way that her parents saw her, so that she could compare it to the way that she saw herself.

On a night when Sasha was out of the country, Amelia went out to the bar with her friends, so she was alone in the house for the first time. Oliver asked her if she wanted to spend the night at his house before she declined his offer since she wanted to take up Dr. Taylor on his challenge that he wanted her to do. She decided that she wasn't going to mope all night in the suite where she made herself get out of bed before she went swimming in the pool. After she got out of the pool, she grabbed a clean towel from the towel holder where she dried her body with it before she went back into the suite to change into a t-shirt and shorts. She grabbed a blanket off of the bed where she went outside by the pool before she took a seat on a pool chair with the blanket over her legs. She looked up at the sky when she said to herself with a smile on her face, "Hello, dad. I know that I haven't talked to you in a while, but things got dark for a long time. I almost died, dad. I'm sure that you knew about that since you stopped it from happening. I was bitter about that for a while, but I know that you were keeping me safe as you always do. Thank you for watching over me. I wish that someone looked after you the same way that you watch over me. I'm trying to be a better person, dad. I really am. I didn't like the person that I was becoming when I was using drugs. She wasn't me. She might have been invincible, but she was the most miserable person in the world. She hated herself more than anyone else. I'm trying not to hate myself anymore. I understand what we were talking about the last time that I talked to you. We were talking about what it means to be dead. I told you that I wanted to be in the cosmos with you since I was already half-way there with you. I meant that when I said that. I'll always want that for us. If you could've responded to me, you would've told me that we're already in the cosmos together. I didn't need to do anything to bring myself to you since we were already there together."

She responded to herself with tears falling down her face, "That's the closest thing that I'm going to get from a response from you. I'm going to keep talking since you're incapable of interrupting me. Did you meet Daxton? I'm sure that you guys are going to get along well with each other since you guys love me so much. This wasn't the way that I saw my life going for me. I'm sure that you never imagined your life going this way either. We were blindsided by life in the worst possible way. I didn't think that I'd make it to twenty years old. I thought that I was going to die when I was thirteen years old. Do you remember when I tried to kill myself? I don't think that anyone else found out about that. That was the night that I read your suicide note for the first time. I was having a horrible day because mom found out that I was self-harming, and I was pissed off at her for taking my razor from me. She tried to tell me that she did that to herself when she was my age, but I didn't want to hear it. I locked myself in my bedroom that night and I went to my hidden spot on the roof to be with you. I tried to tell you about it, but I couldn't stop crying. I took a bottle of pills that I found in the bathroom. I don't know what pills that I took, but I was upset that I woke up puking the next morning for the rest of the day. Mom thought that I had the flu, so I went along with it. They never realized what happened that night. I know that mom thinks that my problems with drugs are new, but we know the truth. Don't we, dad? You'll know the truth no matter what. Thanks for listening to me. You're my favorite person in the world." As she blinked back tears that fell from her face, she wrapped the blanket around her arms as she walked into the suite where Amelia slept on bed before she climbed into the other side of the bed. She wrapped her arms around Amelia where she moved closer to her before she fell asleep for the rest of the night.

CHAPTER TWENTY
(FALL 1963 – HONOLULU, HAWAII)

After she spent a year filming *Ocean's Eyes* in the studio, she left on a press tour with the cast from the movie for five weeks. When they got back to Los Angeles, Sasha met them at the airport since she got back from a work trip in Italy where they went to the house before they had a sleepover together in the living room. She wanted to go on vacation in the time that she was off from working since she hadn't taken any new jobs yet. They decided that they wanted to go on vacation in Europe before she called to ask her cousins in England if they wanted to go on a vacation with them and where they wanted to go. Her cousin Poppy was the only person that was free to go on vacation with them since her other cousins were in school, at work, or they were about to have babies like Audrey was going to. Nina decided to tag along with them since Joseph was in residency for medical school. Anastasia and Damien were in the middle of new parenthood, so they didn't come with them. They went to Greece since none of them had been there before. As she packed for Greece with Amelia helping her pick outfits, Audrey called the house to tell them that she had their nephew Mason Oswald a few days ago when she asked them to visit them in York before they went to Greece on vacation. Once they changed their plans so that they could meet Audrey's baby, Sasha dropped off Isabella and Amelia at the airport where she slept with her head resting on Amelia's shoulder the entire flight before their plane landed in New York. Nina met them at the airport in New York where she spent the night at her parent's house before they got on a plane to London the next morning. She couldn't sleep for the entire flight. When their plane landed in London, her cousin Sean and his girlfriend Polly Turner picked them up from the airport before Sean drove them to York where they met their nephew Mason for the first time. After they spent a few days in York catching up with her family, she got on a plane to Athens with Poppy, Amelia, and Nina. When their plane landed in Athens, Amelia drove their rental car to the hotel where they were staying for a few days before they went to other cities in the country. They got one hotel room since there was plenty of room for them. They spent the first full day in Athens looking at the historical sites. After they spent a few days in Athens going to the nicest restaurants and walking around like tourists, they drove to Mykonos where they spent the next few days at a new hotel that was on the beach. Sasha joined them in Mykonos from Italy where she spent the rest of the vacation with them. For the next month, they went from Meteora to Delphi to Ios to Corfu to Thessaloniki to Molyvos to Kefallinia to Crete to Halkidiki to Athens. By the end of the trip, she didn't want to go back to the states. She wanted to stay in Greece forever. She had to go back home since there was a new movie that she agreed to work on in Hawaii before she left for Greece on her trip. On their flight from Athens to London, she slept for the entire time except for when she was woken up every time that Sasha needed to go to the bathroom on the plane.

On their flight from London to New York, she didn't want to repeat what happened on the last flight, so she sat by the window and not at the end of the row to sleep in peace. When their plane landed in New York, Joseph picked them up from the airport where she spent the night at her parent's house before they got on their flight to California. She made the mistake of taking the end seat with them having to move every time Sasha went to the bedroom. Once their plane landed in Los Angeles, Oliver picked them up at the airport where they went to her house for dinner before she fell asleep in the suite with Sasha and Amelia for the rest of the night. She was immediately thrown into the real world. She was home for a few days before she spent the next few months in Hawaii filming her new movie called *Ukulele Blues*. She was working with Amelia again. She was excited about exploring this new part of the world with one of her best friends. When she told them that they were going to Hawaii to film a new movie, Juliet told her that she wanted to come with them since she wasn't working until the new year. She told them that they were staying at a house that the studio paid for when Juliet told them that her sister had a house in Hawaii that they could stay at for free. This was news for Oliver since he didn't know that Juliet's older sister Maddie owned a house in Hawaii. She called the studio to tell them that they found a place to stay on the main island and that they would only be at the house for only filming purposes. On the morning of their flight to the main island of Hawaii, Oliver dropped off Isabella, Amelia, Juliet, and Posey at the airport where they got on the long flight to Hawaii. As soon as their plane landed on the main island, Juliet's older sister Maddie picked them up at the airport where they went to her house on the beach before she chose a guest bedroom to share with Amelia before Juliet and Posey went into the other guest bedroom. After they spent the first day at the beach, they ate at the restaurant that Maddie owned on the island before they went to sleep for the rest of the night. They filmed the movie five days a week where they got two days off to enjoy themselves. On a weekend when they weren't filming, Oliver and Sasha visited them at Maddie's beach house where they spent most of the day on the beach. As she laid down in a beach chair with Sasha and Amelia sitting in between her, Oliver and Juliet held onto Posey's hands before she let out a scream every time that a wave crashed on them. She tried to read a book that she bought at the airport, but it was too bright outside for her to read any of the words on the page before she fell asleep on the beach chair with a pair of sunglasses covering her eyes. After she slept for a few hours, she was woken up by Posey who was sitting on top of her as she poked Isabella's face until she opened her eyes where Oliver stood behind his daughter with his hands grabbing onto her back. Oliver placed his daughter on his hip when he told her that Maddie had dinner ready in the house where she grabbed her towel and her book off of the chair before she followed Oliver into the house. After they ate a delicious dinner, they grabbed blankets that were hanging off the deck before they went down to the beach to watch the sunset over a campfire.

As she took a seat on one of the blankets in between Sasha and

Amelia, Juliet sat on the other blanket next to Maddie with Posey sitting in her lap as Oliver lit the campfire before he took a seat next to them. They watched the campfire burn with the sun setting in the background as she leaned her head on Sasha's shoulder with Amelia holding onto her hands where Oliver and Juliet had their arms around each other with Posey chasing Maddie around the campfire. When the fire burned out on them, Maddie went into the house to grab more firewood before Oliver chased Posey around the beach with their laughter burning in her ears. Once Maddie returned back to their spot on the beach with firewood in her hands, she threw it onto the fire before she sat down next to Juliet with their arms around each other. As Sasha got up from their blanket with her hand on her shoulder, she asked them if they wanted to go on a walk with her where Amelia got up from their blanket before she shook her head at him when she told them that she didn't want to join them. After Sasha and Amelia left to go on a walk, Maddie went over to where Oliver chased Posey where they grabbed onto each of her hands before they went over to the ocean before Juliet took a seat on the blanket next to her. Once she looked over at Juliet, Juliet wrapped her arm around her as she leaned her head on her shoulder in comfortable silence with Posey screaming in the background. She asked Juliet in a soft voice, "Are you excited to go back to work in a few weeks? It's been two years since you worked last."

Juliet nodded her head at her when she responded to her with a smile on her face, "It has been two years. I can't believe that it's been that long since I've had Posey. It feels like a lifetime ago. Honestly I don't know how I feel about going back to work. Ask me in a few weeks what I think about it. I'm excited. It will be an adjustment for all of us, but I know that Posey will be okay during the day. Did Oliver tell you that we hired a nanny for her?"

She shook her head at her when she responded to Juliet, "No, he didn't mention that. I thought that she was going to go to daycare. What changed? I have a feeling Oliver changed his mind."

Juliet lightly hit her on the arm when she told her with a wide grin on her face, "How did you figure that out, Isabella? He's that predictable, isn't he? Oliver didn't feel comfortable leaving her at daycare even though she only would be going to our church. We had huge arguments about it, but I gave up since he wasn't going to move on from it. Don't get me started on the interviewing process. It was a complete nightmare, but we found the perfect nanny for her. She's an older woman with adult children of her own that Posey got along very well. It's more expensive than daycare would have been, but we only want what's best for her. How have you been?"

She laid down on the blanket with her legs buried in the sand where they stared up at the stars. She let out a shaky breath when she responded to Juliet with her blinking back tears that fell down her face, "I have this memory with my mom when I was a little girl. We were living in England. She used to take me stargazing in the yard of her childhood house with a blanket under us just like this. Even though I was too young to understand her, she told me about every star in the sky. I listened to her in complete awe. She showed me a star in the sky called Polaris. She told me that you can see it everywhere that you are in the world. I remember that I asked why she told me that at that young age. She told me that she wanted me to know that because Polaris represented us. Polaris was where me, mom, and dad were. She told me that no matter where I was in the world that mom and dad would always be with me. It didn't matter how much time passed by or how old I got to be. They would always be with me. In all the places that I've been in the world, I've always seen Polaris in the sky. I know that mom and dad are always with me. I don't know why I said that right now, but I was thinking about saying it all night. I didn't mean to make things emotional, Juliet. I have a habit of doing that."

Juliet shook her head at her when she responded to Isabella in a soft voice, "No, it's okay. That was beautiful. Your mother has a way with words that touches the soul. She has a way about it. When did your mother get into astronomy?"

She responded to Juliet in a firm voice, "Please don't tell her that, Juliet. Her ego is already big enough for the both of us combined. How did she get into it? Her dad was into the stars. He would take her out at night when she was a little girl. He would take her siblings camping and show them the stars. It was the only thing that she had in common with her dad. She talked about the stars with my dad, so it became their thing after her dad died. She doesn't talk about it with anyone, but I know that she got into astronomy more after my dad killed himself. She felt like she was with him when she was with the stars. It was his last promise to us. It was his only promise to me. I feel this sense of duty to keep it going for him. I know that my mom doesn't visit him. I don't blame her since he ruined her life, but she always loved him no matter what happened between them. I never wanted to visit him when I was younger. I thought that I hated him. I was angry at him. I've spent more time with him since I moved to California than when I lived in New York. I didn't feel like I needed to be with him since I had mom. He gets me in ways that mom doesn't get me."

Juliet asked her with a concerned look on her face, "You mean drugs? What do you think that he would understand that your mom wouldn't get?"

She turned on her side to face her when she confessed to Juliet with tears falling down her face, "My mom is incredible. I love her so much, but she's never going to get it like he did. Dad lived that same life before I was born. The secrets. Lying to everyone around you. The white lies that you tell yourself. The rationalizing that happens when you scare yourself. It's not anyone's business what I do. No one can tell me to stop this. I never want to not to feel this way. It's little things like that increasingly get worse over time that people don't see or know about you. Even though you feel horrible all of the time, you can convince yourself that it's worth it. It's not about that you feel like you are always dying. It's about the moments that you are dying that matter. It's really hard to describe such an indescribable feeling, but I know in my heart that it was one that dad knew and desired as much as I do. For only a moment, it means everything and absolutely nothing at once. It was something that I was searching for my entire life. Something I didn't want to lose when I found it. It's the only thing in my life that is mine. I'll spend the rest of my life wanting it. No matter where I am in the world or whoever I become. I'll want it for the rest of eternity. Mom wouldn't get that, Juliet. The only person that I've known that would get that is my dad."

She grabbed onto her hands when she said to Juliet in a desperate voice, "I'm sorry. I didn't mean to scare you, Juliet. It came out of my mouth before I could stop myself from saying it. That doesn't mean that I'm going to do drugs again. I'm looking for that feeling that I get when I'm high. I'm doing well right now. Alright? I was feeling sentimental about my old life. I didn't want to admit this to anyone, but I do miss them sometimes. I'm never not going to miss them. Just because I miss them doesn't mean anything else other than that. You can miss something and not want it."

As Juliet pulled her into a tight hug, she hid her head into her chest when Juliet responded to her with tears falling down their faces, "You're allowed to miss it, Isabella. I'm sorry that I freaked out about it. I don't want it to happen again. It's naive to think that it won't happen again because it will. Oliver tells me that all of the time. I need to stop being so naive about it. I love you. I don't want to lose you. Even though you aren't dead, it feels like you are since you become a completely different person that I don't recognize anymore. We can't be stuck in the past. We need to look up to the future. You are in it or else I'm making you be a part of it."

Once she pulled her head out of Juliet's chest, she sat up on the blanket when she told her with a smile on her face, "I love you too, Juliet. I know where Oliver gets his corniness from. He gets it from you. It makes sense. You're right about the future. When you look up at a star, you are looking into the past. I need to stop looking at stars, so that I can see the future. Did everyone go into the house? Did they leave us here alone with a dead fire?" After Juliet got herself off of the ground, she grabbed onto her hand to help her off of the ground where she shook the sand out of the blanket with the blanket wrapped over her shoulder before she followed Juliet into the house. As soon as they walked into the house, Juliet went upstairs to their bedroom where Oliver already put Posey to bed. Oliver pulled her into a sudden hug where she hid her face into his chest with tears falling down her face. Once Oliver let go of her with a kiss on the top of her head, she followed him upstairs where he went into his bedroom with Juliet and Posey before she went into her bedroom with Sasha and Amelia. When she walked into her bedroom, it was dark with Amelia and Sasha sleeping together in the bed where she got into the shower to get the sand off of her body where she changed into a nightgown before she climbed in between Sasha and Amelia. She slept for the rest of the ni ght.

CHAPTER TWENTY-ONE
(WINTER 1964 – LOS ANGELES, CALIFORNIA)

Oliver, Juliet, and Posey went back to their lives in California. Sasha stayed with them at Maddie's house while she finished filming *Ukulele Blues* in Hawaii. She finished filming *Ukulele Blues* a few weeks later. They packed up their bags to leave Hawaii with the cast for the press tour across the country. On the morning that they left Hawaii; she thanked Maddie for letting them stay with her before Maddie told her that they were welcome to visit her at any time that they were free. After Maddie dropped them off at the airport, she slept with her head leaning on Amelia's shoulder. When their plane landed in Los Angeles, Uncle Stan picked them up from the airport where he pulled them into tight hugs before he dropped them off at their house. After she walked into the house with Amelia and Sasha following behind her, her parents were there to welcome them back home where they pulled her into tight hugs before she took a seat on the couch as she opened up their Boxing Day presents from them. Once she opened up her presents from her parents, she gave her parents presents that she bought for them when they were in Hawaii where they pulled her into a tight hug before they ate dinner together in the kitchen that their personal chef made for them. Her parents left their house after a few days since Isabella and Amelia were about to leave on a five-week press tour with the cast from the movie. Sasha went on a plane back to Italy on the next day after being home for a photo shoot with a luxury clothing brand. Oliver dropped them off at the airport where they got on a plane to Las Vegas. By the end of the press tour, she visited her family in New York for a week before she needed to be in Los Angeles to work on another movie. While they visited their family in New York with Sasha being back from her trip in Italy, Nina and Joseph told them that she was in the early stages of pregnancy with her first child.

On the morning of their afternoon flight to Los Angeles, she visited Daxton's grave with Damien where they brought flowers from her parent's garden that they laid down on his grave. They didn't say anything to each other where they stared at Daxton's grave with tears running down their faces before they left to go to the car when it heavily snowed on them. When it was time to say goodbye to her family, she cried into her mother's chest before Amelia pulled her into her arms where she dragged them onto the plane. She hid her face in Amelia's shoulder with her arms around her for the entire flight back home. Once their plane landed in Los Angeles, she was coaxed off of the plane as Amelia guided them off the airport where Oliver waited for them before his face fell when he noticed that she cried for the entire flight. He wordlessly pulled her into his chest as she blinked back tears that fell down her face before he drove them to her house. Once they got back to the house, they had dinner with Uncle Stan, Thomas, Oliver, Juliet, and Posey before they went back to their houses for the rest of the night. Sasha was in Italy again for another fashion event. On that night, she fell asleep in her old bedroom that she shared with Daxton because she couldn't fall asleep unless she was in her old bedroom. When Sasha got back from Italy, Amelia told her about it even though they couldn't do anything to stop it from happening to her. She was supposed to work on a new movie before she told them that she didn't feel ready to do a new project. Even though they were disappointed that she wasn't going to be part of the new movie, the director told her that they would find someone else to play the leading role in her place. When she told her cousins that she decided to turn down the offer in a new movie, they were concerned about her since she never turned down a role in a movie. Amelia worked on the set of the movie with her co-stars since they were supposed to be doing this together. She didn't know what to say to them. She hid in her bedroom for the rest of the night. She wasn't hungry, nor did she have the energy to do anything. All that she did was lay down in the bed that she used to share with Daxton. She watched television when she wasn't sleeping twenty hours a day. She knew that her cousins told her parents about it, but she didn't have it inside of herself to care about it. She struggled to care about anything. She didn't care about her career. She didn't care about her health. She didn't care about anything. On a third week of refusing to get out of the suite, she woke up to a knock on the door where she jumped awake in the bed. As soon as she opened her eyes, Oliver helped himself into her bedroom before she hid her face into her pillows. Once Oliver took a seat next to her on the bed, he placed his hand on her back where he gently ran his hands up and down her back when he talked to her in the softest voice, "Isabella. Are you doing alright? We are worried about you. You haven't left this room in weeks. Do you want to talk about it?"

Oliver laid down in the bed next to her with his hands resting on her back when he told her with a frown on his face, "That's fine. I'll talk. What's been going on with me? Juliet went back to work a few months ago and it's been an adjustment for us. The nanny didn't work out like we expected it to. Posey is going to daycare at the church. That's going well for her. Posey gets to be with her friends and her teachers while we are at work. Work is fine for me. I had a patient try to escape from the hospital the other day, but we got them into their room again. I'm shocked that's the first time that happened to me. We got a pool at our house since Posey is obsessed with swimming after being in Hawaii, so we don't need to hijack your pool. Posey misses you, Isabella. She keeps asking when we are going to see you. She wants to go swimming with you in her pool. Would you want to come over to see her?"

As soon as she took her face out of her pillows, she blinked back tears that fell down her face when she told him in a broken voice, "I don't want to let her down. I guess so. I miss her too. She's growing up so fast, Oliver. Why is she so big?"

Once Oliver wiped away the tears off her face, he softly chuckled when he responded to her with a smile on his face, "Juliet and I talk about that every night before we go to bed. She's learning how to swim while she's at daycare, so that she can swim in the pool without us holding onto her. She would love to see you. I'll let her know that you'll come by for dinner this weekend. I miss you too, Isabella. It's been weird without you. You know that you can tell me anything. I'd never judge you for anything that you say to me."

Once she laid down on her back with Oliver's arms around her, she stared up at the ceiling as she blinked back tears that fell down her face when she told him in a distant voice, "I don't even know where to begin. I don't know how to explain to myself. It makes me sound like I'm crazy."

Oliver tightened his grip on her shoulder when he responded to her with a serious look on his face, "You're not crazy, Isabella. Stop talking about yourself like that. Start from the beginning. Trust me. I've got all the time in the world. You can spend the rest of time talking to me and I'll always be there to listen to you. I promise."

After she laid her head down on Oliver's chest, he tightened his grip on her arms when she confessed to him in a soft voice, "It started when I was eight years old. It was the first time that I felt like this in my life. It was the day of my dad's funeral. I saw his body in his coffin when my parents weren't watching me. They didn't want me to see him because it would upset me. I snuck into the room where they had his body before the funeral started. I had nightmares about that moment for years. It hit me that my dad was dead. The feeling that I felt in that moment was only one thought. What do I do to be with him? That was the first time that I thought about killing myself. I mean, I was really too young to understand it, but I knew what I wanted. The feeling came back off and on throughout the years. I remember when I acted on it for the first time. Are you sure that you want me to keep going, Oliver? It's going to get worse the more that I talk about it."

Oliver nodded his head at her as he grabbed onto her hands when he responded to her with concern laced in his voice, "Please keep going, Isabella. I need to know this as much as it's going to hurt me. I need to hear it so much."

She nodded her head at him when she openly confessed to him in a distant voice, "As long as you're fine with it, Oliver. I never told anyone this before in my life. I tried to kill myself when I was thirteen. I was self-harming for almost a year before my mom caught me doing it. She was rightfully pissed off at me for doing it. She tried to talk to me about how she did it when she was my age, but I wasn't in the right headspace to hear it. After I stormed into my bedroom, I couldn't stop crying no matter what I did. I didn't want my parents to hear me crying in my bedroom, so I went outside to my hidden spot on the roof where I cried to the only person that would care about me. I wanted to tell my dad about what I was experiencing, but I couldn't stop crying to get any words out of my mouth. I eventually screamed at my dad about how I hated him for doing this to me. It wasn't going to be the last time that I told him that. When my voice was gone from screaming at him, I threw myself off of the roof so many times until I realized that it wasn't high enough of a fall to kill me. I ended up back in the house before I went into the cabinet to take an entire bottle of pills. I didn't know what they were, but I knew that I didn't want to wake up in the morning. When I woke up puking all day the next day, I hated myself even more that I couldn't die. My parents thought that I had the flu, and I wasn't in the mood to correct them. Over the years, I took my parents pills out of the bottles without them noticing it. A pain killer here and a muscle relaxer there before I couldn't get myself to fall asleep with them. I was trapped in an endless cycle of taking pills to get through the day."

She wiped away tears from her eyes before she talked aloud to herself like Oliver wasn't in the room, "I was high at my last dance recital. I was high at my high school graduation. I was high every day for my last year of high school. No one found out about it. I hid the pills that I stole from everyone around me in this bag under my mattress and I would take a few out every day before I left the house. I lied to everyone when I moved to California when they asked if I'd ever been high before when I told them that I wasn't high before in my life. I was getting high for years before it was socially acceptable for me to get high. I didn't try hard drugs until I lived here where it completely changed everything for me. I didn't have any other choice except to hide it. I knew that it wasn't normal that I was high as a teenager every day of my life. I knew that I shouldn't crave them as much as I wanted it. I couldn't live without it, but I wanted to die if I didn't have it.

I'm telling you this because I want it again. I really want to do drugs, Oliver. I dream about it every night. I think about it all of the time. I'm missing how they made me feel. All that I can do right now is lay here in my bed telling myself that I don't need it even though I'll never believe it. If I try to do anything that isn't this, I think about calling my old dealer and buying everything that he has on him before I deadbolt the door to my bedroom to do everything at once. Why am I telling you this instead of you finding my dead body? I'm telling this because I'm fighting against it. I'm trying to fight against it, Oliver. I don't want to do this anymore. I don't want to be this person. I don't want to become another worthless addict like my dad or Daxton was. I want to explore the world. I want to inspire people. I want to fall in love again. I want to have a family of my own. I want the life that you have, Oliver. I want that life for myself. I don't want this life. I can't do this life anymore. If this is going to be my life for the rest of my life, then I wish that I was dead with my dad and Daxton. Maybe I should've died with them instead of trying to stop it. Maybe it's already too late for me to stop it."

Oliver pulled her into his arms as she let out heartbreaking sobs into his chest with him tightly holding onto her. Oliver whispered comforting words into her ear as he ran his arms down her back with tears falling down his face. She slowly pulled her head out of his chest as he let go of his tight grip on her arms before she got off to bed to grab a few bags of cocaine out of the bathroom drawers. After she took a seat on the bed next to him, she placed the bags of cocaine into his hand as he blankly stared at her when he asked her with confusion written all over his face, "Where were you hiding this? We went through every space in this house, and we thought that we got everything that you hid from us. Did you take any of it? Tell me that truth, Isabella. I'm begging you."

She shook her head at him when she told him with a frown on her face, "I didn't take any of it. I promise, Oliver. This stuff was from a few years ago, so it wouldn't be effective. I have a lot of hiding spots that no one knows about in the house. I'm willing to tell you those hiding spots, but you have to trust me. I'm doing what you wanted me to do the first time that I overdosed. I'm telling you before anything horrible happens to me. I thought that we could get rid of them together, so that I don't get tempted to do them. If they aren't in my possession, then I'm not going to try to take them back from you. Do we have a deal?"

Oliver looked at the bags of cocaine in his hands where he was conflicted in his thoughts before he let out a defeated sigh when he told her with a frown on his face, "I believe you, Isabella. Thank you for telling me about it before you almost died this time. How much more do you have laying around the house? I don't know what to say right now. I don't know if I should be thanking you or yelling at you. We can get into that later. We can talk about how you need to go to therapy again too. We need to get rid of this right now before you snort enough of it to make your heart stop beating in your chest. Are you going to tell me where your other hiding spots in the house are or am I going to wait until you're in the hospital?" She got off of the bed with Oliver following behind her as she pointed him out to the spots in the house that she was hiding her emergency drugs. They flashed everything down the toilet in a silent ceremony. Oliver pulled her into a desperate hug where she hid her face into his chest when he told her that he loved her before he kissed her on the top of her head. After Oliver left to go back to his house, she went back into the suite where she cried herself to sleep for the rest of the night.

CHAPTER TWENTY-TWO
(SPRING 1964 – PARIS, FRANCE)

After she flashed all of her drugs down the toilet, she instantly regretted doing it. She thought about it every second that she was awake and when she was asleep at night. She was pissed that she told Oliver to do that even though it was her idea to do it. She thought about yelling at Oliver for doing it before she realized that it wouldn't make anything better. It wouldn't make the drugs come back. They were gone forever like her dad and Daxton were. Even though she pleaded with Oliver not to tell anyone about it, it was a lost cause. Oliver told her cousins about the next day where she hid in the bathroom from them. She didn't leave the bathroom until she thought that Oliver left the house with them before she opened the door to see them staring at her in front of her with looks of concern on their faces. When she realized that they cornered her into not running away from them, she let them drag into the living room where they expressed their concerns to her about her wanting to relapse and trying to kill herself. She tried to deny it even though she admitted it to Oliver last night before without any hesitation. Since she wasn't in the mood to be called a hypocrite, she gave into their questions that they asked her where she answered most of them truthfully since they didn't need to know every detail about her life. After they finished interrogating her in her house, they left her alone for the rest of the night where she watched a movie before she fell asleep on the couch with her head on Amelia's shoulder. She didn't question it when she woke up the next morning in her bedroom with Sasha sleeping on the other side of the bed and Amelia sleeping on the couch. They followed her around the house all day. She told herself that this was for her safety even though she didn't believe a word coming out of her mouth. Her cousins told her in the middle of their interrogation that this was a million times better than her waking up in the hospital. As her cousins walked around on eggshells around her, she regretted telling them about it since they wouldn't leave her alone. She couldn't stand it when they treated her like she was going to break every time that something bad happened to her. Even though she gave them no reason in the world to trust her, she wished that they would leave her alone. She told herself that she wasn't going to do drugs again. This was another lie that she told them that no one believed because the evidence showed the opposite to be true. She was very lucky that they didn't tell her parents about any of this. It could've been a lot worse than them hounding her about it. Her parents were so much worse about everything. She was busy buying time since she had a grand plan when they were in New York for Ivan's high school graduation.

On the night of Ivan's graduation, she was going to disappear when her family was distracted by the party. She would go to the hiding spots in her parent's house because there were drugs in them from the last time that she was in New York. She was going to take them to her old bedroom that her parent's turned into an office, and she would go to the roof where she was going to overdose with no one but the stars to keep her company. She didn't want to think about what the next morning was going to look like. It was the last thing that she wanted to imagine. In the week leading up to her leaving for New York, she felt guilty about everything that she was going to do. She felt guilty about keeping it from Oliver. She promised him that she would tell him if she had anything planned. She tried not to think about her last days with her cousins. She was going to miss this feeling more than anything in the world. She cried herself to sleep every night leading up to the trip thinking about everything that she was going to lose after she died.

She didn't want to do this, but she didn't know what else to do about it. She told her cousins that she was doing better after they got rid of her drugs, but she was doing so much worse than before it happened. She couldn't stop thinking about drugs. She imagined what it would feel like to give into it. She was exhausted because of her worsening depression that got triggered when she got back from Hawaii. She realized that it wasn't her depression that made her so exhausted. The reason that she felt exhausted was because she was fighting the urge to get high every moment of her life. If she gave into it, then she wouldn't feel so depleted. Maybe she would be capable of working or having fun or enjoying herself for once in her life if she gave into the urges that followed her everywhere she went in the world. It was only a dream. She would feel the same way if she was doing drugs. On the morning of their flight to New York, her eyes were swollen from crying all night where she grabbed onto her suitcase with a pair of oversized sunglasses over her face before she walked into the living room. Even though her cousins noticed her distressed demeanor, they didn't have the chance to say anything to her about it before Uncle Stan and Thomas came to drop them off at the airport. Oliver noticed her distressed demeanor as soon as he walked into the airport where Juliet followed behind him with Posey on her hip before they got on the plane where she slept with her face hidden into Sasha's shoulder for the flight. When their plane landed in New York, her parents and Uncle Sam picked them up at the airport where her mother said nothing about her weight loss from not eating or her silence when she pulled her into her arms until she was dragged into the car before Uncle Sam drove them to her parent's house. As soon as Uncle Sam dropped them off at her parent's house, she spent the day hidden in the office where her bedroom used to be where she frantically looked for the drugs that she hid in there.

After she couldn't find them anywhere, she gave up looking for them before she passed out on her spot on the roof for the rest of the night. She woke up in her parent's bed in the morning. She didn't remember coming into the house. For the days leading up to Ivan's graduation, she blended in with her family as much as she could without falling apart before she cried herself to sleep every night in her bedroom. She played the part that her family assigned to her without any effort. By the end of the week, she played her part so well that she forgot why she came to New York. After she was reminded that her goal was to overdose on drugs, she made it her life's mission to find something around the house that could kill her. Her parents got rid of the drugs that she hid around the house the last time that she was in New York. On the morning of Ivan's high school graduation, she was awake all-night counting how many pills that she would have to take in the cabinet that would kill her. She wasn't going to have a repeat of what happened when she was thirteen years old. She would have to take over 300 sleeping pills to kill herself. That sounded like a miserable experience. She resigned herself to throwing herself off of the roof over and over again until she died. She found some of the drugs that she hid under the floorboards of the office. After she found enough cocaine in little bags to make her heart stop beating in her chest, she let out a squeal of excitement as she stuffed it into the pockets of her jacket before she joined her family in the living room. She disassociated the entire time during Ivan's graduation ceremony because she felt the drugs burning a hole in her jacket pockets. She almost snuck away to do a few lines in the bathroom during the ceremony until she remembered that she needed enough tonight to kill herself like she planned to do in the middle of the night. Her plans got immediately derailed when Uncle Sam took them to the airport instead of going to her parent's house like they planned on doing that morning. When she realized that they were dropping off Ivan at the airport and not her, she calmed down again before Ivan asked them if they wanted to go to France with him and Jamie who was already there waiting for him. Even though she really wanted to kill herself, she couldn't refuse Ivan's offer since she didn't ever go to France before in her life. Apparently her cousins already knew that she was going to go with them since they brought her packed bags with them behind her back. Instead of killing herself that day, she went on a plane to Paris with Ivan, Sasha, Amelia, Oliver, Juliet, and Posey. For the overnight flight to Paris, Amelia and Sasha sat in between her to prevent her from getting up from her seat without them knowing where she went on the plane. During the flight to Paris, she thought about killing herself in the plane bathroom. She realized that it would be more poetic for her to die in Paris than in any other place in the world. When their plane landed in Paris, Jamie met them at the airport where Ivan pulled him into a tight hug before Jamie drove them to their studio apartment in the city.

Since there was one bedroom in their apartment, they booked two hotel rooms for them that happened to be right across the street from the Eiffel Tower that Sasha paid for with money from her modeling company. After they changed out of their outfits, they left for the hotel to meet Ivan and Jamie at a restaurant before they went to their hotel rooms for the rest of the night. She couldn't find it in herself to pretend to sleep where Amelia and Sasha slept on their bed together before she smoked a box of cigarettes that she stole from Sasha's purse. As she took a seat on the balcony with the glowing Eiffel Tower in front of her, she brought the lit cigarette to her lips as she inhaled the smoke from it with a blanket around her legs where she closed her eyes with the sounds of the city life below her. As soon as she lit another cigarette, she suddenly jumped up in her seat when she heard the balcony door close in the darkness before Oliver silently took a seat next to her with a look of betrayal on his face. She looked up at him with a cigarette in between her fingers when he asked her with a frown on his face, "Do you think that I'm an idiot? Tell me, Isabella. Don't think for a moment that I can't figure out what's going on in your mind. I know it more than you do."

Her face instantly turned white as she hid her shaking hands in her lap when she asked him with an innocent look on her face, "What are you talking about, Oliver?"

Oliver rolled his eyes at her when he responded to her with a look of anger on his face, "You were going to kill yourself tonight. I can tell by your reaction that I'm right. Try to deny it. I don't believe a word that comes out of your mouth."

After she put out her burnt-out cigarette into the ashtray, she responded to him with an unreadable expression on her face, "You're right. I was going to kill myself tonight. Are you happy, Oliver? What did you expect me to do? I haven't been in the mental state of not trying to kill myself. I was going to take enough cocaine to stop my heart. It's not anything that I haven't tried before in the past. What's your problem with it?"

Oliver harshly smacked her arm as she groaned out in pain to him when he responded to her with anger laced in his voice, "What's my problem with it? How dare you ask me that! You're a fucking asshole, Isabella. I can't believe that we have to have this conversation again. Every time you start self-destructing it's always on me to stop you from killing yourself. Every time that I think that you learned your lesson we are right back to where we started. I'm sick of this song and dance, Isabella. I'm so tired of it. I'm sick of you doing this to yourself over and over again and expecting a different result. I'm not going to watch you do this. I can't watch you get addicted to drugs, and I have to pick up the pieces for you again."

She leaned on the patio chair when she responded back to Oliver with a smirk on her face, "I wasn't planning on getting addicted to drugs. I was planning on dying from a drug overdose."

Oliver harshly smacked her arm again with her groaning in pain to him when he responded to her with his face red with anger, "Oh my god! I can't deal with you! Historically that hasn't worked out for you. I'm not in the mood for this, Isabella. I should be sleeping with my wife and my daughter in the city of love. Not lecturing my cousin whom I love more than life itself about the nuances of killing herself. Do you have drugs on you right now? I know that you do."

After Oliver stared into her eyes so intensely that she couldn't look away from him, she shook her head at him in defeat where she pulled the bags of cocaine out of her jacket pocket before she placed them into Oliver's hand. Oliver looked at her with a softer expression on his face when he told her with a frown on his face, "Thank you for being honest with me. A little late if you ask me, but it's better late than never. I'm not mad at you. I'm frustrated with you. Did you seriously think that your plan was going to work?"

She shrugged her shoulders at him when she told him with a softer expression on her face, "I thought it was going to work, but I couldn't find any cocaine in my parent's house. It's ketamine. It doesn't stop your heart like cocaine does. It would be fucked up if I killed myself in France. I would have waited until we got back to California where I would die in my bed like Daxton did. It's a fucked-up version of Romeo and Juliet except Juliet is incapable of killing herself because of her overprotective cousin Tybalt always stops her. Is that why we're in France? So that I don't kill myself?"

Oliver told her with an unreadable expression on his face, "That's exactly why we're in France, Isabella. You have an unwritten rule that you can't self-destruct in a foreign country for whatever reason that I'm thankful for. You sound so much like your mother when you say that. You know that? Where did that come from? I've never heard you say anything like that before."

They laughed into their hands as soon as they looked at each other before Oliver grabbed onto her hands when she told him in a small voice, "I'm sorry, Oliver. I don't know what's going on with me. I can't blame the drugs for it since I haven't done any despite my own disappointment with it. There's something else going on. Something that has been going on for my entire life. Something that happened to my father. You were right about therapy. I do need to go back to therapy. I didn't want to admit it because it made me feel like a weak person."

As soon as she closed her eyes with her leaning on the chair, Oliver wrapped his arms around her when he responded to her in a soft voice, "There's nothing wrong in realizing that you need to ask someone else for help. You know? There's strength in asking people for help. It shows the world that you can't figure it out on your own. You can't expect yourself to figure it out on your own. Grief is the most complicated feeling in the world. It's anger, sadness, and loneliness wrapped up into one feeling. It can consume you from the inside out if you let it happen."

She told him in a shaky voice, "I'm worried that it might be more than grief. Something that's chronic." Oliver told her with sudden interest in his voice, "What? Is addiction not chronic to you? It's chronic, Isabella. You'll be an addict for the rest of your life whether you like it or not. What do you mean? Like schizophrenia? Or a personality disorder? I'm not diagnosing you with anything, but you're bipolar like your dad."

She responded to him with a confused look on her face, "What? How did you know that my dad was bipolar? I didn't know that."

Oliver looked up at her when he told her with a frown on his face, "My stepdad told me that your dad was bipolar. Your dad was diagnosed when he was a child. I'm sorry. I thought that you knew that. I thought that your mother told you that."

She shook her head at him when she told him with frustration laced in her voice, "I had no idea that my dad was bipolar. My mom doesn't know that either. What else has your stepdad said about my dad?"

Oliver put his hands up in the air when he told her with a defeated look on his face, "We don't need to make this a thing, Isabella. I'm sorry that I said anything to you. I'll tell you about it later."

She held out her pinky to him when she asked him with a wide smile on her face, "Promise me?"

He wrapped his pinky around hers when he told her with a serious look on his face, "I promise. I need to flush this shit down the toilet before you decide to change your mind again. You need to sleep right now. I know that you haven't been sleeping since we left California. I love you so much that it hurts me." Oliver pulled her into a tight hug as she hid her face into his chest before he left to go into his hotel room with his wife and his daughter. After she walked into her room, she placed the pack of cigarettes in Sasha's purse where she laid down in between them before she fell asleep for the night.

CHAPTER TWENTY-THREE
(SUMMER 1964 – LOS ANGELES, CALIFORNIA)

They stayed in Paris for a few more days before they left to go back to the states except for Sasha who stayed in France to work since Ivan and Jamie were modeling with the same company as her. After they said an emotional goodbye to Jamie and Ivan, she got on her flight to New York with Amelia, Oliver, Juliet, and Posey where she slept with her head resting on Amelia's shoulder all night. Once their plane landed in New York the next morning, her parents met them at the airport. Her mother pulled her into a long hug until Oliver walked over to them with their bags in his arms before her parents drove them to her house where they ate dinner together. Oliver, Juliet, Posey went to Uncle Sam's house as Anastasia, Damien, and her one-year-old niece Alina went to their apartment before Joseph and a pregnant Nina went to their apartment in the same building. She later got on a flight to California with Amelia, Oliver, Juliet, and Posey where she slept with her head resting on Amelia's shoulder before Uncle Stan picked them up at the airport. After Uncle Stan pulled her into a desperate hug with her face hidden in his chest, he dropped off Oliver and his family at their house before he dropped her off at her house with her cousin. She slept for the rest of the day in the suite with Amelia laying down next to her. Amelia went back to work on the movie that she was supposed to be on before she called her old therapist Dr. Taylor on Oliver's urging to see him again. It was later in the week that she was at Dr. Taylor's office where she cried to him about everything that she went through in the last nine months. Even though she was hesitant to see Dr. Taylor, she told him things that she never thought that she would tell anyone in her life. She told him the truth about her drug addiction. She told him that she thought about drugs all of the time. She thought about them when she was awake and when she was sleeping. She admitted to him that she thought about killing herself more than she thought about doing drugs. She remained inconsolable for the rest of the day after that. During a session with Dr. Taylor, she asked him if he thought that she was bipolar like her father was before he told her that he suspected that she might've been for a while. She hid her shock from him when he told her that even though her jaw hit the floor. She told him about her magical plan to kill herself before Oliver stopped her from doing it by forcing her to go to France. She couldn't find cocaine and she couldn't look her family in the face while she was planning it. When he asked her what she would have done if she went through with it, she didn't know how to answer that question. She never thought that far into her grand plan to die. She would've felt so guilty that it would have destroyed her. She thought about her mother who she put all her hopes and dreams into.

She didn't have the energy to deal with Amelia or Sasha who was back from her work trip before she hid in the suite for the rest of the night. She woke up in the middle of the night to the sound of the television playing in the background. As she slowly got out of the bed, she grabbed a box of cigarettes and a lighter from the top of her dresser before she walked out onto the balcony where she took a seat on one of the patio chairs. She grabbed a cigarette out of the box where she lit up in between her fingers. After she wiped away tears that fell down her face, she inhaled the smoke from her cigarette where she leaned onto the chair with her eyes closed before she let out a deep breath. She looked up at the stars when she confessed to him in a soft voice, "Hey, dad. I'm sorry that I haven't talked to you in a while. I have so much to catch you up since the last time that we talked to each other. Hawaii was incredible. I didn't want to leave when it was time to go home. I wanted to die in Hawaii. Something changed when I got back from Hawaii. I got really depressed. I almost relapsed. I forgot that I hid drugs in secret places all around the house in case of an emergency like this. Things got out of hand. I was a good girl, dad. I told Oliver about the drugs hidden in the house and my addiction over the years that only you knew about me. After he got rid of my drugs, I was pissed off at myself for telling him about it. Did you hear about how my plan to kill myself backfired on me? It was disaster. I was going to kill myself in New York by snorting enough cocaine to stop my heart. Except that I couldn't find any cocaine at mom's house. Even worse, Oliver forced us to go to Paris where he confronted me about it. I couldn't kill myself in the city of love, dad. It was too on the nose for me."

She lit another cigarette as she let out a shaky breath when she confessed to him in a distant voice, "I know that you're never going to answer me. I don't know why I always wait for you to respond to me. Oliver said something interesting about you. Uncle Nathan told him that you were bipolar. It was news to mom when I brought it up to her when I got back to New York. I might be bipolar too. Dr. Taylor told me that he suspected it almost a year ago. I want to ask Uncle Nathan what else that mom and I didn't know about you. I feel like he would tell me things that he wouldn't tell mom about you. I know he feels protective of mom since you died. It's sweet. Your brother cares about us. I wanted to ask Oliver what else that Uncle Nathan told him, but I know that he won't tell me anything that is going to upset me. He's protective over me like Uncle Nathan is of mom. Do you think that I should call Uncle Nathan? What time is it in England? It's morning there. He would probably be awake at this time. Do you want to listen, dad? Go ahead."

After she put out her cigarette into the ashtray, she ran into the house to grab the phone that was plugged in on the side table before she stretched to take it out onto the balcony where her father could hear their conversation. Once she took the phone off of the hook, she leaned onto the balcony handle with the phone in between her shoulder and her ear before she typed in a number that she knew by heart. With the phone ringing in her ears, she lit another cigarette with her shaking hands at her sides when a groggy voice answered the phone, "Hello? Who is it?"

She let out a shaky breath as she placed the cigarette in between her fingers when she responded to him in a soft voice, "It's Isabella. I'm sorry if I woke you up, Uncle Nathan. I didn't know that you were going to be awake right now. We can talk later since you're in the middle of sleeping."

Uncle Nathan responded to her with concern laced in his voice, "No honey. It's alright. I was about to wake up for work. What's wrong? Did something happen to you?"

She told him with desperation laced in her voice, "I didn't mean to freak you out, Uncle Nathan. Everything is fine. I wanted to ask you about my dad. Oliver said some things that made me start wondering about him."

Uncle Nathan let out a deep breath when he responded to her with concern laced in his voice, "Oliver said something about it to you? That sounds like him. How is he? Tell him to call his mother. She misses hearing from him. What did Oliver tell you honey?"

She let out a shaky breath when she responded to him with a frown on her face, "I'll pass on the message to him when I see him this weekend. Oliver told me that dad was bipolar. That he got diagnosed with it when he was a child. Is that true, Uncle Nathan? Was my dad bipolar?"

Uncle Nathan let out a defeated sigh when he responded to her like he didn't expect to talk about this, "That's true. Your dad was bipolar among other things too. Your grandfather wasn't the most understanding person in the world. He didn't understand why Will was the way that he was. He wanted Will to be more like me. He told him that all the time. 'You need to be more like your brother, Will. Your brother doesn't act this way. Stop acting like that, Will. That's not how a man is supposed to act.' Will felt like a disappointment. He couldn't please him no matter what he did. Your dad tried his best honey. I felt horrible for him since dad was always harder on him than on me."

As she took a seat on the chair with the phone into her ear, she let out a soft sigh when she asked him with a frown on her face, "What do you mean by that? Among other things?"

Uncle Nathan responded to her with sadness laced his voice, "He was an addict. He was diagnosed with schizophrenia as a child after he tried to jump off the roof where he heard voices telling him to do it. There are some other ones that were there, but I don't remember them on the top of my head. I would have to go through my parent's old stuff to know them. He struggled a lot throughout his life, and it hurt me to watch it happen to him. The worst moment of my life was when I was forced to leave him to go into the military. I didn't want to leave him with our dad because I knew what was going to happen to him. It ruined him when I left him. He relapsed the night that I left for the military. He told me about it in a letter. I have it if you want to read it. I can mail it to you. Just make sure that you mail it back to me when you're done with it. I know that your mother wouldn't like it, but you can make your own decisions."

She told him with desperation laced in her voice, "I need to read it, Uncle Nathan. Thank you for telling me about him. It feels nice to talk about him. Like he's here with us. Can we talk about him another time? This is helping me understand myself while I'm learning about him."

Uncle Nathan softly chuckled when he told her with a smile on his face, "It does feel nice to talk about him. I haven't talked about him since he died. I have to get ready to leave for work soon, but I'll call you in a few days when I get home again. We can talk about him more. I'll mail that letter to you. Is your address the same from the last time that I sent you a letter?" She hung up the phone as she put out her cigarette into the ashtray before she took the phone into her bedroom. She threw herself face first into the bed where she pulled the blankets over her before she passed out for the rest of the night.

Chapter Twenty-Four
(Fall 1964 – Los Angeles, California)

After her conversation with Uncle Nathan, she couldn't stop thinking about her father as a young child. She thought about her father when she was awake and when she was asleep where she dreamed of him. She thought about him growing up in a house where no one understood him. It broke her heart that her father wasn't understood by anyone in his life. She couldn't imagine how he went through everything that he did completely alone in the world. She felt so lucky that she had the support of her family that he never had in his life. She hated that her father had to go through his life alone. When Oliver and his family were at her house, she told him about her conversation with his stepdad about her father. He was shocked that Uncle Nathan told her anything about him since he never let anyone talk about his brother. It made her feel a lot better about herself that she was the only person that Uncle Nathan was willing to talk to about her father since he didn't talk about it with his children or his wife. After her conversation with Oliver, Uncle Nathan called her the next night to thank her for telling Oliver to call his mother since she was glowing from their conversation when he got home from work. They talked about her father that night where he told her more about her father's childhood that she was curious about for her entire life. She told Dr. Taylor about her phone calls with Uncle Nathan. She cried about it for weeks and weeks on end. She didn't tell her mother about the conversations with Uncle Nathan since he told her that was a casual conversation with her. Her mother wasn't surprised that she was curious about her father since she was a lot more like him than she was like her. Her mother shocked her when she told her that she was supportive of it as long as it was helping her heal her own trauma. She didn't tell her mother about her diagnoses that she received from Dr. Taylor based on what her father dealt with in his life. It would break her heart if she knew the truth. She talked with Dr. Taylor at length about her father's addiction. They talked about how she felt about this information being kept from her. No one thought that she might want to know about it. It would've helped her feel less alone in the world. She wouldn't have suffered when she was younger if she knew that her father went through the same things that she did. Dr. Taylor told her that her emotions towards her father were always valid to him.

Even though she wanted to be upset with her mother for not telling her anything about her father, she couldn't let herself be upset with her since she knew that her mother didn't know this information about her father. She wouldn't blame Uncle Nathan for not telling her about him since she never asked him about it. She understood why Uncle Nathan was so hesitant to share this information with her. It was something that her father was ashamed of himself. She couldn't fault her father for thinking like that since she was ashamed of her problems too. Her father never told anyone about these things because he didn't want people to look at him like there was something wrong with him. That feeling kept her up at night. No one knew anything about her addiction until she almost died in the club. Even after her overdose in the club, she didn't think that they knew she had a problem until she was addicted to drugs with Daxton. They didn't know about her lifelong anxiety and depression before the drugs came into the picture. They didn't realize that she was doing drugs long before anyone noticed that she was doing them. Her parents never found out about her suicide attempts when she was teenager. Her cousins didn't know about her drug use in high school. Her family didn't know about her self-harming that she did as a teenager. She found herself on the roof of her house except it was a lot higher than the roof on her parent's house in New York. She didn't remember how she got there before she laid down on top of the roof with the stars shining above her in the sky. She cried as she thought about her father in this place from a lifetime ago before she told herself that didn't want to do this. She passed out by the pool that night where she didn't remember how she got there. She disassociated regularly now. She had large gaps of no memories of her days. She hesitated to tell Dr. Taylor about it. Despite her not wanting to admit that there was a problem going on with her, Dr. Taylor told her that she should get evaluated at the psychiatric hospital. That was the moment that she felt like she was her father all over again. She didn't have a choice in the matter since Dr. Taylor already called them to tell her that she would be coming over to the hospital right now. When the ambulance showed up at Dr. Taylor's office, she let them take her to the hospital where she asked them to call Oliver, so that he could tell the rest of her family about it. They already knew who Oliver was since he worked there for a while. They called to tell him on her behalf before they gave her something to make her fall asleep for the first time in a long time. She woke up in a hospital bed with all glass walls surrounding her before everything suddenly came back to her.

She couldn't get off of the bed with her arms and her ankles stripped down onto it. She gave up on escaping before she softly cried to herself until a nurse walked into the room with a tray of food in her hands. Before the nurse left her alone in the room, she asked her if she could see Oliver when the nurse told her that he was working, and he would visit her in a few hours before she cried to herself as she ate the food off of the tray. After she ate all the food on the tray, a nurse walked into the room with medicine to help her sleep until the doctor would evaluate her. She was grateful for it since she wasn't sleeping at home anymore. When she woke up from her morning nap, Oliver sat down in a chair next to her as he held onto her hands not saying anything to her before she threw herself into his arms with her head hidden into his chest. As he moved onto the bed to be closer to her, she sobbed into his chest as he tightened his grip on her arms with her hands grabbing onto his coat. He took off the restraints that were on her wrists and her ankles that the nurse put on her while she was sleeping without her realizing it. After she calmed herself down, she pulled her face out of his chest as he wiped away tears from her face with her hands onto his hands before the doctor walked into the room. As soon as Oliver let go of her hands, he kissed on the top of her head when he told her that he loved her before Dr. Lukas took a seat next to her with a notebook in his hands. After Dr. Lukas got comfortable on the chair, he softly sighed when he asked her with a smile on his face, "Good afternoon, Ms. Foster. I'm Dr. Lukas. I'm going to be taking care of you while you are in the hospital. How about we start with simple questions before we get into the harder ones? Does that sound good?"

She nodded her head at him when he responded to her with excitement laced in his voice, "Great. Let me know if you need a break and we can stop at any time that you aren't comfortable. Let's get started. What does your family look like? Do you have any siblings?"

She responded to him with her nervously playing with the ends of the blanket, "I'm an only child. My family is from England. Most of my father and my mother's family live in England. My mother is an author, and she lives in New York where I grew up. My mum owns a book publishing company, and she lives in New York with my mother. My dad died when I was eight years old, but he wasn't in my life."

Once Dr. Lukas finished writing his notes into the paper, he asked her with a kind smile on his face, "Do you have any other family in the states?"

She responded to him with a smile on her face, "I have an aunt and an uncle that live in New York with my cousins and their families. I live with my cousins Sasha and Amelia. My cousin Oliver and his family live near us. Oliver is like an older brother to me. He's protective over me."

Dr. Lukas responded to her, "I can tell that he's protective over you. I've known Oliver for a few years now. He's really good at what he does. Are your cousins Sasha and Amelia protective over you?"

She nodded her head at him when she told him with a wide grin on her face, "Yes, they are very protective over me like Oliver is. They have always been protective over me, but they are even more now after what happened to me in the last few years with drugs."

Dr. Lukas put down his pen when he responded back to her, "What happened to you in the last few years? I looked at your chart, but I want to hear it in your own words."

She confessed to him with her blinking back tears that fell down her face, "I had two drug overdoses in the last four years. I almost died from them. Since my parents live in New York, my cousins have taken it upon themselves to protect me from drugs. I despised it for a long time, but I've learned to accept that this is the way that has to be. They have gone out of their way and have been supportive of me during my recovery over the years. I appreciate their efforts."

Dr. Lukas responded to her with compassion laced in his voice, "I'm sorry, Ms. Foster. That can be a traumatic experience to go through at any age especially since you're so young. Are you in recovery? When was the last time that you used drugs?"

She let out a shaky breath when she confessed to him with a frown on her face, "I'm in recovery. I haven't used drugs since my last overdose two years ago. There have been moments where I almost relapsed, but Oliver stopped me before I did anything."

Dr. Lukas looked up from his notebook when he asked her with a sad look on his face, "I'm glad that he stopped you. I'm sorry, but we are getting into the hard questions. Let me know if you need a break. Why do you feel like you need to do drugs?"

Her face turned white when she told him in a distant voice, "That's a complicated question. I'll say this about it since I'm sure that you heard some of this from Dr. Taylor. It makes me feel like I'm in control. It's the only time in my life that I felt like I was in control. I could be whoever people want me to be or who I want myself to be without a care. I care too much. It made me not care for the first time."

As Dr. Lukas leaned back in the chair, he twisted his pen around his fingers when he asked her with a frown on his face, "Why do you think that it's a problem that you care too much? Is it because you get hurt when you care about someone else?"

She wiped away tears that fell down her face when she confessed to him in a soft voice, "Every time that I've ever cared about someone they hurt me, or they leave me alone in the world. When I don't care about anything, I'm never going to get hurt by anyone in my life."

Dr. Lukas handed her a box of tissues that she took from him before he put down his pen when he asked her with a serious look on his face, "Did you lose people close to you?"

She looked down at her shaky hands when she told him in a vulnerable voice, "My dad killed himself when I was eight years old. We were estranged from each other, but it changed everything for me. I couldn't allow myself to get close to anyone after he died. I felt this void that he left inside of me that I used anything that I could to fill it up. I used work, drugs, sex, and distractions to convince myself that it would make it better for me. Nothing in the world could replace that feeling though."

After Dr. Lukas grabbed onto her hands, she leaned into his touch when he responded to her with compassion laced in his voice, "I'm sorry, Isabella. The loss of a parent is one that we can never replace even if we didn't have a relationship with them. It's worse that we didn't have a relationship with them since we'll always mourn what we'll never have with them. What about the void scares you? Is it the lack of control or is it the emptiness that comes with it?"

Her entire face turned white again when she told him with tears falling down her face, "It's both. I'm terrified that I'm going to become him. I've been scared of it since he died. I'm scared that it's too late for me. I feel like I'm outside of my body. I'm watching myself do things and I can't stop it from happening. I'm watching myself self-destruct and I can't do anything to stop it from happening."

Dr. Lukas held onto one of her hands as he wrote notes in his notebook when he asked her with a concerned look on his face, "How often does this dissociation happen to you? What happens when you're back in your body?"

She hid her shaky hands into her legs when she revealed to him refusing to look up at him, "A few times a week. I end up in places that I didn't remember going to. Like on the roof of my house or sleeping in a bed that isn't mine. The worst one was when I woke up standing on the ledge of the balcony of my bedroom. I don't remember how I got there. I knew that I didn't want to be up there, but I didn't know how to get down without falling down on the ground. Sasha helped off of the ledge."

Dr. Lukas nodded his head at her when he told her with a serious look on his face, "You had no memory of getting on the ledge? When did this incident happen?"

She confessed to him with a look of terror on her face, "No, I had no memory of it. This was last week. I might have been talking to my dad before I stood on the ledge of the balcony. I talk to him a lot. Sometimes I think that I hear him talking back to me. I wasn't sleeping during this time. I couldn't turn down the voices in my mind, so I stayed in that position on the balcony."

Dr. Lukas leaned forward on the seat when he asked her in a tense voice, "How often can you not sleep? How long has this been going on?"

She looked up at him when she responded to him with tears falling down her face, "It's been going on for most of my life. I've had these problems before I did drugs. Uncle Nathan told me that my father went through the same things. I got this from my dad."

Before Dr. Lukas could respond to her, there was a knock on the door from a nurse telling them that she had visitors when Dr. Lukas told the nurse that they would be done in a few minutes before the nurse went into the hallways again with her softly closing the door behind her. Once they were alone in the room, Dr. Lukas put away his notebook and pen into his pocket as he held onto her hands when he told her with a smile on her face, "Thank you for being so open with me, Isabella. We can talk tomorrow morning. Would it be okay if I spoke to your family when they were here visiting you? I don't want to do anything that you aren't comfortable with. Everything that you told me is confidential information."

She nodded her head at him as he let go of her hands before he went to the hallway to get her family. After she was alone in her hospital room, she wiped the tears off of her face before she softly sighed with a frown on her face. She laid down in the bed while she played with her blanket before her body perked up when she heard the door open to her room. Dr. Lukas walked into the room with her mother, her mum, Oliver, Sasha, Amelia, and Uncle Nathan following behind him. Before she got a chance to say anything to them, her mother pulled her into her arms as she hid her head into her chest before she desperately sobbed into her mother's chest like no one was there. There was eerie silence in the room where her mum and Uncle Nathan had a hushed conversation with Dr. Lukas outside of her room. She slowly moved her head out of her mother's chest where Sasha and Amelia wrapped her into a tight hug with her face hidden in Sasha's chest. As soon as she pulled her face out of Sasha's shoulder, her mum pulled her into a desperate hug with her face hidden in her chest where she almost fell apart again. Once she pulled herself out of her mum's arms, Oliver pulled her into a desperate hug that she didn't know that she needed from him. Oliver only let go of her until Uncle Nathan grabbed onto her shoulders before she threw herself into his arms where she fell apart all over again. Uncle Nathan held onto her until Dr. Lukas asked if he could speak to him in private where he gave her a sad smile before he followed Dr. Lukas out of the room. She laid down in the bed in exhaustion from everything that happened in the last twenty-four hours of her life. She woke up to her mother sitting in the chair next to her with a tired look on her face before her mother grabbed onto her hand with a sad smile on her face. After she spent a few more hours with her family, the nurses informed them that visiting hours were over where she said her emotional goodbyes to them. She didn't miss the way that her mother refused to let go of her until her mum pulled them apart from each other. Once she was alone in her room, she ate dinner that a nurse gave her before they gave her something that made her sleep for the rest of the night. She dreamed about dancing through the cosmos with her dad.

Chapter Twenty-Five

(Winter 1965 – New York, New York)

She spent three weeks at the psychiatric hospital. She talked to Dr. Lukas every morning. She answered his questions with a level of honesty that she never had with anyone else. She slowly got her freedom back where she moved around her floor without any supervision. She got her phone privileges back after a week of being there where she called her family during restricted hours of the day. Even though the call was monitored by the nurses, she was happy that she could talk to her family without seeing the concern on their faces. Oliver visited her during his lunch break, and he visited her after he was done working. He was the only person that could see her outside of the visiting hours since he worked there. They tried different medications that made her feel tired and nauseous all of the time before they found the right combination that worked for her. She didn't care what they had her on because she was able to sleep for the first time in over a year. She slept all day and all night. She was making up for the sleep that she missed the last year. They never told her what they diagnosed her with except for little hints along the way. She never asked them what they diagnosed her with since they weren't going to tell her if she asked them. Even though she was glad that they were protecting her from it, there was a part of her that wanted to know if she was like her father. She made a mental note to ask Dr. Taylor about what they diagnosed her when she saw him after she was discharged from the psychiatric hospital. Dr. Taylor was straightforward with her no matter what she asked him that Dr. Lukas would never be with her. On the morning of her being discharged from the psychiatric hospital, she ate her last meal in her bed with Oliver sitting next to her before the nurse told her that it was time to get ready to go home after Dr. Lukas signed her discharge papers. Once she changed into her regular clothes, her parents came into her room with a wheelchair before she left the hospital with her parents walking behind her as Oliver pushed her wheelchair. On the drive back to her house, her parents picked up her new medication from the pharmacy where she slept with her head leaning onto Oliver's shoulder before she woke up in the driveway of her house. Her parents helped her out of the car before she walked into her house for the first time in a month where Sasha and Amelia pulled her into a tight hug while she hid her face into Sasha's chest. Uncle Stan pulled her into a tight hug where she hid her face into his chest when he told her that he loved her before he kissed the top of her head. Thomas did the same thing after Uncle Stan let go of her before Juliet pulled her into her arms with her three-year-old niece Posey hugging her legs. Once she placed Posey on her hip, she walked into the kitchen to see that her mum made lunch for them. She went into her suite where she slept for most of the day. She would sleep for days if no one woke her up. Her parents told her the next morning that she was going to New York with them a little bit since they wanted to keep an eye on her. She didn't fight them on it since she missed her family in New York.

After Uncle Stan dropped them off at the airport, she slept for the flight to New York with her head leaning on Sasha's shoulder. Sasha came with them since she was off work for a while. When their plane landed in New York, Uncle Sam picked them up from the airport where he pulled her into his arms as she hid her face into his chest until Sasha pulled herself into their hug. Once Uncle Sam kissed them on the top of their heads, Uncle Sam drove to his house where Aunt Valeria waited for them on the porch. Aunt Valeria pulled her into a tight hug as she hid her face into her chest until Sasha threw herself into her mother's arms where she kept them there in her arms before Uncle Sam urged them to come into the house. When she walked through the front door, a large dog latched itself onto her legs where Aunt Valeria pushed the dog into the house. It was news to Sasha that her parents got a dog after Ivan moved out of the house. The large dog named Holly sat at the end of the table when they ate lunch in the kitchen to grab any of the extra food that fell on the floor. She fell asleep on the couch after dinner with her head on Sasha's lap until her parents took her to their house where she slept in their bedroom for the rest of the night. She couldn't get up the next day. After she spent the first few days home sleeping most of the day, she left the house for the first time after Anastasia and Nina invited them over to their apartment for dinner that night. Once she finished getting ready in the bathroom, Sasha picked her up at her house before she drove them over to her cousin's apartment building where they would be spending the night. As soon as she opened the door to her cousin's apartment, Anastasia pulled them into a tight hug with two-year-old niece Alina on her hip before she moved back to let them through the front door. Once Anastasia led them into the kitchen, Damien looked up from where he was preparing a salad where he placed the bowl onto the counter before he pulled her into his arms as she hid her face into his chest until Alina demanded his attention from the floor. She carried Alina into the living room where they played with toys on the floor while Damien mixed up the salad before Anastasia and Sasha caught up in the kitchen with music from the record player playing in the background. She pulled away from her when Nina walked into the apartment with her husband Joseph following behind her where he carried their newborn daughter Bridget in his arms. She placed Alina on her hip as Nina pulled her into a tight hug with her face hidden in her chest until Alina whined in her arms. Once she handed Alina over to Nina who placed her on her hip, she grabbed her niece Bridget from Joseph's arms where she placed the baby on her chest with Sasha standing next to her before she handed Bridget over to Sasha. Anastasia walked into the living room to tell everyone that it was time to eat as she grabbed Alina from Nina before she followed them into the kitchen where she sat at the table next to Sasha. Anastasia talked about the early stages of her pregnancy with her second child where Nina talked about the birth of her daughter. No one asked her about what happened for her to end up in a psychiatric hospital and she was grateful about it. She wasn't ready to talk about it with anyone that wasn't a medical professional.

After they ate dinner in the kitchen, Nina brought Bridget into the living room to nurse her as Anastasia put Alina to bed for the night in her bedroom where she helped Damien clean up the dishes in silence before he went into the living room with Joseph to watch television. She grabbed her purse from the living room with a box of cigarettes and a lighter in her hands as well as a blanket that she grabbed off of the couch before she walked out onto the balcony. As soon as she walked out onto the balcony, Sasha looked up at her with a cigarette hanging out of her mouth where she took a seat next to her before she lit a cigarette from the box with her inhaling the smoke. She inhaled the smoke from her cigarette as she listened to sounds of the city underneath them when Sasha asked her with a smile on her face, "How are you doing?"

After she inhaled the smoke from her cigarette, she shrugged her shoulders at her when she responded to her with a frown on her face, "I don't know. I'm tired. How are you?"

Sasha looked up at her with the cigarette in between her fingers when she told her with an unreadable expression on her face, "I don't know either, Isabella. I think that I'm happy, but I don't know what that means anymore."

After she inhaled the smoke from her cigarette, she looked down at her shaky hands that she hid into her blanket that was around her shoulders when she responded to her, "I get that, Sasha. I've never known what it means to feel happy. Happiness doesn't exist. It's as fake as the American dream, which is also dead. We spend our lives looking for happiness. A happiness that doesn't exist in the world."

Sasha softly chuckled when she told her with a smirk on her face, "You're hilarious, Isabella. Is that what therapy taught you over the years? Happiness is a fairytale."

She smacked Sasha's arm with her softly groaning at her when she responded to her with a serious look on her face, "I didn't mean it like that, Sasha. I think that happiness is possible, but it's rare to find. Like a Jem in the wild. In a lifetime, there are few moments that you will experience happiness. It's like enlightenment from Buddhism. It's a once in a lifetime experience and you die after it."

Sasha lit a cigarette with her inhaling the smoke from it when she responded to her, "Buddhism? Where is my cousin and what have you done with her? Did you learn this in therapy?"

After she rolled her eyes in annoyance at Sasha, she lit another cigarette with her inhaling the smoke from it when she responded to her with a frown on her face, "I didn't learn this in therapy, Sasha. I read books about it when I was in the hospital. What's wrong? Can I not appreciate Buddhism?"

Sasha looked up at her with a softer expression when she told her, "I didn't say that, Isabella. You can believe in whatever you want to believe in. I don't care what you believe in. I'm impressed that you read books since you refused to read anything assigned to us in school. You're being serious. It's been a while since you have been like this. You haven't been like this since we were children."

She tried to hide her offense from Sasha even though she knew that she could see it when she responded to Sasha with an unreadable expression on her face, "That's not what I needed to hear. Just when I was feeling better about myself. I don't know how you want me to act. Should I act like I did when I was high? Should I act like I did when I was trying to kill myself? I know that you hated that. I don't know. I'm too tired to deal with this. You can think whatever you want about me. I don't give a shit."

Sasha's face turned white as she grabbed onto her hands when she responded to her with desperation laced in her voice, "I'm sorry, Isabella. I didn't mean to make you upset. I wanted to spend time with you. Not fight with you. I don't know how to act around you since everything happened with Daxton. It's hard to know how to act."

She let out a defeated sigh when she responded to her with a frown on her face, "It's okay, Sasha. I'm not mad at you. I don't blame you. I don't know how to act with myself either. I feel strange. I'm watching myself do things, but I'm not in control. I've felt that way most of my life. I didn't realize it until it was too late to stop it."

Sasha kept a tight grip on her hands as she inhaled the smoke from her cigarette when she responded to Isabella with a concerned look on her face, "Do you want to talk about what happened? I wanted to know about it, but I didn't want to ask you until you were ready to talk about it."

After she leaned onto the chair with her eyes closed, she let out a shaky breath when she responded to Sasha with tears falling down her face, "It's okay, Sasha. It's hard for me to talk about it. I don't think that I'll ever be ready to talk about it with anyone. What did you want to know about it?"

Sasha wrapped her arms around her shoulder when she asked Isabella, "What did it feel like to be in places that you didn't remember going to?"

She confessed to her cousin, "It was terrifying, Sasha. I can't remember how any of it happened. It was like I was sleeping before I woke up in places that I didn't remember going to. Dr. Lukas told me that I was disassociating. It's my mind's way of protecting myself from overwhelming feelings and thoughts that I don't know how to deal with. It's a coping mechanism. A poor one, but it's a coping mechanism. He thinks that I'm schizophrenic and bipolar. Did you know that my dad was schizophrenic and bipolar?"

Sasha shook her head at her when she responded to her with a frown on her face, "I didn't know that. Who told you?"

Isabella responded to her with tears falling down her face, "Uncle Nathan told me that a while ago. He told me that dad was diagnosed with other things, but he didn't know what they were on the top of his head. I'm disappointing my dad. I can't hide my problems like he did. I'm incapable of hiding it. I get thoughts in my mind that remind me of my dad. Do you want to know one?"

Sasha tightened her grip on her shoulder when she asked her, "What is it?"

She confessed to her in a distant voice, "My life would be easier if no one knew that I had these problems. If I was capable of hiding it, then I wouldn't feel this insistent urge to get out of my skin. People wouldn't look at me the way that they look at me. People wouldn't treat me like I'm going to fall apart. I would be looked at like the unflawed person that I craved. I wouldn't treat myself like I'm going to fall apart.

If I could take back one moment in my life, I would take back when I overdosed at the club. Not because it almost killed me. I want to take back that moment because that was when everything changed for me. No one would've known about who I am if I never overdosed in the club. I'm so envious of people that don't have this shadow following them anywhere that they go in the world. I want that life back. I would do anything to get that life back. That sounds fucked up. I don't care that it's fucked up. You don't know how it feels to live like this. You don't know how it feels to have this shadow haunting you that you can't get rid of no matter what. It's so exhausting."

She threw herself into Sasha's arms as she let out heartbreaking sobs into her chest with her arms tightly around her. She slowly pulled her face out of Sasha's chest as Sasha wiped away the tears from her face when she responded to her with her holding onto her arms, "It's a gift that you can't hide how you feel from the world. My god, Isabella. Look how far that hiding himself from the world got your father. I'm not saying this to scare you, but someone needs to say it. You would already be dead if you hid this from the world. That was what killed your father. He wasn't killed by drugs. He wasn't killed by alcohol. His secrets killed him. Every time that you kept secrets from the world it almost killed you. Why would it be easier if no one knew about this? Would it be easier for you because you would've already died? Tell me how it would be better than this."

After she leaned her head on Sasha's shoulder, she let out a defeated sigh when she responded to her with tears falling down her face, "You're right. Those secrets would've killed me. That was the point of them. I wanted them to kill me. Do you think that things would be better if they did?"

Sasha blinked back tears that fell down her face when she told her in a firm voice, "It wouldn't be better. Where the hell is this coming from? Are you telling me something that you don't want to admit? It's working if that's your goal. Do you want to know what I think about this? You're scared about what's going to happen to you. I don't blame you for being scared. I'm terrified. It's okay to be scared. It means that you care about something. I've watched you not care for so long that it's making me emotional to see you care about something. I'm relieved that you care about yourself. It's been hard to watch what led up to this. You're allowed to be scared, Isabella. I'm terrified for you."

She took her head off of Sasha's shoulder as she wiped away tears from her face when she told her with a frown on her face, "I'm tired. Can we talk about this later?"

Sasha grabbed onto her hands when she responded to her with a smile on her face, "Let's go to bed. We can talk about it later." After she got up from the chair with a box of cigarettes and her lighter in her pocket, Sasha guided them into the darkened apartment since everyone was sleeping in their bedrooms. Once she walked into the guest bedroom, she laid down in the bed where she pulled the blankets on her before she fell asleep for the rest of the night.

Chapter Twenty-Six
(Spring 1965 – Los Angeles, California)

After over a month of her going to Dr. Taylor's office twice a week, he cleared her to come to the office once a week. She told him about all of her fears. She told him that she was afraid of what her life was going to look like in the future. She told him that she was afraid that these moments were going to define her for the rest of her life. Even though no one else would define this way, she would see the worst version of herself. She told him that she didn't want her life to end like her father's life ended. She wasn't going to be the person that she wanted to be. She couldn't hide her problems from the world. She was never going to have a father who didn't kill himself. She was never going to have a mother that wasn't raped by her father. She was always going to be an addict. She was always going to be mentally ill. She was always going to be a serious person. Her parent's actions would always define her. She couldn't take any of it back. She couldn't change what happened to her. She told him about what Juliet told her when they were in Hawaii about her being stuck in the past. When Dr. Taylor asked her what she thought about it, she told him that she didn't know how to feel about it. She was so bitter that she didn't begin to look at what she was telling her. She stayed up all night smoking cigarettes on the balcony since she couldn't get her mind to turn off without doing drugs. She thought about doing drugs when she couldn't sleep at night, but there wasn't anything left hiding in the house. She wasn't in the mood to deal with the aftermath of that. She knew that her cousins wouldn't leave her alone. She just got them off of her back, so she wasn't in the mood to start that up again. She came to a conclusion about it. At the next session with Dr. Taylor, she told him that she needed to stop living in the past. She didn't want to live in the past. She wanted to live in the future. It didn't scare her that she didn't know what that future was going to look like. The future no longer scared her. The past no longer scared her. The present no longer scared her. The only other time in her life that she felt this way was when she was high on drugs. She thought that she would never find this feeling without doing drugs. She told him about this feeling that she was searching for. He asked her what scared her the most. She told him that she was terrified that this feeling would go away and never came back again. She didn't want to lose what she gained from the world. It was a few days after her session with Dr. Taylor that they were preparing to have guests over at the house. They had Oliver, Juliet, Posey, Uncle Stan, and Thomas over for dinner.

After she spent most of the day sleeping in the suite, she woke up to Amelia and Sasha blasting music outside by the pool as she rolled over to fall back to sleep before the maid came into the room to clean the suite like she did every weekend. She went into the kitchen where she grabbed a piece of fruit from the counter before she sat outside by the pool with Amelia and Sasha. While the chef made dinner, she changed into a long dress before she joined her cousins in the kitchen with a glass of wine for her in their hands. She drank wine a few months ago for the first time in years. Dr. Taylor assured her that she could drink occasionally if she showed everyone around her that she was okay with it. After Uncle Stan and Thomas helped themselves into the house, they pulled her into a tight hug where she didn't let go of them until she heard Amelia complaining to the maid about the placement of the spoons. Once she let go of them, she walked into the kitchen to deal with Amelia's problem as she apologized to the maid on her behalf before she excused the maid for the weekend. As soon as she walked into the living room, Oliver walked into the house as Juliet followed behind him with her three-year-old niece Posey on her hip before Oliver pulled her into a tight hug where they didn't let go of each other until Posey ran into her legs. Once she let go of her grip on Oliver, she pulled Juliet into a tight hug as she placed Posey on her hip where they ate dinner in the kitchen. Juliet put Posey to sleep in one of the guest bedrooms before they went into the living room to watch a movie. Uncle Stan and Thomas left to go home since they had to get up early for work. In the middle of the movie, she moved out of the spot in between Amelia and Sasha before she ran into the bathroom to vomit up her dinner into the toilet. She didn't tell her cousins that she was sick every night. She didn't want to make them concerned about her. Once she rinsed her mouth out in the sink, she grabbed a blanket from her bed before she ran into the living room where she laid down in spot in between Sasha and Amelia. Oliver looked over at her with a concerned expression on his face before he focused on the movie with his arm wrapped around Juliet's shoulder. When the movie was done, Juliet pecked Oliver's lips before she went into the guest bedroom where Posey was sleeping for the night. Amelia and Sasha cleaned up the living room as she poured herself a glass of wine before she followed Oliver outside by the pool. After she took a seat on a pool chair, she placed a blanket over her legs as she took a sip of the wine before she set the glass onto the table where Oliver sat next to her. Oliver looked up at her when he asked her with concern laced his voice, "When did you start drinking again? I didn't know that you were drinking."

She shrugged her shoulders when she responded to him with an annoyed look on her face, "A few months ago. Why does it matter if I drink? I'm not going to kill myself by drinking too much wine."

Oliver's face turned white when he responded to her with anger laced in his voice, "I don't know that. Anything is possible with you. Why are you acting so defensive right now? Is there something that you aren't telling me?"

She grabbed her box of cigarettes from the table as she lit one that she discarded earlier in the day before she inhaled the smoke from it. Oliver let out a defeated sigh when he told her with a look of concern on his face, "What is this, Isabella? There's something that you aren't telling me. Do you want to tell me before I guess what it is?"

She inhaled the smoke from her cigarette when she responded to him with frustration laced in her voice, "Jesus Christ, Oliver. You're being direct. I'm not sleeping. That's the secret. Are you happy?"

Oliver's face softened when he told her with a frown on his face, "Shit. I'm sorry, Isabella. I didn't mean to say it like that. Why aren't you sleeping? Does Dr. Taylor know?"

She inhaled the smoke from her cigarette when she responded to him with a smile on her face, "It's okay, Oliver. I'm not upset with you. Of course, he knows. He knows more about me than anyone else. We're trying to figure that out. You don't want to know why I can't sleep. It's a complicated answer that doesn't make any sense."

Oliver looked at her when he responded to her in a stern voice, "I want to know. You don't get to make decisions for me."

She inhaled the smoke from her cigarette when she confessed to him with a frown on her face, "I have these nightmares that wake me up throughout the night. I'm reliving the worst moments of my life until I wake up screaming. I stop sleeping for a few days at a time where I smoke cigarettes on my balcony outside all night. I had this nightmare last night that was so horrible that I couldn't stop puking into my toilet until there was nothing left in my body."

Oliver grabbed onto her hands when he asked her with a concerned look on his face, "What are the nightmares about?"

She shook her head at him when she begged him with a look of terror on her face, "I can't say it. It's horrible. There are things that no one knows about me. Things that I didn't want anyone to know about me. I'm betraying myself if I tell anyone else."

Oliver tightened his grip on her hands when he responded to her in a soft voice, "It's okay, Isabella. You don't have to say anything that you don't want to. Calm down."

As she hid her face into her hands, he pulled her into his arms where she hid her face into his chest. Oliver tightened his grip on her arms as she let out desperate sobs into his chest with him running his hand down her back before Sasha and Amelia ran outside towards them. Oliver shook his head at him before they walked into the house. After she calmed herself down, she slowly moved her face out of his chest with his arms tightly around her. She wiped tears off of her face when she told him in a numb voice, "I'm sorry, Oliver. I don't know where it came from. I haven't been able to sleep for a few days, so I'm more emotional than usual. I didn't mean to scare you. I thought no one noticed it. I forgot that you see everything."

Oliver grabbed onto her hands when he responded to her with a serious look on his face, "Stop it. It's okay, Isabella. You're allowed to be emotional. I only see everything when it's you. I'm not nearly as knowledgeable with anyone else except you. It's different with Juliet than with you. You're my celestial sister and I'm your celestial brother. We're dancing through the cosmos together."

She rolled her eyes at him in fake annoyance when she responded to him with a smirk on her face, "Oliver! You sounded like my mother when you said that! Have you been spending time with her behind my back? What does she say to my celestial brother when I'm not around? Does she wish that I was a boy instead of a girl? Is she disappointed that her only child is me?"

Oliver gently pushed her on her shoulder when he responded to her with sarcasm laced in his voice, "I spend more time with your mother than you do. I'm her favorite child. She told me that I'm easier to handle. You don't want to know what she thinks about your career. She thinks my job is more respected than yours is."

As soon as they looked at each other, they laughed into their hands until they were out of breath where Oliver sat down on the pool chair next to her before she lit a cigarette with her shaking hands. Once she caught her breath again, she inhaled the smoke from the cigarette when she said to him with a serious look on her face, "You're right about my mom. You are her favorite child, Oliver. You were from the moment that you were born. I could never compete with you. I never tried to compete with you. I was always going to lose. She raised you before she raised me. It's okay. I'm not upset about it. You're the son that she never had. Even if I was born a boy, I would never be that to her either."

Oliver grabbed onto her hands when he responded to her, "You know that isn't true. You're her baby girl. You are always going to be her baby girl. Do you remember what she told you when you moved here?"

She responded to him with tears falling down her face, "Of course I do, Oliver. She told me that she loved me. Everything that she went through to get to this point in our lives was worth the pain. She would do it all over again if she had to, so that she could give me a life that she never had. When I was old enough to understand it, she told me the truth about how I was made. She told me that I was born out of rape. I was guilty about that since I was old enough to understand what it meant. That's what I dream about. I dream about my mother getting raped by my father. That's why I wake up screaming every night. I've known about it. Can I tell you a secret that I've never told anyone before?"

Oliver tightened his grip on her hands when he told her with a smile on his face, "Yes, you can. You can tell me anything, Isabella."

She let out a shaky breath when she confessed to him with tears falling down her face, "Daxton would do things to me when I passed out that I didn't remember happening. Things that he didn't do to me when I was awake. He choked me to see how long it would take me to pass out. I didn't know that it was happening until it was too late to stop it. I dream about that a lot, you know? That was why I ended up at the hospital last year. It was crashing down on me. I didn't know what to do to stop it from hurting me. I thought that it would be easier to give into it rather than fighting it. I'm not saying this to upset you even though I can tell that you're really upset by it. I wanted you to be the first person that I talked to about it since you are the most important person in my life."

Tears fell down Oliver's face before she pulled him into a long hug where she hid her face into his chest with his arms tightly around her. Oliver kissed her on the top of her head when he whispered to her like it was a secret between them , "Thank you for telling me that. Daxton is lucky that he's dead because I would kill that fucker myself in an instant. I love you so much that it hurts me, Isabella. No one is allowed to do that to you. I understand why I can't sleep. Do you plan on telling anyone else about it? Like Dr. Taylor? Or your mother?"

She told him with a stern look on her face, "I'm not ready to talk about it. I trust that this is going to stay between us until then."

Oliver nodded his head at her when he told her with a serious look on his face, "I promise. I wouldn't say anything about it unless you do first." She grabbed onto his hand as he pulled her into his arms where she hid her face into her chest. She slowly moved her head out of his chest as she wiped tears off of her face before she followed him into the house before Oliver went into the guest bedroom with Juliet and Posey. She went to her suite on the other side of the house as she closed the door behind her before she laid down in bed. She hid her face into her pillow before she fell asleep for the night.

Chapter Twenty-Seven
(Summer 1965 – London, England)

The nightmares got worse after her conversation with Oliver. She understood what her mother went through with her father. She knew that her mother would understand what she was going through. She didn't want to tell her about it since it would feel real to her. If she never talked about it, then it wasn't real to her. She didn't want to talk about it with anyone. She didn't want them to see her in the way that she saw herself. She understood why her father hid his life from the world. It was easier to pretend that nothing was going on than for her to admit that she was experiencing something that she couldn't deal with on her own. She had a hunger for drugs. Her life was consumed by them. She thought about drugs every moment of her life. She thought about drugs when she woke up in the morning. She thought about drugs when she walked around the house. She thought about drugs when she went to bed at night. Her life revolved around drugs. She didn't have the nerve to reach out to her old dealer to buy drugs from him since she was trying not to do drugs. The only thing that stopped her from doing drugs was that she didn't want to lose the trust that she earned back from her cousins. She couldn't imagine how they would react to any of this information, so she kept to herself in the suite where she left it to grab food for herself in the kitchen or when she went to her sessions with Dr. Taylor once a week. She brought up drugs with Dr. Taylor since she knew that he was the only person that wouldn't have any reaction to it. It was his job to be professionally indifferent to the things that people told him, and this was no exception. After she told him that she couldn't stop thinking about doing drugs, he asked her why she couldn't stop thinking about drugs. She told him about how Daxton sexually assaulted her when she was unconscious. She told him about the nightmares that she had about Daxton raping her like when her father raped her mother. She told him that she couldn't fall asleep without waking up screaming every night. She told him that she couldn't control the way that she felt about her body. She told him that she felt like she was dying. She told him that she didn't know what to do with these intense emotions. When Dr. Taylor told her that this was the reason that she wanted to do drugs again, everything suddenly made sense to her. Drugs were her only coping mechanism to deal with her problems. She didn't know how to deal with her problems without drugs. She didn't think that she was capable of dealing with her problems without drugs. Dr. Taylor told her that she wasn't dealing with her problems when she was doing drugs. She was using drugs to ignore her problems. By suppressing her feelings, she was making her problems worse than they were before. She didn't confront her problems when she ignored them.

She was awake for the rest of the night smoking cigarettes on her balcony until the sun came up the next morning. When she walked into the kitchen to grab some food, Amelia asked her what she did all night where she told her that she was dealing with her problems. After Amelia left for work, she called Dr. Taylor to tell him about her night on the balcony. He told her that he could see her that afternoon where she spent several hours crying in his office about everything that she confronted that night. She slept that night without a care in the world. After her session with Dr. Taylor, she got a phone call from her mother about her cousin Sean and Polly Turner's wedding in London in a month where she asked her if they were coming to it. This was the first time that she heard anything about her cousin Sean getting married, but she told her mother that she would love to go to the wedding since she had nothing better to do with her time. After she dodged her mother's questions about her well-being that she asked her about many times, she asked Amelia and Sasha if they knew about Sean's wedding where they weren't surprised by this news since Sean was Amelia's brother and he told her about it. It was a few weeks later that Oliver, Juliet, and Posey were at the house for dinner that she asked them if they were going to Sean's wedding in London where they told her that they already bought their tickets for the plane. After a few nights of her spiraling in the suite, she worked up the nerve to call her dealer until she realized that his phone was disconnected a long time ago. While they had a movie night in the living room, she laid down on the couch in between Amelia and Sasha with her head resting on Sasha's shoulder when she asked them if they knew that their old dealer's phone was disconnected. She instantly knew that she said the wrong thing since Sasha and Amelia stared at her with a look of fear in their eyes. She told them that she didn't do anything since she couldn't get a hold of him. That didn't make anything better since they knew that she intended on buying drugs from him when she called him. When she realized that she couldn't escape this situation, she caved into herself when she told them about her thinking about doing drugs and her inability to sleep. She knew that this calmed them down a little bit since she was at least being honest with them about it this time instead of them finding out in a worse way like the other times. Even though she reassured them that it was a moment of weakness, she didn't believe the lie that came out of her mouth when she said it aloud to them. They insisted on sleeping in the suite with her that night. She didn't fight against them since she didn't have the energy to do it. They sent Thomas to the house to babysit her during the day while everyone was at work where she walked television in the suite with her head laying on his chest. They made her have a babysitter for weeks after her accidental confession to them. She found Chloe's phone number in Sasha's purse. She didn't know how to ask Sasha about it. Chloe was surprised to hear from her until she asked her if she had the phone number for her dealer. Chloe told her that their dealer was in prison before she asked her that she would talk to Sasha on her behalf since Sasha wouldn't talk to her. She told Chloe that she would talk to Sasha if she gave her the phone number of her new dealer. She knew that Chloe had a new one after their old dealer got sent to prison. Chloe hesitantly gave her the phone number that she was looking for as she promised her that she would talk to Sasha when she got back from her work trip to Colorado.

On the night that she was about to leave to go to her new dealer's house, she was ambushed by her cousins and Chloe who ended up snitching on her where they refused to let her leave the house before she retreated back into the suite for the rest of the night. She ignored her cousins until they were supposed to leave the country for Sean's wedding before her parents unexpectedly showed up at her house. On the night before their flight to London, she spent the night smoking cigarettes on the balcony where she ignored everyone that tried to talk to her except for Posey who was too adorable for her to ignore. When it was time for them to leave for the airport, she made one last ditch effort to look for hidden drugs around the house before she went downstairs with her suitcase in her hand where she followed her family to the car before Uncle Stan drove them to the airport. On the flight to New York, she passed out with her head resting on her mum's shoulder after she took a sleeping pill that her mother gave her for the rest of the morning. After their plane landed in New York that afternoon, Uncle Sam waited at the airport where he pulled her into a long hug that she didn't ask him for with her face hidden in his chest before she walked over to the car. After they ate dinner at Uncle Sam's house, she spent the night smoking cigarettes on the patio with their dog Holly sleeping on her lap. Her parents made her spend the night at Uncle Sam's house. They knew that she didn't hide any drugs at their house like she did at her parent's house. Aunt Valeria woke her up the next morning to tell her that breakfast was ready. After she ate breakfast with her family, Uncle Sam drove them to the airport where they met up with Nina, Joseph, and her nine-month-old niece Bridget who was asleep in Nina's arms. Anastasia, Damien, her two-year-old niece Alina, and her two-month-old nephew Viktor were taking an afternoon flight. Uncle Sam and Aunt Valeria brought their dog Holly with them since no one could watch her. On the flight to London, she sat in between Uncle Sam and Aunt Valeria since she didn't want to be apart from Holly who slept in her lap. She slept for the flight to London with her head leaning on Uncle Sam's shoulder. Her cousins Sean and Tommy picked them up from the airport where she hugged them before she pulled Holly's leash to take her outside. No one stopped her from taking a sudden interest in Holly since it was most normal that she was in a long time. They didn't want to stop her from feeling better. Holly really liked her, so it was an obvious choice to let her take care of Holly while they were in England. After Sean and Tommy dropped them off at their hotel, she pulled Holly's lease as she ran around down the hall into her hotel room that she shared with Amelia and Sasha. Her parents stayed in the room next to them. Oliver's family and Uncle Sam and Aunt Valeria stayed in the rooms across the hall. Nina's family and Uncle Stan and Thomas stayed on the floor below them where Anastasia's family stayed in a room near them. Her family from York weren't flying to London. They chose to drive. It was cheaper since they had to pay for the hotel. During her first day in London, she took a nap on the bed with Amelia and Sasha for the rest of the morning until Anastasia, who landed in London while they were asleep, wanted to go sightseeing. Even though she was exhausted from traveling, she went sightseeing with them with Holly coming with them. After she changed out of her travel outfit, she took Holly from Uncle Sam's room before she explored London with Anastasia, Damien, Nina, Joseph, Sasha, Amelia, Oliver, and Juliet. Their parents watched the children, so that they could spend time with each other. They got back to the hotel after they walked around London. She let Holly sleep in Uncle Sam's hotel room before they met up with Sean, Polly, Tommy, and his girlfriend Lilly Allen at a restaurant where they ate dinner together while they caught up with each other. Sean was in university to be a pastor like Uncle James was and he met Polly there. Tommy moved to London a few months ago to pursue a career as an artist that his parents didn't understand. Tommy met Lilly at an art exhibition that he was holding that her family was sponsoring where they instantly had a connection with each other. Lilly was from an aristocratic family from all the way back to the Middle Ages that owned castles like kings and queens used to own in the past. Lilly promised to show them her family's properties the next time that they were visiting London with her parent's permission. After they got back to their hotel room, she passed out in the bed for the rest of the night. She woke up the next morning to Holly licking her face as she loudly laughed at the dog where she accidentally woke up her cousins who were asleep in the bed with her. She went on a walk with Holly around the city since her cousins weren't free. They had dress fittings for the wedding to attend that she didn't want to be a part of. Uncle Stan and Thomas decided to tag along with her since they had nothing else to do. As she guided Holly with a lease throughout the city, Uncle Stan told her stories about his life in London when he was younger like it happened to him yesterday. Thomas stared at his boyfriend with a smile on his face. Uncle Stan never talked about his life in England. She learned things about London that she didn't know about.

After she woke up from a nap, Uncle Nathan stood in her hotel room with Holly jumping up and down on his legs like she remembered him from the last time. As soon as Uncle Nathan pulled in a much-needed hug, she hid her face into his chest as she blinked back tears that fell down her face while Holly laid down on the bed next to her. Uncle Nathan didn't let go of her until Oliver opened the door with Posey in his arms before he pulled Oliver into a tight hug that she didn't feel like she needed to be in the room for. Once she changed into a long dress, she joined her family in the lobby of the hotel where they ate dinner at a restaurant before they caught up with each other. Aunt Sylvia and Aunt Priscilla talked about how the bakery business was doing in the last year. Uncle Nathan told them stories about passengers that he met and places that he saw while he flew planes across the world. Uncle Sam talked about how his toy factory was doing and how they created a new toy that was a best-selling product. Aunt Valeria and Anastasia talked about how well the hair salon was doing since they started cutting and styling children's hair. Teddy talked about how the construction business was booming since he took over the family company after his father's death. Audrey talked about her pregnancy and her cousins with children talked about parenthood. Ivan and Jamie were flying from Paris in time for the wedding rehearsal tomorrow afternoon. After they got back to their hotel room that night, she smoked cigarettes on the balcony in silence for the rest of the night. She wanted to get a little bit of sleep that morning, but Sasha and Amelia dragged her to the airport to pick up Ivan and Jamie. When they spotted Ivan and Jamie in the crowd, there were two guys with them who they introduced as their boyfriends. Christophe Rue met Jamie a few weeks after they moved to Paris since he was the photographer that took pictures of him. Since Jamie and Christophe liked each other, they introduced Ivan to Antonine Rue who was his younger brother who also was a photographer that took pictures of Ivan for a past photoshoot. Jamie, Christophe, Ivan and Antonine became attached at the hip. They did everything together from working to spending the night at each other's houses to traveling the world for work. Even though they were open with them about their boyfriends, they didn't want the family to know the truth about their relationship except for her parents, Uncle Stan, and Thomas who understood it. She knew that Jamie and Ivan's parents wouldn't get it since they didn't know about Sasha and Amelia's past partners. Most notably Chloe who dated her cousins at different times in the past. They went sightseeing with Ivan, Jamie, and their boyfriends around the city. They met up with the family that were surprised to see Christophe and Antonine. Their parents believed that they were friends from France before they moved on with the dress rehearsal. Since she wasn't at the wedding party, she was pulled with Sasha, Poppy, and her boyfriend Ellis Brown to watch the younger children with George and Alfie helping them. She chased Leo and Mason in the grass field with George, Sasha and Poppy painted Lena, Alina, and Posey's nails while Alfie and Ellis took turns putting Bridget and Viktor to sleep in their arms. When the dress rehearsal was over, they went to a restaurant for dinner where they laughed with each other until it was time to go sleep in their hotel rooms. On the morning of the wedding, she woke up to Posey and Lena jumping up and down on the bed since they became best friends in their short time together before Amelia and Sasha groaned on the other side of the bed. After she pulled Posey and Lena into a tickling session with their laughter filling up the air, she told Sasha and Amelia that they needed to get up if they wanted to go to the wedding where they went into the bathroom to get ready with her.

Once they got to the church that Sean worked at, she joined the girls in a side room where Aunt Valeria and Anastasia did their hair for them as Amelia did their makeup for them. When it was time for the first look, she joined her cousins as Sean saw Polly in her wedding dress for the first time with tears in their eyes. When it was time for the wedding to begin, she joined her family and Polly's family in the church as her cousins walked down the aisle with their partners before they were married by Uncle James who officiated the wedding. After they ate a delicious meal in a pavilion outside of the church, there were football games played by the boys where the girls talked to each other as the children played on the playground. When it got dark outside, most people went inside of the church where they ate dessert in soft conversation with each other. She stayed outside with the children to watch them catch lightning bugs. After Audrey brought Lena and Leo inside with her, she watched Posey as she ran through the grass with a net in her hands to catch bugs while she sat on the picnic bench with a cigarette in her hands. As she inhaled the smoke from it, a figure walked towards her before they took a seat next to her where she looked over to see Uncle Nathan next to her. Uncle Nathan broke the silence when he asked her with a smile on his face, "How are you doing?"

She shrugged her shoulders at him when she responded to him with sarcasm laced in her voice, "I've been great. Things have been great. I haven't been going through anything. Why would something be wrong?"

Uncle Nathan softly chuckled when he responded to her, "You sounded so much like Will when you said that. I'm being serious. Are you doing alright? I heard from your mother that something is going on. Is your mother right, Isabella?"

She lit another cigarette as she inhaled the smoke from it when she responded to him with frustration laced in her voice, "Of course my mother would tell you that. She must be desperate if she got you involved this time. Something is always going on, Uncle Nathan. There's never a moment in my life that nothing isn't going on. I don't want to get into it. I would rather talk about something else."

Uncle Nathan let out a defeated sigh as he leaned onto the table when he responded to her with a serious look on his face, "That's okay honey. We don't have to talk about it if you don't want to. What do you want to talk about?"

She inhaled the smoke from her cigarette when she told him with a frown on her face, "I want to talk about my dad. Can we talk about him?"

Uncle Nathan nodded his head at her when he asked her with a look of uncertainty on his face, "What do you want to know about him?"

She told him with a smile on her face, "I want to talk about when he did drugs. I want to know if he was like me."

After Uncle Nathan lit the cigarette, he inhaled the smoke from it when he confessed to her with a look of fondness on his face, "Will used drugs off and on before I left for the military, but it wasn't anything serious until after I left for the war. He didn't think that anyone knew about it, but I knew that something was wrong with him. One afternoon when he was over at your mother's house, I went into his bedroom to steal cigarettes from him that he stole from our dad. I didn't find the cigarettes, but I found bottles of pills hidden under his bed. I was so angry at him that I got rid of them. When he got home from your mother's house, he was pissed off at me for getting rid of his pills, but he couldn't tell me why he needed them or where he got them from. I knew that he stole them from your grandmother. It had her name on them. Our parents didn't take medicine, so he couldn't take it from them. He told me that he would stop it if I didn't tell them. I believed that he would stop, so I never told our parents."

She tried to hide her shock from him when she asked him, "Dad stole pills from my grandmother? Did she find out that he took her pills?"

Uncle Nathan responded to her with a frown on his face, "She knew that Will was stealing pills from her. She confronted him about it when she realized that her pills were going missing. She thought that Kenny stole them from her before she realized that Will took them. Even though she threatened to tell our parents about it, she didn't tell them about it. She gave pills to him when she realized that she could help him out. They would get high together when no one else was around them."

Her jaw dropped in shock that she couldn't hide from him when she asked him, "My mother had no idea that this was happening. How did you know that this was going on?"

Uncle Nathan brought the cigarette to his lips with inhaling the smoke from it when he confessed to her, "I knew that he was hiding something from me, and I needed to know what it was. He would've never told me if I asked him. The only person that knew was Kenny. He knew everything that I did."

Her jaw dropped when she asked him with a look of confusion on her face, "Uncle Kenny knew that my dad was stealing pills from my grandmother? Why didn't he tell my mother about it?"

Uncle Nathan looked at her like she said something wrong when he responded to her in a tight voice, "You know that wouldn't have made anything better. He didn't want to burden your mother. He felt enough guilt about everything that happened with her that he didn't want to add it to her problems. Kenny knew about Will long before I did. Your grandmother told Kenny everything. He was her best friend. Did your mother tell you about what happened to her when she was a child?"

She nodded her head at him when she responded to him with her lips pressed in a thin line, "She told me a little bit about it. She told me that dad knew about it before she did. She didn't know that until he put it into his suicide note. She talked about how much she wanted to know about that conversation between dad and Uncle Kenny. She wanted to know what was said between them that would make them take their secrets to the grave."

Uncle Nathan put out his cigarette into the ashtray as he pulled out a folded piece of paper out of his pocket before he handed it to her when he told her with a serious look on his face, "You don't have to wonder. This letter should give you answers. It's the letter that I promised that I would give to you. You don't have to read it right now. Read it in your own time. Mail it to me when you're done with it."

Once she took the letter from him, she placed it into her jacket pocket as she threw herself into his arms before he wrapped his arms around her. As she hid her head into his chest, Uncle Nathan tightened his grip on her arms as he kissed her on the top of her head when he whispered into her like it was a secret between them, "Your father would be proud of you, Isabella. He would be shocked how much his daughter was like him. He loved you. He didn't want any of this to happen. He never wanted you to go through what he went through in his life. I love you. I'm sorry for everything. He didn't deserve it, and you don't deserve it either."

Posey ran into her legs as she wiped away tears off of her face before she pulled Posey onto her lap. As Posey hid her face into her chest, she ran her fingers through her hair as she looked up at Uncle Nathan when she told him with a smile on her face, "Thank you. I love you too, Uncle Nathan. I'll read the letter later. Posey wants to sleep, so I'm going to give her to Juliet. I'll see you before we leave in the morning." Uncle Nathan kissed her on the top of her head when he told her goodnight before she carried Posey into the church where she handed her to Juliet and Oliver. When it was time to go back to the hotel, she fell asleep with her head resting on Sasha's shoulder in the car until her parents guided her into the hotel room before she passed out in her bed for the rest of the night.

Chapter Twenty-Eight

(Fall 1965 – Los Angeles, California)

She said an emotional goodbye to her family in England before she got on a flight to the states with her family. After she slept for the flight to New York with her head resting on her mother's shoulder, she stayed at her parent's house for a few days before she went to Los Angeles with her family that lived there. Even though it was hard for her to be apart from Holly who she grew attached to over the past week, she told the puppy that she would see her in a few months even though she knew that Holly had no idea what she was saying to her. On the flight to Los Angeles, she took a sleeping pill that her mother left with her back in England as she slept with her head resting on Amelia's shoulder before she woke her up when they landed in California. After Uncle Stan dropped them off at the house, she went into the suite to sleep for the rest of the day. She woke up in the middle of the night to crickets chirping in the background. She spent the night sitting on the balcony as she smoked cigarettes with her father's letter sitting in front of her like he was taunting her to open it. Tempting her with lies of a better life. She thought about how much easier it would be for her to do drugs than to open the letter that her father wrote to her uncle. She didn't know how she would feel after she read it. At least she knew how she would feel if she did drugs, but the curiosity was eating at her more than anything else. She wanted to find the answer that she was desperately looking for her entire life. It was a question that she could never ask her father since he died before she could ask him about it. Dr. Taylor asked her what she was scared about the most that her father would admit to her. She confessed to him that she was scared that her father was going to admit something that she didn't want to admit about herself. Since she couldn't get her brain to shut off, she was awake on the balcony all night smoking cigarettes. She was unable to get her hands to open the letter that was on the table in front of her. After she was awake all night, she couldn't sleep during the day no matter what she did before she took two of the sleeping pills that her mother gave her in England where she slept for over thirty-six hours straight without waking up.

When she woke up after her long slumber, she didn't realize that she missed over a day of her life before she walked into the kitchen to see that her cousins were concerned that she slept for over a day without waking up. After she got enough food to last her a few days, she camped out in the suite where she didn't sleep for several days until she slept for many days after that. On the nights that she was wide awake, she smoked cigarettes on the balcony where she drank a bottle of wine while her father's letter taunted her as it laid down untouched on the glass table next to her. On the third day of her being awake, she slept for over forty-eight hours in her bed with the blinds hiding the sunlight from her eyes. When she woke up again after two days of sleeping, she saw that things were moved around in the suite like someone else was there when she was sleeping. She thought that the maid was in her suite since it looked like someone cleaned up the room for her before she saw a handwritten note on the bathroom sink from Oliver that told her that she missed her appointment with Dr. Taylor, and he told her to call him when she was awake. She threw the note into the garbage can before she took the phone outside on the balcony with her with a box of cigarettes and a lighter in her hands. After she apologized to him about missing their appointment, Dr. Taylor told her that he was coming over to her house to see her that afternoon since her cousins called him to tell him that they were worried about her. She tried to clean up the suite in the little time that she had left since Dr. Taylor never came to her before in all the years that she saw him. She walked into the kitchen to make herself a sandwich that she quickly ate where she hid food in the suite before Dr. Taylor helped himself into her house. After she took Dr. Taylor to the suite, she laid down in her bed where he took a seat on the couch before he asked her what was going on with her. Even though she didn't want to talk about it, she didn't have much of a choice since he was sitting in her bedroom before she told him the truth for the first time in a long time. Dr. Taylor stayed at her house for a few hours before he left her alone when he felt like she was safe. He told her that the next step was going back to the psychiatric hospital. She didn't want to do it. She woke up in the middle of the night where she smoked cigarettes on the balcony as her father's unopened letter taunted her. As she went to light a cigarette, she inhaled the smoke from her cigarette before she leaned back on the chair.

Once she opened her eyes again, she inhaled the smoke from her cigarette as she let out a defeated sigh when she said looking up at the stars, "Hello, dad. I know that it's been a while since we talked to each other. I've been busy having a mental breakdown. I wasn't trying to ignore you. I didn't know what to say to you. It turns out that you were full of secrets that haunted you after your death. You were a compulsive liar, dad. No one knew anything about you except for Uncle Nathan, Uncle Kenny, and my grandmother. That's strange for me. I don't want to know how they knew these things about you. It's probably in the letter that Uncle Nathan gave to me. Did you know that Uncle Nathan gave me a letter that you sent to him? I haven't read it since I can't work up the nerve to do so. I think about how you would feel about me reading it until I remind myself that you're dead and you don't feel anything. I told Dr. Taylor about the letter, and he told me that it's not that I don't want to read the letter. It's more about that I don't want that to be the last thing that I hear from you. There is nothing that you will say to me after I read it. It's the end of everything. It's the end of you."

She inhaled the smoke from her cigarette as she let out a shaky breath when she responded to herself, "I know that you took your secrets to the grave with you. That's why I resented you when I was teenager. It wasn't fair that you were allowed to take your secrets to the grave. That's why mom resented Uncle Kenny. What was your deal with Uncle Kenny? I don't understand it. What did he have on you to keep you silent? Could you at least tell me that? If you can tell me anything, then that's the only thing that I want to know about you. Uncle Nathan told me that the letter would tell me about it, but you know that's not what I want. I wanted to hear it from you. I resent you for that. You never were brave enough to tell me anything. Your secrets turned you into the biggest coward in the world. You're a fucking coward, dad. I think that you knew that or else why would you kill yourself in the first place."

As she put out the end of the cigarette out into the ashtray, she let out a grunt of frustration as she kicked the metal poles on the balcony until her feet were throbbing with her screaming in pain. She lit another cigarette before she inhaled the smoke from it. She grabbed the letter off of the table as she gently opened it when she said to herself in a threatening tone, "This better be worth it or else I'm going to resent you forever. Here goes nothing now."

As she discarded the letter onto the table, she let out suppressed sobs into her hands. She whispered through her sobs, "Dad. I didn't want to know this about you. Why didn't you tell me this? Why couldn't you tell me? I hate you so much for doing this to me. What am I supposed to do with this? You can't leave me alone to deal with this. I don't want to do this. Can you talk to me?"

She took her head out of her knees as she grabbed the letter off of the table before she read it again to see if it would say something different. She continued sobbing into her hands as she placed the letter down on the table when she realized that it was never going to say anything different. Those were going to be her father's last words. He would never tell her anything again. She wiped away the tears that fell down her face as she attempted to light another cigarette where she couldn't stop her hands from shaking to light it before she threw her lighter and the cigarette onto the table. With her hands still uncontrollably shaking, she grabbed the letter as she slammed the balcony door closed behind her before she threw herself face first on the bed with her dropping the letter on the floor. As she climbed into her bed, she pulled her body under the blankets as she took twenty sleeping pills with water from her nightstand before she passed out for the next seventy-two hours.

October 1939
Dear Nathan,

I still can't believe that you're gone. I had a nightmare last night that I was searching for you in a pile of dead bodies, and I found yours on the bottom of it. I woke up screaming, but luckily I didn't wake up Ella. I didn't want to wake her up since she only fell asleep a few hours earlier. I don't want you to get upset when I tell you this even though I know that it's going to distress you. I smoked meth the night before you left me. Bertha gave it to me. She told me that Ella can't find out about this arrangement since she would hate us if she knew the truth about what was going on between us. I don't care what you think about any of it. You aren't here, Nathan. You don't know how it feels to be the target of our father's aggression. Mum asked me how I felt about you being gone. I couldn't hold it back when I told her that I wish that I could go with you because I couldn't stand living on the same property as them. She told dad what I said, and he punished me for saying such slander in his household. That was a joke since I didn't tell a lie for the first time in my life. After dad punished me, I snuck over to Ella's house to spend the night since her mother worked that night. I stole stuff from Bertha's shed that she gave me permission to take from while Ella was sleeping because I was out of my products. Did I tell you the letter I received from Kenny? You need to tell him to leave me the fuck alone. The audacity of that prick. He wanted to make sure that I wasn't going to say anything to Ella about him when he was gone. I assured him that I have no desire to tell her because I don't want him to tell her about the nature of my relationship with Bertha. He didn't believe me when I told him that, but I don't give a shit if he believed me or not. He should know that I wouldn't do anything to ruin my relationship with Ella. I'm not an idiot. Sometimes I think about when we were younger. I miss those days, Nathan. I miss them more than anything. I would do anything to get those days back. The days before I was mentally insane, and I didn't need drugs to get through the day. I'm fucked up in some many ways that I cannot even begin to put it into words. I'll leave you with a prevailing thought when I found myself on the roof of the barn. Don't ask how I got there. You already know what was going without me having to say anything about it. Do you want to know what I thought about as I stood on the roof of the barn? I thought about us when we were children playing together in the fields. You were chasing me, and I kept tripping since I was a toddler that just learned how to walk. When we were done playing in the fields, we came home to eat dinner that mum made for us before grandpa took us stargazing in our favorite spot on the fields where he told us all about the stars. Stories of gods and goddesses that used to be alive. Stories of the past. A past that no longer exists except in the stars. Do you want to know why I thought of that memory? It was the last time in my life that I felt happy. It was the last time that I went to bed with a smile on my face. I dream about that moment every night. I want to live in that moment for the rest of eternity. I believe that there is a moment in everyone's life that they want to live in for eternity. That is the moment that I want to live in. There is a place in the stars that is meant for us. That is where we will dance in the cosmos.

Love, your brother Will

Chapter Twenty-Nine

(Winter 1966 – New York, New York)

When she woke up in the hospital, she instantly regretted reading her father's letter that led her to take all those sleeping pills. It didn't make anything better that she had bruises on her legs from kicking the balcony railing or that she left her father's letter on the floor. She wasn't surprised that she was here again, but she felt disappointed that the first person that she always saw when she woke up was Oliver. It was a constant reminder to her that he kept her from dying every time that she tried to kill herself. She needed to kill him before she tried to commit suicide in the future, so that she could actually die. The look on her cousin's face told her everything that she needed to know. She knew what she was doing when she took the sleeping pills. Even though everyone knew the truth, she refused to admit it since they would send her to the psychiatric hospital if she told them that it was done on purpose. They didn't give her a choice about it when her doctor told her that she was going to be sent to the psychiatric hospital where she ignored everyone else around her in protest. On the ambulance ride to the psychiatric hospital, Oliver came with her since her parents weren't there. She was fine with that since she didn't want to see them. She didn't want to see Oliver, but he wouldn't leave her alone no matter what she did to get rid of him. After she gave up trying to make him leave her alone, she slept for the rest of the drive to the psychiatric hospital where she woke up in a hospital room with her arms and legs attached to the bed. She didn't acknowledge her parents that sat on either side of her bed before she fell asleep again. She was introduced to Dr. Halley, who was an older woman with a smile on her face as she told her that she was going to take care of her. She didn't look up at her when she asked her if she could get more medicine to help her sleep since she hadn't slept in a long time. When Dr. Halley walked into her room with more medicine, she thanked her before she slept for another day where she woke up the next morning to a nurse bothering her about food that she had no interest in eating. After she ate a few bites of the food, the nurse left her alone where she didn't pretend to eat before she slept for the rest of the morning. When she woke up again in the afternoon, her hands and legs weren't restrained to the bed since Oliver undid them when he was in her room. He told her that it hurt him to see her look like that. She acknowledged Oliver when she asked him what day it was before he told her that it was Boxing day. She nodded her head at him in silence with him before she slept in her bed for the rest of the day.

She woke up the next morning to her parents having a hushed conversation with Dr. Halley that she knew was about her that she had no interest in eavesdropping on. She would've slept for the rest of the day, but they told her that she couldn't lay in her bed before they sent her into a session with Dr. Halley about what they were calling her "suicide attempt". She didn't see it that way. They were determined to find out why she tried to kill herself, but she had no interest in engaging in that conversation since she didn't try to kill herself. When Dr. Halley asked her what she thought that she was doing, she told her that she was trying to sleep since she didn't sleep for many weeks. This didn't make anyone feel better about it since it meant that she was trying to kill herself for over a year. It was clear to her that they weren't going to listen to her. After she blew up into an argument with Dr. Halley about this, she was sent back into her room where she slept for the rest of the day until she woke up in the middle of the night. Since there were a few staff members there at night, she laid down on the nook of the window of her room where she stared up at the stars for the rest of the night. She was told the next morning by the nurse that brought her breakfast that she wasn't allowed to sleep in the window where she rolled her eyes at her before she rolled back to sleep on the same spot. When she woke up again in the afternoon, Dr. Taylor sat down on the bed where she sat down next to him before he asked her what she was doing. Since she was incapable of lying to him, she expressed her frustrations with him in ways that Dr. Halley didn't listen to her while she cried into the pillow with Dr. Taylor's hand on her shoulder. She wasn't under Dr. Halley's care anymore. Dr. Lukas came into her room to talk to her about what happened to her where she fell apart for the first time since she arrived at the psychiatric hospital before she told him everything. After she spent a few days with Dr. Lukas, she was more open with him about what happened with the sleeping pills. She realized it from their perspective for the first time. She understood that it looked bad for her that she made a choice to take that many sleeping pills considering that she knew the effect that it was going to have on her. She admitted to Dr. Lukas that she did try to kill herself even if it was something that she did without her realizing it. She told him that the letter that her father wrote triggered something inside of her to do what she did. Dr. Lukas already knew about it since Oliver gave him the letter when she got to the psychiatric hospital. It confirmed to her that Oliver was the person that found her since he grabbed the letter from the floor of her bedroom when she wouldn't wake up after taking the sleeping pills. She was resentful of Oliver for showing them the letter even though it helped them understand what led to that moment where she took sleeping pills. Her mother was dealing with the repercussions of the letter. Her mum and Oliver visited her every day. She only saw her mother on the first day that she was admitted to the psychiatric hospital. When she asked her mum where her mother was, her mum tightened her grip on her hands when she told her that her mother was dealing with her trauma at Uncle Stan's house. That explained why she didn't see Uncle Stan either. Even though she felt nothing about her apparent suicide attempt, she felt so horrible that her mother found out the truth about her father, Uncle Kenny, and her grandmother this way. She didn't know what to say to her mum to make it better, so she laid down on her mum's lap on the nook of the window as her mum ran her fingers through her hair like she was a little girl again. When the information came out about her father, she revealed to her family that Daxton sexually assaulted her. She wasn't going to hear anything from her mother since Oliver told her that her mother refused to get out of Uncle Stan's bedroom. She got a phone call from Damien who felt horrible that his brother did those things to her. It made her feel better about it since this was the closest thing to an apology that she was going to get from Daxton.

When she was pretending to sleep one morning, her mum and Uncle Nathan got into an argument in the hallway about him giving her the letter that led to what happened after it. Uncle Nathan stormed into the room with her mum following behind him where he pulled her into a tight hug with her face hidden in his chest before he wrapped his arms around her. As she kept her head hidden into his chest, Uncle Nathan told her mum that she wanted to see him even if she didn't want her daughter seeing him. After her mum stormed out of the room, she apologized to him in between her desperate sobs before Uncle Nathan reassured her that it wasn't her fault what happened with her mother. She nodded her head at him like she believed him as she sobbed into his chest with his arms tightly around her. They stayed like that until Dr. Lukas rushed into the room to figure out why her mum and Uncle Nathan got into a screaming match with each other. Uncle Nathan explained to him what happened that led to their argument while she kept her head hidden in his chest. She fell asleep with her head resting on his chest before she woke up alone in her room again where she laid down on the nook in the window to look up at the stars until she passed out again for the rest of the night. After over a month of her being in the psychiatric hospital, she was discharged to the real world where her mum took her to her house to see her cousins who were very happy to see her back to her old self again. Her mum didn't say anything about her seeing her mother since she heard from Oliver that her mother went back to New York with Uncle Stan. She didn't ask her mum where Uncle Nathan was since she figured that she wouldn't be allowed to talk to him for a long time until things went back to normal again. Thomas didn't say anything to her about why her mother and Uncle Stan went back to New York, but she had a gut feeling that it was about her mother's mental breakdown that led to her being in a psychiatric hospital. On the first night back in her house, she slept in the suite with her mum when she woke up hours before she did where she smoked cigarettes on the balcony. She didn't leave the suite for the first few days after she got out of the hospital. She spent time sleeping or smoking cigarettes on the balcony. She asked her mum when she would see her mother again when her mum told her with a serious look on her face that they would see her after she got out of the psychiatric hospital. Even though she wanted to ask her mum about it, she could tell from a look in her mum's eyes that she shouldn't say anything else about it. After she spent another few weeks at her house, she eavesdropped on a phone call that her mum had with Uncle Stan about her mother getting out of the psychiatric hospital. She tried to hide the surprise on her face when her mum told her that they were going to New York since her mother got discharged from the hospital. On the morning of their flight to New York, she hugged her cousin's goodbye when she got on a plane with her mum and Thomas before she slept with her head resting on her mum's shoulder for the entire flight. When their plane landed in New York in the afternoon, Uncle Sam picked them up from the airport where he brought her into a long hug where she hid her face into his chest before her mum came back with their bags in her hands. As soon as she let go of Uncle Sam, she tried to not notice the exhausted look on his face before she fell asleep with her head resting on her mum's shoulder.

When she woke up at Uncle Sam's house, she was attacked by Holly who was more excited to see her than anyone else where she let Holly run all around her before she guided her into the house. As soon as she walked into Uncle Sam's house, her mother and Uncle Stan sat in the living room watching television as Aunt Valeria prepared tea and coffee for them. She sprinted towards her mother as she threw herself into her arms before her mother tightly wrapped her arms around her. As she hid her face in her mother's chest with tears falling down her face, her mother kept telling her that she was sorry over and over again in between her sobs before everyone left them alone in the room to give them some privacy. Once she calmed herself down, she slowly took her head out of her mother's chest as she kissed her on the top of her head when she told her daughter that she loved her so much and she was sorry that she wasn't there for her. Isabella told her mother that it was okay that she wasn't there because she was dealing with her own trauma and that she wanted her to be okay. Once she took a seat on the couch, her mother wrapped her arms around her as she kissed her on the top of her head when she told her daughter that she was her baby girl, and she would always be her baby girl before she sobbed into her mother's chest again. When Aunt Valeria came into the room with cups of tea and coffee on a tray, she grabbed a cup of tea as her mother grabbed a cup of coffee before everyone walked into the living room like nothing happened between them. After they ate dinner with Nina's family and Anastasia's family, she went to her parents' house with Thomas and Uncle Stan who stayed there for over a month. She slept in her parents' bedroom with them as Uncle Stan and Thomas slept in the guest bedroom before she woke up the next morning to Uncle Stan smoking a cigarette on the porch where she smoked with him until her mum walked outside to tell them that breakfast was ready. During the day, she spent most of the day watching television with her head resting on her mother's lap as her mother silently ran her fingers through her hair with her mum occasionally coming into the room to make them eat something. She hadn't found the strength to ask her mother what happened to her. She wasn't on the other side of this before. It felt horrible to be on any side of this situation. It wasn't anything that they talked about to each other. She joined her parents to drop Uncle Stan and Thomas at the airport that morning where she watched Uncle Stan hug her mother for a long time until Thomas told his boyfriend that their plane was going to leave. She listened to her mother crying to her mum through the walls of the guest bedroom that night where she moved away from it when she couldn't stand to hear it. Once she grabbed a blanket from the guest bedroom, she placed a box of cigarettes and a lighter into her pocket where she went to her hiding spot on the roof before she wrapped a blanket around her arms with her sitting down on the roof. As she lit a cigarette with her shaking hands, she inhaled the smoke from it before she laid down on the roof with her eyes closed. Her mother sat down next to her as she inhaled the smoke from her cigarette before her mother grabbed onto her hands. She lit another cigarette as she inhaled the smoke from it when she asked her mother with a concerned look on her face, "Are you okay, mom?"

Her mother tightened her grip on her hands when she responded to her with a smile on her face, "I'll be okay, baby girl. Don't worry about me. That's your mum's job to worry about me. It's not yours to worry about me. Are you okay?"

As she inhaled the smoke from her cigarette, she shrugged her shoulders at her when she responded to her with a frown on her face, "I don't know, mom. I don't think that I've ever been okay. I'm sorry. I didn't mean for it to happen. I feel bad about it."

Her mother shook her head at her as she tightened his grip on her hands when she told her with a serious look on her face, "It's not your fault, baby girl. None of this is your fault. There is nothing wrong with you wanting to know your father. You have every right to know him. It's his fault. It's their fault."

She let out a shaky breath as she looked up at her mother when she asked her with uncertainty laced in her voice, "Do you mean dad or Uncle Kenny? Or do you mean grandma? It's not Uncle Nathan's fault. He didn't do anything wrong showing me the letter. It's my fault that I reacted the way that I did."

Her mother tightened her grip on her hands when she responded to her with a frown on her face, "I know it's not Uncle Nathan's fault. Your mum was the person that was upset with him. I told him that I wasn't upset with him. I don't know who I mean, baby girl. I can't figure out who I should be mad at. I'm the most upset with dad, but I was always pissed off at him more than I was at Kenny. It brought back unwanted feelings to the surface that I haven't felt in a long time. Feelings that I felt towards dad. Feelings that I felt towards Kenny. I have confusing thoughts about it. What's the point of being mad at someone who is dead?"

As she inhaled the smoke from her cigarette, she shrugged her shoulders at her when she responded to her with a frown on her face, "There's no point in being upset with someone who is dead. It's never going to make anything better. Dead people don't give a shit. I spent most of my life being upset with dad. It was pointless. He'll never care about it like I do. I know that you're angry at Uncle Kenny for what he did to you. I feel that way towards Daxton when I remember what he did to me. It doesn't make any sense for me to be mad at him. It's not like he cares. Why should I care about it?"

Her mother wrapped her arms around her when she told her, "When did I raise such a wise daughter? You're so smart, baby girl. I'm sorry about what happened with Daxton. I heard from your mum about it. I'm sorry that you had to go through that alone. You can talk to me about anything."

She laid down on the roof with her mother laying down next to her before she placed her head on her chest with her mother's arms around her. Once she got comfortable on her mother's chest, she asked her with a frown on her face, "Did you read the letter, mom?"

Her mother tightened her grip on her arms when she told her with a neutral expression on her face, "Yes, I read it, baby girl. I don't know how I feel about it. I'm heartbroken, but I'm strangely happy about it. That was the memory that your father wanted to live in for eternity. That was what hurt me the most about it. It wasn't that Uncle Kenny, your grandma, and your father lied to me. It was that it was the best moment of my life with him. I never told anyone about that before in my life. I don't know how he knew that."

She told her mother with a smile on her face, "You never needed to tell him, mom. He knew you better than you knew yourself. I have moments like that with Oliver. It used to annoy me that he knew what was going on with me, but I've embraced it. He won't let me die and he won't let me off the hook. It's good to have people like that in your life."

Her mother whispered to her like it was a secret between them, "It's rare to find that in someone. I'm glad that you have Oliver, baby girl. Never lose him. I imagined what my life would look like with him in it. I thought about how I miss him when I watched you growing up over these years. I thought the pain would go away with time, but it never really does. It turned into a dull ache that will always be in my heart. I always felt his absence. I know that he felt mine when I wasn't with him. A love like that can never be replaced, but it can transform into something so very beautiful."

CHAPTER THIRTY
(SPRING 1966 – LOS ANGELES, CALIFORNIA)

After she spent a few weeks with her parents in New York, she said an emotional goodbye as she got on a plane by herself back to Los Angeles where she slept with her head resting on the window for the entire flight. When her plane landed in Los Angeles that afternoon, Oliver picked her up at the airport as he pulled her into a tight hug that she didn't need to ask from him before they pulled apart from each other when her four-year-old niece Posey ran into their legs. Once she placed Posey on her hip, Oliver grabbed her bags for her where she followed him into the car before he dropped her off at her house. In the first week that she was home, she received a phone call from a director from the studio asking her if she wanted to work on a new movie that he wrote called *Destiny's Choice* before she told him that she would get back to him in a few days to tell him her answer after consulting her family. Dr. Taylor told her that it would help her recovery if she was busy working. After she talked to Dr. Taylor about it, she asked her cousins about working where they told her that it would help her to stay away from drugs if she was working. Her parents told her the same thing since she hadn't worked on a movie in three years. After she consulted with other people around her, she called the director to tell him that she would love to work on this new project with him before he told her that shooting started in a few weeks where he told her the times that she needed to attend fittings and that he would send the scripts to her house. She laid down outside by the pool reading the scripts on the off days that she wasn't having clothing fittings at the studio. Her cousins were relieved that she was back to her old self again. She slept at night due to the medications that she took to help her. On the first day of filming of *Destiny's Choice*, she met the other lead actor movie named Sebastian Brewer who was around her age with a smile on his face every time that he walked into the room. Even though they met each other that day, they were laughing in between every take that they were in a scene together. When she got home from work that night, she had a smile on her face every time that she thought about him. After a few weeks of them filming together, Sebastian invited her to go to an award show with him that he was nominated for a few categories that she instantly accepted from him since she couldn't stand the thought of going to her house without him.

Even though she had little to no time to prepare for the award show, she called Amelia to tell her that she needed her to make her red carpet ready in five hours. That seemed impossible for them to pull off. Amelia called in all the favors that she owed people in the city when she came home to see that there was a full team at the house waiting for her with dresses, hair, and makeup. The team that was pulled together at the last minute made her ready to go on a red carpet. She gave everyone hugs as she thanked them for everything that they did for her before Sebastian's driver picked her up from her house to take them to the award show. As soon as Sebastian's driver dropped them at the award show, Sebastian helped her out of the car as he grabbed onto her hand before they walked out on the red carpet with flashing lights going off around them. Sebastian wrapped his arm around her as he directed them to their seats in the front of the room before she took a seat next to him with other actors sitting at the table with them. Once Sebastian introduced her to the group, she got to know everyone at the table as they talked to each other about projects that were involved in before the waiters brought them plates of food and glasses of champagne. After she toasted her glass of champagne against the other glasses, she drank it in one gulp before she ate the food that was placed in front of her as she had a conversation with the actress sitting next to her. Sebastian stared at her with a smile on his face that she couldn't stop blushing. The host went through the categories that people were nominated for. Sebastian's hand was on her leg with everything happening around them where she smiled at him before she turned her attention onto the award show. After Sebastian won one of the awards that he was nominated for, she gave him a tight hug as he wrapped his arms around her waist before he walked up onto the stage to receive his award where he gave a beautiful speech to the crowd. Once he took a seat next to her, she squeezed his hand with a smile on her face before she turned her attention to the award show. At the end of the award show, Sebastian kept a firm grip on her shoulder as he guided them to the car before they got into his car with a silent agreement that they were going to his house. After the driver pulled up to Sebastian's house, he grabbed onto her hand with her grabbing onto it before he guided them into his house. Once she shut the door behind them, they stared into each other's eyes before she pulled him into an intense kiss. After she pulled apart from him, he grabbed onto her hand as he led them into his bedroom where he closed the door behind him before he pulled her into a desperate kiss that they didn't let go of until she laid down on the bed with Sebastian's body on top of her. They didn't need to tell each other what they needed since their eyes were already telling them that. Even though she knew that they wanted to take it farther than this, Sebastian stopped her when he told her that he didn't sleep with girls on the first date before she asked him if this counted as a date since they weren't alone until they got into his house. Sebastian pulled her into a long kiss that they didn't let go of each other's lips until he told her that he wanted to go on a proper date with her before they slept together. After she let out a fake whine to him, she got off of his bed to change out of her dress into one of his oversized shirts before she climbed in bed with him where she slept with her head on his chest for the rest of the night. She woke up to Sebastian singing after he got out of the shower as she walked into the bathroom to kiss him before she changed into her dress from last night. After Sebastian's driver dropped her back off at her house, she walked into her house to see Amelia and Sasha eating breakfast together in the kitchen before they asked her if she had fun last night. She ignored them as she went into her suite to get changed out of her dress since she had to be at the studio in an hour before she left the house with Amelia to go to work for the day. When she got to the studio, she gave Sebastian a quick glance before they focused on filming for the day.

She went on a date with him a few weeks later. He took them to the movies before they went to a restaurant for dinner. They had conversations with each other about their lives. They wanted this to be a serious relationship. As she told him about past experiences that went through in the last few years, he grabbed onto her hands to comfort her when she didn't realize that she was crying while she talked about it. She took Sebastian to her house because she knew that no one was going to be home that night since Amelia was out with friends at the club and Sasha was out of the country. After she gave Sebastian a tour of her house, she brought him to her suite where they made out with each other for a while until she fell asleep with her head resting on his chest. It was the next morning when she woke up before Sebastian that she smoked cigarettes on the balcony until he came outside to join her. Once they smoked cigarettes on the balcony in silence for a while, they went downstairs into the kitchen where Amelia ate her usual breakfast with her boyfriend Troy Austin who she met a few times since she got back to Los Angeles before she took a seat next to them with a piece of fruit in her hands. Amelia was all over Sebastian who she met for the first time as she interrogated him until Troy stopped her from saying anything else. Once Amelia took Troy into her bedroom, they laughed about it until she took him into the suite with her where they talked for many hours before Sebastian left to go to his house for the rest of the day. Since things were getting serious with Sebastian, she needed to introduce him to her family since Amelia told her other cousins about Sebastian spending the night. On a weekend that she knew that Sasha was going to be home, she told them that they were going to have dinner at her house before she tasked the chef with making a meal for them that would be special for Sebastian. She wore a silk dress that she stole from Sasha's closet from one of her photo shoots before she walked downstairs to see that the table was set with the chef finishing dinner. As soon as she sat down on the couch next to Sasha and Amelia with the television playing in the background, Troy walked into the house as Amelia ran off of the couch to pull him into a tight hug before he sat down next to them. Oliver walked into the house as Juliet followed behind him with Posey on her hip before Posey ran over to her where she pulled Posey into her lap with her face hidden in her chest. After

Oliver pulled her into an intimate hug with her face hidden in his chest, she got up off of the couch with Posey on her hip before she went into the kitchen to check on the food before she grabbed a piece of bread for Posey to snack on since Posey was very hungry. When she walked into the living room, Uncle Stan and Thomas sat down on the couch as they talked to Oliver and Juliet until they instantly went silent when Sebastian walked into the house with a bottle of wine in his hands. As soon as Sebastian walked through the door, she handed Posey off to Juliet who placed her into her lap before she pulled Sebastian into a tight hug where she hid her face into his chest until he kissed her on her lips in front of her family. Once she pulled herself out of his arms, she ignored the shock on Oliver's face as she held onto his hand where she guided Sebastian into the kitchen where Amelia, Troy, and Sasha were sitting at the table talking to each other. When it was time for them to eat dinner, she sat down in between Sebastian and Oliver who were making intense eye contact with each other for the entire meal until she cut the tension between them when she told them about their new movie with Sebastian. She invited everyone outside by the pool where she went into her suite to change into her swimsuit before she jumped into the pool. After she swam for a while with her cousins, she walked out of the pool as she took a seat on a pool chair next to Sebastian where he handed her a towel from the back of his chair before she grabbed it out of his hand. She turned on her side to look over at Sebastian as she heard her cousins fighting over a floaty when she asked him with curiosity laced in her voice, "What do you think of them, Bash? You can be honest with me."

Sebastian responded to her with a serious look on his face, "Your cousins are intense honey. Oliver stared at me all night. Why is Oliver staring at me like I was about to hit him?"

As she lit a cigarette with her inhaling the smoke from it, she grabbed onto his hand when she responded to him in a soft voice, "Don't mind him, Bash. He's harmless. Oliver's overprotective of me. He's like my older brother. Amelia and Sasha seem to like you. It's good that they like you. They hated most of the people that I've dated in the past."

Sasha shouted to her from the other side of the pool where she instantly looked over at her, "Are you talking about us, Isabella? I hope you're telling him how wonderful we are. You have good taste in wine, Sebastian. Can you bring more of that the next time that you come over?"

As she laughed into her hands, Sebastian rolled his eyes at her when he shouted back to her, "Thanks, Sasha. I'll keep that in mind for the next time that I come over to your house. I like you better than Amelia after that comment."

Amelia let out a soft gasp where Sasha splashed her with water that led to a water fight before she held up her towel to keep herself from getting wet as Sebastian did the same thing. After Amelia and Sasha were done with their fight, they placed the towels down onto the ground as Oliver got out of the pool with Posey on his hip before he looked at Sebastian when he told him in a threatening tone, "You better not hurt Isabella or else I'm going to hurt you. She's in a good place and I would hate for you to ruin that for her. Do I make myself clear?"

Sebastian put his hands up in a defensive stance when he told him with a serious look on his face, "I won't do anything to hurt her. I love her. I don't want anything bad to happen to her."

After she looked over at Oliver with a pleading look on her face, Oliver nodded his head at Sebastian as Posey ran over to her mother in the house before he pulled her into a tight hug as she hid her face into his chest with tears falling down her face. Once Oliver let go of her, she wiped away tears from her face as Sebastian wrapped his arm around her before Oliver walked into the house where his daughter ran ahead of him. As soon as Oliver went into the house, she let out a shaky breath as Sebastian tightened his grip on her arms when he asked her with a concerned look on his face, "Do you want to go in the house? It's getting late."

She nodded her head at him as she took his hand before he gently guided her to her suite. Once they were alone in the suite, she softly closed the door behind them as they intensely stared at each other before she pulled him into a desperate kiss where he pulled them towards her bed. When she laid down on the bed with him laying on top of her, she pulled away from him for a moment when she asked him with a confused look on her face, "Stop it, Bash. Did you mean it when you said that you loved me? You never told me that before."

He pulled her into another desperate kiss after he moved away from her lips when he whispered to her like it was a secret between them, "I wouldn't say it if I didn't mean it. I love you, Isabella. Do you love me?"

She pulled him into a long kiss where she pulled away from him for a moment to catch her breath when she confessed to him, "I love you too, Bash. I've thought about that for a while, but I didn't know how to say it. I haven't felt like this. I fell in love with you when I saw you on set for the first time. No one made me feel this way before."

Sebastian moved her hair out of her face when he confessed to her in a soft voice, "You're so beautiful, Isabella. I'm lucky that you want to be with me. You could have anyone, but you want me. Are you ready for this?"

She nodded her head at him as she pulled him into another desperate kiss before he took off her swimsuit top while she took off his shirt over his head. After they finished what they started on their first date, they laid down on her bed under the covers over them with her laying her head onto his chest as he ran his fingers through her hair when she whispered to him with tears falling down her face, "I found the moment that I want to spend an eternity in."

Sebastian tightened his grip on her arms when he asked her with concern laced in his voice, "What do you mean by that?"

She looked up at the ceiling when she confessed to him, "The last thing that my dad told me was the moment that he wanted to spend eternity in. He said that everyone has that moment in their life that they want to spend eternity in. I want to live here for the rest of my life."

Sebastian kissed her forehead as he tightened his grip on her arms when he responded to her in a soft voice, "Your dad was wise beyond his years. That happens when you die young. You become wiser in death. It's the hidden gift inside of it. How old was your dad when he died?"

She sighed when she told him with a frown on her face, "He was twenty-six. He will be remembered as that age. I don't know how I'm going to feel about being there. That's the beauty in it. It's not knowing what's going to look like. I want to get married when I'm twenty-six. Can you propose to me?"

Sebastian responded to her with a smile on his face, "We can get married when you're twenty-six. I'll keep that in mind. We should go to bed." Once Sebastian whispered to her that he loved her with her whispering the words back to him, she fell asleep for the rest of the night with his arms around her.

Chapter Thirty-One
(Summer 1966 – Los Angeles, California)

They spent any free moment that they had together at their houses where they bounced from place to place without a care in the world. When Sebastian was out of town working on another project while they weren't filming *Destiny's Choice*, she called him until the early hours of the morning. Her family warmed up to him over time where Sasha and Amelia asked her where he was when she was alone at the house. Oliver was warming up to him too since Sebastian told her that he loved her in front of him. Oliver invited him to go golfing with Troy, Uncle Stan, and Thomas a few times. When she told her parents about Sebastian, her parents told her that they were happy for her. This was the happiest that she had been in a long time. Her parents told her that they would visit her soon. She told Sebastian that her parents wanted to meet him. He told her that it was time for her to meet his family too. Sebastian didn't have any siblings like her. He had fewer cousins like she did that she got along with that were around her age. Sebastian's family lived in California unlike her family that lived all across the world. She loved Sebastian's parents. They were supportive of their relationship and their careers since they were retired actors from the black and white film days. When they were off from work for the weekend, Sebastian drove them to his parent's house in Northern California where she got to know his parents in an intimate setting before they went back home. After they visited his parents in northern California, her parents stayed with them for a few weeks. They weren't busy with their publishing company because their manager was running it. Even though her parents were initially wary of Sebastian, they realized that they made each other happy. When Sebastian went to his house for a few days to get ready to leave for his other film. Her parents told her that they were happy for her and that they liked that he made feel good. After she spent a few weeks alone with her parents, her parents went home to New York as she filmed *Destiny's Choice* with Sebastian who was back in Los Angeles after he finished working on his other film. She enjoyed every moment that she got with him since they couldn't get a lot of alone time while they worked long days in the studio. Once she left Dr. Taylor's office, she went over to spend the night at his house where they went out on a date before she spent the night at his place until she went back to her house that next morning. When she wasn't spending the night at his house, he spent the night at her house. They were apart from each other while they worked on their projects on the other days.

Even though she missed him when she wasn't with him, she appreciated the alone time that she got with herself. She used to hate spending time with herself. She couldn't stand hearing the thoughts in her mind, but she wasn't in that headspace anymore. She didn't know what was making her feel this way. It could've been her new relationship. Or the pills that she was taking to help her function better. Or it was that she was doing what she loved again. It was all of those things combined since she was actively trying to make her life better. Oliver joked with her one night that she spent the night at his house that the overdoses didn't stick to her like her suicide attempt did. They laughed about it. Even if Oliver only said it to her as a joke, there was some truth in that statement. She didn't take her recovery seriously after her overdoses like she was treating it right now. When she brought it up to Dr. Taylor at their next session, he asked her why she was taking her recovery seriously where she didn't have an answer for him until the end of their hour. She told him that she took it more seriously because she didn't want to live like that. He asked her what the moment was where she didn't have answer until their session the next week when she told him that it was the moment that she read her father's letter that she realized that she didn't want to live like this. It took them many sessions to unpack what her father's letter meant to her. She realized that she lived that moment that her father was in when he wrote that letter to Uncle Nathan. She was in that moment more times than she knew that she was there. It was the moment that she realized that it was the beginning of the end for him when he wrote that letter. If it was a story, then it would be the beginning of his ending that everyone saw coming including him. He refused to acknowledge that it was going to end like that, or he didn't care that it was going to end that way. Dr. Taylor asked her what she thought was her beginning or her end was. She asked him what he thought that it was before he told her that it was when she read her father's suicide note. She thought that it was when her father died. It was poetic to her that the end of her father's story was the beginning of her story. She didn't want to believe that her father's story ended when he died. She continued his story for him. This was all that they were going to be known for. Stories never came to an end. They turned into something else. Something that would be told for centuries after she was dead. People weren't immortal. Stories were what made people immortal. Dr. Taylor asked her how she felt about her father being immortal. That was the only way that she made peace about what happened with him. She was incapable of moving on from him because she thought that she was betraying him. She realized that it wasn't about him not being there with her that didn't want to make her move on from him. She knew that he would be with her until the end of time. It was about how she was terrified that she was going to ruin his legacy. She was responsible for their story until she died someday. She didn't know to make her peace without ruining it. It was the most special thing to her, and she didn't want to destroy it. When she couldn't sleep that night, she pulled out her father's letter that Dr. Lukas gave to her when she got out of the hospital before she read it again on the balcony as she smoked cigarettes all night. She realized that her father didn't write this letter for anyone except for her. This was a few years before she was born, but it meant two different things when he was alive versus when he was dead. When he was alive, it meant that he was lying about his problems, and he hid who he was from the world. When he was dead, it meant that he was being honest about his problems, and he shared who he was with the world. After she sat with this information for a few days, she told Dr. Taylor about it in their next session where he asked her what she thought that would be like for her. If she wrote a letter like this about a moment in her life, then what would it mean when she was alive compared to when she was dead. This led her to testing out this theory where she wrote a letter to herself that she wouldn't share with anyone until she died. As she sat on the balcony in the middle of the night, she smoked cigarettes as she wrote this letter.

I hope that your life is everything that you dreamed that it would be. I hope that you're happy. I hope that you're with someone who makes you feel loved. I hope that you're at peace with yourself. I don't know if you're going to read this letter. You may never read it. My therapist told me to do this. He told me that I need to write a letter to my future self. It's going to help me heal from the past. I want you to know that I've always tried my best. I know that sometimes that's not enough to stop the inevitable from happening. That's all that matters to me. That I tried to be better. I think about dad and mom. I think about the life that was lost. I think about how much that we lost to get here. In all that loss that happened to us, we gained so much. In all the ugliness that we're surrounded in, something more beautiful came out of it. I believe that life is incapable of ending. Our stories are written in the stars. Even when the stars burn out someday, there will be a moment in time that they were there. That's the only moment in time that matters. It's going to last longer than our parents. It's going to last longer than us. It's going to last even longer than our children. Sometimes I think about the life that I want for myself. I want everything that dad never got to have. I want to spend the rest of my life with someone who loves me more than I could love myself. I want to have children that give my life more meaning than I give myself. I want to be remembered by the stories that my children pass on about me. I want it all to mean something more than myself. When we die someday, we will spend eternity in the cosmos. We will have everything that we dreamed of in our lives. We won't get it because we were given it. We will get it because we spent our life working for it. It will make the hardships worth it. All the pain that we went through is going to mean something. It means something to us. We will always have the stars.

She didn't read it before she threw it into an envelope at the back of her desk. She slept for most of the day since she was taking a break from filming and Sebastian was in Maine filming another movie. When she woke up that afternoon, she ran into Sasha in the kitchen before she told her that Jamie, Ivan, and their boyfriends were staying with them for a few weeks since they were off from work. She instructed the chef to prepare French cuisine for them and the maid to clean every room in the house including the guest bedrooms that they haven't used in a long time. She stayed up all night smoking cigarettes on the balcony when she talked to Sebastian on the phone until he went to bed late into the night. Sebastian was stuck in Maine for a few months to film a movie for his friend who was an independent filmmaker. They talked about everything that happened when they were away from each other. Sebastian told her about how much he was enjoying filming his movie and she told him about the gossip that happened in their families while they were away from each other. After she got a few hours of sleep that night, she woke up to Sasha and Amelia coming into her suite as they opened the blinds in the room until she dragged herself out of bed. Once she ate breakfast with her cousins that the chef prepared for them, Sasha drove them to the airport where they waited at the gate for her cousins. As soon as she fell asleep sitting on a chair with her head on Sasha's shoulder, Sasha nudged her awake before Jamie and Christophe held onto each other's hands as Ivan and Antonine held onto each other's hands before another male followed them with their bags in his hands. Once they were closer to each other, she pulled Jamie and Ivan into a tight hug where they hugged their sisters as she kissed Christophe and Antonine on the cheek before Amelia and Sasha kissed them on the cheek. Ivan introduced them as Gabriel Rue who was Christophe and Antonine's older brother. As she kissed Gabriel on his cheek, she didn't miss how Sasha pulled him into a tight hug like she knew him. Once they were at their house, they showed them around the house before they went into the guest bedrooms to sleep for the rest of the afternoon after their long travel day. She fell asleep in her suite for the rest of the afternoon. When she woke up from her nap, everyone sat in the living room as they watched a movie before she joined them in her designated spot in between Sasha and Amelia where she fell asleep with her head resting on Amelia's lap. When she woke up from her second nap of the day, she laid down on the couch all by herself with a blanket on top of her before she joined them into the kitchen for dinner. The chef prepared a meal for them based on her approved list of meals to serve her guests. Amelia and Sasha took Jamie, Christophe, Antonine, and Gabriel to the best clubs in the city where Troy joined them there since it was the night that they always went out together.

Even though they invited Ivan to come with them, he didn't appreciate the nightclub scene since he didn't drink alcohol like everyone else did in the house. Instead of them joining everyone at the club, they spent the night in her suite smoking cigarettes on the balcony while they talked like no time passed between them. After her cousins got home in the middle of the night, Ivan went into the guest bedroom with Antonine as she went downstairs to eat in the kitchen before she saw Sasha and Gabriel making out with each other by the pool. She grabbed the closest piece of fruit there before she sprinted into her bedroom where she hoped that they didn't see her. When she woke up the next morning, she walked into the kitchen to see Amelia and Troy talking to each other over coffee and scrambled eggs as Jamie and Christophe sat across from Ivan and Antonine before she took a seat next to Ivan at the table. When she asked them where Sasha and Gabriel were, Amelia moved away from her conversation with Troy when she told her that they were sleeping in the other suite before she moved back into her conversation with Troy about a new movie that they were working on together. She forgot that Troy was an actor like they were. He was quiet about his career unlike them who were open about it. She moved on from the subject since she knew that she would find out about it soon enough whether she wanted to or not since Sasha would tell her about it. She listened to Christophe and Antonine tell her about their photography business in France that they owned with Gabriel before Ivan and Jamie told her how they met them. She commented about the poetry about it. Amelia left to go to work with Troy at the studio before she packed her bags since they were going to Malibu for the day where Amelia and Troy would meet them there when they were done working for the day. Since Oliver was stuck working a double shift at the hospital and Juliet was in the middle of writing a movie, they took Posey to the beach with them since she knew that her niece was obsessed with swimming after they went to Hawaii. She got permission from Oliver to bring Posey with them since Posey was asking them when she would spend time with

Aunt Isabella. Once she packed everything she needed for a beach day with her family, Sasha and Gabriel waited for her in the living room before she followed them into the car as she got into the passenger seat before Sasha drove them to Oliver's house. As soon as they pulled into Oliver's driveway, she got out of the car as she went into the house to grab Posey from Oliver's arms with her bag over his shoulder before she placed the bag over her shoulder with Posey sitting on her hip. After she pulled Oliver into a tight hug, she walked out to the car where she got into the passenger seat with Posey sitting in her car seat. For the drive to the beach in Malibu, she slept with her head leaning on the window as Posey slept in her car seat while everyone talked with the radio playing in the background.

After they parked the car at one of the public beaches in Malibu, she carried Posey out of the car who was asleep in her arms before she followed them out to their private cabana that they rented on the beach. She didn't wake up Posey until it was time to get changed into her swimsuit where the girl let out a squeal as she put on sunscreen that Juliet packed for her before she ran out into the ocean with her tightly holding onto Posey's hand. After she swam in the ocean with Posey in her arms, she took them back to their cabana where she laid down on the seat with Posey playing in the sand at her feet as Antonine and Christophe had a soft conversation with each other in French. As she helped Posey make a sandcastle with the toys that Juliet packed for her, Sasha and Gabriel came back from the ocean as they held onto each other's hands before they sat down on the seat next to her. Gabriel kissed Sasha on the lips when he told her that he would be back in a few minutes before he walked over to the food stands.

As soon as she was alone with Sasha, she gave Sasha a look that she understood more than anything as they grabbed onto each other's hands before Sasha told her that she couldn't believe that this happened to her. Gabriel came back to their cabana with two slices of pizza when Posey asked Sasha for a bite of pizza before she took Posey to get slices of pizza. After they ate their pizza in the cabana, she took Posey to the ocean where they swam until Amelia and Troy arrived at the beach in the afternoon where she went swimming with Amelia and Troy as Sasha and Gabriel watched Posey when she took a nap in the cabana. Once Posey woke up from her nap, Sasha brought her to the ocean with them where they swam with Posey going back and forth in their arms before they left the beach to go to the hotel to clean up for dinner. The boys wanted to explore the city on their own. After she showered with Posey in the hotel room that she was sharing with Sasha and Gabriel, she changed them into fancier dresses since they were going to an expensive restaurant before they met up with the boys there where they ate a huge meal with a delicious dessert. When they got back to the hotel, Posey was already asleep in her arms as she gently placed Posey onto their bed before she smoked cigarettes on the balcony with Sasha while Gabriel and Posey slept in their beds for the rest of the night. She woke up the next morning. She got Posey ready for their drive home where she got into the car with Amelia and Troy as Sasha and Gabriel took the boys home with them. She slept for most of the drive to Los Angeles since she didn't get any sleep last night. When they were in Los Angeles again, they dropped off Posey at home. Oliver was pleased to see that his daughter had a good time with them before Amelia took them home where she slept in her suite for the rest of the day. It was uneventful for the rest of the time that the boys visited them. On the last few nights of the boys being in town, her family came over for dinner before they hung out outside by the pool for the rest of the evening. This night was no exception except for that Sasha left the country with Gabriel for a photoshoot that he insisted on going to with her. As she laid out by the pool with her towel wrapped around her body, Amelia and Troy splashed each other in the pool as Oliver and Juliet played with Posey in the water. Ivan and Jamie had a diving contest with Antonine and Christophe. After Amelia and Troy went into the house to watch a movie with the boys in the living room, Juliet brought Posey into the house to get her ready for bed before she was alone with Oliver. She lit another cigarette as Oliver took a seat next to her as she inhaled the smoke from it when he said to her with a smile on his face, "Thanks for taking Posey to Malibu with you. She won't stop talking about how much fun she had with you. She keeps asking us when she can do it again."

She responded to him with a smile on her face, "Of course, Oliver. I'm glad that she had a good time. We can do it again. I'll check with Bash to see if he could come with us next time."

Oliver nodded his head at her as he played with the ends of her towel when he asked her with a frown on his face, "Oh yes. Sebastian. Where is he right now? How is that going for you?"

She inhaled the smoke from the cigarette when she responded to him with an unreadable expression on her face, "Bash is in Maine filming a movie. He'll be done with it any day. It's going well, Oliver. We're happy. Why are you looking at me like that?"

Oliver grabbed onto her hands when he responded to her with a neutral look on his face, "I'm not looking at you in any way. That's my face. I know that you don't believe me. I'm happy for you, Isabella. Why are you pulling a face? Do you not believe me?"

As she inhaled the smoke from her cigarette, she let out a shaky breath as she tightened her grip on Oliver's hands when she responded to him with a stern look on her face, "It's not that I don't believe you. I don't think that you mean it. You are saying it to make me feel better. It doesn't make me feel any better about it. I don't want you to be happy about it. I want you to be upset about it. I know that it doesn't make any sense. It's complicated."

Oliver let go of her hands as he wrapped his arms around her when he asked her with a look of concern on his face, "What's complicated about it? You love each other and you want to be in each other's lives. Is there something more going on?"

She shook her head at him when she responded to him with frustration laced in her voice, "He's not the complicated part of it. I'm the complicated part. I love Bash with all my heart, but I can't stop myself from wondering how I'm going to ruin it. I know what you're about to say, Oliver. Your face is telling me everything that I need to know. I'm terrified that I'm going to ruin us."

Oliver tightened his grip on her arms when he asked her in a soft voice, "Are you scared that your addiction is going to ruin it?"

After she lit another cigarette, she inhaled the smoke from it when she told him with her blinking back tears that fell down her face, "It's not my addiction that I'm concerned about. It's everything else. It's a mental illness. It's the trauma with my dad. I'm terrified that I'm going to ruin the best thing that happened to me. If I lose it, then I'm never going to get it back."

Oliver took a seat on her pool chair with her as he pulled her into a long hug where she hid her face into his chest with her letting out a suppressed sob before he tightened his grip on her arms. Once she calmed herself down, she slowly pulled her face out of his chest with his arms tightly around her when he told her in a stern voice, "None of that is your fault, Isabella. You can't help that you experienced those things in the past. Those things are a part of who you are. He loves and accepts those things about you. If he can't handle it, then you'll always have me no matter what happens with Sebastian. I love you."

She responded to him with a smirk on her face, "You're right, Oliver. Damnit! How are you always right? Do you think that Bash loves me like that? Like the way that you do?"

Oliver shook his head at her when he responded to her with a stern look on his face, "That's different, Isabella. He loves you in ways that I can't love you. There isn't one person in the world that will love in the ways that you need. We need different kinds of love to make us feel fulfilled. That was something that I learned from my dad. The love that we crave will be from other people."

Once she leaned her head onto his shoulder, she inhaled the smoke from her cigarette when she asked him with her blinking back tears that fell down her face, "What did you learn from your dad? I hope that it wasn't as fucked up as the things that I learned from my dad."

Oliver tightened his grip on her arms when he confessed to her, "I learned a lot from him. He taught me how to take care of others around me. That's about the only good thing that he taught me. Everything else was bad. There's some stuff that you hope no one learns about you. Well, this is one of those things for me. I understand how it feels. Even though I always had my stepdad, it doesn't make it easier for me. I love my siblings, but they don't understand it. I hate that you understand it, but it feels good to know that I'm not alone."

She confessed to him with tears falling down her face, "The world doesn't need to know everything about you. If you could ask your dad one question, what would it be? I know mine."

Oliver tightened his grip on her arm when he told her, "I would ask my dad why he did the night before he left for the war. He didn't think that anyone knew about it. What would you ask your dad?"

She responded to him with a frown on her face, "I would ask my dad why he thought that killing himself was going to make my life easier. Everything got worse since he killed himself. What did your dad do that night?"

Oliver confessed to her, "He tried to kill himself. It didn't work out the way that he planned it. He still got deployed. My step dad told me that my dad told him that when he was dying. His last words to him. He told my stepdad that he wished that he died before he left for war. He got what he wanted in the end. We have our secrets that we take to the grave with us. His secrets from the world." Oliver pulled her into a long hug as she hid her face into his chest with his arms tightly around her before he kissed on the top of her head. He guided her into the house where he went into the guest bedroom before she went into her suite for the rest of the night.

CHAPTER THIRTY-TWO
(FALL 1966 – PARIS, FRANCE)

She dropped off Ivan, Jamie, and their boyfriends at the airport the next morning before she slept in her suite for the rest of day until she was woken up in the middle of the night by Sebastian. After they made up for lost time, they spent the day in bed before she slept with his arms around her for the rest of the night. The next morning they went back to the studio to film *Destiny's Choice* that had been on hiatus for the past few months because the director was out of the country on vacation with his family. Even though she was disappointed to not have time to herself, she was relieved that she was working again since it meant that she was back to her routine. She finally slept at night for the first time in a long time. She worked so much that she was so tired that she couldn't stay awake when she got home. She went to Dr. Taylor's office where she talked to him about her fears in her relationship with Sebastian. She was learning how to be kinder to herself. That was hard for her since she was never kind to herself. She was learning how to trust herself. That was something she hadn't done either. She thought about drugs and her dad less every day after she met Sebastian. It was always paired together for some strange reason that she didn't understand. She saw a future for herself that was full of life instead of one that was full of death. The future no longer scared her because she went through the worst thing that she was going to go through with her addiction. Nothing could scare her after everything that she went through in her life. She felt happy for the first time in her life. It was a level of happiness that she never thought was possible for her. She waited for it to go away. She lived the life that she dreamed of with Sebastian.

It was a life that her mother dreamed of with her father. It wasn't like she never thought about her father anymore. She dreamed about him every night. He was the first thing that she thought about when she woke up in the morning and he was the last thing that she thought about when she went to bed at night.

She stopped thinking about her father like he was the worst person. He wasn't the worst person. She wasn't the worst person either. They were doing what they thought was best. She couldn't hold it against her father for the way that he reacted to things with the limited knowledge that he had at the time. He didn't know that there was a life out there for him to find outside of himself. He didn't know that his secrets would be the death of him. He didn't know that he would've been supported by people around him if he stopped hiding his problems from the world. He didn't know that drugs weren't going to be the worst thing that happened to him. That was where she understood her father since these patterns were given to her at birth. It was impossible for her to stop herself from doing the same things that he did. That didn't mean that she wouldn't try to stop herself from doing these things. She didn't want to be defined as the worst thing that happened to her. Her father didn't want to be defined as the worst thing that happened to him. She refused to be defined by her addiction. She was always going to have those parts inside of her mind. Once she made her own peace, a weight was taken off of her shoulders.

It was a weight that was on her shoulder since the day that she was born. It wasn't the only thing that she inherited from her parents, but it was the worst thing that she inherited from them. She realized the good things that she inherited from her parents. Her mother's beauty and empathy for others as well as her stubbornness was a gift. Her father's humor and silliness as well as his appreciation for the world.

The more that she thought about her father, the more that she thought about how much her father appreciated the world around him. He loved the simplest beauty found in nature. He loved the vast meanings found within the stars. He loved the lessons that the universe taught him. When she was a little girl living in England, she heard a story about her father that showed this quality about him. Her family told her that he cried if an animal died in the woods. Her father tried to save a baby bird that was left by their mother since it had a broken wing. He nursed it until it was healthy before he left to go in the wild. Uncle Nathan told her that he cried about it for several weeks after he let that bird go since he feared that the bird wouldn't find his family again. Her father didn't want anyone to feel what it was like to be alone. When they went to England for her father's funeral, she went to her father's will reading with her grandparents, Uncle Nathan, and her parents when he told them that he left all that he had in the world to his daughter. Even though he didn't have anything left that he owned, it gave her great comfort that he would've given it to her. It was the only thing that he gave her. He gave her nothing except for him. He might've thought that she would be disappointed that he didn't have anything to give her. She wished that she could tell him that she never wanted anything except for him. Dr. Taylor asked her what he would say to her if she told her that before she told him that he would be devastated that he was the only thing that she wanted from him. It was the only thing that he couldn't give her. They talked about this subject in many sessions after that. It made her consider what her life would've been like if he was in it instead of him being around it. She lived wanting him in her life and not outside of her life. It meant the world to her that he wanted that for them. She didn't feel like she was alone for the first time. Her father made sure that she knew that she was never alone when she was with him. She saw her relationship with Sebastian in a different light. That was the reason that she fell in love with him. Sebastian made her feel like she wasn't alone. She had someone to share her life with. It was a different kind of love that her father would've given her. It was enough for right now. She felt like a person with him. She saw her job and her relationship with other people in a different light. Those things were important extensions of her since they were a reflection of how she treated herself. When she neglected her job or her relationships, she made decisions to neglect herself. She was going to neglect everything else around her for drugs.

On the last night of them filming *Destiny Choice*, she told Sebastian about this. She made him promise her that he would tell her that she was doing this before she recognized that she was doing it. Even though Sebastian didn't know where it was coming from, he promised her that he would keep her accountable to herself, her job, and her relationships. She explained everything to him that led to that conclusion. She didn't give him context when she made him promise her. He called her out when she pushed people away from her. She tried not to spiral even though she knew that it was inevitable that it was going to happen to her. Before she got the chance to spiral, they left for their press tour for the movie where they were gone from home for five weeks as they went across the country promoting the movie that they fell in love working on together. On the morning of their flight to Seattle, she packed her bags before Oliver dropped them off at the airport where she slept for the entire flight. When their plane landed in Seattle that afternoon, a driver picked them from the airport where their driver dropped them off at their hotel. After she got ready in their hotel room, she met with Sebastian and the cast for interviews before she slept in the hotel room with Sebastian's arms around her for the rest of the night. The tour went by faster than she realized before they were at their last stop in New York where she spent a few weeks at her parent's house. Even though her parents met Sebastian, the rest of her family never met him. On the first day of them being in New York, she introduced Sebastian to Anastasia, Damien, her three-year-old niece Alina, and her one-year-old nephew Viktor when they ate dinner at their apartment. She introduced Sebastian to Nina, Joseph, and her one-year-old niece Bridget. After they spent a few days at her parent's house, they went over to Uncle Sam's house for dinner where she introduced Sebastian to Uncle Sam, Aunt Valeria, and Holly who wasn't a puppy. Sasha and Gabriel were in New York at the same time. They were back from their extended stay in Germany where the family met Gabriel. Once they spent a few weeks in New York, Sasha convinced them to go to France since Gabriel had to go home for a gallery with his brothers before they prepared for a flight to Paris.

After she slept with her head leaning on his shoulder for the flight,

Sebastian nudged her awake where she woke up when their plane landed in Paris before she followed him out of the airport. As soon as she saw her cousin's car parked in front of the airport, she sprinted toward them as she brought them into a tight hug with Sasha joining in before Christophe and Antonine drove from the airport to the gallery where they held their event. After the event was a huge success for them, they were dropped off at their hotel that was across the street from the Eiffel Tower where they got ready for dinner before they went to an expensive restaurant to celebrate their gallery. Once they ate at the restaurant, Ivan dropped them off at the hotel where she passed out with Sebastian's arm around her for the rest of the night. Sasha called her early the next morning from Gabriel's house where she had been staying when she told her that Oliver's family, Amelia, and Troy were joining them in Paris. She didn't ask Sasha how she convinced them to come to Paris since she did the same thing with her. Before her cousin's plane landed in Paris, she walked around the city with Sebastian, Sasha, and Gabriel until later in the day where they met up with the boys at a restaurant to eat dinner after they got back from work. After they slept in their bed for a few hours, she was woken up by Sebastian telling her to get the door where someone pounded on the door before she opened the door to see Amelia and Troy standing in front of her with bottles of wine in their hands that they bought at the airport. Before she got the chance to say anything to tell them, Amelia pushed past her with Troy following behind her as they helped themselves into the room that they were sharing with them. Since she was too exhausted to deal with them invading their privacy, she went into the bed as Sebastian wrapped his arms around her before she fell asleep with her head on his chest for the rest of the night. She woke up the next morning to Troy and Sebastian softly talking to each other on the balcony as they smoked cigarettes before she joined them in their smoking before Amelia woke up from her slumber when she told them that she wanted to go get something to eat. They met up with Oliver and Juliet in the lobby as Posey ran over to her where she placed Posey on her hip before she ate breakfast at the hotel with her family. Once they were done eating breakfast at the hotel, they met up with Sasha, Gabriel, and the boys outside of the hotel where they went to the Rue's family estate a few miles outside of the city before they explored the old house for the afternoon until they went back to Paris for dinner at a restaurant near their hotel. After they got back from eating dinner at the restaurant, she opted to stay in the hotel with Sebastian as Amelia, Troy, and the boys went to spend the night at the Rue family estate. Juliet went to bed as soon as they got back from the restaurant. Once they spent some time at the pool in the hotel with Oliver and Posey, she left to go to her hotel room with Sebastian since she knew that this was going to be the only time that they got alone on this trip.

As soon as she closed the door to their hotel room, Sebastian pulled her into a long kiss where she instantly kissed him back before she moved them towards their bed. Once they let go of each other's lips to catch their breaths, she pulled him into a desperate kiss where he unzipped the back of her dress before she took off his dress shirt that she hastily threw down onto the floor. After they made up for lost time on their bed, they laid down under the blankets as she laid her head on his chest with his arms tightly around her before he lit a cigarette for them to share in the bed. Once he passed the cigarette to her, she inhaled the smoke from it when she asked him with a frown on her face, "Are you happy with me, Bash?"

Sebastian's face turned white in shock when he told her with a look of horror on his face, "I'm very happy with you, Isabella. Why are you asking me that? Are you not happy with me?"

She shook her head at him when she responded to him in a soft voice, "I'm so happy with you, Bash. You're the best thing that happened to me. I'm being sentimental about the last time that I was here. Did I tell you about that?"

After Sebastian sat up in bed with her sitting up on the bed next to him, he brought the cigarette to his lips where he inhaled the smoke from it when he asked her with a frown on his face, "What happened the last time that you were here?"

As she took the cigarette from his hand, she inhaled the smoke from it when she confessed to him with her blinking back tears that fell down her face, "I tried to kill myself the last time that I was in Paris. Things didn't go the way that I planned. I didn't have enough drugs to stop my heart and Oliver found out about it before I could do anything. Oliver thought that I wouldn't kill myself in a foreign city.

He dragged me here against my will where he confronted me about it. This wasn't rock bottom for me. Things had to be worse than me killing myself in the city of love. That's what I thought when Sasha told us that we were going to Paris."

Sebastian took the cigarette from her as he tightened his grip on her arms when he responded to her with concern laced in his voice, "You never told me that. If that wasn't your rock bottom, then what was your rock bottom?"

She asked him with a frown on her face, "Which rock bottom are we talking about? The overdose rock-bottom or the suicide attempt rock-bottom?"

After Sebastian passed the cigarette onto her, he nodded his head at her when he asked her with a frown on his face, "How about both of them?"

Once she inhaled the smoke from the cigarette, she laid her head down on his lap as he ran his hands down her back when she confessed to him with tears falling down her face, "I'll start with the overdose story. I was using drugs for over a year with my boyfriend Daxton. Even though things were always bad between us, drugs ruined what was left. When we were left alone in the house, we stopped doing everything that was needed to survive. We didn't have normal conversations. We only talked about drugs. How we were going to get more drugs. How many drugs were left in the house. How long the drugs were going to last that I bought for us. We fucked over drugs, and we fought over drugs. This was our life for months until that fateful day. We took something that was laced with fentanyl, but Daxton took more of it than I did. When I realized that what we took killed him, I knew that I was going to be next since there was no way for me to stop it. That wasn't my rock bottom though. It was when I woke up in the ambulance that I realized what happened was something that I could never take back again. Do you want to know what's the most fucked up thing about it? Despite everything that happened to me, I wanted to do drugs again."

Sebastian lit another cigarette for them as he inhaled the smoke from it when he asked her with curiosity laced in his voice, "When did you decide that you didn't want to do drugs?"

Once she took the cigarette from his hand, she inhaled the smoke from it when she confessed to him with tears falling down her face, "It took a long time for me to not want drugs. There will always be a part of me that wants them. I think about drugs even now. I think about how it would be easier for me to do drugs instead of fighting it every day. I miss the way that they made me feel. I'll never get that feeling back again. The invincibility that it made me feel. It's not that I don't crave them anymore. It's more about that I don't need to feel invincible. In the process of learning how to trust myself, I've learned how to process those feelings instead of shutting down when I feel them hit me. I learned how to do that after I tried to kill myself a year ago. That scared me more than the drug overdoses did. Do you want to know why it scared me?"

Sebastian grabbed the cigarette from her hands as he inhaled the smoke from it when he asked her with a frown on his face, "Why did it scare you?"

She inhaled the smoke from it when she confessed to him in a distant voice, "It scared me because I was doing it to myself. Substances weren't killing me. I was killing myself. It reminded me of my father. He did the same thing. When my dad killed himself, he didn't have any drugs or alcohol in his body. When I was told that, I couldn't believe it since it didn't make sense to me. A sober version of my father would do that without anything in his body. No person would do that without substances in their body. That night on the roof I understood that feeling. The feeling of wanting to let go of the world. The feeling of giving into my darkest desires. I became my father. Even though it was a lifetime ago, we were living in a moment. It felt like he was standing on the roof with me. It was what I dreamed of in my life. I can't remember what happened after that, but I knew that I was never more terrified in my life. It scared me to be in the place that he was in before he died. It was my wakeup call. Something had to change or else I was going to end up on that bridge with him." He ran his fingers through her hair with tears falling down her face. She stayed in bed with Sebastian as everyone went to the beach. Oliver was concerned about her, but Sebastian reassured him that he would stay with her. When Oliver came back from the beach, he spent the day in bed with her as Sebastian arranged for them to fly home since they realized that she was approaching rock-bottom. She was coaxed out of bed by Sebastian until they got on their plane before she slept with her head leaning on Sebastian's shoulder. When their plane landed in New York, she hid in the guest bedroom when they talked about her. She slept on the flight home with Sebastian's arm around her for the rest of the night.

Chapter Thirty-Three
(Winter 1967 – Antananarivo, Madagascar)

She knew that this was going to happen to her. She expected it to happen to her. She was happy for a long time that there needed to be something that ruined it. Since they left Paris earlier than her cousins, she felt horrible that she ruined their exciting vacation together with the untimely return of her depression. Even though Sebastian reassured her that he was okay with going home with her, the depression told her that he was lying to her before she got into an argument with him about it that led to her crying herself to sleep in her suite. It was the morning after their argument that Sebastian came back into the suite to apologize to her where she apologized to him for her outburst before she laid down in bed in his arms for the rest of the day. After two weeks of her being there, her mum went home to New York once her cousins were home again. Her cousins saw that she wasn't acting any different from when they left to go home. It was an unsaid agreement between them that Sebastian stayed at her house with her after they got back from Paris. Even though he had a house to go to at the end of the day, they realized that they didn't want to be apart from each other. They were attached to each other after what happened to her in Paris. Sebastian filmed a new movie in the studio as she went to Dr. Taylor's office twice a week where they talked about everything that she was feeling at the moment. She told him about the nightmares that she was having about her father's suicide when she revealed to him what she told Sebastian about in Paris. She told him that it was the moment that she became her father. She was continuing her father's story for him. She felt like she was standing on that bridge with him. Even though that thought was supposed to scare her into reality, it didn't stop her from thinking those thoughts. It wasn't until she found herself in places that she didn't remember going to that she knew that things were bad again. She stopped sleeping since she couldn't get her mind to shut off at night. She didn't leave the suite since Sebastian brought her anything that she asked him for. This should've told her that things were bad for her since she knew what happened the last time that she refused to leave the suite, but it didn't stop it from happening to her. Once she stopped attending her weekly sessions with Dr. Taylor, he came to her house three times a week to talk to her since it was the only way that she was going to see him. She spent most of the day talking to Dr. Taylor in the suite. He told her that he didn't want to have to get to this point, but the next step was for her to go to the psychiatric hospital. She pretended to be surprised by the news like it was the first time that she heard it. She made a vow to herself that she would do whatever it took to not end up in the psychiatric hospital again. What she meant by that promise she was unsure of what that would like. Her brain would find a way out of this since it found a way out of everything. Since she wasn't sleeping anymore, she smoked cigarettes on her balcony when she came up with ways that she would get out of the prison that she created for herself.

After she didn't come up with a solution to her problem, she went to bed for the rest of the night until she was woken up by Sebastian getting ready to leave for work. She made a last-ditch effort to look for hidden drugs with no success before she slept for the rest of the day where she didn't wake up until Sebastian got back from work that evening. As she laid in bed with Sebastian's arms around her with him sleeping next to her, she thought about how she was going to get out of this, but she came to no conclusions like she did every night. She knew that she couldn't kill herself since Oliver would never let her do that nor would Sebastian who was with her all of the time. She knew that she couldn't get high since that would make everything worse for her. She couldn't overdose on anything since her new dealer was in prison like her last one. She was trapped in this room. After Sebastian left for work at the studio that morning, she packed piles of her clothes into her suitcase from the floor of her closet where she tried to not make it noticeable that she was going away before she left the house once no one was in the house. Once she climbed into a taxi that she called from her bedroom, she told him to take her to the airport. As soon as the taxi driver dropped her off at the airport, she bought a ticket for the first gate that she saw that was boarding right before she got on the plane to an unknown place in the world. For the entire flight, she slept with her head leaning onto the window before she woke up in the middle of Madagascar where she got into a taxi to a hotel before she booked a room at the closest hotel. After she slept in her hotel room for the rest of the day, she woke up in the middle of the night before she smoked cigarettes on the balcony for the rest of the night. Her family was probably frantically looking for her, but she couldn't find it in herself to care. She knew that running away from her life wasn't a good solution to her problems, but it was the only thing that she could think about doing that wasn't killing herself. Whether she wanted to agree with Oliver about it or not, she didn't let herself self-destruct in a foreign country. It was an unwritten rule that she made up for herself. After she spent a few days alone in her hotel room, room service brought food to her room where she ate it on the balcony while she smoked cigarettes all day and all night. On her fourth day in Madagascar, she ventured out of her hotel room for the first time since she got there where she bought more cigarettes before she explored the city. After she ate dinner at an expensive restaurant, she was notified by the front desk that someone came looking for her when she was gone. She gave them money not to tell them where she was before she slept in her bed for the rest of the night. After she was in Madagascar for over a week, she was woken up early one morning when the hotel staff called to tell her that someone was in the lobby looking for her. She let out a defeated sigh when she told them that they could send them up to her room since they weren't going to stop looking for her until they saw her before she got ready to receive her visitor.

There was an urgent knock on the door before she opened the door to reveal Uncle Nathan standing there with an exhausted look on his face like he searched the world looking for her. As soon as Uncle Nathan walked into the room, he pulled her into a desperate hug as she hid her face into his chest with his arms wrapped tightly around her when he told her with a look of relief on his face, "You're okay. We were so worried. We thought that something horrible happened to you."

She slowly moved her head out of his chest as he kept a tight grip on her arms when he shouted at her with anger laced on his voice, "Are you kidding me, Isabella? You can't take off like that and expect people to not panic. What were you thinking? Why the hell are you in Madagascar?"

As soon as she sat down on the bed, she lit a cigarette from the table as she inhaled smoke from it when she responded to him with a smirk on her face, "I didn't ask you to look for me. I was spending time away from everyone. I don't know why you're upset with me. I'm fine. Nothing happened to me. Should I have told you where I was going?"

Uncle Nathan took a seat next to her on the bed before he lit a cigarette that he brought to his lips when he responded to her with a frown on his face, "You're lucky that I'm here and not your mother. She's furious at you. I've never seen her so angry in my life. What did you expect was going to happen when you took off without telling anyone? I'm being serious, Isabella. We had the police looking for you. We thought that you died."

As she inhaled the smoke from the cigarette, she laid down on the bed with her eyes closed when she confessed to him with tears falling down her face, "I'm sorry for scaring you, Uncle Nathan. That wasn't what I was trying to do. I couldn't be in that house. I was going to do something that I couldn't take back. I got on the first flight that I saw at the airport, so that I didn't do something that I would regret doing. This was better than the alternative option."

Once Uncle Nathan laid down on the bed next to her, he inhaled the smoke from his cigarette when he responded to her in a soft voice, "The alternative option is you killing yourself. I know what it feels like to be trapped inside of yourself. What do you think would happen if you stayed there?"

She inhaled the smoke from it when she responded to him with her blinking back tears that fell down her face, "I would've tried to kill myself, but Oliver would stop me like he always does. I would be back in the psychiatric hospital where they would tell me that everything was going to be okay. People would give me that look of pity that I despise more than anything before we would move on with life like it never happened. Oliver would be pissed off at me until he wasn't anymore. He would tell me all the lies that I was told at the hospital. I would believe them until I didn't anymore where I would try to kill myself again. I know what to expect from this. I've done this song and dance before. I was desperate to do something different to see if it would change what would happen instead of the same shit happening all over again. I'm sick of going through this. I never learn anything from it."

After Uncle Nathan tightly wrapped his arm around her, he inhaled smoke from the cigarette when he responded to her in a reassuring voice, "That's mental illness honey. It's what your father's life looked like too. Don't act so surprised that he did this to himself. The cycle is exhausting for everyone involved in it. It's not that way for you. It's like that for your mother, your mum, Oliver, and myself. Do you want to break the cycle? I'll let you in on a secret. The secret to break it is acknowledging it and confronting it. Do you hate the way that it makes you feel? Are you angry about it? Use that anger to fight it. Do you want me to tell you a story?"

She leaned her head on his shoulder as she inhaled smoke from her cigarette when Uncle Nathan confessed to her with tears falling down his face, "I was angry at myself for everything that happened when I got back from the war. I knew that Will was doing drugs. I was angry at him for everything that happened when I was fighting in the war. I didn't know what to say to him. When I married Priscilla, she told me that I should talk to Will since he was reaching out to me. I talked to him at the courthouse a few years later where he apologized to me about everything that happened. Even though I wanted to stay mad at him, I couldn't be mad at him since I knew that he meant it. We talked to each other every day until he suddenly stopped talking to me before he killed himself. I held it against myself for years that I should've tried to get a hold of him. I got a phone call from the police that they found my brother's body in the river. I knew what they were going to say before they told me since I waited for that moment for my entire life. The anger that I held towards him went towards myself. I didn't know what to do with it. I started drinking and I wasn't sleeping anymore.

Priscilla kicked me out of the house for a few weeks since she didn't want me drinking around the children. That was a wakeup call for me since I didn't want to be apart from my children. I went to Will's grave, and I screamed at him before I broke down crying for hours until I lost my voice. I don't know what happened to me after that. I do know that I wasn't angry at myself anymore. I came back home to my family that I missed so much when I realized that was all I needed to do. Even though the cycle ended that way for him, it doesn't have to end that way for you. If you have the sudden urge to run away from your life, then don't go to Madagascar. Go to York to see your father. He can help you feel better in ways that you can never imagine."

After Uncle Nathan pulled her into a desperate hug, she hid her face into his chest as she blinked back tears that fell down on her face. Once she slowly pulled her face out of his chest, he kept a firm grip on her arms when she asked him with a frown on her face, "Does everyone already know that I'm here? Do I have to go home? I don't want to go home. Can we stay here for a little longer?"

Uncle Nathan nodded his head at her when he responded to her with a sad smile on his face, "Everyone knows that we are here. We don't have to go home yet honey. Do you want to go to York with me? You can see your dad when we are there. Your mother can meet us in York. Your cousins miss seeing you, Isabella. I'm sure that you miss them too since you haven't seen them in a long time."

She nodded her head at him when she asked him in a soft voice, "I'll go to York with you. Can Bash come? I miss him."

Uncle Nathan told her, "He can come. I'll tell him to come with your mother. We can stay here for a few days before we go back to York. Should we get something to eat? I'm starving." Once Uncle Nathan talked to her mother and Sebastian on the phone, they ate lunch at a restaurant down the street from the hotel before they slept in her hotel room for the rest of the day. She got on a plane to England where she slept with her head resting on his shoulder before their plane landed in London where her cousin Sean picked them up from the airport. Once they spent the night at Sean's house with his wife Polly and his one-year-old twin girls Alyssa and Ashley, she drove to York with Uncle Nathan, her mother, and Sebastian before she stayed at Uncle Nathan's house with Sebastian and her mother.

CHAPTER THIRTY-FOUR

(SPRING 1967 – YORK, ENGLAND)

Since her cousins Tommy and Alfie moved to London, there was an extra bedroom in the main house for her to share with Sebastian as her mother slept in the guest bedroom across the hall from her cousin Poppy's bedroom. Even though Poppy was getting married to Eilis Brown at the end of summer, she still lived with her parents while she waited to get married to him before she moved out of the house. Aunt Priscilla talked about how she was going to turn their extra bedrooms into housing for their workers at the bakery. Poppy worked at the bakery until she got married to Eilis before she would work on the farm with him that he inherited from his father. Since Aunt Sylvia's house was only a few houses away from Uncle Nathan's house, she went over there with her mother and Sebastian. Her cousin George lived in an apartment. Uncle James and Aunt Sylvia were empty nesters like her parents, Uncle Sam, and Aunt Valeria were. Her cousin Audrey lived a few blocks away from them with her husband Teddy, her six-year-old twins Leo and Lena, her four-year-old son Mason, and her one-year-old daughter Harper. Sebastian was shocked how big her family was since he didn't have this many cousins and none of them had children unlike her large family full of aunts, uncles, cousins, nieces, and nephews. Her cousin Tommy, his girlfriend Lilly, her cousin Alfie, and his girlfriend Debby Hattie visited them from London for a few weeks. Once they went back to London, she took a trip to Cardiff to the inherited family cabin with Sebastian, Poppy, and George. Aunt Priscilla told her that Oliver, Juliet, and her five-year-old niece Posey were coming to visit them since Aunt Priscilla kept persisting on seeing them. She didn't have the heart to tell Aunt Priscilla that Oliver wasn't coming to see her. She told her that she was happy to hear it. She spent the night at a hotel with Sebastian since they wanted some alone time. After they made up for lost time at the hotel, she talked to Sebastian about what happened to her that led to her running away to Madagascar for the first time since they reunited in England. She told him that she ran away from home because she wanted to stop doing the same thing over and over again. It was easier for her to run away to a foreign country than to deal with her problems. She'd rather self-destruct in a foreign country than do it at home since she did that before.

It had nothing to do with him and everything to do with her. Sebastian told her that he knew that it wasn't about him. Oliver reassured him of that when they were looking for her. She didn't want to ask him about that since she didn't want to know what that was like for them when she was gone, but he subjected it to her anyways. Sebastian told her everything that happened after she disappeared to a foreign country. There was a lot of panic with Sebastian and her cousins that later turned into complete hysteria from her parents and Uncle Nathan. The first person that Sebastian called about her being gone was Oliver. Sebastian spent a lot of time with Oliver when they looked for her before Uncle Nathan got involved in it with her mother pleading with him. She didn't know how she felt about Sebastian being best friends with Oliver. The only time that Oliver called her in England he asked her if he could talk to Sebastian after he talked to her. She didn't think that she could get used to it. It wasn't like she wanted them to hate each other. She didn't know how to feel about it. It didn't make her feel better about it.

On the morning their plane landed in England, she drove to London with Sebastian and Poppy who was excited to see her brother. She met them at Tommy and Alfie's apartment since Oliver, Juliet, and

Posey were already picked up at the airport. As soon as she walked into her cousin's apartment, Oliver pulled her into a desperate hug as she hid her face into his chest before he wrapped his arms around her with tears falling down their faces. They didn't let go of each other until Posey threw herself into her legs as she quickly wiped away the tears from her face before she placed Posey on her hip with her face hidden into her chest. As she pulled Juliet into a tight hug, Oliver and Sebastian tightly hugged each other before Oliver pulled his younger sister Poppy into a tight hug. Once they checked into their hotel room for the night, they met up with Tommy, Alfie, Debbie, and Lilly at a restaurant for dinner before she slept in her bed with Sebastian's arms around her for the rest of the night. In the early hours of the next morning, she woke up to Sebastian and Poppy having a soft conversation with each other on the balcony as they smoked cigarettes together before she joined them until they left to drive to York. After they got to York that afternoon, Oliver was pulled into his mother's arms as Uncle Nathan took Posey from Juliet's arms where everyone greeted each other with hugs and kisses before they ate dinner with Aunt Sylvia, Uncle James, her mother, George, and Audrey's family. Oliver chose to stay in his childhood bedroom with his wife and his daughter. Juliet announced to them that she was pregnant with their second child before everyone pulled them into tight hugs as they congratulated them. She pulled Juliet aside to tell her that she knew that she was pregnant since Posey told her at the restaurant last night. No one was surprised that a five-year-old couldn't keep a secret. Oliver spent as much time as he could with his siblings since he didn't get to see them after he moved to the states. Aunt Priscilla spent as much as time as she could with her granddaughter since she didn't see her. She tried her best to ignore any alone time that Oliver might inflict on her since she wasn't ready to talk about Madagascar with him. Oliver got the hint that she didn't want to talk about it since he never brought it up to her. She tried not to get jealous that Sebastian was spending more time with Oliver than she was even though she was ignoring him right now. On the night before Oliver and his family went back to the states, she chose to go spend the night at Eilis's farm with Poppy since she knew that Oliver was going to bring it up to her when she least expected it. She ignored Sebastian's frustration with her as well as Oliver's disappointment that was written all over his face when she left the house with Poppy. Even though Oliver was annoyed with her, he pulled her into a tight hug that she resisted even though she gave into it without any hesitation. She spent the night at Eilis's house spiraling in the guest bedroom since she couldn't sleep. When Poppy walked into the guest bedroom the next morning, she laid down on the bed wide awake as Poppy climbed into the bed before she fell asleep with her head on Poppy's shoulder.

Once they got back to Uncle Nathan's house in the evening, Oliver already left to go to the airport where she ran outside in the grass field to have a panic attack before she hid in the barn for the rest of the day. She fell asleep on a pile of hay inside of the barn until she woke up to her mother standing over her with a flashlight in her hands when she asked her if she wanted to go to the graveyard with her. After she pulled a few pieces of hay out of her hair, she followed her mother to the other side of the farm where her grandparents and her father's tombstones were in a row. Once she took a seat on the ground with her mother taking a seat next to her, she lit a cigarette that she took from her pocket as she inhaled the smoke from it when she asked her mother in a soft voice, "Did you see him before? I haven't been here before. Uncle Nathan has been trying to get me to come here for a while, but I'm glad that I'm here."

Her mother grabbed onto her hands when she responded to her in a soft voice, "I've been here a few times over the years. I'm sorry that I didn't take you to see him, baby girl. I was waiting until you were ready for it. I'm glad that we could be here when you saw dad's grave for the first time. Do you have anything that you want to say to him? He'll always listen to you. He's incapable of interrupting you. Nothing like he was when he was alive. I can leave if you want a moment alone with him."

She inhaled smoke from the cigarette when she responded to her with a frown on her face, "It's okay, mom. You can stay here. I don't want to be alone with him. I've spent enough alone time with him that I can't stand being alone anymore."

She put her cigarette out into the ground as she leaned her head on her shoulder when her mother confessed to her father in a broken voice, "Hello, Will. It's been a long time since I've been here to see you. I brought our daughter with me. You would be so amazed by the women that Isabella has become over the years. You would be as proud of her like I am. I think about us when I can't sleep at night. I think about what our lives would've been. I don't know what to do with those feelings. It comes from a part of myself that I didn't think existed. I can't kill the part of myself that I was when I was with you. It's going to be with me for the rest of my life. Our daughter opened up my eyes to so much about you. Isabella is a lot like you, Will. It scares me that she's like you. I know how things ended for you. I don't know what I would do with myself if that happened to her."

Her mother wrapped her arm around her as she blinked back tears that fell down her face when her mother told her father with anger laced in her voice, "I can't believe how much you kept from me. Why didn't you tell me anything when you were alive? I had to find out everything through Nathan. I'm bitter that Nathan knew this about you, and he never told me. He felt like he was betraying you if he told the world. I have so many questions that I'm never going to get the chance to ask you. You were too much of a coward to tell me yourself. This is going to shock you, but I would've supported you if you told me. If I knew a little bit about what was happening with you, then I wouldn't have been angry with you. I would've done anything for you, Will. I would've done anything for you if you let me into your world. That was all that I wanted from you. I wanted you to let me into your world. You couldn't give me that. I gave you my world and you stole it from me like it meant nothing to you. That's why I took our daughter from you. You took everything from me. You could never take her away from me. She's the most important piece of me. Even in your death, you're trying to take her away from me. She's the best thing to happen to us. She is the best thing that we did. I'm sorry that you didn't see it that way. You missed out on the best thing that you could do in your life. I wish every night that you chose her over the stars. I don't care that you didn't choose me, Will. All I wanted was for you to choose our daughter. You're missing out on the best thing that you created in the world. Isabella is our legacy. She is our destiny."

Once she laid her head down into her mother's lap, her mother ran her fingers through her hair as she blinked back tears that fell down her face when she confessed to her father like they were people left in the world, "I hate you so fucking much, dad. I was never going to be enough for you. All I wanted was to be enough for you. Life humbled me in the last six years. I understand you like I never was able to understand you before. Mom was never going to be enough for you. Uncle Stan was never going to be enough for you. Uncle Nathan was never going to be enough for you. I wasn't going to be enough for you. Nothing is enough for me. That's part of the problem that we have. I wish that I met you before the monsters took over your mind. We would've been the best of friends like you used to be with mom and Uncle Stan. We would've gone stargazing together. We would've nursed sick animals back to health together. We would've taken on the world together. We wouldn't be alone anymore. I'm sorry that you felt alone, dad. No one should live their life alone. I'm not letting my addiction define me. I realized it earlier than you did. I don't want to be alone. I don't want to feel like I'm alone in a crowded room. That was what killed you, dad. The loneliness was what killed you."

As she let out a suppressed sob into her mother's lap, her mother gently ran her hands up and down on her back when she confessed to her father in a broken voice, "I don't know where to go from here. I don't want my life to end like your life did. I'm stuck on that bridge with you. I'm trapped as everything crumbles down around me. I don't want to do this anymore, dad. How do you make it stop? I want everything to stop. That bridge is looking more and more inviting every moment. I know why you did what you did. You thought that it would make everything stop. I'm sorry to disappoint you, but nothing ends. Even after you died, it continued going on inside of my brain. You did this to me, dad. I wouldn't have been this way if you never killed yourself. You would've never been that way if your grandfather never killed himself. Uncle Nathan told me that. Your grandfather killed himself in the old barn. I bet that you didn't think that anyone knew about that. Your secrets don't die with you. They take on a new life after you're dead. I have secrets too, dad. Secrets that I don't want anyone else knowing about. There are things that no one knows about me that will be revealed to my children after I'm dead someday. We all keep secrets from the world. The world keeps secrets from us too. Those are the worst secrets. Those always catch us off guard when we least expect them. Do you want to know a secret about me that I've kept from the world?"

She took her face out of her mother's lap as she lit a cigarette that she inhaled from it when she confessed to him like her mother wasn't next to her, "I'm scared of myself. I've always been terrified of myself, dad. Long before I was an addict I was scared of myself. I care too much about everything that doesn't matter, and I don't care enough about what does matter. One of the first memories that I have is of me being scared of myself. I've never been able to trust myself. I've never been able to like myself. I tried so hard to fight against it. I'm never going to win against it. I've lost every battle that I've been in with myself. I've never come close to winning them. I wouldn't know what to do if I won a battle in the war. Honestly, I would probably die as soon as that happens to me. I've stopped trying to win. It was a lost cause. We are lost causes, dad. We aren't going to win no matter what we do differently in the world. I need to make my peace with it before it drives me to the point of insanity. I'm already dead and I'm watching what could've been my life on a constant loop. My life is going to end like your life ended for you. I don't care about what happens to me. All that we have in the world are our secrets. They become the death of us. When our secrets are revealed to the world, we are gone like they are. We don't exist in the stars anymore. None of it meant anything to anyone. We didn't mean anything to anyone. I don't think that you're anywhere. You aren't under the ground. You aren't in heaven. You aren't in hell. You certainly aren't in the stars like you promised me. I'm talking to the air around me like it's going to tell me anything different than what I'm saying out loud. Thanks for lying to me. I hate you for leading me on like this. I'm done talking to you. I have nothing left to say to you. You disappointed me when you were alive, and you continue to disappoint me in your death. I'll see you in the abyss. I don't care."

Chapter Thirty-Five
(Summer 1967 – York, England)

She woke up to an empty bed the next morning as she grabbed a cigarette from the side table that she lit with her other hand when she inhaled the smoke from it before Sebastian walked into their bedroom with a plate of fruit and a cup of tea in his hands. After she took the cup of tea from him, he fed her pieces of fruit where she laid down in bed with her head leaning on Sebastian's chest before she fell asleep for the rest of the morning. She was alone in her bed while her mother, Uncle Nathan, and Sebastian had a hushed conversation on the front porch about her. She couldn't have cared less about what they were saying about her before she fell asleep for the rest of the day. Once she woke up in the middle of the night, she snuck past Sebastian who was asleep in the bed next to her as she grabbed a box of cigarettes and her lighter before she walked to the barn where she smoked cigarettes for the rest of the night. She woke up the next morning to her mum standing in front of her as she pulled out pieces of hay out of her hair before her mum took a seat next to her when she told her that they were taking her to a psychiatric hospital in London. That was the last place that she wanted to be in. She didn't have the energy to fight against them. She needed to go into a psychiatric hospital when she ran away from home, but she appreciated their efforts to keep her away from it. She slept for the car ride to London with her head leaning on Sebastian's shoulder. When they got to the facility, she hid her face into

Sebastian's chest with his arms around her where her parents pulled her into a desperate hug before she admitted herself to the psychiatric hospital. She had been to a psychiatric hospital before, but this was the first time that she was going to one in England. She slept in her private suite for the rest of the day where she woke up in the middle of the night as she ran into the bathroom to puke up what food that she had in her body before she fell asleep on the bathroom floor. She woke up in her bed the next morning that she was moved into by the nurses before she ignored everyone that talked to her since she wasn't in the mood to talk to anyone. After the nurse bothered her about eating breakfast, she ate a few bites of the food to make them leave her alone where she threw the tray into the garbage before she slept on the bathroom floor for the rest of the day. She woke up in her hospital bed that she didn't fall asleep in as a nurse sat in the corner of the room attentively watching her sleep before she slept for the rest of the morning. She was woken up by a young male doctor named Dr. Tobias. When she realized that he was waiting for her to say something to him, she looked up to him to ask him for more medication to help her sleep before he told her that he would only give her more medication if she would talk to him about what she was feeling. Since she wanted medicine more than anything, she pretended to go along with Dr. Tobias's request where she answered enough of his questions before he gave her the medicine to help her sleep for the rest of the day. When she woke up in the middle of the night, she laid down on the floor of her bathroom as she played with the ends of her sweater. She would kill someone for a cigarette. She would've asked the nurse for a cigarette if she knew that they would give it to her. They would shut her down. She couldn't stop thinking about ways that she was going to get high after she got out of here.

She realized the hypocrisy in it, but she couldn't have cared less about it. She found ways to kill herself without the nurses knowing about it. When all of her plans were a failure, she got off of the bathroom floor when she asked the nurse in the hallway if she could call her parents before the nurse pushed the phone towards her without looking up at her. She had no idea who she was going to call since it was the middle of the night. Her parents and Sebastian were sleeping and her family in the states were at work. After she stared at the phone without doing anything, the nurse asked her if she was going to call them or not before she nervously put in the first phone number that was on her mind into the phone. It was on the second ring when Oliver answered the phone that she instantly hung up on him. She couldn't believe that she called Oliver out of instinct before she ran into her room without saying another word to the nurse who was very confused. After she fell asleep for a few hours, she was woken up by Dr. Tobias who stood in her room when he asked her if she wanted to go on a walk with him before she hesitantly followed him to an enclosed garden that surrounded the hospital. Once they took a seat on a bench, she answered the questions that Dr. Tobias asked her about what was going through her mind before he took her inside to her room where she ate lunch with a nurse watching her before she fell asleep for the afternoon. After she continued this pattern for the next week, Dr. Tobias told her that she wasn't allowed in her room during the day since she slept all of the time. He told her she needed to be in the activity room with the other patients that were in the hospital. She hated the thought of being surrounded by other people, but she complied with his wishes since she wanted to go home for Poppy's wedding. She wouldn't be allowed to leave unless she gave them the impression that she was getting better. She never told them any information that they were going to hold it against her. After over three weeks in an exhausting effort to trick her medical team, Dr. Tobias told her that she was being discharged in a few days since she was improving in their eyes. Even though she wasn't taking any of the medication that they gave her, they thought that it was helping her. They didn't know that she was lying to them. She tricked one of the patients into taking her medicine for her. It shocked her how easy it was for her to trick someone to take her medicine for her without bribing them with money. She was trapped in the activity room until the end of the day. She met an English girl named Jade who was a few years younger than her. In their first interaction with each other, Jade told her that her painting was hideous. She laughed at that since it was the worst thing that she saw in her life before they talked to each other for the rest of the day. On the second day that they met up in the activity room, she made an arrangement with her where Jade took her medicine for her, and she made Jade's doctors think that she was made a friend with someone that was real. None of the doctors found out about their arrangement the entire time. On the morning that she found out that she was getting discharged, Jade told her that she was getting discharged too before they made plans to meet up in London when they could escape away from their families. As soon as she saw her parents for the first time in three weeks, she asked them about where Sebastian was before they told her that he went to the states to work on a new movie. Sebastian would see her again when he came to York for Poppy's wedding in a month. She didn't want to see him right now. After her parents took them to her cousin Sean's house, she slipped out of the house as soon as she knew that everyone was asleep in their bedrooms before she met up with Jade at their meeting spot that they determined that morning. Jade took her to a place that no one would look for them that she blindly trusted her about since Jade lived in London. The secret place ended up being an abandoned park that looked like it had seen better days where they smoked a joint together in a gazebo.

She got high for the first time in five years, and she forgot how amazing that she felt when she was high. She didn't know how Jade realized that she was a recovering addict, but she was never more grateful for someone in her life. After they smoked a joint together, she went back to Sean's house since she knew that her parents always woke up early in the morning before she passed out in her bed for the rest of the morning. When she woke up that afternoon, she felt a craving for drugs that she never felt before in her life. She made the biggest mistake of her life meeting Jade in the hospital. Even though something horrible was happening to her, she pretended that the world wasn't falling apart all around her. She played the part that her parents expected from her. After they spent a few weeks at Sean's house in London, her parents told her that they were going back to York since the family was coming in for the wedding. She told her parents that she was going to stay with Sean in London, and she would come to York with him for Poppy's wedding. Her parents hated the idea, but they weren't going to stop her from staying with her cousin if she wanted to spend time with him. On the night that her parents went back to York, she disappeared in the middle of the night with her bags where she met up with Jade at a hotel that she set up for them to stay in. She didn't say anything when Jade booked a room with one bed. It was implied that they were sharing the bed. There were more drugs that she didn't remember asking her for.

Even though she thought about telling Sebastian about it, she decided that it was better if he didn't know what was happening when they were apart. After they sniffed enough powder off of the counter to kill a small child, Jade dragged her to the bed where they made out with each other for a long time until she reminded Jade that she had a boyfriend. Jade told her that she had a husband and children that lived in the city. She didn't care about them since they were in the room together. She pulled Jade into an intense kiss that only ended because the phone rang on the nightstand. She answered the phone with Jade doing everything that she could do to distract her from talking into it. Sebastian told her that her parents found out that she left Sean's house, and she moved into a hotel room without telling them about it before he asked her what was going on. While she pretended that she wasn't about to scream out in pleasure, she told him that she met a friend at the hospital that she was spending the night with. Sebastian pretended to believe her before he dropped the bomb shell on her that they should take some time away from each other while she was figuring things out in England. Since she was a complete jackass when she was high, she told him that they should take a break from each other where she abruptly hung up on him before Jade prepared lines for them. She passed out with her arms around Jade until the next day. When she woke up in the next afternoon, Jade smoked cigarettes on the balcony without any clothes on as she wrapped a blanket around her before she joined her in on the fun. After they smoked the rest of the cigarettes that she brought with her from Sean's house, they got dressed in between making out with each other before they embarked on the city to get more drugs and cigarettes. Once they got back to their hotel, she was informed by someone at the front desk that her mother was looking for her. She handed him a pile of money to not disclose her location to her mother before she went back up into the hotel room with Jade who was eager to start the night. Before they got completely trashed for the rest of the night, they did a few rounds all around the room before they ate food that they picked up on the way home from their drug and cigarette run. She woke up with her head on Jade's chest before she was interrupted from her sleep by an urgent knock on the door that made them. While they communicated with their eyes to stay as quiet as possible, the knocking persisted until the door was opened up by an older male with two small children in his arms. She realized that this was the husband and children that Jade told her about a few nights ago. She relaxed in the bed with the sheet around her body as Jade quickly got dressed into her clothes before she got into a screaming match with her husband. When their screaming got louder and louder, she tried not to look over at the frightened children crying in his arms or how she was the person that was responsible for their argument. Something inside of her told her that she couldn't be in this room anymore. She was going to be a part of those children's trauma someday.

After Jade attacked the male with her fists, she quickly got dressed into her dirty clothes as she packed up her suitcases at the speed of light before she ran out of the room with the children behind her while Jade punched the male in the face. When she realized that the children were following her, she sprinted into the lobby where she told the staff to call the police. Once the children were gone, she ran out of the hotel faster than ever before. She booked a room in a hotel on the other side of the city where she cried herself to sleep. When she woke up in the middle of the night, she grabbed the bags of drugs that she took out of the room before the police went upstairs to arrest Jade. She didn't want to go to prison in a foreign country for drug possession. After she did a few lines of the powder off of the bathroom sink, she smoked cigarettes on the balcony for the rest of the night where she tried to figure out what to do after this. She considered calling her parents before she realized that wouldn't make anything better. She would've called Sebastian if she didn't cheat on him with Jade. She thought about calling Oliver since he would know what to do until she realized that he was best friends with Sebastian, and he wasn't in the mood to talk to her. She realized that she was alone. This was the last place that she wanted to be in. She thought about how she ended up here. This wasn't what she wanted with her life. She kept ending up in this place over and over again. She would've jumped up off the balcony, but she was only on the fourth floor and that wasn't going to be enough to injure her let alone kill her. When she couldn't come up with any solutions, she decided to do more drugs before she passed out for the rest of the night. She realized that wasn't going to make anything better, but she didn't care right now. In the week before the wedding in York, she needed to sober up for her trip where she would inevitably have to see her family again. She considered ditching the wedding since she didn't want to go. She had to go to the wedding because she promised Poppy that she was coming to her wedding. After she got off of drugs for three days in her hotel room, she packed up her bags for the train ride to York where she only did one line of cocaine in the bathroom before she stayed awake for the rest of the night. Once her train stopped in York, she followed the crowd off of the train before she got into a taxi that she asked to take to Uncle Nathan's house. As soon as the taxi pulled up to the house, she regretted coming here since she was the last person in her family to get there for the wedding. After she paid the taxi driver the money that she owed him, she nervously walked into Uncle Nathan's house where Oliver sat on the couch with Posey sitting on his lap before Sebastian sat next to him with a book in his hands. Once she made eye contact with Sebastian, she dropped her bags onto the floor where she hid in the barn for the day.

When she woke up in the middle of the night, Oliver sat across from her on a hay bale with his arms crossed against his chest before she hid herself into the pile of hay, so that he couldn't see her anymore. It must have worked because she was alone in the barn. She moved her face out of the hay before she slept for the rest of night. She woke up the next morning where Uncle Nathan stood in front of her when he told her that she should shower in the house before the wedding this afternoon. Even though she would've rather died in the barn, she didn't want to miss the wedding. She wanted to know what happened to her suitcases that had her drugs inside of. She dragged herself into the house when everyone was setting up for the wedding on the other side of the farm. She showered for the first time in days when she put on the dress that she picked out before she went into the hospital. She snorted two lines of cocaine off of the sink as she nervously paced around in the guest bedroom before she put on her happy face for the day. Sebastian's eyes burned into the back of her head as she regretted looking up at him before she pretended that he didn't exist again. She left for the after party that was in the barn. She snorted a few lines of cocaine off of the sink in the bathroom before she put on the best face for her family. When she was alone for the first time, she hid at her father's grave since no one would come looking for her there as she laid down on the ground where she smoked cigarettes by herself. After an hour of her hiding from her family, footsteps approached towards her as she looked up at Oliver and Sebastian who stood in front of her before she inhaled the smoke from her cigarette when she asked them in annoyed voice, "What do you guys want? I'm busy."

Oliver rolled his eyes at her as he placed his hands on his hips when he responded to her with restraint in his voice, "What do I want? You can answer that question for me, Isabella. What the hell do I want from you? How about you stop being a jackass? Can you stop disappearing? It would be nice if I knew where you were."

She laughed at him when she told Oliver with a grin on her face, "Fuck you, Oliver! I'm not answering that question. It's none of your goddamn business what I've been up to. That's for me to know and for you to wonder."

Oliver's face turned bright red as he harshly grabbed her off of the ground as she abruptly stood up on her feet when Oliver shouted at her with anger laced in his voice, "Fuck you, Isabella! Can you please be a normal person for two seconds of your life? We know that you're doing drugs again! It's obvious to the world that you're high! What the hell are you doing? Do you know what you're doing?"

As soon as she pushed Oliver off of her, she brushed the grass off of her dress when she shouted at him with hysteria laced in her voice, "I'm having fun! Is it a crime for me to have fun? You're not in control of my life! You have your perfect life in California! Why do you care about what I do with my life? At least you aren't alone like I am! You stole the only person that was mine! Do you feel good about yourself that you took Sebastian from me? Did you poison him against me? He's all yours! I don't want him! I don't need Sebastian, and I don't need you, Oliver! I don't need anyone in my life!"

Sebastian blinked back tears that fell down his face as he grabbed onto her hands when he pleaded with her in a desperate voice, "You don't mean that, do you? Please tell me that you don't mean that. I love you so much."

Oliver shook his head at her when he told her without any emotion in his voice, "Things could've been so different. None of this had to happen. You made the wrong choice, Isabella. You'll regret this someday. I'll always love you. That's my burden to deal with. I want you to be in my life, but not like this. I don't want you in my life if you're going to act like this. I hope that you're happy. You got everything that you dreamed of. You are completely alone. I'm done, Isabella. I'll talk to you when you are better again. I want you to go to rehab, but it's your choice. It was always your fucking choice. You just don't want to see it."

Oliver angrily stormed away from them as they stared at each other until she let out a heartbreaking sob into her hands before Sebastian pulled her into a long hug with her face hidden into his chest. Sebastian wrapped his arms around her as he ran his fingers through her hair when she confessed to him in a broken voice, "I don't want to break up, Bash. I'm sorry. I love you. Oliver's right. I don't like who I'm becoming. I'm becoming someone who I despise more than anything in the world. You have every right to hate me. I hate myself too. Fuck! I cheated on you, Bash. I cheated on you."

Sebastian froze in his spot when he told her with a look of disbelief on his face, "What? Did you say that you cheated on me? When did you cheat on me? I don't believe you, Isabella."

She moved out of his arms when she confessed to him with tears falling down her face, "I met this girl at the psychiatric hospital where we helped each other out of that place. We got high together, and we had sex a few times that night. We only had sex when we got high except for the times that we had sex when we weren't high. She's married to a man, and she has two children, but she was running away from that life. I didn't plan for it to happen, Bash. It just happened out of nowhere. I'm so sorry. I wish that I could take it back. I wish that it never happened."

As Sebastian slowly backed away from her, he shook his head in disappointment when he responded to her in a distant voice, "What the fuck, Isabella? How many times did you guys have sex with each other? Or do you not know that? I can't believe this. You cheated on me with a woman that you met in a psychiatric hospital. What is wrong with you? I would never do that to you. I don't care that you're doing drugs right now. This is so much worse than that. I'm leaving England tonight. I need space from you."

She nodded her head at him when she responded to him in a broken voice, "I get it. I need to go to rehab before we are near each other. I hope that you can trust me to let me into your life again. I deserve this. Please go. I want to be alone." Sebastian walked away from her before she collapsed onto the ground as she let out desperate sobs into her hands. As she got off of the ground, she walked into the house before she passed out in her bed for the rest of the night.

CHAPTER THIRTY-SIX
(FALL 1967 – NEW YORK, NEW YORK)

She woke up the next morning where she remembered everything that happened last night before she wanted to disappear into her bed for the rest of her life. Her mother had other plans for her. Her mother broke into her bedroom when she told her that she was going to New York with them. Since she had no energy left to fight them, she told her mother that she would be ready to leave in an hour as she threw her clothes into her suitcases where she snorted a few lines of cocaine off of the bathroom sink before she went into the living room. Uncle Nathan pulled her into a long hug with her letting go of him where her mother drove to London with her cousin Sean, his wife Polly, and his one-year-old twins Ashley and Alyssa before she slept with her head leaning on her mum's shoulder. When they got to London, she was dragged to the airport with her parents on an overnight flight to the states where her parents slept for the entire flight. She walked past them to snort a few lines of cocaine that she hid at Sean's house before she stayed awake for the rest of the night. She was going insane the longer that she stayed there. She broke a rule to herself when she was in England. She wasn't allowed to self-destruct in a foreign country. She had been self-destructing in foreign countries for the last nine months. She realized that going to England was the biggest mistake of her life, but she hadn't been with a woman in so long. She thought about how amazing she felt when she was with Jade.

It wasn't the drugs telling her that she wanted to be with a woman again. The way that she felt with Jade was something that she didn't feel with anyone else. It was never love since she hadn't thought about Jade after she left her in the hotel room. When their plane landed in New York, her mother woke her up before she followed her parents to where Uncle Stan and Thomas waited for them. While her parents were in the bathroom, she sprinted into the parking lot as she flagged down a taxi from the side of the road before she got into it when she told the driver to take her to the farthest hotel in the city. She had enough hindsight to not to get separated from her bags on the plane since there were drugs hidden inside of them. After the driver dropped her off at her hotel, she handed him money that she owed him as he grabbed her bags out of the back of the car before she paid for the suite on the top floor of the hotel. When she walked into her hotel room, she deadbolted the door behind her as she threw her bags onto the floor before she climbed into the bed where she passed out for the rest of the day. After she woke up in the middle of the night, she snorted three lines of cocaine off the sink. She panicked that she was almost out of the drugs that she stole from Jade in England. As she smoked cigarettes on the balcony for the rest of night, she thought about what she was going to say to Oliver about this situation. The phone rang in of her hotel room early the next morning before she decided that she wasn't going to talk to anyone for the rest of her life.

She didn't want to go to rehab because she didn't want to stop doing drugs. She didn't want to go to California because she didn't want to see Oliver or Sebastian. She didn't want to go to England because she didn't want to see Uncle Nathan. She didn't want to see her parents since they were going to force her to do something that she wasn't ready to do. She woke up in the bed that she didn't remember getting into that afternoon. She was going to get high again until she realized that there weren't any more drugs left. She called Chloe for the first time in a long time. Chloe answered on the second ring when she asked her if she was in New York where Chloe told her that she was living in New York right now before she invited her to come over to her hotel room. It was an unspoken agreement that Chloe was going to arrive with drugs. They were addicts that were cut from the same cloth. After she cleaned up her hotel room, Chloe rapidly knocked on the door as she opened the door to let her into her hotel suite. Chloe pulled out bags of drugs that she bought for them where she instantly pulled Chloe into an intense kiss that she wasn't expecting. As soon as Chloe dropped the drugs onto the floor, she pulled them towards the bed as Chloe laid on top of her when she took her top over her head before she undid the zipper on Chloe's dress. Once they got to know each other, they snorted a few lines of cocaine off the bathroom sink before she laid on the floor with her arms around Chloe. They didn't put on clothes since they were going to have sex again. Even though she knew that Chloe had a million questions to ask her, she knew that she wasn't going to answer them. She passed out for the rest of the morning with her head on Chloe's stomach. She woke up the next morning to Chloe talking on the phone to her modeling agent. Once Chloe was done talking on the phone, she pulled Chloe into a sudden kiss before she went into the bathroom to take her first shower in days. She pretended that she didn't get excited when Chloe joined her in the shower where they made out with each other on the bed before they ate food that they ordered from room service. After she ate for the first time in days, Chloe went to get more drugs for them where she watched the television with her laying down on the bed. When Chloe returned back to their hotel room a few hours later, she pulled her into a long kiss where they ended up together in the bed before they got high for the rest of the night. They repeated this routine for several weeks at the hotel. Chloe left her alone in the hotel room since she was working in a fashion show in France for a week. Chloe didn't need to tell her that she was going to be with Sasha. Chloe told her that her cousin couldn't know that they were doing drugs and having sex with each other. Chloe agreed with her since she was trying to be friends with Sasha, and she needed to have a working relationship with her since they worked on jobs all around the world. For the week that she was alone in her hotel room, she got high by herself every night as she smoked cigarettes on the balcony until she passed out for the rest of the day. She stopped eating since she wasn't hungry anymore. On the day that Chloe was supposed to return back to the city, she was woken up by the phone ringing on the stand next to her before she answered the phone expecting it to be Chloe. It was Sasha on the phone. Sasha yelled at her for being with her ex-girlfriend. Since she was still high from last night's activities, she was a complete jackass to Sasha when she told her that she wasn't dating Chloe since they were only having sex with each other.

As soon as those words came out of her mouth, Sasha screamed at her since it implied that Sasha never had a real relationship with Chloe when they were together. She abruptly hung up on Sasha after she told her that she was going to come to her hotel that she was staying at when her plane landed in a few hours. After she frantically packed her stuff into her bags, Chloe called her from the airport to tell her that they were moving to a different hotel since Sasha was coming to see them before she took a taxi to another hotel in the city that she stayed at before with Daxton. After she got comfortable in the suite in her new hotel, Chloe arrived at the hotel from the airport where they made up for lost time together in the bed before they got high together for the rest of the night. She woke up with her arms around Chloe in the early afternoon where she called down to the front desk to tell them that she would pay them to keep everyone away from their room. They lived in their own world completely uninterrupted for weeks on end before Chloe told her one night in bed that Sasha was demanding to see her since she was in the city again. Even though she wanted more than anything to disappear into her skin, she conceded into Chloe that she would talk to Sasha. She wanted to do it in public since she knew that Sasha was going to kill her if they were alone with each other. On the morning of their fateful meeting, she snorted lines of cocaine off of the bedroom sink. She wasn't going to confront Sasha if she was sober. She knew that her being high would make Sasha even angrier with her, but she didn't give a shit what Sasha thought about it. Sasha should've been grateful that she was coming since she didn't have to come to see her. After she slept in their bed for most of the afternoon, she was woken up by Chloe later that day when she told her that they needed to leave for the restaurant that they were meeting Sasha at before she got dressed for their meeting with Sasha. Once she was ready to leave their hotel room, she snorted one more line of cocaine off of the bathroom sink before she followed Chloe to their taxi before they were drove to the restaurant that they were meeting Sasha at on the other side of the city. As soon as the taxi dropped them off at the restaurant, Chloe handed the driver what he was owed as she grabbed onto her hand before Chloe dragged her into the restaurant where Sasha and

Amelia sat at a table in the back of the room. After she took a seat next to Chloe while she refused to look at them, she lit a cigarette from her pocket as she inhaled the smoke from it when she told Sasha with a smirk on her face, "What the hell, Sasha? Are you trying to confront me? Your plan is failing if that was your intent."

Sasha leaned back onto the chair when she shouted at her with anger laced in her voice, "You are so exhausting, Isabella! The least that you could've done was to not show up high for our meeting! You couldn't give me that! I haven't heard anything from you in almost a year! I had to hear from Oliver that you relapsed in England! He told me that you aren't with Bash! You cheated on him with a woman! I find out from Chloe that you guys are in a drug relationship with each other! What's happening? Can you at least tell me that?"

As she inhaled the smoke from her cigarette, she responded to her with a look of indifference on her face, "It seems like you already know everything about me. Don't you? Why am I here, Sasha? I'm not in the mood for being lectured. I came here to eat some food with Chloe. You made it personal. It didn't have to be this way between us. Things are fucked up right now, but I couldn't be bothered to care about it. If it is only about this, then I'm not interested in being here. Chloe! Let's go!"

Amelia shouted out her name as she turned to face Amelia when she screamed at her with bitterness laced in her voice, "What? What can you possibly say right now to make anything better? You're a fucking dreamer, Amelia! There is nothing that you could say to me that would make me stay in this room any longer than I already have! Come on, Chloe! Let's go back to the hotel! I'm not hungry anymore! They ruined my appetite!"

Amelia slapped her across the face where Chloe pulled her away from Amelia before she could do anything to hurt her. Her ears pounded out of her head as Amelia pushed away Sasha who held her back when Amelia screamed at her with anger laced in her voice, "Look, asshole! We didn't come here to start an argument with you! I know that you don't believe me! You don't have to believe me! We came to see you because we're worried about you! The last time that you acted like this you died! If you're killing yourself, then you're doing a great job at it! You're halfway there! I don't care about this bullshit! I don't care that

Sasha's feelings are hurt that you're with her ex! I don't care that Oliver is pissed off at you for lying to him! I don't give a shit that you ruined your relationship with Bash! I'm here because I'm sick of watching this happen to you! I want you to stop this! If you aren't going to stop it, then I wanted to see you before you died! I'm sorry that your dad died, Isabella! That's not an excuse to act like a suicidal jackass! You need to fucking snap out of it! I'll be here to talk to you whenever you are ready to have an honest conversation! Please leave me out! I don't want anything to do with you!"

Amelia stormed out of the restaurant as everyone in the room stared at them before she ran outside onto the street with Chloe and Sasha following her. Amelia climbed into the back of a taxi when she shouted at her with her hands up in the air, "Fuck you, Amelia! You aren't invited to my funeral! Thanks for embarrassing me in front of the whole restaurant! Go back into the hole that you came from and never come back! We're leaving, Chloe! Let's leave these traitors alone!" They climbed into the back of a taxi before a driver took them to the hotel. Chloe guided her into their hotel room where she snorted ten lines of cocaine off of the bathroom sink before she passed out for the night.

Chapter Thirty-Seven
(Winter 1968 – New York, New York)

She succeeded in taking enough cocaine to stop her heart until she woke up in a hospital bed. She regretted that she saw Amelia sitting next to her since she told her off at the restaurant last night. While Amelia slept in the seat next to her, she spiraled about what happened to lead her to this place. She disappeared into her mind until she heard the door open before she pretended that she was asleep. She opened her eyes where Oliver stood in front of her bed with a look on his face that she hated more than anything in the world. Concern. Oliver hesitantly approached her bed as he grabbed onto her hands before he took a seat next to her without him saying anything to her. Even though she wanted to say a million things to him, she couldn't get any of it to come out of her mouth before she tightly grabbed onto his hands like it was the only lifeline that she had left in the world. Oliver looked up at her with a smile on his face. She smiled at him when they told each other in no words that they would talk about it later before she closed her eyes to ignore the world all around her. She opened her eyes when she heard the door opening again where her doctor walked into the room to ask her questions that she avoided answering for a long time. Once Amelia and Oliver left her alone with the doctor, she was going to be asked if she tried to kill herself even though it was clear that she had a problem with drugs. When the doctor asked her if it was a suicide attempt, she told him that she was an addict. She didn't become an addict to kill herself. There were so many easier ways to do that without doing drugs. Even though she wasn't wrong in her answer, the doctor told her that they were concerned about it because she had so many different types of drugs in her body at the time of her overdose. In the most honest answer that she gave in her life, she told the doctor that in all the times that she purposely tried to kill herself she was always sober. It sounded like something that her father would've told his doctor a different lifetime ago.

When the doctor realized that she wasn't going to give him answers to his questions, he left her alone to sleep for the rest of the afternoon before she woke up in the middle of the night to her parents having a hushed conversation with the doctor. Her parents talked to her doctor about her going to rehab. That was inevitable from the moment that she got high in England. Once her parents realized that she was listening to their conversation about her, her mum asked her if she was going to get better if she went to rehab again where she shrugged her shoulders at her before she slept for the rest of the night.

After she spent a week in the hospital, her parents took her to rehab in Upstate New York where she went to individual and group therapy every day for over a month where she unpacked the problems that she was suppressing during her six-month bender. She met her psychiatrist Dr. Halkin who was a middle-aged male with a bald head that helped her examine the reason for her doing drugs. Dr. Halkin told her that there was a reason why an addict wanted to do drugs that were hidden deep inside of them. It was a secret that they hid from themselves. This was Dr. Halkin's goal for her during her time in rehab. To figure out the root of her problems, so that she could learn how to change the way that she dealt with them. She thought about the moment that she thought of drugs for the first time. She revealed to him that she didn't think about drugs until she took her mother's pills when she was thirteen years old. It was the night that she tried to kill herself by taking her mother's pills that it began. She wondered why she thought about that night so much. Dr. Halkin asked her if she thought that something more than that happened. He implied that her being suicidal as a teenager had something to do with her desire to do drugs. She tried to justify it to him that her being suicidal didn't have anything to do with her drug addiction, but she didn't believe a word that came out of her mouth. When he asked her the reason that she tried to kill herself that night, she couldn't say anything without sounding like a hypocrite before she stormed off to her room for the rest of the day. In their session the next morning, she apologized to Dr. Halkin for abruptly leaving their session yesterday since she felt guilty about the way that she reacted to his comment. They moved on from it like it never happened. He was right about that night. She thought about taking pills for a long time before she found the strength to do it. The first time that she thought about taking pills was the morning of her father's funeral when she was eight years old. She was so young that she didn't understand anything about the world, but she knew when she saw her father's body in a coffin that she would do anything to be with him. Her parents were away on a business trip, so Uncle Sam and Aunt Valeria took care of her. She was in the bathtub with her cousins Anastasia, Sasha, Nina, and Ivan. They were small enough that they took a bath together. Since she was being defiant towards them because her mother wasn't home, she refused to get out of the bathtub when it was time to get dressed for bed before Aunt Valeria left her in the bathroom by herself while she got her cousins ready for bed first. She went underwater in the bathtub for a long time until Uncle Sam lifted her out of the bathtub where she desperately tried to catch her breath before Uncle Sam dragged her out of the bathtub with a towel wrapped around her body. Uncle Sam never told her mother about that since he thought that she fell asleep in the bathtub. Not that she was trying to kill herself by drowning in it. That was nine months before her father killed himself. When her parents got back from California, she was clingy with her mother since she didn't want her mother to leave. After she found out that her father killed himself, she tried to do the same thing in the bathtub that night, but her mother pulled her out of the water before anything bad happened to her. On the night before they left for England for her father's funeral, she laid in her shared bedroom with Sasha where she stared up at the ceiling for the rest of the night before she passed out early in the morning. Her mother carried her in her arms in the airport since she didn't have the energy to walk anymore before she slept in her mother's lap for the flight to London.

She didn't remember much from England since she was disassociated. She remembered every detail of her father's funeral. She remembered the itchy dress that her mother made her wear that she kept trying to take off when her mother wasn't looking at her. She remembered the music that they played in the background of the wake. She remembered the way that her mother cried for the entire funeral in her mum's arms. She remembered the look of sadness on Uncle Nathan's face when he gave his last words to her father. She remembered what suit her father wore as he laid in the coffin that her grandparents dressed him in that made him look like a young child. One thing that she remembered more than anything was how she felt like she needed to run away from that room. Once the funeral was over, she bolted out of the room when her parents weren't looking into the cemetery since no one would look for her there. As soon as she was alone in the church cemetery, she went to where her father was buried before she let out primal screams that came from something deep inside of her. As soon as she lost her voice from screaming out in pain, she let out suppressed sobs into her hands as her body fell onto the ground before she kicked his tombstone until she had bruises all over her legs. In that moment, she thought about how she would do anything to get rid of that feeling that made her want to die with him. She didn't know that the solution to her problems was going to be getting high, but she would soon learn that was the only way that she was going to survive life after that moment. It wasn't that she didn't think those types of thoughts before her father killed himself, but it accelerated the timeline for her. It gave her a little bit of comfort that she would've been an addict if her father never killed himself. She became an addict earlier in her life than she would've been in an alternative world that he didn't kill himself. When she thought about the question that he asked her at their first session, she had an answer for him that he waited for her to tell him. In their last session, she told him that the reason that she was an addict was a series of complicated answers that he would love to know about her. She was an addict because her grandmother and her father were addicts. She was an addict because she didn't have the ability to stop herself from going too far. She wasn't talking about drugs anymore. She was talking about how she was addicted to everything that she did. She didn't know how to live without her vices. It wasn't that the vices that she was using to distract herself were addicting, but she was the addictive component to her vices. She wasn't only addicted to drugs. She was addicted to self-destructing and dying. As soon as she cut out one of the vices, she replaced them with another vices until she ended up doing drugs again. She became addicted to everything that she did in her life. As a child, she was addicted to school and her academics. As a teenager, she was addicted to self-destructing and killing herself. As an adult, she was addicted to drugs, sex, and her work. It felt like a weight was lifted off of her shoulders. She wasn't angry, sad, or frustrated anymore. What power was left from her addiction over her life was slowly diminishing into nothing. She believed what Uncle Nathan told her last year at the beginning of her self-destruction when he told her that she could use that anger and frustration to fight against it. She knew that Uncle Nathan wasn't talking about drugs. This situation was more than a conversation about how she couldn't control herself with drugs. She couldn't control herself with anything that she did in her life. It was a part of a much larger picture that she saw for the first time in her life. She was the artist of the painting, but she didn't know what she was painting until she was done with it. She was in a gallery of paintings that she was going to paint. A galley of paintings that she would never see. After she was discharged from rehab, her parents picked her up from Upstate New York where she slept with her head resting on her mother's shoulder as her mum drove them home. She heard from Uncle Stan and Thomas who were staying at her parents' house that Oliver and Juliet had their second daughter Eleanor Foster a few weeks ago. She called Oliver to congratulate him on his daughter. Oliver thanked her for her kind words before they went into a conversation about how Posey was dealing with her baby sister and Juliet was coping with being away from work since the baby was born. They had an unspoken agreement between them that this wasn't the time to talk about what happened between them. They didn't have anything to talk about except for her time in rehab. She wasn't in the mental space to talk to him about that. She hung up on him when she ran out of things to say to him that wouldn't lead into an unnecessary argument. She grabbed a blanket from her bedroom before she went to her hiding spot on the roof.

As soon as she took a seat on the roof, she lit a cigarette as she inhaled the smoke from it with the blanket around her arms before she laid down on the roof with her eyes closed. Uncle Stan came through the window as he took a seat next to her where she inhaled the smoke from her cigarette before she closed her eyes again. Uncle Stan took one of the cigarettes that was sticking out of her pocket as he lit it with her lighter where he inhaled the smoke from it when he asked her with a concerned look on his face, "How are you doing honey?"

She inhaled the smoke from her cigarette when she told him with a frown on her face, "I don't know if I'll be okay again. Do you want to hear the long version of the answer?"

As Uncle Stan inhaled the smoke from the cigarette, he wrapped his arms around her when he responded to her with a sad smile on his face, "I was the person that asked you the question. I wouldn't ask you the question if I didn't want to know the answer. Go on. Say it. What's your truth?"

She let out a shaky breath as she inhaled the smoke from her cigarette when she confessed to him with her blinking back tears that fell from her face, "I don't know where to begin. I can't believe that everything from last year happened. I feel like it was a fever dream that I can't wake up from. Everything was perfect, and I ruined it. I'm so angry at myself. I was doing so good and suddenly everything fell apart all around me. I wouldn't blame anyone for hating me after everything that I did to them. I really fucked up this time, Uncle Stan. It's haunted me ever since I woke up in the hospital. I'm trying to learn from it and become a better person, but it's so hard to do. I want to fix things, but I don't know where to start to make things better. Maybe it would've been easier if I died, so I wouldn't have to put together the life that I took from myself."

Uncle Stan shook his head at her as he grabbed onto her hands when he told her in a stern voice, "Stop it! You know that isn't true, Isabella! We ruin our lives so much that we don't know how to fix it. I've done that too. I've had these same thoughts that you're having right now after I made terrible choices for myself. I didn't think that I would get out of that moment, but I made it out alive. Even though you feel like you'll be stuck forever, you will make it out. Look at the moments that you made it out of that you didn't think would end. What's your biggest fear?"

She inhaled the smoke from her cigarette when she responded to him in a distant voice, "I'm scared that everyone will hate me. I'm scared that I will die alone. I'm scared that Bash is never going to forgive me for cheating on him. I'm scared that Oliver is never going to trust me again. I'm scared that I ruined my relationship with Sasha from being with Chloe. I'm scared that Amelia will ignore me for the rest of my life. I'm scared that my parents are disappointed in me. I know that you hate me, Uncle Stan. You don't have to say it. I feel it."

Uncle Stan tightened his grip on her arms when he responded to her in a soft voice, "I don't hate you honey. I've been disappointed in you, but I could never hate you. You're too hard on yourself, Isabella. Will was the same way. He was so hard on himself. It made my heart hurt for him. The first step to making things better is to talk about it. Apologize to people that you wronged. If you can't say it to their faces, then write it down for them. Your cousins want to forgive you, but they don't know how to do it. Forgiveness is a two-way street. You can be sorry about something you did, and they never have to forgive you for it. You have to be okay with them not forgiving you. Even though I loved Will with all my heart, I never forgave him for what he did to me. Your mother did and that was her choice to forgive him. She urged me to forgive him after his death, but I can't forgive him for that. Who is to say if Bash will forgive you for what you did to him? That's only up to him. Do you forgive yourself for what you did to Bash?"

She responded to him with a frown on her face, "I can't forgive myself from cheating on him. Even if I was high at the time. It was a choice that I made to betray his trust. I'll give him space to figure it out for himself while I'm figuring out my own life. Why didn't you forgive my dad?"

Uncle Stan grabbed onto her hands when he confessed to her with a serious look on his face, "That's a loaded question, Isabella. There were a lot of reasons why I couldn't forgive him. Loving someone doesn't mean that you forgive them. Even though he wasn't in his right mind when he raped me, he made the choice to do it. No one made him rape me. He made that decision to do that to another person. I know that he felt horrible about it, but it didn't change what he did. He knew that I wasn't going to forgive him. That's why he didn't try to change my mind about it. It took your mother a long time to forgive me after she found out that I was the other person in their relationship. She was rightfully angry at me until we talked to each other about it. I'm so happy that she found it in her heart to forgive me because I love her so much. She's been my best friend for my entire life. It was weird when she wasn't in my life. Your cousins will find their way back to you like what happened with your mother and me. I get to be in your life because your mother has such a big heart."

She leaned her head onto his shoulder when she responded to him with a smile on her face, "I'm glad that mom forgave you, Uncle Stan. I can't imagine my life without you. I do miss my cousins. It's been weird without them. Maybe you're right. You seem to know a lot about this. We will find our way back to each other again. Just like you did with mom. Like you would've done with dad." She followed Uncle Stan into the house where she passed out in the guest bedroom for the rest of the night.

CHAPTER THIRTY-EIGHT
(SPRING 1968 – LONDON, ENGLAND)

After she talked to Uncle Stan on the roof of her childhood house, she thought about what she would say to her cousins to make things better between them. She didn't want to think what she was going to tell Sebastian since she knew that she wasn't ready to open that can of worms for a long time. On the first stop on her apology tour, she started off with Sasha since she was always the first person to forgive her after they fought in their lifelong friendship with each other. Since she knew that Sasha wouldn't take the time to read a letter if she sent one to her, she decided that the best approach was to talk to Sasha on the phone since she never knew where Sasha was at any time. She realized that she couldn't call Amelia to ask her where Sasha was since she wasn't ready to confront Amelia yet. She decided that the safest choice was to call Sasha's boyfriend Gabriel who she knew was living in France with his brothers and her cousins Ivan and Jamie. She wanted to call him that afternoon, but she realized that it would be in the middle of the night for Gabriel, and she didn't want to wake him up to ask him where his girlfriend was. She called Gabriel's phone number that she saved from the last time that she was in Paris with them in the middle of the night for her. Gabriel answered on the second ring since he was shocked that she was calling him when she asked him if he could do her favor before he told her that it depended on what that favor was. After she asked him if he could tell Sasha that she wanted to apologize to her, Gabriel told her that Sasha was asleep on the other side of the bed and that he could tell Sasha to call her when she would wake up in a few hours. She didn't have a chance to respond to Gabriel before Sasha answered the phone when she asked her what she wanted. She barely got out that she was sorry that she ignored her for a year and that she was sorry for the things that she said to her at the restaurant. Sasha told her that she forgave her a long time ago, but she appreciated the apology from her. She wasn't surprised that Sasha forgave her without her saying anything to her. It made her feel a little better that Sasha believed that she was sorry about what happened between them before she asked her when she was going to be in the states again. After they set up a date to meet up in the city, Sasha told her that she needed to get ready to leave for work where she hung up the phone on her before she jumped up and down in her room in victory that Sasha didn't hate her anymore. Once she made her peace with Sasha, she knew that the next person that she had to talk to was Amelia who already knew that she made amends with Sasha before she made amends with her. Amelia and Sasha were competitive with each other about everything including who she apologized to like it meant that she liked one of them more. She helped her mum make dinner in the kitchen when the phone rang before she answered it expecting it to be her mother telling them that she was coming back from the movies with Uncle Stan and Thomas. She almost dropped the phone on the floor when Amelia asked her why she apologized to Sasha before she apologized to her. Even though she saw this coming from them, she pretended to be surprised by Amelia's behavior when she assured her that it wasn't anything personal and that she called Sasha first since she didn't know that she was in France with Gabriel. This calmed down Amelia who was curious about how she was doing since she got out of rehab. Amelia forgave her a long time ago too. She didn't ask her for an apology even though she tried to give it to her before Amelia shut her down every time that the word sorry left her mouth. After she caught up with Amelia on the phone, she told Amelia that she was seeing Sasha in a few weeks if she wanted to come with them before Amelia told her that she was invited by Sasha to be with them. Once she made her amends with Sasha and Amelia, Oliver was the next person on her apology tour since she hadn't talked to him since she congratulated him on his new baby before she decided that Oliver would have more patience than Amelia and Sasha to read a letter if she sent him one. She would've called him to say everything that she wanted to tell him, but she didn't trust herself to say what she wanted to tell him if she heard his voice. Oliver would think that it was odd that she was sending him a letter since she never sent him a letter before, but she wouldn't trust herself to say the right thing on the phone. It was a few weeks later where she was wide awake in the middle of the night where she sat in her parent's office with a blank piece of paper in front of her as she smoked a cigarette before she wrote a letter to Oliver that she never thought that she would write to him.

Dear Oliver,

I know that I've never written you a letter before. It's not the kind of letter that you think that's going to be. I can imagine your face when you open this letter and think the worst happened to me. I'm putting it on the top of the letter that it's not a suicide note, so that I don't give you a heart attack. I'm not pulling a Will. I know that you know me well enough to know that I would never do that to you. I would've called you to tell us this, but I didn't trust myself to say the right words. I'm on an apology tour. Not the kind of apology tour that you go on when you are about to kill yourself. I promise you that I'm not killing myself, Oliver. I'm not making this any better, aren't I? It's the apology tour that you go on when you are in recovery where you make amends to the people in your life that you hurt from your addiction. I never wanted to hurt anyone. Things spiraled out of control and there was no way for me to stop it. Here's the apology that you have been waiting for, but you would never date to ask from me. I'm sorry for lying to you about what was going on in my life. I'm sorry for being a jackass to you. I'm sorry for disappointing you. You were right when you told me that it was a choice. I didn't realize that it was a choice until you told me that. I always had a choice. The problem was that I kept making the wrong choices. I knew that it was wrong, but I did it knowing the consequences of my actions would catch up with me. I was mad at you because you were right. I hate that you're always right about everything. I wasn't ready to hear it, but now I'm ready to hear it. Even though you won't say it to me now that I'm in recovery, I want you to tell me the things that you wanted to tell me back in England. Tell me that I'm a fuck up that can't do anything right. Tell me that I'm ruining my life. Tell me that I deserve to be alone after how horrible I treated everyone around me. You wouldn't tell me this even if I was in the thralls of drug addiction. You never believed any of this about me. That's me projecting my thoughts onto you. Now that I've been out of it, I can see it from your perspective. It would be scary to watch the person that you love get consumed by their addiction. You had a front row seat to it for seven years. My psychiatrist is showing me how to see things from other people's perspectives since I haven't been able to do that. It's hard for me to get outside of myself. Addiction makes me selfish at times. I'm trying not to be a selfish person, but it's a lot harder said than done. I thought of a memory before I overdosed in my hotel room. I thought about when we were children living in that crowded house in York with Audrey and Amelia. We were playing with trains on the floor in the living room where grandma was in the kitchen making dinner. Audrey and Amelia were playing in another room. I couldn't have been more than two years old. I'll never forget it. You looked up at me when you told me that you would protect me from myself. I don't think that we knew what you meant, but you never broke that promise to me. You have spent your entire life protecting me from myself. You saw something in me that nobody else saw. You saw it before I noticed it. That's why I feel so guilty when I let you down because you have invested so much more into me than anyone else. Probably even more than my mother did over the years. I might not be in the mental space to have that conversation with you right now. I would like to talk about it with you someday. We don't need to get into it. I love you, Oliver. Thank you for being my best friend.

Love, Isabella

She placed the letter into an envelope where she placed a stamp on the corner of it as she placed it into her purse to take to the post office before she slept in her bed for the rest of the night. She picked up Amelia and Sasha at the airport for their awaited weekend together. After she hugged her cousins for a long time, she took them to Uncle

Sam's house where they ate lunch with her parents, Aunt Valeria, Nina's family, and Anastasia's family before they went shopping together in Times Square. After they went out to eat at a restaurant, they went to her parent's house where they shared the guest bedroom together as they talked to each other until the early hours of the morning before she passed out in between Sasha and Amelia like when they were children. After Amelia and Sasha went home to California, she was sad that she wasn't going back with them. She reminded herself that she was better off in New York right now than where her ghosts lived. She didn't have to be separated from her cousins for too long since they were meeting each other in London for Tommy and Lilly's wedding. She went to outpatient sessions with Dr. Halkin as well as going to NA meetings twice a week down the street from her parent's company where she helped her parents with their business when she was staying in the city.

On the morning of their flight to London, she got on a plane with her parents, Uncle Sam, Aunt Valeria, Anastasia's family, and Nina's family. Uncle Stan and Thomas were staying in New York to watch Holly since they didn't want to take the dog with them to England. For the entire year that she had dropped off of the face of the earth, she didn't realize that her cousins had more children. Anastasia had three children now who were Alina, Viktor, and Angelina. Nina had two children and one on the way who were Bridget and Eilis. On the plane ride to London, she slept with her head resting on her mother's shoulder where her mum gently nudged her awake when their plane landed in London in the evening before Sean picked them up from the airport. Once her family went to stay the night at a hotel, she stayed at Sean's house with her parents where she apologized to Sean for using him while she was addicted to drugs the last time that she was in London. Sean forgave her when he found out about her overdose in New York three months later before they talked in the living room for the rest of the night.

She woke up the next morning with her head on Sean's legs where she carefully moved past him to not wake him up before she joined Polly in the kitchen for a cup of tea with her two-year-old nieces Alyssa and Ashley who were talking to her in full sentences. After they ate breakfast in the kitchen, she left to go to the airport with her parents where they picked up Amelia, Troy, Oliver, Juliet, her six-year-old niece Posey, and her three-month-old niece Eleanor. As soon as she saw Oliver from the other side of the airport, she sprinted towards him as he pulled her into her arms with her face hidden in his chest where Posey wrapped her arms around her while she held onto her father's hand. She didn't let go of Oliver until Posey asked for her to pick her up as she wiped away the tears on her face before she placed Posey on her hip. After she pulled Juliet into a tight hug, she placed Posey onto the floor as she grabbed Eleanor out of Juliet's arms where she placed the baby on her chest before she pulled Amelia and Troy into a tight hug with the baby crying in her arms. As soon as she handed Eleanor off to Juliet, she grabbed onto Posey's hand where she was about to walk away from the airport before Sebastian walked out of the bathroom with his suitcase. Sebastian pulled her into a desperate hug as she hid her face into his chest before Posey tugged on her hand to take her to the bathroom. Once they pulled away from each other, Sebastian promised her that they would talk to each other later before Posey pulled her into the bathroom. Oliver stood outside of the bathroom with Eleanor asleep in his arms when she asked him why Sebastian was with them before he told her that Sebastian was invited to the wedding since he was friends with his brothers. She wanted to ask Oliver when her ex-boyfriend had time to befriend his brothers before Sebastian appeared at Oliver's side with a bag of food that he bought for them. She stormed out of the airport to get into a taxi to Sean's house before she hid in her bedroom for the rest of the day. In all the chaos that came out from last year, she forgot that Oliver was best friends with Sebastian despite them not being together. After she hid in her bedroom, she went out on the balcony to smoke cigarettes with Sean as she complained about Sebastian until she passed out in the bed. As a small group of her cousins went sightseeing in London the next day, she pulled Oliver aside when she told him that she didn't know that Sebastian was going to be at the wedding, and that he blinded her by not telling her that he would be there. Oliver told her that he should've told her that he was coming with him before he pulled into a tight hug to apologize to her as she instantly gave into it. When she realized that she couldn't avoid Sebastian anymore, she talked to him about his new movie as they ate lunch together at a restaurant across the street from Big Ben. Amelia and Troy looked shocked that she was having a normal conversation with Sebastian like they didn't have a horrible break up nine months ago in the same country. Even though she was pissed off that Oliver didn't tell her that Sebastian was coming with them, she was secretly relieved that he was there since she was looking for a way to get connected with him. She took this as a good sign that he wanted to be around her since he wasn't mad at her anymore. Even though she would never admit this to him, she missed him so much that it made her heart hurt. She was happy to see that he missed her too. When it came time for her to go to Sean's house for the night, Sebastian asked her if she wanted to go to his hotel room with him where she instantly accepted this invitation since she never thought that he would want to be alone with her again.

Oliver and Amelia disappeared into their hotel rooms with smiles on their faces. Sebastian grabbed onto her hand as he guided her to his hotel room where she pulled him into a desperate kiss before he could open the door. As soon as Sebastian opened the door, she slammed the door behind them as he brought her into a long kiss that they didn't let go until Sebastian told her that this didn't mean that he forgave her before she told him that she didn't forgive herself either. After she pulled him into a passionate kiss, he pulled them towards the bed as she laid down on the bed with him laying on top of her before he took her shirt off of her while she unzipped his pants. After they made up for lost time together in bed, she laid down on his chest as he gently ran his hands up and down her back when she confessed to him in a soft voice, "You don't have to say anything, but I want you to know that I'm sorry about cheating on you. I know that I was high at the time, but it was a choice that I made. I know that I don't deserve your forgiveness. I did something horrible to you. I broke your heart and your trust. I never wanted you to feel like that. I've been so guilty about it for so long. You're a great person and you don't deserve someone doing that to you."

Sebastian wrapped his arms around her when he responded to her with a frown on his face, "Thank you for apologizing, Isabella. It doesn't change what happened to us. Nothing in this world is going to change that, but it's a step in the right direction. I can tell that you genuinely mean it. I think that I'm ready to forgive you, but I need you to do something for me. Promise me that you are never going to do that again. I don't mean cheating on me. I mean the drugs too. If we are being honest with each other. That was so horrible for me. I couldn't stand watching you do that to yourself. I was relieved when I found out that you were in rehab. When Oliver told me that you were in the hospital for a drug overdose, I was scared for you. I'm glad that you're okay. How was rehab? Was it different this time?"

She let out a shaky breath when she responded to him with tears falling down her face, "Rehab was long overdue, Bash. There was a lot of crying and uncomfortable conversations with my psychiatrist. It was good for me to feel things that I didn't let myself deal with before in my life. I had a lot of realizations about the life that I was living that made me reconsider a lot of things about myself. It was a huge wake up call for me."

Sebastian gently ran his fingers through her hair when he asked her with a concerned look on his face, "What kind of realizations did you have?"

She blinked back tears that fell down her face when she confessed to him with a serious look on her face, "I realized a lot of things about myself. Some things that people have been telling me for a long time. Other things no one knew about me or had no way of knowing about me since I never told anyone about it. I looked at myself in the mirror and I hated what I saw in front of me. I wanted to change, so I decided that I wasn't going to be that person anymore. I was fucked up long before my dad died. I shouldn't have been so surprised by this, but I was shocked about it. I remembered things about my childhood that I did that were always going to end up with me in this place. I can't promise you that I'll never want drugs again, but I promise that I will try my best to not do them. If I'm being honest with you, I don't know why I cheated on you. It wasn't about love for another person or spite against you. It was only about getting high."

Sebastian told her with a sad smile on his face, "I figured that it was about drugs. You aren't the type of person to do things out of spite. You're too gentle for that. If it means anything to you, I don't think that you're fucked up. You're not broken or damaged like you think that you are. You are a human being that is allowed to make mistakes. We are all allowed to make mistakes. I loved you from the moment that I met you. I never stopped loving you. I loved you after we broke up. I tried to be with other girls, but none of them were you. I kept comparing them to you. You were in my head the entire time that I was with them. Did you feel that way with Chloe? What? Did you think that I wouldn't find out about that? Sasha wouldn't stop complaining about it."

She responded to him with a wide grin on her face, "I knew that Sasha couldn't stand that I was with Chloe. She's such a liar. She told me that she didn't care. I never loved Chloe. I was with Jade and Chloe for drugs. The part that I liked about it was that they were women. I learned that I'm sexually attracted to women. I am my mother's daughter. Don't get jealous of them, Bash. You have something that they couldn't give me. They never understood me like that. You have a massive ego that I love to pick on."

Sebastian pulled her into a long kiss where they didn't go off each other until she told her with a smile on her face, "I love you, Bash. I never stopped loving you. Since we forgive each other, we can try this again. Do you want to start over?"

Sebastian pulled her into his arms with her face hidden in his chest as he kissed her on the top of her head when he said to her with a smile on his face, "Let's do it. I want to show you how much I forgive you if you would let me. Will you let me, Isabella?" He pulled her into a long kiss that turned into a few rounds around their room before she slept in his arms for the rest of the night. She woke up the next morning where Oliver stood in their hotel room over the bed with Sebastian's suit in his hand and cups of tea on a tray on the table as she lightly groaned that Oliver heard them together last night before he sat down on the bed. Sasha walked in from Amelia's hotel room when she told her that her parents sent her dress over for her. The wedding was a bug blur in her mind. Once the wedding started, she took a seat next to Sebastian and her parents where her parents told her that they were happy for them before she smiled at them for a moment. After they sent off Tommy and Lilly on their honeymoon in Greece, she danced with Sebastian's arms around her until she passed out in his arms for the night.

CHAPTER THIRTY-NINE
(SUMMER 1968 – LOS ANGELES, CALIFORNIA)

She got on a plane to the states with her parents, Uncle Sam, Aunt Valeria, Anastasia's family, Nina's family, Oliver's family, Amelia, and Troy. Sasha went to France with Gabriel, Antonine, Christophe, Ivan, and Jamie. She slept with her head leaning onto Sebastian's shoulder until he gently nudged her awake when their plane landed in New York. Uncle Sam and Aunt Valeria took Oliver's family, Amelia, and Troy to their house. She shared the guest bedroom with Sebastian at her parent's house as he helped her pack up her bags that she lived out of in the last year and a half before she fell asleep in his arms for the rest of the night. She hugged her parents for a long time at the airport before Sebastian dragged her onto the plane with her face hidden into his shoulder for the flight to Los Angeles. When their plane landed in Los Angeles, she followed Sebastian with her bags in his hands before they got into a taxi since her cousins weren't coming back to Los Angeles until the next day. After the taxi driver dropped them off at Sebastian's house, he led her into his bedroom where they made up for lost time in their bed before she fell asleep in his arms for the rest of the day. When she woke up in the middle of the night, she smoked cigarettes on the balcony of his bedroom in his oversized shirt where he ended up joining her before they slept in each other's arms for the rest of the night. She slept most of the day until Sebastian woke her up when he told her that her cousins were back in Los Angeles before he asked her if she wanted to go to her house. She shook her head at him when she told him that she didn't want to go back there again before he asked her if she wanted to move in with him. Even though they just got back together, she accepted his offer since she couldn't live in her house anymore before he arranged for his driver to drive them to her house. After they ate dinner in the kitchen that Sebastian's chef made for them, she went to her old house with him to pack up her stuff. When his driver dropped them off at her house, she followed Sebastian into the house as she led them into her suite that looked untouched from the last time that she was there before she placed her clothes into boxes. As soon as Amelia heard them talking to each other in the suite, she sprinted into the room as she asked them what was going on when she told her that she was moving in with Sebastian and that she could have the house that her parent's gave her before Amelia pulled her into a tight hug to thank her for the house. Troy walked into the room asking her what was going on when she told him the same thing that she told Amelia where he pulled her into a tight hug before Sebastian asked her from the walk-in closet if she could come over to him.

She walked into the closest where Sebastian held up a large bag of cocaine in his hands with a look of horror on his face. She grabbed it from his hands when she asked him where he found it before he told her that there were twenty more large bags of cocaine under the floorboards of the closet. She couldn't believe that was where she hid her drugs after all these years of looking for them. At least she wasn't going crazy when she remembered that she hid drugs in her closet. Amelia and Troy appeared in the closet to see what was going on when Amelia asked her how long that was there with a matching look of horror on her face where she grabbed the box that held her cocaine from Sebastian's hands before she brought it into the bathroom. Sebastian and Amelia followed her into the bathroom as she poured the bags of cocaine into the toilet until they were all empty before she flashed them down the toilet.

Sebastian pulled her into a desperate hug as she hid her face in his chest with his arms wrapped around her waist when he told her that he was proud of her for doing that. After she pecked him on the lips, she went back into the closet as she put away her clothes into boxes. As they packed up her clothes away from the closet, Amelia packed up the bathroom in boxes as Troy packed up the rest of the bedroom for her. They packed up her belongings until the middle of the night where they found more drugs hidden in the suite that she didn't realize that she hid there before she flashed her drugs down the toilet. Sebastian was more shocked than anyone else that she had that many drugs on her for many years that no one knew about including her. Once they packed up her belongings in all the boxes that they brought with them, they carried the boxes to the car that the driver cleared out for them before the car was completely full of her last belongings that were left in her old house. She hugged Amelia and Troy as she thanked them for helping her. She got in the front of the car with Sebastian where she fell asleep on the drive to his house until he gently nudged her awake before they helped the driver carry the boxes into one of the guest bedrooms. Once they placed all of the boxes into the guest bedroom, the sun was already coming up as soon as they took a shower together before she slept in his arms for the morning.

Sebastian woke her up in the afternoon with the phone in his hands. When she answered the phone, her mother asked her if it was true that she was moving in with Sebastian where she told her that she moved in with him last night and that she gave Amelia and Troy the house. Her mother told her that she was happy to hear that she was moving in with Sebastian and that she did a kind thing giving Amelia the house before she asked her if Amelia and Troy could pay the bills on the house. Once she told her mother to ask Amelia and Troy about that, she hung up the phone on her mother since she knew that her mother didn't have to say that to her before she hid her face in Sebastian's chest for the rest of the afternoon. When she woke up again in the evening, she was alone in the bed before she walked into the guest bedroom where Sebastian put her clothes into the closet. She joined him in putting her clothes up on hangers where they stopped to eat takeout that his driver picked up for dinner. After they were up all night unpacking her boxes, they moved to the suite where she fell asleep with his arms around her for the rest of the morning. Sebastian went to his first day of filming his new movie since they got back to Los Angeles. Once she slept in their bed until the late afternoon, she transferred her clothes into the suite. She didn't want to go into a different room to get changed. She was half-way through this project when Sebastian got back from the studio where he helped her move the rest of her clothes into his closet before they ate dinner in the kitchen that his chef prepared for them. She almost fell asleep at the kitchen table until Sebastian led her into the suite where she passed out in his arms for the rest of the night.

He went to work at the studio, and she went on auditions for movies that her agent sent the scripts for. She didn't work since she was in the movie where she fell in love with Sebastian, so she decided that she was going to ease into it. While she was looking for a new movie, she did small roles in television shows as well as commercials too. Since they had a busy schedule, they only saw each other when they woke up and when they were going to bed, but they made the most of their time together since they wanted their relationship to work. When neither of them was working, they had her cousins over at the house for dinner and a movie night in the living room before her cousins spent the night in the guest bedrooms. Even though she wasn't attending therapy anymore, she was going to NA meetings since they helped keep her accountable for herself. She was doing well when it came to her cravings for drugs. She rarely thought about drugs since she got rid of the drugs that she hid in Amelia's house. On that night when she found her secret drugs, her first instinct was disappointment that she spent all these years searching for them only for them to be right in front of her face. She was relieved that they were gone from her life. She wished that this version of her didn't exist. Even though she knew how horrible that life was for her, there was this voice inside of her mind that would always want that life. When she shared those thoughts in one of the NA meetings, one of the people at the meeting asked her if she only missed that version of her because she couldn't have it. There was a lot of truth in that statement. She missed the life that she had when she was high. She didn't need to eat or worry about anything except when she was going to get high again. Her life was simpler when she was using drugs compared to when she was sober. When she was in the thralls of drug addiction, she didn't have to worry about anything. Her life was about when was the next time that she was going to get high. Her sober life was so much more exhausting than that. When she was sober, she worried about stopping herself from the need to get high. She cared about her own wellbeing, her relationships, and dealing with the emotions that she didn't want to feel when she wasn't sober. She realized that other people didn't struggle this much to get through the day when she moved in with Sebastian. He never had to think about anything that he did. He went through his day without prevailing thoughts preventing him from being able to move on with his life. She couldn't be up for more than five minutes before she felt like she was too paralyzed with fear to do anything. He got home from work like he breezed through the end of the marathon without breaking into a sweat. She felt like she was struggling to finish the race before she collapsed from exhaustion. He went to bed at night with nothing in his mind and she couldn't fall asleep since there were too many thoughts racing in her mind. She brought this up to him one night in bed with his arms around her when she asked him how he made everything look easy when he asked her what she meant by that. She told him that she felt like she wasn't made for this life. She didn't know how to be a person without her vices. She couldn't get through the day without her vices. She was drowning without them. Sebastian realized that she wasn't talking about drugs. He told her that it wasn't easy for him to get through the day. He had his demons that followed him everywhere he went. When she asked him what that was for him, he revealed to her that he didn't have vices that haunted him, but insecurities about his body that plagued him. Even though she wanted to ask him more, she knew that he wasn't going to talk about it anymore. He was closing the walls around himself before they slept with each other's arms for the night.

Sebastian left for work when she woke up that next morning before she left to go to her commercial shoot for the rest of the day. When she got home from a long filming day, Sebastian sat on the couch waiting for her as she took a seat next to him with his arms wrapped around her when he confessed to her that he used to have an eating disorder that started in his teenage years that ended a few years before they met each other. Even though she was shocked by this, she tried to not scare him as she brought him into a long hug that she didn't let go of until he grabbed onto her hand before he took them to their bedroom. Once they were in their bedroom, she laid her head on his chest as he drew invisible circles on her arms when he told her about his eating disorder that he lived with for over a decade in complete honesty with her. She blinked tears that fell down her face when she asked him why he didn't tell her about it until now. Sebastian told her that he didn't tell anyone about it except for his family who knew about it when it was too late for him. She told him that there are secrets that they kept from others and secrets that the world kept from them. The deadliest secrets are the ones that they kept from themselves. She asked him what kind of secret it was. He told her that it was a secret that the world kept from him.

They would talk about it later before they fell asleep in each other's arms. They didn't talk about it again since Sebastian went to Canada to film a new movie. They were doing a long-distance relationship again. She stayed at Oliver's house with his family while Sebastian was out of the country. Posey was thrilled that she was staying with them since she missed her so much in the time that she disappeared off of the face of the earth. Since she was living at Oliver's house for two months, she became a built-in babysitter for Posey during the day while Juliet took care of Eleanor who demanded her attention all of the time. She was thrilled to be Posey's babysitter since she missed Posey so much when she wasn't in California. After Oliver came home from work in the evening, they ate dinner in the kitchen where she cleaned up the dishes from them before Juliet and Oliver put Posey and Eleanor to bed in their bedrooms. When the children were asleep in their bedrooms, they watched a movie in the living room where Juliet fed Eleanor in their bedroom before she talked to Oliver in the living room until they passed out on the couch. This night was no exception except Juliet went to bed before the movie was done since Eleanor wasn't sleeping in her crib. Once the movie stopped playing on the television, she grabbed a bottle of wine that they opened at dinner from the kitchen as she poured each of them a glass before she placed the empty bottle onto the coffee table. As she took a big sip of her glass of wine, she laid down on top of Oliver's legs with a blanket around her arms before Oliver looked up at her when he asked her with a smile on his face, "How's Bash doing? Is it snowing in the part of Canada that he is in?"

She looked up at him when she responded to him with a wide grin on her face, "He told me that it snowed there the other day. He misses California so much. Other than that, he's doing good. He's almost done filming his movie, so he'll be home again in a few weeks. They cut out his favorite scene from the movie. He was very upset about that last week. I think that he misses you more than me."

Oliver rolled his eyes at her as he lightly kicked her legs when he responded to her in fake annoyance with her, "You're being ridiculous, Isabella. You're his girlfriend. I'm his best friend. He can't miss me more than you. It's impossible for him to do that."

She harshly smacked Oliver on his arms as he softly groaned when she told him with a mischievous grin on her face, "Is Bash your best friend? I thought that I was your best friend. I'm heartbroken. I met you before Bash did. I've known you since the day that I was born."

Once Oliver drank the rest of his glass of wine, he responded to her with a smirk on his face, "You know what I mean. Bash isn't my cousin. You are my cousin and my best friend. That's different, Isabella. You know that."

She sat up on the couch as she drank the rest of her glass of wine before she laid down on the couch with her head leaning on Oliver's shoulder when she asked him with a serious look on her face, "How come we never talked about the letter? Do you hold that against me?"

Oliver wrapped his arms around her when he responded to her with concern laced in his voice, "I never held that against you, Isabella. I don't know why we haven't talked about it. I was waiting until you were ready to talk about it. Do you want to talk about it? We can talk about it if you want to. I've had a lot of questions that I wanted to ask you." She let out a shaky breath when she said to him with a frown on her face, "I do want to talk about it, Oliver. I want to know what you thought about the letter."

Oliver walked away from the couch where he grabbed a piece of paper out of the coffee table before he sat down on the couch next to her. Oliver held the letter in his hand as he wrapped his arms around her when he confessed to her with a serious look on his face, "It was sweet, Isabella. Besides the parts that sounded like a suicide note. Don't be upset, but I showed it to Bash when you sent it to me. I believed that it was a suicide note even though you swore that it wasn't one. Bash assured me that it wasn't a suicide note. I would've called you freaking out if he didn't say that to me."

She grabbed the letter from his hands as she opened it up to read it when she responded to him with a frown on her face, "That sounds like a suicide note. I'm sorry for scaring you, Oliver. That wasn't my intention. It is well written. I can write like my mother. I don't remember writing this. I was dissociated when I wrote this. That's why it sounds like a suicide note. I meant every word. Especially the part about telling me the things that you wouldn't tell me when I was high."

Oliver grabbed the letter from her hands as he pushed it into a drawer under the coffee table when he confessed to her in a distant voice, "It's fine. I'll tell you what I was thinking when I found out that you relapsed in England. When your mother told me that you relapsed after you got out of the psychiatric hospital, I wasn't surprised. I saw it coming from the moment that you ran away to Madagascar. I thought that you relapsed in Madagascar, but my step dad reassured me that you were sober. We don't need to get into how shitty it was for you to disappear like that. You already know how it was for us. When I visited you in England, I thought that you were avoiding me because you relapsed, and you didn't want me finding out. I had Bash look through your bags when you were sleeping because I thought that you were using again, but we didn't find any drugs in your bags. We thought that going to the psychiatric hospital would prevent you from relapsing, but it apparently was the cause of your relapse. We don't need to get into that either. Did you know that Sean told us about your relapse in London? He found cocaine in your bags a week after you got out of the hospital. Your parents flashed it down the toilet, but you kept getting more from Jade. What was your deal with Jade? Was it just about drugs or did something else happen that I was not aware of?"

She blinked back tears that fell down her face when she confessed to him in a soft voice, "It was only about drugs with Jade. It was the same way with Chloe. It was that way with Daxton towards the end of our relationship. I liked how I felt with a woman, but I've never been in love with one. I didn't notice that Sean took drugs out of my bags. I must have been really out of it if I didn't know that he was taking drugs away from me. It feels like a fever dream, Oliver. I couldn't tell you what happened or what was going on in my head. I know that I said and did insane things, but I can't remember what they were for the life of me. Maybe it's better that I don't know what happened during that year. I remember bits and pieces of our argument in York, and my argument with Bash. I don't remember what I said to Amelia and Sasha, but they were hurt."

Oliver grabbed onto her hands when he responded to her with concern laced in his voice, "You told Amelia to climb back into whatever hole she came from, and you told Sasha that she didn't have a real relationship with Chloe. I'm glad that you remember what you said to me. That's nice. It doesn't matter. It's in the past. We forgive you and you forgive yourself. We can move from it except you won't because you never move on from anything. That's what I wanted to tell you in our argument. You are incapable of moving on from anything. I wanted to tell you to stop being a selfish asshole, but you covered that much in the letter that you swore to me wasn't a suicide note. I've never been more upset with you than after our argument in York. I swore that I hated you after that. Of course, I never did, but it felt like that for a while."

She confessed to him in a distant voice, "I hated myself too, Oliver. Don't worry about it. The feeling was mutual. You hurt me when you said that loving me was a burden. I felt like you meant it. You probably did mean it at the time. I think about that moment a lot when I can't sleep at night. Loving me is a burden. You weren't wrong though. Everything that you told me was true. You're incapable of lying to me. I can never lie to you except when I can lie to you. It sounds like you were more bitter about my not-suicide note than anything that I told you in our argument. Tell me why that is."

Oliver let out a defeated sigh as he grabbed onto her hands when he responded to her with a frown on his face, "I was bitter about the letter because I didn't want to forgive you. I didn't want to admit that you were capable of my forgiveness. I tried to be angry at you, but I couldn't be mad at you anymore. It reminded me of what my dad did with my mum when they got into an argument where he wrote her a letter to apologize to her instead of telling her it to her face. It triggered something inside of me. The part of my brain like my dad. I was upset about it since your dad only wrote letters to my stepdad until right before he tried to kill himself. I guess that I'm provoked by letters. Who would've fucking guessed it? The psychiatrist who gets traumatized by letters. The letter was nice, but don't write me a letter again. If you want to tell me something, then tell me it to my face."

As Oliver held out his pinky to her, she attached her pinky to his pinky before she let go of his pinky when she responded to him with a smirk on her face, "I promise you that I'll never send you a letter again. If I do send you a letter, then I will already be dead. Can you elaborate on what you said about your trauma with letters? I can't believe that this was something that I didn't know about you."

Oliver harshly smacked her arm as she lightly groaned in pain when he responded to her with a serious look on his face, "I'll kill you if you try to kill yourself again. I mean it, Isabella. I can't take another suicide attempt from you. The last one nearly killed me. How many times do you think is too much to try to kill yourself? One or two? You're on suicide attempt number four and that's not including the time that you tried to kill yourself when you were thirteen that no one else knows about. There are things that you don't know about me. You don't know everything about me, and I don't know everything about you. If you tell you about the letter stuff, then you have to promise me that you aren't going to kill yourself again."

She nodded her head at him as Oliver wrapped his arm around her when he confessed to her in a serious voice, "Okay, you better not try to pull a fast one on me or else I'm going to tell Bash that you used to pick fights with me when we were children. I'm that serious. This stays between us. No one finds out about this, Isabella. Not even Bash. I don't know if you knew this about him, but my dad was an alcoholic. He got into these screaming matches with my mum until she cried so hard that he felt guilty about it. It happened before they were married, but it got worse after they got married to each other. The yelling turned into hitting which later turned into choking. To apologize to my mum, my dad wrote these elaborate letters to her about how he was a horrible person and that he would never do that to her again. It didn't stop him from doing it again the next night like he never said it to her. Things got so bad that she stopped reading his letters because he didn't do anything that he said that he was going to do. She burned the letters that he wrote to her in the backyard as she screamed at him before he disappeared for the rest of the night. My dad wrote these letters to

Will. I think that he did it to keep him in his place, but my step dad never figured it out. On the night that my dad and my step dad were drafted for the war, Will got into a screaming match with my dad that my step dad had to separate them before they hurt each other. It was about a threatening letter that my dad sent Will. My stepdad didn't know about it. He told my dad to stop sending Will letters or else he was telling Ella about him molesting her."

As she leaned her head on Oliver's shoulder, she responded to him in shock, "That was why he tried to kill himself. Not because he was going to be in the army. Because of Uncle Nathan's threat to him. Did your dad cause my dad to relapse?"

Oliver nodded his head at her when he responded to her with a frown on his face, "Yes, he did. My step dad figured that out too when he got the letter from Will that you read. He wasn't speaking to my dad when he died. They got into many arguments about Will. My step dad's last conversation with my dad was them fighting with each other. It's not my story to tell. It's our dad's stories. They are dead, so there no one left to tell them. My mum refuses to read letters because of what happened with my dad. Uncle Nathan had to read them when your mother sent them to her. Don't send me letters. Especially suicide letters. If you are going to do a fifth suicide attempt, then give me a call." He pulled her into a tight hug as she hid her face into his chest with his arms tightly wrapped around her. She went into the guest room with her closing the door behind her. She crawled under the blankets of her bed with Sebastian's shirt on where she cried herself to sleep before she passed out for the rest of the night.

Chapter Forty
(Fall 1968 – Shasta Lake, California)

She couldn't stop thinking about what Oliver told her about the letters that Uncle Kenny sent her father. When she read the letter that her father sent to Uncle Nathan, her father begged his brother to tell Kenny to stop sending him them. Even though Uncle Kenny was always going to be Oliver's father, Uncle Kenny was the person that molested her mother when she was a child. Uncle Kenny blackmailed her father with that same information. Her father was so afraid to tell her mother about it. Even though Uncle Kenny was dead for over a decade, her father was too terrified to tell her mother what he knew about her. He was scared that Uncle Kenny was going to come from hell to get revenge on him. The more that she learned about Uncle Kenny the more that she realized that her father was right about him. Her mother was so blinded by her love of him that she refused to believe what he was warning her about her brother. She thought about how her father must have felt being in the middle of this situation with Uncle Kenny and her grandmother. Her father was the victim in this situation. He was the victim that turned out to be the abuser. The cycle went on no matter what anyone did to stop it. She realized why Uncle Nathan felt torn about everything that happened with her father. He had a front row seat to watch her father get destroyed by people around him only to destroy himself in the end. This was beginning to change the way that she saw herself. If she was a byproduct of the cycle, then was she always doomed to repeat the mistakes of her parents? Was she already repeating her parent's mistakes without realizing it?

In high school, she dated Trent who was in her homeroom where the farthest that they got with each other was making out since she was worried that he would get her pregnant if they did anything else. Since her mother had her as a teenager, she was determined to not be a teen parent like her, so her relationship with Trent ended after she told him that she didn't want to have sex with him. There were a few people other than Trent, but she was only with those people for drugs. None of it was real. When she moved to California, she met a few guys at clubs that she had one-night stands with, but it wasn't anything serious. Her first serious relationship was with Daxton and that ended up with one of them dying from a drug overdose. She had one-night stands in between meeting Sebastian, but it was nothing serious. Her strange drug relationships with Chloe and Jade didn't mean anything either. Her relationship with Sebastian was her most serious relationship. He was the first person that treated her like she deserved to be treated. He respected her. He believed in her. She was an idiot to lose him, but they found their way back to each other again. He was the first person that she lived with that wasn't from a drug situation. Sebastian was nothing like her bad parts. He was a good person that wanted to do the right thing. He loved people no matter what they did to him. He was the best that she was ever going to do. Even though she was an addict who could be very selfish, they made sense together. He brought her back to earth again and she reminded him to stand up for himself. She learned what kind of partner she wanted to spend the rest of her life with. Her mother ended up with someone who was a caring person like her mum. Aunt Priscilla married Uncle Nathan who was the opposite of Uncle Kenny. Uncle Stan ended up with Thomas after being with her father. Her father would've ended up in a good relationship after he got out of prison, but no one would know if that would've happened to him. Uncle Kenny would've ended up in horrible relationships since he would never learn from his mistakes.

When Sebastian came back from filming his movie in Canada, she was in the middle of a deep spiral. She didn't have the energy to hide it from him. As soon as he saw her for the first time in months, he told her that she needed to go to therapy again. She agreed with him since she knew what happened to her the last time that she was depressed. After Oliver urged her to go to therapy again, she couldn't hold it back anymore before she called Dr. Taylor for the first time in two years. Even though Dr. Taylor was surprised to hear from her, he told her that she was always welcome to see him. She trusted him more than any other psychiatrist. She agreed to see him in a session that week. In her first session with Dr. Taylor, she caught him up on everything that happened in the last two years. She didn't leave out any details since he couldn't help her if he didn't know about it. He wanted to start at a new baseline for her where she was accountable to him for everything. Dr. Taylor meant everything that she was going to do. Since her parents made her a sentimental person, she didn't want to break this promise to him without inflicting pain on herself. She analyzed everything that she did in her day from the moment that she opened her eyes in the morning until the moment that she closed her eyes at night. She wrote down everything that happened into a journal where they talked about what she wrote down in it in their sessions in his office. They examined why she thought like she did. Drugs and killing herself became the same thought. They determined where those thoughts came from. She told him about her fears and the happiest experiences of her life. She told him about everything that happened in her father's horrible situation with Uncle Kenny and her grandmother. She didn't leave out a detail from what she knew from her perspective of the story, and she thought about the impact that it had on her life. Dr. Taylor asked her if she thought that her grandmother knew about what Uncle Kenny did to her mother. She was too stunned to answer his question because she didn't think about that until he brought it up to her before she told him that she wouldn't be surprised if she knew about it. She didn't think too much about it after that. It hurt her too much to think about it. Since she couldn't sleep that night, she sat on the balcony as she smoked cigarettes where she thought about her session with Dr. Taylor before Sebastian came out on the balcony to check on her. Once she reassured him that she was reflecting about what she was talking about in therapy, he pecked her on the lips before he left her alone on the balcony for the rest of the night. She was relieving the moment in her father's life when he realized everything for the first time. She was relieving that memory with him like they were together at that moment. Once she scared herself even more about this situation that she was in, she went back into their bedroom where she crawled into the bed before Sebastian wrapped his arms around her in his sleep for the rest of the night.

Sebastian got ready to leave for the studio the next morning as she pulled him into a long kiss before he broke away from her when he told her that he was going to be late for work. After Sebastian left alone in the house, she wasn't going to sulk around the house all day like she had been doing in the last few months before she called her agent to ask him if there were any new movie offers for her. Her agent told her that he received a call from the studio about a new movie that she would be great in. She asked her agent to send the script over to her house where she did a victory dance in her bedroom before she spent the rest of the day memorizing the script that her agent sent her outside by the pool. When she got up the next morning, she left the house to the studio when she auditioned for the part that she wanted where she was told that she got the part if she wanted it later that day before she accepted it without any hesitation. She called Sebastian from the studio when she told him that she got the lead in a new movie called *Lake Holiday*. Sebastian told her that they were going out to eat to celebrate at their favorite restaurant. Once Sebastian got home from work that afternoon, they left to go to eat dinner with Oliver and Juliet. Amelia babysat the children for them. She made the first move with Sebastian that led to them celebrating all over their bedroom. Sebastian was already gone at work when she woke up the next morning as she packed her bags for Northern California where they were filming the movie for the next six weeks. She took a taxi to the airport to get on her flight. It was only a thirty-minute flight to Shasta Lake where the cast and crew met together. She was driven away from the airport before she was taken to her clothing fittings that were in a trailer off of the lake. After she was finished with her clothing fittings that evening, she ate dinner with the cast and crew of the movie where she went to the cabin that she was staying in with two girls that were in the movie before she passed out in her bed for the rest of the night. They started filming the movie the next morning where she practiced her lines in between different takes where she found her photographic memory to be a gift in this situation. They continued on this schedule for weeks at a time as they got farther and farther into filming their movie before they gave everyone a weekend off from filming since they were almost done filming the movie by the end of the four weeks. When she heard that she was getting a weekend off from filming, she called Sebastian to meet up with him. They booked a hotel room in the city before they explored the city since it was the first time that they had been to that part of California before in their lives. Her weekend with Sebastian was perfect. They swam together in the freezing cold lake. They went out to eat at the best restaurants in the city. They caught up for lost time together in their hotel room. After Sebastian fell asleep with his arms around her, she squeezed out of his grip as she snuck off to the balcony before she smoked cigarettes for the rest of the night. As she lit a cigarette that she inhaled from it, she let out a shaky breath as she looked up at the stars when she said aloud to herself in a distant voice, "Hi dad. I know that it's been a while since we talked to each other. I haven't talked to you until right before I had my European bender. Out of all my benders, it had to be my favorite one since I got to lose my mind all across from Europe. I had a sex with women. You and mom would be so proud of me for that. I did what you guys did. I don't know what mom thinks of it. I haven't asked her about it."

She inhaled smoke from her cigarette as she hid her shaking hands into her lap when she responded to herself with tears falling down her face, "I'm sorry for what I told you at your grave. I didn't mean it. I don't think that you aren't anywhere. I was angry with myself that I wanted you. I know that's not an excuse, but it's the only explanation that I have. I didn't want you, but I couldn't help it. I felt like a little girl that wanted her dad. I feel that way a lot of the time when I'm scared or when I'm too lonely at night. It's natural for a little girl to want her dad. That's why I've always been so fucked up. This is all I'll ever be. I'll always be the little girl that wants her dad. No matter how old I am, that's never going away from me. Did you hear about what happened with Oliver when I sent him that letter? Of course you knew that. You know everything that happens to me. I didn't know about the letter trauma that you guys have. It makes me so sad for you. Sad that you never got the chance to redeem yourself after everything that happened with Uncle Kenny. You two certainly took your secrets to the grave with you, didn't you? I think about how much more secrets you hid from the world. Like a protective blanket that was supposed to protect you. It didn't protect you from anything, dad. It only harmed you. You didn't see that until it was too late to change."

She responded to herself with a sad smile on her face, "I'm sorry that you went through that. It must've been hard for you to know that information and to be powerless to change it. It wasn't fair that the weight was put on your shoulders at a young age. I'm closer to understanding you than I was before. Why you were the person that you became. I know the loneliness that you experienced in your life. I've felt it too, dad. It makes you feel like you're drowning in the middle of the sea. You don't know how to get out of it. You never remembered how you got there. Mom described the feeling as drowning in front of the world and no one notices it no matter what you do to get their attention. She knows that feeling too. I miss the feeling of drowning. Even though I'm not drowning anymore, I wish that I was drowning. At least I would know what to do with myself if I was. I don't know what to do when I'm not drowning. I feel like I should throw myself in the water. I wonder what your last words were to the world. Who did you talk to last? What did you tell them? I've often wondered what my last words are going to be. Who will I talk to last? What will I tell them? I want them to mean something to the world. I want my last words to comfort the people that I leave behind me. I love your last words to mom. They have taken on a new life that you would never imagine in your wildest dreams. They transformed you into who you became remembered as for the rest of time. I don't think that you knew that when you wrote them, but it should comfort you that it's created its own legacy outside of you. You were wrong about a lot of things, but you were right about something. Nothing is real. It doesn't mean anything. Except that you meant something to the stars."

Sebastian walked onto the balcony as he wrapped his arms around her with her face hidden in his chest when he asked her with concern laced in his voice, "Are you okay honey?"

She hid her face farther into his chest as he tightened his grip on his arms when he said to her in a soft voice, "Let's go to bed. We'll talk about this in the morning. Alright?" Sebastian guided her into their hotel room where he helped her lay down on the bed as he climbed in next to her with his arms around her before she slept his arms for the rest of the night.

Chapter Forty-One

(Winter 1969 – New York, New York)

Once they finished filming the movie *Lake Holiday*, she went home to Los Angeles for the first time in two months. She only had a few days at home before she left for her press tour across the country. As soon as her plane landed in Los Angeles, she ran into Sebastian's arms as he pulled her into his chest where Oliver threw himself into their hug before Oliver dropped them off at their house. After they made up for lost time in their bedroom, she laid down on the bed with her head on his chest as he ran his fingers through her hair while they caught up about what happened in their time away from each other. She told him about the journaling that Dr. Taylor told her to do when she wasn't in Los Angeles. Sebastian told her about the projects that he was working on in the city and the adventures that he got into with Oliver. They didn't talk about what happened that night in Shasta Lake. On the night before she left for New Mexico, she spent the night at Amelia's house with Amelia, Troy, Sasha, and Gabriel since they visited them in the states. Since she was going to the airport in the morning, she brought her bags with her and her journal that she took everywhere with her. After Amelia dropped her off at the airport the next morning, she slept for the flight to Santa Fe with her leaning her head on the window until she was woken up by a flight attendant before she got into her car that the studio sent for her. For the six-week press tour for *Lake Holiday*, her hairstylist and make-up artist woke her up every morning from the connecting room next to her where she prepared for her events before she attended the press events that her agent scheduled for her. She repeated this schedule every day no matter what city that they were in until they ended the press tour in New York. At the beginning of the press tour, she made plans with Sebastian to meet up with him in New York at her parents' house, so that they could celebrate Boxing Day a few months later with her family. On the last night of her press tour, she ate dinner with the cast and crew of the movie at the best restaurant in New York before they said their final goodbyes to each other. After she said goodbye to the cast and crew of *Lake Holiday*, she took a taxi to her parent's house outside of the city where they pulled her into a long hug until her mum insisted on making them tea in the living room before she went to bed in the guest bedroom. She climbed on the roof as she smoked cigarettes for the rest of the morning until her mother looked through the office window when she asked her if she wanted to eat breakfast at Uncle Sam's house. She followed her mother into the house where she changed into a warm outfit before her mum drove them to her uncle's house. After they ate breakfast at Uncle Sam's house, she went over to Anastasia's and Nina's apartments where she met her three-month-old nephew Liam for the first time. She spent time with her nieces and her nephews before she spent the night in the guest bedroom after they ate dinner together.

When she went back to her parent's house the next morning, her mother asked her if she wanted to help prepare the food for their Boxing Day celebration before she helped her mother in the kitchen for the rest of the morning. In between her stirring bowls of raw ingredients and rolling out dough for bread, her mother asked her if she wanted to pick up her cousins from the airport before they went back into their cooking. She took her parent's car to the airport with Uncle Sam since her parents and Aunt Valeria were busy cooking dinner. Once they got to the airport, she waited at the Los Angeles gate as Uncle Sam waited at the Paris gate for Jamie, Ivan, and their boyfriends. As soon as she saw Sebastian from the other side of the room, she sprinted towards him as he pulled her into his arms with her face hidden in his chest where they didn't let go of each other until her seven-year-old niece Posey ran into her legs. After she let go of her tight grip on Sebastian, she pulled Posey into a tight hug as Juliet pulled her into a quick hug with her handing her one-year-old niece Eleanor to her when she placed her on her hip before she pulled Oliver into a desperate hug as Posey ran over to her mother. Once she let go of her tight grip on Oliver, she pulled Amelia and Sasha into tight hugs with her kissing Gabriel and Troy on their cheeks where she grabbed onto Sebastian's hand with Eleanor on her hip before she met up with Uncle Sam on the other side of the airport. After she greeted Ivan and Jamie with kisses on their cheeks, she followed Uncle Sam to the car where they got inside of it before he drove them to her parent's house. When they were at her parent's house, she helped her cousins bring their suitcases into the office until they went to their hotel that night where she caught up with her cousins in the living room before they ate in the dining room in soft conversation with each other. After they ate dinner together in the kitchen, they filled every available seat in the living room where they took turns opening up their Boxing Day gifts to each other while the adults drank glasses of wine as the children drank cups of hot chocolate with marshmallows. Anastasia's children, Nina's children, and Oliver's children opened gifts on the floor from their parents, their grandparents, their aunts, and their uncles watching them. Once the children were distracted by their toys, the adults took turns opening gifts that they got each other.

She opened up a beautiful dress that Sasha got for her and records that Amelia got her. Oliver got her a new phone to install in her house since Sebastian didn't have a phone in his kitchen, so that it would ensure that she would never send him a letter. She couldn't stop laughing about it until Posey told her to stop being so loud where she played on the floor. Her parents got her clothes and a necklace with her name engraved on the back of it. She cried when she opened it since it was special to her. Sebastian gave her clothes that she insisted on stealing from him and a necklace that had their names on the inside of it. When she thought that Sebastian was done giving her gifts, she put her gifts away into a box as she turned to face him again before Sebastian stood on one knee with a closed box in his hands. She instantly shook her head as tears fell down her face when she asked him in complete shock, "What? This isn't happening right now! Bash? Is this what I think it is?"

Sebastian grabbed onto her hands as he opened the box when he confessed to her with tears falling down his face, "I love you so much, Isabella. I've never loved anyone the way that I love you. I can't imagine my life without you. I want to spend the rest of my life with you. I want to grow old together as we watch our children grow up. I want to spend every day of my life with you. I want to die in your arms. Isabella? Will you do me the honor of my life by marrying me?"

She nodded her head at him as Sebastian pulled her into his arms with her hiding her face in his chest. At that moment, they were the only people in the world. After she pulled him into a long kiss, she quickly wiped away the tears that were on her face as she pulled out her hand that couldn't stop shaking where Sebastian placed the ring on her left hand before her parents pulled her into a tight hug with their arms tightly around her. Oliver pulled her into a long hug as she hid her face into his chest until she harshly punched him on the arm when she told him with a wide smile on her face, "Did you know about this? I knew that you guys were up to something. Oliver? Did you know about it?"

Oliver placed Eleanor on his hip when he told her with a smirk on his face, "Yeah, I knew about it. I helped Bash pick out the ring and everything. Juliet helped with the size with her hand. Were you surprised? We tried not to give anything away about it when you were in Los Angeles."

She pulled Amelia and Sasha into a tight hug when she responded to them with a smirk on her face, "I had no idea that this was coming. I'm getting married. Did you guys know about it too or was Oliver the only person that was privileged to receive this information?"

After Sasha and Amelia shared a glance, Sasha tightened her grip on her arms when she responded to her with a smile on her face, "Bash told us about him proposing to you a few months ago. I thought that Gabriel and I being in Los Angeles would give it away, but you've been so busy working on your movie that you didn't notice that anything was off."

Once she pulled away from Sasha and Amelia, Aunt Valeria and Uncle Sam pulled her into a tight hug with her other cousins doing the same thing before she left to go to the hotel that Sebastian booked for them. As soon as Sebastian closed the door behind them, she pulled him into a long kiss as he wrapped his arms around her waist before they pulled away from each other to catch their breaths. Sebastian pulled her into a desperate kiss that led to him pulling them towards the bed as he laid down on top of her before she pulled off his shirt where he unzipped her dress from the back. She didn't pull away from him until she told him that she loved him before he told her that he loved her too with him pulling her into another kiss. After they made up for lost time together, she laid down on the bed with her head laying on his chest as he ran his fingers up and down her arms when she said to him in a distant voice, "This is the moment that I want to live in for the rest of eternity. I want to spend an eternity with your arms around me. This is where my destiny lives. You're my destiny, Bash."

Sebastian kissed on the top of her head as he tightened his grip on her arms when he responded to her with a smile on his face, "You're so poetic, Isabella. You are your mother's daughter. I knew that you were going to say yes to my proposal, but it didn't stop me from worrying about you rejecting me. Oliver told me that I was an idiot to think that you wouldn't want to marry me. He is always right, isn't he? We already live together, so it's not going to change much for us except that you will be my wife. You are going to be my wife."

As she hid her face into his chest, she softly chuckled when she responded to him with her voice muffled from her mouth being pressed into the sheet, "Oliver is always right. It's the first commandment in the bible. You are going to be my husband. We need to talk about the wedding, don't we?"

Sebastian ran his fingers through her hair when he responded to her with a frown on his face, "We can talk about the wedding tomorrow. I want to live in this moment with you until we have to face reality again. We could elope to make it easy since we know that we want to be together."

After she took her face out of his chest, she looked up at him when she responded to him with a wide grin on her face, "I know that this is going to sound cliche, but I've always wanted to have a big wedding. We're only getting married once, so let's go out with the production. We can get an orchestra to serenade us down the aisle. The little nieces will be flower girls, and the little nephews will be ring bearers. Oliver will be your best man, and Sasha will be my maid of honor. It will be a wedding that no one will forget about in their lives."

Sebastian responded to her with a smile on his face, "Are you sure that you haven't thought about it? Sounds like you've thought about this. We'll make it whatever you want honey. It's our day, so let's make it one to remember. I want to talk about something else."

As she laid down on top of his chest, she pulled him into a long kiss that they didn't let go until they caught their breaths when she asked him in a soft voice, "What would you want to talk about that isn't the best day of our lives? What's left to say?"

Sebastian wrapped his arms around her when he responded to her with a wide grin on his face, "I want to talk about children. We've never talked about it. I thought that we should talk about it before we get married. It seems like an important conversation. Do you want to have children? I know what my answer is, but I want to hear your answer."

She cupped his face with her hands when she responded to him in a soft voice, "I've always wanted to have children, Bash. I want to have two children, so that they aren't lonely like I was growing up. It's hard being an only child. You don't have anyone to complain about your parents to. What do you think about children?"

Sebastian grabbed onto her hands when he responded to her with a smile on his face, "I always wanted to have children. I want to have four children, but we can compromise with three children. It is lonely to grow up without siblings, so we need to have two children to make sure that they aren't lonely like we were growing up. When do you want to have kids? You'll be the person that gets pregnant, so it's up to you when we start having children."

She shrugged her shoulders at him when she responded to him with a neutral expression on her face, "We'll see what happens. If we end up having children early into our marriage, then that's fine with me. If we don't have children until a few years into our marriage, then that's fine too. I should get pregnant before the wedding. I'd have to get off birth control for that to happen, but it's an option."

As soon as Sebastian flipped her down onto the bed, she loudly squealed as he placed his hand over her mouth when he responded to her in an amused voice, "Let's wait until after the wedding for you to get off of birth control. We don't want people pruning their noses at us because we chose to have a baby out of wedlock. Could you imagine the horror? Someone having a sex without being married? My parent's faith would crumble if that happened. It's a noble idea, Isabella. It's too bold. Even for us."

She affectionately moved his hair out his face when she responded to him with a mischievous look on her face, "I'll wait until we are married to stop taking birth control. It would be funny to shock your parents like that, but I'm not in the mood to be pregnant for my wedding. It would be impossible for me to find a wedding dress that would fit me if I was pregnant. You never know what will happen when I stop taking birth control. I could get pregnant after I stop it, or it could take me ten years to get pregnant. We should practice what we would do to try for a baby to see if we're ready for it. What do you think?"

Once Sebastian pulled her into another long kiss that ended when they were out of breath, he looked up at him when he responded to her with a smirk on his face, "We don't need the practice, but I'm always up for a challenge. Do you think that we could practice for a baby in the shower? You smell like you were in the kitchen. You are practicing being a wife. Spending your days in the kitchen."

She sat up on top of his legs when she responded to him in a stern voice, "I wanted to have children with you until you said that. Get in the shower before I change my mind about marrying you. You better apologize to me. I would never be that kind of wife for you that would slave in the kitchen for you." After Sebastian apologized to her about his off-color remark, she pulled him into the shower where they made up for lost time there until they finished what they started in the bed. She fell asleep with his arms around her for the rest of the night.

Chapter Forty-Two

(Spring 1969 – Los Angeles, California)

After she spent a few more days in New York, she got on a plane to Los Angeles with Sebastian, Amelia, Troy, and Oliver's family. She promised her parents that she would see them when they went wedding dress shopping with her cousins. As soon as they were in Los Angeles again, Sebastian went back to filming a movie in the studio and she went back to filming commercials that her agent set up for her. She went to Dr. Taylor's office for their weekly sessions. In their first session together in six months, she caught him up on everything that happened in their time apart from each other before she shared what she wrote in her journal about what she was processing by herself. She told him that she was worried that she was going to ruin her relationship with Sebastian. Dr. Taylor asked her what she would do to ruin it when she told him that she was worried that she was going to push Sebastian away from her. She didn't want Sebastian to replace the spot that drugs took in her life. She realized that relationships were one of her vices. She became paranoid about her relationship with Sebastian. It was a pattern of behavior that she became addicted to. She had that conversation with Sebastian since they got back together about her being addicted to relationships like she was addicted to drugs. Sebastian wasn't surprised since he knew her better than she knew herself. This fear was ingrained inside of her mind. He asked her if she didn't know how to be alone or if she didn't trust herself when she wasn't with him. Since she didn't have an answer to his question, she left the question unanswered until their session the next week when she told Dr. Taylor that she didn't know how to be alone. When she wasn't in a relationship, she was using drugs or longing for drugs. There was truth in the statement that she didn't trust herself when she wasn't with him. It was more interesting that she didn't trust herself. Sebastian wasn't the exception. She knew that she didn't know what was going to happen to her. What scared her about being alone was that she didn't trust herself to do the right thing. She had enough past experiences to know that she wouldn't do the right thing. She never had a problem being accountable to other people. She knew that they kept her in check, so that she didn't have to do it for herself. She was emotionally dependent on others. There was little that she did that she wasn't using her family as an emotional crutch to get through it. She didn't know when she became this person that was so dependent on everyone around her. She hated that her addiction turned into someone that needed others. She wasn't like that as a child. She was getting away from her mother any chance that she could. She was like that until her father died. That was the moment that everything changed. She was going to end up alone.

It was an odd coincidence that was when she thought about doing drugs for the first time. She didn't want to think too hard about that since she knew that it would cause her to spiral even more than this. She realized that her fear of being alone stemmed from her father's fear of being alone. It was a fear that came from inside of her bones. It was something that she was born with. She was born with a fear of being alone, a tendency to get addicted to everything, and the inability to trust herself. Dr. Taylor told her that it was hard to confront the traits that she was born with since there was little to no chance of them going away. Over her years of going to therapy with psychiatrists, she accepted a lot of things that happened that she couldn't change. She accepted that her addiction killed Daxton. That she was never going to trust herself. That she was never going to see her father. That she was going to be an addict for the rest of her life. That she couldn't change what happened to her parents before she was born. That she wasn't going to the person that she wanted to be. She thought that she wouldn't have to accept anything else. She needed to accept that she was going to have to be okay with being alone. It was hard for her to imagine let alone accept. It was hard for her to think about it since she knew that she would have to put herself in a vulnerable mental space to deal with it. She wasn't sleeping at night after those unwanted feelings came to the surface. She thought about it all night as she smoked cigarettes on the balcony where Sebastian talked to her about it. She told Sebastian that it was hard for her to think about it. It was the last emotion that her father felt in his life. She didn't need anyone to tell her since she felt it from the moment he killed himself. She felt an overwhelming feeling of loneliness every time that she tried to kill herself. That was the reason that she kept trying to kill herself. That feeling of loneliness was there inside of her mind when she took the steps to end her life. She didn't want to die because she didn't want to live anymore. Her only reason that she wanted to die was because she wanted that feeling of loneliness to go away. She told Dr. Taylor the feelings that she talked about with Sebastian. He asked what the most suffocating thing about loneliness was. She told him that she felt like she was trapped in a room with her deepest and darkest fears. She felt like she was standing on the bridge with her father as they fell into the frozen water together to their deaths. It showed to her that she would've rather died than face the reality that she was alone. She was born alone, and she would die alone. Dr. Taylor said that she wasn't scared of the beginning of her life or the end. She was scared of the middle since she didn't know what was going to happen to her. She was so stunned by what Dr. Taylor told her she didn't have a response for him until the end of that session. She revealed to him that he was wrong about one thing. When he asked her what he missed in his assessment, she told him that she was terrified that the only thing that mattered was what happened in the middle and that she wasted her life trying to skip to the end. She was very busy preparing for her wedding at the end of the summer where she spent most of her time outside of work with her wedding planner at their house. She was glad that Sebastian hired a wedding planner for their wedding because she would've been so overwhelmed that she wouldn't know where to start. The most important step for their wedding was picking a venue. They couldn't agree on where they wanted to get married. Sebastian wanted to get married in the states and she wanted to get married in Europe. Sebastian wanted to have a wedding in the countryside, and she wanted to get married at the beach. They decided on a compromise, so that they would get what they wanted. They would get married in the states at the beach. When they agreed on what kind of wedding that they were going to have and what country it was going to be in, they disagreed on where they wanted to get married to each other. Sebastian wanted to get married in California and she wanted to get married in Hawaii. It was hard for them to compromise since Hawaii and California were different places. They chose to get married in California since it was going to be cheaper to get married in their home state.

After they decided that they would go to Hawaii for their honeymoon, it came down to who they wanted in their wedding parties. That was a hard choice since they had so many cousins in their families, and she had so many nieces and nephews to choose from. Sebastian chose Oliver as his best man since they were best friends with his cousins as his groomsmen. He chose the other groomsmen to be Tommy, Alfie, Sean, Troy, and a few of his friends from his childhood. She chose Sasha to be her maid of honor since she promised her that she would be her maid of honor when they were little girls with the other bridesmaids being her cousins Amelia, Poppy, Anastasia, Nina and her sister-in-law's Juliet and Polly. The flower girls for their wedding were going to be her nieces Posey, Alina, Bridget, and Lena. The ring bearers were going to be her nephews Leo, Mason, Jack, and Viktor. When her parents came to visit her in California, she spent a few days going to bridal stores trying on dresses with her parents, Aunt Valeria, Amelia, Sasha, Juliet, Anastasia, and Nina there to help her decide what dress that she was going to buy. It took her trying on over a dozen different dresses for her to find the dress that called to her the moment that she put it on her body with her family in agreement before she paid for her wedding dress with money that she saved. Once her wedding dress was sent away for alterations with the seamstress, she spent the rest of the day at her house with her parents and her cousins Anastasia and Nina who stayed with them for a few weeks. Anastasia brought her two-year-old daughter Angelina with her since she was breastfeeding her. Anastasia was in the early stages of her pregnancy with her fourth child. Anastasia's other two children were at home with Damien who was taking care of them. Nina brought her youngest son Liam with her since he was too small to stay with Joseph. Aunt Valeria stayed at Amelia's house with Sasha and Gabriel who visited with Jamie and Ivan. Their boyfriends weren't with them due to it being a wedding session. After they ate dinner in the kitchen that their chef made for them, Aunt Valeria went to the movie theatre with Uncle Stan, Thomas, and her parents while she watched a movie in the living room with her cousins. Once they put the children to bed in the guest bedrooms except for Posey, they decided to take the party outside by the pool as she laid down in one of the pool chairs with Sebastian lying down next to her where Anastasia and Nina played a competitive game of volleyball against Sasha and Amelia. As Oliver kept score of the game, Juliet pushed Posey around on a bike that they gave her for her last birthday before Juliet asked her to push Posey on the bike since Eleanor was crying for her in the living room. Once she let go of Sebastian's hand, she took the back of Posey's bike from Juliet where Juliet went to calm her other daughter down before she helped keep up Posey's bike for her as she puddled around their yard. After she pushed Posey around the yard for a while, Posey got a few scrapes on her knees after she fell off of her bike on the cement where she placed the crying girl in her arms before she walked over to Oliver to calm down his daughter. Since Oliver was comforting his daughter, she sat down on Oliver's seat as she took the score of the game that was going on before Amelia and Sasha's team won the game in the backyard. After Anastasia and Nina sulked about their loss, they went back into the house to check on their children. She took a seat next to Sebastian who was in the middle of a conversation with Troy before Amelia stole her boyfriend from him. Once Amelia and Troy disappeared into the house, she was laid down on top of Sebastian's lap as she leaned her head on his shoulders when she asked him with a smile on her face, "Did you see that Sasha and Amelia beat Anastasia and Nina? They were bitter about it."

Sebastian pulled her into a backwards hug as he leaned his chin on the top of her head when he responded to her with a neutral look on his face, "I saw that honey. Your cousins are competitive with each other. Mine aren't that way. We let each other win when we play games against each other."

Oliver stood in front of them with an opened bottle of wine in his hand when he asked them with a smile on his face, "Do you guys want to share the bottle? Sasha and Amelia can't know because they will drink it by themselves."

She nodded her head at him when she responded to Oliver with a wide grin on her face, "They don't let themselves enjoy wine. We should go to the suite if we don't want them to know."

After she stood up from her seat, she grabbed onto Sebastian's hand to help him off of the pool chair as they followed Oliver through the back door that led into their suite before she closed the door behind them. Once she made it over to the bed, she grabbed a glass of wine from Oliver as they tapped their glasses together before they took big gulps of their wine. She laid down on the couch at the end of their bed as Oliver and Sebastian laid down next to each other on the bed when Oliver asked them with a goofy grin on his face, "Are you guys excited for the wedding? I'm excited for it and I'm not the person getting married. My best friends are getting married to each other."

She looked over at Sebastian at the same time that he looked at her. She took another sip of her glass of wine when she responded to Oliver with a smile on her face, "You are more excited than we are, Oliver. It feels like we are already married to each other in everything except for in name. We are only getting married because we want to have children."

Sebastian smiled at her when he responded to her in a distant voice, "You read my mind, Isabella. That's why I'm going to marry you. I don't need to tell you anything and you know what I'm thinking. Did you see Isabella's dress, Oliver? She won't show it to me until the day of our wedding. Sasha and Amelia teased me about it earlier."

Oliver lightly hit Sebastian on the arm as Sebastian pretended to be in pain when Oliver responded to him with a smirk on his face, "Yes, I've seen Isabella's dress. She looks like a princess. You can't see it until the wedding, Bash. I don't care what emotional blackmail that you are going to pull on me. It's not going to work. She made me promise her that I'm not going to show it to you. I feel like I'm dealing with a toddler when I talk to you. Eleanor has more patience than you and she's hardly two years old."

As soon as Oliver and Sebastian wrestled each other on the bed, she finished her glass of wine in one big gulp as she pulled them off of each other before Sebastian pulled her on the bed with them. Sebastian pulled her into his arms as she laid her head down on his chest when she told him with sarcasm laced in her voice, "That was a nasty trick to get me on the bed with you. Did you see what he did, Oliver? He pulled me on the bed with him. What do you have to say for yourself, Bash? Tell me that you're sorry and I'll forgive you."

Sebastian pulled her into a quick kiss as she hid her face into his chest when Oliver whispered to Sebastian like she couldn't hear him, "Is she doing okay? You know that she wouldn't tell me if she wasn't doing okay."

She pulled her face out of Sebastian's chest as she looked up at him when she told Oliver with anger laced in her voice, "Jesus Christ, Oliver. She is right next to you and she's doing fine. She doesn't appreciate it when you talk about her like she's not in front of you."

Before she gave Oliver a chance to respond to her, she stormed onto the balcony as she slammed the door behind her where she lit a cigarette with shaking hands before she inhaled the smoke from it. She inhaled the smoke from her cigarette as Sebastian walked onto the balcony when he asked her with a look of concern on his face, "Oliver has a point honey. You do seem a little bit off. Is something going on?" She barely looked up at him as she inhaled the smoke from her cigarette where Sebastian took a seat next to her before he grabbed onto her hands that were shaking in her lap.

She inhaled the smoke from her cigarette when she said to Sebastian with a frown on her face, "If you are wondering about me relapsing, I haven't relapsed. I can be off without relapsing. I know that was what Oliver meant when he asked me that question. I've been stressed with the wedding. Getting married is a lot, Bash. If I knew it was this much, I would've told you that we should elope. We are too deep in it to go back. You know that stuff that I've been talking to Dr. Taylor about?"

Sebastian tightened his grip on her hands when he responded to her with a serious look on his face, "I'm stressed about the wedding too. It would've been easier to elope, but we are too committed to it. What does that have to do with the wedding? The stuff that you're talking to Dr. Taylor about?"

She blinked back tears that fell down her face when she confessed to him in a distant voice, "It doesn't have anything to do with the wedding. I've been thinking about having children. I shouldn't have children because of my problems. I'm worried that our children are going to inherit my problems. I don't want to watch them go through what I had to go through in my life. It would be too hard to watch."

Sebastian drew invisible circles on her arms when he responded to her with a look of fear on his face, "Why do you think that would stop me from wanting to start a family with you? We can't control if our children inherit our problems. Who is to say that they will? You don't know that they will. You're scared that our children will inherit our trauma. It's okay to be scared honey. I'm terrified of that too. Our children are going to become whoever they want to become with or without our trauma getting their way. This seems premature to think about this unless there is something that you aren't telling me."

She leaned her head on his shoulder when she responded to him with a wide grin on her face, "I'm not pregnant, Bash. Don't get those kinds of ideas in your head. It's me freaking out about things that won't happen for a long time. It's nothing new. Even if I was pregnant, I wouldn't tell you this way. It would be much more romantic than me having a mental breakdown. I did stop taking birth control a few weeks ago, but nothing happened yet."

Sebastian harshly smacked her arm as she groaned in pain when he responded to her in a stern voice, "Why didn't you say that you stopped taking birth control? Were you trying to give me a heart attack? Are we trying for a baby before the wedding or after? I'm confused now."

She pulled him into a long kiss as he wrapped his arms around her until she quickly wiped away the tears on her face when she responded to him with a smirk on her face, "What do you think I mean, Bash? Shouldn't we face our fears?"

Sebastian pulled her into a long kiss where he brought them into their bed where she laid down on the bed with him on top of her before she took off his shirt as he took off her shorts. After they made up with each other on the bed, she laid down with her head leaning on his chest as he ran his fingers through her hair when she said to him in a soft voice, "I hope that we made our future tonight. A future that will be brighter than our lives were. I love you, Bash." As soon as Sebastian told her that he loved her too, she fell asleep with his arms around her for the rest of the night.

Chapter Forty-Three
(Summer 1969 – Long Beach, California)

After her family went back to New York, Sebastian filmed his movie in the studio where she filmed commercials that her agent sent her. When they weren't working during the week, they were planning the final details of their wedding with their wedding planner while she got alterations on her wedding dress. When her family from New York visited them, her cousins got their bridesmaids dresses fitted except for Polly and Poppy that got their dresses fitted in England. As they got closer to the day of their wedding, things were getting real to her that she was getting married to Sebastian. It wasn't real to her until they were planning hotel arrangements for their families in Long Beach. There were going to be a lot of people at their wedding. They didn't only invite their families to the wedding, but they invited their co-stars from previous movies that they worked on in the past and people that worked at their acting agencies. When they decided to have a wedding ceremony and to not get eloped at the courthouse, it didn't cross their minds that they knew that many people. Their wedding planner told them that they prepared for two hundred people at the wedding. They didn't realize that they invited that many people to their wedding. This made the wedding more expensive than it already was since they had to feed and entertain over two hundred people with most of them being their families that didn't live near them. She complained about this and other concerns about the wedding to her parents. Her mother offered to pay for the hotels for their families if they paid for the wedding ceremony. They didn't have to pay for professionals to do their hair and makeup since Aunt Valeria, Anastasia, and Amelia were doing it. Uncle James was officiating the wedding for free like them. This left them paying for the venue, the catered meal, the alcohol that they were serving to their guests, the flowers, the decor that their wedding planner curated for them, and the city of Los Angeles orchestra that were playing live music for the wedding and for the afterparty. Sebastian tried to get her to take back her request for live music, but she wouldn't budge about it. It was the only thing that she wanted in the wedding that they weren't going to compromise on. She already compromised enough with Sebastian about having her wedding in the states. The wedding planner added that live music was going to be difficult to do at the beach. She didn't care what her wedding planner thought about it since it wasn't her wedding. By the end of their time, her patience with their wedding planner was growing thinner by the day since she liked to add little comments with her thoughts about everything that they decided to do for their wedding. After Sebastian stopped her from having another argument with their wedding planner, she promised them that she would find a way for the orchestra to play on the beach before they figured out the floral designs that they needed for the chairs. Since she was overwhelmed with the details that were going into their wedding, Sasha and Amelia planned her bachelorette party and Oliver planned his bachelor party. After they found one week that they didn't have anything going on, the girls and Oliver planned their bachelorette and bachelor parties at the same time since it was much easier for them.

She received written instructions from Sasha and Amelia to go to the airport with no knowledge about where they were taking her. Sebastian received similar instructions from Oliver to arrive at the airport. Oliver and Juliet left their children with Uncle Stan and Thomas for the week. After their driver dropped them off at the airport, Oliver blindfolded Sebastian as Sasha blindfolded her before they took them to different gates at the airport. Once they sat down on the plane, Sasha took off her blind fold as she slept for the entire flight with her head leaning on Amelia's shoulder before her cousins woke her up when their plane landed in their mystery destination. After they got off of the plane, Sasha and Amelia blindfolded her again until they got to the hotel where they dragged her out of the airport before they told her that they were in the hotel. As soon as she took off from the blind fold, she saw that they took her to Greece for her bachelorette party where her cousins Poppy, Audrey, Nina, and Anastasia with her sister-in-law's Juliet and Polly were standing in the room. After she came out of her state of shock, she asked Sasha where Oliver dragged Sebastian to for his bachelor party when Sasha told her that the boys were in Mexico City with her cousins and his cousins. She had the time of her life in Greece with her cousins and her sister-in-law's. They followed the itinerary that Amelia planned for them before they took pictures of the trip with Gabriel's camera that Sasha brought with her. She didn't want to go back to the states. She had so much fun in Greece. Sasha reminded her that she had a wedding waiting for her and that was enough motivation to go home. After they left Nina and Anastasia in New York, she got on a flight to California with Sasha, Amelia, and Juliet where their driver picked her up from the airport before she pulled Sebastian into a tight hug at their house. Once they made up for lost time in the suite, they laid in each other's arms as they caught each other up on what happened at their bachelorette and bachelor parties before they slept in each other's for the rest of the night. They spent more time with the wedding planner in Long Beach before their families flew in for their wedding. Her parents came to California early since they were determined to be by her side for the critical weeks leading up to the wedding. She had a nervous breakdown when the orchestra couldn't come to their wedding because they were short a few people. Her wedding planner pulled a miracle out of thin air when she got the conductor to play the instruments that they were lacking in their group. Uncle James came to California early with Aunt Sylvia, her cousin George, and his girlfriend Annabell Heights since he was officiating the wedding for them. He asked them if they were going to do traditional vows or if they were going to write their own vows. This was the only thing that they forgot about out of everything that they remembered to do for their wedding. She argued with Sebastian that night about him wanting to do traditional vows when she wanted to write their own vows. She won their argument by writing their own vows after her mother promised Sebastian that she would help him write his vows. Her mother knew that she didn't need help with that. When she realized that she was writing her own vows, she panicked about it because she had no time to do it. Her writing her own vows gave her more anxiety than anything else that she did. She had to say it out loud to over two hundred people that would be at their wedding.

She wasn't sleeping at night due to this stress as she sat on the balcony with an empty piece of paper in front of her before she smoked cigarettes all night instead of writing anything down. Even though she knew that her mother would help her write her vows if she asked her, she wasn't ready to give up yet. She could write her own vows to Sebastian. She wrote four different versions of her vows two nights before the wedding. That meant that she had less than two days to memorize her vows. It wasn't the most challenging thing for her since she memorized scripts in less time than that. When they decided that they were going to write their own vows, they promised each other that they weren't going to share them with anyone until the day of their wedding. Sebastian wasn't allowed to share his vows with her mother who helped him. On the day before their wedding, she packed up everything that she was taking to Long Beach with her as well as everything that she was bringing on their honeymoon to Hawaii. Most of her family had been at Long Beach for a few days with Sebastian's family. They were the last people that weren't in Long Beach since Sebastian was finishing filming his movie before they would be gone for three weeks on their honeymoon. Once their driver dropped them off at the hotel, Sebastian carried their bags into the hotel room except for her wedding dress and his tuxedo that her parents took with them to Long Beach a few days ago. After they unpacked their bags for the weekend, they joined their families at the beach for the rest of the afternoon where they went to a restaurant that was attached to the hotel for dinner until they went to their hotel room before she fell asleep with his arms around her. On the morning of her wedding, Sasha and Amelia told her that they had a surprise for her before they dragged her into Oliver's room. Oliver gave her something used. It was a jacket that her father wore when he was alive. Her mother didn't know that Oliver was going to give it to her. They cried as soon as they saw her father's jacket in the box that he left it in. After Oliver placed her father's jacket over her shoulders, she didn't take it off for the rest of the day until she got changed into her wedding dress where she put it on for the afterparty that evening. After she ate breakfast with their families at the restaurant, she was separated from Sebastian for the rest of the morning. Amelia put on her makeup, and Aunt Valeria styled her hair for her with her cousins, her nieces, and her nephews walking around the room. Sebastian was in a room across the hotel with his groomsmen, his parents, and his cousins where they got ready for the wedding. When she was in the middle of getting her hair done, her mother gave her something borrowed. It was a brooch that her great grandmother gave her grandmother on the day that she got married to her grandfather. Once her mother pinned the brooch onto her father's jacket, she pulled her mother into a tight hug with her face hidden in her chest. She didn't let go of her mother until Aunt Valeria told her that she needed to curl the other side of her hair. Once Aunt Valeria finished curling her hair, Amelia put on her makeup as she sat in the chair with her eyes closed where Sasha gave her something new that was a pair of diamond earrings that matched her wedding dress before she pulled Sasha into a tight hug. She wanted to hug Sasha longer, but Amelia nagged her about messing up her makeup if she cried too early in the day before she pulled away from Sasha with Amelia fixing the make-up that she already messed up. She wanted Sebastian to be surprised by her wedding dress, so they weren't doing a first look. She was going from her hotel room to the aisle. Once it was time for the wedding to start in the afternoon, everyone in the wedding party took their places that they rehearsed last night where everyone else took their seats that weren't on the beach. That was their final compromise. They would be on the beach with Uncle James, their wedding parties, and the orchestra. After her parents looped their arms around her, the wedding party went on the beach with her walking closely behind them. Their flower girls Posey, Alina, Bridget, and Lena threw flowers over the sand where they sat in the front row with their ring bearers Mason, Jack, and Viktor sitting next to them.

When she looked up at Sebastian for the first time, tears fell down his face with Oliver's hand tightly on his shoulder as she blinked back tears that fell down her face before they walked over to Uncle James.

Her mother kissed her on the cheek as she pulled her mother into a desperate hug with her face hidden in her chest where her mum kissed on the top of her head before she pulled away from her parents. After her parents took a seat in the front row, she wiped away tears that escaped from her eyes as she handed Sasha the bouquet of flowers that were in her hands before she walked over to Sebastian where he grabbed onto her hands. Once Uncle James began their wedding ceremony, she looked up at Sebastian like they were the only people left in the world. When they repeated the words that Uncle James told them to say to each other, Sebastian pulled out a piece of paper from his coat pocket as he held onto her hands when he vowed to her with tears falling down his face that he didn't hide, "Isabella, being with you brought me more joy and happiness that I've ever experienced in my life. It's taken us a lot to get where we are. I'm grateful for the hardships that we experienced because it only brought us closer together. Even though we lost each other for a moment in time, I knew that we would find our way to each other again. I fell in love with you from the moment that I met you on that movie set. You didn't need to say anything for me to never want to be apart from you. I love you so much. It hurts me when you are hurting. Losing you was the hardest thing that I went through. Forgiving you was the easiest thing that I've ever done. I couldn't live without you. I don't want to live without you. You are the air that I breathe. You are my everything. Someday when we're old and we've watched our children grow up in front of our eyes, we will look back at this moment in our lives. We will think about how this was our favorite moment together. We will live in this moment for the rest of eternity. It will remind us of a time in our lives when our love was the purest. Before the children. Before the turmoil of life. Before our death. We will always have this moment. We will always have each other."

Sebastian wiped away the tears that fell down his face as he placed the folded piece of paper into his coat pocket before she let out a shaky breath with her hands tightly holding onto his hand when she vowed to him in with tears falling down her face, "Bash, from the moment that I met you, I knew that I couldn't let you go. You were the first person that treated me with respect. You supported my dreams over the years. You taught me how to love myself. I didn't know what I was doing with my life until I met you. I went through a lot of pain to get here. You supported me no matter how much I hurt you along the way. You forgave me and you let me back into your life. You made me care about life. Before I met you, I used to think everything was meaningless. My life was meaningless. I tried to get out of life. Too many times that I'm comfortable admitting to. I wanted to skip to the end because I didn't realize that the best part happens in the middle. I used to think that nothing mattered. It didn't matter if I lived, and it certainly didn't matter if I died. You showed me that it does matter. It matters if I live, and it matters if I die. I didn't see a future before I met you. I only saw another tragedy waiting to happen. You give me an excitement for a future that I never thought that I would have. I see us raising our children together. I see us giving them the life that we never had. I see us protecting them from the trauma that we went through in our lives. I see us getting old together. I see us dying in each other's arms. We will dance in the cosmos for the rest of eternity. We will always have the stars. That's all that we had. We have that moment in the stars. I love you, Bash. I'll love you until we turn into dust, and we are nothing but a distant memory to the stars."

After she wiped away the tears that fell down her face, Uncle James grabbed onto their shoulders when he pronounced them husband and wife and that Sebastian could kiss the bride. Sebastian pulled her into a long kiss as she leaned into him until she let out a soft gasp when Sebastian dipped her into another kiss before he helped her up onto her feet. As soon as she grabbed onto his hand, she smiled at Sebastian as he smiled at her before they ran down the aisle with everyone cheering behind them. Once they made it to their hotel room, Sebastian pulled her into a desperate kiss as she didn't pull away from him until Oliver and Sasha knocked on the door when they told them to meet them in the ballroom where their guests were waiting for them. After she pulled her father's jacket over her wedding dress with her great-grandmother's brooch attached to it, she followed Sebastian down to the ballroom where everyone cheered as soon as they walked into the room before she took a seat with Sebastian, her parents, his parents, and their wedding party in the front of the room. They ate a five-course meal that was served to them with tall glasses of Italian imported wine while she talked to her cousins and her parents with Sebastian's arms around her. She joined her family for pictures with the wedding photographer on the beach as the sun set in the background. After they finished taking pictures on the beach, she changed into a shorter dress with her father's jacket over her arms where she went into the ballroom before she danced with Sebastian's arms around her with her cousins, nieces, and nephews dancing with her. After they spent most of the night dancing with their arms around each other, Sebastian told her that they needed to get on their plane to Hawaii as she rushed to pack up her bags before she followed Sebastian to the lobby of the hotel room. After she said an emotional goodbye to her parents and Oliver, she got in the back of the taxi with her head leaning on Sebastian's shoulder that she fell asleep in the taxi before Sebastian gently nudged her awake when their taxi pulled up to the airport. She held onto Sebastian's hand as he held onto their bags in his other hand where they waited at their gate to open before she fell asleep with her head resting on his lap. After an announcement that their plane was boarding, Sebastian moved her out of his lap as she grabbed onto his hand while he helped them to their seats before she fell asleep with her head on his shoulder for the rest of the night. She dreamed about the child that they made with their love for each other. After their plane landed in Hawaii the next afternoon, she held onto Sebastian's hand as he pulled them through the crowded airport where he flagged down a taxi before she fell asleep in the taxi ride to the hotel. After their taxi dropped them off at their hotel, Sebastian grabbed onto their bags as she checked them into the king suite at the hotel where she barely closed the door behind them before Sebastian pulled her into a long kiss with their bags being thrown onto the floor. After they made their future in the bed, she told him that she loved him as he told her the same thing before she fell asleep in his arms for the rest of the night.

CHAPTER FORTY-FOUR
(FALL 1969 – LOS ANGELES, CALIFORNIA)

After they spent three weeks in Hawaii on their honeymoon, she was heartbroken when they had to go back to reality again. On the night before they got on a plane to California, she sat on the toilet in their hotel bathroom waiting to get her period since it was long overdue to start on their honeymoon. She realized that she wasn't getting her period any time soon. She almost went into their bed where Sebastian was asleep. A thought entered her mind. She might be pregnant. After she fell asleep with Sebastian's arms around her, she was woken up early in the morning with a sudden urge to vomit as she sprinted into the bathroom where she barely made it into the toilet before she puked up everything that she ate at dinner. As soon as she pulled her face out of the toilet, Sebastian stared at her with a look of concern on his face when he asked if she was okay where she excused it as her hangover before she went into their bedroom to pack up her stuff. Once they finished packing up the rest of their stuff, they took a taxi to the airport as she excused herself to the bathroom where she puked up everything that she ate at breakfast before she joined Sebastian pretending that she wasn't sick. She didn't throw up during their flight to Los Angeles until their driver picked them up from the airport. Their driver was almost home where she yelled at him to stop the car before she puked up what she ate for lunch onto the side of the road. Sebastian was concerned about her because she was so sick.

After she got back into the car, he asked her what was wrong with her where she told him that she might be pregnant before he told his driver to take her to her doctor. Since she wasn't in the mood to push his concern for her, she let him take care of her as he called her doctor from the car before he came to her doctor's appointment with her. She told her doctor that she was throwing up for the last two weeks and she hadn't had her period in over two months. Her doctor ordered tests for her to get done at her office. When her doctor confirmed that she was pregnant, the doctor left them alone for a moment where Sebastian pulled her into a sudden hug before she hid her face in his chest with tears falling down their faces. It wasn't that they couldn't believe that she was pregnant. They have been trying for a child for four months. They were so happy that they were going to start the family that they always dreamed about. She kept her face hidden in Sebastian's chest until her doctor came back into the examination room with additional testing that she needed to get done for her next appointment before they left her office with smiles on their faces.

After their driver dropped them off at their house, she held onto Sebastian's hand as their driver carried their bags in the house where she hid in the bathroom for the rest of the evening since she couldn't keep anything down. When she no longer felt nauseous for the first time that day, she joined Sebastian in their bed with his arms around her where they talked about their baby that was growing in her stomach before they slept in each other's arms for the rest of the night. After she spent most of the week unable to get out of their bed, Sebastian told her that they needed to consider telling people about her pregnancy because she had been hiding ever since they got back from Hawaii. She didn't want to admit that Sebastian was right, but she was going to have to tell her family that she was pregnant at some point. It was only going to be harder for her to hide her pregnancy from them. They decided that they were going to tell their families together that she was pregnant with their child. On the day that Sebastian went to work filming a new movie, she tried to lay low in the house while she watched television in her bedroom before she heard someone knocking on her door that forced her to get out of her bed. As soon as she opened the front door, her parents stood in front of her when her mother asked her why she didn't tell them that she was back from Hawaii where she didn't respond to them before she let them into the house. Before she got a chance to say anything to them, her mother accused her of hiding a secret from them where she couldn't stop the words coming out of her mouth when she told them that she was hiding from them because she was sick from her pregnancy. As soon as she told them that she was pregnant, her mother pulled her into a desperate hug as she hid her face into her chest with her mum's arms around them when her mother told her that she knew that she was pregnant as soon as she opened up the door. After her parents kissed her on the cheek, they wanted to take her to the store to buy baby clothes. She hadn't left the house since they got back from Hawaii. She promised them that they could take her shopping another day when she wasn't sick. Once her parents disappeared into one of the guest bedrooms for the night, she told Sebastian that her parents knew that she was pregnant before she got the chance to tell them where they agreed that they would tell their families when her parents left to go back to New York. For the few days that her parents stayed with them, her parents promised her that they wouldn't say anything about her being pregnant until they were ready to tell the rest of their families where they agreed to her promise on the condition that they could take her shopping for baby clothes. Once she relented to her parents' wishes, Sebastian left for work that day as she was dragged from store to store by her parents looking for baby clothes before she slept on the couch for the rest of the afternoon. Sebastian woke her up in the evening when he got back from work where he guided her into their bedroom before she slept in his arms for the rest of the night. After they dropped off her parents at the airport, they planned to have her cousins, Uncle Stan, and Thomas over at their house for dinner like they did every few months before Sebastian told the chef to prepare for a meal that was friendly with her morning sickness. She hoped that it wouldn't give it away. On the day of the dinner, she spent most of the morning into the early afternoon in their bed since she wasn't able to get out of bed until Sebastian came home from work before they showered together in the bathroom. After she got ready for their guests coming over to their house, she made out with Sebastian in their bedroom before they joined their guests in the living room. Once Oliver saw her for the first time since her wedding, he pulled her into a desperate hug as she hid her face into his chest until Sebastian pulled Oliver into a tight hug with her in the middle of them. After they pulled away from each other, she pulled Amelia into a tight hug as she did the same thing with Juliet and Troy where they ate dinner together in soft conversation. Even though she felt like she was going to vomit only after a few bites of her food, she hid from her family that she felt violently sick before she ran into the bathroom to puke up everything that she ate into the toilet. Everyone stared at her as she took a seat next to Sebastian with his hand on her back when Oliver asked her if she was pregnant where she revealed to them that she found out that she got pregnant in Hawaii. Amelia instantly pulled into a tight hug with her hiding her face into her chest before Uncle Stan and Thomas pulled her into a tight hug that she didn't let go of until she suddenly felt the urge to vomit.

When she realized that it was a false alarm, Oliver pulled her into a desperate hug with her face hidden in his chest. He was relieved that she wasn't secretive with him. He thought that she relapsed on her honeymoon. Even though she knew that it was what Oliver was thinking, he would never tell her that. There was no need for them to say the unspoken words between them. Once she let go of Oliver's arms, Juliet pulled her into a tight hug with Eleanor on her hip as Posey placed her hand on her stomach before they talked about upcoming vacations that they were going on in the future. After they were left alone in the house, Sebastian talked to his parents on the phone in the kitchen about coming over to spend the weekend with them before she called Sasha from their bedroom who was living in France with Gabriel. She wasn't surprised to hear that Sasha already knew that she was pregnant since Amelia called to tell her about it. She complained about her morning sickness to Sasha before Sasha revealed to her that Gabriel proposed to her last night in front of the Eiffel Tower. Sasha made her promise that she wasn't going to say anything about her engagement to their other cousins until she told them about it. Since she took pride in her ability to keep secrets, she promised Sasha that she wouldn't tell anyone about her engagement before Sebastian joined her in their bedroom before they fell asleep in each other's arms for the rest of the night. After she revealed to her cousins in California that she was pregnant, the rest of her family heard about it from her parents as she received a dozen phone calls from her cousins, aunts, and uncles about her pregnancy. Uncle Nathan was the last person to find out about her pregnancy since he was on a long work cycle when he called her when he told her that her father would be excited to be a grandfather. She was inconsolable after he said that her father would've loved being a grandfather. He would've never imagined his baby having a baby of her own someday. It shouldn't have surprised her that she was emotional about this because she was always sentimental about him. She never thought about her father like that until Uncle Nathan said that to her. It gave her more comfort than she could've imagined that it would when she thought about her father being a grandfather. She knew even less about her baby than she did about her father, but they would've been obsessed with each other. There was a part of her that resented her unborn baby because it received more love and kindness from her father than she received from him in her life. It wasn't fair that her unborn baby got to have the relationship that her father didn't get to have with her. The logical part of her mind told her that this resentment that she held towards her father was ridiculous. He chose to not be a part of her life, and she shouldn't care about the relationship that she never had with him. She didn't understand what choices were until the last time that she was sent to rehab. A choice was complicated. A choice was the beginning of a new life. As soon as a choice was made, it brought her down on a new path that led her to the same place that her destiny would always lead her to. Her father's choice to get high opened up a new path that would lead to his death. No matter what he did differently along the way, it was always going to end that way for him. He was always going to be alone. He was never going to be in her mother's life. He was never going to be her father. He was never going to be her baby's grandfather. It didn't matter what he wanted in life. The end was only more nothingness. She was right. The middle was the only thing that mattered.

After Sebastian's parents and his cousins spent time at their house, she would've hid in their bedroom for the rest of her life if it wasn't for Sebastian encouraging her to see Dr. Taylor. He told her that she was falling into a depressive cycle again. She complied with Sebastian's wishes to make an appointment with Dr. Taylor. She didn't want to spend the next seven months of her pregnancy in the middle of a depressive cycle. She wanted to enjoy her pregnancy in the time that she had with her baby in her body. In her first session at Dr. Taylor's office, they talked about how she felt about being pregnant and how her being pregnant made her feel about her parents. She told him that she was terrified that her child was going to inherit her drug addiction and her mental illnesses. Dr. Taylor asked her what was the worst thing that could've happened if her child inherited them. A million thoughts entered her mind that she shared with him that she thought about when he asked her that question. It was over many sessions that they took a deeper look into each of her fears. No matter what happened to her child, they would always have the support of them. That wasn't the only thing that she talked about with Dr. Taylor related to her pregnancy. It opened up a can of worms when it came to things that she never thought about before. She told him about her conflicting thoughts with her father being a grandfather and how she wished that he was there to be in her baby's life. This opened up another train of thought about how she was grieving the relationship that she would never have with her father. He assured her that it was normal for someone to grieve the loss of a relationship with a parent that wasn't there when they were having children. She was surprised that she had undealt with emotions about her father. She thought that she dealt with all of her emotions that she felt about her father after a decade of therapy. There were more things for her to process about him. She was never going to run out of things to feel about her father. Something came up every time that she was in a new stage of life. Dr. Taylor reassured her that what she was feeling towards her father was normal. She felt like there was something wrong with her. That was the thought that kept her up in the last few weeks as she hid on the balcony where she was lost in her thoughts until Sebastian dragged her to bed in the middle of the night. That night was no exception since she was lost in thought on the balcony as Sebastian slept in their bedroom. She sat on her balcony with a blanket wrapped around her. She longed for a cigarette even though her doctor told her that she shouldn't smoke when she was pregnant. She was pulled out of her thoughts when the phone rang in their bedroom before she walked inside to answer it with Sebastian not stirring in his sleep. She hung up the phone after she told Sasha that they were coming to visit them in Paris to celebrate her engagement to Gabriel that was knowledge to their family now before she hid out on the balcony all over again. She leaned back on it with her eyes closed as she placed her hands over her growing stomach when she said aloud to herself with tears falling down her face, "Hello, dad. It's been a while since we last talked to each other. Your little girl got married to the love of her life. She's pregnant with your grandchild. It felt weird getting married without you. I knew that you wouldn't come to my wedding, but it was strange to not have you walking me down the aisle. Mom did a great job at walking me down the aisle. Don't worry about that. She's so excited to be a grandmother. I've never seen her this happy in my life. She calls me every morning to ask about the baby. You can almost hear her say it. 'Is the baby growing? Yes, they are bigger at every doctor's appointment. How is your morning sickness dear? I'm puking every day. Did I tell you that I had morning sickness until the day that you were born, baby girl? Yes, you told me this. Thanks for making me feel worse about it. How is Bash treating you? Bash is treating me like a princess. He should do that because I'm carrying his child.' I could go on forever about it, but you can see it for yourself. Mom has always been overprotective of me, so this is a great excuse for her to be more intense than normal. Don't get me started on Oliver. He's been on my case ever since he found out that I was pregnant. I don't know who is annoying me more between them. Bash is calmer compared to them. He's been gentler with me than he normally is. It's sweet of them to be worried about me. I don't want to sound ungrateful. I'm not ungrateful. It's a lot to deal with."

She gently rubbed her stomach when she responded to herself with her blinking back tears that fell down her face, "Do you want to know what bothers me the most? You aren't here to see it. You aren't here, dad. You have never been here. It doesn't make it hurt any less that you aren't here. I had a dream last night that you were there when I had my baby. I was in the hospital delivering my baby with mom and Bash by my side and you appeared to tell me that everything was going to be okay. I would have this baby, and everything would change for the better. I cried when I realized that it wasn't real. I wanted it to be real. I wouldn't have to think about the reality of it. The reality is that I'm going to have a baby that's only going to have one grandfather. They will have three grandmothers. It's a blessing of its own. Only one grandfather though? No baby should only have one grandfather. Bash assures me that our baby won't know that they are missing a grandfather. They will be so loved by us and their living grandparents. I believe him. A baby doesn't know any better than what they are born into. If I was born after you already died like Oliver's father did, then I wouldn't know what it was like to miss you. I would live my life with my two moms without a care in the world. We were alive at the same time, and it destroys me every time that I think about it. For the shortest amount of time, we existed in the same world. That wasn't the only time that I was with you though. I was with you before that, and I will be with you after that. My baby gets to be with you before they are with me. I'm crying thinking about it. Can you do me a favor, dad?" She quickly wiped away the tears that fell down her face as she let out a shaky breath when she said aloud to herself in a soft voice, "Tell my baby about you. Tell my baby that all that we amount to are the moments that we made life happen around us. Tell my baby that their life is going to be better than your life. Tell my baby that I love them more than anything in the world. Even though I don't know them yet, I will love them for the rest of my life. Like you used to love me. You didn't think that you were hurting me by leaving me alone with mom. You thought that you were protecting me. Just like mom thought that she was protecting me by keeping me away from you. You guys didn't do anything wrong with the way that you raised me. I was going to become who I am regardless of how you guys raised me. I don't want you to think that I blame you. It's not your fault, dad. We were destined to follow different paths in life. You meant to be in the stars, and I was meant to be here. Things turned out okay for us. That was what you meant when you said that we would always have the stars. Everything would be okay. Thank you for showing me that. It was the kindest thing that anyone did for me. I love you, dad. Tell my baby that I can't wait to meet them." Sebastian walked out onto the balcony as he wrapped his arms around her with her face hidden in his chest before he guided her into the house. She fell asleep in his arms for the rest of the night.

Chapter Forty-Five
(Winter 1970 – Paris, France)

She woke up the next morning as Sebastian got dressed for work where she pulled him into a long kiss that they broke apart from each other before Sebastian rushed out of the door to make it to work on time. Once she got dressed for the first time in weeks, she packed her bags for Sasha's bachelorette trip to Italy that Amelia planned for her where they were gone for a week with her cousins Amelia, Sasha, Nina, and Juliet. Anastasia couldn't come with them since she gave birth to her son Tolya Kotov in New York and Poppy was stuck at home with two small children in York. After she finished packing for bags for her trip, she ate breakfast in the kitchen that their chef made for them where their driver packed their bags in the back of the car before he dropped her off at the airport where Amelia and Juliet waited for her. She slept with her head resting on Amelia's shoulder for the flight until Amelia gently nudged her awake when their plane landed in Paris in the evening before she followed Amelia and Juliet over to where Sasha waited for them. Sasha sprinted over towards them as she pulled her into a tight hug with her face hidden in her chest where Sasha grabbed onto her growing stomach before Sasha and Amelia hugged each other while she went into the bathroom to vomit up her lunch. After Sasha drove them to her house that she lived in with Gabriel, she opted out of going to dinner with the family since she was so exhausted that she couldn't keep her eyes open before she slept in one of the guest bedrooms for the rest of the night. She woke up the next morning to puke a few times into the toilet connected to the room that she shared with Amelia where she packed up her suitcase before she joined her cousins in the kitchen. After she pulled Ivan and Jamie into tight hugs with her kissing Antonine and Christophe on their cheeks, she ate breakfast that Gabriel made for them where she grabbed her bags from the guest bedroom before she got on a plane to Sicily with Sasha, Amelia, Juliet, and Nina, who arrived in Paris last night. She slept with her head resting on Sasha's shoulder for the flight to Sicily until Sasha gently nudged her awake where they got off of the plane before they went into a taxi to their hotel in the city.

Since there were over a hundred stairs to get to their hotel, Juliet helped her up the stairs since she was three months pregnant, and she wasn't able to go up the stairs without being short of breath. This was a lot easier to do than the last time that she was in Italy. By the time that they got to the top of the stairs, Amelia and Nina were getting comfortable in their shared hotel room as she got unpacked in her shared hotel room with Juliet where she walked down the hall to see that Sasha was sharing a hotel room with Chloe. She instantly ran into her hotel room where Juliet was surprised to see her back from the bathroom before she told Juliet that Sasha invited Chloe to the trip. Before Juliet got a chance to say anything to her, Sasha walked into her room with Chloe following behind her when Sasha told them that they were going to be late for their boat tour of the island. She intensely stared at Chloe as Juliet grabbed onto her arm before they went down the dreaded stairs from hell to the ship docks. After she spent most of the day ignoring Chloe on the small boat, Sasha took them to a restaurant that served them fresh seafood where they ate in soft conversation. After a while of her silently staring at Chloe, she pulled Sasha aside when she asked her why Chloe was at her bachelorette party where Sasha told her that they were friends with each other before Sasha moved away from the topic like she never brought it up to her. When she had to go back up the dreaded stairs from hell to her hotel room, Chloe offered to help her up the stairs as she let her grab onto her arm when Chloe apologized to her about causing her last overdose and that she was happy to see that she was doing good. She was in the middle of the worst workout in her life, and she couldn't think straight at the moment. She didn't know why Chloe chose this moment to have a deep conversation with her out of all times. She told Chloe that she was glad that she was doing well too. She heard from Oliver that she went to prison for a short amount of time. By the time that they were at the top of the stairs, they were laughing together as she cursed Sasha for choosing a place with only stairs when she was pregnant where they went their separate ways before they went to sleep for the rest of the night. The rest of Sasha's bachelorette's trip was uneventful except for the time that Nina split the back of head when she jumped off of a boat into the ocean before they decided that Nina didn't need stitches on the back of her head. Even though she was weary of Chloe's presence at first, she was glad that Sasha invited her to come with them since she missed having Chloe's friendship in her life before they were inseparable by the end of the week. On their last night in Sicily, they went out to the beach after the sun went down in the sky where they swam in the ocean for hours until they went up the dreaded stairs from hell one more time where they got a few hours of sleep before their flights home in the morning. She said an emotional goodbye to Chloe who was living in Milan as she said goodbye to Sasha who was going to Milan with Chloe before she left to get on a plane to London with Amelia, Juliet, and Nina. The next time that they were going to see Sasha and Chloe was for Sasha's wedding day that was in Paris. When their plane landed in London the next morning, her cousin Sean picked them up from the airport where they stayed at his house for the night before they got on a plane to the states the next morning. While they were in London for the day, she spent time with her nieces Ashely and Alyssa and her nephew Arthur in the living room. Sean spent most of the night talking to his sister Amelia about what was going on in their lives where they ate dinner together in the kitchen before they slept in the guest bedrooms for the rest of the night. Once Sean dropped them off at the airport, she was sick in the bathroom for the flight to New York. Her parents picked them up from the airport where she slept in their guest bedroom for the rest of the afternoon before she joined her parents in the living room for a movie night. They talked about how she felt in the second trimester of her pregnancy. After she spent time with her parents in New York for a few days, she got on a plane to Los Angeles by herself since Amelia and Juliet left to go home early since they had to get back their lives. Once her plane landed in Los Angeles, Sebastian pulled her into his arms with her face hidden in his chest where he placed his hands on her growing stomach before their driver took them home.

Sebastian went back to work at the studio as she kept herself busy while she prepared for the baby's nursery in one of their guest bedrooms. She went to Dr. Taylor's office once a week and she went to doctor's appointments for the baby in between her preparing the house for the baby. It was the week before they were supposed to leave to go to France for Sasha's wedding that Sebastian finished filming his last movie. He spent those days with her in the house as he helped her build the crib in the nursery that she worked on all by herself. They were awake for most of the night building the crib and putting together the stroller for the baby. They stayed in their bed for most of the day as Sebastian talked to their baby as she silently listened to him with a smile on her face before they packed their bags for their trip to Paris. At her last appointment, her doctor told her that she was safe to fly on an airplane as long as she felt comfortable to do it where she told Sasha the news that she could fly in for her wedding since her doctor said that it was fine. Sasha told her that she better fly in for the wedding or else she was going to have to get a new maid of honor in less than a week before her wedding day. She threw up in the bathroom a few times the next morning when she followed Sebastian to the car where their driver drove them to the airport before their driver dropped them off outside of the airport. As soon as they spotted Oliver's family, Amelia, and Troy at their gate, she pulled Oliver into a tight hug as she hid her face into his chest where he placed his hands on her growing stomach to comment how much bigger she was since the last time that they saw each other before Oliver and Sebastian hugged each other in soft conversation with each other. For the flight to New York, she slept with her head leaning onto Sebastian's shoulder until he gently nudged her awake when their plane landed in New York where she pulled her parents into a tight hug once they were out of the airport before her mum drove them to their house with Sebastian and Oliver's family. They ate dinner at Uncle Sam's house where everyone marveled about how pregnant she was since the last time that they saw her. She prepared for their night flight to Paris with Sebastian, Amelia, and Troy since her family were flying into Paris in a few days. She was coming to Paris earlier than the family because Sasha asked if they could come early to help her with the last-minute details of the wedding planning. She really needed to get her dress refitted since she was more pregnant since the last time that she was in Paris visiting Sasha. For their overnight flight to Paris, she slept with her head leaning onto Sebastian's shoulder as he slept with his head leaning onto the window until Amelia woke them up when their plane landed in Paris the next morning. As soon as they got off of the plane, they saw Sasha on the other side of the room as Amelia grabbed onto her hand where she was dragged over to Sasha before she pulled them into a long hug that she didn't let go of until her baby aggressively kicked her stomach. She placed Amelia and Sasha's hands onto her stomach, so that they could feel the baby kicking her where Sasha marveled at how she was glowing in her pregnancy before Gabriel told them that they would be at the car waiting for them. Once Gabriel dropped off Sebastian and Troy at the house, he drove them to an elderly woman's house that was fitting their dresses for them as she changed into her maid of honor dress that was too tight on her where an elderly woman worked on expanding the material around her stomach while she talked in French with Gabriel and Sasha who was fluent in the language after the time that she spent in France over the years.

When the elderly women left with Gabriel to grab dinner, they drank tea that the elderly woman served them as they sat down in her beautifully designed living room when Amelia told them not to tell anyone about it, but Troy proposed to her a few weeks ago. They instantly pulled Amelia into a tight hug as they shouted from excitement about her engagement before the elderly woman shushed them before she walked into the house with homemade pasta in her hands. Once they got to Gabriel's house in the evening, Gabriel walked in the house with his brothers Christophe and Antonine and her cousins Jamie and Ivan following behind him before they told them about Amelia and Troy's engagement. After Jamie and Ivan pulled Amelia into a tight hug with their arms around her, Gabriel grabbed a bottle of wine from 1951 that he was saving for a special occasion that they drank outside by the bonfire. Even though Sebastian didn't like her drinking a glass of wine with her being pregnant, she convinced him to let her have a few sips of his glass of wine as a compromise since she didn't want to be left out of the party. She woke up the next morning with Sebastian's arms around her as she joined Ivan on the balcony where she convinced Ivan to let her bum a cigarette off of him that he took back from her after she got a few puffs of it since Sebastian didn't want her to smoke when she was pregnant. Since their family was flying into the city, Troy and Sebastian were tasked with being a taxi service for them. Sebastian was tasked by Gabriel to take their families to the hotels that they set up for them. They were the only people staying with Sasha and Gabriel at their house since they only had two guest bedrooms that they were already using before she went to the wedding venue with Amelia and Sasha. While Sasha was busy dictating where the flowers went on the tables in French, she helped Amelia set the tables for the afterparty that was taking place in Gabriel's parents vineyard in the outskirts of Paris. After they spent the afternoon at the vineyard, Sasha drove them to the house where she met up with Sebastian, her parents, Uncle Sam, and Aunt Valeria. They were impressed with how well Sasha was doing for herself. She convinced Sebastian to let her drink a sip of his wine before her mother scolded her in front of the table. She slept in his arms for the rest of the night. She woke up on the morning of the wedding as Sasha opened up the blinds in their bedroom where she hid her face into Sebastian's chest before Sasha yelled at her in French to get out of bed. Even though she heard Sasha talking in French, she was shocked that Sasha was so good at it. She knew enough French from the last few days that Sasha called her chienne. It was the word bitch in French. She didn't know whether to be offended or laugh about it.

Sasha drove her cousins and Chloe who was one of bridesmaids despite their family's confusion about their relationship to Gabriel's parents' vineyard where they got ready for the wedding together in the chapel. Gabriel, his brothers, her cousins Ivan and Jamie, Sebastian, and Troy got to the wedding venue where they got ready in the tasting room. Their families were going to meet them at the venue in the evening. After they spent most of the day laughing and chasing each other around the vineyard, it was time for the wedding to start as she grabbed onto Sebastian's arm before they went down the aisle in the grassy field with their families watching them. Sasha walked down the aisle with Uncle Sam's arm around her. Sean officiated the ceremony for them as Sasha and Gabriel said their written vows to each other where they said them to each other in French before they said it to each other in English. As soon as Gabriel dipped Sasha into a long kiss, she cheered with their families as Gabriel grabbed into Sasha's hand where they ran down the aisle before they went into the barn for the afterparty. They ate a delicious meal that was catered by Gabriel's friend that ran the restaurant that they went to last night. Most people danced together where the children ran around the room chasing each other before most adults drank wine and talked to each other about nothing. Once she danced with Sebastian's arms around her for a while, her feet throbbed from being on them all day. She dragged Sebastian to the vineyard where she took a seat on a patio chair before Sebastian took a seat next to her. After she propped up her feet on the unlit fire pit, Sebastian grabbed onto her hand as she leaned her head on his shoulder with her eyes closed when he asked her with concern laced in his voice, "Are you okay honey? It was a long day."

When she opened her eyes, she softly groaned in pain as she leaned back on the chair when she told him with a smile on her face, "I'm okay, Bash. It was a good day. My body isn't used to this much activity. I'm happy for Sasha and Gabriel. I hope that they have a happy life together. Sasha deserves someone who loves her like Gabriel loves her. Did Troy tell you about his engagement to Amelia?"

Sebastian nodded his head at her as he tightened his grip on her hands when he responded to her with a smirk on his face, "He told me about it at the airport before we left for New York. They wanted to keep the news to themselves. That's what Troy told me. I told him that I understood that feeling since we had the baby to ourselves for a few weeks before anyone found out about it. How is our baby doing? Our baby is very active at night. They don't want to let mommy sleep. How do you get any sleep?"

She placed her hands on her growing stomach when she responded to him with a wide grin on her face, "I don't sleep anymore. This little one won't let me sleep. They do acrobatics in mommy's tummy every night. It's okay, Bash. I like to spend time with our baby when they keep me up all night. It's what our future lives are going to look like after the baby is born."

Sebastian placed his hand on her growing stomach when he

responded to her like it was a secret between them, "Looks like someone's waking up. Aren't you, little bee? You can't wait to torment your mommy all night. Who do you think that the baby is going to look like? Me or you? Are you going to look like your mommy, little bee? Or are you going to be like your daddy?"

She shrugged her shoulders at him when she responded to him in a soft voice, "They are probably going to look like you despite me growing them in my body and birthing them into the world. At least they will be handsome like their daddy if they look like you. Little Bee? I love that nickname. It's cute. What do you want to name our baby? I know what I want to name them, but I want you to go first."

They held onto her stomach together when he responded to her with excitement laced in his voice like he was waiting for her to ask him this question, "I have a few ideas for the baby's name. For boys, I like Noah or Benjamin. The nickname would be Benny. There are no good nicknames for Noah. For girls, I like Tabatha or Beatrice. The nicknames would be Tabby or Betts. Or we do Bee as a nickname for Beatrice. Wasn't that your grandmother's name?"

She shook her head at him when she responded to him with a smirk on her face, "My grandmother's name was Bertha, but Beatrice as a middle name would be nice. I don't love Beatrice as a first name. Why does our child need to have a nickname? I don't have a nickname. No one has called me Bella instead of Isabella. Just because you have a nickname doesn't mean that everyone needs a nickname. I hate all of them except for Tabatha and Noah. Tabby is a good nickname."

Sebastian tightened his grip on her hands that were on her stomach when he responded to her with a frown on her face, "Your mother is called Ellie instead of Ella. Our child needs to have a nickname to keep up with the family tradition. If you hate my names, then what names do you like for our child?"

She crossed her arms on her chest when she responded to her in a stern voice like they were in the middle of a business negotiation, "Only my aunts and uncles call her Ellie. My mum has only called her Ella. That's not a valid point, Bash. For boy names, I love the name Archie. I know that it sounds incredibly British, but I happen to be British in case you forgot about that. I love the name Petey. How about

Daphne? There are some nicknames that came out of that."

Sebastian grabbed onto her hands when he responded to her with a wide grin on his face, "Here's the compromise honey. If the baby is a boy, it's going to be named Noah William Foster-Brewer. If the baby is a girl, it's going to be named Daphne Beatrice Foster-Brewer. How does that sound?"

She blinked back tears that fell down her face when she responded to him in a soft voice, "William? That's so special, Bash. I love those names. We'll know what to name our baby when they are born. I hope that it's a boy, so that it will make my mother cry when I make his middle name my dad's name. That would be special for her. We should go back to the house to celebrate our success in finding a name for our baby. What do you think, Bash?" Before she could finish her sentence, Sebastian pulled her into a desperate kiss as she instantly accepted it from him where they didn't let go of each other until they heard the barn door open near them. After he helped her up to her feet, he guided her to one of the many cars in the driveway where he got into the driver's seat as she got into the passenger seat where he drove them to Gabriel's house before she pulled him into a long kiss as soon as they were alone in the house. Once they were in the guest bedroom, Sebastian slammed the door behind him as she pulled him into a desperate kiss that led them laying down on the bed with her on top of him before he unzipped the back of her dress as she unbuttoned his shirt. After they made up for lost time in their bed, she laid down her head on his chest as he wrapped his arms around her when she told him that she loved him where he told her that he loved her too before they fell asleep for the rest of the night.

CHAPTER FORTY-SIX
(SPRING 1970 – LOS ANGELES, CALIFORNIA)

She got on a plane to London with Sebastian, Amelia, and Troy the next morning. She slept with her head leaning onto Sebastian's shoulder before he woke her up when their plane landed in London in the afternoon. After they checked into their hotel for the night, she changed into the only dress that fit her in this late stage of her pregnancy where they ate dinner at their favorite restaurant before she fell asleep in with Sebastian's arms around her. When she woke up the next morning with the sudden urge to vomit, she sprinted towards the toilet where she puked up her dinner that she ate last night as Sebastian held back her hair for her when he helped her off of the ground before they packed their bags for their flight to New York. After they checked out of their hotel in London, they got on their flight to New York where she was sick the entire time. When their plane landed in New York that evening, they took a taxi to her parent's house where they stayed in her parents' bedroom while Amelia and Troy slept in the guest bedroom before they got on a plane to Los Angeles the next morning where she was even sicker than she was before. When their plane landed in California, their driver drove them to her doctor's office. Sebastian was concerned that she wasn't able to keep anything down in the last forty-eight hours. When they arrived at her doctor's office, Sebastian helped her walk into the doctor's office since she was so dizzy that she couldn't keep herself up when her doctor gave her IV fluids in the office before she felt like she wasn't going to pass out anymore. Her doctor wrote her a prescription for anti-nausea medication that was supposed to help feel better where their driver dropped them off at the house before she slept in their bed for the rest of the day. Sebastian checked on her every hour to make sure that she was breathing. After a few days on the anti-nausea medication, she felt better again when she went back to working in the baby's nursery. Sebastian supervised her the entire time to make sure that she wasn't going to pass out like she did in the airport in New York. Sebastian stayed home with her for a few weeks before he filmed a new movie that he started working on before they left for Paris. She decorated the nursery in a bumble bee design that they were obsessed with. Amelia came over to her house to see the nursey with Juliet and her nieces Posey and Eleanor with her where Posey pointed to her large stomach when she asked her how the baby was going to come out of her. Juliet dragged her daughters out of the room since no one wanted to explain the birds and the bees. She was alone with Amelia in the nursery. Amelia told her that she couldn't tell anyone until she told her parents about it. Amelia found out that she was pregnant when they were in Paris where she pulled Amelia into a tight hug before she asked her about what she was going to do about her wedding dress that she picked out in Paris that they took home. Even though her being pregnant on her wedding day felt like the end of the world, Amelia told her that they were going to elope since they didn't have time to plan a big wedding with a baby.

Amelia told her that her parents were coming to California in a few weeks for what they thought was going to be a fitting for her wedding dress, but they were getting married to each other at the courthouse. When Sebastian came home from work in the evening, she told him about Amelia's untimely pregnancy and that Amelia and Troy were going to elope in the courthouse when Aunt Sylvia and Uncle James were in town. Sebastian was surprised about this news. He told her that they would come to the courthouse with her family to support them before he called Troy to ask about what was going on downstairs in the kitchen. She called Sasha from their bedroom that they got back from her honeymoon in Switzerland about if she could come to Amelia and Troy's wedding at the courthouse. Sasha told her that she could be in the states for the wedding if that was what Amelia wanted where she told her to keep it to herself before she fell asleep with his arms around her for the rest of the night. When Aunt Sylvia and Uncle James came to visit them, Sasha and Gabriel stayed with them for a few weeks since they hadn't gone back to work. They kept the wedding from Amelia's parents until the second day there when Amelia told her parents about her pregnancy and that they were eloping at the courthouse that afternoon. Even though her parents were caught off guard, they pulled her into a tight hug as they promised her that it was going to be okay before they met up at the courthouse. Since Amelia, Troy, and their parents were the only people that came into the room with the judge, she waited outside of the courthouse with her hands on a large stomach before Amelia, Troy, and their parents came out of the courthouse with a certificate in their hands. After Gabriel took wedding pictures of everyone in front of the courthouse, Amelia and Troy went to their house with their parents where she went to her house with Sebastian, Sasha, and Gabriel before she slept in their bedroom for the rest of the day. She wasn't sleeping at night with how uncomfortable she was in her pregnancy. When she complained to her mother about how uncomfortable she was, her mother understood what she was talking about since she felt the same way when she was pregnant with her. She wasn't able to bend down. She couldn't tie her shoes since she couldn't see anything over her stomach. Sebastian helped her with everything that she couldn't do by herself. In the last month of her pregnancy, she only left the house for her doctor's appointments, and her sessions with Dr. Taylor's office since she didn't have energy to do anything. She wasn't sick because of the medicine that her doctor prescribed her when they got back from Paris. She couldn't do anything around the house without needing to take a two-hour nap where Sebastian did everything that she didn't get the chance to do. When she went to her last doctor's appointment until the baby was going to be born, her parents went on a plane to Los Angeles where they stayed with them for as long as she wanted them to be there with her. Sebastian was off of work until she felt comfortable enough to be alone at home with the baby without him or her parents at home. On the week of her due date, she got Braxton hicks throughout the night. She ignored them since her doctor assured that it didn't mean that she was in labor. After she had Braxton hicks for several days in a row, she felt things that she never felt before when her stomach suddenly looked low on her body. She was worried that it was time.

Her mother told her that morning at breakfast that she was going to go into labor that day. She didn't want to believe that her mother was right, so she went through her day like she normally did with her doing the bare minimum until she passed out on the couch in the afternoon where she was woken up when she peed all over the couch. She urgently called out for Sebastian and her parents as her parents sprinted into the room with Sebastian following behind them when her mother told her with a smile on her face that it was time to go to the hospital before Sebastian ran over to help her off of the couch. As soon as Sebastian helped her off of the couch, she tightly grabbed onto his hand as she breathed through a contraction with her parents throwing their bags into the back of the car before Sebastian helped her into the car. She worked through a contraction with her mother and Sebastian holding onto her hands. Once their driver dropped them off at the hospital, she screamed through a contraction as Sebastian sprinted into the hospital to grab a wheelchair from the lobby. Her parents helped her into the wheelchair before Sebastian pushed her into the hospital. The nurse took them into their own room where her doctor waited for her. Sebastian called her on the way to the hospital. The nurses transferred her over to the bed before she screamed through another contraction with Sebastian and her mother holding onto her hands. Her mum told her family that she was in labor where she joined them in the room as she placed her hands on her shoulders. She pushed through another contraction with the nurses counting down how long she pushed for until she let out a shaky breath when the contractions went away every few minutes. Her doctor came into the room to examine her when she told her that she was about ready to push out the baby. She cried into Sebastian's chest that she couldn't do it. Her mother told her that she didn't have a choice since the baby was coming out of her whether she was ready or not. Sebastian kissed her on her forehead when he promised her that everything was going to be okay with tears falling down their faces. She looked up at the nurses when she told them that she was ready to push this baby out of her body before the nurses counted down her to start pushing again. She pushed with everything that she had in her for over two hours with

Sebastian and her parents motivating her the entire time. The doctor told her that she saw the baby's head coming out as she told her that she needed to push one more time. She tightened her grip on Sebastian and her mother's hands before she pushed through the last contraction with the last bit of energy that was left in her body. As soon as she heard her baby cry for the first time, she desperately sobbed into Sebastian's chest as he kissed her on the lips with tears falling down his face. The nurse moved her crying baby away from her when Sebastian said to her broken in between his sobs with a smile on his face, "You did it, Isabella. Our baby is here. I love you. We're parents."

She pulled out of Sebastian's chest as her mother pulled her into a tight hug with her face hidden in her chest before her mum placed her crying baby on her chest when her mum said to her daughter, "Good job honey. You did it. Do you want to know what gender your baby is?"

She nodded her head at her mum with Sebastian holding onto her hands when her mother told her with excitement laced in her voice, "You have a baby girl. Congratulations on your daughter, baby girl. What's her name going to be?"

She gently ran her fingers on her daughter's skin as she connected her pinky onto her daughter's pinky when she responded to her mother with a smile on her face, "Her name is Daphne Beatrice Foster-Brewer. Hello, little bee. Welcome to the world. Mommy and daddy love you so much."

Her parents went into the lobby to give them a moment of privacy. She laid in the bed with Daphne peacefully sleeping on her chest where she looked up at Sebastian who was sitting in the seat next to her when she whispered to him not waking up Daphne, "We did this, Bash. Daphne is our baby. You made it all worth it, little bee. This was worth nine months of pain. You got daddy wrapped around your finger. Don't you, little bee?"

Daphne instantly cried from her chest while she shushed her as she brought her baby to her chest where Daphne latched onto it before she gently ran her hands down her back when Sebastian said to her with him grabbing onto Daphne's tiny hand, "Watching you give birth to our daughter makes me love you even more than I thought that

I could. We should have ten more of these. Daphne needs siblings, Isabella. We don't want her to be alone."

She rolled her eyes at Sebastian as she kissed Daphne on the top of her head when she responded to them with a smirk on her face, "Don't listen to your daddy, little bee. He doesn't know what he's talking about. That is the last thing that I want to think about, Bash. I just had our daughter an hour ago. She can be an only child for a while as long as I'm considered. Do you want to burp her while I go to the bathroom?"

Sebastian grabbed Daphne from her chest as he gently hit her on her back to burp her where she slowly got out of the bed before she went to use the bathroom for the first time since she gave birth to her daughter. When she came back from the bathroom, her parents were back in the room with bags of food for them to eat where she thanked her mother before she brought the food counter to the bed with her. Once Sebastian burped Daphne after her last feeding, he handed Daphne to her grandma who was falling asleep on her chest. Sebastian took a seat next to her with his own counter of food before her mother took a seat next to her on the other side of the bed when she said to them with her takeaway food halfway eaten, "She's such a sweet baby. You are lucky that she likes to sleep since you were allergic to sleep at that age. I'm sorry to disappoint you, baby girl. Daphne looks like Bash more than you."

Sebastian laughed into his hands as she shook her head at him when she told her mother with a frown on her face, "She's just a newborn, mom. It's too early to tell who she looks like. You two are a menace together. Remind me to never get you guys alone again. Conspiring against me in front of my own daughter." She finished the food in her takeaway dish and Sebastian's takeaway dish at the same time. Once her parents went back to her house, she fed Daphne from her chest as Sebastian burped her before they placed Daphne into her bassinet next to the bed. After Sebastian pulled her into a kiss, she fell asleep for the rest of the night.

CHAPTER FORTY-SEVEN
(SUMMER 1970 – LOS ANGELES, CALIFORNIA)

She woke up to Daphne crying early in the morning where Sebastian rocked her in his arms before he placed Daphne on her chest. After Daphne latched onto her chest, she gently ran her hands down her back where Sebastian grabbed onto Daphne's hand before a nurse walked into the room to check on the baby. Once Daphne ate from her chest with Sebastian burping her, the nurse took Daphne to the scale to weigh her as Sebastian pulled her into a tight hug with her face hidden in his chest where the nurse placed Daphne onto her chest before Daphne fell asleep again. Her parents walked into the room with Amelia, Oliver, Juliet, and Troy walking behind them where Oliver made a joke about her making it through the dark side before he pulled her into a tight hug with her face hidden in his chest. Oliver pulled away from her when Daphne cried from her chest as she fed her for the second time that morning where Oliver pulled Sebastian into a long hug before she asked Sebastian to burp Daphne. As soon as Sebastian burped Daphne over his shoulder, he handed Daphne over to Oliver who passed her onto Juliet before Amelia and Troy held her in their arms. She took a nap since Daphne was distracted with her aunts and her uncles. Daphne laid on top of her grandma's chest with her grandmum's hand on her back where Sebastian took a nap on the couch. Once Daphne cried for her from the other side of the room, her mother placed Daphne in her arms as Daphne latched onto her chest before her mum placed her into the bassinet once she burped her. Sebastian woke up a few hours later where Daphne slept on his chest. The nurses encouraged him to do skin to skin with Daphne before her parents left them alone for the rest of the night. They spent a few more days in the hospital where Sebastian's parents visited them over the weekend. Uncle Stan and Thomas came to see Daphne on the last day that they were in the hospital. Once they were discharged from the hospital, Sebastian pushed Daphne downstairs in her stroller as a nurse pushed her in a wheelchair before their driver drove them home. After Sebastian helped her out of the car, he carried Daphne into the house where they got emotional about Daphne being in the house before they went into their bedroom with Daphne. It took them a few weeks to get used to their new lives. She fell into the routine of having a newborn baby. She was constantly feeding her, or she was wondering when she was going to feed her again. Daphne slept through most of the night except for a few times that she woke her up to feed her in the middle of the night. Regardless of how much it hurt her, she stuck to breastfeeding. Her mother encouraged her to do it since she did too.

She was glad that her parents stayed with them to help them adjust to having a baby. They felt unprepared for what it meant to have a baby. It was constant work to make sure that Daphne was fed or burped after her feedings. They kept Daphne on a strict feeding schedule to make sure that she was gaining weight that the doctor encouraged them to do. Her cousins visited her a few times a week, but they mostly came over to their house to see the baby. They were fine with that since Daphne was already loved by her family. Sasha and Gabriel visited them from France with her cousins Jamie and Ivan and their boyfriends to meet the baby. Sasha gushed about how cute that Daphne was before Gabriel told her that they would have their own baby soon enough. When she asked Sasha if she was pregnant, Sasha nodded her head at her as she pulled her into a sudden hug that she didn't let go until Daphne cried in Ivan's arms for her before he placed Daphne in her arms to calm her down again. On the last weekend of her parents living with them, they had a date night with Oliver, Juliet, Amelia, Troy, Sasha, and Gabriel.

The boys went back to Paris for a fashion event that Sasha wasn't taking part in since she was taking time off from work during her pregnancy. After they went out to eat at their favorite restaurant, they went to the movie theater to watch a new movie that was all the rage in the film industry where they drank glasses of wine that was served to them with chicken wings in hot sauce. She smoked in the theatre as they watched the movie on the big screen. That was nice since she wasn't allowed to smoke during her pregnancy. Once they dropped Oliver and Juliet off at their house, she said goodbye to Sasha and Gabriel who were getting on a plane back to Paris in the morning where they dropped them off at Amelia and Troy's house before their driver took them home with Daphne waiting for them. When it was time for her parents to go back to New York, she cried in her mother's arms when Sebastian pulled her away from her mother before they left for the airport. After they got back to their house, Sebastian took care of Daphne for the rest of the day except for when she needed to eat where she nursed her in between her naps that she took throughout the day before Sebastian laid down in their bed with Daphne sleeping in the bassinet next to their bed. Once she spent most of the night with Daphne nursing from her chest, Daphne slept in her chest as she gently ran her hands up and down her back in admiration for her before she fell asleep for the rest of the night. She woke up to Sebastian softly talking to Daphne the next morning when he told her that their little bee was crying for her where she nursed Daphne from her chest before Sebastian served her breakfast in bed. By the time that they got out of bed, the sun was setting where Sebastian watched a movie in the living room with Daphne asleep on her chest before she fell asleep with her head leaning on his chest for the rest of the night. Sebastian told her that he wanted to work on a movie where she told him that she could be alone with Daphne. Sebastian told her that he would be home for bedtime before they talked about Daphne grabbing onto her hair that morning.

On the first day that Sebastian went back to work, he woke up Daphne and he gave her a morning bath before he left her alone with Daphne for the rest of the day. She was going to be okay with the baby since all that Daphne did was nurse and sleep. She underestimated how bad a baby's fusing was to deal with. Daphne cried from the moment that Sebastian left the house until the time that he came home from work. When Sebastian walked into the house in the evening, she was having a mental breakdown about how to stop Daphne from crying. She handed Daphne over to Sebastian who screamed louder in his arms before he took her into their bedroom. While Sebastian failed at calming down their baby, she locked herself into the bathroom to get space from Daphne. Her daughter was on her last nerve since she wouldn't stop crying all day. She thought about how she would do anything to get high. She scolded herself since she wasn't allowed to think selfish thoughts like that anymore. She was a mother, and good mothers don't want to do drugs while they take care of their babies. The only mother that she knew that did drugs while taking care of her children was Jade who was in prison for physically assaulting her husband and emotionally abusing her children. After she hid in the bathroom for several hours, she heard a soft knock on the door when Sebastian told her that he got Daphne to fall asleep in their bed when he asked her if she could let him in the bathroom where she opened the door for him before Sebastian pulled her into a tight hug with her hiding her face into his chest. They were only clinging to each other for a few moments before Daphne screamed from their bedroom where she let out a frustrated sigh as she went into the kitchen before she called Oliver to see what to do about this with Sebastian following behind her. She told Oliver that Daphne cried no matter what they did to calm her. Oliver told them that she was probably teething and that they needed to give her something frozen to soothe her gums, where she thanked Oliver for the advice before she ran upstairs to bring down Daphne into the kitchen as Sebastian grabbed a bag of frozen vegetables from the freezer. As soon as she walked into the kitchen with Daphne screaming in her arms, she gently rocked her back and forth in her arms where Sebastian placed the frozen bag of vegetables into Daphne's mouth before her cries were replaced with Daphne softly cooing in her arms. Once they rocked Daphne to sleep in her bassinet, they laid down in their bed with their arms around each other as they watched Daphne sleeping for the first time that day where they softly whispered to each other before she fell asleep for the rest of the night.

Whatever sleep that she thought that she would get was short lived. They woke up to Daphne screaming at the top of lungs in the middle of the night before Sebastian brought Daphne into another room to let her get some sleep. Even though Sebastian and Daphne were in the living room, she could hear her daughter crying from their bedroom where she hit her head on her pillows until she went downstairs where Daphne screamed in Sebastian's arms. They spent the next few hours trying to calm down Daphne where she cried to the point of exhaustion where they slept on the couch that night since they didn't want to wake Daphne by moving her into their bedroom. They didn't get more than a few hours of sleep before he went to work that morning where she was left with a screaming baby. After Daphne cried no matter what she did to calm her down, she called her doctor when she asked him what was wrong with her baby where he told her that she could bring her into the office for an appointment that afternoon before she told their driver to take them to the doctor's office. For the drive to the doctor's office, Daphne cried in her car seat as she gently ran her hands up and down her back to comfort her before their driver turned the music up as loud as possible to drown out the crying baby. When their driver dropped them off at the doctor's office, her baby cried in the lobby as she placed Daphne on her chest to calm her down where Daphne looked up at her with a look of sadness on her face that broke her heart. Once they were called to an examination room, Daphne stopped crying for a moment as she grabbed onto her mother's thumbs before she cried again when she was moved out of their seat. As soon as the doctor examined Daphne, he handed her baby back to her as she placed Daphne on top of her chest. Her cries were muffled into her chest when he told her that Daphne had colic, and her stomach was upset. Her doctor told her that the best way to help with Daphne's colic was to give her a few drops of gripe water to calm her stomach before she nursed her at night and in the morning. After they left the doctor's office with Daphne's prescription, she gave her a few drops of gripe water that the doctor gave her where she nursed Daphne for a long time before she fell asleep in her arms. When Sebastian walked into the living room, he closed the door behind him where she woke her up from her nap as he took a seat next to her on the couch before he wrapped his arms around her when he whispered making sure not to wake up Daphne who was asleep on her chest, "Is she sleeping? What did the doctor give her?"

She ran her hands up and down her back as she looked up at

Sebastian when she responded to him in a soft voice, "She has colic. He gave me gripe water to give to her. I think that it's magic. I don't know what's in it, but it's helping her. How was work?"

Sebastian kissed Daphne in the back of her head as he grabbed onto her hand with his thumb when he responded to her with a look of exhaustion on his face, "It was a tiring day. I missed my girls. I was worried about my little bee. Thank you for taking her to the doctors today. I couldn't take it anymore. I know that you couldn't either. I'm sorry that I left you when she was like this. I didn't want you to feel like I enjoyed it. I was miserable the entire time."

She pecked Sebastian on the lips before she looked down at the sleeping baby in her arms when she responded to him with a frown on her face, "It's fine, Bash. Thanks for staying up with me last night. It would've been so much worse if you weren't there with me. There was a moment at the doctor's office today that she looked up at me with the saddest look on her face. She was asking me to help her. I almost cried. It was so heartbreaking. She's never looked at me like that before."

Daphne fussed in her arms as Sebastian placed Daphne on top of his chest where he grabbed onto her hand before he brought Daphne into their bedroom to sleep for the rest of the night. She blinked back tears that fell down her face with her face hidden into one of the pillows on the couch. Once Sebastian walked into the living room, he hurried over to the couch as he ran his hands up and down her back when he asked her with concern laced in voice, "What's wrong honey? Is it Daphne? Little bee's okay. You don't have to worry about her."

She shook her head at him as she threw herself into his arms with her sobbing into her chest as he wrapped his arms around her when he told her with sadness laced in his voice, "It's okay honey. You don't have to talk about it. You've gone through a lot of changes in the last three months that would overwhelm anyone."

She shook her head at him with her face hidden in his chest when she confessed to him in between her sobs, "That's not what this is about, Bash. I'm glad that Daphne's okay. I never had someone look at me the way that she looked at me at the doctor's office. She looked at me like I was the only thing that mattered to her. It terrified me that I'm going to let her down. When she wouldn't stop crying yesterday, I couldn't stop thinking about how I didn't deserve to take care of someone as fragile as her. Who was I kidding about having a baby? I could never take care of myself let alone someone as defenseless as her. I felt like a horrible mother because I couldn't make her feel better. She was looking for me to help her. I froze in the moment. I didn't know what to do to help her. I've never felt more helpless in my life."

Sebastian let out a shaky breath as he pulled her out of his chest with his hands cupping her cheeks when he told her in a stern voice, "You're a wonderful mother, Isabella. Daphne loves you so much. You are her entire world. It's normal to feel like you do. Being a parent is the most rewarding experience in life, but it also is the most challenging experience too. The important thing is that you got her medicine that made her feel better and now she isn't in pain anymore. We're killing it as parents honey. Don't let your mind tell you any differently than that."

She leaned her head on his shoulder when she responded to him in a distant voice, "I thought about getting high when I was hiding in the bathroom last night. I haven't thought about getting high in a long time. That's why I felt like a horrible mother. I thought about getting high when my baby was crying for me to comfort her."

Before she gave Sebastian a chance to respond to her, she sprinted outside by the pool where she laid down on the ground with her lighting a cigarette in her hands before she inhaled the smoke from it when Sebastian told her in a serious voice with him standing above her, "I'm not upset with you, Isabella. You always run away from me when you think that I'm mad at you. Do you want to know what I think?"

She inhaled the smoke from her cigarette where Sebastian took a seat next to her when he confessed to her with a smile on his face, "I was going to tell you that you're a strong person. You've been through a lot in your life. You're the most resilient person that I know. My love for you has no bounds. I love all parts of you. Even the parts that you hate about yourself. I want our daughter to inherit your resilience, Isabella. She already adores you. You can never do anything wrong in her eyes. You are always going to be her mother. No matter what you think about yourself, we are always going to love you. Do you think that I would be mad at you for thinking about getting high? I'm not upset at you. I understand that it's hard to break bad patterns of behavior. Sometimes I think about starving myself again when I feel overwhelmed. I think about how much easier life would be if I stopped eating all together. I know that it's not true. My life was harder when I was starving myself. Was it like that with drugs?"

She inhaled the smoke from her cigarette when she responded to him with her blinking back tears that fell down her face, "It was a little like that with drugs. I've often thought about how much easier things would be if I was high. My life was a living hell when I was high. I didn't feel anything, nor did I care about anything that happened. I wanted everything to end. I didn't care how it ended for me. We have another thing in common with each other. We know what it feels like to spend a lifetime trying to disappear and forget how to live. Daphne changed a lot for me. My life isn't about me anymore. I don't want Daphne to learn these things from us. If I promise to change the way that I think about drugs, will you promise to change the way that you think about starving yourself? We have to change these parts of ourselves."

Sebastian grabbed onto her pinky before she put out the end of her cigarette into the ashtray where he pulled her into a long kiss until she broke away from him when she told her with a smirk on her face, "We're a mess, Bash. Should we check on our daughter to see if she's sleeping or not?"

Sebastian pulled her into another long kiss that ended because they were out of breath when he responded to her with a wide grin on his face, "She's screaming. I hear her from upstairs. Do you want to go?" She got Daphne from their bedroom as Sebastian got a shower where she got Daphne asleep in her bassinet with Sebastian's arms around her for the rest of the night.

Chapter Forty-Eight
(Fall 1970 – London, England)

She took care of Daphne during the day while Sebastian was at work. Daphne was back to her joyful self. Sebastian noticed that she was falling into a depressive cycle. He called Dr. Taylor on her behalf where Dr. Taylor agreed to meet up with her at his office that week. Before she left for Dr. Taylor's office, she dropped off Daphne with Juliet since she took care of her two-year-old niece Eleanor while her niece Posey was in school. She said an emotional goodbye to Daphne who could've cared less that she was leaving her. Their driver drove her to Dr. Taylor's office on the other side of town where she nervously picked at her fingers until their driver dropped her off at the office. In the first meeting with Dr. Taylor, she caught him up on what happened since she had her daughter where he listened to her with a smile on his face until he asked her what she thought about being a mother. The answer that she had for his question was complicated. She explained to him that she felt overwhelmed by being a mother in many ways that she couldn't say. When he asked her what the best things about being a mother were, she told him that the way that Daphne looked at her with love and devotion in her eyes made her feel like she could do anything. She told him that she felt like she was invincible when she held her daughter for the first time. They stayed on that topic for the rest of the session since she hadn't used the word invincible to describe herself since she was last using drugs before she stopped again from her second trip to rehab. When Dr. Taylor asked her what it felt like to be invincible, she told him being invincible felt like she was untouchable by the world. She couldn't be touched no matter what anyone did to hurt her. She was weightless like she was floating around the world. It was the feeling that she craved when she couldn't have drugs. It was the feeling that she didn't want to lose when she stopped using drugs. In the next session together the next week, Dr. Taylor asked her about the things that overwhelmed her about being a mother when she told him that she felt like she was going to traumatize her daughter the same way that her parents traumatized her. She didn't want her daughter growing up scared of the world like she was. She learned how to be scared from her mother who was afraid of everything around her. Dr. Taylor asked her what she didn't want her daughter to inherit from her before she told him that she didn't want her daughter to be scared of living her life. She didn't want her daughter to be defined by what happened to her parents. They knew that she wasn't talking about her drug addiction or her father's suicide. She defined herself with something even worse than that. From the beginning of her life until the end of her life, she would define herself as the moment that her father raped her mother. Her father was remembered as that person to the rest of the world. When Dr. Taylor asked her what she wanted her daughter to inherit from her, she told him that she wanted her daughter to be curious about people and the life around her. She wanted her daughter to be resilient like her. She wanted her daughter to be stubborn like her grandmother, compassionate like her grandmum, and bold like her grandfather.

The last one made her cry since she hadn't seen her father as bold before. He was the boldest person that was born. They talked about everything starting with how she was raising her daughter to how she felt about doing something that was for her since she was always doing everything for their daughter. Dr. Taylor convinced her to take a night to herself for the first time since she got married to her husband and she started her family. She left Sebastian alone in the house with Daphne as she played with her father on the couch before she met up with Amelia and Sasha at a restaurant to eat dinner. They got farther along in their pregnancies since the last time that they were together. After they ate dinner at their favorite restaurant, they went to their hotel room that

Sasha stayed at without Gabriel who was busy working in France where they talked until the early hours of the morning before they passed out in the bed for the rest of the night. Even though she didn't want their night to end, she missed Daphne who missed her too since she cried for her as soon as she walked through the front door of their house. She easily took on the role of a mother again. When she wasn't in her weekly sessions with Dr. Taylor at his office, she was at home taking care of her baby who was quickly growing up right in front of her eyes.

Daphne no longer suffered from colic, but she did go through a horrible teething period where she ran fevers that kept them up all night as they fussed over her until her fevers passed the next day. Daphne learned how to sit up on her own and she was obsessed with putting anything within her reach into her mouth. It made them more careful to not leave anything dangerous for her to grab off of the table. In the last visit with her parents, her mother got Daphne a wheeled cart that took with her anywhere in the house that she wanted to go, and she was constantly whining for them to put her into it. After Daphne ran over their toes with her cart, they only let Daphne play with it in the yard since no toes could get hurt with shoes on. Daphne wasn't talking to them in words. She talked to them in sign language that she learned from Eleanor who used it with Juliet when she was over at their house. She was happy that her baby was talking to her. She borrowed books from Juliet about how to teach sign language to her baby where she practiced it with her during the day before they showed Sebastian what they learned at the end of the day. She breastfed Daphne even though they were introducing baby food to her. She didn't want to lose her special time with her daughter that she got in the middle of the night and early in the morning. The doctor told her to breastfeed her for as long as Daphne was willing to do it since it was a bonding experience for them to do together. When Daphne was napping during the day, she made a scrapbook for Daphne about her milestones that she was going through since she didn't want to forget anything in her daughter's life. Even though Sebastian scoffed about it at first, he always wanted to know what she added to the scrapbook after he put Daphne to bed where they laughed about what their daughter did before they slept in their bedroom with her. When her parents found out that she was making a scrapbook for Daphne, they came to her house during their next visit with scrapbooks that her mother made for her when she was a baby. Her mother showed her the things that she kept from her childhood that made her mother emotional. That made her emotional about it too. Her mother kept everything from her childhood. Her mother kept her hospital bracelet from the day that she was born.

Her mother kept her baby hair from her first haircut in a small bag. Her mother kept her baby teeth from her childhood that she thought that the tooth fairy kept the entire time. Her mother kept her report cards from school and the drawings that she wrote about her family. The thing that made her the most emotional was that her mother kept the only toy that her father gave her. It was a wooden doll that he bought for her the last time that they saw him in England. She asked her mother if she could keep it. Her mother told her that she could keep it for the rest of her life. She knew how much it meant to her. Her mother showed her the dresses that she kept from her childhood that she wanted Daphne to wear when she was older. She promised her mother that Daphne would wear her old clothes from her childhood when she was bigger where they cried in each other's arms before Daphne woke up from her afternoon nap. Her mother showed Sebastian the artifacts from her childhood, so that he didn't feel like he was being left out since he didn't have a sentimental mother. They placed the clothes that her mother gave her into a bin on the floor of Daphne's closet for when she was older. She thanked her mother for the good memories they had together that she kept over the years before her mother promised her that there were many more things that she had at home when she was in New York. They dropped her parents off at the airport where they promised each other that they would see her in a few weeks for her cousin Alfie's wedding in London. She stayed at home taking care of Daphne as Sebastian filmed his movie in the studio where she left Daphne with Juliet when she went to her weekly appointment at Dr. Taylor's office. She spent the week of the wedding that Daphne napped in her bassinet packing for their trip to London where she struggled to fit their clothes into one bag since she was packing for two people now. She was hesitant about going to England since she never traveled on a plane with a baby. She was traveling to London without Sebastian since he wasn't able to come to the wedding due to his media tour for his latest movie. She talked about it to Sebastian who was upset that he couldn't come to Alfie's wedding. They agreed that she would go to London with her cousins and her parents helping her. Sebastian told her that he would drop everything to be in London with them if he wasn't in a contract that forced him to go on a press tour. She held Daphne in her arms on the morning of their flight to New York as she carried their suitcase down the stairs where she placed Daphne in her car seat before their driver dropped them off at the airport. After their driver dropped them off at the airport, she pushed Daphne in her stroller with their suitcase in her other hand where she met up with Oliver's family, Troy, and Amelia, who had a large stomach, at the airport. She pulled them into tight hugs before she changed Daphne's diaper in the bathroom with Posey insisting on helping her. Daphne slept in her arms for the flight to New York where she only woke up to nurse. When their plane landed in New York that afternoon, her parents picked them up at the airport as her mother grabbed Daphne out of her stroller where she smothered her with kisses until she placed Daphne in her stroller before they drove to her parent's house. While they ate dinner at her parent's house, Daphne was passed along to Uncle Sam to Aunt Valeria to Anastasia and Nina to their older children before Oliver's family, Amelia, and Troy went to Uncle Sam's house to spend the night. She slept in her parent's guest bedroom with Daphne laying down on the other side of the bed. They left for their plane to London the next morning where she placed Daphne in her stroller as her parents placed her suitcase in the back of their car before they drove to the airport to meet up with the family. Except for Joseph, who was at the end of his residency, waited at the airport for them before they got on a plane to London for the rest of the day. Unlike their flight to New York, Daphne refused to sleep where she was passed around between everyone in the family to see who could get her to sleep the longest. Uncle Sam was the only person that got Daphne to sleep for more than a few minutes. Her mother swore that Uncle Sam was the baby whisperer when she was a baby.

When their plane landed in London in the middle of the night, all the children were miserable as they were either crying in someone's arms or they were sleeping in someone's arms. It left the adults depleted dealing with cranky children this late in the night. After her cousin Sean dropped them off their family at a hotel for the night, he took them to his house where she took one of the guest bedrooms with Daphne as Amelia and Troy took the other guest bedroom before she fell asleep for the rest of the night until Daphne's cries woke her up the next morning. She ate breakfast with Sean, Polly, and their children since Amelia and Troy were still sleeping. The twins Ashley and Alyssa woke up Amelia and Troy in the guest bedroom as she dressed Daphne into the only warm outfit that she packed for her before she joined her cousins for a walk around the city. She bought warm clothes for Daphne in the shops that were among the popular streets in the city. They met up with Tommy, Lilly, and their one-year-old daughter Emmeline for dinner. Sasha and Gabriel got into London that day. After she got to Sean's house with Daphne asleep in her arms, she placed Daphne on her bed where she talked to Sebastian on the phone in Madrid before she fell asleep with Daphne in her arms for the rest of the night. On the day before the wedding, she was tasked to be on childcare duties with Amelia and Sasha who weren't involved with the wedding where they took care of their cousins twenty-four children under the age of ten while the family was at the dress rehearsal. A few of her unmarried cousins helped them with the large group of children where they took them to the park for most of the day since they had so much energy that no one knew how to calm them down. When her cousins came back to the hotel to claim their children, Amelia and Sasha told her that they weren't sure that they wanted children anymore before she told them that it was too late for that since they were halfway through their pregnancies. On the day of Alfie and Debbie's wedding, she woke up to her nieces Ashley and Alyssa jumping on her bed as she grabbed Daphne off of the bed where she kicked them out of the room before she got them ready to leave for the wedding venue. Since Debbie's family had ties to the aristocracy like Lilly's family did, they were getting married in a medieval castle that her family owned for centuries. They didn't have to worry about doing any of the work since Debbie's family hired people to do it for them. When she saw the castle for the first time, her jaw dropped in shock since it was so much bigger than she thought that it was going to be where Lilly flagged her down when she told her that the bridal suite was in the back of the castle before Lilly grabbed onto her hand to help her get there with Daphne softly cooing in her arms. Once she met the other girls in Debbie's bridal party, she joined Sasha and Amelia who were in an animated conversation with Chloe and Nina about Sasha's bachelorette trip to Sicily. After she spent most of the morning talking to her cousins and Debbie's friends, she joined the rest of her family and Debbie's family in the throne room before Debbie and her father walked down the aisle. Debbie and Alfie kissed each other in front of their families with them cheering in the background. Debbie and Alfie ran down the aisle holding onto each other's hands. She joined her family in the ballroom for the afterparty where they ate a delicious meal made by a world class chef before she danced with Daphne laughing into her chest for the rest of the evening. After Daphne fell asleep in her arms, she brought her to her mother who held her granddaughter in her arms as she danced with Posey and Oliver until she heard Daphne's loud cries for her before she took Daphne from her mother with her taking them outside for some fresh air. Once she walked outside of the castle with Daphne whining in her arms, she took a seat on a chair outside of the castle as she fed Daphne from her chest while Daphne cooed at her before she leaned onto the chair. She placed her on top of chest where she ran her hands over her arms when she whispered to Daphne like it was a secret between them, "There you go, little bee. Go back to bed. Don't worry about anything in the world. Mommy and Daddy love you so much."

She leaned onto the chair with her staring up at the stars when she said to her father with her blinking back tears that fell down her face, "She's perfect, dad. Thank you for sending her to me. She was exactly what I needed. I can't imagine my life without my little bee. I had a thought after I gave birth to her. Did you feel like this when I was born? I wanted to ask mom about it, but I knew that she wouldn't tell me. She didn't know how you felt when I was born. She never asked you. Do you wish that she asked you how you felt about it? Would you tell her if she would've asked you? I don't think that you would've told her the truth. Maybe you didn't know what you felt. It's okay, dad. Sometimes I don't know how I feel about things. You didn't have to know how you felt. Little bee makes me feel things that I've never felt before. When she smiles at me, I cry about how beautiful it is that this girl looks at me like that. I'm the most important person in the world to her. When she laughs at me, I cry about how much she sounds like Bash. When she cries in pain, I cry in pain too. She's my entire world.

She's the only thing that matters to me."

She ran her hands over Daphne's back when she responded to him in a soft voice, "Mom kept everything from my childhood. I wouldn't be surprised she kept everything from your childhood too. She's a sentimental person. She kept the wooden doll that you gave me when I was six years old. Do you remember that? It was the last time that we saw you in England. On the morning of our last day in the country, mom brought this wooden doll that you left at Uncle Nathan's guest house. She didn't tell me that it was from you until you died. Like she didn't want me to know that you gave it to me. I remember carrying that wooden doll around with me on the day of your funeral. I almost broke it at the cemetery because I was mad at you. I'm glad that I didn't break it. Something stopped me. It was guilt that I was taking back the only thing that you gave me. I couldn't throw it back into your face. I'm not a cruel person."

She responded to him with tears falling down her face, "You were a bold person. I don't know why I never saw that before. There's no difference between being bold and being a coward. I was jealous that you were those things. I could never be that person. I'll never be that person. Being bold requires you to not be scared. I don't know how to not be scared. You have to have courage. I don't have that either. That's what I want little bee to be. I want her to be bold and courageous. You lived an interesting life. You saw people and you did the most amazing things. It wasn't what normal people do. I understand why you did it. You didn't kill yourself to make the pain away. You killed yourself to make the pain take on a new life. Oh boy did it take on a life of its own. It transformed a generation of your family. You didn't know that your pain was going to become your legacy in the world. You probably didn't want that to happen. That's the boldest thing that you did. Your pain becomes your legacy. That takes an amount of courage that mom and I don't have. You did that for us, dad. You did it for me. You did it for mom. You did it for Daphne. I'm proud of you, dad. I hope that Daphne learns from you. I hope that I learn it from you too. I love you. Thank you for the world. Thank you for the stars."

CHAPTER FORTY-NINE
(WINTER 1971 – LOS ANGELES, CALIFORNIA)

She packed up their suitcase the next morning as Daphne slept on the bed until she woke up from her morning nap where she placed her daughter on her hip before she carried their suitcase in the living room. Once she said an emotional goodbye to Sean and his family, she placed Daphne into her stroller as she went into a taxi with Amelia and Troy when their driver dropped them off at the airport where they met up with Oliver's family and her parents. Nina's family, Anastasia's family, Uncle Sam, and Aunt Valeria were staying in London for a few more days. Daphne slept on top of her chest for the flight to New York as she slept with her head leaning onto her mother's shoulder before their plane landed in New York that afternoon. She put Daphne into her stroller as her mother pulled them towards Uncle Stan at the airport before she got in the back seat of the car with Daphne next to her. They made it to her parent's house where Uncle Stan and Thomas stayed to watch Holly for Uncle Sam and Aunt Valeria. She pushed the dog off of them where she went into her parent's bedroom to nurse her daughter before she put Daphne down for her afternoon nap. She sat in the living room with her parents, Uncle Stan, and Thomas as she caught up with them before she brought Daphne into the living room after she woke up from her nap. They ate dinner that her mum made for them, and she went into her bedroom with Daphne asleep in her arms before she placed her into her bassinet. She slept in her bed for the rest of the night. After she slept for twelve hours, Daphne wasn't in the bassinet next to her bed as her mother played with Daphne on the floor where she sat down next to them before Daphne crawled into her lap like she was a master at it. She lifted up Daphne in the air as she kissed her on her face. That was the first time that Daphne crawled in front of them. After they shared Daphne's accomplishment with her mum, she called Sebastian who was in Liverpool when she told him that Daphne crawled for the first time where he regretted missing her achievement due to his job before she reassured him that there was going to be more accomplishments for Daphne. She promised him that they would be together in a few weeks. Daphne crawled around her parent's house as she mocked Holly in her mannerisms when she barked at the mailman, and she laid down in the middle of the living room to get pets like her. Even though it was strange for them, they laughed about it since it was clear that Daphne was her mother's daughter with her larger-than-life personality. For the last three weeks of Sebastian's press tour for his movie, she stayed at her parent's house in New York since she didn't want to go home without Sebastian being with them. Her mother was so excited when she told her that they were staying with them in New York for a few weeks. Her mother kept spoiling her granddaughter until her father was home. She went to Nina and Anastasia's apartments everyday where Daphne played with her cousins as she caught up with Nina and Anastasia in the living room. Daphne was the same age as her cousins Tolya and Liam where they did puzzles on the floor. Daphne showed off her crawling trick to her aunts as she crawled after her cousins Angelina and Eilis around the living room. Anastasia's older children Alina and Viktor were in school.

She didn't want to leave her family in New York. She didn't have a choice since she had to go home. Sebastian expected them to be home with him. She felt so much more confident flying home with a baby. She got on a plane to Los Angeles as Daphne slept for the flight in her arms where Amelia took them to their house from the airport since Sebastian's plane wasn't getting in until late at night. Even though Amelia was about to give birth, she carried her suitcase into the house as Daphne slept in her arms where they sat in the living room for the rest of the afternoon before Amelia went home to see Troy after he got home from work. After she put Daphne to bed in her nursery, she sprinted downstairs when she heard the door open as she threw herself into Sebastian's arms with him wrapping his arms around her before they went upstairs to see Daphne in her bedroom. Once Sebastian kissed their daughter on the top of her head, he pulled her into a long kiss that she instantly accepted from him where they made up for lost time all over their bedroom before she fell asleep in his arms for the rest of the night. Since Sebastian was done working on his last movie, he stayed at home with her as they took care of Daphne together like when she was born seven months ago. Juliet roped her into taking care of her niece Eleanor during the day since she went back to work to help pay for Posey's private school. Juliet was going to have Amelia watch Eleanor for her, but Amelia went into labor in the middle of the night. Amelia was at the hospital having a baby with Troy and Aunt Sylvia who came to the states to support her. After Juliet left Eleanor in her care, she did puzzles with Eleanor in the living room as Sebastian put down Daphne for her morning nap where Sebastian joined them before he brought Daphne into the living room after she woke up from her nap. As Eleanor ran around the living room with Daphne crawling around her, she left Sebastian at home with the children as she was dropped off at the hospital since she wanted to see how Amelia was doing in her labor. She was surprised to see that Amelia already had the baby asleep on her chest. She pulled Amelia and Troy into tight hugs when she congratulated them on their baby. Amelia told her that she had a daughter who she named Katherine Austin after their maternal great grandmother who died when their mothers were young. Aunt Sylvia was emotional about it since none of her other grandchildren were named after her grandmother. She went home with Aunt Sylvia tagging along with her since she wanted to spend some time with Daphne and Eleanor before she went back to England. They ate dinner at their house with Oliver's family after the girls played in the living room. Posey was jealous that her little sister spent time with Aunt Isabella and Uncle Bash when she was in school. Oliver's family went to their house and Aunt Sylvia went to Amelia's house. On the day after Katherine was born, they took Posey, Eleanor, and Daphne to the hospital to meet their cousin for the first time where Eleanor cried to Juliet that Posey got to hold her standing up because she was a big girl. Daphne said her first word of love to Katherine. After everyone in the room got emotional, they left Amelia and Troy alone with her daughter as they went out to eat at their favorite restaurant where Daphne tried a lemon from her plate. Once they dropped off some food to Amelia and Troy who were thankful for the meal, their driver dropped them off at the house as they gave Daphne her bath in the bathroom when she said her second word mama to her where she cried into Sebastian's shoulder that her baby was talking to her. While they were putting Daphne to bed, she said her third word dada to him where he cried into her shoulder before they put her to bed for the night.

Daphne said new words to them every day. Daphne said mama and dada when she wanted their attention. Since Eleanor was over at their house every day, she learned how to say Eleanor's name. It sounded like El since she couldn't say her name. Nevertheless, Eleanor was flattered that her cousins learned her name first out of Posey who became Po to Daphne when she learned how to say it. Daphne had special names for people in their families. She called Juliet Aunt Juju and Oliver Uncle Oli. Oliver couldn't stand it when people called him Oli, but he couldn't get mad at Daphne since she was only a baby. She called Amelia Aunt Mia and Troy Uncle Toy. Troy's name was the funniest to them since Daphne was calling him something that she played with, but he was a good sport about it. She called her cousin Katherine Kitty who she was obsessed with seeing her like she was with Sasha and Amelia. Their daughters were going to be best friends growing up like she was with her cousins. Gabriel and Sasha, who looked like she was about to have a baby herself, visited from France to meet Katherine. Daphne thought that it was funny to call Gabriel Uncle Gabby. It offended him since it sounded like she was calling him a woman's name. Sasha told him that Daphne was a baby, and she didn't know any better. Gabriel realized that he was taking it too seriously. At breakfast, Daphne crawled over to Sasha who was drinking a cup of coffee on the couch when she called Sasha Aunt Sosa. She was taken back by Daphne's name for her before she embraced being Aunt Sosa to the family. Daphne didn't call her grandmother and her grandmum grammy or grandmummy like they expected since she called them by their names Ella and Abby. Even though her parents weren't expecting it, they embraced their granddaughter calling them by their names since there was no confusion who she was talking to when she said it to them. Daphne didn't come up with any more names for other Uncles, Aunts, and cousins. She called them by their names like she did with her grandparents. On top of Daphne finding her voice, she found her love of food. She tried to eat food off of their plates during a meal. She wouldn't eat something if they weren't eating it too. Daphne refused to eat baby food since her parents weren't eating it. Instead of giving Daphne baby food like they were supposed to do, they gave her chewed up or blended pieces of whatever they were eating at the time where she helped herself to it until they took the plate away from her. Since Daphne was eating with them at every meal, she no longer breastfed her during the day. Daphne only nursed in the morning when she woke up and at night before she went to bed purely for comfort since she didn't need it to keep her alive. Juliet dropped off Eleanor at their house for the day as she took care of Daphne and Eleanor who were very hyper all day. She was exhausted by the time that Sebastian came back to the house. He went to an audition for a new movie that he didn't think he was going to get. Once they put down the children for their afternoon naps, they spent some alone time in their bedroom until Amelia called them when she told them that she was coming over to their house since Katherine wouldn't let her put her down to get anything done. When Daphne and Eleanor woke up from their afternoon naps, Amelia walked into their house with Katherine crying in her arms as she took the crying baby out of her arms where Amelia thanked her before she went into a guest bedroom to take a nap for the rest of the afternoon. After Katherine fell asleep in Daphne's old bassinet, she blew bubbles in the yard as Eleanor ran around her with Daphne crawling in the grass where Sebastian had a meeting with his agent in his office. She took the children outside, so that Sebastian could have an uninterrupted meeting with his agent. Their meeting was about a movie that he could work on that wouldn't take him away from his family like the last movie that he worked on did. After Amelia joined her in the yard with Katherine in her arms, Amelia took over bubble duty for the children as she walked into the house to check on Sebastian to see how his meeting went with his agent where she was interrupted by the phone ringing near her before she could make it over to his office.

When she answered the phone in between her bites of her apple, Oliver asked her if they could spend the night at her house tonight since their house was being sprayed for ants by the exterminator where she told them that they could stay at their house as long as they needed to before she tasked the chef with making a meal for them. On her way outside to the yard, she ran into Sebastian who got out of his meeting in the office when she told him that Oliver's family was spending the night at their house since the exterminator was spraying at their house where he agreed with her before they went outside with Amelia who was watching Eleanor and Daphne for them. When she told Amelia about Oliver's family spending the night, she invited herself and Katherine to their last-minute sleepover since Troy was in Texas filming a new movie. After they cleaned up the children from playing in the yard, Oliver walked into the house with Posey who he picked up from school on the way home from work before Posey did puzzles in the living room with Eleanor and Daphne as Katherine took a nap in Daphne's bedroom. Juliet was working all night in the writer's room since she had a deadline to complete a script of her television show. At dinner that night, she sat in between Sebastian and Daphne who was picking up pieces of food off of her plate that they broke down for her. She talked to Posey about her private school this year. They went outside with the children to let them get their energy out from the day. After they put the children to bed in Daphne's bedroom, they watched a movie that Sebastian's agent gave him that wasn't released yet where she grabbed an opened bottle of wine from the kitchen before she sat on the couch in the living room with Sebastian's arm around her. In the middle of the movie, Amelia brought Katherine into the living room with them since she needed to nurse her as she laid down with her head on Sebastian's lap for the rest of the movie. When the movie was done, Amelia brought Katherine into Daphne's room as she went to check on Daphne who was asleep in her crib where she walked into the living room before she laid down with her head on Sebastian's lap. Sebastian looked up at her with a smile on his face as he pecked her lips where he ran his fingers through her hair before Amelia took a seat next to Oliver when Oliver asked them with a smile on his face, "How's parenthood treating you guys? I know Amelia's feelings about it. She called me in the middle of the night to tell me all about it. I never asked you guys how it was for you. Is it everything that you dreamed of?"

She looked up at Sebastian when she told Oliver in a serious voice,

"We didn't get any sleep for nine months and my body will never be the same again. Little bee is a great baby. She went through colic for a little bit, but she grew out of it. She's growing up too fast. Did you see that she was trying to walk? I feel like she learned how to crawl yesterday."

Sebastian ran his fingers through her hair when he said to them with a frown on his face, "I know honey. It was hard to be away from them. I was missing a part of myself. Does it get easier to be away from your children? I was in hell when I was gone for two months."

She grabbed onto his hands to comfort him as Oliver shook his head at him when he responded to him with a look of sadness on his face, "It doesn't get easier to leave them. It only gets harder. I can't lie to you, Bash. What did your agent tell you in your meeting?"

She sat up with her arms wrapped around him where Sebastian grabbed onto her hands when he responded to Oliver with him blinking back tears that fell down his face, "He told me that it would be impossible to find a job that didn't make me be apart from my daughter. If I would open my own studio and make my own rules, then I wouldn't have to comply with what the studio tells me to do. I should stop being an actor. I considered that the last time that I was separated from them, and I missed the first time that my daughter crawled. Do you want to know the worst thing about this? My agent suggested that I shouldn't care that I can't be with my daughter since my job should be above my family. I told him to get the fuck out of my house. I don't know what to do from here. I need some advice if you guys can give me any."

She leaned her head on his shoulder as he kissed on the top of her head when Amelia said aloud to the room with a frown on her face, "I get it, Bash. Troy is having that same problem. He booked this movie before Katherine was born. When he told them that he wanted to stay at home with his daughter, they told him that he had to do the movie since he signed a contract when he got the main role in the movie. They didn't tell him that they would be filming the movie in Texas. He was shocked when they told him that he needed to be in Texas for the next three months. They threatened to sue him if he didn't film it. I wish that I could give you some advice, but we don't know what to do about it."

She got off of the couch with Sebastian following behind her into the kitchen where he held onto her hands when he asked her with a concerned look on his face, "What are you doing, Isabella? Don't do something that you will regret."

She picked up the phone when Sebastian's agent asked her with confusion laced in his voice, "Sebastian? What's wrong? Why are you calling me this late?"

As Sebastian stared at her with a pleading look on his face, she ignored him when she said to his agent with anger laced in her voice, "It's his wife, Isabella. My husband told me what you told him in your meeting. I wanted to be the person to tell you that Sebastian won't be using your services anymore. I don't tolerate anyone talking to my husband like you did. Don't deny it. I know that you told him that his family shouldn't be a priority. His wife would be able to handle it. I'm not a person, but a mere object to you. I know that he already told you what he wanted to say, but I didn't get a chance to say what I wanted to tell you. How dare you suggest to my husband that he not care about his daughter. Are you a father? Would your children like to hear you say that to them? How about your wife? How many other clients do you tell that to? My husband isn't the only one."

Sebastian's agent told her in a threatening tone to make her scared of him like a man could threaten her, "What is your problem? You are basket case, Isabella. My wife and children love me. I'm telling my client what will help them grow in the business. All that I said to him was that it's a part of working in Hollywood. It's nothing personal. I'm sure that your daughter is great. It's nothing against her. If Sebastian can't handle it, then he should get out of the business. It sounds like you shouldn't be in the business. I've seen your films, and they aren't good. If I was your agent, then you would get better roles in movies. Unless you are taking your place in the house, then I can't stop you from quitting."

Amelia and Oliver walked into the kitchen with them when she shouted at his agent in a shaky voice, "You would never be my agent! I wouldn't let anyone talk to me like this! I don't know why my husband let you talk to him like this for all these years! That ends right now!

Don't call this phone number again! If you show your face at our house, I'll call the police!"

She slammed the phone into the counter where it broke on the floor as Sebastian tried to grab onto her before she sprinted outside into the yard. She ran over to their pool where she kicked the chairs into it as Sebastian grabbed onto her to stop her before she punched him in the chest. She stopped punching him in the chest with Sebastian maintaining a tight grip on her arms. She let out a sudden sob into her hands as he pulled her into his chest where she let out a heartbreaking sob with his arms wrapped around her. Sebastian kissed her on the top of her head as he ran his hands down her arms when he said to her in a soft voice, "I don't know where that came from but thank you for standing up for me. You didn't need to do that honey. I would never ask you to put yourself in that place. What are we going to do? I need to make money and now I need to find a new agent."

She wiped away the tears off of her face as she leaned her head onto his shoulder when she told him with a smirk on her face, "You heard the man, Bash. You don't need a new agent. You need to get your own studio. Doesn't what he told us make something clear to you? We need to make a safe place for actors to work that will respect their decision to be in their children's lives. Fuck your agent. Fuck my agent. Fuck Hollywood. It doesn't have to be that way. You don't have to choose your career over your family. You can have your family and your career at the same time. We don't have to quit our careers because we want to have families. What do you say?"

Sebastian kept a tight grip on her arms when he responded to her with a look of disbelief on his face, "This is crazy honey! How are we going to do that? With what money are we going to open a studio? We don't have that much money to throw away."

She cupped her hands around his face when she told him with a wide grin on her face, "I could get a loan from my parents. My mother is a millionaire, Bash. Did you forget about that? She made a fortune off of her books and movies. She still makes money off of them. She doesn't spend her money since she was saving it for something special. This is the thing that's special."

Sebastian nodded his head at her as she pulled him into a long kiss where he kissed her back with wide grins on their faces until they broke apart from each other to catch their breaths when he said to her with a smile on his face, "This is crazy. We are going to do this. We are leaving behind a legacy for our children. We are free from agents in the industry. How long have you been thinking about this? Don't tell me that you didn't come up with this tonight. I know that you didn't do that. You always have a plan for everything." Sebastian pulled her into a desperate kiss as Sebastian almost took off her shirt in the yard before she scolded him that they needed to wait until they were in their bedroom. After they walked into their bedroom, she closed the door behind her as Sebastian pulled her into a long kiss that ended on the bed where she laid down with her head on his chest with his arms wrapped around her before she fell asleep for the rest of the night.

Chapter Fifty
(Spring 1971 – Los Angeles, California)

She called her agent the next morning to tell him that she wasn't going to be working with him anymore. Once they broke up with their agents, they couldn't back away from this decision since they cut the existing ties that they had in Hollywood. After they ended their ties in Hollywood, she called her mother when she told her about their plan, and she asked her if they could loan money to her for their own studio. Even though her mother thought it was a crazy idea, she told them that there was no time like the present to take a chance to do something. Her mother took the same chance when she opened her booking publishing company when she was thirty years old without any experience. Her mother told her that she would loan them as much money as they needed to start their company. Her mother would use her contacts to help her set up everything that they needed to do for their business. They had to go to New York to meet up with her mother's bankers and lawyers to get everything set up for their company. She would go to New York to deal with the bank and the lawyers while Sebastian stayed home with Daphne to use his connections that he had left in Hollywood to create a team for their studio. The biggest problem that they were facing was that they needed to purchase a location for the company and equipment for it. Sebastian had friends in all places that wanted to help him get everything done that they needed to get done in California while she was in New York dealing with the legal side of it. On the morning of her flight to New York, she said an emotional goodbye to Sebastian and Daphne who she was leaving for the first time since she was born. Their driver dropped off at the airport before she read the legal paperwork that her lawyer's in California prepared for her on the flight. When their plane landed in New York that afternoon, she pulled her legal paperwork into her purse as she met up with her mother at the airport before her mother drove them to the bank to meet up with their banker. After they signed the paperwork that the banker provided for them, the banker handed them the bag of cash that they took out of her mother's bank account. Her mother dropped them off at the house where they hid the bag of cash in a safe that was hidden in her parent's bedroom. In the week that she was in New York with her parents, she received a phone call from Sasha that they got back from the hospital after they had their daughter Charlotte Rue where she congratulated them on their baby before she told Sasha about the movie studio that she was opening up in Los Angeles with Sebastian. Sasha was shocked by them opening up a film studio. Sasha told her that she was happy for them that they found something of their own to do that they would leave behind for their children. Sasha told her that Gabriel was thinking about opening up a photography studio in the states since his brothers offered to buy the company from him.

She asked Sasha if that meant that she was moving to the states with Gabriel and Charlotte. Sasha told her that they were considering moving to the states. They wanted to raise their daughter surrounded by her family since they were too isolated in France. When it was time for her to go back to California, she gathered her paperwork into her bags, and she hid the money that she was taking home with her in her clothing pockets. It was a trick that she learned from hiding her drugs in a different lifetime. No one knew that there were hundreds of thousands of dollars hidden in her suitcase. Once their plane landed in Los Angeles in the evening, she grabbed onto her suitcase as she sprinted over to Sebastian where he pulled her into a tight hug that they didn't let go of each other until Daphne said mama from her stroller. She placed Daphne on her hip before Daphne pulled her into a tight hug with her face hidden in her chest. After their driver dropped them off at the house, she put Daphne to bed in her bedroom as they went into their bedroom where she explained to him the documents that she got signed for the business and the money that she got from her mother's bank account. She told Sebastian about everything that she secured for their business on the legal side. He told her about the abandoned building that he bought that was being fixed and the people that he got to work with them at their studio. Sebastian secured a construction crew that worked on renovating the studio for them. He got enough people that were fed up with the industry to work with them. Troy would be coming back from Texas in a few weeks where he worked on his last project with his agent before he would work with their studio. Amelia got over a dozen hairstylists and makeup artists that were sick of the industry to work with them. Juliet got a team of writers including her that were sick of being paid no money for successful projects. Sebastian used his many connections in Hollywood to find groups of actors that were sick of being treated with no respect like their families didn't matter to them. The actors that were going to work for their studio went to their wedding two years ago when they talked about it for the first time. Uncle Stan used his connections with directors that were sick of being treated like second class citizens compared to the executives to work with them. Since they needed to raise their daughter, they hired a manager to deal with the daily problems at the studio that they called Foster Brewer Studios after their own last names. The manager of their studio was an energetic woman named Katie who experienced running other studios in the past before she was forced out of the industry when she had her children, and she wanted to be in their lives. Katie was what they needed for Foster Brewer Studios since she stood for the same values that they did, and she had the experience to execute all the ideas that they had for the studio. Since Katie was busy making sure that the studio was going well, Sebastian focused on creating strong relationships with the actors and the directors that they hired for their films. He was hands-on with all of the productions that they had going on at the studio. She was in constant contact with their lawyers and their bankers to make sure that everything was going well there. It took everything out of them to build their own studio. They were glad that they did it because they were creating something that they could give to their children someday. Sebastian went into the studio to make sure that everything was going well with their productions when she stayed at home having meetings on the phone with their lawyers and their bankers in the office while she took care of Daphne during the day. Juliet and Amelia left Eleanor and Katherine at the daycare that they ran inside of the studio since their employees had children to take care of.

Her mother asked her on the phone what they were going to do for Daphne's first birthday that was coming up in a few weeks where she told her mother that she didn't think about it until she asked her about it. Since they were overwhelmed by the pressures of running their company, she asked Sebastian if they should throw a birthday party for their daughter since she was too young to remember it. Sebastian told her that they had to or else her mother was going to hold it against them for the rest of her life. Her mother wouldn't let it go if her granddaughter didn't get a birthday party for her first birthday. She called an event planner that her new assistant Lucy recommended for her. Lucy used this planner for her children's birthday parties. The event planner met up with them at the house where they discussed what kind of party that they were going to have for Daphne. They let Daphne pick out what she wanted to do at her party based on pictures that she grabbed from the event planner where Daphne chose the theme of to be a rubber ducky themed pool party. Once Lucy provided the event planner with everything that she needed to prepare for the party, she called her mother when she told her that they were having a birthday party for Daphne from the theme that she chose herself before her mother told her that she already invited her cousins that lived in the states to the party. While they prepared to host her family, she received a phone call from Sasha that they were going to stay with them for Daphne's birthday party before she told her that they could stay with them as long as they needed to. On the week of Daphne's first birthday, she went shopping with Sebastian where they bought gifts for their daughter that she would appreciate at her age while Lucy was at the house watching Daphne. After they bought what they wanted to give their daughter, the driver dropped off Sebastian at the studio as she went to the house where she wrapped up the gifts that they got for Daphne during her afternoon nap with Lucy's help. After they wrapped up Daphne's gifts, Lucy prepared her for her daily call with the bank about the studio's finances as Daphne played with blocks on the floor during her meeting. After Lucy left to go home for the rest of the day, she took Daphne with her to the airport where her parents hugged her until Daphne cried out for her grandparents before her mother smothered Daphne with kisses on her face while her laughing into her chest. On the way back to the house, their driver picked up Sebastian from the studio. He was always done filming before dinner no matter how behind they were in their schedules. They ate dinner at their favorite restaurant before they went to bed for the rest of the night. Their families slowly came into town for the party where they stayed at all of their houses. Her parents stayed in one of the guest bedrooms. Sasha and Gabriel stayed in the other guest bedroom. Charlotte shared a room with Daphne as Daphne slept in the crib and Charlotte slept in her old bassinet. Uncle Sam and Aunt Valeria stayed in Amelia's guest bedrooms. Nina and her children Bridget, Eilis, and Liam stayed in two of the other guest bedrooms. Joseph stayed in New York with Holly since he was almost done with medical school. He was taking his final exams to become a cardiologist. Anastasia, Damien, and their children Alina, Viktor, Angelina, and Toyla were staying in Oliver's guest bedrooms. Uncle Nathan and Aunt Priscilla stayed at Uncle Stan and Thomas' house in their guest bedroom. On the morning of her daughter's first birthday, she went into her bedroom where she grabbed Daphne out of her crib as she told her daughter happy birthday. Daphne whined in her arms since she wasn't a morning person. That was something that she bragged to Sebastian about since their daughter didn't take after him. Once she got Daphne dressed in a dress with ducks on it, she put her daughter's hair into pigtails that would be out by lunch before she joined her parents, Sebastian, and Gabriel in the kitchen for breakfast. As Daphne ate scrambled eggs with her hands, her parents talked to Gabriel about helping him set up his photography company while they had conversations about the events for the day.

Since Lucy was off of work on the weekends, they made sure that their daughter's birthday party went well without their assistants or the event planner there. Her mother helped out with the party. She was deeply grateful since her mother was the most effective person in the world. Her mother disappeared in the yard to make sure that everything was in its proper place. She fixed Daphne's hair that was ruined at breakfast as Daphne ran over to Sebastian with his daughter on his hip before he went outside in the yard with her mother and Gabriel who wanted to see what the event planner did with the yard that was top secret. After she ran into Sasha in the living room with Charlotte on her hip, she got into the car as their driver dropped her off at the store where she picked up her daughter's duck themed cake from the bakery before they went into the house with their guests. Once she ran into Amelia and Troy with Katherine on his hip, she pulled into tight hugs where she went into the kitchen where the chef cooked the food for the party. She placed the cake on the counter before she joined the guests in the yard. Daphne chased Eleanor and Posey in the grassy part of their yard as her cousins Nina who was very pregnant, Anastasia, and their children were in the pool with Sasha and Gabriel who had Charlotte in his arms. Daphne ran over to her as she kissed Daphne on top of her head with Daphne on her hip when she walked over to Uncle Nathan and Aunt Priscilla where she talked to them about their company and Daphne's milestones before she handed Daphne over to Uncle Nathan. When Lucy arrived at the party with her children, she left Daphne with Uncle Nathan as she talked to Lucy about everything that they needed to do for the company on Monday morning. Sebastian called for her over to the snack table where he asked her to grab more food from the kitchen before she went into the pantry to get more snacks for the children. Before she left the kitchen with the snacks in her hands, she was pulled into a conversation with Uncle Stan and Katie about a new script that their writers turned in that he wanted to produce into a new movie that has never been done before. She told them to tell Sebastian about it before she went outside to join the party. Once she ran over to her daughter who was chasing her both of her grandmothers in the grass, she pulled Daphne into her arms as she tickled her sides until Daphne was out of breath where she placed her on her hip before she talked to people that came up to her with presents in their hands. When it was time to sing happy birthday, she called everyone to the patio where they placed a smash cake in front of Daphne who was seated in her highchair where she stood next to Sebastian before Sebastian lit the candle on the cake. She told Daphne to blow out the candle after she made a wish. Daphne didn't need help following instructions as she closed her eyes where she made a wish in her head when she blew out the candle on the cake before she smashed her face into the cake. They kissed each of Daphne's cheeks that were covered in frosting where Gabriel took pictures of them. Daphne put cake on their faces with a mischievous look on her face before she changed Daphne into her swimsuit after she cleaned the frosting off of her hands and face. They swam together in the pool with Daphne being passed from her to Sebastian many times before they ate lunch that the chef prepared for them where Daphne ate everything on her plate and anyone else's plate that was left in front of her. They helped Daphne open up birthday gifts from their family and friends wrapped in bright yellow paper to match the theme of the party. Daphne was so good at taking paper off of the gifts that she forgot that she was supposed to look at what was under the paper before she moved onto the next gift in the pile. They thanked everyone for their gifts since she was too young to understand what was going on. Their families stayed at the house until the early evening until everyone went home for the rest of night. Sasha put Charlotte to bed for the night as Daphne helped them clean up the yard until she whined for them to put her to bed where she placed Daphne on her hip before Sebastian followed her into her bedroom. After they walked into Daphne's bedroom, she placed Daphne in her bed after they changed her into her nightgown where she ran her fingers through her hair when she whispered to her with Sebastian holding onto her hands, "Goodnight, little bee. Mommy and daddy love you so much. I hope that you had a great birthday. You are always going to be our special girl. You are the best thing that happened to me. Don't forget that."

Daphne understood what she told her as Daphne looked up at them when she said to him with a look of innocence in her face, "I'm happy."

She blinked back tears that fell down her face as Sebastian wrapped his arms around her where he kissed the top of Daphne's head when he whispered to his daughter with a smile on his face, "We're glad that you're happy, little bee. Do you want to know a secret?"

Daphne instantly nodded her head at him as he grabbed onto her hands again when he whispered to his daughter with tears falling down his face, "I'm happy too. You made me the happiest person by being your dad. What did you wish for when you blew out your candle?"

Daphne grabbed onto her mother's hand when she whispered to them with a smile on her face, "I was with you forever. Is that a good wish?"

She wiped away the tears from her face as she pushed back hair from Daphne's face when she whispered to her daughter with a wide grin on her face, "You did good, little bee. That's what I wished for too. Your wish came true. We'll be together forever. Do you remember the stars?"

Daphne whispered to her mother with a smile on her face, "Yes, mama. Someone was there."

She ran her other hand through her daughter's hair when she whispered to Daphne, "Do you want daddy to read to you?"

After Sebastian read a book to Daphne, she walked into her bedroom where she sobbed into her knees on the floor in disbelief at what her daughter told her. She stayed in that position until Sebastian walked into their bedroom after Daphne fell asleep in her crib. He wrapped his arms around her before she sobbed into his chest with her hands balled into fists. After Sebastian moved her in their bed, she laid down on his chest with his arms around her when she said to him like it was a secret between them, "I never told her about dad or the stars. Do you think that it's real what he said to me?"

Sebastian drew a pattern down her back when he asked her with a frown on his face, "Why else would Daphne know about it? Does it make you feel better?"

She looked at him when she responded to him with a frown on her face, "I don't know how I feel about it. It makes me feel better that my dad wasn't lying to me. I'm confused how she knew about it."

Sebastian pulled her into a desperate kiss until they pulled away from each other when he told her with a smirk on his face, "Give her a few more years before she's telling us everything that we don't know. She's her mother's daughter. That curiosity is going to carry her anywhere she wants to go in the world. Just like it did with your mother. Just like it does with you."

She pulled him into a long kiss that they didn't let go until they were out of breath when she whispered to him with a smile on her face,

"What's my secret?"

Sebastian cupped her face with his hands when he whispered to her, "You are trying to figure out why you are trapped in between the past and the present. You don't know how to live in either of them."

Sebastian asked her with a wide grin on his face, "What's my secret?"

She responded to him with a smile on her face, "You are trying to figure out how to make a difference in the world. One that lasts longer than our existence will in the universe."

Chapter Fifty-One
(Summer 1971 – New York, New York)

Sasha's family were moving to California after Gabriel got the permits approved for his photography studio. Sasha went back to France with Charlotte. Sasha packed up their house with their cousins helping her when she came back to the states after she moved them out of their house in France. Gabriel stayed in their guest bedroom while he looked for a house while he looked for a place for his studio. Sebastian helped Gabriel find a space for his studio where she helped him find a house in the same neighborhood. She took one of the spare rooms in the studio for her office where she gave her assistant Lucy a desk on the other side of the room. Daphne was at daycare with Eleanor and Katherine where the cousins played together before their parents took them home for the day. Sebastian checked on her in the office when they had a few moments to themselves. They talked about what needed to be done after they got home from work. She went to work by herself since Sebastian went home earlier in the day with Daphne who wasn't feeling good. She barely made it through the front door when she heard the phone ringing in the kitchen where she answered with her bags falling down onto the floor. Sasha told her that they were coming to the states with their stuff. Ivan and Jamie were coming with them, so that they could help them move into the house. Gabriel bought the house next to them before it was listed on the housing market. Gabriel was friends with her neighbors in the time that he stayed there. The neighbors were selling their house because they were moving to Texas to be closer to their grandchildren. Gabriel was more than willing to give them more money than they asked for because he wanted to live in their neighborhood. On the morning of Sasha's arrival, she left Daphne at home with Sebastian as her driver dropped her off at the airport before she spotted Sasha on the other side of the room. She pulled Sasha into a long hug until Charlotte whined in her arms as she pulled Ivan and Jamie into tight hugs with their arms tightly wrapped around her. The last time that she saw them was Alfie and Debbie's wedding in London over a year ago. After they placed Sasha's bags into the back of the car, their driver drove them to the new house where Gabriel and Troy waited for them in the driveway. Gabriel pulled Sasha into a tight hug with Charlotte on his hip where they pulled apart from each other when Ivan asked his sister in French where the car keys were before Sasha shouted back at him in French that they were in his pocket. Once Ivan unlocked the car with a smirk on Jamie's face, the boys carried boxes into the house where the girls unpacked the boxes into the rooms that Sasha labeled while she was in France. Sebastian and Oliver joined them in the afternoon after they got back from work as Juliet watched the children at her house. They ate takeout after working for a while as they sat down on the kitchen floor before everyone went to their houses for the night except for Ivan and Jamie that stayed in their guest bedroom.

She woke up the next morning to Ivan and Jamie talking to each other in French in the guest room. She went into Daphne's bedroom to grab her out of her crib. She was excited to see her like she was every day. Daphne ran into Ivan and Jamie's bedroom where they played with her on the bed before Ivan carried Daphne on his hip into the kitchen. After they ate breakfast in the kitchen, the boys went over to Oliver's house as they got his truck that he bought a few years ago where they went shopping at a furniture store to get the pieces that Gabriel purchased while the girls worked on organizing Sasha's house. Juliet taught the children how to swim in their pool except for Charlotte who was too young to do it. After the boys got back from the furniture store, they carried everything into the house. They didn't need a lot of furniture because the previous owners of the house left a lot of their stuff behind for them. Gabriel talked to his brothers at lunch on the phone about his lawyer transferring the family estate and the family business into their names. While Gabriel talked in French, Jamie translated everything for her as he whispered into her ear word for word what Gabriel said into the phone. Jamie suddenly stopped when Gabriel said something so funny that he couldn't stop laughing into her shoulder. When she asked Ivan what Jamie was laughing at, Ivan told her that Gabriel told them that their boyfriends were spying on their conversation and that Jamie choked on himself as much as he choked on Christophe. She didn't know what surprised her the most that Gabriel and Jamie had the same sense of humor or that Ivan said that with a straight face without any reaction. Sebastian rolled his eyes at this interaction. He was annoyed with Gabriel's off-color comments that he made more and more over the past month. The boys went back to work carrying the mattresses up three flights of stairs into the bedrooms. The girls organized the living room as the children ran around them except for Charlotte who was in a carrier on Sasha's chest. Daphne ran around the living room with Eleanor and Posey as Katherine crawled around them. Juliet made the children go outside in the yard to play away from the house. When she was alone in the living room with Sasha who was softly talking in French to Charlotte, she asked Sasha if Gabriel was the only person with a dark sense of humor where Sasha told her that his brothers and Jamie were like that too. Sasha felt like she and Ivan were always correcting the boys. They moved everything into Sasha and Gabriel's house by the end of the weekend. Gabriel and Jamie went to the bar to celebrate their home when Ivan stayed home with them where they watched a movie in the living room after they put Daphne to sleep in her crib. Ivan and Jamie stayed with them for a few more days while they helped Gabriel and Sasha set up the new photography studio. Ivan and Jamie went to New York to visit Ivan's siblings and his parents for a few days before they went to London and York to visit Jamie's siblings and his parents for a few days. Once Ivan and Jamie were home in France, their lives went back to normal as Gabriel worked in the studio with Sasha and Charlotte who were his first subjects to photograph in the states. Sebastian spent a lot of time in the film studio where she worked in her office either at home or at the studio while Daphne was in the daycare. After their studio released their first few successful movies in theatres, that was when their business took off for them. They rejected requests from publications to interview them since they weren't interested in being famous anymore.

There was the level of fame from being an actor in the industry that was bad enough for anyone to deal with. It was a different level of fame when someone became a CEO of a company. There were people that became envious of what you worked on to achieve. When she did interviews during her acting career, she was asked questions about the movie that she was promoting at the time, and they rarely asked her questions about her personal life. She kept her professional life separated from her personal life. She learned that from her mother who established a clear boundary with the press early in her career. She was never going to merge her personal life and her professional life. Sebastian learned the same lesson from his parents who raised him in the industry for many years before the press knew who he was. His parents made the press leave him alone. She had this conversation with Sebastian before they got married to each other. They knew that they would have to deal with it being in the industry. On their first press tour when they started dating each other, they didn't tell anyone from the publications that they were in a relationship with each other until after they were caught together in London before her last relapse and their breakup after that. When the world knew that they were dating each other, they were already broken up where they left alone about it until her public argument with Amelia and Sasha in New York before her public overdose. Even though that was her third drug overdose, it was her first overdose to the world. They didn't know that she was an addict until then. When she found out from her parents that the world knew about her overdose, she was disappointed that she allowed her lives to merge because her mother taught her better than that. After she got back together with Sebastian, she made it her goal to never allow the personal parts of her into the public. When they were engaged with each other, the press didn't find out about it until a few months before their wedding. Sebastian accidentally slipped it out in one of his interviews for a movie. They were forced to move up the date of their wedding to prevent the press from coming. They didn't tell the press about their wedding until they left for their honeymoon. They didn't tell the press about her pregnancy until she was spotted in Paris for

Sasha's wedding when she was late into her pregnancy. The press found out about Daphne's existence after she was born. They knew that they had a daughter, and they didn't know her name. When they opened Foster Brewer Studios, there was a sudden interest in them from the press who wanted to know what they were up to. To make sure that no one would tell anyone to the press about what happened in their family, they made their employees sign Non-Disclosure Agreements to protect the safety of their children and themselves from the press. When Lucy received a request from the New York Times to do an interview with her, she told her assistant that she would ask her lawyer what he thought about her doing an interview. Her lawyer told her that it could be good for their business for her to do the interview before she consulted Sebastian and her parents on what to do about it. Even though Sebastian disagreed with their lawyer that she needed to do the interview, her mother told her that it was smart to get ahead of the story. She convinced Sebastian that it was a good thing before Lucy told them that she would do the interview. She needed to go to New York to meet with the journalist for it. After she packed her bags for the trip to New York, she took Daphne with her since her parents wanted to see their granddaughter before she said an emotional goodbye to Sebastian who didn't like that she was doing the interview. Once their driver dropped them off at the airport, she placed Daphne into her stroller as she pushed their bags in her other hand where they got onto the plane before Daphne slept in her arms for the flight. When their plane landed in New York that evening, she carried Daphne in her arms as she carried her bags and Daphne's stroller in her other hand where she handed Daphne off to her mum when she pulled her parents into tight hugs before her mum drove them to their house for the rest of the night. On the next morning, she met up with her lawyers and her banks for their company while her mum watched Daphne at the house before she came home in the afternoon with her mother putting nail polish on Daphne's fingers and toes. After she was shooed away from the living room, she called Sebastian in the kitchen when she talked to him about her meetings with their lawyers and their bankers. Sebastian asked her if she insisted on doing the interview where she told him that she would think about it. She walked into the living room with Daphne instantly running over to her as she placed her daughter on her hip where she carried her into their bedroom for her afternoon nap. After Daphne was asleep in her bed, she sat down on the couch with her parents where they talked about if she should do this interview. Sebastian made her second guess herself that this was a horrible idea. Once her parents assured her that she made the right decision, she considered calling Sebastian to tell him that she was going to do the interview, but she talked herself out of it. She didn't want to start another fight with him.

They already fought about it enough in the few weeks before she left to go to New York, and she wasn't in the mood for rehashing stuff with him. She prepared the answers that her lawyer cleared her to answer from the list of questions that the journalist sent ahead to Lucy before she left Los Angeles. It was better that the journalist didn't know that she was practicing her answers like she rehearsed a script from a movie because that would ruin the magic. She didn't tell Sebastian or her parents that there were going to be some questions about her drug addiction that her lawyer created responses for her. Daphne was off limits, but she would talk about her drug addiction if it was necessary. On the day of her interview with the New York Times, she left the house with Daphne in her stroller as she walked around the city. She wanted to clear her head before she was expected to be at Aunt Valeria's house. Daphne talked to her the entire time that they walked around the city as she pointed at things when she said the words that she made up for them before they ate lunch at a pizza shop where they shared a slice of pizza. Once they ate lunch at the pizza shop, she pushed Daphne's stroller to the hair salon that Aunt Valeria ran with her cousins Anastasia and Nina where her cousins ran over to her as soon as she walked into the building with their arms around each other. After she took Daphne out of her stroller, Daphne ran over to Aunt Valeria who gave her a tight hug with her three-month-old grandson Owen Sullivan on her hip. Once they left the hair salon in Anastasia and Nina's capable hands, Aunt Valeria drove them to her house as Holly jumped up on her top of her legs with Daphne on her hip where she handed Daphne over to Uncle Sam who was reaching out for her before she took a seat at the kitchen table with Aunt Valeria doing her hair for her. While Aunt Valeria styled her hair for her, Uncle Sam played dolls with Daphne sitting in his lap where Holly slept on the floor. Aunt

Valeria told her that she used to do this for her mother when they were younger. Uncle Sam told stories about her mother when they were growing up in England that made him cry about how much changed since they were children. She knew that he didn't mean that they were old because they had grandchildren. Uncle Sam referred to Kenny and Will. She didn't want to make Uncle Sam emotional about things that he hadn't talked about in decades, but she wanted to know what he thought about what happened when her mother and her father were living in England. This wasn't the time to ask him about it since her daughter was sitting on the floor next to her. Aunt Valeria sent her a disapproving look to stop talking about it. Once they moved onto the subject of Daphne's milestones, the tension in Aunt Valeria's shoulders disappeared into one of happiness before Aunt Valeria told her that she was done with her hair if she wanted to look at it in the mirror. After she left the kitchen with Daphne on her hip, Uncle Sam and Aunt Valeria had a hushed argument with each other about him bringing up Uncle Kenny and her father in front of her. They didn't want to make her relapse like Uncle Nathan had with the letter from her father. Before they caught her eavesdropping on their argument, she placed Daphne into her stroller with the doll in her hands as she sprinted out of the house without looking back at them where she didn't slow down until she made it to her parent's house. After she put Daphne down for her afternoon nap, she hid into the bathroom where she let out desperate sobs into her hands. Even though she stopped crying, she didn't leave the bathroom until she heard Daphne crying in their bedroom as she wiped away the tears from her face where she comforted her daughter who woke up from a nightmare before she played with Daphne in the living room to distract her from what happened with Uncle Sam and Aunt Valeria. Once her parents came home from work, she got ready for her interview that she was going through with after her panic attack this afternoon. After she pulled her mother into a desperate hug that concerned her, she handed Daphne over to her mum before she left the house without saying a word to them. As soon as she was alone in her parent's car, she held back tears that burned in her eyes as she drove to the restaurant in silence.

After she valeted her car at the restaurant, she went into the back of the restaurant to meet up with the journalist. As soon as she spotted the journalist from across the room, she walked over to him as they shook hands with each other where she took a seat across from him when he offered her a cigarette that she gladly took from him before a waiter took their orders. After she ordered the first thing on the menu, the journalist ordered a pasta dish as the waiter disappeared again when he asked her questions from the approved list that Lucy gave to her where she told him the memorized answers that her lawyer prepared for her. Once the waiter gave them their food, they stopped the interview for a few moments as they ate their food before he continued the interview like nothing interrupted them. After she ate her food and she smoked three cigarettes that he offered her, he asked her if her addiction made her life more difficult. Even though she knew that this question was coming, she was caught off guard about how it attacked her. The incident with Uncle Sam and Aunt Valeria from this afternoon was in the front of her mind no matter what she did to stop thinking about it. She wasn't sticking to her script anymore when she told him that her life was harder being an addict. She was programmed to not care if she lived, or she died from the day that she was born. Her answer caught the journalist off guard since he wasn't expecting her to give him an answer that wasn't bullshit like her other answers that she gave him. When he asked her what she meant by her answer, the addict version of herself came out of nowhere when she asked him what he meant by his question. It sounded like he was implying that her addiction wasn't a serious problem. He asked her if it was the kind of problem for her that she would deal with the rest of her life when she asked him if he thought that his alcoholism wasn't that kind of problem for him. She knew that she ruined the interview with the New York Times. She confronted her interviewer about his problems with alcohol to deflect him off of her problems with drugs. He surprised her when he told her that she was right about him that he had addiction problems with alcohol that he inherited from his father. None of them were following their script since they openly talked to each other about living with addiction and the effects that it had on their lives. By the end of their conversation, they cried about what they revealed to each other. She panicked when she realized that she said way too much to him that she was never going to tell him before he assured her that the addiction part would stay between them if she didn't want anyone else knowing about it. She was touched by this act of service that a stranger was doing for her. It sounded too good to be true until the journalist caught her off guard for the third time that night when he told her that she should write a book about her addiction. She didn't know how to tell the guy that her mother was an author until he caught her off guard for the fourth time that night when he told her that he read her mother's books, and he knew that she was a great writer like her. Since she didn't know what to say to him, she excused herself for the night because she needed to get home to her daughter. The journalist shook her hand when he told her that it was a pleasure to meet her and that he hoped to hear more about her in the future. After she escaped the restaurant without revealing any more secrets to him, she drove to her parent's house in complete silence as she tried to make sense of what just happened to her. She walked into the house where her mother typed on her typewriter before she put her purse onto the couch. As soon as she took a seat next to her, her mother took the typewriter off of her lap as she pulled her mother into a desperate hug with her face hidden in her chest. When she pulled away from her mother, she wiped tears that escaped from her eyes as she laid down in her mother's lap with her gently running her fingers through her hair when she asked her with a frown on her face, "I'm sorry, mom. I don't know where that came from. Did little bee get to bed without me? I didn't mean to get back this late."

Her mother smiled at her when she responded to her, "She went to bed with your mum. They are sleeping in our bed. I need to work on my new book, and I wanted to wait for you. How did your interview go, baby girl?"

She responded to her mother in a nervous voice, "I think that it went well. It didn't go like I thought that it was going to. It will turn out better than I anticipated it to be. We'll see what he prints in the article. Let's hope he leaves out the addiction part like he promised."

Her mother stopped running her fingers through her hair when she asked her with a confused look on her face, "The addiction part? What do you mean? This article is about your company. Not your addiction."

As soon as she hid her face in her hands, she shook her head with her blinking back tears that fell down her face when she confessed to her mother with a panicked look on her face, "I realize that it's about my company, mom. Things got out of control. We went off script. When he brought up my addiction, I got defensive about it, and I called him an addict. He was an addict, and we had an honest conversation about addiction. We laughed and we cried. It was a wonderful time until I remembered that it was an interview and not a therapy session. I can't tell the difference between them. It wasn't a complete disaster like I thought that it was going to be. He told me that I should write a book about my addiction, and he was a huge fan of your books."

Her mother held onto her hands when she responded to her with a smile on her face, "It seems like you got the only journalist in this city with any integrity left. You always had all the luck for us. He was right about one thing, baby girl. You should write a book about your addiction. Your story seems to have touched him, and his breed is always greedy for a headline. Would you?"

She looked up at her mother when she asked her with confusion laced in her voice, "Would I what? Would I write a book? I don't know, mom. Why would I do that? What good would that do for me now? The damage has already been done. I did drugs in the past and it almost killed me."

Her mother ran her fingers through her hair when she responded to her with a frown on her face, "What does that have to do with anything? Do you know how many things that I wrote after the damage was done? It didn't matter less because it already happened to you. I would never force you to do anything that you don't want to do, baby girl. I wouldn't make you write a book because I write books. At least be open to the idea of writing a book. It can't hurt to think about it, can it? How would you feel about getting a house in New York? Would that be good for you and Bash?"

She abruptly got off of the couch as she paced in front of her mother when she asked her with concern laced in her voice, "Mom! What are you talking about? We have a house in California. Why would we need one in New York? What are you implying about something bad?"

Her mother pulled her on the couch as she held onto her hands when she told her in a soft voice, "I'm not implying anything bad. I was supposed to tell you with your mum here, but I might as well tell you right now. Your mum and I are thinking about selling the book publishing company. If you want it, then you can have it. I know that you made it clear that you have no interest in it, but people mature with age. Now that you have a daughter, you realize things that you didn't see before. We are past any bitterness that you held towards it, and we have a conversation about it like adults. Someone is willing to buy it for a lot of money, but you know that I don't care about money. I want it to go to my daughter who has been my pride and joy since the day that she was born."

She tightened her grip on her mother's hands when she asked her mother with a frown on her face, "How much money are they willing to pay for it?"

Her mother looked up at her when she told her with a neutral expression on her face, "Three hundred million dollars. We told them that we would think about it after we asked our daughter if she wanted the company. They were respectful about it. I trust the company in their hands, but I always wanted it to go to you. That was my dream from the beginning."

She aggressively shook her head at her when she responded to her in a desperate voice, "Mom! I can't hold you back from that much money. I get that money can't buy you happiness, but it can buy you comfort. A comfort that you didn't have growing up in England. You have to sell it. I can't take it from you. I took so much from you over the years. I don't want to take this from you. You deserve this. After all the hard work that you and mum put into over the last two decades, that money belongs to you guys. Not myself. Bash would say the same thing, mom. You have to take it. What does mum say about it?"

Her mother put a piece of hair behind her ear when she responded to her with her blinking back tears that fell down her face, "Your mum wants to sell it. She would've sold the company on the spot if I didn't stop her. We get into an argument about it every day. You guys want to sell it. It's hard for me. The company became my baby after you moved out of the house. I don't want to let go of it. I'm scared to lose it because I won't have anything to keep me going. You understand that feeling, baby girl."

She pulled her mother into a tight hug as she hid her face into her chest with her mother's arms wrapped around her when she told her mother with a smile on her face, "I can't tell you what to do with your company, mom. The hardest things that I did in my life were the best decisions that I made for myself. Ask yourself this. Am I going to be scared of my shadow and regret that I never did anything? Or am I going to do the bold thing that I would never allow myself to do? The answer comes to you when you think about it."

She leaned her head on her mother's shoulder when her mother told her daughter with a smile on her face, "Being bold? Are you channeling your dad? He was the only bold person that I knew. That's nice that you got it from him. It's what I miss about him the most. Will's boldness. I've been lacking it for a long time. There was a time in my life that I never thought that I would be able to live without it."

She kept her head on her mother's shoulder until she almost fell asleep where Daphne ran into her with her mum running behind her before she pulled into her lap. As Daphne cried into her chest from her nightmare, she gently nudged her mother awake as she jolted awake with her mum guiding her into their bedroom where she got off of the couch with Daphne's muffled cries into her shoulder before she went into the guest bedroom with her. After she laid down on the bed with Daphne laying down on top of her, she kissed her on the top of her head as she ran her fingers through her daughter's hair when she whispered to her like they were the people left in the world, "It's okay, little bee. Mommy is here with you now. I'll keep you safe from the world. No one can hurt you when I'm around. Let's go to bed. I'm sure you're tired. Alright?"

Daphne instantly nodded her head at her when she whispered to her mother like it was a promise between them, "Goodnight, mommy. I love you to the stars."

She kissed Daphne on the top of her head as she blinked back tears that fell down her face when she whispered to her daughter in a soft voice, "Goodnight, little bee. I love you to the stars." They fell asleep in each other's arms for the night.

CHAPTER FIFTY-TWO
(FALL 1971 – YORK, ENGLAND)

After she spent a few more days in New York, she got on a plane to California where Daphne slept in her arms for the flight. Sebastian picked them up from the airport once their plane landed where she pulled him into a long hug that they didn't let go of each other until Daphne cried from her stroller. Once Sebastian placed Daphne on his hip, they walked over to the car where their driver placed their bags in the back of the car before their driver drove them to the house. Once their driver dropped them off at the house, she carried Daphne into the house where Sebastian carried their bags with him following behind her. When they put down Daphne for her afternoon nap, she sat in the living room with Sebastian where she told him about her interview with the New York Times before she told him that her parents were selling their book publishing company for a lot of money. Sebastian asked her how much money that they were offered to sell their company. After she told him that number that her mother told her, Sebastian's jaw dropped in shock as he told her that her parents should sell the company when she told him that was what she told her mother before they moved onto the subject of Daphne. She fell asleep in his arms for the rest of the night. Sebastian worked with Katie on the operations in the studio where she dealt with their banker and their lawyers. Lucy told her a few weeks ago that they sent a sample of the New York Times article to their office that they were publishing a few days where she internally panicked when she asked Lucy to read it to her. As Lucy read the article to her, she bit the end of fingernails as she nervously paced around the room. Lucy finished reading the article where it talked about her and Sebastian being in a marriage about partnership that other couples should aspire to do. She asked Lucy where the conversation was that they had about addiction. Lucy told her that the journalist kept his word that he was going to keep it between them. She sprinted out of the office with the article in her hands as Lucy ran behind her where she ran into Sebastian in the hallway before she handed him the article without saying anything to him. After Sebastian excused himself from the filming crew, he led them into his office until they were alone with their assistants standing there. Sebastian asked her what was going on where she told him that this was the interview that she did with the New York Times before Sebastian sat down at his desk to read the article. As Sebastian read the article with his lips pressed together in a thin line, she nervously paced around the room in circles where Sebastian tightly grabbed onto her shoulders to stop her pacing in the room before she stood in front of him with her biting her lips. Sebastian excused their assistants out of the room as Sebastian pulled her into a tight hug with her face hidden in his chest when he told her that she did an incredible job in the interview and that he should've had more faith in her. She didn't tell him about her off the record conversation with the journalist about their shared experiences of addiction and she didn't plan on telling him about it anytime soon. After they heard a knock on the door from a director looking for Sebastian, he pulled her into a desperate kiss that she instantly accepted from him where they didn't pull away from each other until the knocking got louder before Sebastian ran out of the room to deal with the problem that he had to fix.

When her New York Times articles were released to the public, their assistants were overwhelmed with phone calls from publications that wanted to do interviews with them. They met up with their lawyers when one of the men told them that they should take advantage of the press's interest in them and that they should do as many interviews as possible to promote the company. Sebastian agreed with her that they needed to do interviews for the company. They told their assistants to accept the interviews with the approved list of news publications that their lawyers suggested where they scheduled interviews over the next month that would take them across the country. While they prepared for their trip across the country, her mother called her to tell her that they sold their book publishing company for three hundred and fifty million dollars and that they were moving to California to be with them. She told her mother that she couldn't wait for them to live together. Since they were going to be away from home for several weeks, they made sure that their manager Katie had everything that she needed to run the studio for them where they were going to take Daphne with them. They didn't want to leave her with her aunts or her uncles since they couldn't be apart from her for that long. They got on a plane to their first stop of the trip with their assistants, their lawyer, and their driver that was coming with them. For most of their work trip, she lost track of what she was saying or where they were going since they were in a different city every day. They did interviews every day as Sebastian's assistant watched Daphne at the hotel before they slept in their suite in each other's arms for the rest of the night. While they were on their press tour, her parents sold their house in New York as they packed up their belongings into the car where they drove from New York to California before they moved their stuff into one of the guest bedrooms. Sebastian was excited about her parents moving in with them since it meant that they could watch Daphne during the day while they were at work. She received a phone call from her parents that they made it to California with their belongings. They were in Florida at the time as they sent Daphne home with her assistant Lucy who needed to get back to her children where her parents took care of Daphne while they finished their interviews with the newspaper publications. After a few more weeks on the press tour, they did their final interviews left on the tour while they handled the day-to-day business of the studio where Sebastian called Katie to learn how their productions were doing before she called with the bank about their finances. On the last night of their media tour, she couldn't sleep as she smoked cigarettes on the balcony. She wrote a letter to the journalist from the New York Times where she thanked him for keeping their conversation about addiction to himself and not publishing it in his article to the rest of the world to read about. After they got back to home from being gone for over a month, Daphne ran over to them as they pulled her into a long hug that they didn't break apart from each other until her mother and her mum walked over to them. Once she placed Daphne on her hip, she pulled her mother into a tight hug as Sebastian kissed her mum on the cheek where she pulled her mum into a tight hug with Sebastian kissing her mother on the cheek before they went into the house to unpack their stuff in their bedroom. She received a letter at the studio a week later from the New York Times Journalist. He thanked for her letter, and he asked her what was next for her since he knew that she was a great writer after he read her letter. In her letter back to him, she told him that the chances of her writing a book about her addiction were higher than the last time that she talked to him.

They left Daphne and Katherine at home with her parents. They worked at the studio all day until they got home in the evening where they ate dinner with her parents and Daphne before Daphne's bedtime routine at night. While her daughter slept in the middle of the night, she went into her office to her typewriter that they used for business purposes as she typed up whatever thoughts came into her mind. Sebastian checked on her in the middle of the night where she stopped writing before she fell asleep in Sebastian's arms for the rest of the night. She didn't read what she wrote until the next night where she found herself in front of the typewriter again. That was when she realized that there was something going on here. She wasn't going to write books like her mother's books. Her mother was great at storytelling in a fiction book, but she couldn't do it since she wasn't good at creating a fictional world. She created a self-help book about her personal struggles with addiction. She wrote personal anecdotes from her life that taught her important lessons about how to survive with her addiction and lessons that she learned from her father. When she wrote her book in the middle of the night, Sebastian was the only person that knew about it until she ran into her mother in the middle of the night. She tried to hide it from her that she was writing a book before her mother told her that she knew that she was keeping something from her. After her mother found out about her book, they wrote on their typewriters in the office most of the night where they shared what they wrote with each other before they went to bed in the early hours of the morning. It was nice to have something that she could do with her mother. She hadn't felt that connected to her mother since she was a little girl, and she loved every moment of it. Her mother enjoyed it too since she bragged to her mum about it every chance that she got even though her mum didn't care about it. Her cousin George called to tell them that he was getting married to his girlfriend Annabell and he asked them if they were coming to the wedding where she told him that they would love to come to their wedding. She told Sebastian and her parents about Annabell and George's wedding in York. After she talked to her cousins that were coming too, they made plans to leave the states for a week where Sebastian prepared Katie to hold down the fort when they were gone before she prepared Lucy for taking over her duties with the lawyers and the bank. On the morning of their flight to New York, her parents placed their bags into the back of the car where their driver dropped them off at the airport before they met up with Oliver's family, Amelia's family, and Sasha's family at their gate. For their flight to New York, Daphne slept in her arms as she slept with her head leaning on Sebastian's shoulder until he gently nudged her awake when their plane landed in New York where they went straight from their plane to their flight to London. On their overnight flight to London, Daphne was wide awake as they passed her back and forth from Sebastian and her parents before Daphne fell asleep on her grandmother's chest. When their plane landed in London in the morning, Sebastian carried Daphne who was asleep in his arms as she held onto her niece Eleanor's hand with their bags in her other hand. Sean met up with them at the airport when he pulled her into a tight hug that she didn't let go of until Daphne softly cried near her. Once she grabbed Daphne from Sebastian's arms, she handed him their bags as she held onto Eleanor hand with Daphne on her hip where she followed Sean to his car before she got into the back of the car with her parents and Sebastian. Her cousins Tommy and Alfie took the family to their houses until they met up for dinner that evening. As soon as she walked into Sean's house, her five-year-old nieces Ashley and Alyssa ran into her legs before she pulled them into a tight hug. After she placed Daphne down onto the floor, Daphne ran over to play with her two-year-old cousin Arthur where she kissed Polly on her cheek before she helped Sebastian carry their bags into the house. Once they took a nap for most of the afternoon, she changed into a long dress as she put Daphne into a dress where they met up with her family at their favorite restaurant before they went to their houses for the rest of the night. She met her cousin Tommy's eldest son Charlie and her cousin Alfie's eldest son Weston.

She woke up the next morning to Daphne talking to Arthur on the floor. She gently nudged Sebastian awake who softly groaned at her where they loaded up into Sean's car before Sean drove them to York. Once they got to York in the early afternoon, Sean took them to Uncle Nathan's house where they stayed with him for the rest of the week. She walked into the house with Daphne on her hip where Uncle Nathan pulled her into a long hug that they didn't let go of each other until Daphne whined for Uncle Nathan to pick her up before she handed Daphne over to him. She helped Sebastian carry their bags into their bedrooms as the children ran around them. She greeted her cousin Poppy and her husband Ellis with three-year-old Jack and one year old Madeline in the yard where they hugged each other before she went inside while her daughter played in the living room with Arthur and Emmeline. They went over to Aunt Sylvia's house where Oliver's family and Amelia's family were staying in York. She caught up with her cousin Audrey as her husband Teddy caught up with Oliver where their five children played with their cousins in the living room where they ate dinner in her mother's childhood house before they went back to their houses for the rest of the night. Since they had several days of downtime until George and Annabell's wedding day, she spent time with her cousins where Daphne met most of her cousins that she never met before in her life. Sebastian was in communication with Katie from the studio where he made sure that everything was going well in their absence. She told Sebastian that he didn't need to work while they were on vacation, but he wasn't going to stop working no matter what. She babysat her nieces and her nephews with Amelia, Sasha, Nina, and Anastasia while everyone was at the venue preparing for the wedding. They watched their cousin's children from the ages of ten years old to three months old where they were exhausted by the end of the day before their cousins collected their children at the end of the day. Daphne was surrounded by her cousins that gave her built-in playmates. Daphne refused to nap during the day since she wanted to play with her cousins, so Daphne slept throughout the night. When she wasn't on babysitting duty, she went over to Poppy's farm to see the changes that were made, and she went over to Audrey's house that Teddy expanded for their growing family. While they drank lemonade at Audrey's house, Audrey told her Aunt Sylvia and Aunt Priscilla sold the bakery to Teddy who put it into her name since they were retiring from working to focus on their grandchildren. She wasn't surprised that they were retired. Her parents retired when they sold their book company. On the day of George and Annabell's wedding, they got ready for the wedding where Uncle Nathan drove them to the venue before she was put on babysitting duty once again with Amelia and Sasha who weren't eager about it. While Annabell got ready with her bridesmaids in the church, George got ready in the office with his brothers and his cousins. They watched the children play outside until her cousins collected their children before she followed Sebastian into the church with Daphne on her hip. Once George and Annabell said their vows to each other, Uncle James named them husband and wife as George pulled Annabell into a long kiss with the family cheering in the background where George and Annabell ran down the aisle before they went into the church basement. After they ate a delicious meal that was made for them, she followed Sebastian outside with Daphne on his hip where Daphne chased her cousins around the field before she took a seat on the picnic bench in between Sebastian and Oliver.

Sebastian wrapped his arm around her as she leaned her head on his shoulder when Oliver asked them with a smile on his face, "How have things been for you guys? It's been a while since we talked to each other."

She gave Sebastian a look that told him that she wasn't in the mood for talking as he tightened his grip on her arms when he responded to Oliver with his lips in a thin line, "Life has been very busy. The company is doing well after the interviews that we did to promote it. My mother-in-law's moved in with us. That's been good. We keep Daphne at home during the day with her grandmothers instead of leaving her at daycare. How is Eleanor doing with school? She doesn't stop talking about it."

Oliver responded to Sebastian with a wide grin on his face, "I'm glad that Eleanor talks about school. She's obsessed with her teacher and her classmates. It's a good school for the girls. I'll help you get

Daphne into the school when it's the right time. That's a few years away, but it doesn't hurt to be prepared. I read some of your interviews that you guys did for the company. It was very well done. I would want to work for your company if I wasn't attached to my career. Juliet loves working there. She hated her job until she worked for you. If my wife is happy, then I'm happy too. Isn't that right, Bash? How about you, Isabella? You are being quiet tonight. What's going on with you?"

She lit a cigarette that she got out from her purse as she inhaled the smoke from it when Sebastian said to them with a concerned look on his face, "I'll go check on the girls. They are being too quiet for my liking. I hope that they aren't getting into something that they shouldn't be doing. I'll be back."

Once Sebastian kissed her on the lips, he ran over to where Daphne and Eleanor played with their cousins on the playground as she inhaled the smoke from her cigarette where Oliver wrapped his arm around her when he asked her with concern laced in his voice, "What's wrong, Isabella? Why did you make Bash leave? Is there something that you don't want him knowing about? I can keep a secret."

She inhaled smoke from her cigarette when she responded to Oliver with a frown on her face, "I'm okay, Oliver. I'm feeling sentimental about the last time that I was in York. It's hard to be back in a place where your life fell apart. It was my fault, but it doesn't make it hurt any less. Did Bash tell you that I'm writing a book?"

Oliver shook his head at her as he tightened his grip on her arms when he responded to her with excitement laced in his voice, "He didn't tell me that. That's wonderful, Isabella. I know that you are an incredible writing from the not suicide note that you sent me. What are you writing about?"

She inhaled the smoke from her cigarette when she responded to him in a soft voice, "The book is about addiction. It's a collection of short stories about my personal experiences and lessons that I learned throughout my life. You are never going to guess who told me to write it. It was the journalist that I did the New York Times interview with three months ago. He told me that I should write a book about my addiction after we had an honest conversation with each other."

Oliver ran his hands down her arms when he responded to her with a look of confusion on his face, "That's bold, Isabella. Why didn't I read about that in your article? That would've been more interesting to read about. You're taking your power back from your addiction. It's taken so much from you that it's time for you to take it back for yourself. Can I read your book when you are done with it?"

She nodded her head at him when she responded to him with a frown on her face, "Of course you can, Oliver. You'll be the first person to read it after my parents and Bash read it. Thanks for calling me bold. It doesn't feel like I'm bold. It feels like I'm a coward. I've learned from my dad that being a coward and being bold are the same thing. My mom called me bold. I don't believe that it's true. Since I started writing this book, I can't stop thinking about something. Do you want to know what it is?"

Oliver nodded his head at her when he asked her with a concerned look on his face, "What is that, Isabella?"

She leaned her head onto Oliver's shoulder when she confessed to him in a distant voice, "I can't stop thinking about what my life would look like if I didn't stop what I was doing the last time that I was in York. I get this thought that I wouldn't be alive. There was a moment that I would've welcomed a thought like that. It was before I got married to Bash and I had Daphne. I would've continued on that path if you didn't tell me that it was a choice. I made the wrong choice. No one told me that. Not even my dad told me that. I know that you saved my life many times before, but those words saved my life. That's what I told the journalist when we were talking about addiction. I learned that it was a choice, and I made the wrong choice. That stopped me from going on that awful path that I was destined to go down if I didn't stop doing drugs. I would've died like my dad did. Do you want to know the most fucked up thing? I didn't see this life for myself. I didn't see myself having an engagement, a wedding, or my daughter last time that I was here. If I'm being honest with you, I didn't think that I would live as long as I have been. I never imagined what life would be like if I was alive longer than my dad was alive. I didn't think that I would have a family that depended on me. I didn't deserve to be any of those things that my dad didn't have. Just because he made the wrong choice doesn't mean that he didn't deserve the chance to have any of those things. What makes me so special to have the things that he never had?"

Oliver wrapped his arms around her where she let out heartbreaking sobs into his chest with Oliver running his hands up and down her back. She slowly pulled her face out of his chest as Oliver kept his arms around her when he responded to her in a soft voice, "You deserve those things. Even at the height of your addiction, I thought that you deserved that. I didn't know how you were going to get there, but I had faith that you would find your way. Why do you think that you don't deserve those things? Bash chose you to have a family with. Do you think that he chose wrong?"

She hid her face into his chest when she confessed to him in a distant voice, "He didn't choose wrong. I love the life that I created with Bash and Daphne. It's everything that I thought that I would never have. I couldn't imagine my life without them. I think about the alternative life that I chose drugs over anything else. Life is a series of choices that lead to a moment in time. That moment for me was when I was here in York four years ago. If I could step into a doorway to a different time, I would find myself there. I would be at my dad's grave high out of my mind where you told me that I made the wrong choice and that loving me was the biggest burden in your life. I would be in that moment when I told Bash that I cheated on him with Jade when he broke up with me. I would be thinking about how everything could end that night if I made it stop. I would be successful this time because I was determined to die. I wasn't successful despite my own disappointment, but I wanted to believe that it was possible for everything to stop for me. It's never going to happen. Nothing ever ends. I don't know what I would've done if life went that way. It's not good for me to think about it. That would be a mistake. Don't you get curious about these things? I'm not the only person that thinks about what could've been. Don't you do it?"

Oliver looked down at her with his arms around her when he responded to her with a serious look on his face, "Sometimes I think about what I would do if you died in that club. I think about what I would do if you died when Daxton died. I think about what I would do if you died when you overdosed on sleeping pills. I think about what I would do if you died in your last overdose in New York. None of them are good outcomes for us. When I was younger, I thought about how different my life would be if my dad came back from the war. Do you want to hear my advice as a psychiatrist that I would tell one of my clients? I would say that this thinking is counterproductive. There is a boundary that exists between thinking about what would've been in life and glamorizing the tragedy of it. You've always been leaning more on the side of glamorizing it than being curious about it. If healing is your objective, then you need to learn the balance between these steps. I know that you want to heal and that's why you are writing your book. I'm only telling you this out of love, but you can't balance anything. You've never been able to do it. It's all or nothing with you. In the short term, it keeps life on the edge. In the long term, it's a destructive pattern of behavior that will ruin you. The question isn't how to create a balance in your life. How do you manage balance in your life? It's not your fault that you are like this. You can't help it if you don't know how to do this. No one told you this. I've never walked on eggshells with you. That is what makes our relationship strong. You don't like it when people treat you like you are broken. Not that I think that you are broken, but that's how you would describe it. I don't think that anyone is broken. Do you want to know how to balance it?"

She responded to him with a smirk on her face, "Oliver! How long have you been holding that back? Sounds like you have been storing that for a long time. What do I do to learn how to balance it? I've tried everything, and it doesn't work for me. What's the secret?"

She leaned her head on his shoulder when he responded to her with a smile on his face, "You need to give up control. Not control over your addiction. That's necessary for you to survive. You need to give up the control that you think that you have. You don't have any control on what happens in your life. You can't control who your parents are or what genetic traits that you inherited from them. You can't control who you become. You most certainly can't control what you expect yourself to be. You only get disappointed when nothing goes the way that you plan. I've been holding onto this for a long time. I was afraid to upset you. I didn't think that you were ready. I didn't see it until it happened to you. I learned a lot that I never shared with anyone. I know you won't tell Bash what you told me. It's okay to have secrets. This stays between us as it always does."

Once she looped her pinky onto his pinky, she leaned her head on his shoulder as he ran his hands up and down her back before Daphne and Eleanor ran towards them with Sebastian following behind them. As soon as Daphne ran over to her, she pulled her daughter on her lap as Oliver pulled Eleanor on his lap when she asked Daphne with her running her fingers through her hair, "Did you have fun with Kitty?"

Daphne asked her mother with concern laced in her voice, "We had fun. Are you okay, mommy? Did Uncle Oli upset you? We heard you crying. Daddy made us play somewhere else. I wanted to go to you, but daddy wouldn't let me."

She pulled Daphne into her chest when she whispered to her daughter like it was a secret between them, "I'm okay, little bee. Uncle Oli didn't upset me. He was making me feel better. You know like I do when you are sad. Mommy gets sad about things that happened. It's okay to cry when you're sad."

Daphne asked her with innocence laced in her voice, "Are you sad about grandpa? He feels sad."

She looked over at Sebastian and Oliver who had shocked looks on their faces as she tightened her grip on Daphne when she responded to her daughter with a confused look on her face, "Who told you about grandpa, little bee? Was it Ella and Abby?"

Daphne hid her face in her mother's chest when she responded to her with a frown on her face, "They didn't need to tell me. I already knew who he was. I met him in the stars. You look like him, mommy. Grandma Ella gets sad about him too. You can be sad about grandpa, mommy." She blinked back tears that fell down her face with Daphne in her arms as Oliver grabbed onto her shoulder before he got up from the picnic bench with Eleanor on his hip where he disappeared into the darkness. Once Sebastian took a seat next to her, she hid her face into his chest with Sebastian's arms around her where they stayed like that until Daphne fell asleep in her arms. After she got off of the picnic bench, she walked over to her cousin Poppy's car where Sebastian drove them to Uncle Nathan's house before they fell asleep in each other's arms around the rest of the night.

CHAPTER FIFTY-THREE
(WINTER 1972 – LOS ANGELES, CALIFORNIA)

Sebastian and Oliver had a hushed conversation with each other in the hallway as she pulled Daphne closer into her chest where she ran her fingers through her daughter's hair before Sebastian walked into their bedroom with a plate of food in his hands. Once they ate breakfast with Daphne helping herself to all of their food, Sebastian packed up their bags as she got Daphne dressed into a warm outfit for the airport where she helped Sebastian with the rest of their packing before they drove to London with Sean's family and her parents. She slept with her head leaning on Sebastian's shoulder as he entertained Daphne in the car until Sean dropped them off at the airport where they got their overnight flight to New York. While she slept for the flight, Daphne was having a meltdown that Sebastian had to deal with all by himself. Sebastian gave her the silent treatment where she didn't care about Sebastian's frustration with her. She didn't care about anything ever since her conversation with Oliver in York. When their plane landed in New York later that day, she grabbed onto her daughter who was asleep in Sebastian's arms as she grabbed onto their bags where she flagged down a taxi before the taxi driver drove them to a hotel for the night. Sebastian gave up following them down the street before their taxi disappeared down the street. Once the taxi driver dropped off at the hotel, she paid the taxi drawer the money that she owed him as she carried her daughter on her arms with their bags in her other hand where she paid for a room before she took them to their suite. Once she placed her daughter on the bed, she called Uncle Sam when she told him that she was staying at a hotel with Daphne and that he couldn't tell Sebastian. Uncle Sam didn't feel comfortable being in the middle of their argument. He wouldn't tell Sebastian where they were. She thought about the conversation that Sebastian and Oliver had about her. Sebastian knew why she was mad at him. He knew that she couldn't stand it when people talked about her behind her back. Every time that he tried to do that she got upset with him. The more that she thought about it the more that she realized that she didn't care what they were talking about. It was the act that mattered to her more than their conversation. When her daughter woke up in the afternoon asking where her father was, she told Daphne that Sebastian went home for work as she needed to get work done before they went back home to him. That was enough for her daughter who played with her toys on the floor as she talked on the phone with the bank about meeting with them in person since she was unexpectedly in the city. Once she put Daphne to sleep in their bed for the rest of the night, she got a phone call from Sebastian who was staying at Uncle Sam's house when he asked her why she took off with their daughter in the airport before she told him that he knew better than that to talk about her behind her back to Oliver.

After Sebastian acted like he had no idea what she was talking about, it made her even more angry at him since he didn't want to acknowledge it where she told him that she would talk to him again when he apologized for lying to her before she hung up on him in a fit of anger against him. She woke up the next morning to someone pounding on her hotel room door as she made sure that Daphne was asleep in their bed where she went to open up the door when Sebastian let himself into the room before he asked her if she was high. She wasn't in the mood to entertain that notion, so she told him to leave them alone while she thought about things. Sebastian asked her what things she needed to consider before she told him that she needed to think about her life with him. Even though she didn't mean to be cruel to him, he took it like a personal insult to him as he told her that he was taking their daughter to California with him to make sure that she was safe. She let Daphne go with Sebastian who was confused about what was going on before he took their daughter with him slamming the door behind him. When she was alone in her hotel room, she slid into her comfort position as she sobbed into her knees where she laid down on the floor with her staring up at the ceiling before she passed out for the rest of the night. She woke up the next morning to someone pounding on the door as she stayed in her bed until the pounding on the door got louder before she opened up the door where Oliver stood in front of her. Oliver pulled her into a tight hug that they didn't let go of each other where Oliver brought her over to the bed with her face hidden into his chest. Oliver stayed with her for the rest of the night when he told her that she needed to get professional help where she agreed with him since she knew that the stakes were higher than they used to be with her daughter. Oliver couldn't get her to go to an inpatient place that would cause her to relapse like the last time. Oliver called Dr. Taylor to ask him if he would be willing to see her again when he told Oliver that he would see her at his house where Oliver packed up her bags for her before they got on a plane to Los Angeles. When their plane landed in Los Angeles that afternoon, Dr. Taylor met them at the airport as he pulled her into a tight hug that she instantly accepted from him until Oliver got back with their bags where they went to Dr. Taylor's house before Oliver left her alone with him. Even though this was an unorthodox agreement, it would be best for her to spend as much time as she needed to get better at Dr. Taylor's house since he kept an eye on her without making her go to the hospital again. Once Oliver dropped off her typewriter and her clothes at his house, she got comfortable in Dr. Taylor's guest bedroom as she spent most of her days writing on her typewriter when she wasn't talking to Dr. Taylor about why she was acting like this. She didn't know if the episode came from being in the place of her last relapse or if it was the things that she wrote about that triggered it. It was the closest that she got to relapsing in four years. In her sessions with Dr. Taylor, they talked about everything that led up to the moment that she craved drugs. She told him that being married to Sebastian reminded her of everything that she never allowed herself to have. Being a mother was something that didn't belong to her. She told him about what Oliver told her about being unable to find a balance.

Dr. Taylor asked her what she thought that it meant to have balance where she told him that being balanced meant that she wasn't waiting for the next bomb to drop on her. Dr. Taylor asked her what kind of bombs did that to her. She told him that it was bombs that crept up on her out of nowhere until she couldn't get away from them no matter what she did. Those bombs being her complicated relationship with her father and drugs. She was living in a warzone waiting for the next attack from the enemy except that the enemy was herself and she couldn't run away from herself. That sentiment connected well with Dr. Taylor who understood what she was saying to him since it gave him a chance to teach her the secret to dealing with her mistakes that she made. The secret to deal with the mistakes was to deal with her emotions about what happened to her. It seemed to be an obvious thing to do, but she was shocked by it. It was as simple as Oliver's suggestion in England to give up control in her life. Everything didn't need to go like she wanted it to. Dr. Taylor said that the biggest part of giving up control was that she needed to stop holding onto things that she couldn't change, or she had nothing to do with. She made a professional career over holding responsibility against herself for things that didn't have anything to do with her. She told him that the root of this problem came from her being unable to deal with what happened to her as a child. She took on the weight for everyone around her. If she wasn't taking on the weight, then everyone would suffer from it. The last thing that she wanted was for anyone to suffer if she was there to deal with it. Not only had she taken on the weight of her crimes, but she took on the weight of her father's crimes too. Her father didn't make his peace, and it was her duty to do it for him. Except that there was no peace for him. She decided that there was no peace for her either. That was when she got high for the first time. Dr. Taylor asked her why she felt the need to take on her father's pain when she told him that her father's pain was his legacy and that she didn't want to lose his legacy by letting go of his pain. The pain was the only connection that she had left to him, and she didn't want to lose the only thing that he gave her. Her pain became interconnected with her father's pain. She couldn't tell what belonged to either of them. It was like they merged into one person when he died. The pain was so connected to her identity that she didn't know who she was without it. She didn't know who she was outside of her addiction, her mental illnesses, and her trauma. She found some sense of identity from being a wife or a mother, but it didn't define her like those other things did. She spent several weeks finding the real version of herself under all of the pain. This task was harder than she thought that it was going to be since she struggled to find it. She was awake most nights working on her book while she smoked cigarettes on the balcony of the bedroom where she talked to her father about anything and everything that was on her mind. In her nighttime conversations with her father, she was trapped in this cycle of life and death that was self-inflicted to distract her. She was a byproduct of her surroundings that she grew up in. She learned how to absorb the pain from her parents who were professionals at it. Her parents were absorbing everyone's pain except their own pain that let each other deal with on their behalf. That was why her father was disturbed about Uncle Kenny molesting her mother when they were children because he was dealing with the pain for her. Her father dealt with it by getting high and throwing himself into dangerous situations, but it was his way of dealing with it. Her mother was so consumed with her father being sent to prison that she forgot to deal with her own pain of being raped. Her mother dealt with his pain by going to therapy and processing her emotions on his behalf.

She dealt with everyone else's pain because she didn't want to deal with her own pain. She didn't know what her pain, her mother's pain, or her father's pain was. When she acknowledged her pain for the first time, it came from her parents' pain that became her pain. It was clear why she didn't know how to balance her life because the lines were so blurred that they didn't exist. She didn't have any boundaries with anyone including herself. That meant that she would have to face the reality that she never stood on her own two legs. Since her mother was going through so much when she had her, she didn't have boundaries with her, and her mother didn't have boundaries with her father. Her mother transferred her relationship with her father onto her daughter who took over that role. Her mother desperately searched for someone to fill it. It shouldn't have shocked her that the origin of the relationship with her parents stemmed from her mother's relationship with Uncle Kenny. Uncle Kenny resented her father for taking his place in her mother's life. Uncle Kenny would've been proud of her father for raping her mother because it was something that he did to her. She was caught in between the past lives of her parents and the present of her life. Sebastian was right. She didn't know how to live in the present without being trapped in the past. Suddenly, she was filled with regret for how she treated Sebastian for the past two months where she asked Dr. Taylor at dinner if she could see Sebastian when he told her that they would make arrangements for him to come to the house. Dr. Taylor left her alone in the house a few days later where she nervously paced around the living room until she heard a knock on the door before Sebastian helped himself into the house. As soon as Sebastian walked into the living room, she threw herself into his arms as she hid her face into his chest with his arms tightly wrapped around her where he pulled her into a desperate kiss until they pulled away from each other before she apologized to him. She expressed how she felt horrible for the way that she treated Sebastian on their last day in York and for her taking off in New York with their daughter. Sebastian told her that he was sorry for the way that he reacted to her cry for help that she was asking from him and that he was only worried about her. They had sex with each other in the living room. Sebastian was so remorseful for doing it on her psychiatrist's couch that he wrote him a check to pay for cleaning of the couch before he asked her to come home to her family. She told Sebastian that she would talk to Dr. Taylor about it when he returned home from the bar with his friends where Sebastian went back home before she typed on her typewriter in her bedroom.

Dr. Taylor told her at breakfast the next morning that she could go home to her family if she felt ready to go into the real world again where she thanked him for taking care of her before she pulled him into a long hug that they didn't let go of until they smelled the bacon burning on the stove. Once they ate their last meal together, she packed up her belongings into her bags before Dr. Taylor dropped her off at her house where her parents, Sebastian, and Daphne waited for them. As soon as she got out of the car, Daphne sprinted over to her as she pulled her daughter into her arms with tears falling down their faces. They didn't let go of each other until Sebastian pulled them into a desperate hug. She carried her daughter into the house as her parents pulled her into long hugs. Daphne showed her the new toys that her father and her grandparents got her in the last two months. Daphne wouldn't let her mother out of sight as she cried for her until she pulled Daphne in her arms where Daphne hid her face into her mother's chest before she put her down into her bedroom for the rest of the night. Daphne acted like this in the next few weeks where she worked from home with Daphne following her except for when she left Daphne with her parents during her appointments with Dr. Taylor that Daphne clung onto her for the rest of the day. Daphne didn't act like that with her before she recovered at Dr. Taylor's house for two months. Sebastian told her that Daphne didn't do well with her being away from home. It was so bad that Sebastian took Daphne everywhere with him or else she was inconsolable until he came home. Daphne stopped sleeping in her bed at night where Daphne always ended up in their bed in the morning no matter what they did to encourage Daphne to sleep in her big girl bed that they got for her. They needed to figure out why Daphne was acting like this. Oliver got his co-worker who was a child psychiatrist to talk to Daphne where they waited to get Daphne alone in a room with a psychiatrist until after they got the chance to talk to her. They had a week to themselves in the house since her parents were in New York visiting Uncle Sam and Aunt Valeria. They were celebrating Uncle Sam selling his toy company for twenty million dollars. She needed to stay home to deal with her daughter's emotional issues that she was experiencing when her mother told her to tell their family that they were too busy with the film studio to come with them. Sasha took Charlotte with her to her father's retirement party since Gabriel was so busy with working at the photography studio that he couldn't come with her. She woke up to Daphne sleeping in their bed that morning as she pulled Daphne closer to her as her daughter slept in her arms. Sebastian woke them up when he got ready for work where she pulled Daphne out of bed with her on her hip. Once Sebastian walked into the kitchen to make breakfast, she carried Daphne downstairs where she talked to Sebastian about what was happening at the studio over pancakes that he made for them before Sebastian left to go to work for the day. While Daphne played with her dolls on the couch, she called her assistant Lucy from the office to catch up with her lawyer who was in the office with her before she had her daily phone call with the bank when Daphne took a nap on the couch.

Once she was done working for the day, they ate lunch in the kitchen with Daphne's favorite television show playing in the background where she changed into their swimsuits before she went into the pool with Daphne for the rest of the afternoon. They showered in the bathroom where Daphne played with her dolls as she cooked pasta for dinner when Sebastian kissed Daphne on the top of her head before he pecked her on the lips. Once she was finished making dinner, she set out plates for each of them even though they knew that Daphne was going to eat the food off of their plates. Sebastian talked about his day at work as Daphne shared stories from their time in the pool where she cleaned up the dishes from dinner before Sebastian took Daphne into the shower with him. Daphne didn't need a shower since she got one a few hours ago. Daphne wanted to shower with them every time that they went to go in the bathroom without her. Once Sebastian and Daphne walked into their bedroom, she changed Daphne into her nightgown as Sebastian changed into his favorite pajamas where they laid down on the bed with Daphne in between them. Daphne asked for them to read a story to her. After they read Daphne's favorite book to her, she requested that they read another book to her as Sebastian read her favorite story when Daphne asked him with a pout on her face, "Can mommy read a story to me?"

As she ran her fingers through her daughter's damp hair, she wrapped her other arm around her when she asked Daphne with a smile on her face, "Of course I can, little bee? What do you want mommy reading to you? Do you want to read the bunny book again?"

Daphne laid her head down on her mother's chest when she told her with an innocent look on her face, "I don't want to read the bunny book. I want mommy to make up a story. Grandma Ella does that with me when she takes care of me. Can you do that, mommy? Make it interesting like Grandma Ella."

She looked up at Sebastian who looked as shocked as her about what Daphne told her when she responded to her daughter with a frown on her face, "I'll try to be as engaging as Grandma Ella is. She's hard to compete with, little bee. Mommy isn't a storyteller like she is. Where is this story taking place?"

Daphne told her with her sweet eyes staring at her, "You can do anything, mommy. Don't talk about yourself like that. Daddy doesn't like it. The story is in England."

Sebastian kissed his daughter on the top of her head when he told Daphne with a smile on his face, "That's right, little bee. Mommy shouldn't talk about herself like that. She can do anything that she sets her mind to. Who's in this story? Are we in the story?"

Daphne leaned onto them as her mother ran her fingers through her hair when Daphne responded to them with excitement laced in her voice, "Mommy and daddy are going to be in it. Grandma Ella and Grandma Abby are going to be in it. El and Kitty are going to be in it. Grandpa is going to be in it."

Her face turned white at the mention of her father as she ran her fingers through her daughter's hair when she responded to Daphne with a serious look on her face, "Our story starts in England. Mommy is a little girl like you are little bee. She is born surrounded by the people that love her. That is everyone except for her daddy. Her mommy promises to give her the world. Though none of them know it yet, it will come true for them. Her mommy takes care of her baby like she wished that someone took care of her. She rocks her baby to sleep every night. She's attentive to her needs. She feeds her baby when she's hungry. She soothes her baby when she cries for her. The baby doesn't know it yet, but she is going to miss those moments that she's never going to get back. The baby grows up into a child that is scared of the world. She doesn't know much, but she knows that she's missing something from her life. She sees that her cousins have a mommy and a daddy. She only has a mommy. She asks her mommy why she doesn't have a daddy. Her mommy tells her that daddy can't be with them because he's in prison. Her mommy promises her that they are better off without him because her daddy hurt them. Even though she has more questions for her mommy, she doesn't ask them because her mommy is crying. Her mommy cries a lot about her daddy. She doesn't understand why her mommy is crying. She makes her feel better by hugging and kissing her until she isn't crying anymore."

Daphne hid her face into her mother's chest when she asked her with confusion laced in her voice, "Why is her daddy in prison? Did he steal something from her?"

She put her chin on top of Daphne's head when she confessed to her daughter with tears falling down her face, "Her daddy stole something from her mommy. He stole the most important thing from her. He stole her innocence. Her mommy explains this to her. Even though she doesn't understand what it means, she knows that it's serious. Years go by for her. She grows up without her daddy. She doesn't know her daddy, but she wants to know him. Her mommy promises her that she can know her daddy when he's out of prison. That never happens because they move to the states without her daddy. Her mommy wants to be a writer, so they stay in New York to help her mommy have a career. She moves in with her cousins, her aunt, and her uncle. She doesn't mind living with them because she has someone to play with and her mommy is home with her during the day. In New York, she meets her other mommy, and she has two mommies. When her daddy gets out of prison, she goes to England with her mommies where she sees her daddy. They don't say anything because their eyes tell them everything that they need to know about each other. Her daddy gave her a doll that morning that he leaves on her doorstep. Her mommy doesn't tell her that the doll is from her daddy. She already knows that. Her daddy's eyes asked her if she liked the doll and her eye's told him back that it was the best gift that she received from him. Little does she know that the doll is the only thing that her daddy will give her. She sees her daddy talking to her mommy. She thinks that she has a chance to get to know her daddy now that her parents forgive each other. She goes back to New York with her mommies and her daddy stays in England. Something changes since she has met her daddy. There is a hole missing in her heart that longs for him. Here comes the hard part of the story. Do you want to hear it, little bee?"

Daphne looked up at her mother when she responded to her with her big eyes staring at her, "Yes, mommy. Tell me."

As she wiped tears off of her face, she assured Sebastian who was comforting her with his hand going up and down her back that she was okay when she confessed to her daughter in a soft voice, "That longing gets worse until it erupts into an overwhelming feeling that she can no longer control. She does things to make herself feel better. None of those things work. She's desperate to fill the hole that he left inside of her heart. Little does she know that it's only getting worse for her. When she is eight years old, her mommy tells her that her daddy died and that they have to go to England to say goodbye to him. This breaks her heart. She tells her mommy that she doesn't want to say goodbye to her daddy because she never knew him. She asks her mommy how she can say goodbye to someone that she never knew. That seems to be the straw that breaks her mommy. Her mommy apologizes to her that her baby girl never knew her daddy. She goes to England to say goodbye to her daddy. She sneaks into the viewing room without her mommies, and she sees her daddy. She sees him in a way that no one saw him. She realizes that it's up to her to carry on his legacy. She's responsible for continuing his story from where he left off. She grows up without her daddy. She goes through a lot along the way, and she learns a lot about herself. She'll always be that little girl that wants her daddy. She'll always be that little girl that wanted to know him. Do you want to know the most beautiful lesson?"

Daphne asked her with a frown on her face, "What is it, mommy?"

She grabbed onto one of Sebastian's hands who had tears falling down his face as she grabbed onto Daphne's hand with her other hand when she said to her with a smile on her face, "That something great came out of it. There was a good ending to the story. She could never dream of having a family. She gave her baby what she never had. Her baby would have a mommy and a daddy that loved her. It was the only thing that she needed. Her baby filled the hole in her heart that her daddy left inside of her. Was that a good story, little bee?"

She pulled her daughter into her arms as she ran her hands up and down her back when Daphne said to her mother, "That was a great story. I love you, mommy. I hate it when you are sad. Next time we can do a story that doesn't make you cry."

She kissed her daughter on the top of her head when she responded to her with a smile on her face, "We'll do that next time. Do you want to sleep in your big girl bed? Or do you want to sleep with mommy and daddy?"

Daphne moved into her chest when she whispered into Daphne's ear who was asleep in her arms, "Goodnight. I love you." Sebastian pulled her into a long kiss where they didn't pull away from each other until he whispered to her that he loved her as she said the same thing back to him before they fell asleep in each other's arms for the rest of the night.

Chapter Fifty-Four
(Spring 1972 – Malibu, California)

Their conversation explaining why she disappeared in a childlike manner seemed to work. Daphne slept in her own bed again and she was okay with being apart from during her weekly sessions at Dr. Taylor's office. When her parents came back from New York, they were so shocked by Daphne's sudden change in behavior that they asked her what they did to help her before she told her parents that the only thing that she did was tell her daughter the truth about why she left her. Her parents were shocked that she found a way to explain it to her almost two-year-old daughter in a way that she understood, and Daphne knew what she was talking about in the story the entire time. She didn't tell her parents about how Daphne talked about her grandpa long before anyone told her about him or that Daphne knew that they were in the stars together. Since Daphne was okay with being home with her grandparents, she went back to work in the studio with her assistant Lucy who held down the fort while she was gone. They went to work during the day while Daphne was being taken care of by her grandparents with Katherine and Charlotte. They talked about how they were going to tell Daphne about their pasts when the time would come for her to know about them. There would be a time when Daphne would get curious about their childhoods, and they would tell her about it. Daphne was obsessed with asking them about when she was going to have a little sister. She was jealous of the relationship that Eleanor and Posey had with each other. They weren't thinking about having another child until their daughter brought it up to them one night when they were putting her to bed. This led to many conversations with each other about whether it was time to have another baby or not. They decided that they would see what would happen if they tried for another baby as they would consider what to do after that if it didn't work out for them.

In her weekly sessions at Dr. Taylor's office, they talked about what it meant for her to raise her daughter now that she was aware of what happened to her grandfather. It was hard for her to talk about it, let alone her daughter who she was protecting from it. He asked her what it meant for her to create a boundary between the things that she wanted her daughter to know and the things that she didn't want her daughter knowing about her. He encouraged her to make those boundaries when her daughter was young, so that her daughter wouldn't grow up with the trauma that her parents inflicted onto her. For her to learn how to create those boundaries with her daughter, she needed to learn how to create those boundaries within herself so that she could learn to separate her trauma from her parent's trauma. She thought about the things that she didn't want to think about. She wrote her book in the middle of the night where she felt emotions that never allowed herself to feel before. As she wrote short stories about her addiction, she realized why she felt trapped between the past and the present. She was frozen in the worst moments in her life. The only way for her to get out of those moments was to relive those moments that she didn't want to deal with. She relived the moment in the courtroom with her father where she knew him for the first time. She remembered little things that stuck out to her. She remembered the way that her heart hurt when she saw him walk into the room. She squirmed out of her grandmother's arms to run over to him, but her grandmother's grip on her was too strong for her to win against her. She remembered the look on Aunt Sylvia's face when she saw her father walk into the room like he was a neglected pet on the street. She couldn't forget the look on her mother's face when her father walked into the room like they were walking into a doorway into a different time. As soon as her father looked over at her, she was paralyzed with fear. She thought that it was fear of what he missed in her life. It wasn't fear on what he missed out on, but instead it was the moment that he realized that he made the wrong choice. His eyes told her that if he could go to a doorway into another time, then it was the moment that he raped her mother. That was when he knew that his life was going to end with him killing himself. He saw the life that he could've had with them. He wished that he could tell them that before he never got the chance to say it. The only way that he knew how to say it was to promise the stars. Her father meant a lot of things when he promised them the stars. The stars were a state of mind. It was where the doorway existed that everything would change if they stepped through a different door. If he stepped out of the doorway that he didn't rape her mother, then what would their life looked like for them? Would they have gotten married to each other? Would she have siblings to share experiences with? Would she be a happy person if her parents were together? Would she have this life that she had now with her husband and her daughter? She was more of a writer than she thought was since she imagined the possibilities of what would happen to her. The question that hurt her the most to think about was would her father be alive right now if he chose a different door. She feared it didn't exist. The conversation that her parents had with each other on the steps of the courthouse always lived inside of her mind. It wasn't the things that they said to each other that interested her. It was the things that they never said to each other. Why didn't her father tell her mother about his arrangement with Uncle Kenny? Why didn't her mother tell her father that she cried for him every night since they broke up? Why didn't her father tell her mother about his drug addiction that he struggled with for his entire life? Why didn't her mother tell her father that their daughter longed for him to be in her life? She watched them dance around the truth in a recital that they were in for their entire lives. It was a dance that she knew more than anything. She lived through the same routine with her parents. She was too afraid to tell them the truth about how she felt. She didn't want to hurt them. She spent her life not trying to hurt anyone even though she was hurting herself by doing it. The only times in her life that she expressed that part of herself to the world was when she was high when she didn't care if she hurt anyone around her. Her father told people the truth when he was high. He was afraid to hurt people by what he wanted to say. She missed that when she was sober.

She couldn't tell people the truth about how she felt about anything. Dr. Taylor encouraged her to tell people the truth and she told him that the truth hurt them before he told her that withholding the truth from people was hurting her more than it hurt them.

She decided that she would start this new practice of telling the truth with Sebastian. They got ready for bed one night where she told him that she needed to tell him something before he asked her what was wrong. She told him that she wished that he didn't conspire against her with Oliver and her parents every time that she was in a bad mental space. She couldn't stand it when he treated her like she was a porcelain doll every time that she expressed how she was feeling to him. Even though Sebastian was thrown off by her words, he told her that he didn't mean for it to feel like a conspiracy against her and that he wouldn't do it again if she didn't like it. When she told Dr. Taylor about Sebastian's reaction to the truth, he told her that he was proud of her for standing up for herself and that she could start doing that to other people in her life. They were at Oliver's house with Amelia and Sasha a few weeks later where their spouses played outside with their children when she told them how she felt for the first time. She told Amelia that she didn't appreciate it when she treated her like she was a puzzle that needed to be solved and that she felt like more of a puzzle to her than her cousin. Amelia told her that she didn't mean to make her feel like a puzzle where she assured her that she didn't see her like that again. After she pulled Amelia into a tight hug, she told Sasha that she didn't appreciate it when Sasha assumed that she knew everything about her when she never asked her how she felt about it. Sasha told her that she didn't mean to make her feel like she didn't have autonomy over her emotions and that she didn't make her upset by asking her those questions. She told Sasha that she didn't ask her to protect her and that she couldn't stand it when they treated her like she was made of glass. This left everyone too stunned to say anything. She told Oliver that she didn't like it when he went behind her back with Sebastian in moments of weakness because they didn't trust her to take control over her life. Oliver told her that he loved her to death, but he didn't trust her to make the best decisions for herself because of the past. She paced around the living room when she told Oliver that she thought that she gave him enough time to prove to him that she could make right decisions and that she didn't know when he was going to stop using her addiction against her. Oliver told her that she lost that right for him to trust her after the first time that she overdosed and that he would never trust her again. Even though she knew that was true without Oliver telling her, it hurt her to hear him say it. She pretended that she didn't get offended by it when she asked him how he would feel about being defined as the worst moment of his life by everyone around him. When he didn't say anything back to her, she told him that she worked hard to get where she was, so that she wasn't the person the addiction made her into. Oliver crossed the unspoken boundary in their relationship before she interrupted him when she told him what the point of her was getting better if everyone was going to doubt her before Oliver asked her what he could do to trust her again. Sebastian and Juliet were in the living room since they were screaming at each other when she told Oliver that he could have a little bit of faith in her before she stormed outside to the driveway. Once she got into the back of the car, their driver got out of the car to give her some space as she sobbed with her face hidden into her knees until she heard Sebastian coming into the back of the car. She sobbed into his chest with his arms around her. Their driver brought their daughter over to them as he pulled Daphne in her car seat before he drove them home. After her argument with Oliver, she refused to talk to him for several weeks as she focused on planning Daphne's second birthday party with her assistant Lucy where they played with different options for the party before they decided on having a small intimate party. When they decided that they wanted to do a beach trip for Daphne's birthday, Lucy prepared the plans for them as she discussed them with Sebastian where their family that lived in states could come with them to Malibu. They argued about whether or not to invite Oliver to the party. Sebastian told her that they had to invite Oliver because Daphne wanted Posey and Eleanor at her birthday party and Oliver had a right to be there as Daphne's godfather. Even though she wasn't interested in making up with Oliver, she didn't have a choice in the matter. They had to invite him to the party before she told him that it didn't mean that she forgave Oliver for what he said to her. Sebastian didn't understand why she was still upset with Oliver because he apologized to her a few days after their argument. This led to many fights between them where they didn't scream at each other inside since Daphne was able to hear them.

They went outside to shout at each other until they had make-up sex in their bedroom. When she thought about how much they were arguing with each other, she realized that they weren't arguing about anything that mattered. It was the smallest of things that they did during the day that annoyed each other. She couldn't stand it when Sebastian left for work without cleaning up the dishes. Sebastian couldn't stand it when she put Daphne into an outfit that made diaper changes impossible for him. She didn't like it when he left her to do all the laundry in the evening while he went out with his friends. Sebastian couldn't stand it when she left him to deal with the problems that came from running a successful company while she was at home with their daughter. In a heated argument with each other, he told her that she dealt with things when it suited her and that she expected him to pick up the pieces that she left behind her. She knew that he wasn't talking about the company. It was always about more than the company. Even though their company became a huge part of their lives over the last two years, they used it as an excuse to get out of doing things around the house. They used the company as a facade to talk about their problems in their marriage. Sebastian told her that he hated it when she said or did something selfish without talking about it. He referred to her last mental health crisis where she was at Dr. Taylor's house six months ago. It occurred to her why they spent the last three months fighting with each other. They never had a conversation about what happened in New York. They had an honest conversation with each other about what happened to her. She told him the thoughts that she told Dr. Taylor about, and Sebastian told her about how he felt being left behind from her with their daughter. They made up for lost time in their bedroom until they gave each other long overdue apologies before they fell asleep in each other's arms for the rest of the night. Since she wasn't arguing with Sebastian, she called Oliver that next day where she told him that she was sorry for how she reacted to what he told her and that she didn't want to fight with him anymore. She was relieved that she wasn't fighting with Sebastian and Oliver because she missed them. In the week before their trip to Malibu, she woke up every day with an overwhelming urge to vomit as she sprinted into the bedroom where she got rid of everything in her stomach before she went back to bed for the rest of the morning. By the third morning of her waking to vomit, Sebastian was concerned about her as he held her hair back for her when he asked her if she thought that she was pregnant where she told him that she didn't think that she was before he made a doctor's appointment for that afternoon. Since her parents were in Malibu preparing for Daphne's birthday party, they took Daphne to the doctor's appointment where she went back into the examination room as Sebastian followed behind her with Daphne on his hip when she took a seat on the exam table before Sebastian took seat on a chair next to her with Daphne sitting on his lap. After her doctor walked into the room, she asked her questions about how she was feeling in the past few weeks. Her doctor asked her if she was moody right now where Sebastian instantly agreed with the doctor before she smacked him on his arm in frustration with him. Once she went into the bathroom to pee into the cup that her doctor gave her, they waited a few minutes as her doctor came back into the examination room where she told her that she was pregnant before she left them alone to react to the news. As soon as her doctor left them alone in the examination room, Sebastian pulled her into a tight hug as she hid her face into his chest with tears falling down their face where Daphne colored on the floor before she asked them why they were hugging each other. After they pulled away from each other, Sebastian pecked her on the lips as he placed Daphne on the examination table on her lap where he pointed to her stomach when he told Daphne that mommy had a baby in her tummy. Daphne pointed to her mother's stomach as she repeated the words baby sister to them many times before she corrected her daughter when she told her that they didn't know if it was a baby sister until the baby was born. After they told Daphne to not tell anyone about mommy's baby in her tummy, she left the doctor's office with bloodwork and appointments in the coming weeks where Sebastian told their driver to take them to their favorite ice cream shop to celebrate the baby before they ate ice cream cones on Hollywood Boulevard. Since they didn't trust their toddler to not tell everyone about her pregnancy, she hid them in the house as she packed their bags for their trip to Malibu while Daphne drew pictures of her holding her baby sister before Daphne showed her the drawings with excitement laced in her voice. No one questioned why she wasn't coming into work that week since she told them that she was staying home to take care of her daughter while her parents were out of town. On the night before their trip to Malibu, they talked to her about keeping the baby a secret until her birthday party was over. They promised to give her cake.

When she woke up to vomit the next morning into the toilet, she packed the rest of their stuff while Sebastian got Daphne dressed where their driver placed their bags in the back of the car before their driver drove them to Malibu. After they spent most of the day in the car, their driver dropped them off at their hotel where her parents and his parents met them in the lobby where they gave them tight hugs before they went into their conjoined suite with her parents. Once they met up with the family at the restaurant, she caught up with her cousins Nina, Anastasia, and their husbands Joseph and Damien as Daphne colored at the table. They thought that Daphne was going to accidentally tell them that her mother was pregnant before Daphne talked about how she felt like Eleanor, Katherine, and Charlotte were her sisters. After they ate dinner at the restaurant, they went to their suite as she put Daphne to sleep in their bed where they laid down next to her when they whispered to each other about the baby before they slept in each other's arms for the rest of the night. On the morning of Daphne's birthday, they woke up to their daughter jumping up and down on the bed as Sebastian tickled Daphne's sides with her laughter filling up the room before she sprinted over the bathroom to vomit into the toilet. Once she laid down on the bed with her eyes closed, Daphne laid down her legs with her hands on her stomach as she talked to the baby where Sebastian took Daphne into the bathroom to get her dressed in her swimsuit before her mother walked into the room. They met up with the family at their reserved spot on the beach. She carried Daphne on her hip as Sebastian carried their beach bag over his shoulder where she pulled Oliver, Amelia, and Sasha into tight hugs before she laid down on the beach while Daphne made sandcastles with Eleanor, Posey, Katherine, and Charlotte. She laid down the beach chair with her eyes closed as Sebastian and Oliver had a soft conversation with each other. Amelia talked to Nina and Anastasia about their children with their husbands Troy, Joseph, and Damien talking to each other about sports before Sasha and Gabriel broke into a conversation with each other in French. She stopped herself from putting her hands over her stomach. It would give away that she was pregnant before she got the chance to tell anyone else. Once her parents took Daphne and Katherine into the ocean, she played in the sand with her one-year-old niece Charlotte who kept trying to eat the sand off of her fingers where Charlotte didn't stop putting her fingers into her mouth before Sasha corrected her daughter in French. She handed Charlotte over to Sasha and Gabriel who took her to the hotel for her nap time. She grabbed onto Sebastian's hand as she dragged him into the ocean where he pulled into a long kiss with a wave crashing into them before Sebastian pushed her down into the water. After she pulled herself out of the water, she dunked him into the water until he came up from the water where he pulled her into a long kiss. They would've done it on the beach if their families weren't there watching them since her pregnancy made her want him more than before in their marriage. Sebastian was about to wrap his arms around her stomach as she smacked his hands away from her stomach where she reminded him that they weren't announcing her pregnancy until tonight before they went over to their daughter who was in her grandmother's arms. Once her mother handed Daphne to her, she kissed the top of her head as she tightened her grip on her daughter every time that a wave crashed on them. She placed Daphne in Sebastian's arms when she felt like she was going to be sick before she made an excuse to go into her hotel room. It ended up being a false alarm, but it didn't stop her mother from following her up into their conjoined hotel rooms as she watched her dry heaving into the toilet when she asked her daughter if she was pregnant. Since she couldn't hide it, she told her mother that she was pregnant, but she didn't want anyone to know about it until they announced it after Daphne's birthday.

Her mother promised her that she wouldn't tell anyone except for her mum who needed to know that their daughter was pregnant with her second grandchild. She conceded into her mother's request to tell her mum about her pregnancy before they went back down to the beach. After they spent most of the day on the beach, they went to their hotel rooms to get cleaned up for the birthday party as she changed Daphne into her special dress where they met up with the family on the beach for a sunset picnic with sandwiches and cake. Her parents set out blankets for each family to sit down on as they ate together with the sunsetting in the background before it was time for them to get Daphne's cake from their hotel room. As soon as Sebastian came back from their hotel room with her cake in his hands, he placed the cake in front of them as Daphne sat in the middle of them when she blew out the candles on her cake with Gabriel taking a picture for them. When Eleanor asked Daphne what she wished for when she blew out her candles, Daphne told her best friend that she wished for mommy's baby to be a baby sister. She instantly hid her face into her hands when her cousins asked her if she was pregnant. Sebastian told them that they found out that she was pregnant earlier that week. After her cousins pulled her into tight hugs, she told them that she was surprised that Daphne kept it a secret from them for as long as she did. Sebastian cut a piece of cake for everyone except for Daphne who got two pieces of cake for her keeping her promise. They ate cake in soft conversation before her cousins went into their hotel rooms for the rest of the night. She sat with Sebastian and Daphne with the sounds of the waves crashing in the background. She laid her head on Sebastian's chest as Daphne laid down on top of him with her hands on her mother's stomach when Daphne asked her with a look of innocence on her face, "When do I know if I have a baby sister? Is it going to be a long time?"

As she ran her fingers through her daughter's hair, she looked up at Sebastian who had the same look on his face when she responded to Daphne with a smile on her face, "It's going to be eight months until the baby is born. Can you wait that long, little bee?"

Daphne let out a loud gasp when she responded to her mother with a look of horror on her face, "Eight months? That's too long, mommy! Can't you have the baby sooner? I can't wait that long to know if I have a baby sister!"

She responded to her daughter with a smirk on her face, "You have to wait. Mommy can't have the baby sooner than that. They aren't ready to be born. You were little once. There was a time when you were mommy's belly, and she couldn't wait for you to get out. You have to be patient, little bee. Can you be patient?"

Daphne hid her face into her mother's chest when she told her in her childlike demeanor, "I'll be patient. I don't know if I'll make it until the baby is born."

As she laughed into her hands, Sebastian laughed with his face hidden in her shoulder when he responded to them with a smile on his face, "You're so dramatic, little bee. You'll make it. She gets that from you, Isabella. She's your daughter. What are you going to do if mommy has a baby brother? Are you going to be mad at us?"

Daphne responded to her with a serious look on her face, "I don't know, daddy. It would be nice to have a baby brother. Why can't you choose what baby you have? Did you choose with me?"

She looked over at Sebastian with a look in her eyes that told her that they didn't think they would have to give their two-year-old daughter the birds and the bees conversation yet before she told Daphne in a stern voice, "Why don't we have this conversation later? Go to bed with daddy. Mommy is going to stay outside. Happy birthday, Daph. I love you."

Daphne kissed her stomach goodnight as Sebastian pecked her lips where he took Daphne into their hotel room before she softly laid down on the blanket.

She looked up at the stars when she whispered to herself with tears falling down her face, "Hello, dad. You probably heard it from your next grandchild, but I'm pregnant again. It's been a while since we last talked. I was going through a lot the last time that we talked to each other. Being back in York brought back those unwanted thoughts that I didn't want to think about. Your granddaughter is stubborn like you. She talks about you. I didn't tell you about that before. She remembers the stars. She remembers who you are. I never had to tell her. She already knew about it. She didn't know the details about what happened with you, but she knew that you were there in the stars with her. Do you want to hear something funny? I think that you knew about the stars before you died. I can't figure out how you knew about it, but you knew that it was a real place. That's another mystery that I'll never know about you. How you knew what you knew. People not knowing who you are or what you think until it's too late. Dr. Taylor told me that it's a self-preservation technique to hide yourself from the world, so that you don't get hurt. Of course, you only hurt yourself by doing it, but you don't know that. I'm speaking from personal experience. I learned that lesson the hard way. Do you want to know what I thought about a few months ago? I keep going back to that moment in your letter to Uncle Nathan when you talked about the doorway. You didn't use those words to describe it. That's my own word. It's like what you describe in the moment that you wanted to spend eternity in. There isn't one moment in time that you are stuck in. It's a collection of moments that lead up to the moment that you face your fate. Uncle James preaches that God decides our fates for us, but I don't think that it's true. I don't know if I believe in God after everything that I've been through in my life. I do believe in the stars. Maybe God is the stars, or the stars are God. Those AA and NA meetings know what they are talking about when they say that you need to believe in something bigger than yourself. I wonder if you had programs like that when you were growing up in England. It's a lot of bullshit, but there's some truth. There's a sliver of truth in every moment. That's what they don't tell you in those programs. The truth is objective. You would've hated NA and AA. False promises of a better life that doesn't exist for someone like us. Ironically enough, Oliver was the person that reminded me about that. He would be the person to tell me that. What did you think about in the moment before you died? Did you think about the moment that you described in the letter? Was it the moment in the courthouse with me? Do you want to know what I thought about in the moments before I died? I thought about the doorway. All I had to do was go into it and I would be in the universe. Time didn't exist. Gravity didn't exist. Consequences didn't exist. Nothing mattered except the doorway. We weren't tied down by the weight of the world. We were limitless. I can see peace existing. Never longer than a moment. Nothing lasts forever. Even death isn't forever. This is a secret that I wouldn't trust with anyone other than you and the stars. I almost wrote it in my book, but I stopped myself. We don't owe the world our secrets. It's okay to keep secrets to yourself. I respect your secrets, dad. They are yours to keep from the world. I thought that finding out your secrets would make me feel better, but it only made me feel worse about myself. I promise you that I won't pry into your secrets if you don't want me to anymore. It's better that people won't know about it. Some moments belong to the doorway. Thanks for listening, dad. I love you to the stars." After she brushed sand off of the dress, she grabbed her blanket off of the ground when she shook the sand out of it where she threw it over her shoulder before she went back into the hotel. Once she walked into her hotel room, she grabbed a quick shower as she put on her silk nightgown when she climbed into the bed where Sebastian stirred awake at the sudden moment before he asked her if she was okay. When she assured him that she was okay, he pecked her lips as he placed his hands on her stomach where she hid her face into his chest before he wrapped his arms around her. When she told Sebastian that she loved him, he whispered the same thing back to her before she fell asleep in his arms for the rest of the night.

CHAPTER FIFTY-FIVE
(SUMMER 1972 – LOS ANGELES, CALIFORNIA)

Unlike her pregnancy with Daphne, her morning sickness went away a few weeks after she found out that she was pregnant. She spent more time sleeping than anything else. She fell asleep sitting up in her office where Lucy nudged her awake in the middle of meetings multiple times a day. When she came home from work, she fell asleep on the couch while she was supposed to be playing with Daphne when her daughter woke her up to get her attention. When she told her doctor about her inability to stay awake during the day, her doctor gave her sleeping pills to help her sleep at night. It stopped her from falling asleep all day where she was able to sleep at night. She wasn't able to write her book. It wasn't like she got far in it between her emotional problems and her taking care of a toddler who needed constant supervision. Daphne always got in trouble when no one was watching her. It was a busy time at the studio with new projects being filmed, so Sebastian worked longer hours at the studio. She was home alone with Daphne. Her mother went to New York to get her new book published by the same company that she sold to a year ago and her mum was in England visiting her family since her estranged brother Matthew died. She never met her mum's family since she didn't have a relationship with them. She moved to the states after her divorce with her ex-husband who died from a drug overdose after she moved to the states. She wrote her book during Daphne's naptime where she sat in her office until she heard Daphne calling out for her. Her writing time was interrupted by her doctor's appointments for the baby where she took Daphne with her who was asking about the baby. Daphne asked her mother if it was time for the baby to come before she told her daughter that the baby wasn't ready to come out. They didn't have the birds, and the bees talk. Daphne was content with the answer that they gave her that the stars decided when a baby was ready to be born. Daphne asked them when the stars were going to give her baby sibling where they told her to ask the stars that question. Daphne asked the stars every night about her sibling where she said that the stars told her that the baby would come to her when the doorway was ready for them. She was shocked that Daphne knew about the doorway. She had a suspicion that her mother brought it up to Daphne since her mother knew about the doorway too. Her mother swore that she didn't tell her about it, and she believed her. In her quest to be a more honest person, she hadn't shared this practice with her mother who was the hardest person to talk about anything. She told more information to her dead father than to her mother who was alive, and she saw her in the house. Her living parent knew less about her than her dead parent. She never knew her father. She knew everything about her mother. She knew her mother's strengths and her weaknesses. She knew why her mother struggled to find her place in the world. She knew about her mother's complicated relationship with her grandparents. She knew about her mother's trauma with Uncle Kenny and her father. She knew about her mother's complications with raising a daughter in a world that didn't accept them. She only knew those things because she read her books when she was old enough to understand it.

She never had a conversation with her mother about it. Her mother was only an open person in her books. In real life, her mother was a closed person that didn't give away her trauma. That was what confused her friends and her cousins about her mother growing up because their image of her mother was never what they expected it to be. She wasn't the person that she portrayed herself to be in her books. It was a testament to her mother's writing abilities that they believed that she was the person that she wrote about in her books. That was what her parents had in common with each other. She thought that her mother knew more about her father than she let anyone believe. She wanted her father to believe that his secrets were going to be his secrets. When she told Dr. Taylor that she thought that her mother knew more about her father, he asked her why she came to this conclusion. She told him that her mother was more aware of her surroundings than she wanted her father to believe that she was. She told Dr. Taylor that she couldn't ask her mother about this because she would never tell her about it. He asked her why she was so hesitant to reach out to her mother compared to her father who talked to very regularly before she told him that it was easier to tell her father how she felt because he would never judge her like her mother judged her. Her mother could be discreet with other people's secrets. She kept Uncle Stan and Uncle Sam's secrets for many decades. Her mother had strong opinions about everything that she did. Her mother asked her, "Why would you want to do that, baby girl?"

This judgement extended to everything that she did in her life. From her mother questioning why she wanted to do cheerleading in high school to why she wanted to quit cheerleading her senior year of high school. She told her mother that she wanted to do cheerleading her first year of high school because Sasha was doing it, and she didn't want to be left out of her life if she made new friends without her. She didn't tell her mother that she only wanted to do cheerleading because the girls on the team got invited to the parties. She told her mother that she wanted to quit the cheerleading team her senior year because she wanted to focus on her academics. Not that she got kicked off of the team for failing a drug test that she didn't know that they were doing. She pretended to be her mother on the phone, so that she wouldn't get in trouble with her parents about it. That wasn't the only thing that her mother judged her about her. Her mother tried to convince her not to be an actress and to not move to Los Angeles because life was going too hard for her. Not that her mother knew that her life was hard long before she became an actress and moved to Los Angeles. Acting was the least complicated part of her life. Her mother disapproved of her dating in high school. She made it a point to bring it up to her that she was going to get pregnant as a teenager like she did if she brought a boy to the house. Not that her having a boyfriend in high school wasn't the same thing as her mother getting raped by her father. Every time that her mother thought that she had a boyfriend, it was her latest drug dealer at the time that gave her the pills that she asked for him to bring them where he left out of her bedroom window once the deal was over. Most of the drug dealers that she brought over the house weren't in school anymore, but she didn't want to make it worse by telling her mother the truth about it. She realized in telling these stories to Dr. Taylor that she lied to her mother about pretty much everything that she did in her teenage years. It was no wonder that her mother didn't trust her because she was rarely honest with her. It wasn't her intention to lie to her, but she didn't want it to get more complicated by involving her mother into the shitshow that was her younger years.

One night her senior year of high school, she told her mother that she was going to her friend Emily's house since she couldn't use Sasha as an excuse with her uncle's house being a few blocks away from them. She went to one of the many parties that she went to that year. This party was a few weeks after she almost got kicked off the cheerleading team, but she bullied the cheerleading coach into silence about it. The cheerleading coach was having an affair with the gym teacher, and she blackmailed her with this information. She met up with her friend Emily at the party who was on the cheerleading team with her. She talked about their favorite topic of drugs since Emily was her drug dealer at the time where Emily gave her everything that she asked her for before she got high in a bedroom in the house. Did she fail to mention that Emily's mother was the cheerleading coach, and her parents were married to each other? That's why her secret stayed a secret between them. She left the party early because she was so high that she couldn't stand being near other people. When she went to school the next morning, Sasha told her on their walk into the school that their friend Emily got arrested last night at a house party for dealing illegal narcotics. She was shocked that Emily got caught dealing drugs, but she knew that she wouldn't stay in prison too long since her father was an investment banker that could make it go away for her. With this new information about Emily, she approached the cheerleading coach about her daughter's arrest for drug possession as an extra incentive to keep her quiet about the failed drug test where the coach put two and two together that she bought drugs from Emily. Even though it sounded like a good idea for her to do, it ended up back firing on her since the cheerleading coach told the school about her drug use and she got kicked off of the team. Her couch thought that she turned her daughter into the police. She tried to explain to the coach that she wouldn't tell someone that she bought drugs from, but she didn't want to listen to her. Emily got sent to boarding school for the school year and she broke up Emily's parents' marriage by telling everyone that the cheerleading coach was having an affair with the gym teacher. She was kicked off of the team and she got in trouble with the school for her failed drug test with over two weeks of detention. Her parents found out from the principal about it where she explained to her parents that Emily pressured her to take the pills after cheerleading practice one day. This got Emily into even more trouble with her parents who were in the middle of a nasty divorce. Emily told her later that she ruined her life by what she did to her. When she told Dr. Taylor in a session about this story, he was speechless at what she told him where she assured him that there were a lot more stories like that from her last year of high school. It was the year of destruction for everyone around her since she made it her life's mission to make people's lives a living hell. She didn't care about anything or anyone around her as long as she got the drugs that she wanted from her dealers. She told Dr. Taylor about how she got out of being arrested a week before her high school graduation. By that point in the school year, she went through so many different drug dealers that she couldn't remember any of their names after they went to jail. She was in a bad period of her addiction where she stopped eating and sleeping all together. This was the first time that it happened to her. She was out with other drug addicts that she met at parties where they milled around the streets of New York until one of the boys got a clever idea to steal something out of a bodega when the shopkeeper wasn't looking. This turned out to be a horrible idea since the bodega owner flagged the police down to chase them throughout the streets of the city. She lost her friends down a dark alley as the police cornered her until she was trapped in one of New York's infamous gated alleys before the police pulled her into handcuffs with her face pressed into the ground. Before they made it to the police car, one of her friends lit a police car on fire as the police left her with the handcuffs on her hands before she sprinted away from the police. She didn't stop running until she made it to Uncle Sam's toy factory a block away from the fire.

She knew from Sasha that her father worked an overnight shift at the factory, so she ran into the factory towards Uncle Sam's office on the top floor. When Uncle Sam saw her running into his office with handcuffs behind her back, he jumped over to help her get them off of her arms with a pin from her hair when he asked her what happened before she told him the truth about what happened with the police. The truth that suited her the best at the moment. She was out with her friends from school where one of the boys stole something from a bodega and that she was targeted by the police because her friends rudely ditched her. She didn't tell Uncle Sam how they scored drugs from all of the wrong places in the city or that her friend stole a lighter so that they could smoke the joint that they bought from a stranger in Central Park. Uncle Sam asked her if her mother knew that she was out at this time as she didn't respond to him before a worker from the factory appeared in the office to tell him that there was a fire near the police station that was spreading to the other cars on the street. When she ran outside with Uncle Sam ahead of her, there were lines of cars that were on fire as she couldn't look away from it where Uncle Sam pulled her into the car before he drove away from the rapidly spreading fire in the city. As Uncle Sam sped away with the firefighters getting rid of the growing fire, the police officers had arrested her friends that caused the destruction where she swore that she would never talk about that night ever again. She didn't plan on telling anyone about these stories. She knew that this wasn't the person that they saw her as over the years. Dr. Taylor didn't have a stake in these people that weren't in her life. Once she told Dr. Taylor about this side of herself, he asked her what would happen if she told her mother about this where she told him that she wouldn't know where to start before he told her that she should start from where it began for her. She told Dr. Taylor that she was going to be bold and take a chance with her mother. It was a lot easier said than done to reveal the secrets that she kept from her mother. If she was going to tell her mother about this side of herself, then she was opening up a can of worms that she couldn't take back once she said it. It was a few weeks after her session with Dr. Taylor that she decided that she was going to be bold when her mother came back from a press tour for her new book. Her mum came back from York a while ago after seeing her family for the first time since she moved to the states. When she went to the airport to get her, her mother brought Uncle Sam and Aunt Valeria with them before she drove them to the house. On the first night, she wasn't going to ambush her where they played games in the living room before they went to bed for the night. On the second night, she didn't tell her since her parents went out on a double date with Uncle Stan and Thomas. She had a bonfire with her cousin's families, Uncle Sam, and Aunt Valeria before they went back home.

On the third night, she was going to tell her mother about it. They were alone in the house for the first time. After she spent the day playing with Daphne in the pool, they ate dinner that her mum prepared for them while her parents asked her about her pregnancy where she talked about her baby with her hands over her growing stomach before Daphne got everyone's attention by pouring her milk all over the table. Once Sebastian cleaned up the mess that Daphne made on the table, she placed her daughter on her hip as she carried her into the bathroom to give her a bath where she put Daphne into her favorite pajamas before they put Daphne in her bed for the night. Sebastian went into the bathroom to get a shower as she went into the living room with a cup of hot chocolate in her hands where her mother sat on the couch proofreading the drafts of her newest book that she started working on a few weeks ago. Her mum went to bed early in their bedroom since she was struggling with the time zones from being in the states again.

As soon as she took a seat on the couch next to her, her mother looked up from the papers in her hand as she grabbed onto her hands when she told her daughter with a smile on her face, "How have you been? Bash told me that things with the company are crazy and that he's hardly home. You are glowing, baby girl. Pregnancy suits you more than it did me. What's your doctor saying about the baby?"

She leaned back on the couch when she responded to her mother with a smile on her face, "Thanks, mom. I'm feeling a little bit sick at night, but it's not too unbearable like my pregnancy with Daphne. I'm so tired. The doctor is saying that the baby is measuring on the smaller side, so they want me to go over forty weeks if I don't go into labor until then. Everything else is fine. We are attempting to potty train

Daphne, but it isn't working for us. Bash and I want her to be potty trained before the baby is born, so that we don't have two children in diapers. If you could help us with that, that would be wonderful. You potty trained not only me, but Oliver, Amelia, and Audrey. Aunt Sylvia and Aunt Priscilla told me that you are a professional at potty training, so I'm in luck since you are my mom, and you live with me."

Her mother tightened her grip on her hand when she responded to her with judgement laced in her voice, "It would be my honor to potty train my granddaughter. I'll potty train my other grandchild when they are old enough. Oliver and the twins were easy to potty train. I told them what to do and they did it. It was hard to potty train you because you didn't listen to anything that I told you to do. There were a lot of accidents to get you to learn how to do it, but you figured it out in your own time. I'll start working with Daphne tomorrow. She always listened to me better than you. You guys are too soft with her. You need to be firmer or else she'll grow up to be a spoiled little girl."

She paced in circles around the room when she responded to her mother with anger laced in her voice, "That didn't last long before the judgement came out. She's two years old. What do you expect us to do to make her understand how punishment works? She's smart, but she's not that smart. This was what I wanted to talk to you about, so thank you for bringing it up. When I told you guys that you could move in to help us with Daphne, I didn't ask for your advice on how to raise my daughter. Why are you so worried about my daughter being spoiled? You didn't care about that when you were raising me."

Her mother let out a shaky breath when she responded to her daughter with a look of disbelief on her face, "What are you implying, baby girl? I didn't spoil you. It wasn't my intention if I ended up spoiling you. I never thought that I would have that much money when you were born. Things happened along the way."

She took a seat on the couch next to her when she responded to her mother with a frown on her face, "You didn't spoil me, mom. You did the complete opposite of spoiling me. I'm not trying to argue with you. Daphne will be okay. I promise. She will have all the love and care that she needs without being spoiled. I want to talk about something else. I've been wanting to get it off of my chest."

Her mother leaned back onto the couch when she asked with a frown on her face, "What is it?"

She propped her feet up onto the coffee table as she placed her hands on her stomach when she confessed to her mother in a distant voice, "I've been taking a new approach to life. I'm telling people how I feel without being worried that I'm going to make them upset. Dr. Taylor told me that I need to stop being concerned with taking on everyone's pain. Part of this process is coming clean about the things that I hid from everyone. I love you, but you are impossible to go to when I have a problem. It's not that you're an uncaring person, but you have a judgement about everything I tell you. For my entire life every time that I tried to tell you anything, you always came from a place of judgement instead of coming from a place of understanding. There were a lot of things that I didn't tell you because I knew how you would react if I told you about it. I didn't tell most people about anything because I was scared of your reaction. It made me not able to trust anyone. You made me feel like I was always doing something wrong. You showed me that it is better to keep it to myself than to tell anyone else what I was going through in my life."

She got off from the couch as she nervously paced around the living room when she confessed to her mother with tears falling down her face, "The first time that I thought about killing myself was when I was eight years old. It was before dad killed himself. I tried drowning myself in the bathtub, but Uncle Sam pulled me out of the water. On the night that we found out that dad killed himself, I tried to drown myself and I was unsuccessful. I thought about getting high for the first time at dad's funeral. I sprinted out of the church to throw myself off the roof, but it was too low to the ground to do any lasting damage. I got high for the first time when I was thirteen years old. I took all of the pills in the medicine cabinet to kill myself. It was an accident that the medicine made me high. I knew it was a mistake as soon as it happened, but I never went back after that moment. I have always craved that feeling since then. I resisted the urge a few years before I found myself in that place where I was high again. Sasha and I got invited to our first high school party our first year of high school. The football team invited the cheerleading team to the party. Someone gave me something that dissolved on my tongue that I learned was called

LSD. For the first time, I could take on the world without any fear. I lost my virginity that night. It was a guy that I went to school with that was older than me. It was pretty unmemorable except for when he told me that he could get me more drugs if I loved them so much. I told him that I loved drugs over and over again until I convinced him to be my dealer. I think that his name was Dylan. Dylan gave me pills every weekend at parties for the rest of the school year. By the time that summer came, Dylan got busted by the police and he was sent to jail for dealing drugs. Ironically, Dylan's father was the state prosecutor in New York at the time. I stopped getting high for a while since the experience with Dylan freaked me out. It didn't take me much to get hooked on narcotics again. This time it was different for me. I couldn't quit no matter how hard I tried to stop it. I wasn't addicted yet. That was the summer before my last year of high school."

As she wiped away the tears off of her face, she took a seat on the couch next to her when she confessed to her mother with tears falling down her face, "I went through a lot of dealers over my high school years, but none of them were more magnetic to me than Emily. Do you remember Emily from the cheerleading team? She was dating Sasha when I met her our second year of high school. I didn't realize that Sasha was dating Emily until Emily told me about it. I was so jealous of Emily because she took Sasha away from me. I wanted to do something to sabotage their friendship, but my plan backfired. I tried to get Emily to think that Sasha was replacing her with me, but Emily became my friend. When the school year started, we went to parties without Sasha since Uncle Sam grounded her for pranking Ivan over the summer. Emily also happened to be a drug dealer. That was what really solidified our friendship. She gave me narcotics and I gave her attention that Sasha didn't give her. We would only have sex with each other when we were high, but Sasha never found out about it. I know that this is going to shock you when I tell you this, but I was high everyday my last year of high school. I was shocked when I found out that I was graduating from high school because I didn't do any work. I paid other people to do the work for me. I was busy finding my next high to care about school. Emily and I kept up with this arrangement until the cheerleading team incident in the late fall."

Her mother's jaw dropped in shock as she grabbed onto her hands when she asked her daughter in a soft voice, "What cheerleading incident? The one where you quit the team during a game?"

She paced around the living room when she confessed to her mother in a distant voice, "That was the one, mom. Except I didn't quit the team. I was kicked off the team because I failed a drug test. This is where it gets interesting. Did you remember that Emily's mom was the cheerleading coach? Emily's mom called the house to tell you about my failed drug test. I pretended to be you on the phone since you were in California for your movie. When I learned of the incident, I went to the cheerleading coach the next day to blackmail her into letting me stay on the team with the information that she was having an affair with the gym teacher. This kept her silent about it. I didn't plan on quitting the team in the middle of the game, but I got into an argument with Emily about Sasha finding out that she was cheating on her. Sasha didn't know that it was me that Emily was with, but Emily threatened to tell Sasha if I didn't quit the cheerleading team. I couldn't explain this to Sasha who was mad at me. I would be implicating myself for worse crimes against her. Things got out of control when Emily got arrested for possessing drugs and her mother thought that I was the person that turned her into the cops. I later found out that Sasha turned her into the police. Sasha found out that she was a drug dealer, but I got blamed for it. I got in trouble by the school for the failed drug test, Emily got sent to a boarding school, and Sasha dated Emily's sister Samantha a few weeks later. Sasha never found out about us, and Emily hated me for ruining her life."

Her mother responded to her daughter in complete shock, "Holy shit, baby girl. I don't know how to respond to this. Did you feel bad about it?"

After she took a seat next to her mother on the couch, she shrugged her shoulders at her as she wiped away the tears that fell down her face when she responded to her mother, "I didn't feel proud of it. I was so high that I didn't give a shit about anything that happened. I could've killed someone, and I wouldn't care about it. I was on a path of destruction where I left as many casualties as possible that I could behind me. I was shocked that you let me move to Los Angeles. I thought that everyone realized what was going on and that I didn't do a good job hiding it from the world. I'm telling you this now because I never got the chance to tell you about it. I wanted you to know that being in Hollywood didn't turn me into this person. I was always going to be this person regardless of where I was in the world. I thought that I was the master at hiding this version of myself, but I wasn't as good as I thought that I was. It was about surviving, you know? I didn't have any meaning or any purpose outside of it. I lived that way long before anyone else realized it. It's easy to look back on it and see how ridiculous it sounds, but that was the life that I saw for myself. This normal family life never seemed to be for people like me until the last few years with Bash and Daphne."

Her mother pulled her into a tight hug with her face hidden in her chest as she blinked back tears that fell down her face when her mother responded to her in a soft voice, "Thank you for telling me that. I figured that you were going through something, but I didn't know the depth of it. I understand why you didn't tell me about it. I wouldn't have understood it. I get it now. You were going through so much by yourself that you didn't know how to handle it. I'm sorry if I hadn't been emotionally available for you over the years. I didn't want you to feel like you couldn't talk to me about anything. I wish that I was there for you. Like I wish that I was there for dad when we were growing up. I love you, baby girl. I've loved you since the day that you were born, and I'll love you until the day that I die."

Once she pulled herself out of her mother's arms, she quickly wiped away the tears from her face as she got off of the couch when she told her mother with a smile on her face, "Thanks for the apology. I love you too, mom. There's a lot that I want to tell you that I never got the chance to tell you. I'm glad that I can tell you about it before you read about it in my book. It's always better coming from me. I want you to do the same with me if you want to. We can do this for each other. You tell me about yourself, and I can tell you about me. It will be fun for us. Mum might get jealous when she finds out about it. We should let her do it with us. I'm sure that she also has a lot of stuff to share with us." After she said goodnight to her mother, she went into her bedroom where Sebastian was asleep on his side of the bed as she went on the other side of the bed before he wrapped his arms around her in his sleep.

Chapter Fifty-Six
(Fall 1972 - Big Island, Hawaii)

After she told her mother about the secrets that she kept from her, they got together in the living room every night where they talked about the things that they never used to talk about with each other. Her mum joined them in their discussions where she learned about her mum's childhood in England since the wound was re-opened by her brother's death. She told her parents about the stories that she never thought that she would tell them. Her mother told them about memories with her father that made her miss him. Her mum told them about her relationship with her ex-husband. It felt nice to be connected with her parents. She realized that it was as hard for her parents to talk about their problems then it was for her to talk about her problems. When she told Dr. Taylor about her conservations with her parents, he told her that he was proud of her for doing something bold. She told him that she wanted to have this kind of relationship with her daughter when she was grown up someday. Even though it terrified her to think about her daughter being an adult, Dr. Taylor told her that it was good that she was excited for the milestones in her daughter's life like her parents were with her over her life. She told him that her mother was excited no matter what stage of life that she was in. As much as she wanted her daughter to be innocent forever, she was excited for every chapter that was to come in her daughter's life. She was excited for her daughter to go to school and learn what she wanted to do with her life. She was excited for her daughter to fall in love and learn how to let someone else in her life. She was excited for her daughter to bring her friends to the house to play in their pool and have sleepovers where they talked about the people that they had crushes on. She was excited for her daughter to find her own path in her life about where she wanted to live and who she wanted to be. She was excited for her daughter to fall in love with the person that she would marry and have a family. She was excited for her daughter to have a life that she gave her when she was born. She felt the same way towards her unborn child. She wanted the same things for them that she wanted for Daphne. It was a promise that her mother told her when she was born. They were going to give their babies the world. Maybe the world didn't look like what they imagined that it was, but it was better than the one that they had. That promise was inbred into every mother's mind when her baby was born. It was a mother's instinct to give her baby the world. They were stuck in a cycle of raising those children in a world that they wished that they had for themselves. She could see how a mother would learn to resent her child that took advantage of everything that she worked towards to give them for the child only to throw it back into her face. Dr. Taylor asked her what her grandmother would think about the world that her children created after her death a long time ago. She told him that her grandmother wouldn't recognize the world that her children left behind them.

Her mother made a life in New York for her daughter that she never had for herself. She didn't think about how her mother felt about leaving her life behind the only place that she knew to be in one of the biggest cities in the world. Her mother must have been scared coming into this world. She didn't know if she would make it out alive. Her mother made a successful career as a writer. Uncle Sam took the biggest chance by leaving his life behind to get out of the war that killed his father and his brother before he made a life for his family to the states. Uncle Sam and Aunt Valeria had nothing when they moved to New York where he struggled to make ends meet for them while they lived in tenement housing. Anastasia was born into a world that she didn't know anything better than the life that her parents had in the states. She forgot that her cousins Anastasia, Sasha, Nina, and Ivan were born and raised in New York unlike Oliver and Amelia that were born and raised in England. When Uncle Sam got the chance to open his own factory after being in New York for almost a decade, he took a chance to do it, so that he would have a legacy to leave behind to his children. Even though Uncle Sam sold the factory to a privately owned manufacturing company, he created a name for himself in the city where he ran for local office and won in the past two decades. Aunt Valeria did the same thing when she opened up her hair salon in the city where her daughter Anastasia was prepared to take it over for her when she retired someday. Sasha used her father's influence to create a very successful career as a model for herself that let her explore the world before she found Gabriel, and she created a life with him. Ivan took the biggest risk out of his siblings since he moved to France where he learned a language that he didn't know while he lived in a culture that he didn't grow up in before he met his partner through his very successful modeling career. The same thing could be said about Aunt Sylvia and Uncle James' family because their children were all over the world just like Uncle Sam and Aunt Valeria's family were. Audrey and George lived in the same town that they were born in. Sean created a life for his family in London. Amelia moved to the states to create her own life for her family in Los Angeles. Jamie was the person that took the biggest chance when he moved to France with his best friend Ivan where he met his partner, and they created their life together. Oliver had his own family in Los Angeles while he helped people every day in his career. It would've shocked her grandmother to see her grandchildren to be so successful in their lives and being spread in different corners of the world. She helped Sebastian in the studio with the increasing workload as her parents watched Daphne during the day. With her mother's magical abilities, Daphne was officially potty trained where the only time that she used a diaper was at night when she was sleeping where they stockpiled diapers for their baby that was on the way.

Daphne was more excited about the baby in her stomach that got larger by the day. By the last few months of pregnancy, she went to her doctor's office once a week to make sure that she was okay and that the baby was okay before she was sent to get more bloodwork done to make sure her levels were good. At this stage in her pregnancy, she was uncomfortable in any position that she was in except for when she laid down with her legs tucked into her stomach. Sebastian told her how strange it was every morning when he saw her sleeping like that before he told her that she could sleep in any position that she wanted to do as long as she was happy with it. She struggled to fit into most of her clothes. She didn't keep any of her maternity clothing from when she was pregnant with Daphne. Her assistant Lucy went shopping at the mall with her pushing Daphne in the stroller where she bought maternity clothes that she needed to buy before they went out for ice cream after Daphne asked for it while they were shopping at the mall. After Daphne was covered in ice cream, her assistant Lucy dropped them off at the house where she put Daphne into the bathtub as soon as they got into the house before they played with dolls on the couch in the living room. Once Sebastian came home from work in the evening, they ate dinner that her mum made for them where her parents put Daphne to bed while they left the house to go on a date at the movie theater before they walked around Hollywood. As they walked down the crowded street hand in hand, they talked about everything from what films that they were going to work on in the studio to what places that they wanted to take Daphne. They wanted to go on a vacation before the baby was born in three months where they met up with their driver before they dropped off at their house for the night. Their assistants made the plans for their family vacation as she packed their bags for their trip to Hawaii where Sebastian prepared their manager Katie for dealing with the studio while they were away on their vacation. They wanted to go to Hawaii with Daphne because she hadn't been there since after her honeymoon. Since her falling out with Juliet's sister Maddie that lived in Honolulu, they were going to Big Island that they had never been to. The biggest problem with getting to Big Island was that it was hard to get to because there were no direct flights there. Their flight would take them to the Honolulu airport where they would go on a ferry that would take them to the island. On the week before they left for their vacation, she was in the nursery for the baby while Sasha and Amelia helped her paint on the wall. They chose a farm animal theme for the baby's nursery because they called the baby their little critter due to the baby being very active in her stomach all night. After they called the baby their little critter, they thought that a farm animal theme would be the theme for the baby's nursery since it went well with Daphne's bedroom. Daphne helped them paint straight lines on the wall until she got bored of it where she pulled out the baby's clothes from the dresser with Katherine and Charlotte who had the time of their life making a mess. While she was in the middle of painting a pig, Katherine asked her mother when her baby was going to be born where she instantly looked over at Amelia when she asked her if she was pregnant. Once Amelia told her that she was pregnant, she pulled Amelia into a long hug where Sasha joining in on their hug. She joked with Amelia that was what happened when you entrusted your secrets with a toddler before Daphne told her that Katherine told her about her baby sibling last night. No one was surprised that toddlers couldn't keep secrets, but they were surprised that toddlers kept secrets between themselves. Not from adults. When Sebastian got home from work that evening, she told him that Amelia and Troy were expecting another baby where Sebastian told her that Troy told him about it at the studio because Amelia called to tell him that their toddler spilled the beans about the baby. She showed Sebastian the progress that they made on the nursery where they almost finished painting in the rest of the farm animals on the wall. Sebastian pulled her into a long kiss to thank her for working on the baby's nursery before Daphne ran into the room with her blanket around her. They put Daphne to bed in her bedroom before they went to bed in their bedroom for the rest of the night. On the morning of their flight to Honolulu, their driver put their bags into the back of the car where she hugged her parent's goodbye before their driver drove them to the airport. After their driver dropped them off at the airport, she pushed Daphne in her stroller with Sebastian carrying their bags where they walked into the crowded plane before they started on their journey. Daphne slept in her arms for the flight to Hawaii where she slept with her head leaning on Sebastian's shoulder before he nudged her awake when their plane landed in Honolulu. She carried Daphne off of the plane with Sebastian carrying her stroller and their bags. Once they got into a taxi to their hotel, she placed Daphne on the bed to sleep as she joined Sebastian in the shower to celebrate their journey before they slept in the bed with his arms around her for the rest of the night. After they packed up from their hotel the next morning, she pushed Daphne in her stroller as Sebastian carried their bags where they went onto the ferry to Big Island that took an hour to get there. Once they got into their hotel room, she changed Daphne into her swimsuit as she walked down onto the beach with her holding onto her daughter's hand where Daphne tried to squirm away from when they put sunscreen on her before Sebastian took Daphne into the water with him. She laid down in her chair on the beach most of the day until Daphne begged her to go into the ocean where she grabbed onto Daphne's hand before her daughter dragged her into the water.

They went to their hotel room to clean up as she changed Daphne into a dress where she pushed Daphne in her stroller to the restaurant that they ate dinner at before they went back to their hotel room for the rest of the night. The rest of their vacation went by too fast. They went snorkeling in shallow water where Daphne grabbed the fish out of the water with her bare hands before they swam away from her. They went on hikes to beautiful waterfalls and non-active volcanoes where Sebastian jumped into the water off of the 25-foot cliff as she walked back down to join him in the water. He taught Daphne how to golf for the first time. Sebastian wanted to go golfing when they were in Hawaii, and she gave in to him because he let her go shopping while they were golfing near the waterfalls. They got ice cream every night after they ate dinner at a new restaurant since it was Daphne's favorite place. She woke up when the sun came out as she sat on the beach with her hands on her growing stomach when she talked to her little critter until Sebastian came to join her on the beach with Daphne. On their last day on Big Island, she woke up early to watch the sunrise with Sebastian and Daphne as they ate breakfast in the hotel lobby until they went to their hotel room to get dressed for their last hike of the trip before they walked to the national park. When they made it to the top of the waterfall a few hours later, they took a picture of themselves with the camera that Gabriel gave Daphne for her birthday where they ate lunch at the hotel cafe before they spent the rest of the day at the beach. While she was in the ocean with Daphne, Sebastian took pictures of them laughing since he was taking pictures of their entire trip for the memories to look back on one day before he joined them in the water. As the sun set in the sky, they went back to the hotel to get cleaned up for dinner where they went to their favorite restaurant for the last time before they went to the beach. Even though the sun already set hours ago, they wanted to spend their last night on vacation at the beach until they would have to go back to the hotel room. She laid down on their blanket with her head leaning on Sebastian's shoulder as Daphne sat in Sebastian's lap with her grabbing onto her mother's growing stomach when she asked them with excitement laced in her voice, "You are so big, mommy. Does that mean that the baby is almost here? I've been patient waiting for them. I told Kitty how hard it is to wait for a baby sibling. They take forever to grow in our mommies' bellies."

She ran her fingers through her daughter's hair when she responded to her with a wide grin on her face, "You have been so patient, little bee. Mommy and daddy are so proud of you. It's hard to wait for things that you are excited for, but you've done good. Little critter will be here soon, and we will become a family of four."

Daphne gave a pouty face as she let out a defeated sigh when she responded to her mother with a frown on her face, "I'll wait a little longer. Baby will be here soon, and we'll be happy. I'm going to play with my toys in the sand. Can you play with me?"

They helped Daphne shovel sand into her plastic toys as she looked up at him when she asked Sebastian with a smile on her face, "Are we still good with names? Did you want to add anymore to the list before the baby is born?"

As Sebastian poured the sand onto the ground with Daphne giggling at him, he shook his head at her when he responded to her with a smile on his face, "I think that we are okay. We were going with Noah if the baby is a boy and Mia if the baby is a girl. What do you think that the baby is?"

She shrugged her shoulders at him as she filled up one of Daphne's plastic toys when she responded to him in a soft voice, "I don't know what I think, Bash. Some days I think that the baby is a girl and other days I think that the baby is a boy. I would be happy with either way, but we'll see what happens in a few months. Isn't that right, little critter? You are going to be part of our family soon. I can't wait to not be pregnant anymore. It's so uncomfortable, Bash."

After Sebastian pulled her into a quick kiss, he pulled away from her as he placed his hands on her stomach when he responded to her with a serious look on his face, "I'm so grateful that you are willing to put your body through this. No, don't give me that look, Isabella. I'm being serious right now. Thank you for giving me our children. It's the best thing that I was given in my life. I love you so much. I don't want you to forget about that."

She pulled him into a long kiss that they didn't let go of each other until Daphne threw herself into her mother's chest when she responded to Sebastian with her arms tightly around Daphne, "You're so sweet. Thank you. I love you too, Bash. Our children are lucky to have you as their father. You work so hard to provide for us. What do you think, little bee? Isn't daddy great?"

Once Daphne took her face out of her chest, she pulled pieces of hair out of her daughter's face when Daphne responded to her mother with an innocent look on her face, "Daddy is the best. I love you so much, daddy. You taught me how to golf, and you gave me ice cream."

Sebastian kissed his daughter on the top of her head when he responded to her with a smirk on his face, "Is that all I'm good for? Golf and ice cream. You are silly, little bee."

Daphne hid her face in her father's chest as he ran his fingers through her hair when she responded to him with a smile on her face, "Those aren't my favorite things about you, daddy. You are good at cuddling, and you read better than mommy."

She pretended to be offended when she told her daughter with a wide grin on her face, "What's that supposed to mean? Why can't mommy tell you good stories? I've told you plenty of good stories. What makes daddy better than me?"

She hid her face into her mother's chest when she responded to her, "You are a good storyteller, mommy. Daddy does voices for the characters. I love them, but they are sad. Grandma Ella tells me happy stories. Will the baby get to hear the stories too?"

She ran her fingers through her daughter's hair when she responded to her with a smile on her face, "Of course the baby can hear the stories. I get it, little bee. I'm not mad at you for not liking my sad stories. At least I like my sad stories. Are you ready to go to bed?"

She placed Daphne on her hip as Sebastian grabbed the blanket off of the ground with Daphne's sand toys in his other hand before they went to their hotel room. Once she changed Daphne into her favorite pajamas, she placed Daphne on the bed when she whispered to her daughter, "Goodnight, little bee. I love you to the stars." She pulled Daphne into her arms with her face hidden in her chest before they fell asleep in each other's arms for the rest of the night.

CHAPTER FIFTY-SEVEN
(WINTER 1973 – SANTA FE, NEW MEXICO)

She woke up the next morning as Sebastian tickled Daphne's sides with her infectious laughter filling up the room where she joined Sebastian in their tickling session before they packed up their bags while Daphne helped them by throwing things into a bag. Once they finished packing up their stuff, she pushed Daphne in her stroller as Sebastian carried their bags where the taxi took them to the marina before they got onto the ferry that took them to the main island. Once their ferry docked in Honolulu, she pushed Daphne in her stroller as Sebastian carried their bags where they flagged down a taxi that took them to the airport before they got on a plane back to Los Angeles. Daphne slept in her arms as she slept with her head leaning on his shoulder while Sebastian read a book that he bought on Big Island. Once their plane landed in Los Angeles, Sebastian nudged her awake as he grabbed their bags off of the plane where she carried Daphne in her arms who was asleep before they met up with her parents in the airport. After she pulled her parents into tight hugs, she handed Daphne over to her grandmothers as they smothered her with kisses on her face where she walked over to her parent's car before they got into the back of the car. When her parents made it back to their house, they took Daphne into their bedroom with them. They slept for most of the day before Katie called Sebastian to tell him about a filming delay for one of their movies. Sebastian went to work at the studio. She went into the studio for her meetings with their lawyers and their bankers where she spent the rest of the week at home with Daphne and her parents while they prepared for the baby's arrival in a few short months. Daphne played in the yard with her grandmothers in the afternoon while she worked on her book that she had been working on for over a year. She was so close to finishing it. She had conversations with her mother's editors and publishers about when they would get the completed draft. She struggled to come up with the ending of the book that wasn't too complicated to understand. She decided on a name for the book. She called her book *The Trials and Tribulations of An Addict*. It was what people could expect from it. It was a book of short stories about the mistakes that she made in her lifetime of addiction. *There are things that you think will define your life that you can't let control you. You are better than your addiction wants you to think.* This was a lesson that she learned from her father after he killed himself. She learned a lot about herself that her father didn't get the chance to learn. She didn't like thinking about that too much. It made her sad to think about the life that her father never got to experience before he died. Someone told her that she was defining herself by the things that she thought that she deserved instead of defining herself as the things that she deserved from the world. It was probably Oliver.

This was the final message in the book. It was so fitting to describe the nuisances of addiction that way everyone would be able to understand it. She realized that there were a lot of nuisances in life, but there were more nuisances in addiction. She described a lot of these nuisances throughout the book since it was a part of dismantling that part of herself that she didn't want to be anymore. She wouldn't move on from the undesirable behavior unless she acknowledged it, and she took accountability for it. She was ignorant to the nuisances of addiction. She didn't want to take responsibility for what she did. She ruined a lot of people's lives because of her addiction. She ruined Emily's parents' marriage and Emily's chance at a normal life. She ruined the trust that Oliver had for her. She ruined the chance of connecting with her parents as a teenager. She ruined her youth by growing up faster than she should've grown up. Some of that was due to her father's death, but everything that happened after that was her fault. She ruined Damien's chance of having Daxton in his life. She ruined Daxton by introducing drugs into their relationship. She ruined her chance at having a normal life with her family. Out of everything that she took responsibility for over the years, the thing that was the hardest to take responsibility for was the time that she spent waiting for life to happen to her. She let drugs steal the best years of her life from her. The birthdays, weddings, vacations, births, and graduations that she missed out on because of her addiction. It was a loss of what she could've had if she made the right decision. She dedicated her book to her father, "Always my muse and my inspiration. The man that I wished that I knew in life. The man that I wished that I didn't know in death. If there was a door to a different time, I'd go there with you. I'll miss you forever. I love you to the stars."

When she showed her mother the dedication, it made her mother cry. She shared it with Uncle Nathan when he came to visit her in Los Angeles. He thought about it for a long time, but he couldn't find the right words to say it. This book was the only thing that she gave to her father that meant anything to them. Even though she couldn't take back the lost time that she would never have with him, she was able to have this connection with him that she wanted to share with the world. Once she finalized the details of her book, they prepared for a media tour of her book as they made it a light schedule since she was almost eight months pregnant. They were only going to bookstores in New York, San Francisco, and Los Angeles. On the morning of her flight to New York, she said an emotional goodbye to her mum, Sebastian, and Daphne as she got on a plane to New York with her mother where she slept with her head leaning on her shoulder before her mother gently nudged her awake. They stayed at Uncle Sam's house as her mother went to her book signings with her where they went back at the house before she slept in her bed for the rest of the night. When it was time for them to go back to California, she said goodbye to her family in New York as she led them to their gate with her mother carrying their bags where they got on the plane to San Francisco before she slept with her head on her mother's shoulder. In the middle of the flight, she woke up to a strong pain in her stomach as she moved past her mother who was asleep with her head on the window where she went into the bathroom before she felt like a gush of water came out into the toilet. She instantly panicked since her water broke into the toilet, and she was currently on an airplane. It was too early for her baby to come out of her. It wasn't good that she was in labor. Before she got off of the toilet, an intense contraction hit her out of nowhere as she grunted in pain where she frantically went to get her mother's attention before she fell down on the floor when another intense contradiction hit her out of nowhere.

As soon as a flight attendant walked in front of her, she flagged her down when she told her that she was in labor, and they needed to get her to a hospital where the flight attendant sprinted into the pilot's cabin to tell him about it. After she shockingly made it back to her seat, the plane was told that there was someone in active labor on the plane and that they were rerouting to the nearest city. As her mother ran over to her with her the flight attendant behind her, her mother pulled her into a frantic hug as she tightly grabbed onto her mother's hands when she pushed through another contraction where the flight attendant told them that they would be landing in Santa Fe, New Mexico in ten minutes before her mother told the flight attendant that they needed to get there faster. After their plane landed in Sant Fe four minutes later, the flight attendant opened up the emergency exit door as two paramedics helped her onto a stretcher when they instantly gave her medications to slow down her labor with her mother holding onto their bags that the pilot gave to them before the ambulance sped to the hospital. As soon as they pulled into the hospital, the paramedics pulled her stretcher into the labor and delivery room where her mother followed her as long as she could when the doctors shut the door in her face before her mother asked the receptionist in the lobby for a phone. She told Sebastian and her mum to get to New Mexico as soon as possible. While her mother was explaining to her husband and her mum that she was in labor, she was on a bed in the middle of an operating room with a dozen doctors and nurses looking at her as they frantically tried to stop her labor where she screamed through every contraction before the pain hit her out of nowhere. She couldn't believe that this was happening to her. Once the nurses failed at calming her down, the doctor looked at her when he told her that they did everything that they could to stop her labor, but they would have to perform an emergency c-section on her. She asked the doctor why they needed to perform a c-section on her in a break in-between her contractions. The doctor told her that the baby was coming out of the wrong way and that the cord would wrap around their neck if they didn't operate to save her life and the baby's life. As soon as she nodded her head at the doctor in silent confirmation, he prepared her for surgery as a nurse injected a numbing medication into her spinal cord, so that she wouldn't feel them taking out the baby or cutting her stomach. They performed the surgery on her when she told them that she couldn't feel anything below her stomach. The surgery itself took them a few minutes as she laid down on the bed as still as possible with her blinking back tears that fell down her face. She heard the sounds of her baby crying for the first time before she let out a desperate sob into her hands. After they placed her baby onto her chest, she looked up at the nurse when she asked her with tears falling down her face, "What is it?"

The nurse kept a grip on her baby when she responded to her with a smile on her face, "You have a baby boy. Do you want to say something to your son before the doctor checks on him?"

As she wiped away tears from her face, she looked up at her son as he stared up at her with wonder in his eyes when she said to him in a gentle voice, "Hello, Noah. I'm your mommy. I love you so much, little critter. I promise you that I'm going to give you the world. Your daddy and your sister love you. You'll be okay, Noah. You have to be okay. Please take him to the doctor. Please save him."

The nurse took Noah over to the doctor where they did what was necessary to keep him alive. She let out a desperate sob into her hands as one of the nurses placed her hand on her shoulder when the nurse told her that they needed to sew her back up before they put her into a recovery room. Since she was incapable of saying anything to them, she nodded her head at him as one of the doctors went to work putting her back together again. She laid there with her eyes closed from being suddenly dizzy when she heard more nurses running towards her before she passed out in the operating room. She wasn't in the operating room after she woke up as she tried to get up from her bed until someone gently pushed her into the bed again where she looked up to see Sebastian sitting next to her before he grabbed onto her hands when he said to her with an exhausted look on his face, "It's okay, honey. Don't get up. You'll pop out your stitches."

She tried to get up again as Sebastian gently pushed her down on the bed where she blinked back tears that fell down her face when she asked him with desperation laced in her voice, "Bash? Where's Noah? Is he okay? Is my baby okay?"

After Sebastian pulled her into a tight hug, she let out heartbreaking sobs into his chest where he ran his fingers through her hair when he responded to her with concern laced in his voice, "Noah's okay honey. I promise you that he's okay. He has his own room in the NICU. We can see him in a few hours after he gets out of surgery. I got here as soon as I could. I'm so sorry honey. I know that you didn't want this to happen to him."

Once she took her face out of Sebastian's chest, he quickly wiped away the tears from her face as she shook her head at him when she asked him in complete shock, "What are you saying? Noah is in surgery. What kind of surgery? Why is my baby getting surgery?"

Sebastian kissed her on the top of her head as he pulled her into a desperate hug with her face hidden into his chest when he responded to her in a soft voice, "He's having heart surgery. He was born with a hole in his heart. The doctor is confident that they can fix it. You weren't conscious when they found it, so I told them that they could do it. After you lost all of that blood during your surgery, you were in and out of it for a few days. You're okay. I knew that you were going to be okay."

As soon as she took her face out of Sebastian's chest, she laid back down on the bed with Sebastian holding onto her hands when she responded to him in a distant voice, "A few days? It didn't feel like any time passed by. Noah's okay. He'll get through his heart surgery, and he'll grow stronger in the NICU. I'm sorry that you weren't there, Bash. I know that you wanted to be there. I shouldn't have gone on this stupid book tour because now my baby has to have heart surgery and has to be in the NICU for a long time."

Sebastian tightened his grip on her hands when he responded to her in a stern voice, "Stop it, Isabella. It's not your fault what happened with Noah. The book tour didn't have anything to do with this. I don't blame you and he doesn't blame you. We'll be okay. He will be okay.

You need to focus on your own healing and the doctors will work on healing Noah. He's like you. He's stubborn as hell."

Sebastian ran his hands up and down her arms when she asked him with a frown on her face, "Where's Daphne? I hope that she's far away from this shitshow. Did you tell her about Noah?"

Sebastian grabbed onto her hands again when he responded to her with a neutral expression on his face, "She's with your parents at the hotel. She knows that she has a baby brother, but she can't see him yet. She wants to see you. Do you want to see her? She's been begging me to let her come to the hospital. Your parents should be here soon. I told them that you woke up and they are eager to see you."

She nodded her head at him as she tightened her grip on his hands when she responded to him with a smile on her face, "Yeah, I want to see Daphne. I don't want her to get upset about not being able to see me. Are they going to be here soon? I want to take a nap before they get here. I'm so exhausted."

Sebastian kissed her on the top of her head when he responded to her with a smile on his face, "Yeah, it's okay, honey. Take a nap. I'll wake you up when they get here. I'm going to check with the doctor to see if you can see Noah when he gets back to the NICU. I love you. I'm so relieved that you are okay. We are all so happy that you are better now. I'll see you in a few hours, okay?"

It didn't take her long to fall asleep with all of the pain medicine that she was on where she dreamed about holding Noah in her arms. She woke up to her parents having a soft conversation with Sebastian where Daphne ran over to her as soon as she opened her eyes. Once Daphne failed to jump up onto the bed, Sebastian placed Daphne on top of her legs as she wrapped her arms around her daughter with her face hidden in her chest where she ran her fingers through her hair when she told her daughter in a gentle voice, "Hey, little bee. Mommy missed you too. Did daddy take you to meet your brother?"

Daphne kept her face hidden in her mother's chest when she responded to her with tears falling down her face, "Daddy didn't let me meet Noah. He said that he's sick. I don't want my brother to be sick. Are you sick too, mommy? Is that why you are in the hospital?"

As she looked over at Sebastian, she kissed Daphne on the top of her head as she ran her fingers through her hair in a comforting motion when she responded to her daughter with a frown on her face, "Noah will get better, little bee. The doctors are taking good care of him. Mommy is okay now. I had surgery to get Noah out of my stomach. Do you see the marks on my stomach? You have to be careful with my stomach for a few weeks while I'm healing from it. I know that you want to meet Noah. We'll meet him together. How does that sound? Are we allowed to see Noah, Bash? What did the doctor say?"

Sebastian placed his hand on Daphne's back when he responded to them with a smile on his face, "The doctor said that we can go to Noah's room right now. He's awake from the anesthesia. Let's get mommy a wheelchair from the nurse's station. Okay, little bee?"

After Sebastian disappeared with Daphne on his hip, her mother took a seat next to her as her mum grabbed onto her hands when her mother said to her with a concerned look on her face, "I'm glad that you are okay, baby girl. You scared me when you went into surgery. I was relieved to learn that you were okay and that my grandson was okay too. Things happened so quickly. Anything could've happened if we weren't as fast as we were at getting to the hospital. Noah is such an angel. He looks so much like you. He has your eyes."

She leaned back onto the bed before she hid her face into her mum's hands when she responded to her mother with a frown on her face, "I know, mom. It could've had a worse outcome. I'm relieved that the pilot was fast at re-routing us to land. Almost like he had to do this before. Thank you for being so incredible. You guys are taking care of Daphne while Sebastian is with us at the hospital. I love him so much, mom. He's worth all of the pain that I'm feeling."

Sebastian came back into her room with a nurse pushing Daphne in the wheelchair as her mum placed Daphne on her hip when Sebastian and the nurse helped her off of the bed into the wheelchair where she groaned in pain before she sat down in it. As the nurse pushed her in the wheelchair over the NICU, she laid back on the wheelchair with her eyes closed from being dizzy as Sebastian kept his hand on her back until the nurse told them that they made it to Noah's room where Sebastian pushed the wheelchair into the room with her parents and Daphne following behind them. As soon as the nurse attending to Noah moved away from his small bed, Sebastian pushed her closer to him as she placed her hands into the sides of the bed with Sebastian doing the same on the other side where Daphne sat on her lap looking over at Noah when she softly asked them since Sebastian already told her that she couldn't talk loudly in his room, "Is this baby brother? He's so tiny, mommy. Hi, Noah. This is your big sister Daphne. I love you so much."

As she blinked back tears that fell down her face, she grabbed onto one of Noah's tiny hands as she gently stroked it back and forth when she whispered to him like they were the only two people left in the world, "Hi, little critter. I haven't seen you since you were born. I was the first person that you met. You're my special boy, Noah. You are my Noah William. You are my miracle."

Her mother let out a soft gasp as she held onto her mum's hands when she whispered to her daughter with tears falling down her face, "I love it. That's so sweet, baby girl. Noah William. Your dad would be honored to have his grandson named after him. I can see it. He's definitely a little William. He's our William."

She smiled at her mother before she turned her attention back to Noah who was staring at them with his wide eyes full of life when she whispered to them with a smile on her face, "Bash, look over here. He's staring at us. He knows that we are his parents. We love you much, Noah. Mommy and daddy love you so much. You are the sweetest boy. You were worth the wait, little critter. You are everything to me." A nurse came into the room to tell them that they needed to check on Noah's vitals again. Sebastian pushed her wheelchair out of the NICU into her hospital room where she took a nap for the rest of the afternoon before she was woken up by a nurse bugging her to eat dinner that was placed in front of her. She ate dinner with Sebastian alone in her room since her parents took Daphne back to the hotel with them. Sebastian left her alone for the night as a nurse came into her room to update her on Noah's status, and she gave her pain medicine to help her sleep before she fell asleep in her hospital bed for the rest of the night.

CHAPTER FIFTY-EIGHT
(SPRING 1973 – LOS ANGELES, CALIFORNIA)

She only spent a few days in the hospital, but Noah had a long way to go until he was ready to go home. They moved from their hotel to a rental house that her mother got them in a few streets away from the hospital. Even though Sebastian wanted to stay with them while Noah was in the NICU, someone still needed to run their company for them. Sebastian spent the weekdays in Los Angeles, and he flew back to Santa Fe on the weekends to be with them. She spent any moment that she could in the hospital with Noah. She helped the nurses take care of him in any way that she could connect with him. Since he was too tiny to nurse from her chest, she pumped milk for him to drink through bottles that he learned how to drink from his feeding tube where the nurses fed him his bottles during the day. She took the time to appreciate that she got to hold Noah. She could only see him for a few hours a day because he was under lights for the rest of the day. It was hard for her to put him into his bed since she couldn't hold him again until the next day. When she was alone at night pumping milk, she cried that she shipped the milk to the hospital for the nurses to feed him instead of her. Things weren't easy for her after Noah was born. There was a hole in her heart where he was supposed to be with her. She didn't have this experience when Daphne was born. Daphne was in her arms all of the time when she was a newborn. She never put her down except for when she was asleep, but Daphne slept in her arms most of the time anyways. She wanted to hold Noah for the rest of his life if it meant that he was never taken away from her again. Her heart broke every time that she handed Noah back to the nurses. She acted like everything was okay and it wasn't affecting her that she couldn't be with her baby. The facade cracked in the least expected way. She got back from the hospital after being with Noah all day. She fell apart for the first time since Noah was born. She cried for a long time in the car until a security guard knocked on the window of her car when he asked her if she was okay. She confessed to him that she was visiting her son in the NICU every day for three weeks and that she couldn't handle it anymore. After the security guard gave her a comforting squeeze on her shoulder, he asked her if she needed anything from him. She told him that she was okay before she drove back to their rental house. It made her feel better for only a moment.

As she went to the NICU without Sebastian, her mental health got worse in the coming weeks. She was so happy that Noah was getting better, and he was gaining weight like the doctor wanted him to. She was still heartbroken that this was happening to her baby because she couldn't keep him in her body for five more weeks. Her parents and Sebastian told her not to blame herself for what happened with Noah's birth, but old habits died very hard. She couldn't get rid of that part of brain that told her that she was a horrible mother from leaving her daughter behind at home to be with her son in the hospital. Her parents assured her that Daphne was okay with her being at the hospital, but it didn't make it feel any better for her that she was choosing her son over her daughter. She felt like she was being selfish by being upset about this when her son was in the hospital fighting for his life. There was a conservation that no one had about how Noah almost died when he was a few days old, and she was here thinking about herself yet again. She thought that she learned this lesson by writing her book to not be selfish anymore, but that opened up a can of worms that she wasn't ready to deal with. What was she going to do about her book tour? She forgot that she wrote a book and that she was on a book tour promoting it. When she asked Sebastian about it in the NICU with their son laying on his bare chest, he told her not to worry about it and that Lucy handled that for her by telling everyone that it was postponed since her son was in the hospital. The press was sympathetic to her newborn son being in the hospital because no one blamed her for being with her son when he needed her while his heart healed, and he gained weight. After Noah was in the NICU for over a month, he didn't need to be under the lights during the day where they held him for as long as they wanted to except for when the nurses did their hourly check on him. It was around that same time that the doctor told her that she could start trying to breastfeed Noah since he wasn't on a feeding tube anymore. On the first day of her trying to breastfeed her son, Noah almost latched a few times where he couldn't keep the milk in his mouth before she gave Noah a bottle of her milk instead. This was the pattern for over a week of her trying to breastfeed Noah before she gave him a bottle because it wasn't working for them. In the next week of her trying to breastfeed her son, the nurses got a lactation expert to help them with this task. She was so emotionally exhausted from seeing the sad look on her son's face when he couldn't latch onto his mother's chest. After her day with the lactation expert, they finally got Noah to latch to her as she softly cried to herself when she rocked Noah back and forth in the rocking chair where he cooed from nursing her chest before she thanked the lactation expert for helping them. It was part of their new routine for Noah to nurse from her chest during the day every two hours where the nurses gave Noah bottles of her milk at night. She cherished this time that she got with Noah. She was the only person that fed Noah during the day. Noah looked up at her when she was nursing him like she was his favorite person. The look on her son's face told her everything that she needed to know. Noah told her that he loved her, and she was special. She hoped that he would always feel that way about her because she never wanted that feeling to go away in her heart. It reminded her that the horrible feelings that she felt and the mistakes that she made in her life was worth it. This was one of the moments that she was going to spend in eternity with Noah. It made the pain, and the heartbreak mean something more than life. This was a feeling that she craved with drugs over the years that she felt without drugs and only with her children. It was the feeling of being invincible. She could do anything. She was in the stars with her father, her mother, Sebastian, and her children. When she started nursing her son, she produced more milk than she did with Daphne since she pumped to give him the milk at night. Noah's doctor told her that this was a good thing that she was overproducing milk. Noah ate more milk, and he gained more weight, so that he could be discharged from the hospital. There were whispers from the doctor and the nurses about when Noah would be able to go home. They didn't want to give them a date without knowing the details. She was desperate for her son to go home because she couldn't stand being apart from him at night. She cried herself to sleep since he wasn't there with her. Nursing made it worse since her body ached for him and she didn't know what to do without him.

On the week before Noah was discharged from the hospital, they met with Noah's doctors that felt comfortable letting him leave the hospital if he gained a pound in a week before they considered letting him leave the hospital. She nursed Noah every hour that she was at the hospital where the nurses fed him every hour throughout the night to make him gain more weight. While she was doubtful of the doctors discharging Noah from the hospital, Sebastian already made plans for them to go to Los Angeles with Noah. He wanted to spend a large amount of their money on a private jet since he felt that being on a crowded plane in the airport would be bad for a pre-mature baby. She didn't disagree with his point that Noah couldn't go home on a crowded plane after he went through a dirty airport, but she told Sebastian that they should drive home. Sebastian didn't think that was a good idea because they didn't know how being on a long car ride would impact him. She thought that he didn't make any sense because a plane ride wasn't going to do him any good. They got into a public argument at the hospital before Sebastian stormed out of the hospital leaving her without a way back to the house. After she got a taxi to their rental house, Sebastian was on his way back to Los Angeles where she stewed in anger towards him for the rest of the week until he came back to Santa Fe the next weekend where he pretended that nothing happened. They were fighting a lot more than they did before in their relationship. They took turns starting new arguments with each other that ended up with her being stuck at the hospital with their son and Sebastian retreating back to Los Angeles for the week. Their arguments were about Noah and Daphne where the root of it was the bitterness that they felt towards each other. She wouldn't have been so bitter towards Sebastian if he was there with her to deal with their son being in the

NICU. When she expressed to him that she felt like she was doing this alone, he got defensive about it because she told him that he chose his career over his family. This was something that she didn't believe about him, but he put those words into her mouth. He told her about how he took care of their daughter when she had her mental breakdown in New York, and this was the universe's way of showing karma to her for being an absent mother. She forgot what their argument was about since it turned into such a shitshow after that. When they got the news from the doctor about Noah being discharged from the hospital, they got into a screaming match with each other in the car on the way back from the hospital about how Sebastian spent fourteen thousand dollars on a private jet that they didn't need since she thought that they were driving Noah home. Sebastian already set everything up without telling her about it. She told him that she should have autonomy about what happens to their money where he reminded her that he was making the money for the last two months before she told him that it was her mother's money that started the company. The argument ended at the rental house on their last night at Santa Fe where she slept in Daphne's bed since she proved to Sebastian that she wasn't an absent mother. Sebastian went to a hotel for the night. On the day that Noah got discharged, her parents packed up their stuff into the car.

Her parents promised to meet her at the hospital with Daphne before she left to go to the hospital by herself. She wasn't surprised to see that Sebastian wasn't there since he knew that she was coming in first thing in the morning to get Noah ready to go home. Sebastian told her after their explosive argument last night that he would meet them on the private jet. After she nursed Noah from her chest for the last time in the hospital, the nurses got rid of the rest of the cords off of his body as she placed him in his stroller with a blanket around him where she thanked all of the nurses and the doctors that nursed her baby back to health before she met up with her parents and Daphne in front of the hospital. Once she got Noah in his car seat in between her and Daphne, her parents drove them to the private jet as he met them outside of the private jet with the pilot where she carried Noah in her arms while Sebastian placed Daphne on his hip before they got on the plane together. Even though she was very angry about what Sebastian said to her in their argument last night, she acted like she always did with him as they kissed each other on the cheek at the airport. They talked to their children instead of each other since she knew that they would fight again, and they didn't want to fight in front of their children. For the plane ride to Los Angeles, she was busy nursing Noah and comforting him to pay attention to anyone else while Sebastian played with Daphne in their seats on the other side of the plane. When their private jet landed in Los Angeles, her parents drove to Uncle Stan and Thomas' house for the night since they had a retirement party for Uncle Stan before their driver dropped them off at the house. After they got back to their house for the first time in two months, she got Daphne to bed in between her constant feedings for Noah as Sebastian went into the office to do some work that he claimed that he needed to get done that night. She wasn't in the mood to deal with him, so she left him alone for the rest of the night. Once she put Daphne to bed, she took Noah into their bedroom as she nursed him from her chest until he fell asleep on her chest where she left him sleeping on top of her chest since she wanted this moment more than anything in the world. Noah would've slept all night on her chest if she didn't wake him up to nurse him since she kept him on the same strict nursing schedule that they had him on at the hospital.

When she woke up in the early morning to Noah crying in his bassinet, she placed him on top of her chest as he instantly stopped crying where she nursed him before he fell back to sleep in her arms. She didn't see Sebastian until that evening at dinner where he talked about planning a birthday party for Daphne who was turning three years old in a few weeks where she told him to handle the party for her since she knew that they were going to get into an argument about it. After Sebastian was content with this information, he told Daphne that he would do whatever birthday party that she wanted where Daphne told them that she wanted to have a unicorn themed party at the house before Sebastian told her that he would have his assistant set it up for him. She stayed up all night with Noah for his feedings while her parents got Daphne up in the morning as Sebastian went to the studio all day where Sebastian took Daphne to bed for the rest of the night. Her parents went out most nights with Uncle Stan and Thomas' friends. She didn't want her parents hearing their arguments that they had with each other. Since they were late planning Daphne's birthday party, they could only have the party after her birthday where they had a small celebration at home. She got up out of the bed to wake up Daphne after she just fell asleep with Noah where she pulled her daughter into a tight hug as she kissed her lips when she told her happy birthday. Sebastian was supposed to be there with her, but he was too angry at her from their argument last night. Once she put on Daphne's unicorn dress that she picked out at the store, she took them into their bedroom where she nursed Noah from her chest while Daphne talked to her about everything that she wanted to do for her birthday before they went downstairs to eat breakfast with her parents. Her mum made Daphne pancakes with sprinkles on it. Daphne was so obsessed with them that she kept trying to give them to Noah before she reminded her daughter that Noah was too young to eat sprinkle pancakes. She played with Daphne in the living room for most of the day as she went back and forth from nursing or burping Noah before he fell asleep on her chest while her parents prepared the house for Daphne's birthday party. Once Daphne helped her grandmothers put up decorations, she went into their bedroom to take a needed nap since Noah didn't sleep for more than forty minutes at a time.

She was woken up when Daphne told her that daddy was home from work. Once she changed into a white dress, she joined her cousins Oliver, Amelia, and Sasha and their families in the living room as they pulled her into a tight hug when they asked her how she was adjusting to having two children. She told them that everything was fine before she let them hold Noah. Oliver didn't seem convinced by that answer, but he let it go for the moment before he moved into a conversation with Sebastian about the studio. After they ate a delicious meal that her mum made for them, she went into her bedroom to nurse Noah as an excuse since she wanted to be alone to cry for a moment before she joined her family in the living room. Daphne opened up her presents with no help from them until it was time for the cake. Once her mother lit three candles on the cake, Daphne closed her eyes as she blew out the candles on the cake. Daphne told everyone that she wished that her baby brother was going to be healthy where everyone got emotional for a moment before Sebastian cut pieces of cake for them. Daphne fell asleep in Sebastian's arms as he took her up to bed for the rest of the night while she went into her bedroom to nurse

Noah where she put him to bed in his bassinet before she joined her cousins and their spouses in the living room. When Sebastian walked into the living room, he took a seat next to Oliver as she rolled her eyes in annoyance at him where he gave her stern look before he stormed off into the yard with her following behind him. After she walked into the yard, she sprinted over to Sebastian who paced back and forth in circles when she asked him with anger laced in her voice, "What's your problem, Bash? This party was your idea, and you are acting like you can't be bothered to deal with it."

Sebastian gave her a venomous look when he responded to her with a frown on his face, "That's not true. I didn't realize that I needed to get work done. You wouldn't understand that feeling."

She shouted at him with a look of disbelief on her face, "Here we go again! I don't know what work is so important that you don't engage with anyone on your daughter's birthday! She only turns three years old once and you couldn't have been bothered to be there! How dare you say that to me! I don't know what it is like to work. You forget that I had a career before I met you and we had children! In the work that I did as an actress, it's never come close to the work that I do as a mother! You'll never know what that is like to do my job! It might not give me wealth and status, but it gives me more happiness than you will know! I'm up all night with our son! I take care of our daughter all day and I try to make time for you! You wanted nothing to do with me since our son was born! The studio is an excuse! It's only an excuse! You don't get to say that to me! I get it, Bash! I don't think that you get it!"

Sebastian stood in front of her with his hands on his hips when he shouted at her with anger laced in his voice, "Do you think that about me? That I want nothing to do with my children? I love my children! They are the best thing that happened to me! This isn't about them! You make everything about the children when it's just about us! It's about us being so sick of each other that we can't stand to be together! You're right! I can't stand how you act holier than God when you say, and you do things! Like I'm destined to fail because I'm not God's chosen child! You can't do anything wrong! You are Saint Isabella! I'm always the bad guy! Bash must have done something wrong to make Isabella cry because she would never do anything wrong!"

She was livid at him when she shouted at him with tears falling down her face, "Stop it, Bash! That's not true! You are the only person that thinks that! I'm not a perfect person and you aren't either! I'm not a saint or God! I've made a lot of mistakes in my life, okay? I can't tell you all of them because there's so many of them! I've ruined my own life and other people's lives! Sometimes when I wasn't trying to and other times when I was trying to! You're right that this isn't about the children! This has always been about that fucking studio and what it means to you! I know that this might come out as a shock to you, but I don't care about the studio! I only cared about it because you care about it. I don't care if it fails, or if it succeeds! The only thing here I care about is our marriage! Do you want to know what I think? You care about the studio more than our marriage! It breaks my heart to say this, but I think that you care about that studio more than our children! Maybe I already knew that a long time ago, but I didn't want to admit that to myself! I want you to care about me! I want you to care about us! I can't make you care about us! I'm going to ask you a question that we have been skirting around for three months. Do you want to be with me anymore?"

Sebastian shrugged his shoulders at her when he responded to her with tears falling down his face, "It might be better for us to not be with each other. At least for a little bit while I figure out what's going on with me. I'm trying to be the person that everyone needs me to be when I don't know who I am. I don't think we know each other. We've been living separate lives for so long that we don't know how to live with each other. This divide between us started a long time ago. Before Noah was born. Before Daphne was born. This has been coming for a long time. We took our time getting to this crossroads where we have to decide what to do from here. I love you, Isabella. I love our children. We've been avoiding this for a long time."

She wiped away the tears that fell down her face when she responded to him with desperation laced in her voice, "Avoiding what? Getting divorced? Bash? What are you talking about? Where the hell is this coming from? We just had our son! This is ridiculous! We're only fighting! It doesn't mean that we need to get divorced!"

Sebastian grabbed onto her hands as he blinked back tears that fell down his face when he said to her with a frown on his face, "We're not getting divorced. I need to go into treatment. That's what I mean. I have an active eating disorder. I relapsed the day that Noah was born."

She pulled away from him as she moved back away from him when she asked him with a shocked look on her face, "What did you say? You are binging and purging again? This isn't about the company. You have been using it to hide this from me. I'm sorry that I didn't notice it. I was so consumed with Noah that I didn't realize what was going on. Is that why we have been fighting? Were you mad at me for not saying anything about it? You should've told me, Bash. You should've told me before it got this bad between us. How dare you keep this from me."

Once she punched Sebastian in the chest to get her frustration out on him, she noticed that he was a lot thinner than she remembered him being before Noah was born until he grabbed onto her hands to stop her from hitting him when he responded to her with a softer look on his face, "Stop it. I'm sorry that I've kept this from you. I didn't know how to tell you about it without coming off as defensive. It backfired on me. Did you think that I was asking you for a divorce? Why would I do that?"

As soon as she pulled him into a desperate kiss, they broke apart from each other when she responded to him in a confused voice, "Jesus Christ, Bash. I don't know why I thought that you wanted to get divorced. It felt like you hated me or something. You didn't want to be with me anymore. I didn't know what to do about it. It was all very confusing to me. Just to clear the air. We aren't getting divorced. You don't hate me. You are going to get treatment for your eating disorder while I what?"

Sebastian placed his hands over her hands when he told her with a smile on his face, "No, we aren't getting divorced, and I don't hate you. I'm sorry for the mess that I created. I didn't mean to drag you into my shit. What are you going to do when I'm in treatment? What you always do honey. You are going to take care of our children and our company that I wasn't having a secret affair with. Were you jealous of the company? Really, Isabella? It's not a real person. How would you react if I cheated on you with a real person? Would you be asking me if we should get divorced then?"

After she hit Sebastian on the shoulder with him groaning in pain, she pulled him into another desperate kiss until they were out of breath when she responded to him with a smirk on her face, "I would kill her with my bare hands. That's what I would do if you cheated on me. I was jealous of the company. Don't act like a prick about it. You made me think that the company became your mistress and not the eating disorder that you hid from me. I don't know what's worse to be jealous about a company or an eating disorder. Am I going to be replacing you as CEO of the company? What would the studio do with a woman's input about our films?"

Sebastian pulled her into a long kiss that they didn't separate from each other until they heard the back door open when Oliver asked them if everything was okay where she shouted at him that they kissed and made up before Oliver closed the door behind him. Once he pulled her into another long kiss, she unbuttoned his shirt as he unzipped the back of her dress where he pulled them towards their tent that Daphne made her grandparents put up in the yard before he pushed her onto the ground. After she pulled him into a compassionate kiss, they broke apart from each other when he responded to her with his hands doing things to her that made her want to scream, "The company will be fine in your capable hands. No woman will know me like you know me. I trust you, Isabella. No one could replace you. Don't forget that."

After they were done making up with each other, she laid down with her head laying on his chest as he ran his fingers up and down her back when she whispered to him like it was a secret between them, "I'm sorry about everything that I said to you. I didn't mean it. I love you, Bash."

Sebastian kissed her on the top of her head when he whispered back to her, "I'm sorry too. I didn't mean it either. I love you, Isabella. I'm leaving for treatment tomorrow. Oliver is taking me there, so that you can stay home with the children."

She shook her head when she responded to him with a smirk on her face, "You told Oliver before you told me about it? I saw that coming. He's so good. He knows what's wrong before you tell him. I'll pay the mistress a visit tomorrow. Noah can meet the staff too."

Sebastian let out a frustrated sigh as he tightened his grip on her arms when he responded to him with a frown on his face, "Please stop referring to our company as the mistress. People are going to get the wrong impression. They are going to think that I cheated on my wife with a mystery woman."

Sebastian pulled her into a long kiss until they broke apart from each other when Oliver said to them, making them sit up on the ground, "You two are worse than teenagers! I think that the whole universe heard you guys go at it with each other. Are you okay? I got wounds from your argument, and I had no stake in it."

As she hid her face into Sebastian's chest, she responded to Oliver with sarcasm laced in her voice, "We're okay, Oliver. Bash is going to treatment tomorrow and I'm going to visit the mistress. Is Noah awake? Does he need to be fed?"

Sebastian hit her in the arm for calling the company his mistress. Oliver looked at them when he responded to them with confusion written all over his face, "Okay. Right. I don't want to know what kind of sick inside joke that you said to me, but I want absolutely nothing to do with it. Noah is with Juliet. She said that he's hungry, so you need to go inside to feed him. Everyone else left when you guys were screaming at each other. Please just come into the house. Noah is screaming for you, Isabella. You can stay here all night, Bash. Isabella needs to be in the house making the baby quiet because no one can sleep over it. I need to take this idiot to treatment in the morning. Come on, idiot number two. Let's go inside now or else I'll scream too." Once Oliver helped her off of the ground, she zipped up the back of her dress with Sebastian following behind them where Oliver didn't let go of the strong grip on her hand until they were in the house again before Juliet rushed over to her with Noah screaming in her arms. As soon as Juliet placed Noah in her arms, she gently rocked him as Noah's cries slowly calmed down where she held Noah to her chest before he drank from it. Oliver and Juliet went upstairs in their guest bedroom where Eleanor and Posey were asleep, and Sebastian went into their bedroom while she was nursing Noah on the couch. After Noah fell asleep in her arms, she walked into her bedroom where Sebastian waited for her before she joined him in their bed. As soon as Sebastian wrapped his arm around her, she laid her head on his chest until she fell asleep in his arms for the rest of the night.

Chapter Fifty-Nine
(Summer 1973 – Los Angeles, California)

She woke up early the next morning while Sebastian was packing his bags for the treatment center when he pulled her into a long hug that they didn't let go of until Noah cried for her on the bed before she followed Sebastian outside in the driveway where Oliver waited for him. After she pulled Sebastian into a desperate hug with Noah in her arms, he kissed her on the lips once more as he kissed Noah on the top of his head where he handed his bags to Oliver who put them into the back of the car before he got into the car. Once Oliver and Sebastian drove away from the house, she went into the house with tears falling down her face where she hid in her bedroom until it was time to get Daphne up for the day. After they ate breakfast with Juliet and her daughters, Juliet drove her daughters to their house with her as she got Noah and Daphne dressed in cool outfits before their driver took them to the studio for the rest of the day. Everyone in the studio knew that she was coming in since Sebastian told everyone in their weekly meeting that he was stepping away from the studio for a while to be with his mother who was sick. It wasn't a lie that her mother-in-law was sick because she had cancer for several years and everyone already knew that about her. As soon as she dropped off Daphne at the daycare center, she carried Noah in her arms as she moved throughout the studio catching up on what she missed out on in the last five months. Lucy followed her around the building with papers that she needed to see about every movie that they were filming at the time. She took a break to feed Noah in her office every two hours.

She went to their studio every day of the week. She went into it on the weekends since that was when their editors and producers worked on final cuts of the movies that she needed to approve of before it got sent to the movie theaters. Noah came with her everywhere that she went since she wasn't apart from him since he got discharged from the hospital. Daphne stayed at home with her parents unless her parents were on a trip with Uncle Stan and Thomas where she took Daphne to the daycare at the studio. On the weekends that her parents weren't in town, she took Daphne into the studio since nothing was filmed on those days. Daphne ran around the studio as much as she wanted to without her breaking anything. Sometimes she took Daphne into the booth where they edited the movies as Daphne watched their producers work on the final cuts of the movies. Daphne didn't question why her father was gone from their lives. She told her daughter about daddy being with grandma in San Francesco who had cancer, and he was helping her get better like when Noah used to be sick. This was something that Daphne understood more than most children her age since her brother was in the hospital when he was sick, and she couldn't be with him for a long time. In Sebastian's absence, she let Daphne sleep with her in the bed. Daphne missed him like she missed him. He called her once a week where he told her about his steps towards recovery as she told him about how their children were doing and that the company was doing great in his absence. They never talked about the unspoken things that they weren't saying to each other. The unspoken things were louder than the spoken things between them. They didn't talk about what their marriage was going to look like after he got back home or that they would never be the same after Noah's birth. They didn't talk about the impact of the things that they said to each other in their arguments over the last three months. Even though they were angry with each other, there was some truth in what they said to each other. She might not have agreed with the way that she told him about it, but she was telling him the truth no matter how much it hurt him to hear it. She knew that Sebastian meant it when he told her that she was an absent parent to Daphne when Noah was in the hospital. It didn't hurt her that he said that to her. She felt it in her heart. It only hurt her because he knew that he was comparing her to her father because he abandoned her before she was born. Even though she wanted to tell Sebastian that she didn't abandon her daughter, it wasn't different from what her father did to her. She was pawning her daughter off to Sebastian or her parents, so that she didn't have to deal with it. It wasn't that she didn't want to deal with her daughter's emotions, but she didn't know how to deal with them. She didn't have the capacity to deal with her emotions. That was the reason why she couldn't deal with Sebastian's emotions. It was hard for her to understand anything at that moment. During a routine appointment for Noah's six-month check-up, his doctor asked her if she was feeling okay as she tried to come up with an answer that wouldn't overcomplicate an already complicated situation. His doctor suggested to her that it sounded like she had postpartum depression before she instantly dismissed it since it would imply that she wasn't capable of taking care of her children. She thought about it a lot at night when she was awake feeding Noah where the doctor might have been onto something with this postpartum depression thing before she called Dr. Taylor asked him if she could come see him at his house. Once Dr. Taylor told her that he would be home all weekend if she wanted to come see him, she left Daphne with her parents for the day as she went to his house with Noah in her arms since she didn't want to be apart from him before he let her into his house. Since this wasn't a therapy session, they were informal with each other as they caught up with each other since she knew him for over a decade, and she considered him to be her friend even if he didn't see her that way.

Dr. Taylor cuddled with Noah on the couch when she rambled to him about her self-destructing relationship with her husband and her suspicion that she might have postpartum depression from Noah's traumatic birth. She didn't call Noah's birth traumatic because he put the words into her mouth. When Dr. Taylor asked her what she was fighting about with Sebastian, she told him everything that they fought about in the last three months before he went to the treatment center that she opened up about. She couldn't talk about his eating disorder with anyone else except him. Between their children and the company to the point that they couldn't stand being around each other, there was a lot of ground to cover that she spent the whole next day at Dr. Taylor's house talking to him about it. There was one thing that she didn't want to talk about that kept coming up in their conversations. She didn't want to talk about how she was becoming her mother, and Sebastian was becoming her father. The cycle that she worked so hard to break was being continued without them realizing it. They were driving each other to the point of insanity, and they didn't know how to stop it from happening. She grew to resent Sebastian because he had everything that she couldn't get back again. Even though everything changed for her when she had her children, nothing changed for Sebastian. He got to go to the parties in Hollywood and have the glamorous life that she used to have. Sebastian could go to work all day and not have to worry about where his children were or what they were doing when he wasn't with them. He could go out to the bar at night with his friends until the sun came up without any consequences. He represented everything that she could never have. She chose to have her children, so she shouldn't be upset by this, but didn't make it better. She wasn't allowed to have that life. She couldn't go to work without worrying about who was going to watch Daphne, so that she didn't have to take her with her. She couldn't stay out past eight pm since she needed to put Daphne to bed. She couldn't travel without Noah because his food came from her body. There wasn't a world that she was only an actress without being a wife and a mother before it. She used to be an actress. Now she was only known as Sebastian's wife and Daphne and Noah's mother. She wasn't allowed to be Isabella anymore. If she knew that having a family would take away her ability to define her life, then she would've chosen a different door. A better door.

When Dr. Taylor told her that she needed to find herself without being a wife and a mother, she asked him how she could do that when she was trapped in her life before he told her that she needed to go out in the world to see who she was without her children. That sounded like an impossible task since Sebastian was in the treatment center and she was proving to him that she could raise her children without pawning them off on her parents. Once she asked Dr. Taylor how she was going to do that, he told her that she should finish the book tour that she put on hold when Noah was born. He hadn't seen her that happy in a long time. She told him that she would take Noah with her since Daphne hardly noticed her absence. He told her that it would be good for her to step outside of herself for a few weeks since she wouldn't get a chance like this again. She didn't know if he was implying her time away from her husband who she had problems with or her daughter that was used to being apart from her. She didn't want to know the answer. She told her assistant Lucy that she wanted to continue her press tour that was put on hold when Noah was born. Lucy had been bothering her about it every day for the last month. She was going to bookstores in San Francesco and Los Angeles like she planned on doing before her water broke in Santa Fe where Lucy added dates in Las Vegas and Denver since she only wanted to go to places on the west coast. Since Sebastian bought a private jet that was sitting at the LAX airport, Lucy coordinated the information to the pilot as they prepared for their trip to San Francesco where she agreed to see her mother-in-law since she felt bad for using her as a scapegoat without asking her about it. She accepted that Daphne was better off with her grandparents than with her own parents. Neither of them could be there to emotionally support her like she needed from them. She saw the complete hypocrisy in doing what her mother did with her when she got famous from her books, but she couldn't have been bothered to care about it. When she told Daphne that she was going away for a few weeks on a book tour, Daphne wasn't fazed by it since she was going to be with her grandparents, and she spent most of her time with them. Daphne didn't ask her why Noah got to come with her since she realized how indifferent her daughter was to it because she didn't care that Noah was going with her. She didn't let herself get into that black hole of a thought since she wouldn't be able to find her way out of it.

On the morning of her leaving for the book tour, she pulled Daphne into a tight hug that she only let her hold onto for a few moments before she ran over to play with her grandparents on the floor. She tried not to act upset as she got on their private jet with Noah asleep in her arms where Lucy handed her tissue before she took it from her hands. The book tour was a big blur in her head. They went from city to city on the west coast where she did book signings with the large crowds that came out to see her before they did it all over again the next day. They took a few days off in between going to a new city where she left Noah with Lucy in the hotel room for several hours where she went on new adventures by herself. She went on a hike with the sun rising in the sky. She jumped off a boat into the Pacific Ocean with people that she met for the first time from the booking signing. She swam in the ocean in the middle of the night with the moon glowing in the sky. She rode a bike all through Denver with the sun setting in the sky. She found a version of herself that she would've been if she chose a different door. It wasn't a person that was defined by her parents. It wasn't a person that was defined by her addiction and her father's death. It wasn't a person that was defined by being a wife and a mother. She was someone who was enjoying her life instead of life happening around her. She was someone who was living in the moment instead of always being trapped in the past. She was someone that lived without any fear of the world instead of being too scared to take any chances. She was someone that believed that there was some kindness left in the world for her instead of believing that the world was a cruel place. While she jumped off of a cliff into the Pacific Ocean, there was a moment that she was flying through the air into the water when she felt like she was in the doorway with her father. Even though she used to be so scared of this moment, she realized that she wasn't scared of it anymore. She knew that he was in the water with her. Like they were together in a different time where everything was yet to be told by the universe. She stayed under the water with him longer than she should have before she was pulled back to the shore by one of her new friends. When they asked her why didn't swim up from the water, she told him that she was in the doorway with her father, and she told him to make a different choice. She was telling him to make the right choice. They didn't get it, so she stormed into her hotel room with her son and Lucy who was talking on the phone to her children. She carried Noah out on the balcony with her as she cried like she never did before where she wrote her father a letter that she never sent him.

I know that you are never going to read this letter. You're dead. You have been dead for twenty-two years. I never got the chance to write you a letter before you died. After all of the letters that you sent to people in your life, it's only fair that you receive a letter from your daughter. A wise person told me to start from the beginning. That wise person was you. I'm going to tell you things that I never got to tell you. You leaving me with mom was the worst decision that you made in your life. I've never been angrier at anyone than I was at you. I think that you thought that you were protecting me by leaving me. You didn't want to hurt anyone else in your life like you hurt mom. I hate to break it to you, but you hurt me more by leaving me. I wasn't hurt by anyone more than you. You never gave me a chance to tell you how I felt about it. You assumed that you knew how I felt without asking me. I wasn't that hurt by you dying because you were already gone. Gone. What a dark and desolate word. Gone, but never forgotten. That's what your grave says. I don't know who came up with that one, but they were a genius. The foreshadowing on that one. It was probably Uncle Nathan. I learned about what choices are and how we make right or wrong choices that decide where our life is going to lead us someday. If we make the wrong choice, we are stuck dealing with the consequences of it for the rest of our lives. We know a lot about wrong choices, don't we? It seems like I have a lifetime full of them. I don't think that I've ever done anything right. I know that you felt like that too. No one will know the depth of that feeling like we feel it. I was told a lot of things in my life that made me upset. Do you want to know what some of those things are? One of them was when Oliver told me that I made the wrong choice in York after my last relapse. Another one was when Oliver told me that loving me was a burden. That was the same conversation. Poor guy wouldn't give me any moment to breathe. The worst one was when Sebastian told me that I was abandoning my children. That one hit home for me because it's a familiar feeling.

I thought about it for a really long time. Am I abandoning my children when I'm not with them? I don't think that I am. I'm still in their lives and raising them. Sebastian doesn't know what it means to be abandoned. It means to be left alone forever. He wasn't left alone by anyone in his life. The only time that I left him was when we were having problems with each other like we are right now. I don't know what I think about that word. Abandoned. It sounds so isolating and lonely. Mom wouldn't let me feel like that even though you made her feel like that. Sometimes I forget that you didn't just abandon me. You abandoned mom too. Neither of us asked for this life that you chose for us. I think that only abandoned people have the capacity to abandon others. Who abandoned you? Was it your father who didn't understand you? Was it Nathan who tried to protect you from the world? Was it your grandfather who raised you in the earliest years of your life? I understand you, dad. I'm the only person that has ever understood you. I'm your daughter. We share one mind. We've always shared our minds with each other. I know what it's like to be abandoned by the person that you want to be with the most in the world. I know what it's like to be raised by an emotionally unavailable parent. You are always trying to compare your living parents to the parent that left you. You don't mean to do it, but you can't stop yourself. It's easy to compare your emotionally unavailable mother with your father who never got the choice to disappoint you. She's never going to compete with him. It's already too late for her to change your mind. My biggest fear is that my children are going to see Bash and I like I saw you and mom. I'm always going to be a disappointment to them because their father never got the chance to disappoint them first. I love Bash, but things are complicated with him. Things were always complicated with him because we are very different people. It's not a bad thing that we are different. I don't want him to be like me. I wouldn't be able to stand it otherwise. We wouldn't have been married for as long as we have been if we were the same person. Here's another thought that scares me. I wonder which parent I'm going to become to my children. I have a horrible feeling that it's not the person that I want it to be. You know who I am referring to. You always know what I'm talking about no matter what's happening to me.

One parting thought before we leave each other. I went cliff diving for the first time today. It was so exhilarating. I felt like I didn't live until I jumped off of that cliff into the Pacific Ocean. There was a moment where I was underwater that you were there with me. It was like we were at the doorway when you made that fateful decision to jump off of the bridge. I realized that I was there because I've stuck there with you since then. I thought about all the times that I tried to stop you from doing it and every single time I failed to stop you except for this time. You told me that you didn't want to make this choice. You were sick of making the wrong choice over and over again. As you grabbed onto my hand, we went through the doorway together. When I was pulled up above the surface of the water, I saw it all for the first time. You turned away from the bridge. You went to Nathan's house where you told him everything that you never allowed yourself to tell him. You called mom to tell her that you were sorry for hurting us and you wanted to see us again. You went to New York to meet mom and I for the first time in two years. You pulled me into your arms when you told me that you loved me and that you were sorry for abandoning me. You told me that you would be with me for the rest of time. You and mom never got back together, but you stayed in New York with us. We celebrated birthdays and boxing days together. You were there when I fell in love for the first time. You were there for my first break up. You were there when I graduated from high school. You were there when I moved to Los Angeles. You were there when we watched my first movie together. You were there when I fell in love with Daxton. You were there when I lost Daxton. You were there when I fell in love with Bash. You were there when I got engaged to Bash. You were there on our wedding day. You were there when your granddaughter was born. You were there when your grandson was born. You were there every step of the way. Even though none of it was real, it felt real to me. You told me a long time ago that it means everything because it's real to you. I'm sorry for what happened to us. I fear that this is going to happen to Bash and I. We are doomed to repeat the mistakes of the past. I hope our story doesn't end that way for us. It would break my heart if that happened to us. I don't think that it's going to though. Bash and I want better for our children. We want to be better than our parents. That's all we have left in this world. Our deepest and darkest secrets. No matter what happens to us, I know that we are going to be okay. If we fail, then we fail in being better people. If we succeed, then we succeed in happiness. Nothing matters except the stars.

She went into her hotel room with the letter in her purse where Lucy slept in the other bed before she fell asleep with Noah laying down next to her. When she got on her private jet back to Los Angeles the next day, she got a phone call from Sebastian that he was being discharged from the treatment center where she told the pilot to take a detour to Oakland where the treatment center was located. After their private jet landed in Oakland, she nervously paced back and forth in circles as Noah crawled around her on the floor where she didn't stop pacing until Lucy appeared with Sebastian walking behind her before Noah crawled over to Sebastian at the entrance of the plane. As soon as Sebastian pulled Noah into his arms, he sprinted over to her as he pulled her into a tight hug with her face hidden in his chest until Noah whined for her in his arms where Sebastian handed Noah over her before they took a seat next to each other. For the flight back to Los Angeles, she laid down on the couch in the private jet with Noah asleep on her chest while Sebastian laid down next to her with him running his hands up and down her back. They didn't know what to say to each other that would make it better. They were waiting to have the conversation that they needed to have with each other until they were alone at their house that night.

Once their land landed at the LAX airport, she placed Noah on her hip as Sebastian carried their bags with Lucy leading them to the car where Sebastian put their bags in the back of the car before their driver drove them to their house. After their driver pulled into the driveway, she placed Noah on her hip as Sebastian helped their driver grab their bags from the back of the car where she didn't make it into the house before Daphne ran into her legs. As soon as she placed Daphne on her other hip, Sebastian wrapped his arms around them as Daphne hid her face into her father's chest where they stayed like that until Noah whined to be put down on the floor before she placed Noah on the floor with him crawling over to his grandparents. Once she handed Daphne over to Sebastian as she talked to him about everything he missed when he was gone, she went over to grab Noah from her mother who was whining for her where she went upstairs in her bedroom to nurse him before she went in the kitchen for dinner. After they ate dinner that her mum made for them, she fed Noah in their bedroom as Sebastian gave Daphne a bath where she was about to join them in the bathroom before Daphne ran towards her wrapped up in a towel with Sebastian following behind her. As soon as she placed Noah on the bed, Daphne crawled into her lap as she tightly wrapped her arms around her when she asked her daughter with a smile on her face, "Did you have a good bath with daddy?"

Daphne grabbed onto Noah's hand who was making squealing noises next to them when she responded to her mother with a childish look on her face, "Yes, I did. We played with my water toys. I missed daddy so much. I missed you too, mommy. I missed you, Noah."

Once she kissed her daughter on the top of her head, she tightened her grip on her arms when she responded to her daughter with a smile on her face, "We missed you, little bee. Noah missed his big sister so much. You can teach him how to walk now that he's crawling. How about you let daddy get you dressed into your pajamas, and we'll meet you in your bedroom for a bedtime story."

Sebastian picked up Daphne from the bed as he carried her into her bedroom where she looked down at Noah who was staring at her as he grabbed onto her finger with his hand when she whispered to him, "Hello, little critter. How are you doing? You are the happiest little boy. Do you want to read a story with your sister? You are my Noah William. You are my special boy." After she got up from the bed with Noah on her hip, she walked into her daughter's bedroom as Sebastian grabbed a book off of the shelf with Daphne sitting in his lap where she took a seat next to them with Noah sitting up on her lap before Sebastian read the book to them. Once he read the first book to Daphne, she asked for him to read another book as Sebastian read aloud from it while she rocked Noah to sleep on her chest until it was time to put Daphne to sleep in her bed. Even though Daphne fought them about going to bed, they reminded her that they would be there in the morning where Daphne agreed to go to bed. She got a shower while Sebastian played with Noah where she walked into their bedroom with a towel wrapped around her before she changed into her pajamas. As soon as she laid down on the bed, Noah crawled over to her as she pulled him into her arms where she nursed him from her chest in silence. Once Noah fell asleep on her chest, she laid her head down on Sebastian's chest as he ran his hands up and down her arms when she asked him with a frown on her face, "Should we talk about it?"

Sebastian told her with nervousness laced his voice, "We can talk. Where do you want to start?"

She confessed to him with her blinking back tears that fell down her face, "Let's start when Daphne was born. That's where this started. That was when the resentment started growing in me. I've resented you for so long, Bash. I couldn't stand it that my life changed as soon as our daughter was born, and your life didn't change. I think about everything that I gave up for my children. Don't get me wrong. I would do it again. I used to be someone before we got married and we had our children. I was an actress. I had a career. I lost that as soon as I had Daphne. You got all of the glamour and admiration in our marriage. I've always been stuck living in your shadow. I'm not Isabella anymore. I'm Sebastian's wife. I'm Daphne and Noah's mother. Do you know what that feels like? To be cast out into the dark because you don't fit into their definition of who you are supposed to be? I want to be someone again. I want to be my own person. This book has reminded me that I am my own person outside of this family. This family isn't going to define me to the world."

Sebastian tightened his grip on her arms when he responded to her with a frown on his face, "Thanks for clearing the air, honey. I didn't know that you felt like this. I don't understand what that feels like because nothing changed for me. You're right. I've been so busy living my life thinking that nothing changed between us that I forgot to ask you how you felt about it. I didn't realize that I was hogging all of the light. I thought that you didn't want that life after Daphne was born. You want that life. Where does that leave us? How can we make things better between us?"

She blinked back tears that fell down her face when she responded to him in a distant voice, "I don't know, Bash. I don't know what to do. We can't take back the things that we said to each other. We can't undo the mistakes that we made. All that we have left to do is to forgive each other. Forgive, but never forget. Why do you resent me? You never told me why you resent me."

Sebastian ran his hands up and down her back when he confessed to her with tears falling down his face, "Forgive. Is it that simple? If this relationship has shown me anything, it's that nothing is simple. Do you want to know the answer to that question? I'll tell you. I resent you because you represent something that I can't stand. You were given this beautiful life from your mother, and you are constantly shitting on it. You had everything that you needed, and you tried to get the one thing that you could never have. You wanted it so much that you didn't care about losing everything else to get it. That's what drew me to you at first, but I grew to resent it over time. All these things didn't mean anything to you if it wasn't about you getting closer to your dad. I was jealous of him because he got a part of you that no one could have. He didn't deserve it. You were better off without him in your life. It's hurtful to say that, but we're being blunt with each other right now. You had a beautiful life without him, and I can't stand it when you romanticize him like he was a fucking saint. No one could be better than him. Did it occur you that you didn't fucking know him? What you knew about him was stuff that you projected onto him about yourself. Maybe you didn't know him. Have you thought about this? You're never going to know him? I'm not trying to be a prick about it, but I can't handle it. I love you and I want to spend the rest of my life with you. I didn't ask to spend the rest of my life with him. You have to choose. Do you want to be with me or with your dad?"

After she lowered Noah into his bassinet, she sat up next to him on the bed as he grabbed onto her hands when she responded to him with a soft voice, "You're right. Don't look so surprised, Bash. I had revelations of my own when you were gone. I went on a trip to find myself. I do romanticize my father. I've always done that. It's easier to long for the things that you don't have then it is to accept the things that you do have. I loved the life that my mom gave me. She worked so hard to give it to me and I didn't spit it back into her face. I don't think that you understand what it's like to be missing something. Even though I had all of the money and comfort, it wasn't enough to fill up the hole that he left behind. Nothing is going to be enough. Here's another thing that you got right. I didn't know him, and I'll never know him. I've spent my whole life trying to find out why he did it. I never thought that I would figure it out. I realized it when I went cliff jumping in San Francisco. It gave me the closure that I've been longing for. Before you assume that you know everything about someone, don't judge a book by its cover. People are more complicated than you think. Your problem is that you oversimplify things. It's easier for you to understand it. No one is who you think that they are. To you, my dad was an addict that was a coward. He's always been more than that to me. He was a person that deserved a good ending just as much as we do. Read this letter. It will show you everything that you need to know about him."

As soon as she threw the letter at him, Sebastian caught it before it fell down onto the floor as he laid back on the bed where he read it while he bit his lips. Once Sebastian was done reading the letter, he placed it down onto the bed as he looked up at her when he asked her with confusion laced in his voice, "What's this supposed to mean? You almost drowned yourself to write this letter that you weren't going to send to anyone? Explain it to me."

After she grabbed the letter off of the bed, she placed it into her side table drawer as she grabbed onto Sebastian's hands when she responded to him with tears falling down her face, "I didn't drown, Bash. I was swimming in the ocean with strangers. This isn't the point. The letter was my way of telling my dad that I forgave him for everything he did to me. Abandoning me. Killing himself. I realized that I couldn't move on because I didn't forgive him. I resented my dad for doing what he did to me. I resented you for implying that I was capable of doing what my dad did to me to our children. It's hard to forgive someone when they are the first people to break you. Whether you want to admit it to or not, it impacts you for the rest of your life. I love the life that I created with you, Bash. I don't regret it, but there's always going to be a piece of myself that will be tied to him. He was my dad. He will always be special to me. You need to accept this or else we will resent each other for the rest of our lives. I'm not asking you to give up your connection with your father. Why are you asking me to do it? I forgave my dad, but I'll never forget him. If you can't accept that, then we should get divorced. It's clear this marriage isn't going to work if you don't get over this. I've asked for nothing in our relationship. I've given you everything that I had to give you without asking for anything in return. Please let me have this one thing. I want to remember my dad. I don't care what kind of person that he was to you. He'll never be that person to me. He'll always be my favorite person. Nothing is going to change that."

Sebastian nodded his head at her as he placed his hand on her cheek when he responded to her with a smile on his face, "You can have him. I didn't understand it. We have someone like that in our lives. I forgive you, Isabella. For everything that I used to resent about you. You are allowed to have your own life outside of our family. If you want to go back into acting, I'm not going to get in your way. I know that you miss it. This wasn't your dream. It was my dream. Sometimes I forget that we are allowed to have different dreams from each other. If you want more things from our marriage, ask me about it. I promise that I'll listen to you."

Sebastian pulled her into a desperate kiss where they didn't pull away from each other until they were out of breath when she whispered to him, "Thank you, Bash. I forgive you too. I'm sorry for making you feel like I was replacing you with my dad. He could never replace you. Nothing could replace you. You are everything to me. I love you so much. I want to act again. It's what I've been craving for a long time.

I'll keep it in mind the next time that I want something from you."

Once she pulled Sebastian into a long kiss, he wrapped his arms around her as he laid them down on the bed where she undid the buttons in the front of his shirt before he unzipped the back of silk pajamas. After they made up for lost time together on the bed, she laid down her head on his chest as he comfortingly ran his hands up and down her arms when she asked him with a smirk on her face, "Was that the first time that we've had sex since you left for the treatment center? Wow, talk about long overdue. It was nice. I didn't realize how much I missed you." As he pulled her into another long kiss, she didn't pull away from him until she heard Noah crying in the bassinet next to the bed when she placed Noah on her chest where she ran her fingers through Noah's hair before Sebastian turned off the light. Once she was finished nursing Noah, she placed him back in his bassinet where she laid down in the bed with Sebastian's arms around her for the rest of the night.

CHAPTER SIXTY
(FALL 1973 – LOS ANGELES, CALIFORNIA)

She woke up the next morning to Sebastian whispering something to Noah who laid on top of his chest as she pulled Sebastian into a short kiss where he handed Noah over to her before he went into the bathroom to get ready for work. Sebastian carried Noah downstairs where her parents were getting Daphne ready for preschool before she got ready for her audition. Even though she owned the studio, she needed to audition for the part since Sebastian didn't want people to think that he gave his wife the part over everyone that auditioned for it. As soon as she joined her family in the kitchen, they ate   breakfast together that Daphne helped her grandmother make for the special day. Noah ate cut up oranges as a way of introducing food to him. Sebastian pecked her on the lips as he kissed his children on the top of their heads where he got into the car before their driver drove him to work. As her parents cleaned up the mess that the children made at the table, she grabbed Daphne's backpack from the living room as she held onto Daphne's hand with Noah on her hip before she took them to her parent's car.

When she buckled up her children in their car seats, she got into the driver's seat as she drove them to Daphne's new school. It was the same school that Oliver and Juliet sent their daughters to. Oliver helped them get Daphne into their school. There was a long waiting list to get into the school that was impossible to get into unless you knew someone in the administration. Oliver knew all of the people in the administration. After Daphne ran over to her teacher, she drove to the studio where Sebastian was waiting for them since she had her audition. After she dropped off Noah with Lucy, she joined Sebastian and their top executives into the screen-testing room for her audition before the executives told her that they would tell her if she got the part. She did better than she thought that she was going to since she got the script that morning. It was silly since they knew that she was going to get it since she co-owned the studio, but that was one of their formalities. One of the studio executives came into her office around lunch time to tell her that she got the part. She acted surprised even though everyone in the room knew that she was going to get it where she thanked him before she went into filming the movie that day.

She was at the studio five days a week filming her movie *The Kingdoms Keeper* with her co-stars and the crew that she worked closely with in the last three months. Noah was at home with his grandparents where they spoiled him since Daphne was at school during the day. Sebastian checked on her a few times a day in between filming breaks where he caught her up on the problems that needed her attention. She dealt with those problems before she finished filming for the day. After they came home from work in the evening, they ate dinner together as a family as Daphne told them about school where Noah ate little bits of their food off of their plates before he was covered in food. Noah refused to eat baby food because he only wanted to eat what they were eating. She didn't mind Noah eating off of her plate since it meant that they weren't wasting money on baby food that he wasn't going to eat like they did with Daphne when she was his age. When she was off work on the weekends, she went to Dr. Taylor's house with Noah. Daphne ran around at the studio while Sebastian got his work done. Since they no longer had a client and therapist relationship, they were friends with each other. She called him by his name Jacob instead of his professional name. She secretly called him Jacob for over two years, but she was allowed to call him by his first name since she wasn't his client. Jacob told her about himself for the first time in over a decade of knowing each other. Jacob was originally from England where he met Oliver at university in London. He was friends with Oliver and Juliet in London, and he went to their wedding at the courthouse. When Oliver told him that they were moving to the states after graduating from university, he followed them over to the states a year later where he started his own practice out of the living room of his house before he got his own office to see his clients. He worked in his office four days a week and he was at the hospital seeing clients in an in-patient setting two days a week. On his only day off in the week, they hung out at his house where they talked about what happened to them during the week. He invited her to go to a gay bar with him one weekend. It threw her off since she didn't realize that Jacob was gay. It made sense why Sebastian didn't get upset with her for hanging out with him since there was no competition for his affection like with other guys from the studio. As Daxton told her a long time ago, she was always the last person to realize the most obvious thing in the room. Since her parents offered to watch the children, she decided that her night out with Jacob included her cousins that were in the city. Her cousins Jamie and Ivan were visiting the states with their boyfriends for a few weeks, and she knew that Jacob would get along well with them. They even invited Uncle Stan and Thomas to come with them for good measure since they knew the best gay bars in the city. They declined the invitation since they weren't that fun anymore. As she got ready for their night out in the bathroom, Noah crawled on the floor around her as he grabbed onto the counter to get himself on his feet before he fell down on the floor. He tried it again with the same result happening to him. Noah was determined to walk no matter how many times that he fell onto the floor. After Noah fell onto the floor for the hundredth time, he broke into a desperate cry as she placed him on her hip where she did the final touches on her hair before she joined her cousin's downstairs. Sebastian talked to Oliver and Jacob after she finished getting ready in the bathroom. Once she handed Noah to his grandmother, her mum brought Daphne over to her as she pulled her daughter into a tight hug where she did the same thing with Noah before her cousins piled into their car. Her parents watched Posey, Eleanor, Daphne, Noah, Katherine, Charlotte, and her three-month-old nephew Christian who she met for the first time.

Once their driver dropped them off at the gay bar, Jamie and Ivan and their boyfriends waited for them in the front of the building as she pulled her cousins into tight hugs with her kissing Antonine and Christophe on their cheeks where she grabbed onto Sebastian's hand before they walked into the bar. She realized that a gay bar wasn't much different than a regular bar except that they were the only girls there, and it was full of guys not wearing clothes. As the bartender got drinks for her cousins and their partners off of the menu, she hadn't drank since Daphne was born and she didn't want to start that up again. She found herself in a compelling conversation with a stranger at the pool table. She was looking for the bathroom since her children ruined her bladder control before a gay guy who introduced himself as Paul told her that he read her book about addiction and that it made him get sober for good. When she asked Paul what a sober person was doing at a bar, he asked her the same question that caused them to start uncontrollably laughing until Sebastian and Jacob came looking for them with drinks in their hands.

After she introduced Jacob as her former therapist with awkward silence following after that, Paul and Jacob had an intimate conversation with each other as Sebastian dragged her into the center of the room where he wrapped his arms around her before they danced with her cousins around her. She looked over at Jamie and Christophe who were dancing so filthy that it looked like they were having sex with each other. She shouted at them to get a room as Jamie rolled his eyes at her where Christophe grabbed onto Jamie's hand before he took his boyfriend into the bathroom. She didn't want to go to the bathroom since she was going to see something that she didn't want to see. Ivan and Antonine disappeared into the bathroom a few minutes later while Jacob appeared on the dance floor with his arms around Paul before she winked at him. She was a good wing woman for getting him laid. She stayed on the dance floor with Sebastian's arms around her until things got heavy between them as he grabbed onto her hand where he dragged her outside of the building before he pulled her into a desperate kiss. He told her that they were going to the car as he dragged her over to the car where the driver went outside to smoke before he pushed her down on the back seat of the car. They joined her cousins and their partners in the gay bar until they were forced to leave when Sasha got so drunk that she fought with the bartender as Gabriel held her back from throwing another punch. They left the gay bar with everyone laughing at Sasha's bar fight. Jacob stayed at the bar with Jamie, Ivan, and their boyfriend's since they didn't have children to get home to. On the way to the house, their driver went to a fast-food restaurant before their driver dropped them off at their house. They checked on Daphne and Noah who slept in their bedrooms where Sebastian dragged her into their bedroom before they had a second round in their bed. They took a day trip to the beach with the family as Daphne played in the sand with her cousins where Noah tried to eat the sand off of his fingers before she carried him into the water to stop him from eating it. This plan backfired on her since Noah tried to drink the ocean water where she decided that Noah eating sand was better than him drinking saltwater. While she took a nap on a beach chair, she was woken up by Eleanor, Daphne, and Katherine pouring a bucket of cold water on top of her head as she let out a loud scream from the sudden shock where she chased the girls around the beach when she grabbed onto Daphne's arms before she submerged her into the ocean to get revenge on her. As Daphne let out an infectious laugh, she couldn't stop laughing with her daughter until she was out of breath where she carried Daphne out of the ocean before Daphne ran over to Sebastian to tell him about her funny prank.

On their day trip as a family of four, she took them to Griffith Observatory where she showed Daphne and Noah the stars in the large telescope as Daphne asked her questions about them before she explained the creation of the constellations to her like her mother explained to her when she was the same age as her daughter. Even though Noah was too young to verbalize his interest in it, he squealed when they saw new constellations in the sky where they stayed until the observatory closed for the night. Daphne talked about that trip so much that they went back there only a few weeks later when it was the two of them since Sebastian worked an overnight shift at the studio with their editors and Noah was at home with his grandparents. As she laid down on the floor with her arms around Daphne, she animatedly described the history of the constellations to her as she pointed to them in the sky where Daphne suddenly pulled her into a tight hug when she told her that this was the moment that she wanted to spend an eternity in with her. Daphne didn't know what that was without hearing it from her grandmother. She waited to hear that from the moment that

Daphne was born. She told Daphne that she was grateful to spend an eternity with her in the stars when Daphne told her that they were already there. At this point, they cried to each other as Daphne hid her face into her mother's chest where they stayed in each other's arms until the observatory closed a few hours later. On the drive home from the observatory, Daphne fell asleep in her car seat as she held onto her daughter's hands until their driver pulled into the driveway where she carried Daphne in her arms before she placed her into her bedroom. As soon as she placed Daphne on her bed, she didn't stir awake from her sleep as she gently moved a piece of her hair out of her face when she whispered to her daughter with a smile on her face, "Goodnight, little bee. Mommy loves you. You are always going to be my little girl. No matter how big you get, you will always be my baby. I hope that you dream of the stars. It's where we belong together."

After she kissed Daphne's forehead, she quietly closed the door behind her as she walked into Noah's bedroom where Noah slept in his crib before she grabbed onto his hands when she whispered to him with a smile on her face, "Goodnight, Noah. Mommy loves you. You are always going to be my little boy. Have good dreams, Noah William."

Once she kissed Noah on the top of his head, she quietly closed Noah's bedroom door behind her as she walked into her bedroom where she changed into her silk pajamas before she walked out onto the balcony. As soon as she took a seat on the balcony, she grabbed a cigarette out of her pocket as she lit it with her shaky hands where she inhaled the smoke from it when she said aloud with a frown on her face, "Hello, dad. It's been a while since we talked to each other. I don't smoke anymore, but I couldn't resist it. I always feel happy when I smoke with you. It's a tradition to smoke together. Did you read my letter that I never sent to you? I hoped that you got the chance to read it. It came from my heart. You would be flattered to have your grandson named after you. Noah William reminds me so much of us. Daphne is Bash in her appearance and her personality. Noah reminds me of a younger version of us. He's so sensitive. I wish that I could protect him from the world. A world that was so cruel to you. I'm trying to be the best mother that I can possibly be for my children. It's not easy to be a parent. You're watching your children make the same mistakes that you made in your lifetime. I don't want my children to think that I wasn't a good mother to them. I'm being emotionally available for them. Mom wasn't emotionally available for me when I needed her the most. I used to hold that against her, but I understand it now that I have children. It's hard to be a mother when you're going through so much. She had a complicated first decade of parenthood because of you. She doesn't hold it against you anymore. I used to hold it against you, but something in me shifted the last time that we talked to each other. Do you want to know what it was? I forgave you. Who knew it was so simple? If you would've told me a decade ago that all that I needed to do was to forgive my dad, then I would've laughed in your face in disbelief. How could it be that simple to do? Do you want to know why I didn't see it?"

She inhaled the smoke from her cigarette when she responded to herself with her blinking back tears that fell down her face, "I didn't want to see it. In a cruel and dark world, it couldn't be so obvious that forgiveness was the only option. You know that I've never been good at realizing obvious things. It hurt me that I didn't see it. Everything has to be complicated. I miss it when it's simple to understand. When you think about it, most things are pretty simple to understand. The truth is that I will always be an addict no matter what I do to act like that life never happened to me. I'll always be your abandoned daughter. I'll never know you and you'll never know me. You'd find this funny, dad. Bash told me that I project what I'm feeling onto you. I'm never going to know you except for the image that made up of you. Let's add that to the list of the most offensive things that anyone told me. It hurt me to hear him say it. He intended to hurt me. I'm upset about it. I don't know why I'm upset about it. None of this is real. You're not real. This moment isn't real. Hell, I'm starting to think that I'm not even real. That I died a long time ago. That I'm watching what would happen if I took a different door. Who is to say if anything is real? I was wrong about a lot of things. Do you want to know what I was wrong about?"

As she wiped away tears from her face, she inhaled the smoke from her cigarette when she responded to herself in a desperate voice, "I was wrong about everything. You were wrong. We thought that the world would mean more than it was. That's why we were let down. We put our hopes and our dreams into a reality that didn't care about us. We tried so hard to be the people that the world wanted us to be. We did things to make things right for the people that we wronged. We tried to make things right. I tried so hard to make things right. That was what took so much away from me. Trying to make things right. It was all in vain. Sure, we can forgive each other. Maybe we could learn to forget each other if we tried hard enough. The truth is that nothing is going to make this right. Nothing is going to be okay. That's what we have to forgive each other about. We have to forgive each other that nothing is going to be okay. Our mistakes are always going to be our mistakes. Our wrong choices are always going to define who we are. We can't run away from our wrong choices more than we can run away from an avalanche of snow. I ran away from my wrong choices for a long time. I'm never going to get away from them. I'm never going to win. I'm not running away from them. I'm done running away from my choices. I felt that under the water with you. I didn't only forgive you that day, but I also forgave myself. That was the simplest truth that I missed. All that I needed to do was forgive myself. Thank you for showing me that, dad. I wouldn't see that without you. You saw that in your final moments. Look at everything that happened to you. I can't wait to see the world. I don't know what it will look like, but I know that it made everything worth it. The stars were worth it to me. The stars are the only thing that matters to me." After she put out the end of her cigarette onto her ashtray, she wiped away the tears off of her face as she walked back into her bedroom where Sebastian laid down in the bed reading a book before she laid down on the bed next to him. As soon as he wrapped his arms around her, she leaned her head on his chest as he ran his hands up and down her back when he asked her if she was okay where she told him that nothing was okay, but she was okay with it. She told him that she forgave herself for her wrong choices that she made in her life. They fell asleep in each other's arm for the rest of the night.

CHAPTER SIXTY-ONE
(WINTER 1974 – YORK, ENGLAND)

While she filmed her movie called *The Kingdoms Keeper*, her mother got a phone call from Uncle James that Aunt Sylvia's health was declining where she spent the last few weeks in and out of the hospital. Uncle James asked her mother if she would go to England to see her. Her mother packed up her bags and her mum's bags came to England with her. Her cousin Amelia and her husband Troy were going to England with their children since Uncle James told Amelia that she should see her mother before she lost the chance to see her again. Uncle Sam and Aunt Valeria were joining her parents and Amelia's family on their trip to England since he wanted the chance to see his sister. Even though she didn't know how serious Aunt Sylvia's health problems were, she realized that they must be pretty serious if her family was going to England to see her in a rush like this. On the morning of her parent's flight to New York, she pulled her mother into a long hug where she didn't let go of her until their driver told them that they needed to leave for the airport before she hesitantly let go of her mother when she promised her that she would call them if they needed to get over to England. When her mother was in England, she struggled to keep her head above water as she worked on her movie while she took care of her children when she wasn't at work before she hid in Sebastian's arms for the rest of the night. Even though her mother didn't tell her whether Aunt Sylvia was dying or not, she felt it in her heart that her aunt was almost there with her father and Daxton because her mother was radio silent with her. The only time that her mother was radio silent with her when she was traumatized by her father's letter to Uncle Nathan after her suicide attempt on sleeping pills. She was concerned about Amelia since she wasn't answering her phone calls either. Every time that she called Uncle Nathan's house where she was staying at, Amelia was never able to answer the phone for a laundry list of excuses that Aunt Priscilla made up for her. She apologized to Aunt Priscilla for bothering her so much where she asked her if she would tell her if anything happened to Aunt Sylvia since Amelia and her mother weren't talking to her. After Aunt Priscilla promised that she would tell her if anything happened to her, she sobbed into her hands until Daphne ran into her bedroom from her nap where she pretended like she wasn't crying before she played with Daphne in the living room. Daphne knew that she was upset, and that something was going on because her grandparents weren't home, and her mother was sobbing alone in her bedroom. Daphne pulled her into a long hug as she softly cried into Daphne's hair until she heard Noah squealing from his bedroom before she went upstairs to get Noah up from his last nap of the day before he went to bed.

After almost three months of radio silence from her mother, she got a phone call in the middle of the night as Sebastian lightly groaned from the sudden noise where she sat up in her bed with her rubbing her eyes before she answered the phone with confusion laced in her voice, "What's wrong, mom? It's the middle of the night."

Her mother said to her in a serious voice, "Aunt Sylvia died last night. Can you, Bash, and the children come to England?"

She promised her mother that she would be in England where she hung up the phone before she frantically threw a pile of her clothes into her suitcase. Once Sebastian was alarmed that something happened, he pulled her into his arms as she let out heartbreaking sobs into his chest when she told him that Aunt Sylvia died and that they needed to go to England to be with her family. Sebastian told her that they should go to bed and that they would figure it out in the morning where she followed him back to the bed before they slept in each other's arms. She woke up with Sebastian's side of the bed empty the next morning as she remembered everything that happened last night where she fought off the urge to cry before she went into the closet with Sebastian packing their bags. After Sebastian pulled her into a desperate hug, he told her that they were leaving for the airport in an hour and that he packed the children's stuff where she thanked him for taking care of her before she went into her children's bedrooms to wake them up. When she told Daphne that they were going to England, Daphne was excited about it despite knowing that something was wrong before they went into Noah's bedroom to get him up. Their driver put their bags and the double stroller into the back of the car before they drove to the airport where they met up with her cousins. After they were dropped off at the airport, she pushed Noah and Daphne in the stroller as Sebastian carried their bags where Oliver pulled her into a desperate hug with her face hidden in his chest before they pulled away from each other when they boarded onto their plane. On their flight to New York, she slept with her head leaning on Sebastian's shoulder as Noah slept in her lap where Sebastian entertained Daphne until she passed out in his arms. When their plane landed in New York that afternoon, they went on their flight to London before the children slept for the night in their arms while she was awake all night. After their plane landed in London the next morning, she carried Noah and Daphne off of the plane as they slept in her arms with Sebastian carrying their bags and their stroller where she pulled her cousin Sean into a long hug that didn't let go of each other until Daphne whined for her uncle to hold her. Once Sean placed Daphne on his hip, she told him that she was sorry for his loss and that his mother was a special person where Sean pulled her into another long hug before they moved away from each other. As soon as they put their bags and stroller into the back of Sean's car, she joined his wife Polly and their children Ashley, Alyssa, and Arthur in the back of the car as she slept with her head leaning onto the window for the drive to York where she dreamed about her father's funeral when she was eight years old. She remembered exactly how she felt on the day of her father's funeral. It was one of the worst days of her life. She spent her life running away from it. Not that she could get away from it. It crept up on her when she least expected it. She walked through the doorway. She stood there with her mother tightly holding onto her hand as she held onto her doll in her other hand where she watched them pour dirt onto her father's coffin that was in the ground. The sound of dirt hitting her father's grave was engraved inside of her memory. The plunking noise played inside of her head for months after his funeral. She heard it everywhere she went in the world. She heard it in her sleep. She heard it at school. She heard it at home. She heard that plunking noise so long that she thought that she would never have peace from it. She only stopped hearing it because her mind became fixated on how to get high instead of hearing noises that weren't happening around her. She was terrified of hearing that noise at Aunt Sylvia's funeral. She didn't know what to do with herself if she heard that noise. When she went to the only other funeral that she went to in her life, she ran into the church before she heard the dirt hitting Daxton's coffin. She couldn't handle that on top of the guilt that she already felt about what happened with him.

When they got to York in the early afternoon, Sebastian woke her up as she grabbed Noah out of his car seat with Sebastian getting Daphne out of her car seat before they walked over to Uncle James outside of the house. Uncle James pulled her into a tight hug where they didn't let go of each other until Noah whined from on her hip. Once they let go of each other, she handed Noah over to Uncle James as he talked to Noah with a smile on his face before she walked behind Sebastian and Daphne into Uncle James' house where the family waited for them. As soon as she walked into the living room, Amelia sprinted over to her from the couch as she pulled Amelia into a desperate hug with Amelia sobbing into her chest where she ran her hands up and down Amelia's back before Audrey pulled herself into their hug. Audrey hid her face behind her sister's back as she tried to comfort her inconsolable sister until they broke apart from each other when Uncle James handed Noah back to her. Once she placed her crying son on her hip, she pulled Amelia into another hug to calm her down before she handed Amelia over to Troy before he pulled his sobbing wife into his chest. After she escaped from the living room, she walked into the kitchen with Noah on her hip where Sebastian had a conversation with her parents and Uncle Sam who had his arm around her mother while he comforted her before Daphne ran over to her. As soon as she pulled Daphne on her other hip, she handed Noah over to Sebastian before she pulled her mother into a tight hug with her mother softly sobbing into her chest. Once her mother cried harder into her chest, her mum pulled her mother into her arms as her mum pulled them into a bedroom for some privacy. Daphne asked her if Grandma Ella was okay where she told her daughter that she was going to be okay before she pulled Daphne into a tight hug to reassure her. After she placed Daphne onto the floor with her running into the living room, Uncle Sam pulled her into a tight hug with her face hidden his chest as she blinked back tears that fell down her face when he asked her if she was okay where she asked him the same question before they softly chuckled about it. Uncle James yelled for everyone to come into the living room for a family meeting as she grabbed Noah from Sebastian's arms with Sebastian placing Daphne on his hip where they stood next to Oliver's family and Sasha's family. Uncle James told everyone that he was grateful to have the family together to celebrate Sylvia's life and that there was going to be a wake for her at the church tomorrow and the funeral was in two days. Uncle James told them that Sylvia's lawyer was here to read her will, so he was going to be calling names for people that needed to meet in the office that were mentioned. He called out Audrey, Amelia, Teddy, Sean, Polly, Jamie, George, Annebell, Sam, Ella, Priscilla, and Isabella. As soon as she heard Uncle James say her name, she froze in shock at what he said to her as her mother grabbed onto her hand when she led them into the office down the hall where they were the last people in the room before Uncle James closed the door. As she adjusted Noah on her hip and fell asleep on her chest, she stood in between her mother and Amelia who grabbed onto her hand when the lawyer took a seat in the desk next to Uncle James before the lawyer listed off assets that Aunt Sylvia gave to the family. He looked over at Audrey and Teddy who were standing next to each other hand and hand when the lawyer told them that her mother left the title of the bakery business to them and a sum of money for her grandchildren Lena, Leo, Mason, Harper, and Edward when they were old enough to inherit it. Audrey thanked the lawyer with a smile on her face before he turned his attention over to Amelia and Troy who stood next to her. The lawyer told Amelia and Troy that her mother left her favorite dresses and money for her grandchildren Katherine and Christian when they were old enough to inherit it. Amelia nodded her head in response to him before the lawyer turned his attention to Sean and Polly standing on the other side of the room. The lawyer told Sean and Polly that his mother left her car with clothes for Polly and money for her grandchildren Ashley, Alyssa, and Arthur. Sean thanked the lawyer for that information.

The lawyer turned his attention onto Jamie and Christophe who stood in the corner when he told them that his mother left him her land that her father bought in France during the First World War. Their jaws dropped in shock as they looked over at Jamie who was too stunned to say anything to them before the lawyer explained how Aunt Sylvia found out about her father's small plot of land in France that he bought with Will and Nathan's father. Nathan made a joke that his father sold it for more alcohol that would kill him. Once everyone got over that startling information, the lawyer turned his attention to George and Annabell who were holding their daughters Zoe and Sofie in their arms when he told them that his mother left them the deed to the house in her will that was agreed upon by James and some money for her grandchildren. This surprised them since no one in the family expected that Aunt Sylvia was going to give the house to her youngest son George over her son Sean who also lived in England. George pulled his father into a tight hug. The lawyer moved onto Aunt Priscilla and Uncle Nathan when he told them that Sylvia left behind her favorite dresses and the recipes that they made over the years in a special book that she got published before her death. They could pass it onto their children and their grandchildren after they were gone. Her mother admitted to them that they were working on a book in the last year of her life as a surprise for her death before Aunt Priscilla pulled her mother into a tight hug when her mother handed her the book that they worked so hard to publish. The lawyer moved onto Uncle Sam and Aunt Valeria who were stunned by the recipe book when he told them that his sister left him their father's pocket watch with his war uniform that they recovered after his death and their brother Kenny's military necklace that was found after his death. This left Uncle Sam inconsolable in her mother's chest with Aunt Valeria's arms around him where he cried even harder when the lawyer handed her grandfather's military uniform to him and Uncle Kenny's military necklace with a picture of him in it. They gave Uncle Sam and her mother a few moments to calm down. The lawyer turned his attention to her mother when he told her that her sister left her the photo albums from their childhood that their parents made and a mystery box of items that belonged to their mother that she didn't have the heart to get rid of when she died. The lawyer handed her mother the box of her grandmother's last earthly belongings and the photo albums from her mother's childhood. The lawyer turned his attention onto her as she tightened her grip on Noah when he told her that Aunt Sylvia left her letters that her grandparents wrote to each other and other people from their lives and a special item from her parent's past lives. After the lawyer handed her a box of letters with a framed photo on the top of the pile, she handed the box over to Amelia who placed it onto the floor as she turned photo over to see that it was a picture of her parents when they were young at a fair in front of the Ferris wheel where she showed it to her mother before her mother whispered to her with everyone in the room hearing them, "I thought that Sylvia got rid of that picture of us when we broke up. That was our first date. We went to the fair." They thought that the lawyer was done shocking them with surprises that Aunt Sylvia was saving for them.

The lawyer looked over at Uncle James as he told him that there was one more surprise that was left for him where Uncle James tried not to cry even though he was on the verge of tears before the lawyer handed a book that she handmade from their letters from when he was fighting in the Second World War. Aunt Sylvia was a sentimental person that saved these artifacts that she collected in her lifetime. Aunt Sylvia named her book of letters *The Love Story of Sylvia and James* where she wrote a dedicated message to Uncle James saying to him, "To the love of my life. To my soulmate. I couldn't imagine my life without you. Read this to remember me when I'm gone."

The lawyer left them alone in the office as the spouses filed out of the office behind him except for them and Sylvia's children where they pulled their sobbing father into a group hug before Isabella, Uncle Sam, Aunt Priscilla, Uncle Nathan, and her mother joined them in the hug before they cried tears of happiness. While everyone was crying in each other's arms, Noah said his first word as he shouted out to them with a smile on his face, "Baha!"

As soon as Noah made a sheep noise, everyone laughed into their hands as they pulled away from each other when she said to Noah who stared at her with a smile on his face, "You're so funny, Noah William. This was the perfect time to say your first word. What does Baha mean?"

Everyone stared at him when Noah responded to her with a wide grin on his face, "Baha!"

They filed out of the room when Uncle Nathan told them with his arms around her, "You are so much like your grandfather. You're so silly, Noah William. He's always going to make us laugh. Isn't he, Isabella?"

After she agreed with Uncle Nathan with a smile on her face, she kissed Noah on the top of his head as she joined her family in the kitchen where they ate dinner before Uncle James and Uncle Sam told everyone about how Noah's first word was Baha while they cried in each other's arms. She went over to Uncle Nathan's house with her parents and Oliver's family as they bathed their children together in the bathtub where they put the girls to sleep into the guest bedroom when they took Noah into their bedroom with them before they fell asleep with their arms around each other for the night. When she woke up on the morning of Aunt Sylvia's wake, Noah and Daphne wrestled on the bed as she separated them from each other where Daphne sat in her lap with Noah sitting on top of Daphne. Once she put Daphne into her black dress with Noah in his black suit that he kept trying to take off, she changed into one of black dresses that she brought with her as she carried Noah on her hip with her hand holding onto Daphne's hand where she let go of Daphne once they were living room before she joined her parents, Sebastian, her aunts, her uncles, and her cousins. After they ate breakfast together that Aunt Priscilla made for them, they piled into cars as she got into Uncle's Nathan's car with Noah, Daphne, Sebastian, Poppy, Ellis, and their children Jack, Madeline, and Millie. Once Uncle Nathan parked the car, Noah and Millie slept in the car seats as they carried their children into the church while Sebastian carried Daphne in his arms with Ellis holding onto Jack and Madeline's hands. As soon as she walked into the church, Uncle James pulled her into a tight hug as she hid for her face in his chest until they pulled apart when Amelia ran over to her father with Christian on her hip before Uncle James pulled Amelia into a tight hug. She walked over to her parents who talked to people from the church. Her mother pulled her into a tight hug with her face hidden in her chest. Her mother bragged about her daughter to other people before she was introduced as Ella Foster's elusive daughter. After her mother bragged about her grandchildren, she took that as her cue to leave as she walked away from her mother where she didn't stop until she made it over to Aunt Sylvia's coffin on the other side of the room before she froze in front of it unable to look away. Once Sebastian realized that she was having a panic attack, he sprinted over to her as he left Daphne with Oliver, Juliet, and their children Posey and Eleanor where he pulled her into a private room before he closed the room behind them. As soon as he pulled her into his arms, she let out a suppressed sob into his chest as he comfortingly ran his hands up and down her back until Noah interrupted them as he made barking noises where they softly chuckled at him before Sebastian pulled her into a desperate kiss with her hands around his hips. After Noah made more barking noises, she joked with him that they didn't have a son. She accidentally gave birth to a puppy instead of a baby where they finally acknowledged Noah before they went back into the church. She stayed in the church for the wake before she went to the picnic area while their children played on the playground.

They shared their stories of Aunt Sylvia as they passed a joint around for everyone except for her. Audrey shared a story of her mother when she was in the hospital getting her tonsils out. Amelia shared stories of her mother when they were getting ready for her dance recitals. Sean shared stories of his mother when she was taking him to his speech therapy. Jamie shared stories of his mother about his school plays. George shared stories of his mother going to his football games. Poppy shared a story about how Aunt Sylvia was with her when she got her period for the first time. Oliver told them that Aunt Sylvia taught him how to drive when he was sixteen years old. Tommy told them that Aunt Sylvia took him and the boys camping where she taught them how to fish. Alfie told them that Aunt Sylvia took him to the movies every Sunday night where they watched the famous pictures. She told them that Aunt Sylvia always called her on Saturday mornings after they moved to New York to catch up with her. They went to the house to eat dinner at George's house where they put their children to bed before her cousins went out to the bars for the rest of the night. Oliver and Sebastian stayed at the house with her since the boys hadn't gotten a chance to talk to each other in a while. Oliver and Sebastian went to the barn to hang out before she went into her mother's bedroom to help her write her eulogy for Aunt Sylvia's funeral.

When the boys came back from the barn, she helped her mother make the final touches on her speech where Sebastian dragged her into their bedroom with Noah asleep on the bed before she fell asleep in his arms for the rest of the night. When she woke up on the morning of Aunt Sylvia's funeral, she felt nauseous as she struggled to keep down her breakfast that she forced herself to eat. She knew that Sebastian and her parents would be worried about her if she skipped a meal. She got the children ready for the funeral before they left to go to the church in Uncle Nathan's car with her parents and Oliver's family. After Uncle Nathan parked the car, the nauseous feeling took over as she tried to ignore the burning feeling in the back of her throat when she walked into the church where she excused herself into the bathroom before she vomited up her breakfast into the toilet. Once she cleaned off her face, she walked to their seats in the second row as she took a seat next to Sebastian where she grabbed Noah from his lap with his face hidden in his mother's chest before Sebastian asked her if she was okay. She lied to him that she was feeling okay, but she knew that he didn't believe her. Sebastian went back to his conversation with Eleanor and Posey about the best horse breeds where Oliver looked over at her with a worried look on his face before he asked her if she was okay. Before she got the chance to respond to him, Uncle James got up from his seat in the front row as he stood up at the podium when he thanked everyone for coming to celebrate Sylvia's life and that she was so loved by everyone before he welcomed his oldest daughter Audrey. After Audrey got up from her seat with Teddy squeezing her shoulder, Audrey took her place in front of the podium as she placed a few pieces of paper in front of her when she said to the room never looking away from her mother's body in the coffin with tears falling down her face, "I didn't mean to come up here crying. My siblings volunteered me to speak for them. I don't mind doing this. I'm their older sister and it's my duty to take care of them. I learned that from mum. She took care of everyone else before herself. She would do anything for anyone if they asked her to. You did a good job, mum. You treated us like we were the most important people in your life. We were your babies. Now that I have my five beautiful children, I know that feeling more than anything else. The look that you gave us was priceless. You were always there for us when we needed you. No matter what was going on in your life, you would drop anything to be with us. It didn't matter to you that we weren't children with families of our own. You did that for us. Thank you for showing me love and kindness. Thank you for showing me how to be a better person. You were the best person that I knew. I'll always strive to be just a little bit like you. I love you, mum. I'll always love you. Thank you for everything. Rest easy, mum."

Once Audrey wiped tears off of her face, she walked back to her seat in the front pew as Teddy wrapped his arm around her when Aunt Priscilla walked up to the podium with a piece of paper in her hands before she said aloud to the whole room with her blinking back tears that fell down her face, "Sylvia was the most incredible person that I've met in my life. I was so lucky to call her my best friend. Even though we weren't blood, she made me feel like I belonged in the family. It was the first time that I belonged to anything that mattered. She always thought of everyone else above herself. When Kenny died in the war, I thought that I lost everything. I wasn't going to be a part of the family anymore because my husband was dead. That didn't happen though. Sylvia insisted that I stay a part of the family. That I stayed in their home with them. We were doing the impossible thing. Sylvia, Ella, and I were raising our children together in a loving family. I'm so happy that Oliver got to grow up alongside his cousins because he never knew what it was like to not belong anywhere like I did. Sylvia treated Oliver like he was her own son. It was the kindest thing that anyone did for me. Thank you for the memories, Sylvia. I'm so glad that I joined your family. It's brought me so much enjoyment and happiness in my life. I love you, Sylvia. I'll never forget the gift that you gave me. Rest in peace."

After Aunt Priscilla walked back to the third pew with Uncle Nathan wrapping his arms around her, Uncle Sam walked up to the podium with no papers in his hand when he said aloud to the room with tears falling down his face, "I never thought that we would be here. I thought that we were going to live forever. I didn't think that you would be the first person to leave us. You were one of the most important people in my life. You were my first best friend outside of Kenny and Ellie. I taught you how to do everything. You followed me around the house with that torn up blanket that you insisted on taking everywhere with you. You were upset when I went to school without you. You cried in mum's arms for hours until I came home again. It broke my heart to leave you when I did. It was the right thing for my family, but it hurt me to do it. You were so supportive. You know why we had to leave, but I didn't want to leave behind my little sister. Even when I was gone, you made sure that I was there. I love you, Sylvia. Thank you for everything that you did for me. I'll never forget you. Rest easy angel."

As soon as Uncle Sam took a seat next to Aunt Valeria with her tightly grabbing onto his hands, her mother walked up to the podium as she placed her papers on it when she said aloud to the room with her blinking back tears that fell down her face, "I wrote a hundred different versions of this, but it never gets easier for me. I'll give you the short version of the speech. Sylvia was more than my older sister. She was my best friend. She was my co-parent. She was my greatest comfort during the hard years after Isabella was born. She was always there for me no matter what was going on in her life. Her bed was a safe haven from the world. I could tell you a million stories about my sister, but I'll tell you one story that I thought of last night. Isabella and I were re-writing this speech. I told her when I knew that I loved my sister. We were playing with our wooden dolls in the living room. I wasn't even two years old, and Sylvia turned three years old. We were talking to each other in our made-up language. I could tell you what we were talking about with each other. Something about how our dolls needed dresses for their weddings. There was a moment where I looked up at Sylvia when I saw it. The look on her face showed me that she was always going to protect me. I was her baby sister. Nothing significant happened in that moment, but it's one that I would spend an eternity in with her. Thanks for being there to protect me. I love you so much, Sylvia. I can't wait to be with you in the stars."

As soon as her mother walked away from the podium, her mum

stood at the bottom of the stairs waiting for her as she pulled her mother into a tight hug with her mother hiding her face into her mum's chest where she pulled them back into their seats next to them before she wrapped her arms around her mother. Once Uncle James walked up to the podium, he looked over at Aunt Sylvia as he blinked back tears that fell down his face when he said aloud to the room in a shaky voice, "I can't believe that you are gone. The last few days don't feel real to me. I keep looking for you when I walk into a room. You know that I'm not good at this. Bearing my heart out for the world to see. I'd do anything for you, my love. To the world, you were lots of things. Loving to your family. Caring for those in need. Devoted to our children. You were those things and so much more to me. Meeting you was the best day of my life. You were in grade four and I was in grade five. Sam introduced us to each other. When I looked at you, you told me that my tie was crooked, and I was obsessed with you since then. Our life has been one that I could never imagine having with anyone else. You and the girls were my only source of hope when I was fighting in the war. I couldn't wait to go home to you. There were moments when I thought that I wouldn't make it home to you guys. I loved raising our children with you. I loved every moment that I spent with you. My life isn't going to be the same without you. I'll spend the rest of my life missing you. I will always love you. You were the best part of me. The only part of me that means anything to the world. I'll be with you again someday."

Uncle James went into his seat with Audrey and Amelia pulling their father into a tight hug. George walked up to the podium when he thanked everyone for coming to celebrate his mother's life where he told them that there were refreshments in the basement before he told them that the family needed to join them outside for the burial. As soon as everyone filed out of their seats, she excused herself into the bathroom with Noah on her hip as she sprinted into the bathroom to vomit where she left the bathroom before she joined her family outside in the church graveyard. When Sebastian asked her if she was okay with a worried look on his face, she brushed it off as only nerves where he wrapped his arm around her before Uncle James called everyone over to the large hole in the ground. As they lowered down Aunt Sylvia's coffin into the ground, she tightened her grip on Sebastian's hand as he ran his hands up and down her back where she heard her mother and

Amelia sobbing in the background before Uncle James, Uncle Sam, Uncle Nathan, Sean, Jamie, and George threw dirt on her wooden casket. Even though she felt like she needed to vomit again, she held it back as she handed Noah over to her mother until she heard the plucking noise of the dirt hitting the coffin before she vomited on the ground. She knew that she couldn't hide it since she vomited in front of her family while they buried her aunt into the ground. Sebastian and Oliver sprinted over to her where they pulled her in their arms with her letting out heartbreaking sobs in Sebastian's chest. Once they pulled her away from the crowd, Oliver held onto her arms as she sobbed into Sebastian's chest where they didn't say anything to her until her sobbing slowed down when Oliver asked her with concern laced in his face, "Are you okay, Isabella? Should we call a doctor? How long have you been feeling like this?"

She told Oliver in between her sobbing, "I'm okay, Oliver. It's nerves."

Sebastian pulled her face out of his chest as he cupped his hands around her face when he responded to her with a look of terror on his face, "It's not nerves, Isabella. You're puking blood. Answer his question. How long have you been puking up blood?" She pushed them off of her as she puked up blood onto the ground where she heard Oliver shouting for someone to call an ambulance before she puked on the ground on her hands and knees. As she tried to get up off of the ground, she felt so dizzy as her body fell down onto the ground before everything turned to black.

Chapter Sixty-Two
(Spring 1974 – Los Angeles, California)

When she woke up in the hospital a few days later, she was reminded of what happened at Aunt Sylvia's funeral. She made a fool of herself in front of her family. She tried to get up from the bed where she felt intense pain from her abdomen before she laid back down on the bed. Since she was alone in her hospital room, she looked around the room to get some clues about what happened as she messed with her IVs that were hanging off of her hands where she reached over to grab her medical chart that hung off of the side of her bed before she read the words, "Isabella Foster-Brewer. Aged 31 years old. Came into the hospital with fever, nausea, and vomiting blood. Pancreatitis. Unknown Cause. Surgery to close the tear and remove the gallstones. Blood transfusions were given due to blood loss. Medicines are antibiotics and morphine." Before she got a chance to react to the news, the doctor walked into the room with a nurse following behind him when he asked her how she was feeling where she told him that she felt like she had her stomach cut into before he told her that she was funny. After he asked her if she remembered having any pain before she was admitted into the hospital, she told him that she didn't remember anything except that she felt nauseous and that she was throwing up blood before he told her that it was rare when people didn't feel gallstones passing through their bodies. Once they cleared the air about what happened, she asked him where Sebastian was when he told her that Sebastian was at home since it was the middle of the night. He asked her if she wanted him to come before she told him that he could see her in the morning. The nurse gave her pain medicine to fall asleep for the rest of the night.

She woke up the next morning to two people having a soft conversation with each other. Sebastian and Oliver sat on either side of her bed with them grabbing onto each one of her hands where she told them that she felt better now that she wasn't vomiting blood before they laughed at her joke that she made to lighten up the mood. Once she stopped laughing because her stomach was hurting, she saw the look of exhaustion in their eyes from Aunt Sylvia's death and her body's desire to punish her. She asked Sebastian about how Daphne and Noah were doing before he told her that Daphne and Noah were being taken care of by Uncle Nathan and Aunt Priscilla the last few days. She didn't want to cry about how much she missed her children. She asked Oliver how long she was staying in the hospital as he pulled her into a tight hug when he told her that the doctor said that she could be discharged by the weekend.

She blinked back tears that fell down her face when she told them that she was sorry for scaring them and she didn't mean for this to happen. Sebastian insisted that it wasn't her fault like she predicted that he was going to do. She tried to believe him even though she struggled to accept it. Most of the time it was her fault that she ended up in the hospital because she took too much of something that she knew was going to kill her. Whether it was pain killers, sleeping pills, or drugs, she was ingesting it with the intention to kill herself. The only other two times that she ended up in the hospital without trying was when Noah was born five weeks early and when her pesky pancreas tried to kill her at a funeral. She asked Sebastian when they were going to celebrate Noah's first birthday where he reassured her that they would celebrate his birthday when they got back to the states before she told him that she wanted to take a nap. Once she was left alone in the room, she tried to sleep, but she couldn't stop thinking about the plucking sound on Aunt Sylvia's coffin from the dirt hitting it where she remained awake before she passed out when the nurses gave her medicine to help her sleep. For four days that she was in the hospital recovering from Pancreatitis, she couldn't stop hearing the plucking noise. She thought about how it felt to be buried. It must be dark and claustrophobic to be confined in such an unappealing space. She never thought about it when her father died because she was too young to understand a concept like that. It must be lonely to be trapped in the ground for the rest of eternity with only the worms to keep you company. There was a whole life going on above you that you can never participate in again. Sure, dead people didn't have feelings, but that didn't make it okay to leave them there. She needed to visit her father's grave before they went back to the states because she wanted to know if he liked being in the ground. She tried to remember if they buried her father at the church or at Uncle Nathan's house because there was a conflict in her memory about that day. She remembered him being buried at the church when she was frustratedly kicking his grave in anger towards him, but now she didn't know if that was true or not. Maybe her father was buried at Uncle Nathan's house, and she was mixing up that memory with another one from a different day. She didn't know what was true or not because her memory was hardly reliable with little details. Her mind always tried to play tricks on her. Did something happen to her or was it a fabricated story that she told herself over the years? She questioned this over a million times. There were a lot of reasons why she was like this. She was mentally ill and misremembering things was a part of the course. She ruined her brain from the heavy drug use in her life. She was traumatized from it like she was with other things that she didn't remember over the years.

When she first saw Jacob over a decade ago, they had a conversation with each other about how the brain remembers traumatic experiences and how it often doesn't match up with reality. She was too early in her healing journey to understand it, but she appreciated it now. Jacob told her that the way that her brain remembered traumatic moments was like a child telling a story to their parents. She didn't get that comparison until she had her own children. It was the best analogy that he could've used for it. The objective of the child was to tell their parents the most important parts of the story. The child failed to tell their parents what happened in between the important parts of the story. How did they get into that situation? No one knew the answer to that. The most important part of the story was the ending.

Her brain told her that her father died when she was eight years old, and she went to his funeral at the church. What her brain failed to tell her was that she got to the funeral in her uncle's car. Her mother held onto her hand the entire time or else she was going to run away from her. What made her the most upset was that she didn't remember what anyone said about her father. Who talked at his funeral? What did they say about him? She didn't know the answer to that question. It was like she wasn't there when they talked about him. She always thought that her mother said the unspoken things that they never said to each other, but she wasn't sure of that. She didn't think that her mother was capable of saying them to him. Even in death, they couldn't be honest with each other. Her father's suicide note said even less than what her mother said at his funeral. It felt like a lot to her because she didn't know anything about him. This was where her memory confused details together. Where did she hear the dirt hit his coffin? Was it at the church cemetery? Was it at the Heartley farm? She spent her entire life believing that it was at the church, but she didn't think that it was true. It was on the Heartley farm where his grave was and where he would spend the rest of eternity. If it wasn't her father's grave at the church, then whose grave did she kick? She felt horrible for what she said to his grave. It was his final resting place, and she bothered him with her problems. She had the nerve to tell him that it didn't mean anything. That he didn't mean anything to her. She knew that it was a lie because he meant something to her. Everyone in the universe knew that she was lying to him. Hell, she didn't believe herself when she said it to him. She lied to herself about a lot that she didn't admit to anyone else. Lying always came easy to her because she spent a lifetime lying for her addiction. She could tell any lie to any person without any consequences except for her father. She was always incapable of lying to him. She didn't want to lie to the only person that couldn't correct her. The lying in of itself became an addiction of its own that always ended up as horrible as her benders did for her. She became addicted to the feeling of telling a lie to someone because lying gave her a power that the truth could never give her. It let her be in control of her own destiny. She was controlling the narrative that her story was being told in for the rest of the world to see. She understood why her parents never told the truth about how they felt about each other. After someone spends a lifetime lying to everyone around them, they don't know where to begin to tell people the truth. Her parents had their own reasons for lying to each other that they justified a long time ago. There wasn't a universe where they weren't constantly lying to each other. They knew that they were lying to each other, but either they didn't care about it, or they made their peace with it. She didn't know which one that it was, but it worked for them. They could lie to each other, themselves, and the rest of the world without feeling the consequences of it. She used to have that ability before she realized that the lies were killing her. She stopped doing it because she didn't know how to live with her secrets without them eating her alive. She was buried underground with the worms in a lonely and dark place.

On her last night in her hospital room, she paced across the room in the darkness as she suddenly froze in front of the window when she remembered one of the most important moments of her father's death. Her grandfather William went first to talk about her father. He told everyone that he couldn't believe that his son did this to himself. That was a lie because her father tried to kill himself many times before in his life. Uncle Nathan went next to tell everyone about how he wished that he could've been there to help her father get through life. That was the most truthful thing that anyone said about her father. Who wouldn't want that for someone who killed themselves? To be there for them? Her mother went last to tell everyone about the beauty in her father's death. Her mother didn't believe a word that she was saying about him because she was only saying what he wanted her to say to him. Her mother saved the real eulogy for later that night when they moved her father's coffin from the church to the Heartley farm. Uncle Nathan and her mother were drunk when they did it. They didn't want him to spend an eternity with people who didn't love him like they loved him. She caught her mother and her uncle pouring dirt on his coffin. She heard the plucking noise for the first time. She was furious at them for doing that to him. For putting him back into the ground to be alone like he was in life. She ran away from them since she couldn't stand hearing the plucking noise anymore, but that wasn't enough to stop her from seeing it. The coffin moved into the ground. The sound of the dirt hitting the wooden coffin.

The sounds of her mother and Uncle Nathan hysterically laughing with a bottle of rum in their hands.

The sounds of her mother and Uncle Nathan crying with the empty bottles of rum on the ground. The next night she stormed over to her father's grave where she went to dig him up out of the ground with a shovel that she stole from the barn before she hit a sharp piece of rock that was on top of it. Her grandparents put it there after they found out about her mother and Uncle Nathan moving her father's body to the farm. They weren't upset about it because they wanted him close to them. She threw the shovel onto the ground. She kicked her father's tombstone as hard as she could until she couldn't feel her feet. It didn't make her feel better about it, but she didn't want to die anymore. She woke up the next morning from her emotional hangover when the doctor told her that she was getting discharged from the hospital in a few hours before she changed into clothes that Sebastian bought for her. Daphne sprinted over to her as soon as she saw her from the hallway before Sebastian pulled her onto the bed since she couldn't lift more than four pounds for a few weeks. Once Sebastian helped her into a wheelchair, he placed Noah and Daphne on her lap as he pushed them outside of the hospital into the car. Uncle Nathan and Aunt Priscilla pulled her into tight hugs before Sebastian helped her into the back of the car with the children in between her. She spent a few weeks at Uncle Nathan's house recovering from her surgery where she played with Daphne and Noah in the living room while she laid down on the couch. Sebastian was on the phone with the studio during the day when he wasn't helping Uncle Nathan and Aunt Priscilla on the farm. Everyone including her parents went to the states a few days after she had her surgery. Sebastian surprised her when he told her that he got the permit for their private jet to fly over international waters since she was stressed about flying home after her surgery. Once she was cleared by the doctor to carry her children, she didn't put down Noah except for when he was asleep at night. That was the longest time that she went without holding her son since he was born a year ago in the hospital. Uncle Nathan drove them to the airport that he used to work at before he retired a few years ago where their private jet waited for them on the tarmac before they got on their flight to the states. Since they took their private jet home, they went from York to New York.

They made a stop in Dallas to refuel the plane where they stayed at a hotel for the night before they made it back to Los Angeles the next day.

Once they were home, Sebastian ran the studio while she worked on filming a new movie called *A Ballerina's Last Dance* that she didn't have time to audition for due to her surgery. Daphne went to her private school, and she left Noah with her parents during the day. Her mother worked on a new book as soon as they got back from England where she rarely saw her during the day and at night since she hid in her bedroom all of the time. Her mum took care of Noah by herself during the day. He was becoming more independent now. He ate all by himself and he walked all over the house. They baby proofed everything in the house since Noah got into all of the drawers in the kitchen and the bathroom where he threw everything on the floor like it was a game to him. Noah talked to them non-stop since they got back from England where he repeated what they said to each other in a conversation before he made himself laugh from it. Daphne was her serious child much like her who was always concerned about making people upset if she said something to them. Noah was so much more like Sebastian in his personality. He was always making people laugh. Noah was the funniest child that she met in her life. He was obsessed with making animal noises. He grabbed onto her nose to make a honking noise before he made himself laugh over and over again. When she wasn't filming her movie *A Ballerina's Last Dance*, she was in her office at the house while she planned Daphne and Noah's joint birthday party that they were having at the zoo. They decided that the theme of the party was going to be zoo animals. The zoo actually let them rent the entire zoo for a private event where they invited everyone from the studio to come to the party and their families that lived in the states. They invited Daphne's classmates from school to the party. It was the week before the children's birthday party that she got her costume designer from the studio to make an outfit for themselves and the children that was a different animal at the zoo. She chose a lion for Noah, a cheetah for Sebastian, a panda for Daphne, and an elephant for herself. Sebastian told her that she didn't have to go all out for the children's party. She insisted on it because she made up for not being able to celebrate Noah's birthday with her being in the hospital. Due to the time crunch, she told their costume designer that the outfits didn't need to be over the top because Daphne would keep it on all day and that Noah wouldn't keep it on for more than five minutes.

In the coming days to the children's birthday party, her family that lived in New York came into town. Uncle Sam and Aunt Valeria stayed home since he hadn't been feeling well enough to travel and Aunt Valeria stayed at home to take care of him. Her cousins Anastasia and Nina came into town by themselves with their children. Joseph was busy at the hospital and Damien was busy with his job as a real estate agent. She hasn't seen Anastasia and Nina since she had Pancreatis in England during Aunt Sylvia's funeral. They told her when they saw her that they were glad that she was feeling better and that her body knew how to make a production out of everything. Her body always made her problems a public attraction for the world to see. Nina and her five children nine-year-old Bridget, seven-year-old Eilis, five-year-old Liam, three-year-old Owen, and one-year-old Rose stayed at their house. Anastasia and her four children eleven-year-old Alina, nine-year-old Viktor, seven-year-old Angelina, and four-year-old Tolya stayed with Sasha and her family. Bridget and Eilis shared Daphne's bedroom. Liam and Owen slept in Noah's bedroom since Noah was sleeping in their bedroom. Nina and Rose slept in their only guest bedroom that was right next to her parent's bedroom. When she wrapped up her filming for the day, their costume designer told her that the outfits were ready when she followed her into the costume department before she saw their costumes for the first time. Once she told her that the costumes were perfect, she showed them to Sebastian where he told her that he would be caught dead in a cheetah suit before she told him that he was going to do it for his children. He changed his mind when he told her that he would wear it for the pictures before he would change into his normal clothes. She told him that it was fine if he changed out of it after they got their pictures done because Noah wouldn't keep it on for longer than that. When she woke up on the morning of the party, Daphne pulled her mother into a tight hug where she pulled Noah into their hug before she pulled away from them when Sebastian walked into their bedroom with a tray of food. After they ate breakfast in bed with Noah throwing eggs all over the floor, she carried the children into the bathroom as she got them dressed in their costumes. She put

Daphne in her panda dress and Noah in his lion suit before she got changed into her elephant dress. She put Daphne's hair into pigtails that looked like panda ears. Daphne was obsessed with her dress as she ran down the hallway into her grandparent's bedroom to show them her outfit. Noah had the opposite reaction before he tried to take it off of him as soon as she put it on him. As Noah tried to break out of his indestructible suit, she got ready in front of the bathroom mirror. Noah got bored of trying to undress himself when he wandered over to where her makeup sat on top of the counter before he almost threw it into the toilet. As soon as she pulled her makeup products where he couldn't reach them, she called for Sebastian to watch Noah while she got ready where Sebastian walked into the bathroom in his cheetah printed suit before she pulled him into a long kiss to thank him for playing along with her. Once she was ready to leave the house, she carried Noah on her hip with Sebastian following behind her as he carried Daphne in his arms where they got into the back seat of the car before their driver drove them to the zoo. Everyone was already at the zoo waiting for them. They were late to the party because they had sex with each other in their closet while Noah played with her makeup on the bathroom floor. They weren't proud that they were having sex with Noah right next to them, but something inside of her broke when she saw Sebastian in a cheetah print suit that she had to be with him in that moment.

Sebastian told her that they should wait until their son wasn't next to them where she told him that Noah wouldn't know what they were doing when they agreed that it was the right decision to get it out of the way before the party took over their day. After their driver dropped them off at the zoo, she put Daphne and Noah in their double stroller as Sebastian pushed their children into the zoo with an attendant letting them through the gate where they stopped in the entrance of the zoo before everyone jumped out yelling surprise to them. As soon as they let out Daphne and Noah from their stroller, Daphne ran over towards the panda enclosure as Noah ran towards the lion enclosure when he shouted rawr to them where everyone laughed at him before the attendant took them on a tour of the zoo. While they were on the tour of the zoo, Daphne held onto Katherine and Eleanor's hands as she ran over to each animal in the fenced areas. They held onto each of Noah's hands when he shouted out animal's noises at each animal that they passed by before they took Noah to get a closer look into the enclosures. By the end of their tour, the children were grumpy from overdue naps as the younger children slept in their strollers while the older children played in the jungle gym that provided them entertainment. When Noah woke up from his afternoon nap, she went into the jungle gym with Noah as he went down the slide next to his cousin Rose who Nina pushed down the slides. After the children wore themselves out by running around the zoo, they moved into a pavilion where they ate a delicious meal that was catered by the zoo until it was time for everyone to gather together for dessert. They put Noah and Daphne in two seats next to each other as they placed their cakes in front of them with Noah's cake having a lion design and Daphne's cake having a panda design where they sang happy birthday to them. Daphne blew out the four candles on her cake as she helped Noah blow out his one candle after they made a wish. Gabriel took a picture of them together before they divided up the cake to their guests that wanted a piece of cake. Daphne opened up her presents by herself as they helped Noah open up his presents. He was more interested in eating wrapping paper off of the ground instead of the gift inside of it before Daphne opened the rest of Noah's presents for him as he tried to undress himself in front of everyone. When the sun went down in the sky, everyone left the zoo to go back to their houses as her parents gathered the bags of presents into the car when they went back to the car where Noah fell asleep in his car seat. Once their driver dropped them off at the house, Sebastian gave Daphne a bath with Noah joining her when he woke up from his nap where they got the children into their pajamas before they moved into their bedroom for story time.

As she sat up in the bed with Noah sitting up in her lap, Sebastian read her current favorite book about cows sharing grass with each other with Daphne sitting in his lap when she asked her with an innocent smile on her face, "Thank you for the party, mommy. It was fun. Can you read a story? Daddy's read to me too many times."

She ran her fingers through her daughter's dampened hair when she responded to her with a wide grin on her face, "You're welcome honey. We are glad that you had a good birthday party. Thank you for sharing your special day with Noah. He had fun too, didn't you, Noah

William? Did you have fun, silly boy? Sure, little bee. What do you want me to read to you?"

After Noah let out a squealing noise followed by a rawr from a lion, they laughed at him as she kissed Noah on the top of his head when Daphne responded to her with a smirk on her face, "I want mommy to read a made-up story to me. Don't make it sad though because I don't want to be sad. It needs to be a happy story."

She ran her fingers through her daughter's hair when she told the story to them with excitement laced in her voice, "A happy story? You got it, little bee. Our main character is named Kylie. The story takes place in New York City at Christmas. Kylie's mommy asks her to write a list of what she wants to get for Christmas. Kylie's list looks a little bit different each year. Sometimes she wants dolls. Other times she wants cars. She always wants more dresses and more shoes to wear to school. One year, Kylie asks her mommy if she can get a special present. Her mommy asks her what kind of special present she wants. Kylie tells her mommy that she wants to do something that she never tried before. Her mommy sees that this is a reasonable request. Her mommy asks her what she wants to do. Kylie tells her mommy that she wants to go to New York City for Christmas. Her mommy doesn't know if she can do it, but she tells her that she will try her best to make it happen. Kylie patiently waits for Christmas until her mommy tells her that they are spending Christmas in New York City. Kylie pulls her mommy into a tight hug when she tells her that she's excited to go to New York City. Kylie and her mommy get on a bus early in the morning that takes them to New York City. They see the Christmas tree in Rockefeller Plaza. There's over a million lights on it. It's magical to Kylie because she never saw a Christmas tree so big in her life. They see the Rockettes in Radio City Music Hall. They see a Broadway Musical where Kylie and her mommy sing along to the songs. They go to the biggest store in the world with eight floors where Kylie's mommy buys a doll for her. Kylie gets to meet Santa Claus and get a picture with him. Kylie's mommy keeps that picture on the fridge for years. They go ice skating together in Central Park. It is everything that Kylie dreamed that it would be. When they have to go home, Kylie is sad because she doesn't want to leave New York City and the magic that it brought her. Her mommy promises her that they can come back next year. This time they will take her grandma with her. Kylie can't wait for next Christmas. She counts down the days in a calendar on the wall until she can go to New York again."

As she rocked Noah to sleep in her arms, Daphne climbed into her lap when Daphne asked her mother with curiosity laced in her voice, "Does she do it, mommy? Does she go back to New York next Christmas with her grandma?"

She nodded her head at her when she responded to her daughter with her blinking back tears that fell down her face, "I was getting to that part, little bee. Kylie does get to go back to New York City next Christmas with her mommy and her grandma. They don't go on a bus. They get on an airplane. It's Kylie's first time on an airplane. Kylie tells them that she's scared. Her mommy and her grandma assure her that she'll be safe, and she believes them. They stay in New York City for a week. They go to places that they didn't go to the last time that they were there. They go to the World Trade Center. It wasn't there the last time that they were there. They can see all of the city from the top of the building. They are on top of the world. They go to Carnegie Hall to see the Nutcracker. Kylie loves ballet, so her mommy knows that she'll love it. They take a ferry to Ellis Island to see the Statue of Liberty. Her grandma stays behind as Kylie and her mommy go to the top of Lady Liberty's torch. People look like ants to them. They can see a ship docking at Ellis Island with immigrants coming to the states for a better life. Kylie asks her mommy if that was how she came to the states when she was a little girl. Her mommy tells her that she came to Ellis Island on a big boat with her grandma that they rode on for over two months When they made it to Ellis Island, her grandma told her mommy that they were home. Her mommy told her grandma that it was the most beautiful thing that she saw. Her grandma told her mommy that this was the beginning of the greatest chapter of their lives. Kylie asked her mommy what she thought of this place when she was a little girl like she was. Her mommy told her, 'Kylie, the world is yours. Do what you know is going to make you happy. Become anyone that you want to be. I'll always be proud of you. This life is my gift to you. Take this gift and make something beautiful out of it. Something more beautiful than I can give you.'"

Sebastian grabbed onto her shoulder as she wiped away tears that fell down her face when Daphne asked her with a frown on her face, "Mommy! This sounds real. Is this story about you and Grandma Ella? I'm not mad. I'm only telling you that I figured it out. What happened next? Did Kylie get what she wanted?"

She responded to her daughter with a wide grin on her face, "You're so smart, little bee. I can't get anything past you. Kylie got everything that she wanted and more than she imagined in her wildest dreams. She'll never forget that moment with her mommy. It's one that she wants to spend an eternity with her. That moment that she looked at the city changed her life. Sometimes she looks back on how much changed since she saw the city and she wonders to herself how she found so much beauty in such a dark place. There were times in her life that she thought that place represented something dark about her. She forgot that there was beauty there before there was pain and loss. It reminded her of something that she heard at her daddy's funeral. Her mommy told her that there was pain in beauty and there was beauty in pain. A place can bring you so much beauty and yet bring you so much pain. Two things can always be true at the same time. When there is pain in the world, there is beauty to see in it. Does that make sense?"

Daphne responded to her with a smile on her face, "I understand. That was a good story. It wasn't sad like your other stories. What's the beauty in it for you?"

She pointed at Daphne's chest as Daphne grabbed onto her hand when she responded to her daughter, "You are the beauty, my love. You and your brother are beautiful. My life was dark before you came into the world. You reminded me of the beauty that I saw in New York. You and your brother showed me that there was a better way to live my life. I'll show it to you." She kissed Daphne on the top of her head as Sebastian carried her into her bedroom for the night where she laid down on the bed with Noah sleeping on her chest before Sebastian came back into bed with him wrapping his around her. She fell asleep in his arms for the rest of the night.

CHAPTER SIXTY-THREE
(SUMMER 1974 – NEW YORK, NEW YORK)

Daphne finished up preschool where they got dressed up to attend her graduation at the school before they went out to eat together at their favorite restaurant. They invited her cousin's Amelia, Oliver, Sasha, their spouses, and their children to come with them since Daphne wanted to be there with her cousins to celebrate her first school milestone. With Daphne home from school during the summer, her mum stayed home with the children on the days that she wrapped up filming on her latest movie where she was about to leave on a press tour around the country. Her mother rushed to New York to be with Uncle Sam who was in the hospital for pneumonia. Her mother was staying in New York to help Aunt Valeria take care of him when he got home. Sasha left with her mother to go to New York to see her father in the hospital without Charlotte who stayed at home with Gabriel. Before she left for a three week long press tour, she said goodbye to her children who were upset that she was leaving them where she promised them that she would be back in a few weeks. Sebastian and her mum promised to take good care of the children before she was driven to the LAX airport. She saved money by letting everyone use their private jet. It was more expensive to pay for plane tickets for thirty people than to use their own private jet. Once she met up with the cast and the crew at their private jet, the pilot flew them to their first stop at Las Vegas, Nevada where they did their press events for a few days before they went off to the next city on their press tour. When she was alone in her hotel room in Kanas City, she got a phone call from Sasha who was sobbing when she told her that her father got diagnosed with stage three lung cancer and that his doctor gave him only a year to live. She tried to comfort Sasha the best that she could from a phone call before she asked Sasha how her mother was taking the news about Uncle Sam's lung cancer. Sasha told her that her mother locked herself in Aunt Valeria's bedroom. Sasha assured her that her mum and Uncle Stan were with her to make sure that she was okay even though that didn't make her feel any better. Once she hung up the phone on Sasha, she called her mother from Aunt Valeria's house where Uncle Stan answered the phone when he told her that her mother wasn't able to talk because she was in Uncle Sam's bedroom. After Uncle Stan offered his sympathy to her about her uncle having cancer, she hung up the phone on him as she let out heartbreaking sobs into her knees where she didn't stop crying until someone aggressively knocked on the door before they let themselves into her room.

Jacob entered her room because he was in the room next to her as he pulled her into his arms with her face hidden in her chest. Jacob was in Kanas City for a medical conference around the same time that she was there for her press tour where he told her that he could stay at the same hotel as him, so that she got away from the cast. She was glad that she took him up on his offer. She didn't want anyone seeing her like this. He saw her like this more times than they could remember. Once she told Jacob about Uncle Sam's stage three lung cancer diagnosis, he told her that he was sorry that her uncle was going through that where she didn't say anything back to him before she hid her face into his chest for the rest of the night. She had an honest conversation with Jacob and Sebastian who was talking to them through the phone that she should stay on the press tour until the end. She would go to New York to see her family after the press tour was over. Her mother needed space to figure out her emotions before she came to see her when she was at her lowest. Uncle Stan and her mum would make sure that her mother was okay. She told herself that she wasn't going to worry about what she couldn't change. It was Jacob's advice, but she wasn't going to give him credit for every decision that she made in her life. She wanted to think that she would've come to this conclusion without him. Once they went to their last stop on the press tour in Boston, she took their private jet back to Los Angeles to drop off the cast at home. Sebastian met them at the airport with Daphne and her three-year-old niece Charlotte who she was taking to New York with her. Sasha missed Charlotte in the last few weeks of being apart from her. She thought if she brought Daphne with her that it would make her mother feel more like herself again. She didn't know how her mother was going to react to it. After she said goodbye to Sebastian and Noah, she carried Charlotte on her hip as she held onto Daphne's hand where she walked them over to their private jet. The girls colored in their notebooks before the pilot flew them to New York. Since it was an overnight flight, she slept on the bed with the girls until their plane landed in New York the next morning. She carried Charlotte and Daphne off of the plane who slept in her arms. As soon as she saw Sasha from across the room, Sasha ran over to her as she pulled Sasha into a tight hug with Sasha's face hidden in her chest until Charlotte cried for her mother before Sasha placed Charlotte on her hip. After Sasha drove them to Uncle Sam's house, she carried Daphne into the house as Holly attacked her legs when she walked through the front door with Sasha yelling at her to stop in French where she pulled Aunt Valeria into a tight hug before Daphne jumped out of her arms. Before she realized that Daphne was gone, Daphne ran into her grandparent's bedroom as she sprinted after her daughter when she apologized to her parents for waking them up before they pulled her on the bed with them into their group hug with Daphne in her lap. She didn't leave her parents' bedroom until it was dinner time where Daphne fell asleep with her head on her mother's chest. They ate dinner in the kitchen with Uncle Sam who was acting like he always did even though he was really sick before she fell asleep in Sasha's bed with her and the girls for the rest of the night. She woke up the next morning to Aunt Valeria smiling at them when she told them that they used to share a bed when they were little girls and that it was sweet to see them together again. She didn't tell Aunt Valeria that she slept in the same bed as Sasha until they were married to their husbands. She wanted to take Daphne, Sasha, Charlotte, and her parents to Ellis Island to see the Statue of Liberty. Her parents and Sasha loved the idea since it was a great way for everyone to get out of the house. Uncle Sam, Aunt Valeria, and Uncle Stan wanted to go with them too. They got into two cars to the ferry stop where they parked their cars before they got onto the ferry. Sasha took the girls on the top of the ferry as they carried their daughters on their hips when they showed them the city where they sat at the top of the ferry for the boat ride. After their ferry docked at Ellis Island, she placed Daphne onto the ground as she held onto her daughter's hand with her parents walking behind them where they stopped at Grand Central Station that was empty. Her mother commented to her that it didn't look like this the last time that they were here where she laughed at her mother's comment before Uncle Sam and Aunt Valeria called for them ahead to where the museum was located within the island. Their next stop was the museum where it showed the immigration process of how people came to the island to live in the states from all around the world. They didn't need to wonder how it worked since they lived through it themselves, but it was a great time to share with the girls how their family got to live in the states. Even though Charlotte was too young to understand it, Daphne was intrigued as her mother, Uncle Sam, and Aunt Valeria told her about what it was like to move to the states where the first thing that they saw was Ellis Island. After they spent the rest of the morning in the museum, they stopped at the only restaurant that was on the island for lunch as they sat on the stairs by the front of the building where they ate deli sandwiches. Their last stop was the Statue of Liberty. Uncle Sam and Aunt Valeria opted not to climb up into the Statue of Liberty since it was steep.

She told Daphne to be careful as they made their way to the top of the torch where she placed Daphne on her hip before she looked out at the city when she said to her mother with a smile on her face, "It's like I remembered it being when I was a little girl. Peaceful and Beautiful. Chaotic and Painful. At the same time."

Her mother wrapped her arm around her shoulder when she responded to her daughter with her blinking back tears that fell down her face, "You're missing something, baby girl. Possibilities. Endless possibilities."

After her mother squeezed her shoulder, her parents and Uncle Stan made their way back to the ground with Sasha and Charlotte following behind them as she looked at Daphne holding onto her hand when she asked her daughter with a frown on her face, "What do you think, little bee? Is this everything that you dreamed of?"

Daphne nodded her head at her mother when she told her with wonder in her eyes, "It's more than what I dreamed of. I love you so much, mommy. You have to show Noah."

She pulled her into a tight hug with Daphne hiding her face into her mother's chest when she responded to her daughter with tears falling down her face, "I'll show it to Noah when he's older. We can come here with daddy and Noah. I love you, little bee. How about we go back on the ground? I see the ferry coming towards us."

As soon as Daphne grabbed onto her hand, she led them down the narrow stairs until they were back on the ground as her mother grabbed onto her hand where she placed Daphne on her hip before she followed them onto the ferry off of Ellis Island back to the mainland. Ellis Island disappeared in the background with the Statue of Liberty always staring back at them. The doorway was right in front of her. She was in Uncle Sam's arms on the top deck of the ferry as she watched Ellis Island disappear behind her and New York City appear closer to her. It was the beginning of her life in the states. It was the end of her life in England. If she could go through that doorway again, she would choose a different path for herself. She would choose this life over her past life. She would choose this over her father. What was the word that her mother used for it? Possibilities. Endless possibilities. It was simpler than she thought it was. Everything was so simple. She wasn't upset about it anymore. She made her peace with it. What were the words that she used to describe the city? Peaceful and Beautiful. Chaotic and Painful. It was the perfect storm. It was a storm that she felt like she lived in her entire life. The world of addiction was chaotic and painful, but there were moments of peace and beauty within it. The feeling that she felt in the beginning of a high. The silence in her mind. The invincibility that she felt in that moment. It was like anything was possible. It never lasted for more than a few minutes. It never was supposed to last longer than that. That feeling was instantly replaced with that chaos and pain all over again. She lived for those moments when she was at the height of her addiction. Her life revolved around those moments of peace and beauty. Those were the moments that she felt like everything was going to be okay. Even though her life was falling apart, everything was going to be okay. She felt that peace right before she almost died every time that she overdosed on drugs. Her father knew those moments too. She hoped that he realized that life wasn't supposed to be like that for him. Everyone didn't live for those moments like they did. There was more to life. There was a life outside of that world. A beautiful world. A world full of endless possibilities. When they got home from Ellis Island that afternoon, she put Daphne and Charlotte down for an overdue nap in Sasha's bedroom as she grabbed her father's suicide note from her mother's suitcase that her mother carried with her. She took a seat on the balcony when she read it like she was reading it for the first time. The line stuck out to her when he wrote to her, "I hope that your brother would've come to the same conclusion as us." She couldn't see where her father said what that conclusion was. That was another mystery from the universe. Would she go on another wild goose chase looking for this answer? She didn't want to do that. It took so much out of her. She didn't think that she could do it again. The world was better off without knowing what her father's conclusion was. Her mother reminded her that some things are meant to stay a secret. She'll never know what would've happened to her life if she chose a different door. She was okay with that now. She didn't need to know anything anymore. She didn't want to know now.

Chapter Sixty-Four
(Fall 1974 – Los Angeles, California)

After they spent another week in New York, they went back to Los Angeles as Sasha worked at the photography studio with Gabriel while Daphne, Katherine, and Charlotte went to private school together. Her mother went back to writing her book at night where her parents watched Noah during the day. She wanted to write a screenplay about what she was passionate about. Juliet helped her write it since she had experience writing screenplays. They worked on it at the office, and they met up at Oliver's house in the evenings where she acted out parts that they wrote that day. Her screenplay was about a family in the twentieth century that came to Ellis Island to escape Russia during the October Revolution. She drew inspiration from Aunt Valeria's story and the story of Uncle Sam and her mother moving to the states. The story was about a young girl Alya and her family coming to the states. Alya's father Dima was a doctor in Russia, and he refused to support the Communist Party when they overthrew Czar Nicholas II, and they killed the Romanov Family. Alya escaped to the states with her father and her sisters Mariya and Victoria. Alya's mother died when she was two years old, so her sisters raised her. Alya and her family made a new life in the states. Dima went back to medical school because his degree didn't count in the states. Alya and her sisters took up odd jobs to help support the family. Her older sisters worked in the sewing mills to help make ends meet while Alya worked in the most dangerous factories in the country since they were jobs that a child did. Alya got hurt working in the factory and it left her disabled for the rest of her life. The story followed Alya's struggle with being disabled and her family's pursuit for justice. When she pitched the idea to Sebastian and Juliet, they told her that this wasn't a story that was told before in Hollywood. A story about an immigrant family trying to find the American Dream to find out that the American Dream was dead. The underlying message from her movie was that the American Dream never existed. Even though she wanted to go out in full force with that message, their lawyers advised them that would be a way for their backers to pull out their funding from the studio. That was something that no one wanted to happen. Least of all for her that depended on their backers to keep their studio profitable. She agreed to tone down the message in her screenplay about being against the American Dream. Juliet came up with a better way to express that message in their screenplay that wasn't going to compromise with her morals. They settled on the message of the screenplay being that the American Dream only happens to the luckiest people and that the only way that the American Dream would happen was if someone worked very hard to get it.

They changed the ending of their screenplay that they called *Russian Doll* with Alya and her family finding their own paths of success in their lives by doing what was right. Even though Alya was disabled for the rest of her life, she didn't stop fighting for what was right no matter what the challenges were. Her lawyer's told her that their financial backers were content with that version of the story. Sebastian gave his green light on it, and she was a producer on her movie. Since she was the producer of the movie, she gave Juliet the credit for being the writer on the movie even though they wrote it together. Juliet deserved nothing less than everything that she gave her. She decided that she wasn't going to act in the movie. She was going to be the director of the movie alongside her favorite director to work with named Laurence who she worked with for over a decade now on different movies. Laurence was the only person that she could think of to work with on her first movie that she wrote where he told her that he would work with her on anything that she gave him. The process of casting was long since they were looking for Eastern European actresses and actors and that was hard to find when the world was against Russia. After Sebastian cashed out the favors that he owed people in the city, they found the right group of people that were sick of playing a stereotype and they were ready to play a character that was going to have a real impact on the world. As soon as they started filming *Russian Doll*, she sat behind the camera for the first time in her life. She saw everything from a different perspective. She wasn't worried about what would happen if she missed the timing on her lines or what they were going to do when she missed her cue. Instead, she told everyone else where their cues were or what lines to start the scene on. She was worried about where the camera played in the room so that they wouldn't miss anything from the scene. She made sure that they finished the backgrounds of the scenes before they were scheduled to film them that day. Everything had to be perfect that was in the shot of the camera. There wasn't room for mistakes in her movie and everyone that worked with her knew that because she drilled it into their heads from the beginning of production. There were a few people that didn't understand that requirement that she had to fire, but everyone understood her loud and clear that she wasn't going to be challenged by anyone on this issue. Her co-director Laurence was refreshed by her desire to make a movie that was going to have an impact on the world. He always complained that he felt like the other producers or directors never cared to do that. She didn't tell him that she wanted to make this work out for her because she was the person that was paying for it since the studio belonged to herself and her husband. There was more to it than that because she cared about other things besides money. Even though she didn't want to waste her money on a movie that wasn't going to be successful, it wasn't about the vanity for her. Money didn't mean anything to her if she didn't make a difference in the world. That was something rare to find in Hollywood. Someone who wasn't greedy and made movies that they knew weren't going to make them wealthier. Laurence and her lawyers told her that she was brave for making something that mattered. She didn't want to tell them that she spent her life being a coward.

She wanted to be brave like her father because she had too many brushes with death for it to mean too much to her. In her sessions with Juliet when they wrote *Russian Doll*, she told her that she wanted to make something that meant something to her. She was sick of doing things that didn't mean anything to anyone. She wanted to make everything mean something to the world because none of it mattered. This was something that she struggled with for a long time because she was always questioning herself if anything that she did meant something to the world. It was what her father struggled with for his entire life. How do you find any meaning in this painful experience called life? There were a million ways to define this, but she always saw it being something that was very personal to her. Nothing in the world mattered unless it mattered to her. What always mattered to her was that there was justice in the world and that her life was going to amount to something more than to herself. That's why she wanted to become an actress. She wanted to do something that would mean something to the world. She had this conversation with Sebastian many times in their relationship. How would she complete this impossible task? Her mother wrote books that mattered to the world. They were books that showed people that there was a beautiful world outside all of the pain. Her mother immortalized herself when she wrote her book *Colliding Fates,* and she knew that when she did it. No one needed to tell her to know that because her mother felt it the moment that it happened to her. She always longed for that moment that she was going to be immortalized ever since she looked up to the stars on the television. She dedicated this dream to her father who became immortalized in the worst possible way. His light wasn't gone because she was carrying it on for him. It was her duty as his daughter to finish what he started. Her mother carried on one part of his dream, and she would carry on the rest of the dream. This world did everything that it could to stop her from doing what she was meant to do, but she wasn't going to let it win. She was done losing the battle. Even if she never won the war itself, she would at least win the battle. Her winning the battle was more than what her parents won in their lives. She was at home alone with the children for over a week since Sebastian was in New York with her parents for a work trip. She went through her clothes in the closet that didn't fit her after she had her children. She went through the children's old clothes a few weeks ago where she cried when she placed their clothes into a donation bag to her cousins that needed baby clothes. They decided after Noah's birth that they weren't going to have any more children because her doctor told her that it would be too dangerous for her. She was sad because she always wanted to have more than two children. Sebastian got a vasectomy a few weeks after Noah was born because he didn't want anything bad happening to her. That was before they argued with each other, so they made that decision together. She spent most of the day going through her clothes with Daphne helping her fold the clothes into piles on her bed before Noah knocked them onto the floor where Daphne yelled at him. Noah did it over and over since he thought that it was a funny game for him to play with her. Daphne wasn't amused with him before Daphne and Noah fought with each other with her separating them. This was the first time that they fought, and it wasn't going to be the last time. They would fight for the rest of their lives. Once Noah was distracted making a mess in her bathroom, Daphne helped her fold the rest of her clothes on the bed as they put them into a bag. She placed it with the several bags of clothes that she got rid of from the children. She asked Daphne to make sure that Noah wasn't breaking anything in the bathroom before Daphne ran into the bathroom to yell at Noah who was about to break the glass soap container by throwing it onto the floor. As soon as she was about to leave her closet, she bumped into a box as she groaned in pain with her toes throbbing where she picked up the box from the corner of her closet before she took a seat on the floor. She opened it to see that it was a box of letters. She let out a soft gasp when she remembered that this was the box of letters that Aunt Sylvia gave her in her will between her grandparents. She read a letter in the pile that said:

June 1939
Dearest Richard,

It's been two weeks since you got deployed to Germany. I can't believe that you are gone. I know that we haven't been in a good place for a long time, but I want you to know that it doesn't mean anything to me. You are always going to be my husband no matter what we do to hurt each other. You are the father of our children. She doesn't mean anything to me. Things haven't been the same since Camille entered our lives. She was a great distraction to you for many years. This is going to sound morbid, but I'm glad that you were called to fight in the war. She can't distract you anymore. Camille stopped by the house after you were deployed overseas. I had the pleasure of telling her that you were gone, and you weren't coming back to her. Kenny told me that I need to be kind to Camille because she's going through a lot. I told our son that we're all going through a lot. Our son had the audacity to tell me that I looked like I was having a party and not grieving anything. I slapped our son across the face for him saying that. He had to be lying to me. We've had our fair share of problems over the years, but we've always found our way back to each other. I've looked past your parade of discarded women, and you looked past my questionable relationship with young William. I hope that you've thought of me. I think of you every morning when I wake up with young William. We used to be young once, didn't we, Richard? Those were the days. The sex compared to nothing in this world. Young William is a lot like you in bed, so it's good to know that I'm not missing that much without you. The children asked about you. Sylvia told me to ask dad if he's feeling homesick. Sam asked if you would send him a letter about how you are doing in the military. He might be interested in joining you when he's old enough to. Kenny doesn't ask about you. Ella doesn't either. Please send them a letter because I know that they want to hear from you, but they don't know how to ask you about it. What else am I missing dear? I got promoted at the sewing mills, so that's extra money for the house. One more thing before I let you go. Did you know that Camille is pregnant? Priscilla and I saw her at the store with a large stomach. I believe the child is yours. I wasn't going to tell you about it, but you have a right to know about it. If it even is your child. She's been sleeping with Caleb Tucker, so it could be his. Ask her about it if you want to. Let me know what she says. I'm dying to know who knocked Camille up between you two. I'll write to you soon.

From, Your dearest Bertha

August 1939
Dearest Richard,

    Looks like I was right about Camille's child being Tucker's baby. He moved her and the baby into the house with James and Haley. When Priscilla and I went to book club at the church, Haley was so furious at him that she couldn't look at anyone except Camille and the baby. Could you believe that Camille would show up to book club with Tucker's child while his wife was there? That man has a set of balls on him. If you did that to me, I would murder you in your sleep. Not that you would do that. Compared to him, you are husband of the year. I told Haley that she should divorce him. She's considering it. She's worried about James, and I understand that. I'm so glad that Camille moved on from you. I'm sure that she was fun, but it never lasts, doesn't it? I don't need to tell you this. You are probably already doing this but find some young German or French girl to remind you that you are better off without Camille. What else did you miss? Priscilla is getting bigger by the day. The baby is coming soon. Kenny's worried about the draft. His friends at the coal mines got drafted and he's worried that he's next. I'm reminding him that there's millions of young men to choose from and that the military is fine without him. He told me that he doesn't believe me. They are recruiting for the military. If he doesn't sign up for it, then he fears that he's going to be forced into a position that he doesn't want to be in. We don't talk about the war with the children because we don't want to scare them. Ella is too young to understand it. Speaking of Ella, she's struggling. I don't know why she is because she won't tell me. She never tells me anything. I fear that I'm never going to know what's going on with her. Young William knows even less than I do about her. She doesn't tell him anything either. I hope that you are well and that you'll win the war for us. I think about you every morning when young William and I smoke meth together outside of the house. Meth is nice. You should try it. Send me some drugs when you get the chance. Send us some cocaine this time. It's young William's favorite. Thank you so much dear.

From, Your dearest Bertha

November 1939
Dear My Angel Son,

My heart breaks that God has separated us from each other. Even though it's for the good of the country that you are gone, I feel like I'm missing a piece of myself. I pray for you every second of every day for your safe return to me. I don't know what would happen to me if you didn't come home. I would die with you. I hope that you and Nathan are protecting yourselves from the Germans. Priscilla and I heard from the ladies at book club that they have better planes than us thanks to the Japanese for loaning zeros. Please let me know if that is true. Priscilla's ready to have the baby. The doctor says that they will be here in a few weeks. To have a baby in the house again. We haven't had a baby in the house since Ella was born. I'm going to touch on a serious subject if you will entertain it. Young William approached me with an ultimatum of sorts about the delicate issue. You know which one I'm talking about. He told me that he's going to tell her about it. He's sick with guilt about it because she's been having nightmares at his house. I tried to tell him that he needs to let sleeping dogs lay down, but he won't listen to me. He told me that you aren't here to stop him anymore because you are in France. What I'm going to ask you to do isn't pretty, but you need to stop him. I don't care how you do it, but just do it. I know that means that I have to stop seeing him. I'm very upset about it, but he'll understand why I'm ending our affair. I'm sure he felt weird sleeping with his mother's girlfriend, so he'll be relieved that it's over with us. I can find someone to replace him. Everyone is replaceable. Your father who is the most replaceable person. When you tell young William about it, don't mention that I told you to do it. He's going to know that I told you about what he said to me. That's only going to make things harder for him. I'll leave him with a parting gift to make him not upset with me. Camille and Tucker already got divorced. It didn't work with him like she thought that it was. Camille came to my doorstep crying about her divorce. I don't know why she thinks that we're friends, but I took your advice on being nice to her. I stopped myself from saying funny things to her because I was trying to be a good person. After I asked her why she came here to talk to me, Camille told me that she wanted to tell me that the baby is Richard's son, and he always was Richard's son. I wasn't surprised when she told me this considering that he was identical to you and Sam when you guys were babies. I asked her what she was going to do about the baby. She told me that she wanted to give the baby to someone who would take care of it. Camille tried to pawn her baby off onto me where I shot her down since I wasn't going to be raising my husband's bastard child. I tried to give her a list of couples in the church that could take care of the baby, but she wanted the baby with me. I wasn't explaining to my children that their father had a child out of wedlock. It would ruin our family. Here's what I told Camille to do instead of her giving the baby to us. I told her to take that baby as far away as possible and make a better life for herself. It could be Scotland or Wales or Australia. I didn't care where she took the baby. I told her to get *as far away from this hellhole as possible before it robbed her of her life. Camille was gone the next morning with her son. A month later Camille sent me a postcard from Sweden thanking me for everything I did. I felt bad for how horrible that I treated her over the years. She's a good person. I used to be that person too. Before I met your father and sold my soul to Satan himself. I was just another Camille. I should've run away to Sweden with you when I had the chance to. I'm sorry that I didn't leave your father when I could. Sometimes I think that if there was a different door, then I would go through that door with you. I never regretted anything more in my life. Please forgive me, my love. I'm sorry that my best wasn't enough for you. I'm sorry that your father and I weren't enough for you. Don't become your father. Don't lose Priscilla and your child. I wouldn't know what to do with myself if you did that. I was going to say that I would die, but your father killed me a long time ago. I hope that if one of you has to die in this war that it's him. I don't want to see him again. He's hurt me so much. More than you can imagine and he's never going to apologize to me like I do to him. Be a better man, Kenny. Don't be your father. I love you so much.*

Love, Your Adoring Mother

She didn't know what she was more upset about between her grandma having an affair with her father when he was a minor or her grandma begging Uncle Kenny not to become like his father. She was heartbroken for her grandma that she was stuck in a loveless marriage to a man that barely tolerated her existence. The loneliness that her grandma must have felt in her life. No wonder she was so drawn to her father. He was one of the only comforting people in her life. How lonely her grandma must have been when she lost her father and Uncle Kenny. She knew that feeling that her grandma was describing to Uncle Kenny. She wished that she could tell her grandma that she didn't have to feel that way. Daphne ran into her closet with Noah running behind her where she shoved letters back into the box that she put back in its place in the corner of the closet. Daphne pulled her into a tight hug when she asked her mother with a frown on her face, "What's wrong, mommy? Why are you crying?"

She smoothed her hair around her ear when she responded to her daughter in a soft voice, "I'm okay, little bee. I get sad for people who aren't here anymore."

Daphne grabbed onto her mother's hands when she responded to her with a frown on her face, "Noah broke the soap container. There's glass all over the bathroom floor."

As she looked over at Noah who had a guilty look on his face, she gently pulled him into her arms as she kissed him on the top of his head when she said to them in a calm voice, "It's okay, Noah William. I'm not mad at you. You guys are going to stay on the bed while I clean up the glass off of the bathroom floor. We are going to sleep in my bed with many stories to come. How does that sound?" After Daphne and Noah nodded their heads at her, she got up off of the floor as she carried Noah onto her bed with Daphne silently sitting down next to him where she cleaned the broken glass off of the bathroom floor before she joined her children in the bed. Once she read them stories that they took turns choosing the books, she changed her children into their pajamas as she laid down in bed with her arms around them before she fell asleep with her children in her arms for the rest of the night.

Chapter Sixty-Five
(Winter 1975 – New York, New York)

Once they finished filming *Russian Doll* in the studio, she spent several weekends with the editors in their booths while they worked on the final edits of the movie before they sent the final version of the movie to theaters. Sebastian secured contracts for them to show their movies in Europe and Central Asia while he was in New York with her parents. This was the first movie from Foster Brewer Studios that was going on the international market. They were going on their first press tour outside of the states. They decided to use their private jet for the trip to Europe and Asia before they ended the press tour in the states. The movie premiered in theaters across the world. She prepared for her press tour in Europe and Central Asia. Her mother and Sasha rushed to New York to be with Uncle Sam who had surgery to remove the tumor out of his left lung after he went through chemotherapy that wasn't working for him. She was presented with a dilemma of whether she should drop her tour to be with Uncle Sam or she should continue on with it. Uncle Sam told her that he would never forgive himself if he was responsible for putting her career on hold for him. It gave her the answer that she was looking for. She told Lucy and Sebastian that she was going through with the tour. They left for their first stop in Austria with their second stop being in Hungary. Crowds showed up at the movie theaters for their question-and-answer sessions and their afterparties where they talked to people about the movie. Sebastian and Lucy told her that they reached the highest records for this movie than any other movie done by their studio. She didn't need them to tell her that her movie made an impact on the world. People told her during their premieres that this movie changed their perspective on the American Dream and how it was a sales pitch by the states to get immigrants to move to their country. Whatever message that her lawyers wanted her to diminish from the movie became useless. People saw the message loud and clear without her saying anything. In her interviews with the press, they asked her how she made a movie that told the truth that the states didn't want the world knowing about. She told them that she was saying the unspoken things that no one wanted to admit out loud to the rest of the world. She knew a lot about how the unspoken things could do more damage than the spoken did. She was tired of her country lying to the world. She didn't know that these interviews were printed into newspapers that were distributed across the world.

When these publications caught up to the states, she received a frantic phone call in the middle of the night while she was in Singapore from her lawyers. They were upset about what she told the international press about the meaning of her movie *Russian Doll*. She explained to her lawyers that she never said those words that they were putting into her mouth. She repeated what people told her about after they watched the movie. This made things worse with her lawyers since they told her that they were concerned that their audience in the states was going to boycott the movie. She told them that they should ask Sebastian what their audiences in the states thought about the movie before they made assumptions about their viewers at home. She hung up the phone before she gave them a chance to respond to her. She didn't care what they had to say to her. In the middle of the night that the next day, she was in Japan when Sebastian told her that he fired their lawyers and that he replaced them with new lawyers that believed in their message. When she asked him how *Russian Doll* was doing in the states, Sebastian told her that they broke the box records for the year above other movies that came out in the last few months and that they had the movie play in more theaters across the country since it was sold out everywhere. Sebastian told her to do more interviews in Central Asia before the press tour started in the states. After she spent another week in Central Asia island hopping after doing a dozen interviews, they left from South Korea to go back to the states where she was treated like royalty as soon as her plane landed at the LAX airport where she started her press tour for *Russian Doll* in the states in Los Angeles where she ended up in New York by the end. She took Lucy and Noah with her for the last leg of their press tour. Her mum had to go to New York with her mother and Sasha because Uncle Sam was in the hospital after he developed pneumonia from a cold. Her mum took Charlotte with her since Sasha wanted to be with her daughter. Sebastian took care of Daphne at the house where she went to school during the day while he worked at the studio. On the second to last stop in her press tour in Boston, she received a frantic phone call from her mother that she needed to go to New York to see Uncle Sam who was dying in the hospital. After Lucy cancelled her last press events in Boston and New York, she paid for Lucy to get on a flight to Los Angeles where she went on her private jet to New York with Noah before Sebastian and Daphne were on their way to New York to be with them. After her private jet landed in New York, her mother took them to the hospital where Sasha pulled her into a tight hug in the hallway by his room where her cousins Anastasia, Nina, and Ivan stood in the hallway with swollen eyes from crying before Aunt Valeria walked into the hallway to tell her that she could come into the room.

Once she handed Noah over to Ivan who placed his nephew on his hip, she followed Aunt Valeria into the room as she stood by the door until Uncle Sam motioned for her to come towards the bed where she walked over to his bed before she took a seat on the bed with Uncle Sam grabbing onto her hands. Uncle Sam told her that he was proud of the woman that became and that he loved her from the moment that she was born. She pulled him into a desperate hug with her face hidden in his chest where he wrapped his arms around her when she told him that he was the father that she never had and that she loved him so much that it hurt her. She pulled out of his arms as Aunt Valeria grabbed onto her shoulder where she pulled out her tight grip before she sprinted out of the hospital without looking back at her parents or her cousins standing outside of his room. She didn't stop running until she made it into the parking lot where she curled onto the ground before she let out heartbreaking sobs into her hands.

Once she heard someone walking towards her, she looked up to see Ivan staring at her with tears falling down his face when she pulled Ivan into a desperate hug where she let out soft sobs into his chest with his arms tightly around her. Ivan grabbed onto her hand to help her off of the ground where she followed him into the hospital before Anastasia handed Noah over to her with Noah on her hip. When she asked her cousins if Uncle Sam was gone, Nina sobbing in Anastasia's arms was enough of confirmation to her that Uncle Sam was dead. Before she got the chance to say anything, Sasha pulled her into a tight hug with Charlotte on her hip as she hid her face into Sasha's chest before she wrapped her arms around Ivan with his face hidden in her back. Aunt Valeria walked out of his room with her parents on either side of her where Anastasia and Nina pulled their mother into a desperate hug before her mum asked them if they wanted to go to the house. After she let go of her grip on Ivan and Sasha, her parents wrapped her arms around her with Noah on her hip where they guided her to their car before her mum drove them to the house. She went into her bedroom without saying a word to her parents before she cried herself to sleep for the rest of the night. She woke up the next morning with Sebastian sitting down on the bed. He pulled her into a desperate hug with her face hidden in his chest as he ran his fingers through her hair where he kissed her on the top of her head before he asked her if she wanted to eat breakfast with her family. Once she shook her head at him, he told her that he would be in the living room with Daphne and Noah if she wanted to join them where he left her alone in her bedroom before she spent the rest of the day laying down on her bed. Sebastian urged her to eat lunch and dinner where she told him that she wasn't hungry before he left her alone for the rest of the day. She wanted to spend the days until Uncle Sam's wake hiding in her bedroom, Sebastian had other plans for her. Oliver came on the third day where he pulled her into a desperate hug before she laid down in his arms for the day.

On the morning of Uncle Sam's wake, her mother dragged her out of her bed since she wanted to go through what speeches that they were saying at Uncle Sam's funeral. She didn't know that her mother volunteered to talk at the funeral before she asked her mother why she thought that she wanted to talk at the funeral. After she gave into her mother with that persuasive look on her face, she moved onto what speeches they were going to write about him where her mother pulled her into an impromptu writing session before they left for the church. Once they spent two hours writing eulogies, Sebastian walked into their bedroom with the children in his arms as she changed Daphne into a black dress and Noah into his black suit that he was trying to escape from. She put on one of black dresses that Sebastian brought with him before they left to go to the church with her parents, Sasha's family, and Aunt Valeria. She tried to avoid people as they tried to talk to her about her uncle. She wasn't about to have a mental breakdown in front of strangers. She let them ask her about her family, her book, and her movie *Russian Doll* that was a huge hit. She forgot it existed until someone brought it up to her as soon as she walked into the church. She excused herself out of a conversation with a stranger about how her uncle touched their life. She sprinted towards a bench that overlooked Central Park as she took a seat on the part of the bench that wasn't covered in snow where she lit a cigarette from her purse before she inhaled the smoke from it with her hands shaking from stress. As soon as she inhaled the smoke of her cigarette, Aunt Valeria sat down next to her as she offered her a cigarette to her where Aunt Valeria took it from her hands before she leaned onto the bench. They sat together in silence for a while until it snowed on them again where Aunt Valeria helped her off of the bench before she followed Aunt Valeria into the church. After they spent the rest of the afternoon at the church, her mum drove them to the house where she ate dinner with her family before she went into her bedroom to work on her eulogy. She was torn about what to say about her uncle. She didn't want to say the wrong thing to a crowd of people that she didn't know except for her family. She knew what her mother was going to say about her uncle and that was enough to stop her from saying a lot of what she wanted to tell him. She learned a long time ago that she was good at saying the wrong thing at the wrong time. There were so many moments that she wanted to include in her eulogy that she didn't feel like she had the right. She learned from her father that she needed to respect the secrets of the dead because that was all that was left. She didn't want to rob anyone of their secrets. She knew how it felt for the world to take that away from her. There was no dignity in dying, so the least that she could do for her uncle was give him his secrets since no one would take that away from him. She wrote two eulogies to her uncle. The one that she shared with the world and the one that she shared with him. It was what her mother did for her father when he died. She gave him a eulogy for the world to hear and one for him to hear. She wasn't below recognizing when her mother had a good idea. Her mother had some good ideas. Like writing a book that she resisted for most of her adult life until she found it to be a good idea. Her mother would rub it in her face if she found out that she gave her credit for an idea. She was going to do it in secret like the universe intended it to be.

On the morning of the funeral, her mother told her to get ready because Uncle Sam's lawyer was here to go through his will. She changed into another black dress where she met up with her family in the office before she closed the door behind her. Inside of the office was Uncle Sam's lawyer, Aunt Valeria, her parents, Anastasia, Damien, Sasha, Gabriel, Nina, Joseph, her niece Rose, Ivan, and Antoine. His lawyer looked over at Anastasia and Damien when he told them that her father left them the hair salon that was in her mother's name to her since her mother retired after her father's death and a large sum of money from his sale of the factory for his grandchildren. Anastasia was surprised by this since her mother didn't say anything to her about retiring from the salon. She pulled her mother into a tight hug when she thanked her for leaving her the hair salon and the money for her children. His lawyer told Sasha and Gabriel that her father left her his shares in the stock market for General Motors worth three million dollars and some money that was set aside for Charlotte. He looked over at Nina who had Rose on her hip and Joseph when he told them that her father left the family house and some money for her children. No one expected Uncle Sam to give them the house. Aunt Valeria told them that she was going to live with them if they were okay with it before Nina pulled her mother into a tight hug when she softly thanked her. Once Aunt Valeria and Nina pulled away from each other, his lawyer looked over at Ivan and Antonine when he told them that his father gave him his stock in French companies worth five million dollars. He looked over at Aunt Valeria where he told her that her husband gave her the rest of his wealth and their beach front property that they owned in Italy that he bought for their twentieth wedding anniversary. No one knew except for Sasha and Ivan that stayed there before that Uncle Sam owned a property in Italy including Anastasia and Nina who asked their mother if they could visit the property with her. Aunt Valeria promised them that she would take them to their Italian beach house. His lawyer looked at her and her mother when he told them that Uncle Sam left them a surprise in his will that was seen in the picture that he presented to them. After she grabbed the photo from his hands, she kept it close to her mother as they looked at the picture of a woman and a baby boy who looked like they were in Sweden because of all of the snow. Before she stopped herself from saying it out loud, she shouted out that it was Camille and her son as everyone in the room instantly looked over at her with confused looks on their faces. They had no idea what she was talking about. She asked Aunt Valeria how Uncle Sam found out about Camille and his half-brother. Everyone let out shocked gasps when Aunt Valeria ignored them when she told them that Uncle Sam found out about his half-brother Jason James after he visited them when Camille died in Sweden. When she asked the lawyer what the surprise was about Camille and Jason, he told her that Jason died ten years ago, and he left his estate to his half-brother Sam. Uncle Sam was left the estate to her and her mother because he knew that they would appreciate the beauty in it. She didn't know what surprised her more, whether she was one of the only people that knew about Camille and Jason's existence or that she owned a house in Sweden that her uncle owned for a decade. Her mother asked her how she found out about this where she told her that it was in the letters that Aunt Sylvia gave her before her mother stormed out of the office with her mum following behind her. Everyone filed out of the office as she looked at the picture of Camille and Jason in the photograph with the house behind them. She turned over the photograph to see a taped envelope on the back of it before she opened it up to see what was inside of it. The envelope had a key to the house pictured in the photograph and it also included a letter from Jason to Uncle Sam that said:

March 1965
Dear Sam,

I want to thank you for everything that you did to help me after my mother died. I know that you didn't like keeping secrets from our sisters, but you did it for me. I wanted to tell you this in person, but I'm too sick to make it to New York. I was diagnosed with ASL a few years ago and I was given a few months to live. They didn't know that I would live years after that. I'm crippled now. I am confined to a wheelchair, and I can't take care of myself anymore. I've talked about it with my doctor, and he agreed to kill me with a lethal dose of morphine. Euthanasia is legal in Sweden now. Since I'm not married and I don't have children, I have no one to give my estate to except you. You are my only family left in the world. Please take care of it for me. My mother's family built that house with their own hands. It's special to me. I want you to give it to Willie's daughter Isabella. I've always had a soft spot for Willy. She deserves something as beautiful as it. I love you, my brother. I've always loved you to the stars.

Love, Your Brother JJ Johnson

She stuffed the letter and the key into the envelope as she placed it into her purse where she joined her family into the living room before she followed her parents and Sebastian with Noah and Daphne on their hips. When they pulled up to the church, she walked into the church with Noah on her hip as she took a seat in the second pew in between Sebastian with Daphne on his lap and Oliver with Eleanor sitting on his lap where the preacher thanked everyone for coming to the funeral before he asked Anastasia to come up to the podium. Once Damien squeezed his wife's shoulder, Anastasia walked up to the podium with a piece of paper in her hands when she said aloud to the room with her blinking back tears that fell down her face, "He was a good man, my dad. He was the best person that I knew. My dad was so hard-working. He was determined to do the right thing. He wanted the world to be a beautiful place. When I was a little girl, he took me to work with him. He showed me where his office was, and he told me that this place didn't give him enjoyment like what my sisters and my brother gave him. We went on so many adventures over the years. He told me that I was more than what I thought that I was. I shouldn't allow anyone to treat me like I'm less than them. I couldn't tell you how many times someone tried to talk down on me, and I told them what he said to me. He'd say, 'Anastasia, you are everything to me. You are my sun, and I orbit around you. Even though I will be gone someday, you will shine for the both of us.' Thank you for everything. I love you, dad. I'll miss you for the rest of my life."

Anastasia walked to her seat in the front pew with Damien grabbing onto her hands. Sasha got up from her seat next to Anastasia as Gabriel grabbed onto her shoulder where Sasha stood at the podium with a piece of paper in her hands when she said aloud to the room with her blinking back tears that fell down her face, "My dad and I struggled with our relationship over the years. We fought when I was a teenager. We were too similar. I didn't want to admit that my dad was right. I needed to stop being stubborn. I didn't understand until I had my daughter Charlotte. She showed me that it's hard to be a parent to someone who is like you. We reconciled our differences four years ago and I've never been happier. I've tried to make up for lost time with him. I didn't have forever with him. When we were in the hospital on his last day, he said that he longed for this feeling since we were children. All of his children together and unified towards their love for him. It was bittersweet since it was his last moment with us. I'm sorry for not making things right sooner than I did. It's my biggest regret. I'll always love you, daddy. Thank you for being so patient with me."

Sasha took a seat next to Gabriel as he tightly grabbed onto her hands. She handed Noah over to her mum who placed him in her lap as she walked up to the podium with two speeches in front of her before she decided what speech she was going to say. She placed both pieces of paper onto the floor when she said aloud to the room with her blinking back tears that fell down her face, "I wrote two versions of this eulogy. I didn't know which one I wanted to read. I realized coming up here that I wanted to read neither of them. I wouldn't be telling you the truth. Uncle Sam deserves the truth. Not a lie or secret to be hidden from the world. I'm not capable of telling another lie. Uncle Sam was one of the most important people in my life. He treated me like his own daughter. He didn't need to do that because he already had three daughters of his own, but he still did it. He was the father that I never had. I told him on his deathbed that he was more of a father to me than my real father was. He told me that he didn't want me feeling like I was missing something in my life because my dad was dead. I think that was what broke me. He died believing that it was enough. I never got the chance to tell him that he wouldn't be enough. I didn't want to break his heart any more than my dad broke it when he killed himself. There was a lot that I never got the chance to tell Uncle Sam. I know that there was stuff that he kept from me. He died with his secrets like I'll die with my secrets. If he would've known those secrets about me, then would he love me the same way? Would I have been special to him if he knew the truth about me? I'd like to think that nothing would change between us. I would tell him my secrets and he would tell me that he still loved me. That he would love me for the rest of time. I'm sorry for making you believe that it was enough for me. I should've told you that it wasn't going to be enough. That nothing would be enough for me. You were a good person, Uncle Sam. I'm never going to be a good person like you, but I'm trying to be. I want to be a better person for you. I want to be the person that you thought that I was. Even though I'm never going to win the war, at least I'm going to win the battle. Thank you for showing that to me. I love you, Uncle Sam. We'll always have the stars."

She let out heartbreaking sobs into her hands as her mother and Sebastian rushed over to the podium where he pulled her into his arms with her sobbing into chest before her mother whispered into her ear with her arms around her, "You did a good job, baby girl. I'm proud of you. He would be proud of you."

After Sebastian pulled her over to their seats, Oliver wrapped his arms around her as she softly cried into Sebastian's chest with his arms wrapped around her when her mother said aloud to the room in between her sobs, "I'm sorry. I didn't mean to cry. I can't help it, but cry when my baby girl cries. I loved my brother so much. He was my best friend. I didn't think that I would be the last one left out of my five siblings. I'm saying five because I had a half-brother that lived in Sweden that Sam didn't tell me about. I've never been in a world without my brother in it. He changed my life in the best possible way. He gave my baby girl and I a life in New York. A life that we could start over after what happened with Will. It was the best gift that I received in my life. All of the money and the fame that came from being an author didn't mean anything without him. He believed in me before I believed in myself. He believed in our dream before it happened. My baby girl and I always have had the same dreams. Sam had that dream too. We wanted to make this world a better place. We did it, Sammy.

After a lifetime of sacrifice, look at the beautiful world that we made together. I couldn't have done it without you. None of this would be here without you. Thank you for everything. I'll love you until my dying breath. Until we meet again in the stars."

Her mother took a seat next to her with Oliver sliding down to let her into the pew. She pulled her mother into a desperate hug as she hid her face into her chest with her arms tightly wrapped around her. Aunt Valeria said aloud to the room with tears falling down her face, "I'm heartbroken that you aren't here with me. I haven't been away from you since we got married in 1941. It was the best thirty-four years of my life. It was the honor of my life to be there by your side as we conquered the world together. New York didn't know what was coming when we moved here. We were going to cause an avalanche that no one had seen before in their lives. Ella was right. We did it. We beat the odds, and we made something beautiful out of an ugly world. I know that you didn't see it that way. You only cared about helping people and making justice in the world. That's what I loved the most about you. Your desire to make things fair. You didn't want me to feel like an outcast because I was a Russian immigrant in an English-speaking country. For the first time in my life, you made me feel like the world belonged to me. You taught our daughters to not be limited by the possibilities that the world determines for them. You taught our son that he was responsible for his destiny. You taught your niece that her adversities make us stronger people. Not weaker like society teaches us. You taught me that the world can be a beautiful place. Thank you for always taking care of us. I couldn't imagine my life with anyone else. I promised you on the day that we got married to love you for the rest of my life. I'd do it again."

Aunt Valeria took a seat next to Anastasia and Nina who pulled her into a tight hug. The priest thanked everyone for coming to celebrate Sam's life and that they would bury him outside where her mother dragged her with the family before she looked at the open hole in the ground with Noah asleep in her arms. Oliver, Ivan, Jamie, Sean, George, and Tommy carried the coffin over to the hole as they lowered it into the ground where they threw dirt on top of Uncle Sam's wooden coffin. As she heard the plunking noise hitting Uncle Sam's coffin, she thought about what her mother told her father in her eulogy to him after they moved his grave to the farm. Her mother told her father that everything that she told him at the funeral wasn't true. She didn't want to say it in front of the world. Her mother felt like her father was giving up on everything that they could've had with each other. He was giving up on their dream because he didn't believe in it. Her father didn't believe in that life. That was the biggest betrayal to her mother. Not cheating on her with Uncle Stan. Not lying to her about his substance use disorder. Not running away from her when she needed him. Him raping her didn't come close. She couldn't believe that he gave up something that could've been beautiful. If he let it happen to him, then he could've seen it. The world would've been more beautiful without him. He'd done enough damage to the world, and he didn't want to do any damage to it. She couldn't take it. She handed Noah over to her mum where she sprinted towards Central Park before she dry heaved with her hands on the ground. Sebastian stood above her with a concerned look on his face as he helped her off of the ground where he wrapped his arms around her with her face hidden in his chest before he asked her if she was okay. She ignored him by not saying anything to him until he told her that they should go back to the church where they eventually left in the car before he came back for them. Once Sebastian came to the car with her parents and Daphne, her mum drove them to the house where she hid into her bedroom until Sebastian put the children to sleep in their bed before she fell asleep with Noah sleeping on her chest for the night.

CHAPTER SIXTY-SIX
(SPRING 1975 – STOCKHOLM, SWEDEN)

They helped Nina and Joseph move into their house that Uncle Sam gave them in his will. They went back to Los Angeles on their private jet with her parents, Oliver's family, Sasha's family, Amelia's family, Uncle Stan, and Thomas. The girls went to their private school during the week. Sebastian spent his days at the studio where she stayed at the house with her parents during the day. She stepped away from work to focus on her family. Since her mother was busy working on her book, she helped her mum potty train Noah. It wasn't working like they wanted it to because he thought that it was a funny game. When they first introduced the toilet to Noah, he told them that it was a garbage can and not a place to go to the bathroom. He was talking in full sentences, so that he could talk to Daphne, and he always told them the most unexpected things that made them laugh at him. This sentence about the toilet being a garbage can is one of his famous sentences. He wasn't wrong in his analysis with the toilet being a garbage can of human waste. Sebastian came home from work asking about how Noah's potty training was going for them. She told him that Noah refused to go to the bathroom where the garbage was going. She explained to him that reverse psychology failed him before Noah told his father about how mommy lied to him to make him go to the bathroom on the toilet. They tried everything that they could think of to make Noah want to use the toilet that didn't work for them.

She begged for her mother's magical touch to help with Noah because she was at her wits end with him. Her mother told her that Noah would use the toilet by himself in less than a week. It didn't surprise her that her mother was right because Noah was fully potty trained in less than a week. He was no longer referring to the toilet as the garbage trap. She struggled to have patience with him to understand where this comment came from in his mind. Since Noah was potty trained at the age of two years old, this meant that they were no longer buying diapers. This was most of their budget that they bought more than anything else for the house.

The next task was to get Noah to stop trying to undress himself as soon as they got home from being out in public somewhere. Daphne caught Noah taking off his pants in the car where she scolded Noah by telling him that he couldn't be a nudist before he told her that he was born naked, so why did he have to wear clothes. She knew that Noah wasn't wrong in his comment, but she couldn't reward him for being right all of the time. She missed it before Noah could talk to them because he was a lot more to handle than Daphne was at that age. At least Daphne didn't try to undress herself in public or try to call everything right that was wrong in society. Daphne required a lot less supervision than Noah because Daphne worked on one coloring book all afternoon and she only had to check on her once until Daphne found her when she was done with her pictures. Noah was everywhere in the house. If she didn't watch him every second that he was awake during the day, then he got into something that he wasn't supposed to get into. Noah broke so many of their glass pieces that were in their house that they apologized to their interior designer for their son breaking all of her one-of-a-kind pieces that she sent them from London where she lived with her own family. Sebastian sent them to get fixed by their repair guy and he sent them back to them in better condition than they received them in. They put their expensive decor away into storage to put out when Noah was out of the vandalism phase. Noah broke their glass table by banging his cup on it so hard that the table shattered into little pieces on the floor. They got rid of any glass furniture pieces in their house. After Noah broke something in the house, he cried that he was sorry for doing it when they told him that they weren't angry with him before they replaced the object that he broke. She wanted to write a screenplay based on the letters that she read from her grandma over the years. In her moments of peace where Noah took a nap or played with her mum, she hid on the floor of her closet where she read the letters that her grandma wrote to people in her life. She was shocked to find out that her mother kept in touch with Camille and Jason when they were living in Sweden. She couldn't believe that she owned Camille's house. Her mother sent Camille letters up until her death in 1945. She saw a series of letters from Camille who was worried if something bad happened to her. No one told her about her grandma's drug overdose. Aunt Sylvia later wrote a letter to her that her mother died from a drug overdose. Camille never wrote back to her because she didn't want anyone else finding out her secret. The conversations that her grandma had with Camille were intimate. It was a conversation between lovers. Her grandma was in love with Camille. She could never be with her because the world would never accept them. Camille and her grandma never signed the letters with their names. They had code names for each other that they used. They never uttered people's names in the letters. After she looked through the letters, Aunt Sylvia thought that these letters were between her parents and not her mother and her secret woman lover. Why else would she give them to her if it wasn't for this reason? Camille called her grandma Lilly Jean, and her grandma called Camille Poppy Seed. They used code names for everything that they were talking about. They didn't want anyone to know that they were in a relationship with each other. Not even their children knew the truth about them.

This was the spark that ignited her next screenplay that she called *Yellow Carnations* that told the story of two women who were deeply in love with each other in the 1920s, but they were forced to hide it from the world. Evelyn lived in London with her husband Francis who was a politician in the House of Commons. Evelyn struggled to conceive, so they didn't have any children. Francis was disappointed about it because he wanted to have a son to take his place in the government. Evelyn met her secret lover Irene when she was on holiday with Francis in Sweden where they shared their first kiss after they went horseback riding. Irene inherited her father's wealth after he died since she didn't have any other siblings to pass it onto. She remained unmarried as an aristocratic woman in Sweden. After Evelyn went to London with her husband Francis, she wrote letters to Irene who she called her yellow carnation. They didn't see each other for a long time because Evelyn was pregnant with Francis' child where she is presented with a new dilemma. Did she stay with Francis to raise her child to be a politician in England or did she run away to live her dream life with Irene? Evelyn took her son Daniel to Sweden with her to spend the rest of her life with Irene. When she presented *Yellow Carnations* to her lawyers, they told her that it was something that was going to be hard to sell to the public. It was a queer love story, and Hollywood didn't make those kinds of stories. Sebastian screamed at them that they were going to find a way to make this movie or else he was going to fire them. Their lawyers rushed out of the room to make frantic phone calls about the issue of the script. They had sex with each other in the middle of the conference room before their lawyers walked into the room with the news that they could make this work. They looked for specific women to cast into the parts of Evelyn and Irene and the child that they wanted to play the part of Daniel. After she found the perfect actors for the roles, they started filming the movie. They had conversations about where she wanted to film the part of the movie that was in Sweden when she told them that she wanted to film the movie at her house in Sweden that she inherited from Uncle Sam's will. This meant that they needed to go to the place to scout for the place for themselves. She took Sebastian, her children since Daphne was on a week break from school, her parents, and Sasha's family with her. She needed Gabriel's help getting photographs of the place for the studio. They left on their private jet with members of their production team before they saw her house in Sweden for the first time. Like Jason's letter told Uncle Sam, the house was everything that she thought that it was going to be. Her grandma's lover spent her lifetime making this house her own. She followed Gabriel around the house while he took photographs of everything that he was drawn to. Sebastian, her parents, Charlotte, Daphne, and Noah played with the horses in the stable before Sasha insisted on Gabriel taking photographs of her in the house. After Gabriel was distracted by Sasha's impromptu modeling session, she joined the children by the stables where she taught everyone how to ride horses. Sebastian asked her who taught her how to do it. She told him that her mother taught her how to do it when they were at the farm in England after her father died before they went home. She filmed for her movie *Yellow Carnations* in the studio for the scenes that took place in London. When she wasn't filming her movie, she was at Jacob's house with Lucy and Sebastian planning Daphne and Noah's joint birthday parties. They were going to have a surprise party since Daphne's friend had one and Daphne asked her if she could have a surprise birthday party. This proved to be a hard task because they couldn't talk about it at the house because Daphne was going to overhear them. Jacob told her that they could plan their children's birthday party at his house without the children overhearing them. After they bounced themes for the birthday party, Jacob recommended that they have a horse themed birthday party since Daphne was obsessed with horses after they went to her house in Sweden. She asked them if the surprise should be that the party would be in Sweden before Sebastian told her that it could be possible to do that if they did it on the weekend. Once she left Lucy to handle the planning for the party, she invited Oliver's family, Amelia's family, and Sasha's family to go to Sweden with them where they agreed to meet them at their private jet. She took a trip to her house in Sweden to see the developments of their renovations on the house that they were doing for the movie and the area of the house that was reserved for the party. Since Daphne had no idea that they were leaving the country, she waited to pack their bags until the middle of the night when her daughter was asleep in her bedroom. She was going to do a bigger surprise with her children. She planned the deals of the surprise with Lucy who was in Sweden for the week.

On the morning of her children's birthday party, she woke up Daphne and Noah in their bedrooms where they ate pancakes for breakfast as she told them that they were going on a trip. Daphne bombarded her with questions about where they were going before she told her that she would figure it out after they got there. Daphne was upset that she didn't know where they were going. She told them that they needed to be out of the house as soon as Sebastian placed their bags in the back of the car where she placed the children in their car seats before their driver drove them to the airport. As soon as their driver dropped them off at the airport, she held onto Daphne's hand with Noah on her hip as Sebastian led them to their private jet where they greeted everyone with tight hugs before their pilot flew them to

Stockholm. When their plane landed at the Stockholm airport, she told Daphne and Noah to stay on the plane until it was time to get off of it as they held onto each of their hands. They told them it was time to get off of the plane where Daphne ran ahead from Noah who hung onto her legs before Daphne shouted out that they were in Sweden. They got into cars that took them to the house as Lucy greeted them on the front steps when she told them that everything was set up for the surprise before everyone went into the horse stables where they were horseback riding for the rest of the afternoon. The sun set in the sky as they ate dinner in the grass that consisted of finger sandwiches and biscuits that Sebastian joked was the most English style meal before it was time for dessert where Lucy brought out two cakes for Daphne and Noah that they placed in front of them. Daphne blew out the five candles on her cake and Noah blew out the two candles on his cake. Gabriel took a picture of them as they kissed their children's cheeks with Daphne making a funny face at the camera where Noah stuck his tongue out to the camera before they gave everyone a piece of cake. Noah sat in her lap as she helped him open up his presents as Daphne got help opening up her presents from Katherine and Charlotte. When it was time for the surprise, she winked at Lucy who rushed over to grab the lighter from her pocket before she told everyone to look up at the sky. As soon as everyone looked up at the sky, Lucy lit the end of match that set off fireworks that exploded in the air as she pulled Daphne on her lap where Noah sat on Sebastian's lap with his hands over his son's ears. Daphne shouted to her over the cracking noises that this was the best surprise party before she pulled Daphne into a tight hug with her face hidden in her chest. Once the fireworks were done, she laid down on the blanket with Daphne and Noah laying in between them as Daphne laid her head down on her mother's chest where she pointed up at the stars when she asked her with excitement laced in her voice, "There's Polaris, mommy! You are right! It is everywhere!"

She tightened her grip on Daphne's arms when she responded to her with a smile on her face, "Good job, little bee! You found it by yourself. Do you remember what I told you that Polaris means?"

She grabbed onto her daughter's hands when Daphne responded to her with a look of innocence on her face, "It means that mommy and daddy are always with us. I love you, mommy. I love you, daddy. I love you, Noah. Even though you are annoying."

Noah wrestled with Daphne where they rolled around on the blanket before they separated them from each other. After Daphne was in Sebastian's arms with Noah in her arms, she ran her fingers through Noah's hair as he sat down in her lap when she told him in a stern voice, "Noah William. We don't hurt our sister. That's not right. You guys can play with each other, but I don't want anyone getting hurt. Tell Daphne that you are sorry for pulling her hair."

Noah let out a defeated sigh when he said to Daphne refusing to look at her, "I'm sorry for putting your hair, Daphne. That was bad of me."

She pulled Noah into a tight hug as she peppered his face with kisses that led to him smiling at her when she responded to him with a smirk on her face, "That's good, Noah William. Be responsible for your actions. I think that it's time to give you a haircut, little critter. It's almost as long as Daphne's hair. How about that? How does that sound?"

Sebastian asked Daphne with a smile on his face, "What did you wish for, little bee? A horse?"

Daphne grabbed onto her father's hands when she responded to him with a frown on her face, "No, I wish that we don't have to go to funerals anymore. I don't want anyone else to die. Can I have that wish, dad?"

As Sebastian looked over at her, she grabbed onto Daphne's hands when she responded to her daughter with a serious look on her face, "I'm sorry baby. We can't promise you. People get sick and doctors can't heal them. They can't fight sicknesses like they used to. Does that make sense?"

Daphne placed her head on her mother's lap when she asked her with a frown on her face, "Is that what happened to grandpa? Was he sick like Uncle Sam and Aunt Sylvia were?"

Her face turned white as Sebastian grabbed onto her hands. She didn't know how to answer her daughter's question. She didn't think that she'd have to explain what happened to her father. Sebastian struggled with what to say about Daphne's question because his eyes told her that they needed to retreat from this. She ran her fingers through her daughter's hair when she responded to her with her blinking back tears that fell down her face, "Your grandpa struggled a lot in his life. He didn't know how to handle things. Do you remember when I told you that mommy used to be involved in bad things? Grandpa did those things too. Except grandpa didn't stop like mommy did. Look, Daph. Sometimes people die without being sick. Grandpa wasn't sick when he died. At least with physical sickness. He was mentally sick. His mental illness killed him. He did everything that he could to stay with us, but he couldn't handle it anymore. Mommy isn't mad at him for what he did to her. I got over it a long time ago. You can be upset about it if it upsets you. Does it upset you?"

As Sebastian adjusted Noah who was asleep on his chest, Daphne shrugged her shoulders at her when she responded to her mother with a neutral look on her face, "I don't know if it upsets me, mommy. I think that it doesn't upset me, but I'm not sure. Why would you be mad at him? Did he hurt you like he hurt Grandma Ella?"

She looked over at Sebastian when she responded to her daughter with tears falling down her face, "Yeah, he hurt me baby. Not the same way that he hurt Grandma Ella. There are different ways that people can hurt each other. There are different levels of pain that people inflict upon each other. Sometimes they mean it and other times they don't mean it. Your grandpa hurt me by not being in my life. He didn't think that he could hurt me if he wasn't with me. I used to be mad at him because he left me alone in the world. He didn't want to do that to me. He spent a lifetime alone. He didn't know that he was hurting me. He didn't mean to do it. I don't know if he cared about me or not. He never told me anything about him. Daph. Don't let yourself do something like that. It's not worth it. Trust me when I tell you that mommy learned it the hard way."

Daphne hid her face into her mother's chest as she softly cried into her daughter's hair when Daphne asked her with her voice muffled by her dress, "Did you try what he did to himself?"

This conversation was far beyond anything she imagined telling her five-year-old daughter, but she was too deep into it to turn back now. Sebastian was too speechless to say anything to help her out of this situation. Out of all of the thoughts that were racing in her mind, she said in full confidence to her daughter, "Yes, I did. I tried it a few times. It didn't work. Your grandpa was right about a lot of things, but he was wrong about that. It didn't do me any good to do that. It won't do you any good either. I love you, little bee. I'm only telling you this so that you don't make my mistakes. I wish your grandma told me this when I was growing up. I didn't know that I needed to hear it until it was too late to stop it. It would break my heart if something happened to you or your brother."

After Daphne nodded her head at her, Sebastian let out an exhausted sigh as she looked at him with a silent look on her face where he carried Noah into the house who was asleep in his arms before she followed him into the house with Daphne in her arms. Once they put their children in their bedrooms for the night, she changed into her silk pajamas as she laid down in the bed with her head leaning on Sebastian's chest where he wrapped his arms around her when he asked her with uncertainty laced in his voice, "Why did you say all of that to Daphne? You didn't have to do it."

After she looked up at him with her elbows standing up on his chest, she let out a shaky breath when she responded to him with a frown on her face, "I'm not lying to our daughter, Bash. I had to tell her. I didn't have a choice. She was going to find out about it at some point, so it's better if she hears it from me. It's better that she knows. I didn't know that when I was her age. No one bothered to tell me about it when I was child. It's the least that Daphne deserves."

Sebastian pulled her into a desperate kiss where they didn't pull away from each other until they were out of breath before she laid her head down on his chest with his arms tightly around her. She broke the silence between them when she said to him with a smile on her face, "For the record, I'm not disagreeing with your point, but you were wrong about something. Daphne can handle it. She's stronger than we think that she is. She's better than us."

Sebastian nodded his head at her when he responded to her with a smirk on his face, "You're right. Daphne is stronger than I thought that she was. She's like her mother. She's smart, stubborn, and strong. I love you so much. You are the strongest person that I know. Daphne will be okay like us." After Sebastian pulled her into a long kiss, they pulled away from each other with smiles on their faces where they told each other goodnight before she fell asleep in Sebastian's arms for the rest of the night.

Chapter Sixty-Seven
(Summer 1975 – Stockholm, Sweden)

They spent two more days in Sweden exploring the property and she taught the children how to ride horses. They went home to Los Angeles to go back to their normal lives. Daphne and the girls had a few more weeks left of the school year. They made plans to spend the summer in Sweden. Sebastian came every other week because he needed to run the studio in their absence. Once they were done filming the scenes of *Yellow Carnations*, their production team prepared for their transition to film the rest of the movie in Sweden. Daphne was finishing school as her mum stayed home with Daphne and Sebastian while she went to Sweden with Noah and her mother. She was in the process of working on a new book since she published her other book a few months ago. Her mum and Daphne would join them once she was done with school. She had a fun summer planned for them when they weren't filming her movie on the other side of the house. The filming days went by quickly because she was worried about what direction the camera was going in or she was concerned if something that wasn't supposed to be the background was in the frame of the camera. They didn't need to get any props for the 1920s and 1930s because Camille's house was designed like a house from that time period. Something told her that Camille was an elegant woman throughout her life. That was why she was confused how Camille ended up in a small town like York when she could've been anywhere in the world. Clearly Camille was a wealthy woman because this house was worth over a million pounds in the 1940s. She was curious about Camille's backstory. She didn't know how an elegant woman ended up being the mistress of a poor worker in the coal mines. Being in the house where Camille lived for most of her life was surreal for her. She felt like the spirit of Camille was there with her. No one was alive to tell the tale of Camille, so she wrote that part for herself. This was the exciting part of writing screenplays. Finding out the reason that her characters were the way that they were. How did her character Irene live such an elegant lifestyle? Why was her character Evelyn so drawn to Irene? Was it Irene's energy that she put out into the world? Was it Irene's desire to know the human heart? What made Irene so drawn to Evelyn? Was it Evelyn's tenderness towards her? Was it Evelyn's love of nature more than other love in the universe?

She based characteristics of Irene and Evelyn on her and Sebastian. That was one love that she knew better than any other. She wanted people to feel it when Irene and Evelyn realized that they loved each other. She wanted people to be heartbroken when Irene and Evelyn realized that they could never be together because the world would never accept them. She wanted people to know what it felt like to long for something that you could never have. The desperation that you would do anything to get it. She projected this feeling onto Irene and Evelyn that she felt towards her father. The desire to know him and to have him in her life blinded her from anything else. This feeling towards him wasn't healthy. It took her a long time to recognize that. It was the first thing that she became addicted to. Long before she was addicted to drugs. She was addicted to that desperation that her father made her feel in her heart. The longing for a relationship that she could never have with her father. The desperation for justice in the world because of the injustice that her father experienced in his life. Correcting the wrongs that her father inflicted on the world because he wasn't there to correct them. She realized that it was all in vain.

None of it mattered. She spent a long-time spiraling about it. It didn't mean anything. His sacrifice didn't do anything. His death didn't mean anything greater to the world. It was hard for her to accept that it was for nothing. How could that pain and suffering that she went through not mean anything? How did her parent's pain not mean anything? It was easier for her to believe in the fantasy. It justified to her why her father wanted to kill himself. If her father knew that his death held a greater purpose, then he would've loved to do it. He'd do it again for them if it meant something in the universe. If she believed in God, then it might mean something to her. She never believed in God. It didn't mean that she didn't believe in anything. She believed in the stars. She believed in her father. She didn't know why she believed in her father. He gave her no reason to trust him. He lied to her about everything that happened to him. He was a distant figure in the background of the photograph. Never in the mainframe, but her eyes saw him when he briefly appeared in front of her. She never cared what was left to see in the photograph. She was always looking for him. When she missed what was happening around her, she was too busy looking for him. She spent a lifetime looking for him and he never once looked for her. He would never look for her because he was always looking for himself. He never cared about her the same way that she cared about him. Oliver tried to tell her that a long time ago, but she didn't want to hear it. The world never cared about her. Her father never cared about her. Sebastian, Daphne, and her mum joined them in Sweden for the next month. That was a much-needed distraction from her current mid-life crisis. She spent her free moments with Sebastian and her children. Daphne told her that she was going to brag to her friends at school that she spent the summer at her mother's house in Sweden with her horses. She told Daphne that she didn't want to make other children feel bad about themselves where Daphne responded to her that she didn't care what other people thought about her. She was shockingly proud of her daughter for being so confident about herself because she wasn't that confident in herself. By the middle of the summer, they were done filming her movie *Yellow Carnations*. Their production team left the house. She left Daphne and Noah with her parents while she went back to the states with Sebastian before she worked with the editors in the studio for a few weeks. She told them to wait on releasing the movie until they were back from Sweden. They were going on an international press tour for the movie that Lucy was planning for them. The reason that they waited to release the movie was because their lawyers were in the middle of contracts with the movie theatres. The contracts said that they wouldn't stop showing their movies if they pushed them to show *Yellow Carnations* in theatres.

They couldn't show any movies in theatres until they had signed contracts from them, and many owners were dragging their feet about not signing it. She didn't care what their excuses were for not signing the contracts. She instructed their lawyers to do whatever they needed to do to make sure that they signed those contracts by the end of the summer. She told them that she didn't want to know what they did to make it happen. Sebastian knew that it was important for the future of their film studio to have these safety nets in place for any movies that she was going to make that might be controversial that the theatres wouldn't like to show. It felt like someone was watching her. She tried to get over it, but she couldn't shake the feeling. She walked around the house looking for something to distract herself from her spiraling mind while Sebastian and the children swam in the pool. Daphne begged her to join them in the pool, but she told her daughter that she would join them after she took a nap. She tried to take a nap in their bedroom, but her mind wouldn't shut off no matter what she did to make it quiet. She got up to get a glass of water in the kitchen when she tried to take a nap after that. She intended on fulfilling that promise before she walked into Camille's office. Camille's old office that looked like it hadn't been touched in over twenty years. She messed with the drawers in the desk that had blank pieces of paper in it before she found out that the bottom drawer was locked. After she tried for several minutes to get into the locked drawer, she let out a defeated sigh as she was about to walk away from it until she felt a taped key under the bottom drawer where she put the key into the hole before she heard a click when she unlocked the drawer. Once she placed the key back under the drawer, she opened up the drawer to see stacks of letters that Camille sent to her grandma after she moved to Sweden with Jason. Once she grabbed the letter on the top of the pile, she let out a soft sigh when she whispered with a frown on her face, "Let's see what Camille had to say about grandma. I've never been more curious in my life." After she opened the letter from the envelope, she read it as she sat down on the floor with her legs crossed.

May 1940
To my dearest Lilly Jean,

I'm sorry that Popeye died overseas. I heard from my friends about his death. They told me that you weren't taking it well. It explains why you haven't written back to me for three weeks. I was worried that something happened to you, but I understand it. Take all of the time that you need to write back to me. I know that you had a complicated relationship with Popeye, but you always loved him. I felt the same way. Popeye was special to me. He was the only man that I loved in my life. I'll be here waiting for you when you are ready for me. We don't have to make this serious if you aren't ready for it. No matter what decision that you make I want you to know that I'll always support you no matter what. My love for you knows no bounds. If you are feeling lost in the world, you can always come to me. I'll be there to hold you in the middle of the storm. I hope that you are well, my love. Here's to being reunited again.

With Love, Your Poppy Seed

March 1943
To my dearest Lilly Jean,

Spending this time in Sweden with you were the best days of my life. Waking up with your arms around me. The smell of your hair. The delicate touch of your skin. The tenderness of your hands. If I died tomorrow, I would die the happiest woman in the world. I miss you so much. Ever since you left me to go to England with your children, my heart aches for you like it's ached for no one else. JJ asks about you every morning. I told him that you had to go home to your family. He doesn't understand that you have a family that isn't us. He's only four years old, so he doesn't know better than that. It's better for us to be apart from each other. People would suspect that something was going on between us. We would never want anyone finding out the truth about us. The world wouldn't be able to handle it. They aren't ready for us. I dream about a world where I hold your hand in public and I exclaim to the world that you are the person that I love more than life itself. I fear that the world won't be there when we are around. Someday it will be there. For our children. For their children. I want my JJ to tell me about the world after I'm gone someday. I want him to tell me that everything that I did meant something. I made a difference in the world. If it didn't mean anything, then I know that it meant something to us. We mean something. Even though the world refuses to acknowledge that we exist, they will see it someday. Everyone will know about us, my love. We'll become famous because we did the thing that no one was brave enough to do. We loved each other without any hesitancy. We embraced our love for each other.

With Love, Your Poppy Seed

May 1945
My Dearest Poppy Seed,

This is the last letter that I'm going to write to you. I'm about to do something that will shock you and my children. It might shock the world. I'm going to overdose tonight. I've been planning to do this for several months. It was the right time. I bought pills from my dealer and I'm going to take the whole bottle. No one knows about my plans except for you and Willie. Neither of you can stop me because you live in Sweden and Willie is in prison in England. I don't know why I decided to only tell you two about it, but it felt fair since you guys were the only people that I loved in my life. I can't take it anymore. The lying is killing me. The secrets are drowning me. It breaks my heart that I can't be who I am to the world. I'm not just talking about being in love with you. It's the drugs. My children know that I'm using drugs again and they know that I'm lying to them. I'm sick of letting them down. I feel like all that I've ever done for anyone is let them down. I can't handle that feeling of guilt that's inside of me. It's consuming what is left of my soul. The part that Popeye didn't rob from me. The part that I gave to you. Please know that this decision wasn't because of you. You were the best thing that happened to me. You'll always be a part of me. Even after I'm gone from the world, I'll be there with you in the stars.

I love you. Your Lilly Jean

She placed the pile of letters onto the floor as she let out a defeated sigh when she whispered to herself with devastation laced in her voice, "Fuck you, grandma. You gave dad the idea, didn't you? Did he only kill himself because you did it first? These secrets are like a poison that leaks through the ceiling. In the beautifulness of this house, there's a dark truth hidden inside of it. The truth is that nothing ever changes. I was always going to be the person that was meant to become like my dad and my grandma. I wonder what happened to Camille. I wonder if she survived or not after this." Once she grabbed the letter at the bottom of the pile, she read the last letter that Camille wrote to her grandma.

March 1955
To My Dearest Lilly Jean

It's been almost ten years since you killed yourself. It's been four years since Willie killed himself. He visited me when he got out of prison. It was after his custody hearing with Ladybug and Butterfly. Willie told me that he wanted to see them one last time before he killed himself. Instead of him killing himself in 1949, I made him stay in Sweden with me for almost a year until his brother showed up looking for him. Bigfoot thought that I was keeping Willie hostage here, but I told him that it was the other way around. I was keeping him safe. JJ's gotten very attached to him. He cried when Willie went back to England with Bigfoot. JJ told me that he wished that Willie was his father. I told him that he was a father to a baby girl that he wasn't involved with. I hurt JJ when I said that to him. It made him sad for her. Willie confessed to me that he felt so bad for leaving his daughter behind after he saw her for the first time. He told me that he cried himself to sleep for years after that. When we weren't talking to each other about our deepest regrets, we were talking about our fears. I told him that I was scared that it didn't mean anything. The life that I had with you. Willie expressed the same thought towards Ladybug and Butterfly. This led us to a lot of existential questions. Did we even mean anything? How about our mistakes? Did they mean anything? How about our choices? Did they mean anything? The more questions that we came up with the more that we realized that there's no way for us to know the answers. I expressed to Willie that I wanted to believe in something, but I don't believe in God. Who was I supposed to believe in if I couldn't believe in God? Do you want to know what Willie told me? He said to me, "Camille, there's no one else to believe in except for the stars. They can't judge us like God does. They don't determine what is right and wrong in the universe. They are detached from the world. We can't define ourselves by God's standards. The universe doesn't care what we do. We choose our path in life and that's the door that we go down." He was right, my love. The minute that I believed in the stars it made me feel freer than I've felt before in my life. I met a girl named Olga and she's everything that I've been looking for in a long time. No one could replace you, but she's good for me. Olga treats JJ like her own son and JJ is obsessed with her. They have a special bond with each other. This is the last time that I'm writing to you. I'm not dying any time soon, but it's time to move on without you. I've resisted this for a long time because I didn't want to lose you. I wasn't ready to lose you. These letters were all that I had left from you. Writing to you made you feel alive to me. JJ tells me that it's not healthy to do this to myself. Obsessing over what I can't have. I should've learned from Willie that it only ends one way when you do that to yourself. I don't want to leave JJ behind. I've always stuck around for him. There would be no one to raise him if I left him alone in the world. Someday when JJ has his own life I can leave him. Just not right now. The stars will be okay without me. You and Willie will keep each other company while I'm gone. You guys have always been good at laughing together. I'll give you some advice. Life is like a hike where you spend what feels like an eternity to get to the top. While you are making your way to the top of the mountain, all that you can think about is how you feel like this is never going to end. You are never going to make it to the top of the mountain. You start to question yourself if it's worth it or if it's possible to get to the top of the mountain. The mountain isn't real and I'm doing all of this work to get there for nothing. You are about to give up until you see the peak of the mountain in the distance. You can't give up now. You are so close to the top. Something happens to stop you from getting to the top of the mountain. A tree falls in your path, and you have to go the longer way to the destination. When you see the mountain peak in front of you, you spirit towards it like there isn't a tired bone left in your body. You see it for the first time. You see the valley in between the mountains. The view is breathtaking. It's more beautiful than any painting in the world. It was worth it. It was worth everything that it took to get here. You sacrificed everything. You went through a lot of pain and suffering. It's worth the view. When I want to die, I say, "You didn't get to see the view. There are so many steps until we get to the top of the mountain. Don't you want to see the view?" That stops me. Damn, can't I wait to see that view? I can't wait to see it. All that matters to me is the view.

With Love, Your Poppy Seed

As she let out suppressed sobs into her hands, she placed the last letter onto the floor as she angrily kicked the desk when she yelled to herself with desperation laced in her voice, "Goddamnit, dad! You can't do this to me! I can't find out the truth this way! You can't ignore me only for me to find out that you died thinking about me! Why did you come to Camille over me or mom? Why couldn't you come to us instead of her? This isn't fair, dad! All of this time of me thinking that you didn't want me! None of it was true! I can't believe this! I need to get out of this house or else I'm going to hurt myself!"

She sprinted out of Camille's office with her slamming the door shut behind her. She ran into the yard where Sebastian sat by the pool alone since the children took their evening naps as he tried to approach her before she ran away from him. She sprinted towards the horse stables as the attendant threw a horse towards her where she got on the horse's back before she sped away from him. She steered her horse at full speed with the sun setting in the sky as she got to her destination with Sebastian following far enough away from her that she didn't feel like he was cornering her. After she got off of her horse at the top of the mountain, she held onto her horse with her other hand when she shouted out loud over the mountain with a smile on her face, "Look at that view! I would kill myself after I saw something as beautiful as this! I understand you, Camille! I think that we are the same person! It can't be this simple, can't I? I can't believe this!"

As soon as Sebastian ran over to her with his horse closely following him, he pulled her into a desperate hug as she hid her face in his chest when he asked her with concern laced in his voice, "Are you okay, Isabella? You're not going to throw yourself off of the mountain, are you? I didn't bring back up with me to stop you."

She pulled her face out of his chest as she responded to him with a wide grin on her face, "No, I'm not going to throw myself off of a mountain, Bash. That would be too painful. This is where Camille told me where to go to stop myself from killing myself. I needed to see the view to remind me of everything that was worth living."

Sebastian raised his eyebrows in confusion when he asked her with a frown on his face, "Who is Camille? What did she tell you? How did she tell you that?"

She kept a tight grip on her horse's harness when she responded to him with an annoyed look on her face, "It's complicated, Bash. I can explain it to you later. She was out here saving lives. Even after her death she's saving lives."

Sebastian's face softened as he grabbed onto her hands when he responded to her with a sad smile on his face, "Camille as in the house used to belong to her? What did she tell you that saved your life?"

She leaned onto his chest when she responded to him with excitement laced in her face, "It's that Camille. She said to my grandma years after her death that she had a trick to keeping herself alive. She couldn't die before she saw the view. The view was worth all of the pain and suffering that it took to get there. This is what is keeping me alive. After I find out that my dad thought about me before he died, this stops me from wanting to kill myself." Sebastian tightened his grip when he responded to her in a stern voice, "We can talk about this later. I don't feel comfortable with you standing on top of a mountain declaring that you feel like you want to kill yourself. We need to go home before one of us does something that we might regret. That person wouldn't be me. It's you. Ride down to the house with me." After she rode down the mountain with Sebastian's horse leading them, they left their horses in the stables with the attendant as he kept a tight grip on her hand like she was a child that was going to run away from him where he let go of her once they were in the house before she ran away from him with Sebastian running behind her. Once they were in their bedroom, he told her to get ready for bed as she complied with his request because he made those concerned eyes at her that made her skin crawl where he got into the bed with her before she fell asleep in his arms for the rest of the night.

Chapter Sixty-Eight
(Fall 1975 – Los Angeles, California)

Sebastian packed up their bags when she asked him why he was packing their bags since they were supposed to be in Sweden longer. He told her that they were going back to the states early before she disappeared into Camille's office for the rest of the morning. She brought a bag from her closet to stuff the letters into because she didn't want to leave them behind in Sweden. She was pulled out of hiding by her mother who was confused why they were leaving so soon. She shrugged her shoulders as she placed her bag of letters in the back of the car where she got into the back seat of the car in between her children who were more confused than her about what was happening before their driver dropped them off at the airport. Once they got on the private jet by themselves, Sebastian didn't explain to her why they were going on home after she asked him about it three times where she did puzzles with Daphne and Noah on the table before they fell asleep on either side of her for the rest of the flight. After their private jet landed at the LAX airport the next morning, she carried Noah on her hip as she held onto Daphne's hand with Sebastian leading them to the car where she got into the back of the car with her children as Sebastian took a seat across from them before their driver dropped them off at the house. As she walked out of the car with Noah on her hip, she saw Jacob's car in the driveway as she gave Sebastian a look of confusion that he didn't look up at her where she walked into the living room with Jacob sitting on the couch waiting for her before she stared at him unable to move away from the door.

Before she got the chance to say anything to him, Jacob ran over towards her as he pulled her into a tight hug with her face hidden in his chest until Noah whined to be put down on the floor where she placed Noah on the floor with him running to his toys on the couch before she asked Jacob what he was doing at her house. Jacob gave Sebastian a look that she didn't appreciate when he asked her if she wanted to talk in her bedroom where she accepted his request before she followed Jacob into her bedroom. She didn't feel like they were giving her any choice in the matter. As soon as she closed the door behind them, she got irritated with him because he wasn't saying anything to her. She asked him if he had a question that he wanted to ask her or was he going insane by staring at her. Jacob took a seat next to him on the bed before she complied with his instructions because she didn't have a choice. Jacob found the courage to ask her if she was feeling suicidal right now. She let out a frustrated sigh because she knew that this was what it was about. She responded to him that she thought about killing herself in Sweden, but she stopped herself from doing it before Jacob asked her what stopped her from doing it.

She grabbed the letter that Camille never sent to her grandma that she hid in her pocket as she handed it over to him where he raised his eyebrows in confusion before he read the letter. Jacob handed the letter back to her when he asked her who Camille was where she told him that she would explain the context to him later as she asked him what he thought about the last paragraph of the letter before he asked her if that was what stopped her from killing herself. It was a confirmation to him that it was true. He asked her how she felt about what Camille said about her father before she pulled out a cigarette from her pocket to smoke it on her balcony even though she didn't smoke anymore. She told Jacob that she was angry at her father for not coming to them over Camille who didn't know him. He challenged her when he asked her how she knew that her father didn't know Camille just because she didn't know anything about it. She told him that she didn't want him to know her because it meant that Oliver and Sebastian were right. She didn't know anything about him. She would never know anything about him. They talked about how Camille's letters made her feel about what she thought that she knew about her father. When Camille said that JJ wanted Will to be his father, she wanted to scream at Jason that he wasn't his father. He never belonged to her. She wanted him to belong to her like she belonged to her mother, or their children belonged to them. He was supposed to belong to her. She was his flesh and blood. Her father belonged to her grandma, Camille, and Jason. Not Isabella or her mother. Her father belonged to these strangers over his family. It hurt her that he wanted to belong to these people over them. Her father was more comfortable with her grandma, Camille, and Jason than with his real family. They were more accepting of him than they would be of him. Her father let them into his life because he felt like they were the only people that he could trust. They were the only people that understood him. They were the only people that saw him for who he was. They were like him. Outcasted from society. Left with no one to hold onto except each other. A cruel and uncaring world left them to die alone and scared. She saw the real side of her father that he hid from the world. The honest side of him. The part of himself that wasn't tangled in a web of lies. No matter how inappropriate her grandma's relationship was with her father, they understood each other on a deeper level than anyone else. They knew what it was like to be trapped by the burdens of the world. The addiction that plagued their lives from the moment that they were born. The way that their brains couldn't stand to live in the world after it only hurt them. The injustice that they experienced from everyone else. The loveless relationships that didn't fulfill them like they were supposed to. The darkness that followed them everywhere that they went in the world. The suffocating feeling of being trapped in moments that they could never move on from. Those were feelings that she understood more than anyone else. This was why she was impacted by those letters. She felt every word of them. She never read anything that she understood as deeply as those letters. Like she was the person writing those words on paper in a different lifetime. That was why Uncle Sam left her the house and the treasures hidden within it. He knew that she would understand it more than anyone in the family. Now that these emotions existed inside of her, she didn't know what to do with them. What was she supposed to do after this? How could she move on if these feelings were inside of her? There were two doors for her to choose from that appeared in front of her. One doorway was the path that her grandma and her father chose that led to their self-destruction in the end. The other door was the path that Camille chose that led her to the path less traveled despite only seeing pain in the world.

She wasn't able to sleep at night as she smoked cigarettes on the balcony where she thought about what she was going to do after her world shattered around her. She was at a crossroads where she was presented with the choice of what door that she wanted to go into that was going to determine what her life was going to look like after this. Was she going to choose the path of self-destruction? Or was she going to choose the path that was less traveled? Was she going to become a Will or a Camille? She'd been in this place before in her life. The crossroads that an addict always found themselves in. The path of self-destruction or the path of uncertainty. It was never easy when she found herself in this place. She was torn on which one to choose. After she smoked more cigarettes than she did in five years, she came to the conclusion that she would see what path was chosen for her. She reminded herself of the view and it stopped her from thinking about killing herself. After she spent a few days mopping around the house, she was brought back into the real world again when their lawyer's called her to tell them that the last movie theatre signed the new contracts where they told her that it was time to premiere the new movie. She kicked herself into high gear preparing for her international press tour. On the same week that she left for two months on her press tour, Daphne had her first day of school as her parents returned back to the states from their trip to England after visiting their family before Sebastian took over duties at the studio. After she said goodbye to her family, their driver dropped them off at the airport where she met up with the cast before they went to their stop on the press tour to Perth, Australia. This was her first time in Australia, and she was obsessed with it from the moment that she stepped foot off of the plane. She didn't pack accordingly because it was the middle of summer, and she brought clothes for winter where she bought new clothes with Lucy at the best boutiques. They did a similar format to their last international press tour where they watched *Yellow Carnations* at the movie theaters before they asked them what they thought about it after they watched it. While they went to a new European city every two days, her movie *Yellow Carnations* was premiering in the states at the same time where it was already setting records. There were whispers that *Yellow Carnations* was going to be nominated for an Oscar, but they wouldn't know until she got back to the states after her press tour was done. They were being ambitious with this press tour because this format worked with their European and Asian audiences. They loved to feel like they were special by getting to meet the people that were a part of the movie. No one else in Hollywood was doing this, so this was more special to them. This wasn't the way that American audiences wanted to experience their entertainment. They were interested in being left to their own devices to consume the movie. This was based on research that her team did during the last movie. They wanted to do what would work best for their different audiences from all around the world. She knew from working as an actress that she was only going to succeed if she sold herself correctly to the world. The world would only like her if she sold them the image that they wanted from her. She was a professional at this because her addiction taught her how to sell herself a long time ago. That was only a part of the complicated reality of being an addict. It was required for her to learn to survive in the world. That's why she was so drawn to acting when she was growing up because she was already doing what they were doing on the big screen. The only difference between her and the actors on the television was that they got paid for what they did, and she wasn't getting paid for it. She couldn't tell any of this to her parents that she wanted to be an actress because she wanted to get paid for her performances. They didn't need to know the truth about it. They were better off without it. The world was better off without the truth. She stopped thinking about her father, Camille, and her grandma during the day. She was so busy with the press tour that she barely had a moment alone with her thoughts. The only time that she thought about them was when she was alone in her hotel room at night where she drove herself insane about it until she passed out in her bed for the rest of the night. She did this no matter what city in the world that she was in. She forgot that she could never run away from herself. Even though she was spiraling in her mind, she put on her best act for everyone to see because they didn't need to know what was going on with her. The only person that was with her that knew that something was wrong with her was her assistant Lucy. They had more important things to focus on than her crumbling mental health. She was a movie producer that was proud of her revolutionary movie that was changing the world.

She got an urgent phone call from Oliver that his mother had a heart attack and if he could leave the girls with them for a few weeks while they were in England. She told him that she would have to ask Sebastian if the girls could stay with them. Oliver told her that he already asked Sebastian that question and that he said that they could stay with them. She told Oliver that she would see the girls when she got back to the house in a few days where Oliver thanked her before he hung up the phone on her in a hurry to leave the house. When her private jet landed at the airport, Daphne pulled her mother into a tight hug as she pulled Noah into their group hug where she pulled the children away from her before Sebastian pulled her into a passionate kiss that she wasn't expecting from him. As soon as they pulled away from each other, her thirteen-year-old niece Posey pulled her into a tight hug with her seven-year-old sister Eleanor pulling herself into their hug. Posey thanked her for letting them stay at their house while their parents were in England before she told her that she would do anything for Oliver. Once their driver dropped them off at the house, Posey watched Noah in his bedroom as Eleanor and Posey played with barbies in her bedroom. They made up for lost time in their bed before they laid there in each other's arms until Noah stormed into their bedroom with Posey running behind him. She dropped off Posey at the middle school before she dropped off Daphne and Eleanor at the elementary school where she stayed home with Noah all day. Her parents were in England with Oliver and Juliet after Aunt Priscilla's heart attack where she was in the hospital recovering from it. Noah was a wild child that caused complete carnage around the house, but she was too depressed to care about it. She didn't clean the house anymore. Posey cleaned the house for her during the weekend when she wasn't in school because her mother had her clean at home. She didn't mind having a teenager in her house. Posey took care of Noah, and she played with Eleanor and Daphne when she took her afternoon nap. She joked with Posey after the children went to bed that she could stay with them if she wanted to after her parents got back from England. Posey told her that she didn't think that her father would like that, but she could babysit Noah and Daphne when she wasn't busy with school. They made jokes with each other until she went to bed in her bedroom for the rest of the night. Sebastian was out of town for several weeks while she was alone with the girls and Noah. Posey helped her keep the house going without Sebastian. She put Noah to sleep in his bedroom and she put Daphne and Eleanor to sleep in Daphne's bedroom one night where she went into Posey's bedroom to tell her that she needed to go to bed soon. Posey told her with her face out of her book that she would be sleeping in ten minutes after she finished reading the chapter. After she walked into her bedroom, she went into the bathroom to take a shower as she changed into her silk pajamas where she walked out onto the balcony before she lit a cigarette with her inhaling the smoke from it. She was only smoking at night where she gave into some relief that the world had to offer her.

After she sat in silence for a while, she lit another cigarette as she inhaled the smoke from it as she rested her feet on top of the railing when she said aloud to herself with a frown on her face, "Hello, dad. It's been a while since we last talked to each other. I learned a lot about you. I know about your relationship with grandma. I thought that it was about drugs. I was surprised to learn that it was more than that. You guys had a deep emotional bond with each other. You had a better relationship with her than her children did. Maybe not Kenny. I know that they had a deeper bond with each other. I was surprised to hear about your relationship with Camille and JJ. They cared about you. That's good. There weren't enough people that cared about you. I am glad that you had them. I thought that you died alone. It turns out that you weren't alone. It made me feel better. That was something that I never thought that I would tell you. I'm happy that you weren't alone. I'm glad that grandma was good to you. Even though I don't agree with some parts of your relationship, she loved you for who you were. Not the person that you wanted people to think that you were. The person that you were deep inside of your heart. Do you want to hear a twisted thought? I wish that I was the person that everyone thought that I was. It would be easier if I didn't have to pretend anymore. I told Uncle Sam at his funeral that I was done lying to the world. I didn't mean that I was done lying to myself. I'm never going to be able to stop lying to myself. It's hard to not lie to myself. I've spent a lifetime doing it. Once an addict, always an addict. Right?"

She inhaled the smoke from her cigarette when she responded to him with her blinking back tears that fell down her face, "I found out a lot more about you in Sweden. I found out a lot about myself too. You are going to laugh at me for saying this. I always do this thing that I can't stand more than anything. I find myself in this place where I'm trapped in between the person that I used to be and the person that I want to be. There's this doorway where I have to make a choice between which one I'm going to choose. The problem is that I don't know where either of them lead me. How am I supposed to make the right choice if I don't know what I'm choosing? It's an impossible task to ask someone to do. I want to do the right thing for myself and my children. Sometimes I don't know what that is. I can't tell what's a right decision between a wrong decision. That's a part of being an addict. Not being able to tell between right and wrong. You know that feeling, don't you? It's hard to tell the difference between them. There isn't one version of right and wrong in the world. The truth is full of nuisances and bullshit. That's what makes life exciting, right? The highs and lows of learning what is right and wrong for you. It's the world's most complicated game that you are never going to win. There aren't any winners. There are only losers in the game of life. We live and we die in a world that doesn't mean anything to us. There is no mercy for the wicked. I've heard Uncle James say it from the Bible. I wonder who God is referring to when he says the wicked. He means people like us. The addicts. The liars. The cheaters. The crooks. People who take advantage of other people. Not like I believe in God because I don't believe in him. He never believed in me. Why should I believe in him? No one believed in me. I don't believe in myself. It's a sad world. A woman that doesn't believe in anything and no one believes in her. That should be my next screenplay about a woman that no one believes in because she's so lost to the world. Lost forever in the stars."

She inhaled the smoke from her cigarette as she let out heartbreaking sobs into her hands when she responded to herself, "I'm not mad at you for not coming to me, dad. I wouldn't come to me either. What was I going to do to make it better? Get high with you? That's not a solution. That was only going to make the problem worse for you. I understand why you went to someone like Camille. Who had open arms for you. Who listened to you when you poured your heart out to her. Who held you in her arms as you cried to her about your fears. She sounded like a wonderful woman. She was the person that you needed at the time. Someone who cared enough about you. To make you feel like it was worth it. The scary thing is that I have my own Camille in my life. I have Oliver, Sebastian, and Jacob. They make me think that it's worth it. We knew that it was a lie, but we chose to believe in the lie. The lie that there is meaning in the world. The lie that what we do means something to someone other than us. That it means something to the stars. Sometimes I spiral when I think about this. I think about how easy it would be to give up and do what you and grandma did to myself. I stop myself from doing it. Camille said to us, 'You can't give up before you see the view from the top of the mountain. When you get there, you'll see it. The view is breathtaking. It's more beautiful than any painting made in the world. It was worth everything to you. It's worth the sacrifices. It's worth the pain and the suffering. It's worth disappointing the world. Damn, that view is worth anything.' I think about that moment where I see the view for the first time. I know it's going to be worth it. I hope you saw the view before you died. You climbed up to the top of the bridge. You looked down at the water below you. You thought to yourself that this is the moment that you've been waiting for your entire life. You saw the view. It was the most beautiful thing you saw in your life. Everything made sense to you. All of the pain and suffering was worth something to the world. That view was worth it to you. Everything ended for you after that moment. That view though. It was fucking worth it. You are spending eternity in the stars looking at it."

After she sobbed into her hands on her balcony for a while, she put out the end of her cigarette onto the ashtray as she got up from her seat where she walked into her bedroom before she laid down on the bed with her face hidden in her pillow. She kept her face hidden in her pillow until someone climbed into the bed next to her where she pulled her face out of her pillow before Daphne laid down next to her. Once she pulled Daphne into her arms, Daphne let out heartbreaking sobs into her chest as she ran her hands up and down her back where she pulled the blankets over them before she told her that she loved her with her kissing her daughter on the top of her head. Once Daphne told her that she loved her too, she told her that they should go to bed where Daphne listened to her before she fell asleep with her daughter in her arms for the rest of the night.

CHAPTER SIXTY-NINE
(WINTER 1976 – YORK, ENGLAND)

After they spent two more weeks at their house, Posey and Eleanor went home with Oliver and Juliet. Aunt Priscilla recovered at home with Uncle Nathan and Poppy taking care of her. Sebastian came back from his business trip in New York at the same time. He stayed at an apartment unit in Damien's apartment building while he worked in the city. They didn't talk about what happened in Sweden. They were ignoring each other. It wasn't like she needed to explain herself to him. He knew her well enough to know what happened to her. She had a manic episode followed by a depressive episode. It wasn't anything that she didn't experience before. This was part of living with bipolar disorder. She couldn't hide anything from Sebastian. He knew her better than anyone else. When her parents got home from England, she went into the studio with Sebastian running it smoothly after they were gone for long periods of time. She was in her office on the phone with their bankers as Lucy ran over to her with the newspaper in her hands where she hung up the phone. She read the newspaper that Lucy shoved into her hands before she asked Lucy what she was supposed to be looking for. Once Lucy pointed out the section on the bottom corner, she let out a frustrated sigh as she looked at the Oscar nominations where she jumped up into the air when she saw that her movie *Yellow Carnations* was nominated for five Oscars. Lucy pulled her into a tight hug with her hiding her face into her chest. She heard the door opening as she pulled herself out of Lucy's arms when Sebastian asked her what was wrong where she handed him the newspaper before he read it with a frown on his face. He realized that *Yellow Carnations* was nominated for five Oscars including best produced movie and best written movie. He pulled her into a tight hug with her face hidden in his chest where they stayed like that for a while until their lawyers walked into her office with the newspaper in his hands asking them about the Oscars before Sebastian called a meeting to share the news with the rest of their staff. After they shared the news of their nominations with their staff, people congratulated them before they went back to work again. Everything that she was doing at the studio didn't seem important anymore. She needed to prepare for the Oscars. Lucy called in her favors that people owed her. Even though she went to the Oscars on her first date with Sebastian, she wasn't nominated for any awards. He was the person that won the awards. This was the first time that she was nominated for an Oscar award. She never won any awards for her acting. She was going to win awards for her writing and the production of her movies. Sebastian told her that there was a chance that she wasn't going to win and that she couldn't determine the outcome of it. She understood where he was coming from since he experienced disappointment from not winning in the past. She wanted to believe that this was when she was going to be recognized by Hollywood for her talent after the years of her giving the industry her heart without receiving anything in return.

On the day of the Oscars, she spent the afternoon at her house with her team of makeup artists and hair stylists led by Amelia helping her get ready for the show. Daphne sat down next to her with Noah sitting in his mother's lap before Sebastian got home from work to get ready for the show. Since she required a lot more work to get ready for the show, Sebastian's hair was fixed into a high fashion hairstyle as he changed into his designer suit where he played with the children in the living room until Posey made it to their house. She changed into her designer dress with her parent's help because it was impossible to get into by herself. Her parents told her that they would watch the Oscars on television with the children and Posey. Sebastian helped her into the back of the car because she couldn't move in her dress as he got into the seat next to her before their driver dropped them off at Santa Monica

Civic Center where the show took place. This wasn't where it was the last time that they went to the Oscars. They moved the event a few years ago after public pressure to change it. Once their driver dropped them off at the red carpet, Sebastian grabbed onto her hand where they walked towards the building with them stopping every other step to have their photographs taken by the magazines before they walked into the building. Sebastian led them to their seats in front of the room where they sat down with the director and the leads of *Yellow Carnations* that were also nominated for awards before they broke into a conversation about how excited they were for the show. They were served a five-course meal with plenty of champagne that she opted out of because she wanted to be sober. The lights darkened in the room as the host of the Oscars introduced himself to the television crowd as everyone clapped for him where he introduced each category from cue cards before he listed off the various other actors and actresses that were nominated in each category. When they introduced her category of best producer, she perked up in interest as they read her name aloud since she was the only woman on the list of males where the actor announced from the cue card her name before Sebastian pulled her into a tight hug with her face hidden in her chest. As soon as Sebastian pulled away from her, he pecked her lips as she walked onto the stage where the actor handed her the trophy before she said her speech to the crowd and the camera that was in front of her. She thanked her team that made the movie possible and her husband Sebastian who supported her in everything that she did. She thanked the audience for being a part of her world. Once she took a seat next to Sebastian, they moved onto the next award as another actor walked on the stage where the host announced the nominations for best writer in a movie before he announced her name again. She pulled Sebastian into a tight hug until he pecked on her lips where she ran onto the stage with the actor handing her the trophy before she said her second speech of the night. It was only fitting for her to mention that she was glad that she wrote a woman told story that so many people connected to so much. Her studio took a huge risk with this movie. It was worth it because she told a story that was never told before in Hollywood about a different kind of love. She was about to walk away when she felt the urge to say one last thing. She dedicated this award to her mother, her mum, her grandma, and Camille who showed her that love conquers all. In the face of true adversity, our love transpires anything else in the universe.

She got a standing ovation as Sebastian whispered into her ear that it was an incredible speech before they moved onto the next categories with an actress coming on the stage. *Yellow Carnations* won the awards for the best actress and the leading movie of the year. They posed with their trophies in their hands as photographers took pictures of them with Sebastian's arm tightly around her waist. They said goodbye to their team at the studio where Sebastian led them to their car before their driver drove them to their house. Since they got home in the middle of the night, Sebastian pulled her into a desperate kiss before she closed the door behind them where she pulled them into their bedroom when they had a few rounds celebrating in bed. Sebastian told her that he was proud of her and that he loved her when she told him that she loved him before she fell asleep in his arms for the rest of the night. Whatever excitement that her winning two Oscars had made, there was a crash that was about to happen to her. She was at the house one evening a few weeks later where she heard someone knocking on her door when she excused herself away from Sebastian and the children who were icing sugar cookies at the table before she opened the door to see Oliver standing in front of her. Before she got the chance to ask him what was wrong, he pulled her into a desperate hug as he sobbed into her chest with her arms tightly around him where she asked him what was wrong before he told her that his mother died from a heart attack. She tightened her grip on his arms as she dragged him towards her bedroom with Sebastian asking her what was wrong where she told him to leave the children downstairs while they were upstairs before she guided them into her bedroom. As soon as she closed her bedroom door behind her, she guided them over to the bed as Oliver hid his face in her chest with him sobbing in her arms. He pulled away from her when he asked her if this was how it felt for her when her dad died where she couldn't think of anything to say to him before she pulled him in her arms with Oliver sobbing in her chest again. She laid in her bed with her arms around Oliver until he fell asleep with his head leaning on her shoulder. Sebastian walked into their bedroom after he put the children to sleep as he laid down next to them before he looked over at Oliver with a frown on his face.

Sebastian told her that Juliet called them when he was putting the children to bed when she asked him if Oliver was with them where he told her that he was with Isabella in their bedroom. Juliet told him that they should stay with him because he found out that his mother died and that he wasn't taking it well. While she stayed in the bed with her watching Oliver sleep on her shoulder, Sebastian packed their bags for their trip to England in the morning where Sebastian joined them in bed in a few hours once he packed their bags and the children's bags before they slept in their bed for the rest of the night. She woke up early the next morning to Oliver and Sebastian having a hushed conversation with each other on the balcony where she grabbed her robe off of the back of the bathroom door. She joined them out on the balcony with Oliver's bloodshot eyes staring at her before she pulled him into a silent hug with her face hidden in his chest. They stayed like that a while until Sebastian told them that their plane was leaving in an hour. They pulled away from each other where Oliver left to go to his house to pack his bags before she got ready to leave for the plane. Sebastian dressed the children into warm outfits for winter in England. She got into the back of the car with her children and Sebastian when Daphne asked her if they were going to England because someone in the family died again. She explained to Daphne that Aunt Priscilla died yesterday before Daphne asked her if she was sick. Once she told Daphne that Aunt Priscilla died from a sudden sickness, Daphne didn't ask more questions for the rest of the drive to the airport. Their driver dropped them off at the LAX airport where they met up with her family before they got on their private jet. She was on grief duty with Juliet, Sasha, and Amelia. Sebastian and Troy took care of Noah and Christian who were wreaking havoc on the plane. Her parents and Gabriel watched Daphne, Charlotte, Eleanor, and Katherine play barbies on the floor while Posey read a book on the other side of the airplane.

When their plane landed in York the next morning, she woke up Daphne as she slept on her lap as she carried Noah on her hip who was asleep in her chest when she followed Sebastian where Uncle Nathan waited for them before Oliver gave his stepdad a tight hug that they needed from each other. Oliver pulled his sister Poppy into a tight hug as Uncle Nathan pulled her into a desperate hug with her face hidden in his chest until Noah whined from her hip before she placed

Noah on the ground. Noah ran towards his four-year-old cousin Millie who screamed his name. After she pulled away from Uncle Nathan, her parents tightly hugged him as she pulled her cousin Poppy into a tight hug with her six-year-old niece Madeline hugging her legs until Daphne stood next to her where she placed Daphne on her hip before she followed Poppy over to the car with everyone got into the cars. After they got to Uncle Nathan's house, she got out of the car with Noah asleep in her arms as Sebastian held onto Daphne's hand where her cousin Tommy pulled her into a tight hug with his one-year-old son Damon on his hip before her cousin Alfie pulled her into a tight hug with his one-year-old son Sunny on his hip. Noah played in the living room as she went to look for Oliver since she didn't see him walk into the house where he sat in the barn before she sat down on the ground next to him. They sat in comfortable silence for a long time until their fingers were cold where they went back into the house before they ate dinner in the kitchen. Her family and Oliver's family stayed at Uncle Nathan's house. Poppy's brothers Tommy, Alfie, the children, and her husband Ellis stayed at their house. Her parents stayed at George's house with Amelia's family and Sasha's family. The rest of the family stayed with Audrey and Teddy since they had the most space for them. She put on one of her black dresses the next morning where she changed Daphne into her black dress and Noah into a suit that he wasn't escaping from. They ate breakfast in the kitchen before Uncle Nathan called for family members to meet them in his office for Aunt Priscilla's will reading with their lawyer. Uncle Nathan called out for Oliver, Poppy, Tommy, Alfie, Ella, James, Valeria, and Isabella. Her mother guided her into the office as Uncle Nathan closed the door behind them where Uncle Nathan stood in front of the room. The lawyer looked over at Oliver who held onto Juliet's hand when he told him that his mother left him the sum of her property on the farm that wasn't built on and some money for her granddaughters. The lawyer looked over at Poppy who held onto Ellis' hand when he told her that her mother left her the rest of the farm that she didn't give to Oliver and some money for her grandchildren. Poppy and Ellis already knew that her parents were leaving the farm to them. The lawyer looked over at Tommy who held onto his wife Lilly's hand with her three-year-old daughter Annie on her hip when he told them that his mother left him a sum of a million pounds of artwork that she inherited from her mother and some money for their children. Tommy thanked the lawyer for telling him about the paintings that no one knew about. The lawyer looked over at Alfie who held onto his wife Debbie's hand with their three-year-old daughter Piper on her hip when he told them that his mother left him many priceless artworks and money for his children. The lawyer looked over at Aunt Valeria who leaned her head onto Uncle James' shoulder when the lawyer told them that Priscilla left them all of the books in her collection that her children or Nathan didn't want to keep where they nodded their heads at him. The lawyer looked over at her and her mother who grabbed onto her hand in dread for what he was going to tell them. The lawyer told them that Priscilla left her mother a collection of the stories that she wrote over the years before she moved to New York. Her mother grabbed onto the book of short stories that she wrote before she thanked him for giving this to her. The lawyer looked over at her when he told her that Aunt Priscilla left her a collection of photographs from her mother's youth that she accepted from him without her finding the right words to say to him. He looked over at Uncle Nathan who nervously played with the ends of his suit. The lawyer told Uncle Nathan that Priscilla left him the rest of her wealth and the letters that they wrote to each other after they got married to each other. This made Uncle Nathan emotional since he hadn't read any of these letters in decades where his children pulled their father into a desperate hug before she left them in the office. She knew what it was like to put her grief on display, and they didn't want to do that.

Once Uncle Nathan and his children walked into the living room, she got into a car with Poppy's family where she carried Noah in her arms into the church before she interacted with people that came up to talk to her. The most common comments that people made to her was that they saw that she won four Oscars for her last movie and that they were sorry for the loss of her aunt. When she couldn't handle it anymore, she left Noah with his grandparents as she went outside into the graveyard to smoke cigarettes where Oliver joined her where they didn't say anything to each other before they joined their family into the church for the rest of the afternoon. After they left to go to the house for the night, she ate dinner with her family where she put her children to sleep in their bedroom before she smoked cigarettes on the balcony for the rest of the night. She didn't come into the house until Sebastian made her after it heavily snowed outside and that she was going to frostbite if she stayed out there any longer. She wasn't in the mood to argue with Sebastian that she was born in this country and that her blood was resilient to cold temperatures. She fell asleep in his arms for the rest of the night. She woke up on the morning of Aunt Priscilla's funeral to Daphne crying in Sebastian's arms that she didn't want to go to another funeral as he looked over at her to help him. She pulled Daphne into her lap when she explained to her that they needed to say goodbye to Aunt Priscilla before Daphne gave up on not going to the funeral. After she got the children dressed for the funeral, she carried Noah on her hip as Sebastian carried Daphne in his arms where they got into the car with Uncle Nathan, Oliver, Juliet, Posey, and Eleanor before Uncle Nathan parked the car at the church. As soon as she walked into the church, she was reminded of her father's funeral. She forced herself not to think about it. She took a seat in the second pew with Noah sitting in her lap. Sebastian sat down next to her with Daphne sitting in his lap and Oliver grabbed onto Juliet's hand like it was his only lifeline. Once Uncle James thanked everyone for coming to celebrate Priscilla's life, he invited her son Tommy to come up to the podium as Tommy grabbed onto Lilly's hand with their five-year-old son Charlie sitting in her lap where he made his way to the front of the room with pieces of paper in his hand before he said aloud to the room with tears falling down his face, "Alfie and I argued about who was going to talk at our mum's funeral, but he backed out of it last minute. He couldn't do it. I told him that I would say what we wanted to tell her. On behalf of my brother, he wants to say that he's heartbroken that mum is dead. He loves her and that he will miss her for the rest of his life. I'm so heartbroken that mum is dead. She struggled to recover after her last heart attack. I didn't see the second one coming. I don't think that anyone did. Mum was the strongest person that I knew. She taught me so much about the world. She taught me how to live with myself. She showed me that there is love after a heartbreak. There was love for her after Kenny died with my dad. There was love for me after my Rosie died when we were only fifteen years old. Mum was there for me more than anyone else after Rosie was killed in the accident. I felt like the world ended when Rosie died, but mum reminded me that it wasn't the end of my life. The end of one life is only the beginning of a new life. A life full of love and happiness was waiting for me on the other side. You were right, mum. There's the beauty of it. The life that you got to see for yourself. I love you, mum."

Tommy wiped tears away from his face as he took a seat next to Lilly who tightly grabbed onto his hands where Poppy got up out of her seat in the first pew with Ellis grabbing onto her shoulder before she walked up to the podium with pieces of paper in her hands. Poppy said aloud to the room, unable to look away from her mother's coffin, "Mum, this world is a lot darker without you. You brought so much light to the world. It was your special purpose here. To make it a brighter place. I didn't get it until I had Jack, Maddie, and Millie. You need to create the world that you want your children to live in. The world that you left behind for my brothers and I was nothing short of extraordinary. You showed us that anything is possible. You did it with your love for us. Thank you. I love you, mum. I'll miss you forever."

After Poppy took a seat in the front pew with Millie crawling into her lap, Oliver got up from his seat next to her as Juliet grabbed onto his shoulder where he walked up to the podium with a piece of paper in his hands when he aloud to the room with him blinking back tears that fell down his face, "I struggled with what to say about my mum. I'm not a master at words like my sister or my brother is, so I had to get some help with it. Thank you for helping me, Isabella. I love you so much. My mum was a special woman. She had me when she was only nineteen years old. My dad was fighting in the war. She had to do it all by herself. My dad died when I was ten months old, and it changed our lives forever. Mum was a single mother with a baby to take care of. She didn't know how she was going to survive to the end of each day, but she did it for her baby. She woke up every morning to leave her baby behind at home with his aunts while she worked to support her family. I was raised by all women for most of my life. It shaped me into the man that I am today. I learned to understand others. To be compassionate towards others. I wouldn't have become a psychiatrist if it wasn't for them. My mum and I loved helping people. We would do anything to help someone in need. No matter what was going on in the world, mum would tell me, 'Oliver, you have to make people feel like they are special to you if you want to show them that you love them. Do what you can do to help them. Listen to them. Care about them.' This carried onto my profession later in life where I listen, and I care about my patients. I do that with my family. I'm so happy that Posey and Eleanor got to know the woman that I called my mum. They are going to grow up into the women that she would be so proud of. I'm proud of them too. They are so compassionate and loving to like her. Love goes a long way in the world. When we have nothing else left in this world, we have our love for each other. That's all that we ever needed. I love you, mum. Rest easy."

As soon as Oliver sat down next to her, she pulled him into a tight hug as he softly cried into her chest with Juliet's head pressed into his back. Oliver took his face out of her chest where Eleanor and Posey pulled him into tight hugs before he tightly wrapped his arms around his daughters. Once her mum gently squeezed her mother's shoulder, her mother walked up to the podium with no paper in her hands as she let out a shaky break when she said to the room with tears rapidly falling down her face, "Priscilla was one of the most special people in my life. Even though she wasn't my blood sister, she was my sister. She treated me like her little sister. She taught me how to be a better person. She taught me how to be a better mother to my baby girl. I got to practice on Oliver before I had my own baby. Out of everything that we created together, I'm so glad that our children are so close to each other. Oliver and Isabella have always been best friends. It's a beautiful representation of our love of each other. We could transmit that onto our children. Losing Kenny was hard for everyone in the family. It was the hardest for us. Obviously for different reasons, but his death bonded us for the rest of our lives. You were there for me after Kenny died. Even if no one knew the truth about him, I'd like to think that we knew it from being with him. We never needed to tell each other about what he did to us. We always understood each other. You saw it in my eyes like I saw it in your eyes. The look of pain that he inflicted on us. The look of betrayal that he did to us. It all amounted to something though. When I was at my lowest, you reminded me that there was light in the world. You showed me that there was love left for me. You didn't realize what you were doing, but I knew you were. I loved the life that we had together with Sylvia and our children in

England. I never wanted it to end. Nothing lasts forever though. It was the simplest years of my life. It gave me reassurance that I was going to be okay. After everything that happened with Kenny and Will, you gave my hope for the future. The future was going to be bright for me and my baby girl. Thank you for everything that you did for me. I love you, Priscilla. Rest in peace."

As soon as her mother took a seat next to her mum, her mother grabbed onto her hand for a moment where she grabbed onto her mum's hand for a moment before Oliver grabbed onto her hands with tears falling down his face. Uncle Nathan walked up to the podium when he said aloud to the room with tears falling down his face, "I don't know what I'm supposed to say about this. You dying before me wasn't part of our plans. You were supposed to outlive me. I smoked every day since I was thirteen years old. I'm heartbroken that you are gone. It was God's time to take you away from me. I never thought that I would fall in love with you. You were with my best friend for as long as I knew you. I used to say that Kenny was lucky to have someone as wonderful as you in his life. It hurt me when he took advantage of you. I was relieved when he died. That sounds cruel, but we weren't getting along before he died. I was surprised when you kissed me. I felt the magic flowing between us. It was so infectious that I thought that the world was going to catch it. Our life was a dream. Raising our children on the farm. Watching them live their best lives without us. Spending every night in your arms until our last night. You told me that there aren't many things worth dying for in this world. Love was the only thing worth dying for. Our love was worth it to me. I would do it again. I love you, Priscilla. Rest with Will and Kenny. Tell them that I miss them."

Uncle Nathan took a seat in the pew with Poppy and Tommy pulling their father into a tight hug with his face hidden in his shoulder. Uncle James told the family to come outside for the burial. She wasn't going to risk hearing the plunking noise before she sprinted out of the church without looking behind her. She didn't stop running until she made it to the bridge that her father killed himself on as she stared down at the bottom of the river with her holding onto the wooden pillars where she sat down on the bridge before she let out desperate sobs into her hands. She stayed in that position after there were no tears left to cry. She pulled her face out of her hands when she asked Oliver with a look of exhaustion on her face, "How did you find me? Did my mom tell you where I was?"

Oliver wrapped his arms around her when he responded to her with a frown on his face, "Your mom didn't have to tell me. I figured that you were here. I know that you don't like it when you hear people getting buried into the ground. I don't like it either. It's okay."

She leaned her head on his shoulder when she responded to him in a distant voice looking down at the water rushing down below them, "Thank you. Are you okay?"

Oliver shrugged his shoulders at her when he responded to her with tears falling down his face, "I'm not okay, Isabella. Both of my parents are dead. I don't think that I'm going to be okay again. It's okay that it's not okay. I tell my patients that they have to be okay with that. It will be better someday. My mum will always be dead, but at least I had a good life with her. You know?"

She let out a soft sigh when she responded to him with her intensely staring at the rushing water below them, "Right. I guess that's all that matters. That you had a good life with her. I'm thinking something very morbid right now. This all began at this bridge. I think that it ends here too. Life always ends where it begins. How do you be okay with something like that?"

Oliver tightened his grip on her arms when he responded to her in a serious voice, "You have to be okay with the things that make you sad. It's simple." She shrugged her shoulders at him as she got up from the bridge with her helping Oliver to his feet when they walked into the church where Sebastian waited for her with a concerned look on his face before he guided her back to the car. They ate dinner in the kitchen as everyone went into their bedrooms for the night where Sebastian got the children ready for bed before she slept in his arms.

CHAPTER SEVENTY
(SPRING 1976 – LOS ANGELES, CALIFORNIA)

Once they were back in California, everyone went back to their normal lives. The girls went to school where she went into the studio with Sebastian while Noah was at home with his grandparents. She wasn't working on a screenplay because she wasn't sure how to write about what she was feeling right now. She was torn about her loyalty to her father or to the world. She didn't feel like she was supposed to share those thoughts with the world. She had nightmares about the bridge every night since they got back from England. She stood there looking down at the water questioning why she found herself in this place. The nightmare ended differently every night. Sometimes she jumped off of the bridge. Other times she walked away from the bridge. The scariest version of the nightmare was when her younger self stood on the bridge with her. It was her when she was eight years old. Her younger self looked over at her when she asked her if she was going to do it. It took her a few moments to understand what her younger self was referring to before she asked her younger self if she was going to jump off of the bridge too. Her younger self laughed at her when she asked her why else she would be standing on a bridge if it wasn't going to jump off of it. She asked her younger self why she was standing on the bridge if she wasn't going to jump off of it. Her younger self told her that she was here to see the view. After she asked her younger self what view, her younger self pointed down below them beyond the water when she told her that she should see it for herself. As soon as she looked down at the view, she jolted awake in her bed with her heart pounding out of her chest and unable to catch her breath. She didn't tell anyone what her nightmares were about. Not even Sebastian who knew that she was waking up from nightmares every night. It wasn't that she was intentionally hiding it from him, but she didn't know how to explain it to him without making him worried about her. How was she supposed to tell anyone about her nightmare of being trapped on the bridge in York with her younger self for the rest of eternity? It made her look like she wasn't mentally there even though she convinced herself that she was okay. She didn't have a choice except to be okay. If she wasn't okay, then she was convincing herself of a lie. Whatever the case was for her, she was okay with either outcome from this situation. The moment that she stepped on that bridge in York, she knew that this was the place that she was stuck in for the rest of her life. Oliver told her that she had to be okay with not being okay. She was trying to be okay without being okay. It was hard for her to imagine any other moment except for the bridge in York.

She tried to move on from it. Every time that she thought that she was over it, she wasn't over it. Jacob told her a long time ago that being over something didn't mean that she was ready to move from it. There was a possibility that she was never going to move on from it. She wasn't meant to move from it. There was a reason that she was stuck on the bridge after all of this time. When she realized that she wasn't going to get over it any time soon, she knew that she had to do something productive with it or else it was going to destroy her. That was when she decided to write her new screenplay about that moment on the bridge. No one was going to tell her that she couldn't write about it. Her mother wrote about so many things that happened in her life, and no one batted an eye at her. This new screenplay proved to be difficult for her to write because she was writing about emotions that she locked up a long time ago. She wanted the bridge to be the center of the story. She didn't want it to take place in England because that would be too disrespectful towards her father's story. She decided that the bridge that she was using for the screenplay was going to be the Golden Gate Bridge in San Francisco. She heard some statistics from Lucy that three people killed themselves jumping off of it every day in the last five years. She didn't know if it was true or not, but it was interesting to her that people chose to die in that particular place. This sent her on a spiral to learn everything about the Golden Gate Bridge. It couldn't be a consequence that this bridge was a common place of death. After she did her research about the Golden Gate Bridge, she found out that it was the place of death since it opened up to the world in 1937 and the rest was history after that. Her new screenplay called *Golden Shi* was based on the Japanese concept for the cycle of death. It was about three stories of people that lived in San Francesco in the 1950s. The first character story was about an investment banker named Charles Harper that lived in the city with his wife Lauren Harper and his two sons Alex Harper and Owen Harper. Charles lived a normal life with his family where he drove home from work on the Golden Gate Bridge when he saw someone about to jump off of the bridge before he pulled his car over to stop them from jumping off of the bridge. This introduced the second character story about a young man named Frank Barker that was a struggling drug addict that found himself in an unfortunate position after his girlfriend Cassidy died from a drug overdose. After Charles convinced Frank not to jump off of the Golden Gate Bridge, he took Frank to his house to stay with him since Frank was homeless where he gave Frank a job at his office to help him out. Charles and Frank developed a close friendship with each other over the years where Frank eventually moved into his own house to create his own family with the third character story about Hannah Smith who he saved from jumping off the Golden Gate Bridge like Charles saved him all those years ago. Hannah and Frank fell in love with each other where they got married to each other before they started a family of their own like they always dreamed of with their daughters Ophelia and Rosalind. Inspired by their own experiences, Frank and Hannah told Charles that they should start a foundation that supports people after they tried to jump off of the Golden Gate Bridge. At the end of the movie, it was fifteen years after Charles and Frank first met each other that their families came together to have a memorial service for those lives that were lost jumping off the Golden Gate Bridge over the years. The last scene of the movie was Charles holding Lauren in his arms as Frank held Hannah in his arms when they said to each other that it all started with his bridge, and it would always end here too.

After she showed Sebastian her new screenplay for *Golden Shi*, he was so overwhelmed with emotions when he told her that was the most beautiful screenplay that he read where she asked him if he thought that it was good enough for the world. Sebastian told her that it was the most real thing that she shared with him, so why couldn't they share it with the world. It was inspiring and it had a good message. People could relate to being that place where they were about to give up on everything before something stopped from making that choice. Since *Golden Shi* was about suicide and drug addiction, they knew that it was going to be a tough sell to their lawyers because this wasn't a topic that people made movies about in Hollywood. Their lawyers told them that they could make this work despite the difficult subject matter discussed. They created a cast for the movie, and she hired people to make the sets in the studio except for the Golden Gate Bridge that they were planning on filming those scenes on location. She was excited to be working on a movie. Nothing made her feel more alive than working on a new movie that was going to have an impact on the world. It made her feel like she was doing something productive with her feelings. While they were in the middle of preparing for production of her screenplay *Golden Shi*, her mother's health took a turn for the worst as she struggled with intense pain in her stomach that she thought was part of her stomach being upset until the pain got so bad that she couldn't get out of the bed. After she urged her mother to go to the hospital with her mum backing her up on it, her mother gave in as her mum called for an ambulance to come to the house where she helped her mother out of the bed before she noticed that there was blood all over the bed. Since she couldn't hide the fear from her mother, she asked her if she knew that she bled on the bed where her mother shook her head at her in confusion before she told her mother to stay there until the ambulance got to the house. When the ambulance arrived at the house, she rushed over to the paramedics when she told them that her mother bled all over the bed and her mother had intense pain in her lower stomach that prevented her from getting out of bed. The paramedics rushed over to get her mother on the stretcher before they pushed her into the back of an ambulance with her mum coming with them. She told her mum that she would meet them at the hospital after Sebastian and the children got home from the park with Amelia, Sasha, and their children. Once Sebastian came home from the park, he knew that something bad happened because she nervously paced around the living room until he pulled her into a desperate hug as she cried into his chest that her mother was in the hospital where he told her to go be with her mother while he stayed at home with the children. After she thanked him for staying at home, she ran outside to her parent's car as she drove to the hospital as fast as she could where she sprinted towards her before her mum pulled her into a desperate hug with her face hidden in her chest until a doctor appeared in front of them. As the doctor pulled them away from the waiting room, her mum grabbed onto her hand when the doctor told them that they stopped her mother's heavy bleeding, but they needed to do more tests to see what was causing it. He told them that they were admitting her mother into the hospital. After the doctor led them to her mother's hospital room, they rushed over to her mother who was sleeping in her bed with them sitting on either side of her as they held onto her hands. They sat in silence for a while until her mother woke up from her nap before she asked them what was going on. Her mum told her mother that they were figuring it out, but that she was going to be okay. Her mother believed her until the doctor walked into the room with a serious look on his face. The doctor told them that they got the test results back and that her mother tested positive for ovarian cancer, but they caught it early because it was only stage two. No one said anything for a while since they were in too much of a state of shock to say anything to him. Her mother broke the silence when she asked him what her chance of beating the cancer was when the doctor let out a defeated sigh before he told her it was less than a thirty percent chance. She didn't break down until she heard that her mother had less than a thirty percent chance of living. She sprinted out of the room without looking back at her mother who called out baby girl to stop her before her mum told her that she would check on her. She didn't stop running until she was out of the hospital where she suddenly fell down onto the ground. She let out heartbreaking sobs into her hands before her mum pulled her into a desperate hug with her face hidden in her chest. They stayed like that for a long time after she was done crying into her chest until her mum told her that she could go home if she needed space to process everything where she walked over to the car before she drove back to her house in complete silence except for the sound of her breathing in the background. By the time that she got home, it was well past the children's bedtimes. She didn't want Noah and Daphne seeing her like this.

When she walked into the dark house with her hands shaking in her pockets, Sebastian ran over to her from where he was reading a script on the couch as she let out heartbreaking sobs into his chest with his arms tightly around her when she told him that her mother had stage two ovarian cancer with a thirty percent chance of beating it. Sebastian told her that her mother was a fighter and that she was the strongest woman that he knew. She didn't have the energy to argue with him before he dragged her to their bedroom. After they showered together, she changed into one of his oversized shirts where they got into bed before she slept in his arms for the rest of the night. It took her a few days for her to work up the nerve to see her mother in the hospital. Her mother was starting her first dose of chemotherapy since the doctor wanted to get rid of the cancer as quickly as possible before it spread to other parts of her body. She sat with her mother at the hospital while she got chemo treatments as she edited her screenplay *Golden Shi* since they were filming in a few weeks, and she wanted everything to be perfect. They didn't talk about her mother having ovarian cancer because it was too soon for her to talk about it. Her mother wasn't processing what was happening to her. Instead of talking about death, she told her mother about her screenplay *Golden Shi* as her mother listened to her. Uncle Stan spent the rest of the day with her mother where he pulled her into a tight hug before she went home to her children. Her mother was supposed to spend five weeks in the hospital until she was healthy to come home where she got her chemo treatments at an outpatient center. The children were wondering about Grandma Ella. By the week mark of her mother being at the hospital, they told the children about it when they were alone at the house while her mum was at the hospital with her mother. She was nervous about how the children were going to react to it. Noah wouldn't understand what was going on, but Daphne knew what it meant. She was old enough to know what it meant to have cancer. When they were laying down in bed with Noah and Daphne in between them, Sebastian gave her the look that they needed to tell them as she tightened her grip on her children's arms when she told them that Grandma Ella was in the hospital because she was sick with ovarian cancer. Noah didn't say anything because he didn't know what to say to her. Daphne asked her if Grandma Ella was going to die where she told her daughter that Grandma Ella might die before Sebastian assured Daphne that she was getting medicine to heal her. Daphne didn't seem interested in Sebastian's answer before she asked her mother if Grandma Ella was going to die. She told her daughter that she was going to die before Daphne sprinted into her bedroom as she loudly cried to herself. Sebastian gave her a stern look as he ran after Daphne to comfort her where she pulled Noah into her arms with his face hidden in her chest before she softly cried to herself into his hair. Sebastian stayed in Daphne's bedroom with her as she fell asleep, and Noah slept on her chest. They kept Daphne home from school because she couldn't do anything except cry in their arms. Neither of them was able to go into the studio since Daphne wouldn't let them out of her sight. She let Daphne and Noah come to the hospital with her to see their grandmother since Sebastian needed to get work done at the studio. Daphne sobbed into her grandmother's arms as Noah ate snacks off of his grandmother's food tray that she was too nauseous to eat from the chemotherapy. Once Daphne went back to school, she went into the studio to film her movie *Golden Shi*. She was determined to work on it despite the news of her mother's cancer. She poured that energy into making her movie something special that no one saw before in Hollywood. She visited her mother on the days off from filming her movie where she told her about the progress that they made in the time that they were apart from each other. Her mother stayed in the hospital for a few more weeks than the doctor thought that she needed to stay there. Her mother's body wasn't responding to chemotherapy, so they had to do extra sessions to kill the cancer. Her doctor was going to attempt to operate on the tumors. They were stuck playing the waiting game.

Her mother was stuck in the hospital for Daphne's birthday, so they brought the party to the hospital as they opened Daphne's presents on her mother's bed until they went back to the house to eat cake where her mum left to go back to the hospital to give her mother a piece of Daphne's cake before they got the children ready for bed that night. While Sebastian gave their children a bath in the suite, she read her screenplay with a pen behind her ear as she pulled it out to make changes where she put it back behind her ear before she went back to her screenplay. As soon as she placed her screenplay onto the bed, Daphne ran towards her from the bathroom in her favorite pajamas as she pulled Daphne into her lap with her face hidden into her mother's chest when she told Daphne with her running her fingers through her daughter's hair, "My big six-year-old. I'm sorry that we didn't get to do anything special for your birthday. Did you have a good day, Daph?"

Once Daphne pulled her face out of her chest, she leaned her head onto her mother's shoulder when she responded to her with a frown on her face, "It's okay, mommy. It was a good day. Noah didn't get a birthday party when he turned three. I'm not upset. Is that your new movie? What is it about?"

She responded to her as she picked up her screenplay off of the bed, "That's good, baby. I'm glad that you aren't upset. This is my new screenplay. It's about the Golden Gate Bridge. Do you know where that is?"

Daphne nodded her head at her when she responded to her mother with excitement laced in her voice, "It's in San Francisco. Are you going there to film? Can I come with you?"

She kissed Daphne on her cheek when she responded to her daughter with a wide grin on her face, "You can come with me. You shouldn't have school while we are in San Francisco. I'm sure that daddy will be okay with Noah. It's time for another Daphne and mommy adventure."

Daphne laid down on her lap as she ran her fingers through her hair when Daphne asked her with nervousness laced in her voice, "Can I ask you a question, mommy?"

She nodded her head at her when she responded to her daughter with a reassuring smile on her face, "Sure, baby. You can ask me anything."

Daphne bit her lip when she asked her with an uncertain look on her face, "Is Grandma Ella going to be around for when I turn seven next year?"

She tightly grabbed onto Daphne's hands when she responded to her daughter, "I don't know, Daph. No one knows the answer to that question. I want her to be here next year for your birthday, but that's not up to us to decide what happens to her."

As Daphne sat up across from her, she wrapped her arms around her as Daphne nervously bit her lips when she asked her mother with a frown on her face, "Who decides what happens to us? Bridget told me that God determines that."

She affectionately moved pieces of hair behind Daphne's ears when she responded to her with fighting the urge to cry, "Bridget can believe in God. You can believe in anything. God. Buddha. Nothing. As long as you are happy."

Daphne stayed silent for a few moments before she asked her mother with curiosity laced in her voice, "What do you believe in, mommy?"

She pulled Daphne into a tight hug with Daphne hiding her face into her chest when she responded to her daughter with tears falling down her face, "I don't believe in God, Daph. I believe in the stars. I don't think that anything decides our future. We determine our futures. We make choices that lead us to the doors that we are destined to go inside of. There are a million different doors to choose from and it leads us down a path in our lives. From the moment that you walk into the door, you can see it in front you. The life that you could've had for yourself. The life that you could've had if you made the right choice. Grandma Ella is going to be okay. She will be okay no matter what happens to her. We'll be okay no matter what happens to her. I don't want you to worry about her. She's at peace with whatever direction that the stars want with her. You can't worry about the things that you can't control. It will make you go insane. I learned that lesson a long time ago."

Daphne nodded her head at her when she responded to her mother with a frown on her face, "Okay, mommy. I'll try not to worry about what's going to happen to Grandma Ella. She'll be okay. The stars will take care of her. Where's daddy and Noah? They are going to miss story time." As soon as she got off of the bed with Daphne following behind her, she walked over to Noah's bedroom as Sebastian rocked Noah to sleep in the rocking chair where he smiled at her before he placed Noah in his bed to sleep for the rest of the night. Once Sebastian followed them into Daphne's bedroom, he read her a few books that she chose off of her bookshelf with her sitting in in his lap as she sat in the rocking chair next to them where Sebastian laid down Daphne in her bed when she was asleep in his arms before they went into their bedroom. After Sebastian turned out the lights, he climbed into the bed next to her as he wrapped his arms around her with her face hidden in his chest where they said that they loved each other before she fell asleep in his arms for the rest of the night.

CHAPTER SEVENTY-ONE
(SUMMER 1976 – SAN FRANCISO, CALIFORNIA)

After her mother spent two months in the hospital, she was discharged after the doctor was satisfied with the size of her tumors. Her mother was going to have a surgery in a few months to remove the tumors out of her ovaries. She was glad to have her mother at home because the children missed her so much. Daphne and Noah were always in their grandmother's bedroom before they kicked them out of the room to let her mother sleep. Her mum took on the full duties of taking care of her mother. She needed help with her basic needs. Uncle Stan came over to the house to help when her mum needed a break. With her mum taking care of her mother, they couldn't leave Noah with them. She took Noah into the studio with her while they filmed indoor scenes of the movie *Golden Shi* on set. She acted in the movie because the actress that was going to play Hannah dropped out of the movie. They reshoot scenes with her as Hannah that they already filmed for the movie. This made them behind from their filming schedule, but everything was set for them to film in San Francisco. Once they filmed the scenes in the studio, she left with the production team to go to San Francisco a few weeks ahead of filming. She made sure that they got the right permits that they needed to film parts of the movie. Lucy told her that the police didn't allow anyone to walk on the Golden Gate Bridge at night. She told her lawyers that they needed to film those scenes at night because it was going to have the biggest impact on her characters considering the end of the movie. She was afraid that the movie would lose the emotion on her if she wasn't standing on the Golden Gate Bridge in the middle of the night. Their lawyers promised her that they would figure something out with the police where they would get a permit to film at night. She acted like she didn't have a panic attack in front of the company lawyers. Their lawyers gave her permits to film on the Golden Gate Bridge at night like she asked them where she thanked them for doing it. The next task for her was to go to San Francisco to see the Golden Gate Bridge during the day since they could be there at night when they filmed the movie. After Daphne was finished with first grade at her private school, she took the children to San Francisco with them. Her niece Posey came to help them to watch the children while they filmed their movie. Oliver and Juliet were okay with Posey spending the summer in San Francisco with them. It kept her from doing nothing all summer while her sister Eleanor was at her sports camps. They paid Posey on a weekly basis because it was only fair that she got paid for her services. Posey wanted to save money to buy a car for her sixteenth birthday in two years that her parents wanted her to work for. After she said an emotional goodbye to her parents and Uncle Stan who stayed with them for the whole summer, their driver drove them to the LAX airport where they got on their private jet with the production crew and the cast of the movie before they were in San Francisco for the rest of the summer. Once they were in their rental house in the downtown area, they left Daphne and Noah alone with Posey who played in the pool with them as their driver dropped them off at the Golden Gate Bridge where the production crew waited for them before they tested angles that they were going to film in that night. When it was a few hours from getting dark outside, they went to the house as she ate dinner with her family in the kitchen before they left for the Golden Gate Bridge for the first night.

They started with Charles and Frank on the bridge when they met for the first time. Before they got the chance to film, police officers visited them as they asked them what they were doing where she told them that she was the producer of this movie and that they were filming the movie with the necessary permits. As soon as the police officers dismissed her permits, Sebastian firmly told them that he owned this studio and that his lawyers got permission from the judge to film at night where the police officers apologized for causing them any trouble before they drove away from the bridge. She told the actors that they were filming again as Sebastian whispered into her ear that he was calling their lawyers to tell them to come fix this where she nodded her head at him before she called action for the actors to say their lines on the cue. They filmed until the next morning where she told everyone that she would see them tonight before everyone went home to go to bed. They worked on this schedule for several weeks until they got the perfect takes for the scenes with Charles and Frank on the Golden Gate Bridge before it was her turn to film her scenes with Frank. Before her most important scene of her career, she thought about her father standing on the bridge in York before he jumped into the water. She imagined what his last thoughts were. Was he thinking about how it felt to fly? Was he thinking about everything that he never did? Was he thinking about the things that he should've told them? Was he imagining what it felt like to reach the end of his life? Was he regretting everything that he did wrong? She wanted her performance to feel like she was going to jump off at the Golden Gate Bridge. She put herself in the mindset that she was in when she read her father's letter before she overdosed on sleeping pills. She wanted to be in the mindset that she was in when she stood on the ledge of her balcony at her old house in Los Angeles. She wanted to be in the mindset that she was in when she was on the mountains in Sweden after she read Camille's letters to her grandma. She wanted to be in the mindset that she was in before she overdosed on drugs. She wanted that feeling like she didn't care about the consequences of her actions. She wanted that feeling of invincibility. Sebastian knew what she was doing to prepare for the role of the character Hannah. He made his disdain for it obvious when he asked her why she felt the need to do this where she told him that she was the only person that could do it. She knew what it was like to be that place. Even though he didn't approve of her doing this, he was coming to watch it being filmed because he wanted to support her regardless of if he agreed with her. On the way to the Golden

Gate Bridge, she was withdrawn from Sebastian where they didn't say anything to each other until their driver dropped them off at the same location that he always did before he told her that he would watch her from the other side of the railing. As soon as she got out of the car, she went over to the stunt director who put bungee cords on her body to make sure that she wasn't going to fall too far off of the railing before the actor that played Frank caught her. When they asked her if she was ready to film the scene, she nodded her head at him even though she was nervous as she pecked Sebastian's lips one more time where she told them that it was time to go before they filmed her getting on top of the railing of the Golden Gate Bridge. As she stood on the railing of the Golden Gate Bridge, she delivered her lines to Frank who tried to stop her from jumping off of it where she let out a shaky breath before she jumped off of the bridge.

As soon as she jumped off the Golden Gate Bridge, she let out a desperate sob with her hands out at her side until she suddenly wasn't falling anymore. The actor playing Frank caught her where he pulled her back into the safety of the bridge before she sobbed into his chest. Her sobbing wasn't part of the original script because they were supposed to cut as soon as she got on the bridge. The director kept filming it because it was raw emotion that came from her. They improvised the kiss between their characters Frank and Hannah. The actor playing Frank pulled her into a desperate kiss that she was surprised by because she wasn't expecting it. The director yelled cut after their impromptu make out scene with her crying in his arms. They pulled away from each other as everyone gave them a standing ovation. The director told her that was an incredible performance before he asked her if she could do that a dozen more times. They did it a dozen more times until it got realer and realer to her that she couldn't stop crying after the director cut the scene. Sebastian dismissed everyone from filming for the rest of the night before he pulled her away from them with her sobbing in his arms. Once their driver dropped them off at the house, he gently guided her into their bedroom where he laid down in the bed next to her before she fell asleep in his arms for the rest of the morning. They took a few days off of filming. She was too emotionally exhausted to get out of bed, let alone film more emotional scenes like that for their movie. While they took a week off from filming, the director visited them at the house where she told him that he could come into their bedroom even though Sebastian didn't agree with her. The director asked her if he could show her that first take of her jumping off of the Golden Gate Bridge. She told him that she was interested to see how it turned out where he set up the movie projector in their bedroom before he played out the scene for them. She sat in her bed nervously biting in her lips with Sebastian's arms tightly around her as she let out a shocked gasp when she watched herself jump off of the Golden Gate Bridge. She couldn't look away from herself falling down towards the water before Frank caught her with her sobbing in his arms. She wiped tears off her face when she told the director that she wanted to do something different in the scene where he asked her what she wanted to change before she told him that she wanted to touch the water. Sebastian instantly told her that they weren't doing that because she could die if they do that. The director told her that they could do it if they had the help of the coast guard to place a safety net on top of the water before she told the director to do that. He walked out of their bedroom with his film and his projector. Once she was alone with Sebastian, he angrily stared at her where she was trying to tell him that it made the movie more emotional if she almost died from jumping into the water before he stormed out of their bedroom. She took that as a sign that he didn't want to hear it. He disappeared before she told him about why she wanted to do it.

Regardless of how pissed off Sebastian was at her; he came to watch them film the scene where she jumped off of the Golden Gate Bridge with her touching the water. Every time that she jumped off of the railing into the water, she felt like her father was there with her as they flew in the air together. She landed on the safety net where the coast guard helped her back to land from the boat before she went onto the bridge to do it again. After they tried this new version of the scene, it made more sense for the story for her character Hannah to almost die to make her change her perspective on her life. They kept the crying scenes in and her kissing Frank's character. It was so passionate that it evoked raw emotions from anyone that watched it. By the end of her doing her own stunts, she was covered in bruises, and she dislocated her shoulder on the last take. She screamed out in pain that she knew that they kept in the movie before Sebastian rushed down to her with her laying down on the boat. After a member of the coast guard put her shoulder back into its place again, Sebastian pulled her into a desperate hug with her face hidden in his chest. He told the director that they weren't doing this anymore. The director told him that they got everything that they needed for the scene before Sebastian carried her off of the boat.

They spent more time on that scene than they anticipated. They cut out the minor scenes from the movie because they weren't relevant to the story anymore. They filmed scenes with Frank and Charles during the day while she watched them from behind the camera as she gave them directions. The only scene that was left to film was the scene with everyone at the bridge having a memorial service for the victims. The other last scene of Hannah and Frank looking down at the bridge after the memorial service was over. This scene required a lot of extras, so they invited members of the community to come to their filming for the night. This required new permits with the judge and the police had to be there to make sure that everything was okay. They didn't fight the police on this because the police gave them so much grace by letting them use the coast guard. They told the police officers to blend in with the movie. They needed a lot of children for the scene. Sebastian told her that they could have Daphne be one of her daughters where they asked Daphne if she wanted to be in the movie before Daphne told them that she was so excited to be in the movie. They explained to Daphne that being on camera was a serious job and that she needed to listen to the director when he told her what the right time was to do something. After Daphne promised them that she was going to be on her best behavior, they left Posey and Noah at home as they took Daphne to the Golden Gate Bridge where they got changed into their costumes for the scene before they took their places in the scene. As soon as the director shouted out action, everyone said the lines as she leaned into the actor playing Frank with Daphne and another little girl in their arms where she said her lines to Charles and Frank before the director called cut on the scene. After they filmed that scene a dozen more times, the director thanked everyone for helping them make this scene come true and that the only people that were needed for the filming tomorrow was Isabella and Greg who was the actor that was playing Frank in the movie before he dismissed everyone to go back home. Even though it was hours past Daphne's bedtime, she was wide awake as she talked about how exciting that it was to be in a movie where they told her that they would talk about putting her in more movies if she wanted to before Daphne slept for the rest of the morning. While Sebastian slept in the bed next to her, she couldn't sleep as she thought about the last scene in the movie that she needed to film where she talked to Frank about why she wanted to kill herself on the night that they met each other. This was something that she added after they decided to have her almost die in the water. She wanted to explain something that was missing in the movie. On her last day of filming *Golden Shi*, she woke up in the early afternoon to a pit in her stomach as she pushed that feeling back into herself until she was on the Golden Gate Bridge where she went there the rest of the day like she normally did before she left for the Golden Gate Bridge with Sebastian. As soon as she stepped foot on the Golden Gate Bridge for the last time, she let out a shaky breath as she prepared for her scene in her trailer until an attendant told her it was time to film where she followed them to where everyone waited for her before the director asked her if she was ready for this. After she nodded her head at him with a fake smile on her face, the director told everyone to get into their places as Greg playing the character Frank wrapped his arms around her with her leaning her head on his chest where the director called out action when Frank asked her character Hannah with a frown on his face, "I never did ask you honey. Why did you jump off of the bridge when we met each other?"

Acting as her character Hannah in that moment, she cupped Frank's face with her hands when she responded to him with a smile on her face, "Ah that. I wondered when you were going to ask me that question. If I tell you why I did it, then will you tell me why you didn't do it?"

Frank nodded his head at her with him holding onto her arms when he responded to her with a frown on his face, "Why didn't I do it? It was a mistake. I looked down at the water and I thought about how it felt to hit the water. How being in that water wasn't the last thing that I wanted to feel. I was sick of making the wrong choices. I wanted to make the right choice for once. There's my reason why I didn't jump. Why did you jump, Hannah?"

As she blinked back tears that fell down her face, she walked away from Frank to the railing where she looked down at the water before she turned around to look over at Frank when she confessed to him in an uneasy voice, "I didn't care about life. I thought that the world would be better without me. After all of the people that I hurt in my life, I thought that I was doing them a favor by leaving them alone. Frank, that feeling that I felt when I was in the air. It was something that I spent my entire life looking for. That feeling of invincibility. Like I could do anything. Even though it was there for the briefest moment, I felt like I could have that feeling forever. If I had died at that moment, I would've died with that feeling in my bones. That was until I touched the water. The water suffocating me reminded me of how I felt before I jumped off that bridge. Trapped in an endless cycle of pain. Stuck in between a place of life and death. Not knowing how to be a person. It didn't mean anything. None of it meant anything. I was ready to give up. I was prepared to die, but you did the unthinkable. You pulled me out of the water. You gave me a reason to live again. For you. For our daughters. It felt like the old version of myself died the moment that I touched the water. I became your Hannah. I'm so glad that I jumped. It showed me what my life could be. I made the right choice for once."

After she pulled Frank into a desperate kiss with his arms around her, they looked down at the water as they held onto each other's hands when Frank said to her with a smile on his face, "To life."

She leaned her head on his shoulder when she said to him with a smile on her face, "To our lives together. Goodbye, Golden Gate Bridge. Thank you for saving us. Are you ready for this, Frank?"

As soon as they walked away from the bridge together hand in hand, the director yelled cut once they were off of the bridge where Greg pulled her into a brief hug with her face hidden in his chest before Sebastian pulled her into his arms with her face hidden in his chest. Once she pulled away from Sebastian, she grabbed onto his hand as she led them towards their production team where she made a speech thanking everyone for working on the movie and that they were going to make history with this movie before everyone left to go to their houses for the rest of the night. She guided Sebastian over to the middle of the bridge where they sat down on the ground as they leaned onto the railing before she leaned her head onto his shoulder. As he ran his hands up and down her arm, she broke the silence between them when she said to him in a distant voice, "We did it, Bash. We made our movie. It's going to be a hit. People are going to connect to it from all around the world."

Sebastian kissed her on the top of her head as he tightened his grip on her arms when he told her with concern laced in his voice, "You did it honey. I'm so proud of you. Even though you scared the living shit out of me, I'm glad that it turned out good. Please don't do this to me again. Doing your own stunts. Jumping off of suicide bridges. Dislocating your shoulder. The nightmares that I had about you falling and getting hurt. It was enough to give me a heart attack."

She pulled him into a desperate kiss where they pulled away from each other when she said to him with a serious look on her face, "I promise you that I won't do it again. I love you so much, Bash. I'm sorry for scaring you. I scared myself too. I needed to do this to feel better about him. In order to move on from him, I needed to feel what he felt in his last moments. I understand how he felt at that moment. The thoughts that he had. The things that he felt before he touched that water. It was like I was with him. I don't know how to describe it."

Sebastian let out a defeated sigh as he pulled her into his arms when he responded to her with a frown on his face, "I thought that this was about him. I'd rather you do this than do what he did. If this is your way of moving on from him, then I'm not stopping you. That's all I've wanted you to do for a long time. Do what you need to get over him. What did it feel like when you were falling?"

As she let out a shaky breath, she leaned her head on his shoulder as she blinked back tears that fell down her face when she responded to him in a distant voice, "That's what was confusing to me. I didn't feel anything until I hit the water. As soon as I landed in the water, I saw him. I didn't tell you this, but I've had nightmares since we got back from England about the bridge. I'm there with myself as an eight-year-old and we stood on the bridge. My younger self told me that I need to see the view. Every time that I'm about to see it, I wake up in our bed. I never got to see the view. The moment that I hit the water I understood what she meant by it. The view isn't a thing that you see like water or mountains. It's a feeling that you get when your life flashes in front of your eyes. You see the moment in your life that you chose the wrong door. There it is. It's the view from the doorway." After they sat on the Golden Gate Bridge for a while, Sebastian helped her off of the ground as he held onto her hand where he guided her to the car before their driver drove them to the house. Once their driver dropped them off in the driveway, she followed Sebastian into the house as she went into their bathroom to take a shower where she changed into her silk pajamas before she walked into their bedroom. As soon as Sebastian pulled her into a desperate kiss, they didn't break apart from each other until they were out of breath where he pulled her towards the bed. Sebastian laid down with her head on top of his chest as he ran his hands up and down her back when she told him that she loved him with him saying the same thing where he wrapped his arms around her before she fell asleep in his arms for the rest of the night.

CHAPTER SEVENTY-TWO
(FALL 1976 – LOS ANGELES, CALIFORNIA)

They spent the last weeks of summer in San Francisco where they went to places in the city with Posey and the children. On their trip to Los Angeles, Posey pulled her aside from her reading other people's scripts when she told her that she enjoyed her summer with them where she told her niece that she could be with them whenever she wanted to before Posey asked her if they could go on their next trip with them. She told Posey that she could come with them the next time that they went to Sweden. Posey pulled her into a tight hug until Daphne ran over to them with a drawing in her hands before they went over to where Sebastian and Noah played together on the floor. Once they were in Los Angeles the next day, Posey went home with her family where her mum sat with her mother in the living room before she pulled them into tight hugs with their arms tightly around her. When they asked her about how filming went on the Golden Gate Bridge, she told them that it was very therapeutic for her and that she would show them the movie once they finished the final edits where her mother told her that she was so proud of her before she asked her mother how her treatments were going. Her mum helped her onto the couch as she held onto her hands when she told her daughter that her mother's chemo treatments were slowly progressing over the summer. The doctor thought that he could operate on it after a few more months of chemo treatments. She pulled her mother into a tight hug with her face hidden in her chest. Daphne shouted for her upstairs as her mother quickly grabbed onto her hand where she ran upstairs to Daphne's bedroom before she saw that her parents and Uncle Stan redecorated her bedroom while they were gone. Her mum helped her mother into Daphne's bedroom as Daphne pulled them into a tight hug when her mum told them that they had some free time with them gone where her mother told Daphne to look at Noah's bedroom before she followed Daphne into Noah's bedroom. Her parents redecorated Daphne and Noah's bedrooms over the summer. Daphne's bedroom looked like the Swedish countryside with horses and mountains and Noah's bedroom looked like the zoo with animals all over it. She thanked her parents and Uncle Stan who came out of hiding in his bedroom for doing this for the children. Her mother told her that they did something to their bedroom too as she raised her eyebrows in confusion to her mother where she walked into the suite with Sebastian standing there in shock when Noah ran into her legs before she placed him on her hip. Her parents and Uncle Stan redecorated their bedroom to look like an old Hollywood movie with the wallpaper, carpets, light shades, and golden designs in the room.

As she pulled her parents into a tight hug with her face hidden in their chests, she asked them when they had to time to do this where her mum told her that they were bored without the children to entertain them, and they thought that they would do something to surprise them after her working so hard on her movie. They went into the kitchen where they ate dinner with Oliver, Juliet, Posey, Eleanor, Uncle Stan, and Thomas while they caught her up on what happened when they were gone when Oliver asked her about how the filming went for the movie. Sebastian commented that she threw herself off of the Golden Gate Bridge so many times that she was covered in bruises and that she dislocated her shoulder. Everyone in the room stared at her as she gave Sebastian an irritated look when Oliver asked her why she was doing that where she told him that it was for the movie before Daphne told everyone that she got to be in the last scene of the movie. Everyone moved their attention onto Daphne as her mother told Daphne that she was excited for her when Uncle Stan changed the subject to about her mother's recovery before everyone forgot about Sebastian's comment. On the way out of the door, Oliver pulled her into a tight hug with her face hidden in his chest when he whispered into her ear asking if she was okay where she nodded her head at him before he walked out of the house. After they put Daphne and Noah to sleep in their bedrooms, she waited for Sebastian on their bed as she read screenplays that they needed to approve of where she placed her screenplay on the bed before Sebastian took a seat next to her. Sebastian claimed that he had a headache. She chose to believe him even though she didn't believe a word that he said to her before they went to bed without touching each other. Despite the growing tension between them, their lives went back to normal as Daphne went into second grade with Noah starting preschool at the same private school where they went to the studio during the day. Her parents spent most of the day at the hospital getting her mother's chemo treatments done every other day. It was nice that Noah was going to school because she didn't have to worry about who was going to watch him. While Sebastian spent his time in his office in meetings with their lawyers and their bankers, she spent her time in the editor's room helping him put together the movie through the hundreds of takes that they did until they created the final version of the movie. She walked into Sebastian's office to hand him to the movie. She didn't wait to hear his response before she walked out of the room when she shouted out to him for everyone in the office to hear that she hoped that he enjoyed watching her throw herself off of the Golden Gate Bridge. Sebastian shoved the film into his assistant's hands as he asked her to contact the movie theaters and to contact Lucy to set up the press dates where he followed her into her office with him slamming the door behind him before he pulled her into a sudden kiss. They made up with each other on her meeting table. They didn't care if the office heard them having sex with each other because they owned the place, and their workers couldn't complain about it. They were no longer at each other's throats. Once it was time for her international press tour in Europe and Central Asia, she got emotional about leaving Daphne and Noah at home with her parents and Sebastian because she spent so much time with them over the summer. Sebastian reminded her that she needed to do this for them.

On the morning that she left for a month-long international press tour, she pulled Daphne and Noah into a long hug as she told them that she loved them where she did the same thing with her parents and Sebastian before she got into a car with Lucy. After their driver dropped them off at the airport, she followed Lucy to their private jet where the production team and the cast were waiting for them before they left for their stop in Paris, France. They used the same format that they used for their last two international press tours because it worked well for them. They made an effort to go to new places that they didn't get to go to before. While they went across Europe and Central Asia doing events in a new city every other day, the movie *Golden Shi* premiered in theaters across the states where they were doing a press tour in the states when they got back from Europe and Central Asia. Sebastian called her when they were in Warsaw, Poland to tell her that their movie *Golden Shi* was doing great in the states and the rest of the world. He was being asked to do interviews about the movie with her when she was home before she promised him that she would do the interviews with him. People told her at the movie screenings that they connected to the message of the movie. No one talked about addiction and mental illness in Hollywood like her. She made this movie for her father because he never got the chance to have the life that he deserved to have after he killed himself. Her father killing himself defined her life since she was eight years old, and this was her way of making something beautiful. She needed to make something beautiful out of it or else she was going to lose herself in it. When a journalist asked her why she made this movie, she told the journalist that she promised her uncle at his funeral that she wasn't going to lie to the world. She was sick of lying to the world about what happened to her when she was a child. She wanted to do something that her father would be proud of if he had the ability to tell her anything. This message connected even more for people than the message of the movie. Everyone knew someone in their lives that was lost to them and the world. They mattered to the world. She closed her interview by saying that everyone wants to matter to someone because it gives us purpose to keep going on. When the journalist asked her what she kept going on, she told them her husband, her children, her parents, and her cousins. Most importantly, she was going on for her father. She was living the life that he never got the chance to have. The interview that she did with the journalist for a newspaper in Spain quickly spread across the world. She woke up one morning to her face on the cover of *The New York Times* with the story that she did a week ago. She didn't know what surprised her the most about the fallout of *Golden Shi* that her movie stroked so many hearts of strangers that she never met or that she was becoming the main story in the press over her successful movie. She was happy that her message was being spread by the best means possible because that was the goal of her making it. Not to win awards or get famous from it. She wanted to make a difference in the world. She was trying to make a world that she wanted her children to live in. Like what Poppy said at Aunt Priscilla's funeral that stuck with her ever since then. When she came home after her international press tour, she only had a few days before she had to leave for her press tour across the country where she spent as much time as she could with her children. She missed them when she was away from them. Sebastian was going on her press tour with her. Uncle Stan stayed at the house to help her mum take care of her mother and the children while they were gone. She got on the private jet with Sebastian, his assistant Kathy, and her assistant Lucy where their first stop was in Las Vegas. They did joint interviews for newspapers and magazines before they left to go to Denver the next few days later. She attended watch parties in the movie theaters where Sebastian did media appearances for newspapers before they did joint interviews together when it was requested for them to do it. On their last stop of the tour, they received a phone call from her mother that they were going to do surgery to remove the tumors in her ovaries because they were small enough to operate on. She promised her mother that they would be home for it before she told Lucy that they needed to wrap up their tour for good. Once they were home for the first time in three weeks, they pulled Daphne and Noah in their arms as they told them that they loved them and that they missed them so much. Noah got her attention when he told her to see his artwork from school.

After she joined Noah in his bedroom, he explained his artwork to her where she asked him if he had any drawings of their family before Noah pulled out a picture of their family that he painted in school. Noah pointed out each family member to her with his fingers as he went over mommy, daddy, Daphne, Noah, Grandma Ella, Grandma Abby, and one more person that was in the background. When she asked him who the last person was in his picture, Noah told her that it was grandpa when she told Noah that grandpa was dead where Noah told her that it didn't mean that grandpa wasn't with them. She stopped herself from crying because Noah didn't like it when she cried in front of him. She told him that he was the sweetest boy and that he was named after his grandpa when Noah asked her if his name was Noah too. She kissed the top of his head before she told him that grandpa's name was William after his middle name. Noah told her that he liked being named after him because he had a special connection to him. She cried as soon as Noah said that because that was the sweetest thing that her son said to her. She was doing something right with raising him. Sebastian pulled them out of Noah's bedroom to tell him that Grandma Ella was going to the hospital if they wanted to see her where she carried Noah downstairs. After her mum left for the hospital with her mother, they got the children ready for bed as Daphne asked about Grandma Ella's surgery when they tucked her into bed where she told her that she would see her in the morning before Daphne slept for the rest of the night. Once they put Noah to sleep in his bedroom, she followed Sebastian into their bedroom where he wrapped his arms around her before she slept in his arms for the rest of the night. When she woke up the next morning to Daphne and Noah jumping up and down on the bed, she tickled their sides with the room full of their laughter until Sebastian walked into the room with a tray of breakfast for them to eat in their bed. Once she changed the children into comfortable outfits, she carried Noah on her hip as Sebastian held onto Daphne's hand where they got into the back of the car before their driver dropped them off at the hospital. She walked into the hospital with Noah sitting on her hip as Sebastian followed behind her with him holding onto Daphne's hand where the nurse directed them to her mother's room before Daphne gave her grandparents tight hugs with her mum placing Daphne on her lap. As she placed Noah on the bed with Grandma Ella, she pulled her mother into a tight hug with her mother's arms wrapped around her until Noah pulled her oxygen tubes off of her where she placed Noah onto the floor before she sat down next to her mother with Noah running around the room. Sebastian placed Noah in his lap to keep him from running away as her mother talked about how she felt after she woke up from her surgery where she grabbed onto her mother's hand giving her mother all of her attention before Daphne announced to the room that she had to go to the bedroom. Sebastian took her to the bathroom with Noah coming with him because he had to go too. She leaned onto the chair when her mum asked her with a smile on her face, "How was your press tour honey? I've read your interviews, and they are impressive."

She grabbed onto her mother's hands when she responded to her mum with a frown on her face, "Thanks, mum. It's been great. I'm relieved that it's over, but I'm sad too. I'm worried that I have to do something new after this that is going to top it. I don't know if I can top what I did with that movie."

Her mother cupped her hands over her face when she responded to her daughter with a serious look on her face, "Hush, baby girl. You'll do something better. Every movie that you write gets better and better. I know that this movie was special to you. You put your heart and soul into it, but you can do that with a new movie. You aren't going to top jumping off the Golden Gate Bridge, but you can do anything that you set your mind to. Your mum and I watched the movie with Uncle Stan and Thomas in the movie theaters. How much did it hurt jumping off of the Golden Gate Bridge? It looked painful watching it."

She grabbed onto her mother's hands when she responded to her with a smile on her face, "It hurt so bad, mom. You have no idea. We did it so many times that I thought that it was going to kill me. I dislocated my shoulder on the last take. That was one that they used in the movie. I was screaming in pain from it. Poor Bash was so freaked out about it. It was okay. I had to wear a sling for a few weeks, but it was worth it. Thanks for believing in me, mom. You too, mum. None of this would be possible without you guys. I love you."

As her mother pulled her into a tight hug with her face hidden in her chest, her mum pulled herself into their hug where they didn't let go of her until Sebastian walked into the room with the children holding toys from the gift shop in their hands where Noah ran over to her to show her his teddy bear before she placed him onto her lap. Daphne handed her grandma Ella flowers from the gift shop as her mother took them from Daphne's hands when she said to her with a smile on her face, "Thank you, Daph. These are so pretty. Did daddy help you pick them out?"

Sebastian placed Daphne on the bed as he ran his fingers through her hair when he responded to her with a smirk on her face, "We went into the gift shop for flowers. These little heathens convinced me to get them stuffed animals. Like they don't have any room for stuffed animals at home. Don't give me that look, Isabella. You would've done the same thing." Noah talked about his teddy bear where Daphne talked to her grandmother about her challenge between choosing from a stuffed horse or a teddy bear before she chose the horse to add to her growing stuffed horse collection. Her cousins Sasha, Amelia, and Oliver visited them at the hospital while Sebastian played outside with the children at the playground with their spouses until they went to the house where they got the children ready for bed before they changed into their favorite pajamas. Once they read bedtime stories after Daphne and Noah fell asleep in her arms, she placed Noah into his bed as Sebastian tucked Daphne into her bed where she followed him into their bedroom before he laid down in the bed next to her. After he told her that he loved her and that he was so proud of her, she told him that she loved him too and that he believed in her where he wrapped his arms around her before she fell asleep in his arms for the rest of the night.

CHAPTER SEVENTY-THREE
(WINTER 1977 – NEW YORK, NEW YORK)

After her mother spent a week in the hospital, she recovered from her surgery at home where the doctor required her to go to his office every two weeks to test her blood, so that they could see if the surgery was a success or not. Sebastian observed their movies that were being filmed where she helped their editor create the final cut of the movies before Sebastian shared the movies with the movie theaters across the country and to the rest of the world. She didn't find any motivation for her next screenplay even though she was desperately looking for it. She was concerned that she would never make anything more important than her movie *Golden Shi*. Nothing would be as special to her than what she did at the Golden Gate Bridge. Her mother reassured her that it wasn't true. She was going to find her muse again and it was going to be greater than anything that she did before. She didn't believe a word coming out of her mother's mouth, but she pretended that it was enough for her. She spent time at Jacob's house on the weekends with his boyfriend Trevor who owned a gay night club. She was hesitant to say anything in front of Trevor because she didn't know him. It didn't take her that long to trust Trevor like she trusted Jacob. They talked about personal things with each other. She told them that she was sick of pretending that it was enough, and she didn't want to lie to people. Jacob asked her what she was pretending that was enough before Trevor made a joke that his therapist side was coming out. After they laughed about it, she told Jacob that she was pretending that it all was enough. Working at the studio. Being a mother. Being a wife. Writing and filming her movies. Being celebrated in Hollywood for those movies. The glamorous lifestyle that came with it. She realized that it should be enough for her, but it wasn't enough for her. Nothing was going to fill the void inside of her. She knew that fame wasn't going to be the answer to her problems. She was going to be the same empty person with or without fame in Hollywood. It hurt her that she thought that it would be enough for her. She desperately wanted it to be enough for her because it meant something so much worse to her. If the fame and success in Hollywood wasn't enough for her, then nothing would fulfill her. She sobbed into Jacob's arms when he told her that she was trapped in the aftermath of addiction where drugs were the only thing that mattered to her. Nothing was going to make her feel like drugs made her feel like. She was never the same after she got high for the first time. She chased that feeling only to find that nothing was going to feel like that again. She thought when she was younger and naïve. She believed in the world. She believed that there was greater meaning in her life. She believed in other people. She believed in the magic of Hollywood. She believed in herself. It was naïve for her to have faith. They were never going to give her the feeling that she desired. She didn't care. She wouldn't have believed it if someone told her that it wasn't true. She wanted to believe in her delusions. It comforted her from reality. Her delusions protected her until they were hurting her. Not that she cared that they were hurting her. She was willing to die on that hill.

Jacob told her not to be so hard on her younger self because she didn't know what she knew now. This was another delusion that she believed from him. That it didn't matter. She told him that she didn't want to talk about it anymore. She didn't want to uncover these thoughts. Her mind became a desolate place. A barren desert that didn't get any rain for over a decade. An abandoned house in a deserted neighborhood. Pompei after the volcano erupted in the year seventy-nine leaving ashes and debris in their wake. As much as she didn't want to confront these thoughts, she couldn't stop thinking about it no matter what she did to stop it. She dreamed about it at night. She thought about it during the day when she was working at the studio. She thought about it when she was with her children when they got home from school. She thought about it when she smoked cigarettes on her balcony at night. She couldn't escape it no matter what she did to run away from it. It followed her no matter where she was. She went to the doctor's office with her parents where he told them that her mother's cancer was in remission before she pulled her parents into tight hugs in shock at what happened. They went to their favorite restaurant to celebrate her mother being cancer free. Posey went home with the children after they ate their dinner where they went to the movie theater to see a movie that their studio released last week. Something inside of her broke when she watched the movie. It wasn't anything that the movie said that provoked her emotions. She saw herself in this place a long time ago. She hid her crying from her parents and Sebastian until she couldn't take it anymore where she sprinted out of the movie theater without looking behind her before she went into the bathroom. She let out heartbreaking sobs into her hands as she sat down on the floor with her knees in her chest. She thought about a movie that she saw when she was five years old. It was her first time watching a movie in the theaters with her cousins. It was her birthday present from her parents. She didn't remember what movie it was. It wasn't what was important to her. When she looked up at that big screen, she saw herself inside of it. She believed in Hollywood. She believed that this was going to fill the void in her heart. This movie marked the beginning of a dream that she was never going to have. It wasn't fame or fortune. It wasn't being immortalized on the big screen. She was going to find meaning from being an actress. She had a funeral for herself. She grieved a dream that wasn't coming true. She grieved the little girl that she used to be. She grieved the little girl that believed in the magic of Hollywood. She grieved the little girl that believed that there was greater meaning to her life. For the person that used to believe in the world. It shouldn't have taken her this long. All that mattered was that she was doing it. She let go of the person that she used to be. She let go of the person that she was never going to be. She let off the pressure to make it mean something. She let go of the drugs. She let go of her dreams. She let go of her father. He was an important part of the delusion that she believed in. He was the last thing that she needed to let go of. She needed to let go of the part of her that waited for him. He was never coming back. He didn't want to be in her life. Not because he was fulfilling a secret destiny that she needed to complete for him. He was gone. That part of her that wanted him was gone. She realized it when she jumped off of the Golden Gate Bridge. As she was in the water, she saw that she needed to let go of him because he let go of her a long time ago. She spent the rest of the movie sobbing on the bathroom floor. Sebastian banged on the door when he begged her to open the door where she unlocked the door for him before he pulled her into a tight hug with her face hidden in his chest. He didn't ask her what was wrong, and she didn't ask him why he wasn't bothering her. That was a conversation for them to have with each other later.

Once Sebastian guided her to where her parents were waiting for them, she didn't say anything to them as she got into the back of the car where they followed her into the car before their driver drove them to the house. When their driver dropped them off at the house, her parents went into their bedroom as Sebastian guided them into their bedroom where she sat down on the bed with him holding onto her hands before he asked her what happened at the movie theatre. She told him that she didn't believe in the delusion anymore before he asked her what she meant by that. She walked onto the balcony as she lit a cigarette with her inhaling the smoke from it where he took a seat next to her leaning on the railing before he asked her why she always did this. With a scowl on her face, she asked him what he meant by that where Sebastian looked over at her with a face that she hated more than anything before he asked her why she always acted like this after she got off of a high. He was referring to her depressive episodes that she went through after a period of mania. She told him that she didn't know why she did it, but she didn't like it. He told her that he could predict that this was going to happen after they got back from San Francisco. She tried to defend herself by saying that she couldn't help it if she was like this because of her bipolar disorder. It turned into a horrible argument between them when he told her that he didn't mean it like that and that she knew what he was talking about where she shrugged her shoulders at him as she smoked her cigarette before Sebastian stormed into their bedroom. She stayed on the balcony smoking cigarettes until she ran out of them where she walked into their bedroom when she laid down in the bed next to him before they slept for the rest of the night without touching each other. This argument lasted between them for several months where they said passive aggressive comments to each other at the office. They pretended to get along with each other in the presence of her parents and the children. Even though they were actors, no one around them was buying it that they got along with each other. She didn't understand why Sebastian was upset with her. He didn't know what she was upset about at the movie theaters during her emotional breakdown. She never got the chance to tell him about it because he already made up his mind about it. She couldn't stand it when he did that, and he knew that she couldn't stand it. The resentment that they got over four years ago didn't have an impact on them. They had new resentments for each other that grew between them over the years. Sebastian only talked to her about things concerning their company or the children. She vented about her problems to Oliver and Sebastian did the same thing as her. Oliver told her multiple times that this would be so much easier if they talked to each other, but neither of them wanted to hear it. While she was busy on her campaign to ignore Sebastian, her parents rushed to New York with Sasha since Aunt Valeria was hospitalized for kidney failure where her mother promised to tell her when she needed to go to New York to say goodbye to her if things got worse. She was okay with that deal because her mother always stayed true to her word. After a few weeks of them being in New York, her mother called her to tell her that she needed to get to New York as soon as possible since Aunt Valeria got worse where she promised her mother that she would be there in the morning before she packed her bags to go to New York.

When Sebastian came home from work that evening, he asked her where she was going as she rushed to put the last pair of boots into her suitcase when she told him that she was going to New York to say goodbye to Aunt Valeria who was dying in the hospital. Sebastian didn't have any idea what she was talking about because they didn't talk to each other in months. He tried not to act like he wasn't hearing about it for the first time before he told her to bring the children with her, so that they could see their cousins. After Sebastian disappeared in his office, she went into the children's bedrooms to pack their bags where she smoked cigarettes on the balcony until Sebastian turned off the lights in their bedroom before she joined him on the other side of the bed. When she woke up to an empty bed, she hid the disappointment that she felt in her heart as she got the children ready for the day. They were confused about where they were going when she told them that they were going to New York to see their cousins before Daphne asked her why daddy wasn't coming with them. She told Daphne that daddy had to work and that he would join them when he was done working. Daphne didn't believe her when she told her that it was fine before Noah changed the subject about sledding in New York where she told him that they would if it snowed there. After she did her customary kiss for Sebastian with him pulling the children into tight hugs, she got into the back of the car with the children where they made a trip over to Sasha's house to pick her six-year-old niece Charlotte to take her with them before their driver drove them to the airport. They got on their private jet for a flight to New York that took them most of the day to get there where she entertained the children with puzzles and books until the children played by themselves with her taking a nap in the afternoon. When their plane landed in New York that same evening, she carried Noah off of the plane as Charlotte and Daphne held onto each of her hands. She ran over to Sasha who was happy to see Charlotte with her before she pulled Sasha into a desperate hug with Sasha's face hidden in her chest. As soon as they pulled away from each other, Sasha pulled Charlotte into a tight hug with her face hidden in her mother's chest as Sasha affectionately spoke to her in French where she followed Daphne to the car before Sasha drove them to Nina's house. Once they walked into Nina's house, she pulled Nina into a tight hug with her four-year-old niece Rose hugging her legs as she placed Noah on the floor to play with Daphne and his cousins Liam and Owen in the living room where she joined her parents, Ivan, Joseph, Eilis, and Bridget who were helping their mother make dinner in the kitchen. After she pulled her parents into a tight hug, she pulled Ivan into a tight hug with her face hidden in his shoulder until Daphne called out for her where she kissed Joseph on the cheek before she ran into the living room. She separated Noah from Owen who fought with him over the same toy. She carried Noah into the girl's bedroom as he screamed in her arms with him kicking his legs where she placed him on the bed with her hands tightly on his legs to prevent him from getting away from her. It was silent between them until Noah stopped trying to squirm away from her with her tightly holding onto him when she asked him if he was proud of himself for acting like that where he shook his head at her with his hands crossed on his chest before he asked her why he was getting in trouble. She looked at him when she told him in a stern voice that he was getting in trouble because he hit Owen with a toy car where Noah tried to tell her that Owen hit him first before she told him that he was lying to her and that she didn't appreciate it. Noah wasn't in the mood to play games. He told her that she lied to daddy all of the time where she restrained herself from something that she might regret before she told Noah that it was their business what they said to each other and that he wasn't allowed to lie to them. Noah knew that she was pissed off at him when he told her that he was sorry and that he would apologize to Owen. As she kissed Noah on the top of his head, she told him that she loved him and that she was saying this to him because she wanted him to grow up to be a gentleman like daddy was where Noah nodded his head in understanding with her before she carried him into the living room. Once Noah apologized to Owen for hitting him with a toy car, Owen wasn't bothered by it as he played with Noah again like nothing happened between them where she went outside on the porch for a moment alone before she noticed that Ivan followed her there. They didn't say anything to each other, but Ivan understood what her eyes said to him because he looked at her with a concerned look on his face. She would've smoked a cigarette, but she couldn't stop her hands from shaking inside of her pockets. They stood outside on the porch in comfortable silence until Nina opened the door as she told them that it was time for dinner where she walked into the house before she sat down in between Daphne and Noah who fought over who got to have the biggest portion of mashed potatoes. Since she wasn't in the mood for it, she gave them a stern look that stopped them from fighting where Daphne handed the plate of food to Noah who accepted it from her before they ate dinner with the family. Everyone had soft conversation with each other except for her since she was obsessing over what Noah said to her in the girl's bedroom. She was so caught up in her mind that she didn't realize that everyone was done eating as she placed her dirty dishes into the sink with her ignoring everyone in the room where she called out for her children to get ready for bed before Daphne and Noah followed her into their bedroom. After she put the children to sleep in their bed, she sat on the balcony as she smoked cigarettes for most of the night where she obsessed about what Noah said to her before she went to bed when she couldn't feel her fingers.

She woke up the next morning to an empty bed as she walked into the living room to see Sebastian sitting at the kitchen table drinking coffee with her parents and Joseph while Noah and Daphne played with their cousins in the living room where she kissed Sebastian's cheek before she told them that she was going to meet them at the hospital. Before Sebastian or her parents got the chance to say anything to her, she grabbed her coat off of the back of the door as she ran outside to see Nina coming back from a walk with Holly where she told her cousin that she was going for a run before she sprinted away from the house. She didn't stop running until she made it to her childhood house that someone else was living in as she blinked back tears that fell down her face before she ran to the nearest bus stop where she got on the bus to the hospital. After the bus dropped her off at the hospital, she let out a shaky breath as she walked towards Aunt Valeria's room where she didn't stop running until she was inside of it before Aunt Valeria laid in the bed with tubes attached to her. She was in a medically induced coma. Once she sat down on the chair next to her bed, she grabbed onto her hands as she blinked back tears that fell down her face when she told Aunt Valeria everything that she never got the chance to tell her where she didn't stop talking until a nurse entered the room looking surprised that she was there. As soon as she told the nurse that she said everything that she needed to say to her aunt, the nurse nodded her head at her with a confused look on her face as she grabbed her coat off of the chair before she walked out of the room. She didn't stop walking until she made it onto the subway. She got on the subway to Central Park where she got off when it was her stop before she ran over to a bench that wasn't covered in snow as she sat down on top of it. She didn't know how long she sat on the bench until her mother sat down next to her where she looked up at the sky to see that it was dark outside before her mother guided her to the car to go to the house. When she walked into Nina's house with her mother following behind her, Nina cried in Joseph's arms as Anastasia cried in Damien's arms where she walked past them without saying anything to them before she silently went into her bedroom. She walked in her bedroom expecting to see the children sleeping or playing. Instead, she walked into an empty room with the bed perfectly made like she didn't sleep there with her children last night. Once she sat down on the bed, there was a handwritten note on the nightstand where she grabbed it off of it before she read it aloud to herself. The note said that Sebastian took the children to stay in a hotel for a few days while they were in New York and that they would see her at the funeral. She didn't know what surprised her more that her cousins were burying their mother so quickly or that Sebastian had the balls to take the children away from her. She was more upset about Sebastian taking the children away from her. That meant that he didn't trust her with them right now. In a complete fit of anger against him, she went out on the balcony as she placed the lighter to the piece of paper where she watched it burn in front of her before she kicked the ashes off of the porch. She smoked a box of cigarettes on the balcony until her hands froze from being outside in a snowstorm before she laid down in her bed as she stared up at the ceiling all night.

On the morning of Aunt Valeria's wake, she wasn't able to get out of her bed as she hid under the covers like it was a defense from the world. Her mother barged into the room when she asked her why she wasn't dressed for the wake before she told her mother that she wasn't going to the wake. Her mother was at a loss of words of what to say to her because she wasn't going to miss her aunt's wake before her mother asked her what was going on with Sebastian. When she didn't respond to her, her mother let out a defeated sigh as she told her that they left a car at the house if she changed her mind where her mother left her alone in her bedroom before she pulled the covers over her. She woke up in the evening to no one in the house since everyone was eating dinner at Anastasia's apartment. She walked into the kitchen to grab the car keys that her mother left for her on the table as she walked over to the car where she drove to the only place that she could stomach being at right now. She pulled up to the graveyard that Uncle Sam was buried in, and that Aunt Valeria was going to be buried in the morning. Even though there was a sign on the gate that clearly said no trespassing, she broke the lock off of the gate without a care as she parked the car in a hidden area that no one would know where she was before she walked through the dark graveyard until she got to Uncle Sam's grave. She sat down on the ground next to his grave as she stared at the open hole that was for Aunt Valeria's coffin in the morning where she laid down in it as still as she could with her eyes closed and her hands crossed on her chest. She stayed like that until the night security guard shouted at her when he asked her if she was okay when she didn't respond to him before she got up from the ground where she walked to her car like she wasn't covered in dirt. After she made a last-minute decision to ditch the car in the cemetery, she walked throughout the city covered in dirt from the cemetery until a police officer stopped to ask her if she needed any help where she shook her head at him before she walked throughout the city like she didn't come back from the dead. She passed out on a bench in Central Park for the rest of the night. She woke up the next morning with someone shaking her when a police officer told her that she needed to go home where she asked him how she was going to get home before Oliver told the police officer that he would take her from here. She didn't know what upset her the most about this situation, that she didn't succeed in freezing to death in Central Park or that the first person that the police called was Oliver and not Sebastian. After Oliver thanked the police officer for taking care of her, Oliver reached out to grab onto her hand where she took it from him before he guided her to the car on the street. Once they were in the warm car with Oliver's coat wrapped around her shoulders, he didn't say anything to her as he drove them to his hotel where she almost fell asleep in the car before Oliver smacked her awake to tell her that she wasn't allowed to sleep with a concussion. She didn't know that she had a concussion. She was about to ask Oliver what he meant by that until she looked down at her hands and legs. They weren't covered in dirt. They were covered in blood. She crashed the car into the fence at the cemetery since she couldn't pick the lock on it. She got too frustrated and that was why she crashed the car into the fence. She didn't realize that the fence was going to be so hard to go through with her car. It wasn't her car that she crashed. It was Nina's car. She crashed her cousin's car in the cemetery gate. She must not have been that injured to walk out of the car and to lay down into Aunt Valeria's empty grave because she didn't know that she was hurt. After the security guard kicked her out, she managed to walk all the way to Central Park where she passed out on a park bench until a police officer told Oliver to take her home.

When they got to the hotel, Oliver found the nerve to talk to her as he pulled into the parking lot when he asked her in a soft voice, "We're here. Do you need help getting out of the car?"

She shook her head at him as she got herself out of the car where Oliver grabbed onto her hands before he led her into his hotel room. They took the elevator because she lost her balance on the first step where he dragged them over to the elevator before he opened the door to their room. As soon as he closed the door behind him, she limped over to the closest chair as Oliver grabbed a pile of clothes when he told her with concern laced in his voice, "Bash brought these over for you. You can take a shower in my bathroom. Everyone else is at the funeral, so it's only us. Do you need help in the bathroom? I'll help you if you need it." She shook her head at him as she walked into the bathroom with the clothes in her hands where she closed the door behind her before she placed the pile of clothes onto the floor. Once she took off her clothes that were covered in dried blood and dirt, she threw them away into the garbage as she stared at herself in the full-sized mirror until tears fell down her face where she hurried over to the shower before she turned on the warm water with her letting a light groan from the pain in her shoulder.

When she got all of the blood off of her, she put on her clean clothes as she struggled to get her sweater over her injured shoulder where she looked at herself in the mirror onc last time before she walked into the room to see Oliver reading a book on the bed. As soon as Oliver noticed that she was out of the bathroom, he placed his book onto the nightstand as he patted down on the bed next to him when he told her with a smile on his face, "Here, sit down with me."

She hesitantly walked towards him as she sat down on the bed next to him with trying not to wince in pain every time that she put pressure on her right arm. Oliver lifted her sweater over her head to get a better look of her shoulder before he told her in a gentle voice with his lips pressed together, "It doesn't look like your arm is broken, so that's good. I think that it's only bruised, but we can still get a doctor to look at it to be safe."

When she didn't say anything to him, Oliver let out a defeated sigh as he helped her into her sweater without hurting her arm when he asked her in a frustrated voice with a frown on his face, "Are you going to be mute for the rest of the day? Normally I can't get you to shut up. I'm not used to this. Can we talk? Why did you do it?"

She leaned back on the bed not putting pressure on her right arm when she asked him with a frown on her face, "What do you mean by that? Why did I do what?"

Oliver let out a frustrated sigh as he crossed his arms around his chest when he responded to her in a stern voice, "You know what I'm talking about, Isabella. Why did you crash Nina's car into the cemetery gate?"

She lightly groaned in pain as she touched her right shoulder when she responded to him in a distant voice, "I don't know why I did it, Oliver. I wanted to feel something. It's better than crashing into a river, isn't it? Is Nina mad about it?"

Oliver kept his arms around his chest when he responded to her with a serious look on his face, "Yes, Nina is pissed about it. Why would she not be upset about it? It's her car that you crashed. I don't appreciate the jokes, Isabella. This isn't the time. That's a stupid reason to crash our cousin's car. I don't believe you. What's the real reason?"

She sat up on the bed groaning in pain when she responded to him in a frustrated tone, "I'll buy another car for Nina. She'll be okay. Why don't you believe me, Oliver? Do you think that I had other motives?"

Oliver got off of the bed as he paced back and forth around the room when he responded to her with desperation laced in his voice, "Why don't I believe you? You're an addict, Isabella. You are incredible at thinking that people believe you aren't lying to them. I want to understand why you are doing this. I want to help you. I don't want you to be like this any more than you hate it. Help me understand it. Why would you do this?"

She looked up at Oliver as she blinked back tears that fell down her face when she responded to him with frustration laced in her voice, "I'm telling you the truth, Oliver. I did it because I wanted to feel something. I was sick of feeling like it didn't mean anything. I don't mean anything. I resorted to the only way that I feel anything. I laid down in Aunt Valeria's grave and I felt like I was already dead. That's why I did it. Are you happy now? Did you get the answer that you wanted me to tell you?"

Oliver sat down on the bed next to her as he grabbed onto her hands when he responded to her in a soft voice, "I believe you. I never stopped believing in you. None of us stopped believing in you. They don't know how to handle you when you are like this. It's hard to know the right thing to say. We don't know how you are going to react to it."

She let out a loud laugh that hurt her ribs as she placed her hands on her chest when she responded to him in a sarcastic tone, "You mean that Bash doesn't know how to handle it? I figured it out the moment that he didn't let me say anything to him after my emotional breakdown at the movie theaters. He didn't say anything to me. He knew what I was going to say before I said it to him. I'm not mad at him for not knowing what to do because I don't know what to do either."

Oliver grabbed onto her hands when he responded to her with a sad smile on his face, "I know that this is hard for you. It's not your fault that you do this, Isabella. You can't control what you are. You only control what you do about it. Crashing cars isn't a good way to deal with it. Putting yourself in danger is the worst way to deal with it. What were you upset about at the movie theaters?"

As she tried to laugh without remembering her bruised ribs, she laid down on the bed when she confessed to him with her blinking back tears that fell down her face, "We were watching one of our movies. I don't remember which one. Something broke me when I watched that movie. I felt like I was five years old. It was the first time that I believed in something when I watched that movie in the theaters. Like it all meant something more than me. Not that I thought that being in movies would make my life better. I thought that it would give me a purpose in the world. It didn't give me any purpose. Nothing gives me purpose. That's what scared me in the movie theater. Everything that I wanted to fulfill me is never going to fulfill me. My job isn't going to fulfill me. My family isn't going to fulfill me. My father isn't going to fulfill me. That's what triggered it, and it spiraled out of the control after that to where it is now. Nothing was going to make me feel content."

Oliver pulled her into a loose hug to not hurt her as she let out a heartbreaking sob into his chest with his arms around her before she pulled away from him. She gently laid down the bed as she held onto her chest that was burning when she said to Oliver with desperation laced in her voice, "I need to see a doctor. My ribs hurt so bad that I can barely move."

Oliver kissed her on the top of her head with his arms around her as he reached over to grab the phone off of the nightstand where he talked into it before he hung up the phone promising her that the doctor was coming soon. The doctor came ten minutes later as he examined her ribs with Oliver watching from the corner of the room until the doctor moved away from her when he told her that she broke her right ribs, and she tore muscles in her right shoulder before he told her that she should go to the emergency room to get x-rays of her chest. Oliver helped her off of the bed as she leaned heavily on him where they were about to walk out of the hotel until Sebastian walked into the lobby with Noah in his arms and Daphne holding onto his hand. Daphne ran over to her before Sebastian could stop her as she almost fell down on the floor where Oliver caught her in his arms before Daphne ran into her legs when she cried to her with tears falling down her face, "Are you okay, mommy? Why are you hurt?"

After Oliver helped her onto a chair in the back of the lobby, he ran outside to pull the car in front of the door as she ran her fingers through Daphne's hair with her face hidden into her mother's chest when she responded to her with a fake smile on her face even though she wanted to cry out in pain, "I'll be okay, Daph. Mommy got into a car accident. Uncle Oliver is going to take me to the hospital to get me better."

Daphne pulled her face out of her chest as she wiped away the tears on her daughter's face when Daphne asked her with a frown on her face, "Is that why we couldn't see you, mommy? Because you got into a car accident?"

She looked over at Sebastian who looked like he felt guilty about leaving her alone last night. She breathed through her pain when she told Daphne with her biting her lips, "No, that's not why I couldn't see you. I'll explain it to you when we get home. Bash, take the children to the hotel room. I don't want them to see this."

Once Sebastian heard her the third time that she told him, he pulled Daphne towards him with Daphne crying in his arms where he rushed the children into the elevator before Oliver appeared in the lobby with Ivan to help him get her into the car. After Oliver and Ivan got her into the car without causing a scene, Oliver drove them to the hospital as Ivan held onto her hands until Oliver pulled up to the hospital where they helped her into a wheelchair before Oliver took her into the emergency room with Ivan parking the car. At the hospital, they did x-rays to make sure that she didn't have any broken bones, and they put a sling on her right shoulder to help her get the pressure off of it. They gave her pain medicine that helped her calm down. She apologized to Ivan for missing his mother's funeral when he told her that his mother knew that she loved her. She didn't get the chance to grieve for her aunt because she was busy having a mental breakdown. Oliver and Ivan assured that no one was upset. Nina wasn't mad at her. She was in the hospital. She passed out in her hospital room for the rest of the night.

Chapter
Seventy-Four
(Spring 1977 – Stockholm, Sweden)

She was discharged from the emergency room the next day with a sling on her right arm and her ribs were put back into place. Oliver dropped them off at the hotel as she walked into Sebastian's hotel room where he packed up the children's bags before he stopped when he noticed that she was standing there. He pulled her into a desperate hug with her hiding her face in his chest where they didn't let go of each other until Daphne ran into the room with Noah following behind her before Daphne shouted out to her mother. As soon as she pulled away from Sebastian, she lowered herself onto her knees as she pulled Daphne and Noah into a tight hug with their faces hidden in her chest. Daphne asked her if she was going home with them before she told Daphne that she was going home. Once Daphne and Noah were distracted by something else, she pulled Sebastian into a desperate kiss where they didn't let go of each other until she groaned in pain from Sebastian hitting her ribs before he apologized for hurting her. She told him that she needed to go over to Nina's house to apologize to her as he nodded his head at her when he told her that he got the money out from the bank to pay her back for the car where she thanked him. She went into Oliver's hotel room to ask him to drive her there because she couldn't drive for over six weeks. After Oliver drove them to Nina's house, he asked her if she wanted him to come with her as she shook her head at him when she told him that this was something that she needed to do by herself when she walked out of the car before she knocked on Nina's door. As soon as Nina opened the door, she pulled her into a sudden hug as she loudly groaned in pain with Nina letting go of her when she asked her if she was okay where she chose not to respond to her before she handed Nina the envelope of money. Nina pushed it back to her when she told her that she didn't need to be repaid for the car where she pushed the money towards her again before she told her that this was her apology for crashing her car. Nina refused to accept the money because it was a pride thing to not take money from her family. She told Nina that she wasn't in her right mind when she crashed her car and that she felt guilty about it. Nina told her that her being injured from the car accident was hard for her to accept out of everything that happened. Not that she crashed her car or that she walked around the city injured without knowing it. It was that she was hurt from her own actions. As soon as Joseph appeared in front of the door, she realized that Joseph was the person that was mad about it and not Nina who could never be upset with her when she handed the money to Joseph who took it from her hands before he disappeared into the house. After Nina told her to call her when she was feeling better, she nodded her head at her as Nina slammed the door behind her where she undoubtedly fought with Joseph about him taking the money from her before she went back into the car with Oliver who was watching it happen in front of him.

Once Oliver asked her if she was okay, she nodded her head at him as he grabbed onto her hands before Oliver drove them to the hotel where Sebastian and the children waited for her. Since she was useless at helping Sebastian pack their bags, she played with Daphne and Noah on the floor of their hotel room until Sebastian told them that it was time to leave for the airport where she held onto Noah's hand with Sebastian holding onto Daphne's hand where they got into the car before Oliver drove them to the airport. As soon as Oliver returned his rental car to the airport, they got on their private jet with Oliver's family, Amelia's family, and her parents. Sasha and her family were staying in New York for a few weeks to be with her sisters and her brother. For the flight to Los Angeles, she took a painkiller that the doctor prescribed to her where she slept in one of the bedrooms before Oliver and Sebastian checked on her every hour with Daphne and Noah tagging along with them to make sure that she was breathing. When their private jet landed at the LAX airport the next morning, Oliver woke her from the long flight home where she didn't wake up once before she followed them off of their private jet. As soon as she got into the car with Sebastian and the children, Oliver promised to check on her before their driver drove them to the house. Her parents spent the night at Uncle Stan and Thomas' house since they knew that she needed space to figure out things with Sebastian. After their driver drove them to the house, Sebastian carried their bags into the house as she followed Daphne and Noah into the living room where they went into their bedrooms to play with their toys before she went into their bedroom. She fell asleep for the rest of the afternoon where she walked into the kitchen to see Sebastian eating dinner with the children before he asked her if she wanted to join them. As soon as she took a seat next to him, she made a plate of food as Daphne told her about the adventures that they got into when she was gone where she listened to what her daughter told her before Noah asked her if it hurt getting into a car accident. Even though she was caught off guard by his question, she told Noah that it hurt when Noah laughed at what she said before Sebastian changed the subject by asking them if they were excited to go to school. After they put the children to bed for the rest of the night, Sebastian prepared a warm bath as he helped her into the bathtub where he got into the bathtub with her before he wrapped his arms around her being careful of her injuries. They didn't say anything to each other as Sebastian gently washed her with her leaning her head on his shoulder where he helped her out of the bathtub before she changed into her silk pajamas in her closet. As soon as she joined him in bed, he wrapped his arms around her with her head leaning on his chest while he ran his hands up and down her back where he asked her why she did it before she answered his question the same way that she answered Oliver's question in New York. She crashed the car into the cemetery gate because she wanted to feel something. Sebastian didn't know how to respond to her until he broke the silence when he asked her if this was about what happened at the movie theater before she told him that it had everything to do with what happened at the movie theater.

Sebastian felt guilty about how he reacted to it because he wasn't saying anything to her. She told him that she didn't blame him for not reacting to the situation well because there was no good way to react to it. This made Sebastian feel a little bit better about it because he knew that she wasn't upset with him about it. Sebastian asked her if she intended to do something worse than crash the car into an iron gate.

This comment threw her off because not even Oliver found the nerve to ask her about if she was trying to kill herself or not. Since she was revealing the truth to him, she told him that she was trying to kill herself and that she intended on crashing Nina's car into the Hudson River. Sebastian was silent for a long time before he asked her what stopped her from doing it. She looked up at Sebastian when she told him that she thought about how she was going to miss out on the view. It was a moment that they were living in since she walked out of the movie theater. Sebastian went to work in the studio as the children went back to school where she stayed at home recovering from her car accident. Her doctor went to the house to see her once a week to see how she was healing from the accident where he figured out how it happened before she made up a story that stopped him from bothering her. She wasn't in the mood to explain her mental illness and her suicide attempt to her doctor. It was none of his business what she did to cope with her life. She couldn't run away from her almost suicide attempt because Oliver was asking her about it. Every time that Oliver brought it up to her, she asked him not to ask questions that he didn't want to know the answers to where he left her alone until the next time that he went over to the house. They were the only people that asked her about it. She only would tell them the truth out of anyone else in her family. They were the only people brave enough to ask the question. Her mother never asked her about it because she never asked her the hard questions. It wasn't that her mother didn't trust her, but her mother had enough hindsight to know the answer to those kinds of questions. No one else knew that it was another one of her suicide attempts except her mother, Sebastian, and Oliver. She didn't want the world knowing that about her. There were some secrets that they would never know about her. Since she had unlimited free time during the day, she wrote for the first time in a long time. She wasn't writing a new screenplay or a book like she did when Noah was born. She wrote in a journal. Jacob would've been so proud of her for going back to her roots. She didn't write diary entries. She wrote letters. Letters to herself. Letters to her father. Letters to her mother. Letters to her mum. Letters to Oliver. Letters to Sebastian. Letters to her children. She never intended on sending these letters. This wasn't an exercise on what she was going to say to them after she killed herself. This was about what she would say to them if her life unexpectedly ended one day that was out of her control. She would share these letters to people after she died. It was her gift to them. A world that she left behind for them. Since her near death experience in New York, she thought about the impact she was going to have on the world. How was she going to be remembered? Would she be known as the person that she was? Or would she be known as the person that she wanted people to think of her? She had too many close encounters with death not to be concerned about this. This was long overdue for her to think about this when she wrote in her journal. She considered showing a few of her letters to Sebastian, but she stopped herself from doing it. It would make him treat her like she was broken. It would defeat the point of her being treated like a normal person after being a broken person. They couldn't help it when they treated her like that because it was their nature to do that. Oliver was never going to stop treating her like that. He forgot about it because she made him forget about it. Sebastian would always treat her like that, and she was learning how to live with it. She couldn't stand it when he treated her like she was a broken person. She wouldn't forget it, but she would learn to forgive him. What else could she expect from him? A husband that was worried about something bad happening to his wife who was the mother of his children. She understood why he was that way with her. He didn't want their children to not have a mother. It wasn't what she wanted for her children either. She didn't want them to grow up like she grew up without her father. The damage that it did on her wasn't what she wanted Daphne and Noah to feel. She questioned what the purpose was of her life after all of this pain. She pretended to be a different version of herself.

The version of herself that she would be if she walked through a different door. Sometimes she was Isabella who chose to stay in New York to be an author. Other times she was Isabella that chose drugs over the world. She could be anyone that wanted to be in her journal. Most of the time, she was Isabella who lived in England. Where her mother married her father. Her parents had a family together. She had a brother and a sister to take care of instead of doing drugs and killing herself in her youth. Her father was a veteran of the war, and her mother was a stay-at-home mom. Her father loved his children more than anything in the world. This was her favorite world that she created for herself. The world where everything went the way that they wanted it to go for them. It was so perfect. Her father called her his butterfly. He took her fishing with her brother. He took her to see the stars with her sister. Her mother showed her how to be a good and loyal person. Her father taught her how to drive when she was thirteen years old because they lived on the farm, and she was eager to help them with the work. Her younger siblings complained to their mother that it wasn't fair that their father spent extra time with her. She told them that they had a special relationship with each other. He took care of her like he wished that his father took care of him. When she wasn't in that world, she was so upset. She felt like the door was right in front of her, but she could never reach it. It was floating in front of her as it taunted her with what she could never have. It told her that this wasn't the world that she wasn't supposed to live in. It was a world that belonged to a different Isabella. She would never leave that world if she got inside of the door. There would be no need for her to come back to her world because it was where she got everything that she wanted. She would miss Sebastian, her mum, and her children who weren't in that world with her, but it would feel like she never needed to do anything to feel complete. The world would be enough for her. They would be enough for her. This led to her writing letters in her journal to herself about how one choice changed the course of her life. It was a choice that she never got the chance to make because her parents made it on her behalf. Everything always went back to the moment when her father raped her mother. Everything broke for them. She wasn't born before the world broke her. She wasn't trapped between the past and the present. She was trapped in between to two different doors one where her father never raped her mother and the other door where her father raped her mother. She was stuck there for so long that she didn't realize that she was trapped in it. It was her own prison where she was torn between which world to choose. Would she spend an eternity in a world that she was never going to have? Or would she spend an eternity in a world that she was never going to accept? Each world came with its own caution that she wasn't going to like what she saw in it. That wasn't enough to stop her from looking into it. What she couldn't have would always be more appealing to her than the world that she deserved. She didn't think that she deserved any of this. She didn't deserve the fame and the success in Hollywood. She didn't deserve her wealth from it. She didn't deserve to have this life with her husband and her children. She didn't deserve the world that she was living in. It wasn't because her father didn't have that world. It was because she robbed her chance of a good life the moment that she chose drugs. She would always choose drugs no matter what world that she was living in. Whether she was a wealthy only child living in Manhattan, or she was the oldest daughter in a poor farming family, she would choose drugs over anything in the world. This was her prison. A lifetime full of disappointment that nothing was going to be enough for her. No matter what she did to escape from it, she couldn't run away from it. She could run away from everything else in the world except for that. She uncontrollably sobbed in her bedroom with her face hidden in her knees. They always ended the same way every time that she wrote them. It always ended up with her alone in the world. It was a curse that she wasn't able to break no matter what she did. She was never going to be fixed. She could ruin a perfect world by just being there. She was incapable of being more than a thing that would hurt her.

Before her latest manic episode in New York, this didn't scare her because she at least had her delusions that she still believed in at the end of the day. She didn't have her delusions to make her feel better anymore. The only thing that she had left in the world was this feeling that she wasn't meant to be fixed. She understood why her father jumped off of that bridge. He realized that he couldn't be fixed. The delusions weren't true. It wasn't like he gave up on the world. The world gave up on him. She felt that at the movie theater. The world gave up on her. The feeling of that pressure off of her to be fixed by the world. Even though she struggled to deal with this reality that became her life, she acted like everything was okay and that she wasn't in the middle of the worst realization in her life. She was working again like the car accident never happened to her. No one asked her about it, and she didn't bring it up. Sebastian acted like he never mistrusted her with their children, and she pretended not to be upset with him. Oliver pretended that she didn't try to kill herself and she forgot why she crashed Nina's car. These were her new delusions that she believed in. She realized that she needed to believe in something or else she was going to go insane. She believed that what happened in New York didn't mean anything. It wasn't real if she didn't acknowledge it. She forgot about the journal that she neglected in her bedroom. It lost all meaning to her. The world lost its meaning to her. She pretended to be the person that she needed to believe that she was in order to live with herself. Even though that feeling of satisfaction lasted for only a moment in time, she chose to live inside of those moments instead of the real world. The delusions were the only world that mattered. Since she was busy proving to the world that she was a mentally stable person, she forgot to prepare for the children's birthday parties in Sweden. She tasked Lucy with making the last-minute plans for her before she packed up their bags for them. This party wasn't a surprise because Daphne and Noah knew that they were going to Sweden, and they were excited about it. Sebastian and her parents bought birthday presents for the children as she wrapped them in the middle of the night when she couldn't sleep instead of moping on her balcony smoking cigarettes all night. Since the children were off from school for spring break, they spent a week in Sweden while they rode horses in the meadows, and they hiked up the mountains. For the first few days in Sweden, she was alone with the children since Sebastian worked at the studio. She took the children on a hike to the top of the mountain that Camille told her to go to in her letters. Daphne squealed once they got to the top as she carried Noah on her back who was too tired to walk anymore before Daphne shouted down the mountain thinking that someone else was going to respond to her where she told Daphne that no one was going to respond to her. After Daphne and Noah chased each other at the top of the mountain, she led them down the mountain with Noah ending up on her back again because he said that his legs hurt from all of the walking. She promised him that they would come back up here with horses next time before Daphne asked her how a horse could get up the mountain. She explained to Daphne that horses ran faster than humans for the rest of the walk down from the mountain. She went into Camille's office after she put the children to sleep in their bedrooms where she read the letters that she didn't get the chance to read the last time that she was there. She stumbled upon a letter that her father wrote to Camille. After she placed the other letters into the box, she held the letter in hand as she gently ran her fingers over the page before she softly read it aloud to herself in a shaky voice.

August 1951
Dear Camille,

I've considered what you told me the last time that I saw you in Sweden. I thought about it for a long time, but I have to decline your offer. I'm sure that I could have a beautiful life with you and JJ in Sweden. We could get into the best laughs together. We could see the best sunsets of our lives. We could be whoever we wanted to be. I could start all over without them. Like Ella and Isabella did in New York. It's not that I don't want it. I want that life more than anything in the world. It's just that I don't deserve it. You don't agree with me. I know that. You don't have to agree with me. Deep down within yourself, you know that I'm right. There are people like you that try to make the world a better place. There are other people like me that try to undo the world that they created. It's one thing to create a world that is deserving to be lived in. It's another thing to destroy a world that no one deserves to live in. As much as I destroy that world, I'm never going to succeed. What happened cannot be undone. We can't take back the hurt that we caused in the world. There are limits to human existence. We can do a lot of things, but we can't do everything. I know that we like to think that we can do anything. That's what our society teaches us. We can do anything that we set our minds to. I used to believe in it when Ella told me that. As much as I loved her, she was never going to understand it. She lives in a different world than me. She lives in a world of dreams and possibilities. I live in a world of broken promises and mistakes. I don't hold it against her for living in that world. After everything that I took from her, I'm happy that she believes in the world. It's not Ella that I'm worried about anymore. I'm worried about Isabella. She doesn't live in her mother's world. I fear that my daughter is all alone in the world. That is what keeps me up at night. I think about my butterfly being alone. I don't have the heart to tell Ella about this. She wouldn't understand how I know that about our daughter. I don't know her, and she doesn't know me. Why would I say that? This is what Ella would say to me. The look on her face would instantly stop me from saying it to her. Ella will find out for herself when Isabella gets older. I fear that it would be too late for me to do anything to stop it. Isabella will figure it out for herself. If she's anything like me, then she will find it out the hard way. I wrote a letter for my butterfly that I want you to send to her if anything bad happens to me. You know what I'm talking about. I'm not going to see her again and I couldn't leave her without saying anything to her. She would never forgive me if I didn't say goodbye to her. I'm sending the letter in this envelope, but you will need to send it in a new one to the address that I wrote down for you. You'll know when to send it to her. I trust your judgement. Thank you, my friend.

Sincerely, Willie

She leaned her head onto the desk from being suddenly dizzy until she didn't feel like she was going to pass out. She went through the rest of the letters in the box before she didn't find what her father was referring to in his letter with Camille. In a fit of anger, she dropped the box of letters onto the floor as she tore them up into little pieces until she found one of the last letters that she didn't destroy where she wiped the tears away from her face. She let out heartbreaking sobs into her hands with her face hidden in her knees when she whispered in a soft voice, "Why didn't you tell me this? Why did Camille never send this letter to me?"

She placed her father's letter in her pocket where she read a message written on the back before she read aloud to herself, "Thank your dad for talking to you. He must know that you need to hear from him." It was gone in the blink of an eye like it was never there. Sebastian knocked on the door where she stuffed the letter into her pocket when he asked her with a concerned look on his face, "What's wrong? Why were you crying? Why does it look like a bomb went off in this room?"

She ran over to him as she pulled him into a desperate hug with her face hidden in his chest where he wrapped his arms around her before he whispered to her in a soft voice, "Are you okay, Isabella? You're scaring me. Did you do something?"

She let out a shaky breath in between her sobbing when she whispered to him like it was a secret between them, "I was going to do something, but he stopped me. He finally talked back to me after all these years." Sebastian knew that this conversation wasn't going anywhere as he gently guided her into their bedroom where he got into the bed with her before she fell asleep in his arms for the night.

To my butterfly,

I'm sorry honey. I'm sorry for everything that happened to us. I know that it's hard without me in your life. Your mother is doing what is best for you. Your life in New York is what is best for us. Growing up in York would've destroyed you. Your mother knew that and that's why she left with you. You are young right now and there is a lot about your life that you don't understand. Just know that I love your mother so much. I would've done anything for her. She was my best friend. Even though you love someone, it isn't enough to make it work with them. I hope that you don't have to know what that feels like. It's the worst feeling that I've ever felt in my life. Not being enough for her. Your mother is a wonderful person. She is a light in the dark. She is safety in a storm. I know that you are being raised by the most incredible person. That's not what I worry about. You carry my darkness inside of you. Maybe you already know that or maybe you don't. I do know that it's not too late for you. You don't have to know the darkness that I knew in my life. The world hasn't been decided for you yet like it's been decided for me. I know what my ending is going to be. It doesn't have to be your ending. A wise person once told me that we are more than who we believe that we are. Your grandmother told me that when I was a teenager. Like most people in life, she couldn't take her own advice. Butterfly, whatever you believe about yourself, stop believing in it. I don't care what it is. It's not true. None of it is true. The world that you see around you isn't real. We aren't real. I'm not real. You aren't real. The world is a dark and scary place full of monsters that want to hurt you. I'm not talking about fairytale monsters from books. These are real monsters. Scarier than people. Your mind is the real monster. It will take away the world from you. It will take advantage of you until the day that you die. It will rob you of any joy that you had in your life. It makes you become someone that you don't recognize in the mirror. It takes everything from you until there is nothing left in you. The monster becomes you in every way. I didn't know about it until it was too late. I became a monster before I could stop it from consuming me. This monster is in everyone. It starts out as a little voice in your mind that lies to you. It doesn't seem intimidating. It's so weak that it can't hurt you. This is the farthest thing from the truth. This little voice turns into a monster that takes control of you. It makes you do things that you never wanted to do. It makes you believe in a world that isn't real. It makes you think that the only way out of this world is to leave it. It's right about some things, but it's never right about the end. The ending is up to you. You are the writer in your story. You control your own destiny. It doesn't have to end the way that they want it to. Promise me that you wouldn't let it control your ending. Do whatever you need to do to stop it. Believe in the world. Believe in God. Believe in the stars. Believe in me. You have to believe in something. You're stubborn like your mother. Use that stubbornness. Only you can control your ending. Make it beautiful. Make it perfect. A tragic story needs a good ending. Tell yourself this when you feel like you want it to end. The stars aren't ready for you. I close my eyes on the ledge, and I see the stars. As I fall to the ground, I see us.

I love you forever, Your father.

Chapter Seventy-Five
(Summer 1977 – Los Angeles, California)

The children's birthday party was a huge success. Daphne declared on the top of the Swedish mountain top that she was never happier in her life. As Daphne blew out the seven candles on her cake, she closed her eyes to make a wish that she told them later that night that she wished that she could live in this moment for the rest of her life. When Sebastian asked Noah what he wished for when he blew out the four candles on his cake, he told him that he wished that mommy wouldn't be sad anymore. She fought off the urge to cry before she told him that he was so sweet and that she loved him so much. Noah asked her if his wish was coming true like Daphne's wish where she put on her bravest face when she told him that they would see it for themselves soon enough. That was enough to make Noah drop the subject. They stayed in Sweden a few more days. She made it up to the children for being so upset for most of the trip where they explored Stockholm for the first time before they saw the landmarks in the city. They were sad about it when their trip came to an end. No one wanted to go back into the real world. Daphne told them on the drive to their private jet that she wanted to live in Sweden when she was a grown up where they told her that was fine as long as she was happy before Noah told them that he wanted to live in New York when he was a grown up. No one talked for the rest of the car ride where their driver dropped them off at the airport before they got on their private jet. When they got home to the states, they got the children dressed into their uniforms where Sebastian dropped them off at school before he went into the studio. Her parents were on vacation in Mexico. She was alone in the house. She read her father's letter over and over again until she memorized it before she wrote a response to him in her neglected journal. She wrote different responses to him. Some of them were angry at him. Others were appreciative of him. The worst ones were her telling him that he was wrong about her because it was too late for her. She couldn't stop thinking about the words that her father said to her in the letter. Her father told her that the monster becomes you in every way. Even though she never heard anyone use the words to describe it like that, she completely understood what he meant by it. She became the monster before she knew that it was there. She was too late to stop it from taking control over her. She always had a little voice in the back of her mind telling her lies about herself and the world around her. That little voice in the back of her mind told her that everything was going to fall apart. She couldn't stop herself from self-destructing. The world was a cold and uncaring place that didn't owe anything to her. She was alone in the cruel world. She knew the truth about it. The world wasn't what her mind told her. It was her mind that was this place. Her mind was a cruel and uncaring place. Her mind self destructed itself. Her mind made her feel like the loneliest person in the world. Her father was right. It was impossible to tell between where she started to where her mind began. They were the same person. She didn't know who she was over who the monster was. She understood why her father spent his whole life being so scared of himself. He was the person that he ran away from in his nightmares. She was the person that she ran away from in her nightmares. The scariest face in the world was her face. She was her worst enemy. No wonder she was so scared of everything. The monster stared back at her in the mirror.

This gave her an idea to write something that she never wrote before. She wanted to write a screenplay about someone that was so scared that they ran away from the monster. They went on an adventure doing everything that they needed to do to make the world not a terrifying place. They made peace with the world. They helped people around them. They tried to make the world a better place. Every time that they thought that they were safe, the monster came back again like it never left them. They did everything in their power to get rid of the monster. They became better people. They treated people like they deserved to be treated. They created a world that they didn't grow up in. It suddenly became clear to them. The monster wasn't the world. They were their own monsters. The monster was their mind. The delusions that they believed along the way was to protect them from finding out the truth. As soon as they didn't believe in the delusions anymore, they saw the truth for the first time. She took a lesson that she learned from her father. The monster that you know was worse than the monsters that you didn't know. This was the concept of her new screenplay called *In the Shadows*. She wrote a horror movie about a group of teenagers that were locked in a mansion at the Hollywood Hills over a weekend. They had to figure out who the monster in the shadows was and how they were going to stop it from killing them. They worked together to find out who was the killer. She created lots of creative ways for the killer to kill each of the characters because she didn't want to write a stereotypical killer in her movie. Some of the characters fell in love with each other. Other characters fell out of love with each other. There was drama, love, and excitement. Everything that a good Hollywood movie needed to be successful. The twist at the end of the movie was that none of it was real. Nobody died. There was no killer hunting them in the house. They were dreaming of it. The message stayed the same though throughout the movie. They didn't need to look far to find the killer because the killer was right in front of them. The killer was each character in the house. It warned the world what happens when you let the monster inside of you win. There was only death and heartbreak to follow after that. She presented her screenplay for *In the Shadows* to Sebastian one night while they were in bed. He asked her why she wrote a horror movie where she told him that she felt inspired by what her father said to her in his letter before Sebastian asked her if he could read the letter. After she handed Sebastian the letter from her nightstand, he quietly read it to himself with his lips pressed together in a thin line where he handed it to her before he asked her where she found this letter. She told him that she found it in the desk of Camille's old office where he told her that's why she was sobbing that night before she told him that was where her screenplay came to her. They met up with their lawyers a few days later about her screenplay. They told her that this movie was the least controversial thing that she wrote in her life. Their lawyers told them that they didn't have anything to worry about with the movie. She worked on casting the actors and actresses with Sebastian overseeing it. She tasked her costume designers with making the set for the movie before she tasked her costume department for getting the clothes and the props ready for the movie. Since this was her first time working on a horror movie, she asked for help from their horror movie director Fred to make this movie come together. Fred was more than willing to help her make this movie happen before he prepared the camera angles on the set. Within only a few weeks, they were filming her movie *In the Shadows.* The actors and actresses got direction from the director Fred where she helped put together the scenes that were filming that day. Like all movies in Hollywood, it was filmed out of order. The actors and the actresses quickly adapted to the changes.

She told Fred that she wanted the last scene to be the last thing filmed for the movie. She wanted it to set a tone for the ending that she desired for the movie. Fred promised her that he would find a way to make it happen. He was in control of the filming schedule that they followed like it was the Bible. If they didn't finish filming the scenes for the day, then they stayed in the studio until they finished their work. Fred was willing to work like this because this was how great movies were made in Hollywood. Since she spent long days in the studio, she missed most of the afternoon and the evening with Sebastian and her children who asked where she was if she wasn't home for dinner. She understood what sacrifice was. She spent decades on her craft as an actress and a shorter amount of time after that on being a director and writer of movies. Sebastian understood why she wasn't home. He treated the industry the same way that she did with dedication and hard work. Her children were old enough to understand why their mother wasn't home. This was part of her job and that she would be home with them once the movie was over. Daphne told her that she bragged to her friends at school about how her parents were successful actors and actresses. That wasn't much of a flex in Los Angeles because most of Daphne's friend's parents worked in Hollywood, but she was glad that Daphne was proud of them. One night she surprised the children by coming home to eat dinner with them where Daphne and Noah sprinted over to her with Sebastian and her parents stopping their conversation about politics before she pulled them into a tight hug with their faces hidden in her chest. As soon as she let go of them, she walked into the kitchen as Sebastian pecked her lips where she sat down in between Sebastian and Noah before she ate dinner with them. Once everyone ate dinner in the kitchen, her parents cleaned up the dishes in the sink as they went into the bathroom to bathe the children. Daphne talked about how she wanted to be an actress when she grew up before Noah told them that he wanted to be a writer when he grew up. After they bathed the children, Sebastian got the children dressed in their pajamas as they joined her in Daphne's bedroom where Sebastian read them bedtime stories with each of the children sitting on their laps before they put them to sleep in their bedrooms for the rest of the night. Sebastian went into his office to read scripts while she went into the living room where her mother read someone else's book for once before she sat down next to her. Her mother placed her book down on the couch as she grabbed onto her hands when she told her daughter with a smile on her face, "It's nice that you got the night off from filming. I feel like I haven't gotten a chance to see you since you got back from Sweden. Bash told me that you're filming a horror movie. What inspired you to write that, baby girl? You hated horror movies growing up. You were scared of them. You always went into our laps."

She looked over at her mother when she responded to her with a frown on her face, "Sweden is what inspired the horror movie. Something that I read gave me inspiration to make something beautiful out of it." Her mother tightened her grip on her hands when she asked her daughter with curiosity laced in her voice, "What was that, baby girl? What did you read?"

As soon as she moved away from the couch, she grabbed her father's letter from her bedroom as she walked into the living room again where she sat down on the couch next to her before she handed her mother the letter. Once her mother grabbed the letter from her hands, her mother quietly read it with a confused look on her face where she let out a soft gasp before she handed her the letter that she quickly placed into her pocket. Her mother told her daughter with a look of horror on her face, "I don't understand, baby girl. Where did you get this? I didn't know that your dad wrote this letter. What does it have to do with Sweden?"

She hid her shaking hands into her lap when she responded to her mother in a distant voice, "I found it in Camille's desk. Dad sent it to her before he killed himself. He told her to send it to me when it was the right time, but Camille never sent it to me. She didn't want to burden a little girl with the weight of her father's death. It wouldn't have done me any good to read it then. I'm glad that I found it. He knew that I needed it. What do you think about it?"

Her mother grabbed onto her hands when she responded to her with her blinking back tears that fell down her face, "What? The letter? It sounds like Will. The way that he talked to me. His humor. His sarcasm. It took me back to when we were children. He spoke about this feeling to me every once and while. I was so young that I thought that he watched a scary movie with Nathan. I didn't understand what he was talking about. He was suffering on a deep level. Deeper than anyone understood. Do you feel like he described in the letter?"

She leaned her head on her mother's shoulder when she confessed to her with tears rapidly falling down her face, "Sometimes I feel like that. I've spent a long time feeling like that. I didn't know what to do with it. All those negative feelings. They consume you from the inside out. It makes you feel like nothing means anything. The feeling of nothingness. It's terrifying. Like you let it win. It doesn't feel good. Winning. It feels like you already lost before you got the chance to start. Dad said that he didn't know what it was until it was too late. It already won before he could stop it. That's a defeating feeling. To lose something that you were never going to win against. Like the outcome is decided for you before you get the chance to change it."

As her mother wrapped her arms around her, she hid her face in her mother's chest when she responded to her daughter with a sad smile on her face, "I know that feeling, baby girl. It's horrible. There's no good solution. Nobody wins in the end. Things never change around you. People never change. I appreciate that he thought that I believed in the world after what he did to me. He comforted himself with that thought. The truth hurts more than the lie. It's easier to believe in the lie than in the truth. Lies don't hurt you like the truth does."

Once she pulled her face out of her mother's chest, her mother grabbed onto her hands when she asked her with tears falling down her face, "What do you believe in, mom? Do you believe in the world?" Her mother wiped away tears from her face when she responded to her daughter with a frown on her face, "Hell no, baby girl. I don't believe in the world. I don't know what I believe in. When I was a little girl, I used to believe in God. That didn't last long after Kenny died. I believed in Will. I didn't know what to believe in after Will. I struggled to find my purpose. I believed in you. That's what kept me going through that time period. I put my faith into you, and you didn't disappoint me. You never once disappointed me. What do you believe in?"

As soon as her mother kissed her on the top of her head, she leaned her head onto her shoulder when she responded to her in a soft voice, "Thanks, mom. I love you. What do I believe in? Daphne asked me that question too. I told her that I believed in the stars. Daphne said that she believed in us. Bash and I never thought that someone would believe in me. When I was a little girl, I believed in you and dad. I get why Daphne believes in us. All children believe in their parents when they are young until they believe in something else. Something a lot scarier than their parents. They believe in the world. Something robs the world from us. We can't believe in anything. We were foolish to believe in it. It never believed in us. We were fucked from the beginning. Damned if you do and damned if you don't."

Her mother wrapped her arms around her with her hiding her face in her chest as she kissed her on the top of her head when she told her with a smile on her face, "I'm so proud of you. You've done so much good in the world. People see themselves in your movies. They don't have to hide who they are. It's worth all of the pain in the world. Knowing that you made a difference. I love you too, baby girl." She got into the bed with Sebastian before she fell asleep in his arms for the rest of the night.

Chapter Seventy-Six

(Fall 1977 – Los Angeles, California)

After they spent a few more weeks filming her movie *In the Shadows*, they made it to the last scene in the movie. She nervously bit her lips when the director yelled action where the actors and the actresses took their places in the living room that was previously covered in blood before they delivered their lines. When the director yelled cut one last time, she told them that she was proud of them, and that this movie was going to be a hit before the director dismissed everyone off of the set. Sebastian pulled her into a desperate kiss with her sitting on her lap where she was about to take off his shirt until an actor walked onto the set to grab his jacket before he ran outside pretending that he didn't see them. They finished where they left off in Sebastian's office where they weren't interrupted this time before she went into the basement to work with the editor while Sebastian went back to his investor calls. She spent the next few weeks with the editor as he put together her movie. She was there until late into the night before she came back into the studio to do it again. She was home less than she was during her filming days. It was a long process that needed a delicate touch. While they worked on the final version of her movie *In the Shadows*, Lucy put together her international press tour where they included as many new cities as possible. They wanted their studio to spread to every part of the world. Once they had a movie to share with the world, she handed the completed version of *In the Shadows* to Sebastian who hung up the phone when he asked her how she got done with the movie so quickly where she told him that she was determined to finish it before Sebastian told her that he would make copies to share with the movie theaters. Since she only had a week to prepare for her international press tour, she spent as much time with the children as possible until she left them for a month. She packed her bags in any free time that she had during the day before she talked on the phone with Lucy about the interviews with newspapers that she was doing in Europe and Central Asia. She didn't miss the children's first day at school for the new school year. After she dropped off the children at school, their driver drove them to the airport where she pulled Sebastian into a tight hug when he promised her that he would call her every night before she followed Lucy on her private jet with the cast and crew of her movie. It was a tradition that they used her private jet to travel across the world for their press tours. They purchased an additional private jet because there were so many people coming with them. Sebastian surprised her with it the day before they left the states. Lucy told him that they weren't going to be able to fit everyone on the plane with them. She was on the newest private jet with Lucy and the other executives from their studio. The international press tour was a blur to her where they were in a new city every night before they had screening parties with people at the movie theaters. She always enjoyed this part of the tour the most where she heard how her movies connected with the viewers. It made her feel like everything that she did to get here was worth it. Sebastian called her every night where they talked about how her movie was doing in the states before he told her about how the children were doing at home. Noah wasn't bothered by her absence since he was lost in his own world. Daphne wasn't taking her absence well. She asked to talk to her when Sebastian talked to her where he handed Daphne the phone. Daphne told her about school to her ballet practices that she went to after school to how she had nightmares that her plane crashed into the ocean. She reassured Daphne that her plane wasn't to crash into the ocean and that she was watching too many scary movies with her grandmothers.

Daphne told her that anything could happen to her. She told Daphne that she had faith in the stars that she was going to be okay.

Daphne understood what she meant by that. After she traveled across Europe and Central Asia, their private jets took them home. She had a few days to herself at home before they left for the press tour across the country with the cast and crew. Once she said goodbye to her children and her parents yet again, their driver dropped them off at the airport where she got on their newest private jet with Sebastian, Lucy, and the cast before they left for their first stop in Las Vegas, Nevada. They spent every night in a new city as they watched the movie with the viewers where they answered questions that they asked them before they heard what the viewers thought of the movie. People across the world told her that she made a good horror movie for someone that never made a horror movie. They were sick of horror movies about things that weren't real. It was refreshing to watch a movie about something different. She did joint interviews with Sebastian about the movie. She didn't hold back in what she said in the interviews. She made good on her promise to her father and Uncle Sam that she was going to be honest with the world. She talked about her father's suicide note that never got sent to her. She said that he talked about the monsters in his mind that took over his life and how he didn't want that happening to her. When the interviewers asked her if it happened to her, she told them that it didn't because she was here to fight another day and that she wasn't going anywhere anytime soon. Sebastian was happy to hear that because he was worried about her for a long time about that. She said this to the world in Florida where she said it for the rest of their stops on the tour. When they got to New York, she brought her journal with her for the press tours. She wrote about this feeling that she experienced in New York in her hotel balcony at night. She gave up on the unsent letters path since it was too on the nose with what her father did. She wrote about prompts that made her question why she was feeling that way. Why did she feel like she was drowning? Why didn't her brain understand that she moved on from what happened in New York? She wasn't talking about the latest mental breakdown that she had a year ago. She was talking about everything that she did in New York. Her senior year bender where she got into trouble every night of the week. Her destructive relationship with Daxton that blew up in her face. The last six months of her European bender where she had an affair with Chloe while they lived out of hotels. Her suicide attempts here in her life. Being in New York wasn't what triggered her to do these things.

It was memories that existed that made her think about it. She saw the bar where she met Daxton. She saw her old house where she jumped off of the roof so many times. She saw the hotels where she self-destructed. It was like she could open a door, and she would be in those moments again. She felt like it was everywhere in the world. In Los Angeles, it was the house that Daxton died in and the house that she killed herself in. She couldn't go into Amelia's house for more than a few moments without feeling like she was there in those moments. Even though Amelia and Troy changed everything about the house, it was like she was a doorway away from walking into that moment. In London, it was the hotels that she self-destructed in and her cousin Sean's house where she overdosed twice. She felt like she was there in those moments. She felt Jade's presence around her like she felt Chloe in New York and Daxton in Los Angeles. The ghosts of the past. The ghosts of her old life haunting her when she went to those places that reminded her of them. The worst place for her to be in was York. She felt her father everywhere that she went, especially on the Heartly Farm where she felt him the most out of anywhere in the world. Or the bridge that he jumped off of that haunted her nightmares. She struggled to think about it without breaking down. She felt her grandma and Camille with her when she was in her house in Sweden where she wished more than anything that she could open the door. Her father's suicide note told her that he was scared of the monster in his mind. Even though she was terrified of the monster in her mind, she was more scared of the ghosts of her past. They reminded her of the life that she could've had if she chose another door. She wondered what that would look like for her. She wrote about it in a journal until she questioned her sanity. She told herself that this wasn't productive to do. She made herself crazy over thoughts that weren't real, and she let it control her life for too long. This was what her father talked about in his letter to her. She can't spend her life wishing for the life that she didn't have. She couldn't think about the choices that she wished that she made in her life. It was part of the monster's distraction, so that she would let it take over her mind. Imagining a person that she would be if she didn't know what it meant to not know the consequences of her actions. Imagining the person that she would've been if she wasn't trapped in this doorway. She didn't say any of this in her interviews. It wasn't something that she wanted the world to know about her. She didn't tell Sebastian about it. She professed to him how well that she was doing that she didn't want to disappoint him. Jacob told her that she was going to have periods of her life that she felt good about herself and then she was going to have periods where she felt horrible about herself. It was a part of having mental disorders that she accepted a long time ago. She was never going to be the person that was capable of being the same. Sebastian knew this about her before they got married to each other. He didn't understand it like her parents or Oliver understood it. She knew why they understood it because this was the way that her father was, and Uncle Nathan engrained this into Oliver's brain from a very young age. That it was okay to not be okay. On the last night of their press tour, they were at a gala in New York where she socialized around the room before Lucy hurried over to her when she whispered into her ear that her mum needed to talk to her. She pulled away from the conversation that she had with people from another studio. She grabbed onto Lucy's hand as she dragged her through the crowd where Lucy handed her the phone from a side hallway when she asked her mum what was wrong before her mum told her that she needed to sit down to hear this news. She took a seat on an antique chair that she wasn't supposed to be sitting on as she let out a shaky breath when she asked her mum if something happened to the children where her mum assured her that the children were fine. She let out a soft gasp in relief before her mum told her that her mother was in the hospital and that the children were at Oliver's house. She broke the silence between them when she asked her if her mother's cancer was back where her mum told her that she had new tumors in ovaries before she asked her mum if they needed to come home. Her mum told her that they didn't need to come home because her mother didn't want them missing out on their events. She told her mum that she would talk to Sebastian about it before her mum told her that she would call them in the morning after she slept. After she hung up the phone onto the receiver, she didn't look up at Lucy when she asked her to send for their car where she walked away from Lucy without looking back at her.

She sprinted towards Sebastian who was talking to one of their directors and an executive from another studio. As soon as he saw her from across the room, he excused himself from their conversation as he ran over to her where he pulled her into a desperate hug with her face hidden in his chest before he pulled them in front of the building. Before she could explain anything to him, Lucy sprinted over to them as their driver pulled the car in front of them where Sebastian guided them to the car before they sat in silence for the drive to their hotel. After their driver dropped them off at the hotel, Sebastian grabbed onto her hand as he guided them to their room on the top floor where he sat down next to her on the bed with him holding onto her hands when he asked her with concern laced in his voice, "What's wrong, Isabella? You're scaring me. Did something happen to the children?"

She blinked back tears that fell down her face when she responded to him in a distant voice, "No, the children are fine, Bash. It's my mom. Her cancer is back. Mum told me that she is in the hospital. It's not good."

Sebastian wrapped his arms around her with her face hidden in his chest when he responded to her with compassion laced in his voice, "I'm so sorry, Isabella. Your mom doesn't deserve that. She's a wonderful person. Where are the children right now?"

She pulled her face out of Sebastian's chest as he wiped away the tears that fell down her face when she responded to him with a frown on her face, "The children are at Oliver's house. Mum told me that we don't have to rush back home, but I wanted to see what you thought about it before I made the final decision about it."

Sebastian tightened his grip on her arms when he responded to her with a sad smile on his face, "I think that we have to go home honey. There isn't another choice. We can cancel the rest of our events in New York, so that we can be with your parents and the children. I'll have Lucy arrange for us to be home by tomorrow afternoon."

As she pulled Sebastian into a desperate kiss, they didn't pull away from each other until they were out of breath when she told him with her arms wrapped around him, "Thank you for taking care of me, Bash. I love you so much. I'll start packing our bags."

He grabbed onto her hands as she looked up at him when he told her with a serious look on his face, "I'll do it, Isabella. Don't worry about it. Take a bath and have a moment to yourself to process this. I'm sure that you're overwhelmed. It would be good for you to think about it alone. I love you too honey." After Sebastian went into the closet to pack their bags, she grabbed her journal and her pair of silk pajamas from the bed as she walked into the bathroom where she left the door cracked a little bit to let Sebastian know that he could join her when he was done before she ran warm water in the bathtub. Once she hung up her gown and shawl on the back of the door, she turned off the water from the facet as she got into the water with her head and her arms sticking out of the bathtub where she lit a cigarette that hid in her journal with her inhaling the smoke from it before she closed her eyes in relief. As she sat up in the tub with her smoking a cigarette, she thought about the last time that her mother had ovarian cancer. It shocked her so much that she felt like her world was falling apart. She didn't know what she was going to do without her mother in her life. Even though all of her cousins lost one or both of their parents, she still had her mother and her mum in her life, and she didn't want that to change anytime soon. She stayed like that for a long time as she sat in silence in the warm water smoking a cigarette. She was pulled out of her thoughts when her journal fell down onto the floor off of the edge of the bathtub before she picked it up off of the floor with her cigarette being disregarded onto her ashtray. As she looked at page after page that she wrote in her journal, the last page of the journal had something written on it that she didn't remember writing where she looked at it.

In the doorway, I see it. It's the life that I never had. If I made the right choice, I would find myself there. I would be in a world where I didn't damn generations of my family to the pain that I inflicted onto them. I would be in a place where I found the happiness that I looked for. I would've found that my happiness didn't come from other people. That happiness came from within me. I wouldn't regret what I never did. I wouldn't regret the things that I never got the chance to say. I would be at peace with myself and the world. The more that I look into the doorway, the more that I realize that it's not my past. The doorway is my future. A future that exists in dreams. A future that exists in death. I see the doorway, but I can't catch the doorway. It's reminding me of my death. As death gets closer to me, the doorway gets closer to me. Like it's about to shallow me in one bite. I can't enter the door until I'm on the bridge. I see it there looking back at me. The door is wide open, and it is ready for me to enter it. As I enter the doorway, I see it for the first time. I see the stars. They are right in front of me. I can almost touch them. A bright halo approaches me. I welcome it into my body. I feel invincible. I feel like a brand-new person. The mistakes are melted off of me. The heartbreak is erased like it never happened. I am no longer defined by the mistakes of my past. I am no longer limited by the world. I am at peace until I do it all over again. The mistakes. The heartbreak. The pain. The limitations of the world. This time I will change it. I am everyone and I am nobody. I become the person that I truly meant to become. I am free.

As she wiped tears away from her face, she placed the journal onto the edge of the bathtub where she read it again to figure out who wrote it before she saw it on the corner of the page. This was written by her father. It was in his same messy handwriting. It was a prophecy that he discovered over a lifetime ago. He knew what was going to happen to him before anyone knew about it. That's what he was running away from. He was running away from his prophecy. He was running away from his fate. As soon as she read it again, it said something different on the page where it originally had her father's name on it. The same message was written by her on the day that her father killed himself. Like she knew that this was her destiny too. Sebastian walked into the bathroom with a robe in his hands as she looked over at the last page of her journal to see that it was empty. She let out heartbreaking sobs into her hands before Sebastian pulled her out of the bathtub with the water going cold a long time ago. As soon as he wrapped the robe around her, she sobbed with her face hidden in his chest as he tightly wrapped his arms around her where he drained the water in the bathtub before he guided her onto the bed. Once she sat down on the bed, Sebastian went into the bedroom to grab her clothes and her journal as he handed them to her where she changed into her silk pajamas before she placed her journal into her purse. As Sebastian laid them down on the bed next to her, he wrapped his arms around her with her face hidden in his chest where he told her that he loved her with her saying the same thing back to him before she fell asleep in his arms for the rest of the night.

CHAPTER SEVENTY-SEVEN
(WINTER 1978 – YORK, ENGLAND)

She instantly remembered getting the worst news of her life that her mother's ovarian cancer was back. She almost forgot that she read the poem that she wrote when her father died. She stopped herself from crying when Sebastian suddenly woke up next to her. She followed Sebastian out of the hotel as Lucy met them in the lobby where Lucy pulled them into tight hugs before they got into the back of their car. Once their driver dropped them off at the airport, Sebastian held onto her hand as Lucy carried their bags where they went on their private jet before their pilot took them to Los Angeles. Sebastian read scripts as Lucy read reviews for her movie while she wrote in her journal about the poem that she read last night where she fell asleep on the couch before Sebastian woke her up when their private jet landed in Los Angeles. As soon as she walked off of their private jet, Oliver stood near them with Noah on his hip as Daphne sprinted over to them where she pulled Daphne in her arms before Sebastian wrapped his arms around them. Noah ran into her legs where she placed Daphne onto the ground before she placed Noah on her hip with his face hidden in her chest. Oliver pulled her into a tight hug with her face hidden in his chest until Noah told her to put him down where she placed Noah onto the ground as Posey placed him on her hip before she pulled Juliet and her nieces Posey and Eleanor into tight hugs. After Posey handed Noah over to her, she followed Sebastian to the car with him holding onto Daphne's hand where she got into the back of the car with Noah asleep in his car seat before their driver drove them home.

Sebastian was at work and the children were in school. She was in the attic looking through boxes of stuff from her childhood. She was looking for the poem that she saw in her journal that disappeared after she read it. This proved to be an impossible task. She didn't know where she was supposed to find it or how she was supposed to determine if it was real or not. After she couldn't find it after several days, she asked her mother about it when she visited her in the hospital. Her mother asked her what she was looking for in the attic. She told her mother that she was looking for something that wrote when she was a child where her mother told her that she would find it in the box labeled stories and poems before she thanked her mother for helping her. She spent most of the day with her mother while she got her chemo treatment. She picked up the children from school as they told her about their days until she told them that they were going to look at boxes in the attic where Daphne told her that she wanted to find her toys before Noah told her that he was going to find more toys than Daphne. Everything was a competition between Daphne and Noah. They were always outdoing each other. Oliver assured her that it was normal for brothers and sisters to be like that. Poppy and Tommy competed with each other their entire lives. She told Daphne and Noah to be careful with the stuff in the boxes because it was old, and it couldn't be replaced. They promised her that they would be careful with the boxes where Daphne sprinted over to the box labeled toys with Noah following behind her before she looked for the box labeled stories and poems. After she stopped Daphne and Noah from fighting over a toy, she continued her search as she found the box labeled stories and poems where she went through her mother's old stories and poems when she was younger before she placed them into a neat pile on the floor.

Once she finally got to the bottom of the box, she grabbed a photo album that her mother labeled Isabella's drawings and stories where she opened it up to the first page to see a drawing of herself as a little girl, her mother, and her father before she felt tears falling down her face. As soon as she wiped away tears from her face, she looked at the album where she saw drawings that she made, writing her earliest stories in school, and pictures that her mother took of her. She always held her father's doll in her hand like it was her only lifeline to him. Daphne ran over to her with Noah following her when Daphne asked her why she was upset when she wrapped her arms around them before she told them that she was crying about the past. Once she kissed Daphne and Noah on the top of their heads, they fought over the toys in the box as she looked at the album. She let out a soft gasp before she ran her hands over the page like she was going to break it. It was the same poem that she read in her journal except for one difference. It said, "I am free. I am home." Since she was alone in the attic, she let out heartbreaking sobs into her hands as she placed the album onto the floor when she saw the date on the paper that she wrote on it. It was three weeks before her father died. On the last page of the album, there was the same letter that her father sent to her mother that she wrote her version of the poem. She remembered that day like it happened to her yesterday. Her parents were in California preparing to work on a movie. Uncle Sam and Aunt Valeria took care of her. She had a nightmare the night before. She woke up screaming for Uncle Sam. He asked her what the nightmare was about. She refused to tell him because it would terrify him. Uncle Sam tucked her into bed, but she didn't go to bed. She snuck into her mother's bedroom to grab a piece of paper from her desk. That was where she wrote the poem for the first time. She cried the entire time that she wrote it. She tucked it away into her dresser to hide it from her family. She went to school that day like nothing was going on. She got home from school where she opened her mother's mail for her. Her mother told her to open her mail in case something urgent came when she was gone. She placed the bills in a different pile to tell her mother about on their call. She found a letter from her father at the bottom of the pile. She didn't think that anyone else knew about it because it was stuck in between two pieces of mail. She read the poem that her father sent to her mother. She was so shocked that she wrote it when she couldn't sleep. She didn't know what he meant by it until she saw his final line of the poem. It wasn't I'm home like her last line was in her poem. It said, "I'm free. I'm dead." She knew that her father was going to die for three weeks before anyone found out about it. She hid the poem from her mother because she didn't want her to know about it. She tried to kill herself in the bathtub that night. Her father killed himself and she couldn't talk about it with anyone else.

She didn't realize how hard that she sobbed until she heard her mum helping her catch her breath again where she listened to her mum's voice before she wasn't out of breath anymore. As she hid her face in her mum's chest with her arms tightly around her, her mum asked her if she was okay where she handed her the album before her mum read her father's poem and her poem. Her mum asked her what this meant with a look of horror on her face. She pulled her face out of her mum's chest when she told her that she knew that her father killed himself before he did it because he sent this poem to her. Her mum asked her why she didn't say anything about it. She didn't know why she didn't say anything to them. She told her mum that she was protecting her mother from the truth. She was protecting herself from the truth. When her mum asked her what that truth was, she told her that the truth was that it was inevitable. Her mum told her that they couldn't tell her mother about this until it was the right time where she asked her mum when they would know what the right time was going to be before her mum told her that she knew what she was talking about. She nodded her head at her where her mum kissed her on the cheek before they joined the children in the living room. After she put the children to sleep that night without Sebastian, who was on a business trip to Spain, she stayed up all night smoking cigarettes on her balcony thinking about what her mum said to her. Those were the same words that her father used to Camille in his last letter. She knew what he was talking about. She couldn't tell her mother about the truth of her father's death until her mother died. This sent her on a new train of spiraling thoughts. She didn't know what was worse to talk about her being the first person that knew that her father was going to die or that her mother couldn't know the truth until she was dead. She imagined her mother being dead. Even though she spent a lifetime thinking about her father being dead, she never thought about what it would feel like when her mother died. The thing that she was scared of the least was death. Death never scared her. It excited her beyond any other feeling. It made her feel like she was more alive than anyone else. She had a new fear. She was scared of her mother dying. She was so angry at her mum for saying it without any emotion in her voice. Like it didn't hurt her. She knew that her mum loved her mother, so it couldn't be that she didn't care about her. Her mum had emotionally detached herself from it because she knew how painful it was going to feel when her mother died. They didn't talk about death the last time that her mother had cancer. No one even dared to utter that word. The only person that said that her mother was going to die was her and she didn't realize what it meant the last time that she said it. No one wanted to say that word because it was so permanent that it couldn't be taken back. After her father killed himself, no one wanted to use the word dead for him. They used more colorful words like passed on or tragically gone. Like it made them feel better about it. Every time she said that her father was dead at his funeral, her mother gave her stern look to stop it where she said it to her again until her mother pulled her away from everyone else before she told her that she needed to stop making people feel uncomfortable. She wanted to ask her mother why it was her responsibility to make people feel comfortable after her father never felt that way, but she never found the courage to do it. Instead of telling her mother any of this, she stormed away from her to her father's grave that they dug him in where she kicked it until she had bruises all over her legs before she walked over to the bridge to be with him. As she looked down at the water, she heard her father's poem playing in her ears on repeat where she almost got the nerve to jump off of the bridge before Oliver shouted out her name in the distance with her running over to him. Like she almost didn't do what her father did a few weeks ago. She never told anyone about the poem or what happened to her on the bridge. She didn't want people to know the truth about them. They were going through the same door. It was who they were meant to become.

She didn't know how to move on. She put on a good front for her children before she hid in her bedroom for the rest of the day. She slept all day until her alarm woke her up to pick up the children from school. She laid there until she felt like she didn't want to die anymore. This was the person that Sebastian returned to when he got back from his business trip in Spain. Not the Isabella that was happily socializing at galas in New York. Not the Isabella that was working on her latest movie. He came home to the Isabella who was questioning the will to live. It didn't surprise him considering that her mother was dying from cancer. Sebastian knew that this was worse than her mother dying from cancer. This was about how she realized what it meant for her mother to be dead. She was trapped in a world that already happened and a world that was still yet to happen. Sebastian tried everything in his power to make her feel better. He knew what the alternative was, and no one wanted that to happen anymore than she did. When Sebastian's plans didn't work, he called Jacob to figure out what to do about it where he told him that they would have to let her accept that her mother was going to die before Sebastian asked him what he was supposed to do. As she pretended to sleep in their bed, Jacob told him that the only thing that he could do was make sure that she was going to be safe where Sebastian said to him that he could do that for her. Jacob meant that Sebastian should make sure that she didn't do anything to hurt herself. She knew that it wouldn't do anything for her. She stopped seeing her mother in the hospital for several weeks where her mum begged her to see her mother with her before she agreed to go with her because she brought Daphne and Noah with them. At the hospital, her mother pulled her into a tight hug with her face hidden in her chest when she asked why she stopped coming to see her where her mum took the children to the cafeteria to get lunch before she told her mother that she realized that she was going to die like dad died. She didn't want her to die. This made her mother cry. She wasn't her adult daughter. She was her baby girl that didn't want to lose her mother. They cried in each other's arms until her mum came back with the children with bags of food in their hands where she excused herself before she smoked cigarettes outside of the hospital with her hiding her shaking hands in her jacket pockets. She stayed outside for the rest of the visit as her mum came outside of the hospital with her holding onto Daphne and Noah's hands where she asked her if she was going home with them before she followed them to the car. She withdrew in her bedroom in the evening until Sebastian forced her to hang out with Oliver, Sasha, and Amelia who were there for dinner with their families where she changed out of her three-day old clothes before she put on best happy face for their guests. Her cousins knew that she was depressed about her mother dying and they left her alone. Even

Oliver left her alone. That shocked her because he never left her alone about anything else before in her life. Jacob must have said something for him to leave her alone. Her cousins came over because they tried to distract her from her mother dying. It was a noble effort on their part because she momentarily forgot about it until she remembered the poem that her father wrote about them, and she sobbed all over again. Her cousins rushed over to her as they pulled her into a tight hug before she sobbed in Oliver's chest. They left Sebastian to take care of her where he pulled her into their bedroom before she fell asleep in his arms for the rest of the night.

She would've remained hidden from the world, but her mother came home to the hospital for the first time in months. She got her chemo treatments at the outpatient center every other day where Uncle Stan went with her. It was hard for her to mope around the house about her mother dying when she walked around the house. She put on her best act for the children that she wasn't questioning her whole life before everyone else believed that it was true. Everything went back to normal like no one was dying until she got a frantic phone call from Amelia in the middle of the night that her father had a stroke, and he was in a coma. When Amelia asked her if she would come to England with her, she knew what it was like to lose a father where she told her that they would leave in the morning before she packed her bags for England. When Sebastian woke up an hour later asking her what she was doing, she told him that Amelia called her to tell her that Uncle James was in a coma after having a stroke and she was going to England to be with her where Sebastian told her to take the children with her before she nodded her head at him with him rolling back to sleep in bed for the rest of the night. Since she was up all night packing their bags for England, she drank too many cups of coffee to keep herself awake. Her parents asked her why she was so buzzed this morning before she told them that Amelia told her that Uncle James was in a coma after he had a stroke. Her mother told her that she wished that she could come with them, but she was too weak from the chemo treatments. Her mum told her that she would go to England with her before Sebastian said that he would stay home to take care of her mother. After her mum packed her bags in their bedroom, she got the children dressed in their warmest clothes where Daphne asked her why they were going to

England before she told her that Kitty's grandpa was sick with Daphne moving on from the subject as she put on her winter boots like she was going on a ski trip. She pulled Sebastian into a tight hug with her face hidden in his chest until he pulled the children into a tight hug where she pulled her mother into a tight hug before her mum told her that they needed to leave for the airport. After they got into the back of the car, their driver drove them to the airport where Amelia and her family waited for them as she walked out of the car with Noah on her hip before Amelia pulled her into a tight hug with Christian asleep in her arms. Once they pulled away from each other, she kissed Troy on the cheek as Daphne and Katherine held onto each other's hands where she got on their private jet before the girls played on the floor with the boys sleeping in their arms for the flight.

When their private jet landed in York, she held onto Noah's hand as Amelia followed behind her with Katherine asleep in her arms and Troy holding onto Daphne and Christian's hands where they met up with Jamie at the airport before he pulled them into a tight hug with her face hidden in his chest. They pulled away from each other when Noah tugged on her leg to get her attention where they pulled away from each other with her placing Noah on her hip before Jamie pulled Amelia into a tight hug with her face hidden in her brother's chest. Once she pulled Audrey into a tight hug with her arms around her, she got into the back of the car with Amelia, Troy, and the children where Audrey drove them to George's house before she parked the car in the driveway. As soon as she got out of the car with Noah on her hip, George pulled her into a tight hug with her face hidden in his chest until Noah whined to be put down on the ground where she placed Noah onto the ground before Noah ran inside of the house after Katherine and Daphne who ran towards the toys in the living room. After she followed the children into the house, she pulled Sean into a tight hug with her face hidden in his chest until Daphne shouted for her where she ran into the living room before she stopped Noah from hitting his one-year-old cousin Henri with a toy car. As she carried Noah out of the living room with Noah kicking and screaming in her arms, she brought him into Zoe and Sofie's bedroom as she placed him on the bed with Noah squirming away from her where she kept a grip on his arms and legs before she asked him why he was going to hit his baby cousin. She let out a defeated sigh when she asked him if he was proud of himself where he shook his head at her before she asked him if daddy would be upset with him. Noah told her that daddy would be mad at him where she told him that he knew better than to hit his cousins before he nodded his head at her. After she kissed Noah on the top of his head, she told him that she was proud of him for owning up to his mistakes where he told her that he was being a good man like daddy was. Once Noah knew that he wasn't in trouble anymore, he ran into the living room to play with Daphne and his cousins where she went into the kitchen before she helped Audrey and Annabell put dinner on the table. As Daphne and Noah sat in between her at the table, everyone helped themselves to their own plates of food where Noah provoked a fight with Daphne over the last dinner roll before she told them that they could share it with each other. Even though Daphne and Noah weren't excited about it, they silently nodded their heads at her as she broke the dinner roll in half for them where she listened to her cousin's conversations with each other about Uncle James and his constant progress in the hospital. After everyone ate dinner in the kitchen, she helped Annabell and Polly clean up the dishes in the sink where Annabell offered her Uncle James' bedroom to sleep in before she thanked her for thinking of them. Once she got the children cleaned up for bed, she changed them into their pajamas as she read them a bedtime story before her children fell asleep on the bed. She woke up the next morning to Daphne and Noah fighting over one of old toys that they took from the attic. She scolded them that they shouldn't fight over toys that don't belong to them where they didn't listen to her with them pulling the toy back and forth before they broke the toy in half. As she saw the head of her wooden doll fall off that her father gave her, she stopped herself from losing it on them as she silently grabbed the head off of the floor where she asked them in the calmest voice to hand her the doll before Daphne rushed it over to her with Noah hiding in complete fear behind her sister. Daphne and Noah nervously stared at her when she told them with tears falling down her face that this was the only toy that grandpa gave her where this made them to feel worse about it before Daphne told her that they could get it fixed for her. She didn't know what to say to them. Daphne grabbed onto Noah's hand as she guided them out of their bedroom where she laid down on the bed with the broken wooden doll cradled deep into her own chest.

Amelia came into their bedroom where she sat down on the bed next to her with her running fingers through her hair before she asked her if she wanted to come to the hospital with them. Amelia walked out of her bedroom when she told her that she left the children with her at the house while everyone else was at the hospital before Amelia left her alone in her bedroom. She would've stayed in that room for the rest of her life, but she needed to watch her children and her cousin's children. She walked into the living room to see the children playing on the floor before she asked them if they wanted to go on a walk. Since it was the middle of winter, this was a hard sell until she mentioned sledding to them where Noah asked her where they were going to go sledding like he knew anything about York before her five-year-old niece Zoe told her that her parents took her sledding on the hills on the Heartley Farm. After she instructed the older children to get their snowsuits on by themselves, she helped the younger children into their snowsuits and boots as Zoe grabbed the sleds from the attic where she grabbed onto Noah's hand with Henri on her hip before the older children followed her over to the Heartley Farm. As soon as she let go of Noah's hand to knock on the door, Uncle Nathan opened the door as he pulled in her into a tight hug with her face hidden on his chest until Sofie asked him if they could go sledding with Jack, Maddie, and Millie where he told them that they could always go sledding before she told him that she would meet him on the hill. Once she made the long walk up the hill, she placed Henri onto the ground as she grabbed one of the sleds from Zoe where she got on it with Noah and Henri in her lap before Daphne and Katherine pushed them down the hill. She let out a joyful scream as she went down the hill with her arms tightly around Noah and Henri where they let out infectious laughs before their sled landed at the bottom of the hill. When she asked the boys if they wanted to go again, Noah told her that he wanted to go down with Christian as she carried Noah and Henri to the top of the hill where she helped Noah and Christian onto the sled before she pushed them off of the hill with their happy screams filling the air. She went down the hill with Daphne and Katherine a few times and Noah and Henri too. Uncle Nathan suddenly threw a snowball at her. As soon as she threw a snowball back at him, the children threw snow at each other where everyone was soaked with the cold melted snow before Poppy came over to invite everyone inside for hot chocolate and warm tea. After they made the walk to the house, she changed the younger children out of their wet clothes where they walked over to Poppy's house before she sat down next to the fire with Noah and Daphne sitting on her lap. When her cousins came back from the hospital, most of the children were asleep on the couch or on other adults from their tiring day where Amelia asked her if she had a good time before she told her with Noah and Daphne asleep on either side of her that it was a day that she would never forget. When she asked Amelia if he was dead, she nodded her head at her as she grabbed onto her hand when she told her that she was sorry for her loss where Amelia sadly smiled at her before she carried Katherine and Christian to the car to drive to Audrey's house for the night. Once Daphne woke up from her nap, she carried Noah to George's house with Daphne holding onto her hand where the children slept in her bed before she sat on the balcony smoking cigarettes for the rest of the night. When she woke up the next morning to Daphne and Noah still asleep in between her, she kissed them on the top of their heads as she went into the kitchen to see George sitting at the table where she took a seat next to him before she grabbed onto his hands with him smiling at her. They stayed like that until Annabell walked into the kitchen with Henri in her arms where Henri reached for her before she placed him in her lap. After Annabell disappeared with Henri to get the girls awake, she finished George's cup of coffee that he stopped drinking a while ago as she went into her bedroom where she got the children dressed for the wake with Daphne in her black dress and Noah in his black suit before she changed into her black dress. She joined George, Annabell, and the children in the kitchen for breakfast where they went into the car before George drove them to the church. As soon as she walked into the church with her holding onto Daphne and Noah's hands, Daphne ran over to Katherine and Charlotte as she placed Noah on her hip where she talked to people that came up to her before they asked her where her mother was. Once she told them that her mother wasn't well enough to travel right now, they asked what was wrong with her as she fought off the urge to cry when she told them that her mother had ovarian cancer where they told her that they would pray for her before she excused herself to a conversation with another person about the same thing. By the fifth time that someone asked her where her mother was, she couldn't take it anymore. She left Noah with Oliver and Juliet where she ran into the cemetery before she vomited onto the frozen ground.

She would've hid in the cemetery all day if it wasn't for it being freezing outside where she wiped away the tears from her face before she put on her happy face for the rest of the wake. When she made it to his house for the rest of the day, they ate dinner in the kitchen where she told the children that they were going to bed before they followed her into their bedroom. Once she changed the children into their pajamas, she put them to sleep in their bed before she went to the balcony to smoke cigarettes for the rest of the night. When she woke up on the couch with a blanket around her the next morning, she didn't question it as she pushed it off of her where she went into her bedroom before she got dressed in a new black dress for the funeral. After she woke up the children who slept for over twelve hours, she changed them into their black clothes for the funeral where she walked into the kitchen with the children following behind her before she ate breakfast that Annabell prepared for them. George drove them to the church as she held onto Daphne's hand with Noah on her hip where she walked into the church before she took a seat in the second row in between her mum and Amelia grabbed onto her hand. George got up from his seat in the front row as Annabell grabbed onto his hands with Henri sitting on her lap where George stood in front of podium before he said aloud to the room with tears falling down his face, "My dad was my hero. He taught me everything that I knew about life. He taught me how to be a good person. He taught me how to be a father and a husband. He taught me how to be myself. Being a pastor was everything to my dad. He told us when we were children that he wanted to do something that made a difference in the world. He wasn't talking about fighting to protect our world from fascists. That was the bravest thing that he did, but it was more than that. My dad wanted to do something that would touch people's lives. It's safe to say that he did that because look at everyone here. He had fulfilled his destiny. He once said to us, 'Look at what you guys became. You guys made my life complete. Thank you for giving me a purpose.' That was the last thing that he said to us before he died. You gave me a purpose. I think that we're all looking for purpose and not all of us find it in the end. I want to find my purpose. I want to feel confident about it until my last breath. I've found my purpose here at the church. With my family. With my friends. Thank you for showing me my purpose. I love you, dad."

Once George took a seat with Annabell grabbing onto his hands, Audrey got up from her seat in the front pew as Teddy grabbed onto her hands where she stood at the podium with a piece of paper in her hands before she said aloud to the room with tears falling down her face, "My dad was my best friend. He called me every morning and every night. We talked about everything. Even though we didn't live far away from him, he came over to our house every day. He called me to see how I was doing in our time apart from each other. He called me his Water Lilly. It was his favorite flower. They come into bloom at springtime, and he would take me to the pond in the morning to show them. He did this when I was four years old after he got back from the war. He told me that there was no beauty in war and that he found it in the most unusual places in Europe. The designs of broken glass. The fallen pictures in the mud. The ashes falling onto the ground. He told me that he never found any flowers. There was only blood and sorrow. He appreciated flowers. He planted as many as he possibly could in the spring. He gave me flowers any chance that he got. When he was in the hospital, I gave him flowers from my garden. I told him that they were his favorite. Water Lillies. He wasn't awake to see them. I told him that I would always remember the Water Lillies. I'm so glad that my children got to love you. I love you so much, dad. Rest well."

After Audrey took a seat in the front row with Teddy's arms around her, Amelia got up from the seat next to her as Troy gently squeezed her shoulder where she walked up to the podium before she aloud to the room with tears rapidly falling down her face, "Leaving my dad was the hardest thing that I did in my life. I knew that my life wasn't in York anymore, but I couldn't bring myself to leave it. Dad sat me down and he told me, 'Mia, you're never going to forgive yourself if you don't do this. This is your chance to do something beyond your wildest imagination. I don't want you to leave me, but you aren't happy here. You need more in life. More than what this world can give you.'

I took his advice. I took a leap of faith. I moved to California. It has been everything and more than what I dreamed of. I never would've been happy with myself if I didn't do it. He was right. My life there with Troy and my children is special to me. I wouldn't trade that for all of the money in the world. He knew that I was happy. In our phone calls, he asked me about how the children were doing before he asked me how I was doing. I always told him the same answer. I said to him, 'Daddy, I'm living the dream.' I didn't feel like that when I told him that, but it was still true. I am living in a dream. A dream that is full of heartbreak and loss. A dream that is full of so much joy and happiness. That was how life worked for us. There are good and bad moments where you decide what you're going to do with your life. To make the right decision or the wrong decision. To be the better person or the worst person. I think that we made the right decision. I'll always love you, daddy. I'll never forget the dream."

Once Amelia took a seat next to her, she grabbed onto her hands as Troy wrapped his arms around her where her mum got up from next to her before she walked over to the podium. As soon as her mum placed her pieces of paper down on the stand, she wiped away the tears from her face where she let out a shaky breath before she said aloud to the room unable to look away from Uncle James' closed coffin, "This might seem strange when I say this, but James was the first person that I loved in my life. We were neighbors all of our lives. His parents had a cattle ranch, and my parents were animal breeders. Our families were close to each other because they did business together for a long time. We didn't have any siblings, so I considered James to be my older brother. He took care of me when my parents got divorced. I was eight years old, and I didn't understand what it meant to have your family torn apart. I didn't understand why my mum wanted to leave my dad, but I understood it when I was older. I was at his house more than my house. My mum died when I was twelve years old, and my dad moved into the house with me. My dad was drunk. He understood why I didn't want to be near my dad. He asked his parents if they could adopt me, so that I didn't have to live with him. It didn't work, but I thanked him for trying. I moved out of the house when I was sixteen years old. I married the first boy that gave me any attention. James begged me not to do it because he knew what would happen to me if I left with him.

James told me that he would marry me to keep me there with him, but he was already engaged to Sylvia at that point. I left with my husband who later turned into an ex-husband. I found out that I was pregnant with his child only after being with him for a few weeks. James took me to a place to get an abortion. He paid for it too. I was only fifteen years old at the time and I wasn't ready to be a mother. He promised me that he would never tell anyone until one of us died. I realized that I was gay long before I told anyone about it, but James was the first person to know about it. He always supported me no matter what. He told me that he would help me get married to Ella even though it is illegal. It was sweet of him. As my partner once said, we have different kinds of soul mates in our lives. James was one of those to me. He was my platonic soul mate. Thank you for everything that you did for me. I'll never forget it. Rest in peace, my angel."

After her mum took a seat next to her, she pulled her into a desperate hug as her mum hid her face into her chest with tears falling down their faces. They pulled away from each other when George thanked everyone for coming to celebrate his father's life before he told the family to meet them in the cemetery for the burial. She wasn't in the mood to see another person that she loved buried into the ground. She left Daphne and Noah with her mum as she walked towards the bridge before she looked down at the rushing water underneath her. She sat there in complete silence for a long time where she pulled out her broken doll from her coat pocket before she let go of it with it instantly falling down into the water. As soon as her broken doll hit the water, she watched the water consume it as she blinked back tears that fell down her face when she said to herself with a frown on her face, "Here's to letting go. I'm letting go of the life that I'm never going to have. I'm letting go of the dreams that are never going to be mine. I'm letting go of you, dad. Take this doll as my peace offering to you. I'm done being trapped between doorways. I'm over it. I'm over you, dad. Thank you for showing me the poem. It helped me see things in a new light. This is our destiny. I'm free. I'm home."

As soon as she got up from her spot on the bridge, she looked down at the water one last time as she blinked back tears that fell down her face when she said aloud to herself with a smile on her face, "I messed it up, didn't I, dad? It's not that. I'm free. I'm dead. I like my version of the poem better. Your poem is too gloomy. I'm not seeing the stars yet. Maybe someday I'll see them. Maybe that's when the door will finally open up for me. A world so beautiful that I'm not going to know what to do. A world without any pain or suffering. A world without any heartbreak. A world without any fear. That's where we are free. Free from the world. Free from the universe. Free from the cosmos. Goodbye, dad. I'll see you in the doorway." She walked away from the bridge without looking behind her as she ignored the tears that fell down her face where she sprinted back to the house before she ran into George pulling up the car into the driveway of the house. Before he asked her how she got home so quickly, she ran into the house as she went into her bedroom with the door shutting behind her where she laid down on the bed staring up at the ceiling before she passed out in her bed for the rest of the night.

Chapter Seventy-Eight
(Spring 1978 – Stockholm, Sweden)

She got on her private jet with her mum, her children, and Amelia's family where she slept for the flight home before her mum woke her up once they landed in Los Angeles. Sebastian pulled her into a tight hug with her face hidden in his chest until Noah tugged on her legs where she placed Noah on her hip before Sebastian pulled Daphne and Noah into a tight hug with their faces hidden in his chest. Once their driver dropped them off at the house, she went into her mother's bedroom as her mother woke up from a nap where she pulled her mother into a sudden hug before her mother tightly wrapped her arms around her with her face hidden in her chest. They stayed like that until her mum walked into the room with cups of tea in her hands where she sat down on the bed before she took a cup of tea from her mum's hands. She broke the silence between them when she asked her mother if she knew about what her mum said at Uncle James' funeral where her mother grabbed onto her hands before she told her daughter that she knew more about her mum than anyone else. She leaned her head onto her mother's shoulder where she stayed in there with her parents until Daphne shouted for her before she ran into Noah's bedroom to stop him from climbing on top of his dresser. Their lives went back to normal after that. Her mother went to the hospital every other day for her chemo treatments with her mum or Uncle Stan. Daphne and Noah finished up the rest of the school year. She worked on editing the final cuts of their movies in the studio. Her cousins and their families came over to the house once a week for dinner and drinks where they talked to each other before they went home for the night. It was like nothing changed except for the deaths of her family members. No one talked about being left behind by their parents. It was too soon to have that conversation. It was always going to be too soon to talk about it. She didn't bring up the conversation with her cousins because she didn't want to upset them. They were living in their delusions, and she didn't want to be the person that took it away from them. She talked to Jacob about these thoughts. He knew what it meant to have your delusions taken away from you before you were ready to accept them. She told Jacob that she let go of her father in York before he told her that he was proud of her. He asked her what she did to let go of him before she told her father that was letting go of him. Jacob asked how she felt after letting go of him. She told him that she felt like a weight was lifted off of her shoulders. She wasn't looking for him. She told him about the journal incident in New York. She told him about her finding that same poem. She told him about her knowing that her father died three weeks before anyone found out. She didn't want to tell her mother about her father's death. Jacob told her that the weight that it had on her was so enormous that she didn't know what to do with it. She told him that she tried to kill herself that night after she found out that her father was going to die. He asked her why she didn't tell anyone else. She told him that she didn't feel like it was her place to share his secret until he was ready to. She wanted to protect his secrets like he would've done with her secrets. This led to a conversation with Jacob about whether or not it was fair for her father to put this huge secret on his daughter. She didn't see it that way before Jacob brought it up to her.

She wanted to think that her father meant for her mother to see the poem. She knew the truth without anyone saying anything to her. She knew that poem was only meant for her. It was the same thing with her letter that her father never sent to her. The poem that he sent her was his suicide note to her. Not the letter that was never sent to her. Her father didn't mean for Camille to send that letter to her after he killed himself. He meant for Camille to send her that letter after she overdosed on drugs. Camille died a few months before she overdosed in the club, so she could never send it to her. Jason couldn't send it to her because he didn't know anything about it. Camille didn't tell Jason about it until after she died. Jason went to New York to show the letter to Uncle Sam asking him what to do about it. Uncle Sam told him not to send it to her because she was recovering from her overdose, and he didn't want to make it worse by showing her that letter. That was why Uncle Sam left her the house in Sweden. He wanted her to find the letter on her own when she was ready to read it. His last wish for her was to get closure from her father. That was his gift to her. With her knowing about her father's letter, everything went the way that it was supposed to. Her father knew that this letter was going to save her like how his poem that he sent her saved him. She didn't understand the power of words for the longest time. Even though she grew up with her mother preaching about it, she didn't believe her until she read her father's poem. Nothing saved the world like words did. It showed us a greater path in our lives. It gave us purpose in the world. It gave us comfort in times of pain and suffering. It gave us happiness in times of sadness. It reminded us of the world that we could have if we chose a different door. The imagination of words. It created worlds out of nothing. It brought worlds to life that didn't exist. It made the nonexistent things feel so real. The world would die without words. Her world would end without words. After all of this time, she found her purpose. Her purpose was to create worlds with her words. To create places in the world that became real. She wouldn't have anything without words. She wouldn't have known joy, sorrow, or pain without the impact of words. It was her father's purpose. It was her mother's purpose. It was her purpose. None of it meant anything. Her addiction didn't mean anything. Her mental illnesses didn't mean anything. Her pain didn't mean anything. The only thing that mattered were her words. What impact were her words going to have on the world? What impact did her words have on her? What impact would her words have on the generations after her? This gave her an idea for a new project to work on. She wrote a book about the letters and the words that she wrote in her journal. She called her book *All of the Things that I Never Got the*

Chance to Say. She used the letters that she wrote to people where she wrote what she wanted to say in those moments that she never said. She started from the beginning with the moment that she was able to talk, and she ended the book with where she was now. She didn't use the names of her family members, but she used code names to talk about them. They would understand when they read it. She wanted a space where she could talk to people that she wasn't able to talk to again because they were dead. She wanted a space to talk to people that were alive telling them things that she never found the strength to tell them in real life. She didn't tell anyone except her parents and Sebastian that she was writing a book because she didn't want anyone knowing about what she was writing about. Not that they would object to her writing a book about it, but she didn't want to tell them until she was completely finished working on it. When she wasn't working on her book, she went to her mother's chemo treatments with her because her mum was in the hospital with Uncle Stan.

Uncle Stan was admitted in the hospital with pneumonia, but the doctors found out something worse on the second day. They found out from a blood test that Uncle Stan tested positive for HIV. When they found out that Uncle Stan was developing Aids, the doctors urged Thomas to get tested too since it was likely that he got the disease from him. Thomas refused to get tested because he didn't want to believe that it was real. There were so many people in the country dying from Aids and he didn't want to be one of them. Thomas didn't want to believe that Uncle Stan had Aids either, but he begged his boyfriend to get tested just to be safe. After Thomas conceded to his boyfriend's request, he went into the clinic to get his blood tested where he found out that he tested positive for HIV too. She visited Uncle Stan in the hospital after her mother's chemo treatments where they talked about everything except for the elephant in the room. The word got out to the rest of the family about Uncle Stan and Thomas having HIV. They got phone calls about it from her cousins that were worried that she was going to catch it before she told them that Aids wasn't contracted in the way that they thought that it was. Most of them stopped bothering her. Audrey didn't stop bothering her where she called her a few times a week asking her if she gave her children Aids before she hung up on her. She didn't tell anyone else about what Audrey said to her because she didn't want to upset her parents and Sebastian. When Lucy reminded her that Daphne's birthday was in a few weeks, she asked Lucy if they had enough time to plan a birthday party where she told her that it was doubtful that they could pull a party off in a little bit of time before she told Lucy that she would come up with something for the children's birthday parties. Even though Noah's birthday was in the winter, they celebrated it in the spring with Daphne. It was easier for them to do one party a year instead of two parties. Daphne and Noah liked having their parties together. They told them about how much they looked forward to it every year. With everything going on with her mother's chemo treatments and Uncle Stan being in the hospital, she told Sebastian that they should have an intimate party for the children where he agreed with her because he wasn't up for a party either. When they asked the children about a party, Daphne told her that she wanted to go to Sweden as Noah told them that he wanted to ride horses where she looked over at Sebastian before she told them that they were going to Sweden. After she tasked Lucy with preparing for their weekend trip to Sweden, she asked her mother if she felt good enough to come with them where her mother told her that she would do anything to spend time with her grandchildren before she told her mother that she would have Lucy make plans for her to come with them. They invited some of her cousins to come with them with their spouses and their children where they told her that they would love to come to Sweden with them. She packed up their bags with warm clothes since it was cold in Sweden where Sebastian wrapped up the presents that Lucy bought for them before they fell asleep in each other's arms for the night. They woke up the next morning to Daphne and Noah jumping up and down on their bed before they pulled the children into a tickling session with their laughter filling up the room. Once Sebastian took the children into their bedrooms, she helped her mum carry their bags and the children's presents into the back of the car where they ate breakfast in the kitchen before they got into the car. After their driver dropped them off at the airport, she pulled her cousins into tight hugs where they got onto their private jet. Once their plane landed in Sweden that afternoon, she carried Noah off of the plane with Sebastian carrying Daphne in his arms before they got into cars that took them to the house. Once they placed their bags into their bedrooms, she told them that they were going to ride horses until the sun came down where they would have a picnic on the lake before they were going to watch fireworks. Everyone went outside to the stables except for her parents who helped their chef make dinner. They went around the property a few times before the sun went down where she told everyone to meet them on the lake.

Once she met up with her parents in the kitchen to see if dinner was done, her mum told her that the servants set it out for them on their blankets where she thanked her parents for helping her before she went outside by the lake with the servants setting out food for them. After their families took a seat on the blankets, they helped themselves to the food where they gathered the children on one blanket before Daphne and Noah opened their presents in excitement. Daphne placed her gifts in a pile while Noah threw them into a messy pile where she asked the children to thank everyone for the presents with them repeating the words that she said before her parents brought over two cakes. Her mother placed the cake with eight candles in front of Daphne as her mum placed the cake with five candles in front of Noah where they closed their eyes making wishes before Gabriel took a picture of them together with smiles on their faces and their arms around each other. After the children ate their pieces of cake with frosting all over Noah's mouth, she wiped his face with a napkin as he fought her tight grip on him where Lucy asked her if it was time before she nodded her head at her with her letting Noah run away from her over to Christian's blanket. As soon as Lucy put off the fireworks, everyone looked up at the sky in excitement as she placed Noah on her lap with Sebastian placing Daphne on his lap where he pecked her lips before Daphne told them that they were gross. The fireworks went off for twenty minutes until it was dark outside where she told the children that it was time for bed before Sebastian told them that it was way past their bedtime. After they put the children to sleep in their bedrooms, she joined her cousins by the fire where she grabbed a marshmallow from the patio before she took a seat in between Sebastian and Oliver. Once she placed her marshmallow over the fire, she propped her feet up on bricks from the fire as Sasha and Amelia talked about their favorite brands of clothes that they got their children. She had an intrusive thought that made her stop focusing on her marshmallow before Oliver shouted at her to get her attention with him grabbing her marshmallow stick from falling into the fire, "Isabella! Your marshmallow!"

As soon as she grabbed the stick from him, she placed the melted marshmallow in between the graham crackers and a piece of chocolate where she took a bite of it before she leaned onto her seat with her eyes closed. Oliver broke her out of her trace from the fire when he asked her with concern laced in his voice, "You seem distracted. What's going on, Isabella? You're never this quiet."

As soon as she opened up her eyes again, her cousins and Sebastian stared at her as she lit a cigarette off of the fire with her inhaling the smoke from it when she responded to him with a frown on her face, "Why is everyone staring at me? I'm fine, Oliver. I've been thinking about Uncle Stan. I feel horrible for him and Thomas. I can't imagine what that feels like. Having a disease that the world is scared of, and no one can cure it."

Amelia grabbed onto Troy's hand when she responded to her with a sad look on her face, "I feel horrible for them too. That must feel so helpless. How are they taking it?"

Once she inhaled the smoke from her cigarette, she responded to Amelia with Sebastian grabbed onto her hand, "Uncle Stan is taking it well. He's being optimistic even though the doctors are certain that it's only going to get worse for him. Thomas isn't taking it well. He is drinking a lot and Uncle Stan is concerned about him, but he can't get through to him. Thomas' disease isn't as progressed as Uncle Stan's disease, so I can see why he's worried."

Oliver grabbed onto Juliet's hands when he responded to her with a frown on his face, "I could talk to Jacob and see if he could help him. Jacob knows what that is like. His boyfriend has Aids too. I know that he will help us. I get it. He doesn't want to watch the man that he loves die in front of him. How's your mom taking it? Is she doing okay with her chemo treatments?"

She blinked back tears that fell down her face as she inhaled the smoke from her cigarette when she responded to him, "The doctor isn't happy about how her tumors aren't getting any smaller. He wanted to do a surgery to remove them, but he told us that it would be too dangerous to do that. He doesn't think that she's going to get it out this time. Mom is okay with it. She told me the other day that she's ready to die. Even though she doesn't want to die, she'd be okay with it. She stopped chemo treatments a few weeks ago. The doctor gave her a few months to live. Mum is looking into hospice for her. She asked me to help her, but I couldn't do it. I told her not to tell me anything about it. I don't want to think about that. We haven't told Daphne and Noah about it. I don't know how to tell them without scaring them."

As Sebastian pulled her into a tight hug with her face hidden in his chest, they pulled away from each other as she took a seat on the ground with her face hidden in her knees where Troy and Juliet left them alone before Oliver wrapped his arms around her. Once she let out heartbreaking sobs into his chest, he ran his hands up and down her back until she wasn't crying where he helped her off of the ground before she sat down on her seat with Sebastian grabbing onto her hand. She stared at the dying fire like it was the only thing keeping her alive right now. Sasha broke the silence between them when she said aloud to the room with tears falling down her face, "I guess that we never talked about it. Having dead parents. How do we feel about it? I don't think that I felt much when my mom died because I was so numb to it. My dad was a different story. It hit me as soon as he died. It wasn't like I was close to him, but it hurt me more when he died. I could never take back what I didn't have with him. There was a lot of guilt and regret. I understood how you felt when your dad died, Isabella. It's hard to move on from what you never had with your dad. I wish that I spent more time with him. I wish that he knew me. Not this fake version of me. The real me. The person that Gabriel and Charlotte know me as. The person that I am."

Once Amelia grabbed onto Sasha's hands to comfort her, she blinked back tears that fell down her face when she responded to Sasha in a soft voice, "Thanks, Sasha. That means a lot to me. I hate that you get it, but I'm glad that you don't feel alone. I wish that I could tell you that feeling goes away, but it doesn't leave you. You spend the rest of your life living with that regret about what could've been with him. The only way that it goes away is making your peace with it. You have to make your peace with that you are never going to get that back again. You aren't supposed to have it. You have to be okay with not being okay."

Oliver responded to her with a smirk on his face, "You took my advice. I'm glad that you listened to me. I was right, Isabella."

As soon as she lightly smacked him on his shoulder, she responded to him with a wide grin on her face, "Stop looking so smug. Yes, you were right, Oliver. Are you happy? Were you waiting for me to say that to you?"

Oliver grabbed onto her hands when he responded to her with a look of pride on his face, "I'm happy, Isabella. Thank you for acknowledging that I was right and that you listened to me. It feels good to be right."

As soon as she rolled her eyes at Oliver, Sasha looked over at her with Amelia's arms around her when Sasha asked her with tears falling down her face, "How did you get over your dad? How long did it take for you to do it?"

She let out a shaky breath when she responded to her with her blinking back tears that fell down her face, "It took me thirty years to get over him. Thirty years too long if you ask me. Trust me, Sasha. I know it's not going to take you that long to get over your dad. How did I get over him? Isn't that a big question? I found his letter that he wrote me that wasn't sent to me, and I knew that he died thinking of me. That's all I needed from him. To know that I meant something to him. I stood on the bridge in York where he died, and I let go of the doll that he gave me when I was a little girl. I watched it fall into the water. I told him that I was done looking for him and that he wasn't going to define my life anymore. I told him that I was moving on without him. He didn't object to it. He let me walk away from the bridge and he told me to never look back. I always tried to find out the reason why he did it. It didn't matter why he did it."

Amelia said to her with a smile on her face, "I'm speaking for everyone here when I say that we are happy to hear you say that. We've waited a long time to hear you admit that to us. Oliver assured us that you would learn that in your time. I thought that the drug overdoses were going to teach you that. What taught you that?"

As she lit a cigarette while inhaling the smoke from it, she let out a shaky breath when she responded to Amelia in a soft voice, "I'm glad that you guys knew it all along. Do you want a medal or something? I'm joking. I'm not upset. Thanks for giving me the space to figure it out for myself. I'm sure that it wasn't easy to do that considering that you guys are obsessed with control. What made me see it? Nothing you guys said or did that's for sure. I don't know what made me see it. It was a combination of everything between my dad's letters, the poem that he sent me the day that he died, and the moments in the water with him. It was something that I needed to move on from him. You'll see the poem in my book. My poem is the beginning of the book, and his poem is the end of my book."

Her cousin's jaws dropped in shock as soon as she mentioned her book. She inhaled the smoke from her cigarette when she told them in a soft voice, "'In the doorway, I see it. It's the life that I never had. If I made the right choice, I would find myself there. I would be in a world where I didn't damn generations of my family to the pain that I inflicted upon them. I would be in a place where I found my happiness that I spent a long time looking for. I would've found that the happiness didn't come from other people. Happiness came from within me. I wouldn't regret what I never did. I wouldn't regret the things that I never got the chance to say. I would be at peace with myself. The more that I look into the doorway, the more that I realize that it's not my past. The doorway is my future. A future that only exists in dreams. A future that only exists in death. I see the doorway, but I can never catch it. It's reminding me of my death. As death gets closer to me, the doorway gets closer to me like it's about to shallow me in one bite. I can't enter the door until I'm on the bridge. The door is wide open, and it is ready for me to enter it. As I enter the doorway, I see it for the first time. I see the stars. They are right in front of me. I can almost touch them. A bright halo approaches me. I welcome it into my body. I feel invincible. I feel like a brand-new person. The mistakes are melted off of me. The heartbreak is erased like it never happened. I am no longer defined by the mistakes of my past. I am no longer limited by the world. I am at peace until I do it all over again. The mistakes. The heartbreak. The pain. The limitations of the world. This time I change the outcome. I am everyone and I am no one at the same time. I become the person that I truly meant to become. I am free. I am home.'"

Oliver responded to her with a sad look on his face, "That's beautiful. Did you write that?"

She put out the end of her cigarette into the ashtray when she responded to Oliver with a wide grin on her face, "Yes, I did. I wrote it when I was eight years old before my dad died. It was three weeks before anyone else found it. I knew it because he ended his poem with I am free, and I am dead. The rest of the book is things that I never got the chance to tell him. It's everything in between when I received the poem until I understood the poem. That's what made me get closure from him." She fell asleep in his arms for the rest of the night.

CHAPTER SEVENTY-NINE
(SUMMER 1978 – YORK, ENGLAND)

They went back to their lives in Los Angeles. The children finished up their school year where she worked on finishing up the final edits on the book before she sent it off to her publishers. When she got the phone call that she waited for from them, she packed her bags for her trip to New York. They met up with her publishing team where they talked about the timeline for their release and public events that she was attending across the country. She called her mum to tell her mother that she was going to get her book published. All of her excitement disappeared when her mum told her that her mother was at the hospice center where she hid the disappointment in her voice before she told her mum that she would tell her about it after she saw her again. Once her mum promised her that she would tell her mother about it, she hung up the phone as she let out a heartbreaking sob into her hands where she passed out from exhaustion on her bed of her hotel room before she woke up to the phone ringing in the middle of the night. She completely ignored it as it rang three times until she finally answered it. Her mother told her that she was proud of her for her book where she told her mother that she was surprised that things were happening so fast ignoring what she said to her. Her mother didn't say anything to her for what felt like an eternity before she said to her, "I'm sorry, baby girl. Things don't work out like we want them to, don't they?" She hung up the phone on her mother. She couldn't bear to hear the utter calmness in her voice. She sobbed with her face hidden in her pillows before she passed out the rest of the night. They were in New York for the rest of the week working out the details for her book release where she struggled to focus on anything that was happening around her. She couldn't unhear her mother's voice telling what she told her over the phone. *Things don't work out like we want them to, don't they?* It was like her father's words that haunted her for most of her life. She heard her mother's words anywhere she went in the world regardless of what she was doing. She heard them in New York at meetings with her publishers. She heard them in the silence of her hotel room. She heard them on the flight home. She heard them in her sleep. She heard them at home when she played with the children. She heard them when she woke up in the morning. It wasn't the content of the words that scared her. Her mother said a lot more imitating things over the years that they didn't bother her. It was the way that she said them to her that scared her. Like there was nothing left inside of her mother anymore. It scared her because that was what she sounded like in the height of her addiction. She had so many questions that she wanted to ask her mother, but she didn't ask them. She wouldn't be able to forget them if she found the nerve to ask her mother about it. The innocence of her not knowing the truth was the reason that she didn't ask her mother. If she could do it, then she would've asked her mother what it felt like to be so close to the door. She would've asked her how she felt being so close to death. Was it what her father felt in those moments? Being so close to the door that he could touch it, but he had to pretend to keep on living like nothing was there. She learned a long time ago that her knowing things never made anything better for anyone. Least of all herself who couldn't move on from anything. She assured herself that her mother was probably writing it down right now for her to read after she died. Her mother was waiting until she was gone. She waited to tell her mother about the truth of her father's death until long after she died.

The secrets that they kept to themselves. With her mother getting closer to death every day, she thought about what secrets that she was going to die with. She was going to take the night that her father died to the grave with her. She was going to take the night that she overdosed when she was thirteen years old. She was going to take the day that Daxton died with her. No one needed to know the truth. Another moment that she was going to take with her was when she got high the summer before her senior year of high school. She wondered what memories her mother was going to take the grave with her. It was memories with her father and Uncle Kenny who her mother never talked about. Even if her mother wasn't writing it down to tell her, she knew what her mother would've said to her in a letter. She would say that she loved her. She was sorry for everything that happened to them. She was doing what she thought was best. She wanted to do more to help her. She wished that she understood her when she grew up. She wasn't mad at her for choosing drugs over her. She understood why she did it. She knew that life was hard. It was hard to know what door to choose. No one knew when they were making the right choice or the wrong choice. She didn't have to be so hard on herself. She couldn't control her destiny was determined for her the moment that her father raped her mother. She was sorry that she didn't stop her father from killing himself. She should've done more to help her. Her mother would say to her that the world was a dark place, but there was a moment of light inside of it. The light was impossible to catch. It always disappeared before she could grab it. She spent her life looking for that light and all that she got from the world was darkness. She held onto that light like it was the only thing keeping her alive. Hoping and praying that she would get a chance to see the light. Every time that she didn't see the light she was disappointed all over again. She struggled to believe in the light. She questioned if it was real or if it was a dream that she made up in her mind. Right when she lost hope in the light, she saw it sneaking out from a dark corner. She chased it until she couldn't find it anymore. Suddenly, she turned around with it staring right at her. She grabbed onto the light, and she saw it all for the first time. That was the feeling that her father described in his poem. That was the feeling that Camille described in her letter to her grandmother. They all had different names for it. Her mother called it the light. Her father called it the stars. Camille called it the view. It was all the same things. It was what they were waiting for. It was their version of Heaven. This inspired her to write a new poem. She wanted to honor all of them. Her mother. Her father. Her grandmother. Camille. The people that taught her all about the world. This was her newest poem that she wrote down in the middle of the night. She placed this paper into her desk drawer until she felt another piece of paper stuck in the back of the drawer. As soon as she grabbed it out of the drawer, she realized that it was the letter that she wrote to herself after her last overdose where she put her poem that she wrote that night before she placed it into an envelope. She wrote out the envelope in Oliver's name with his address on the corner where she pulled out a piece of paper from her desk before she wrote to him a letter with a frown on her face.

You step through the door. You see the life that you wished that you had. You step through another door. You see the life that you deserved to have. One door leads to another door. You are in your worst nightmare. You are in your paradise. You are surrounded by people who hate you. You are surrounded by people who love you. You don't know how you got to be here. In a place where you are lost amongst doom already happening to you and dreams ready to come true. If you chose the wrong door, you are trapped in the moment that you made the wrong choice. If you chose the right door, you are surrounded by a paradise. No matter how different the doors are, they end up going to the same place. You end up inside of the moment that you have been chasing when you are born. The stars. The light. The view. Your version of Heaven. You dance in your Heaven for the rest of eternity. You are dancing in the stars.

Dear Oliver,

I know that I promised you that I would never write you another letter. I wouldn't break your promise if it wasn't this important. You aren't going to like this, but there is a reason that I'm sending this to you. If something were to happen to me, I would want Bash and the children to know what happened to me. There's two pieces of paper in this envelope besides this one. The first one is a letter that I wrote to my future self a long time ago. I haven't read it since I wrote it, and I want you to do the same thing. When the time is right, you need to show it to Bash and the children. Don't address it like you are the person sending it. Send it like I'm sending it to them. Use your address. I only ask you to put my name down instead of yours. The second one is a poem that I wrote around the time that my mother was dying. It inspired me to do this. The poem is something that I want read at my funeral. I want you to read it. I trust you to convey this message to the family. Once you read it at the funeral, I want you to drop the poem off of the bridge in York. I want my poem to be part of the river for the rest of eternity. My father planned what he sent to me before he died. I want to do the same thing for Bash and my children.

Do you know how I know what is going to happen to me? Because my father told me about it a long time ago. After everything that went wrong in my life, this is the only thing that is going to go right for me. I'm entrusting you with this responsibility because I know that you are going to do it. There is no one else in the world I ever trusted as much as I trusted you. I trusted you with my life too many times to count. When you get this letter, don't ask me about it. I will still be alive when you get this and I'm not going to talk about it. This secret is going to stay between us. Hide this from the world until it's time. You know what I'm talking about. I'm trusting you to do what I couldn't finish doing in life. If you get this letter, it doesn't mean that I'm going to kill myself. It only means that I know that I'm not going to live to be an old woman. It has nothing to do with anything else. It will be peaceful. It will be the end.

Love you always, Isabella.

After she sealed up the envelope, she placed it into her purse as she snuck past Sebastian who slept in the bed where she drove to the post office before she waited until they opened early in the morning. As soon as she walked into the post office, she handed her letter to the worker who placed a stamp on it when she asked them if she could request for the letter to be sent on a particular date. The post office worker asked her what date that she wanted it sent out before she told them that she wanted it sent on a date in ten years. The post office worker was shocked by what she said because they never heard anyone say that before where she asked the post office worker if that was possible when the worker told her that they would have to check with their manager. After the post office worker disappeared into the back office, she smoked a cigarette in the lobby even though the sign said no smoking where the post office worker told her that they were able to do that for a price before she handed them a pile of one-hundred-dollar bills. The post office worker didn't correct her for smoking in the post office because she gave them so much money where they asked her if she needed anything else before she grabbed a box of stamps off of the rank. Once the post office worker charged her for her book of stamps, she thanked them as she walked out of the post office where she got into her car before she drove to the house since she was going to miss her flight to New York. She walked into the living room to see Sebastian and the children eating breakfast at the table as she kissed Daphne and Noah on the top of their heads where Sebastian asked where she was before she told him that she needed to leave for the airport soon. Sebastian didn't bother her about not answering his question as he pecked her lips where she kissed the children before she disappeared in her car. After her driver dropped her off at the airport, she met up with Lucy who waited for her where she got on her private jet before the pilot flew them to New York. This was the beginning of her press tour for her book *All of the Things that I Never Got the Chance to Say*. She did book signings at bookstores in the city until she left for the next city a few days later before she did it all over again. She forgot that her mother was dying from cancer or her scary dreams that made her write that letter to Oliver. She wasn't a wife. She wasn't a mother. She was a writer that published their second book, and she was enjoying every moment of the success from it. She talked to people from all kinds of backgrounds that related to her book. They understood feeling trapped between the doors. People told her about their resentments over the years over the doorway. She realized that this was a universal experience that most people felt in life. It was good to be validated by these different people because she didn't have to be alone. They were all stuck in the doorway with her.

She got a phone call in the middle of the night from Oliver. She initially panicked because she thought that he was going to yell at her about the letter. The post office worker remained true to their word when they told her that they weren't going to send that letter for ten years on that day. Oliver told her that Uncle Nathan dropped dead from a heart attack this morning in Cardiff where she asked him if he wanted her to come to England with him in the morning before he told her that he was getting on a flight to New York. After she hung up on Oliver when they announced that his plane was boarding, she called Sebastian who answered the phone when he asked her what was wrong where she told him that Uncle Nathan was dead and that they needed to go on their private jet to York. Once Sebastian asked her if she needed anything from the house, she told him to bring some black dresses for her and her journal from her dresser where he told her that he would see her in England before she asked him if her parents were coming with them. Sebastian broke the silence when he told her that her mother discharged herself from the hospice center to go to the funeral where she tried to hide her surprise in her voice before she told him that she was so glad that her parents were coming with them. She hung up the phone on Sebastian, so that he could pack their stuff as she packed her bags with her clothes laying everywhere in her hotel room. She went into the shower to ignore that bad feeling burning in the back of her mind before she softly cried to herself in the shower. She sobbed in the shower for two hours until the water was frozen where she wrapped herself up in a robe before she tried to get a few hours of sleep. After she got two hours of sleep, she was woken up by someone pounding on her door before a distraught Oliver stood in front of her. Once she pulled him into her arms, Oliver sobbed into her chest with her arms tightly around him where she dragged them over to the bed before they laid down on the bed. She broke the silence between them when she asked him if he wanted to order room service where he nodded his head at her before he took a shower while she talked into the phone. When Oliver came out of the shower, they ate breakfast with them wearing robes from the hotel where she placed their empty dishes into the hallway for the staff to get before she told him that they should probably leave for the airport soon. Oliver carried their bags as she went into Lucy's room to apologize to her about ending the book tour early where Lucy told her that they could always reschedule once they got back from England before she joined Oliver in the lobby with him flagging down a taxi for them. As soon as their taxi driver dropped them off at the airport, she paid him more money than what she owed him as she followed Oliver to their private jet where she slept in the bed. When their plane landed in York that evening, she followed Oliver off of her private jet as he sprinted over to his sister Poppy who pulled him into a tight hug with her face hidden in his chest where they pulled away from each other before Poppy pulled her into a tight hug with her face hidden in her chest. Once she got into the back of the car, Poppy drove them to the Heartley farmhouse as she dropped them off at the front of the house where she followed Oliver out of the car before Poppy sped away without looking back. As soon as Oliver unlocked the front door of the house, she followed him into the living room that was untouched from the last time that they were in York nine months ago where she went into one of the bedrooms before she closed the door behind her. She laid down on the bed with her face hidden in the pillows where she pretended to not hear Oliver sobbing in the room across from her before she pressed her face into her pillows with her letting out a scream into it. After she almost lost her voice, she got up from the bed as she kicked the dresser over and over again until her legs were covered in bruises where she wiped away the tears that fell down her face before she sprinted towards the barn. She unlocked the doors by hitting it with a metal stick where she helped herself into the abandoned barn before she laid down on a pile of forgotten hay that was on the ground. She wanted to scream at Poppy for selling the Heartley Farm.

They couldn't get rid of the only thing that reminded her of her father. It was the only thing left. If the farmhouse was gone, then that meant everything was gone. None of it was real. It didn't mean anything. He didn't mean anything. She knew that Oliver was upset about it too because Poppy didn't mention it to them when she picked them up at the airport. She talked about everything else except for that they were selling their father's farm. She was woken up the next morning by a stray dog licking her face as she sat up on the ground with the dog sitting in her lap where she ran her hands up and down their fur coat before the dog ran away from her after they heard another noise. Once she pulled pieces of hay out of her hair, she walked to the house with the sun coming up in the sky. She walked into the kitchen as Oliver ate a can of peaches at the kitchen table where she sat down next to him before she took some peaches from his can. They didn't say anything to each other until Oliver ate the last peach where he placed the empty can into the garbage can before he told her that they were going to Poppy's house to talk to her. She got dressed into one of her floral dresses before she walked over to Poppy's house with him. They didn't talk to each other on the walk over to Poppy's house where Oliver helped himself into the house with her following behind him before they found Poppy sitting at the table eating breakfast with Ellis and their children except for Jack. As soon as Poppy saw the serious looks on their faces, she excused herself from the table as she grabbed Madeline and Millie's hair when she walked outside of the house before she asked them what was wrong with them. She let out a frustrated sigh as she looked over at Oliver who shook his head at her when he asked his sister when she was going to tell them about her selling their father's farm. Poppy let out a defeated sigh before she told her brother that they weren't going to tell them because they were going to stop them from doing it. This made Oliver even angrier at his sister as he paced around in circles. He asked her when she got so selfish before Poppy defended herself by saying to him that he wasn't there with her and that he had no right to call that. Oliver told Poppy that it wasn't her right to make that decision before she told him that he wasn't his real dad. This made their arguing instantly stop as Oliver was too stunned to say anything to her. She broke the silence when she asked Poppy why she was getting rid of her father's legacy where Poppy turned around to look at her before she told her with a scowl on her face that she didn't want that legacy for herself. She was too stunned to say anything to Poppy as Oliver asked her what happened to her where Poppy got in Oliver's face before she told him that she could say the same thing about him. As soon as Poppy said that to him, Oliver shook his head in disappointment at her as he asked her if this was worth losing her family over where Poppy didn't say anything for a long time. She broke the silence between them before she said to him that Tommy and Alfie agreed with her. She wasn't talking about the farm anymore. Oliver stormed away from her without saying anything else with her following behind him as Poppy stormed into the house where they didn't stop running until they made it into a pub before Oliver walked inside of it with her following behind him. After Oliver ordered a pint of beer for himself, she told the bartender that she wanted a cocktail as he disappeared to get their drinks where the bartender placed their drinks in front of them before Oliver handed him the money that they owed him. They didn't say anything to each other as they silently drank their drinks in peace where they placed their empty glasses onto the table before Oliver led them to a local grocery store to get some food for the house. She pushed the cart as Oliver placed food inside of it where they bought the food before they carried it to the house.

When they got back to the house again, they were starving after they put the food away as Oliver made something for them to eat where she grabbed a broom from the kitchen to clean up the house before Oliver told her it was time to eat. After they ate lunch together in silence, she lingered at the table for a few moments until Oliver asked her if she was going to go to the funeral where she shrugged her shoulders at him with a frown on her face before he told her that they could do anything that they wanted to do. She told Oliver that he was sounding a lot like her when she was manic. Oliver didn't say anything to her before Sebastian walked into the house with her parents and the children where she walked into the living room to greet them before Daphne and Noah ran into her arms. After she pulled away from Daphne and Noah, she pulled Sebastian into a desperate hug with her face hidden in his chest when he asked her what was going on where she told him that she would tell him about it later before she helped her mother onto the couch with her mum holding her up on the other side. Once her mother was comfortable on the couch, she walked into the kitchen where Oliver was on the phone with Juliet telling them not to come to York before she took a seat across from him. After Oliver explained everything to Juliet, he took a seat across from her as Sebastian stood behind her with his arms wrapped around her. Oliver told them that they weren't going to the funeral where Sebastian asked why they weren't going to the funeral before she ignored him by saying to Oliver that they needed to stop Poppy from selling the farm. Her parents were in the kitchen as her mum let out a shocked gasp when her mother asked her why Poppy was selling the farm where she turned around to look at Sebastian before she asked him if they could buy the farm from Poppy. Sebastian asked her how they were going to buy a farm in a country that they didn't live in where she told him that they would pay people to take care of it before Sebastian walked outside to think about it. Her mum helped her mother into their bedroom as she wrangled the children into the living room to tell them that they weren't going to the funeral where Daphne asked her what they were going to do before Oliver said to them that they were going to have their own funeral for him. Even though the idea was completely insane, she told Oliver that it was a great idea as she went into her parent's bedroom to tell them about their impromptu funeral for Uncle Nathan. Her mother thought that it was a great idea before they prepared for the funeral in the yard. Since she didn't want to waste the black dress that Sebastian packed for her, she put on the black dress that he brought with him as she changed Daphne into her black dress and Noah into black suit where she followed the children into the living room before she followed them to the graveyard with her holding onto Noah's hand. Sebastian held onto Daphne's hand where Oliver stopped them at the graves before everyone lit a candle that they placed on top of the graves. Oliver didn't look away from the candles lighting up the graveyard as he blinked back tears that fell down his face when he said aloud to the comforting stars in the sky, "Here's the real funeral for you, dad. Not the fake one that your other children want to have for you. Thank you for being the father that my dad could never be for me. Thank you for loving my mum when no one else would ever dare to love her. You treated me like your son and it's more than anyone else has ever done for me. I'm happy that you are with mum again. She was getting lonely without you. There's only so much pain that one person can take in their lifetime. I think that you took more than most people took from the world, but you didn't let it affect your life. You were determined to live your life no matter what happened to you. I love you so much, dad. I always will."

As she wrapped her arm around Oliver's waist, she looked down at the candles as Oliver blew out one of the candles where her mum helped her mother out of her wheelchair before she handed her one of the candles. Once her mother held onto one of the candles, she looked down at the graves when her mother said aloud with her blinking back tears that fell down her face, "Nathan, I miss you so much. You were one of the best men in my life. Your compassion for me and my baby girl knew no bounds. You were always there to help us no matter what happened. More than anyone was there for us. I appreciate every moment that we spent together. I loved every moment of it. Even the painful moments after Will died. You were the only person that understood what it felt like to lose him. The emptiness that followed after his death was so blinding that we thought that it was going to consume us. We were stronger than we thought because we made it on the other side. We did the impossible, Nathan. We made a life without him. I don't think that we could've imagined what it would look like without him. How beautiful that the world became. Not because Will was dead. Will was living inside of us. His light didn't go out. We carried on the torch for him. The torch is in Isabella. Someday the torch will be in Daphne and Noah. As I blow out this light, my time has come to an end. Our time has come to an end, Nathan. It's up to Isabella now to finish what we started. Goodbye, Nathan. We'll be together soon."

As soon as her mother blew out the candle with her mum's help, her mum placed it onto the ground as she grabbed onto her mother's hands where she grabbed the last candle off of the ground before she said aloud with tears falling down her face, "Mom messed me up by what she said. All that I can say is that I'm sorry. I'm so sorry, Uncle Nathan. This wasn't what I wanted to happen to you. You didn't deserve to die alone like dad did. No one deserves that no matter how much they ruined the world. You blamed yourself for what happened with dad. Even though it was a choice that he made, you always felt responsible for it. I don't blame you for feeling that way. I blamed myself for it too. He wouldn't want us to blame ourselves for it. I know what that pain feels like to lose everything that you cared about. Losing yourself for a long time. Trying to escape from it. The monster consumes you from the inside out. That's what dad said in his letter to me. You had that monster inside of you too. You knew what it felt like to have your life taken away from you. To not know where the monster began to where you started. The world can be a place of joy and happiness. It can also be a place full of pain and sorrow. I'm thankful for everything that you did for me. You reminded me of the wonder. You reminded me of the joy."

As soon as she blew out her candle, Sebastian wrapped his arms around her with her face hidden in her chest. Daphne called out for her where she pulled her face out of his chest before her jaw dropped in shock from the swarm of lightning bugs. As she grabbed onto Oliver's hand, the children and Sebastian chased them when he whispered into her ear, "Looks like he's here with us now."

She caught a lightning bug in her hands where she stared at it in wonder before she responded to him with a smile on her face, "I know what to do. Thank you." She grabbed onto Oliver's hand with smiles on their faces. The children slept in their beds before she slept in Sebastian's arms for the night.

CHAPTER EIGHTY
(FALL 1978 – LOS ANGELES, CALIFORNIA)

She woke up before the sun came up as she got dressed into a floral dress where she met up with Oliver in the kitchen who finished his banana before she followed him outside for a walk. When they got to the bank, she asked the banker that she wanted to take money out of her account where they asked her how much money that she needed before she told them that she needed a million dollars. The banker was too stunned to say anything to her until Oliver asked them to hurry up where the banker ran into the vault to grab the money for her before they handed her the money without saying another word to her. After they stopped at the real estate office to talk to Poppy's agent, she kept the cash in her purse and the piece a paper that the real estate agent gave them in her purse where they walked to the church in comfortable silence. As they were about to walk into the church, Oliver asked her if she was ready for this as she nodded her head at him where she followed him inside of the church with everyone stopping to look at them before Oliver sprinted over to Poppy who had an intimate conversation with Audrey. Poppy stopped her conversation with Audrey to ask them what they wanted from her where Oliver silently handed her the envelope with the cash and the paper inside of it before she opened it to look at it with a frown on her face. Poppy's face turned white when she realized what it meant when she asked them where the rest of the money was before she told her that they gave the money to someone that needed it.

This left Poppy with more questions than answers and she didn't ask them about it. She knew what they were talking about right now. Poppy handed the paper back to her. She was about to put the money into her purse before Oliver said aloud for everyone at the wake that the money didn't belong to her because the farm doesn't belong to her. This stopped all conversation in the church as Poppy stared at them with hatred in her eyes when she asked Oliver what he was talking about where Oliver revealed that the farm belonged to Isabella. The money was their way of getting her to admit that she stole the farm from her. Tommy and Alfie came over to see what the commotion was about as she forced the deed to the farm and the cash out of Poppy's hands where she placed it inside of her purse before Poppy asked them who told them about it. She maintained eye contact with Poppy when she told her that Uncle Nathan told her about it. She didn't look away from her until she looked over at Audrey who looked like she saw a ghost before she told her with everyone intrigued by their conversation that she didn't have Aids. She sprinted out of the church with Oliver following behind her where they didn't stop running until the church was a distant memory before they laughed about it in relief with each other. They left England that night.

When they were on the way to Los Angeles, her mother asked her if they could stop in Florida to go to the beach where she instructed their pilot to reroute them to Palm Beach. Oliver called Juliet and his children Posey and Eleanor to tell them to meet them in Florida. They stayed at Palm Beach for two weeks where they had the vacation that they deserved to have together with no one there to judge them.

The children had to the time of their lives as they played in the water with Posey and Eleanor while she laid down on the beach with the sounds of the waves putting her to sleep. She didn't know what was going to happen after they got home. She tried to enjoy this moment before things got worse for them. In her mind, she was always going to be at Palm Beach with Oliver, his family, her parents, Sebastian, and their children. No one asked why they were in Palm Beach because everyone knew why they were there. This was the last place that her mother wanted to go to before she died in the hospice center. The children went back to school as Daphne went into fourth grade and Noah went into first grade where she dropped off the children at school before she visited her mother in the hospice center. Sebastian went to work at the studio during the day. She finished the last stops on her book tour in California before she worked on renovating the farmhouse that Poppy badly neglected before she let George in charge of overseeing it for them. She trusted George to take care of her property because he knew how important the farm was to her. She would've gone to England to oversee it herself, but she had to be home with her children that needed her in their lives. Her mother's health declined as she received daily updates from her mum that she was getting weaker and weaker by the day. She didn't spend any energy thinking about that because she knew that it would destroy her. She thought about the farmhouse most of the time. She called George once a day to ask him about the renovations before he told her about every little detail that the builders did to the house. George updated her on everything going on with her cousins in England even though she expressed to him that she didn't care to know anything about them. He told her that Poppy called the police on George several days in the beginning of their building project. She didn't like that she lost control of the situation. George told her and the police several times that he was supervising this project for his cousin who lived in the states before Poppy stormed off to her house. Oliver wasn't upset by his siblings deciding that they were too good for him. He was happy for the first time in a long time. Like the burden wasn't placed onto him anymore. She was happy that Oliver got the answer that he was looking for with him cutting off communication with his siblings. Her mother's lawyer came to the hospice center to certify her last will and testament. Her mum asked her not to come on that day. She didn't fight against her mother's wish because she completely understood it. She got her last will and testament certified by her lawyer in secret because the nightmares were still haunting her. The nightmare where she was on the bridge with her father. She looked at a reflection of herself when she was a little girl. Her father asked her if it was worth it. She asked him what he meant by that. He told her that she knew what he meant by that. She got chills that went down on her arms and legs when he said that to her. She asked him if she was dead. He always told her the same answer. He told her with a sad smile on his face, "Butterfly, you know that's too late to do anything to stop it." She asked him what was going to happen to her. He looked over at her one last time when he told her you'll see it for yourself soon enough. She always woke up before she saw what he was talking about.

She knew that it had something to do with that date. The one in ten years that she couldn't stop thinking about. He told her enough to know the truth about it. He was right. She knew what was going to happen to her. She patiently waited for it to happen. Her father told her not to rush into it. You can't take back what you forced to happen. You can't stop it once it started. It wasn't her mother's impending death that triggered her to think like this. It was a tidal wave that she ran away from. She couldn't stop the waves from getting to her. She was going to lose against them. She didn't tell anyone about it. Not Sebastian who would tell her that she needed to talk to Jacob again. Not Oliver who didn't know anything about the letter that was going to be sent to him. Not that her mother was almost inside the doorway. It wasn't that she tried to keep it from them, but she didn't want them to know what she couldn't escape from in her nightmares. It wasn't her death that scared her. It was what was going to happen after she had died. She had conversations about it with her mother during their daily visits at the hospice center. What was it going to feel like when her mother died? Where was her mother going to go when she died? Who was she going to be with in death? Would she be a better person than she was in her life? Would she be happier in death than she was in life? Her mother had many answers to those questions. She mentioned the stars to her. The light. The view. Whatever made her mother feel better that day. She didn't stop her mother from believing in anything. Her mother could believe in whatever that she wanted to believe if it made her feel better. She knew that her mother would do the same thing for her if she was in this situation. She would lie to her about anything if it made her feel better about her impending doom. She used to believe that lies were destructive things that ruined people's lives. Lies ruined her father's life. Lies ruined her own life. Lies ruined the world. She didn't know if she believed that it was true anymore. Lies didn't always destroy lives. Lies could save people's lives. It could pull someone out of the darkness. It could make them see beauty. She thought about the times that lies saved her. Her father's letter to her mother. Her father's letter to her. The words that Sebastian said to her at their wedding. The promises that she told her children. Those lies made her feel like it was worth it. It didn't amount to anything. She knew why her parents believed in the power of lies. The power that a lie had over you could make your life better or worse in a blink of an eye. Like her mother told her, two things can be true at the same time. Lies destroyed her life. Lies saved her life. She wanted to tell her mother about her revolutions with lies, but the doctors told her that her mother wasn't able to get visitors. She was so sick now that she was bedridden. Her mum couldn't even visit her because of this rule that the hospice center had about patients being sick. After a few weeks of no one being able to see her mother, her mum had enough of it as she marched into the hospice center with the family lawyer falling behind her where the staff prevented them from leaving the lobby before her mum demanded that the staff let her take her mother home. She told the staff that their lawyer was prepared to sue them if they didn't let her mother go home with them where the staff hesitantly told them that it was their decision to discharge her before she followed her mum and their lawyer into her mother's bedroom. As soon as her mother saw them, she asked them what they were doing there where her mum told her that she was going to die at home before her mother smiled at her mum with the staff packing up her stuff into her bags. Her mother was at the house that afternoon. She hired medical staff to take care of her mother in their downstairs bedroom. They told the children the truth about her mother's condition before Daphne told her that they already knew about it from when Posey told them. She made a note to thank Posey for telling the children about their grandmother dying. She focused on her project at the farmhouse in England where George assured her that the renovations were almost completed now. She promised her mother that she would show her the farmhouse before she died without knowing if she could fulfill this promise to her. There were a lot of hushed conversations between her mum and Uncle Stan about when it was going to happen. She listened to them through the wall before she pretended that she didn't know. She couldn't stop thinking about her mother's death. She didn't want to miss when she died because she was asleep, or she was working at the studio. The nurses that came into the house wore grave expressions on their faces that she saw them passing her in the hallways where she tried to ignore them to the best of her ability before she pretended that she didn't see the look on their faces.

The face they made when someone around them was about to die. A look of horror. A look of emptiness. A look of nothingness. She didn't know what scared her the most either that she was about to become an orphan or that she didn't know when her mother was going to die. The timing scared her more than anything else. She was about to complete her parents biggest dream by taking control of her father's farmhouse. She wasn't going to have parents left to share it with. She was going to be alone in the farmhouse. There were moments where she doubted herself by wondering if she should sell the farmhouse. She didn't have anyone to share it with that would appreciate it. To everyone else, it was a house that was abandoned by the world. To her, it was so much more than that. This house was where her father and Uncle Nathan raised each other. Her mother and her father grew up in that house where they learned how to do everything together. They gained so much in that house. They lost so much in that house. There was so much more to the story. She didn't want it to end. It was a place where lives were destroyed. It was a place where so much beauty took place inside of it. She spent her life letting the darkness control her so that she forgot to look for the light. Nothing could prepare her for what was going to happen to her. She got the children ready for school where she dropped them off at school before she went into the house to check on her mother. Her mother was a little more out of it than usual, but she told them one comprehensive thought out of what they could piece together from her rambling. Her mother said that she wanted to get married to her mum. Her mum was shocked by this because they never talked about getting married to each other. They were married in their hearts and that was enough for them. Her mother told her mum that she wanted to be married to the love of her life before she died. This made everyone in the room cry because that's all what anyone wanted. They wanted to be with the person that they loved with their entire hearts. Uncle Stan told them that he got a marriage officiation license a few months ago when their friends got married to each other. Once Uncle Stan rushed to his house to find his papers, she helped her mother pick out a dress to wear to their wedding as her mum left to go the store to get rings for them. She called her cousins that lived in the neighborhood asking them to come to her parent's wedding before they promised her that they would be there that afternoon. She went into her bedroom to pick out something to wear at the wedding until she came across the dress that she wore when she was fifteen years old while she modeled in New York. She ran her fingers through the material as she closed her eyes with tears falling down her face where she imagined herself in that moment. She felt like it was right in front of her. She heard the chatter from everyone on the set. Sasha helped her into the dress as she looked at herself in the mirror with a smile on her face. Sasha told her that looked beautiful before she told her that she felt beautiful for the first time in her life. She could see the flashing lights in front of her as the camera men took pictures of her laying down on the velvet couch where they gave her instructions for her to make faces at them before she did what she was told to do. She thought about what her father would tell her. She felt herself crying before she dismissed herself into her dressing room for the rest of the photoshoot. She didn't tell anyone about it. Sasha held onto her arms. They didn't say anything to each other as Sasha ran her fingers through her hair with her numbly staring at the ceiling. Sasha never asked her what happened that day. If she asked her about it, she would've told her that she was thinking about the darkness. She couldn't think of the light without thinking of the darkness. The darkness was always there to tell her that the light wasn't real. The world in the light wasn't real. As soon as she let go of the dress, she wiped away tears from her face where she placed the dress into the closet before she grabbed the dress that was the nearest to her. She distracted herself for the rest of the morning by reading her new book to her mother who silently slept where she pretended that her mother was listening before she closed the book when she knew that it wasn't doing anything for her. She laid down in her mother's bed with her head leaning on her chest while her mother peacefully slept next to her where she blinked back tears that fell down her face before she fell asleep with her. Her mum woke her up when she got back from the store with their rings in her hand where she ran her fingers through her hair before her mum asked her if she was okay. She didn't say anything to her mum as she held onto her mother's hand who was still asleep next to her where her mum told her that she would pick up the children for her before she softly thanked her with a smile on her face.

Once she was alone with her mother, she thought about saying something to her to fill up the silence, but she didn't know what she was supposed to say to make this better. She chose to not say anything as she held onto her mother's hand until her mum, and the children walked through the front door where she kissed her mother's hand before she joined them in the living room with the children telling her about their days at school. Her mum went upstairs with her mother to get her dressed for the wedding as she took the children into their bedrooms to get them changed into their fanciest clothes where Daphne asked her if they were going to a restaurant before she told Daphne that their grandparents were getting married to each other. Daphne grabbed onto Noah's hand as she dragged them into her grandparent's room where she went into her bedroom to change into the dress that she grabbed from her closet. Sebastian walked into the house with a cake in his hands. After she pecked him on the lips, Sebastian placed the cake onto the kitchen table as he went into their bedroom to change into his suit where she went into her parent's bedroom before Noah ran into her legs with a bouquet of flowers in his hands. As she grabbed the bouquet of flowers from him, she kissed Noah on the top of his head as she placed him on her hip when she told him that they were beautiful where he told her that they were for her before she kissed him on his cheek to thank him. She placed Noah on the bed with him sitting on his grandmother's lap where she went downstairs with the flowers in her hands before she placed them into a vase with water from the sink in it. Oliver walked through the front door with his family behind him as she pulled him into a tight hug with her face hidden in his chest until Sebastian called for him where she pulled Juliet and her nieces into a tight hug before she did the same thing with Amelia and her family. Sasha's family, Thomas, and Uncle Stan made it to the house a few minutes later where she pulled them into tight hugs before she walked into her mother's bedroom. Even though her parent's bedroom was very crowded at this point, they managed to fit everyone in the room. Uncle Stan took his place in front of the bed with her mother laying on the bed while her mum stood next to her with her standing up on the other side of the bed. As Uncle Stan read the lines out of the book that he was given at the courthouse, her mum held onto her mother's hand who sat up on the bed propped up by pillows where Uncle Stan told her to give them to the rings before she handed the box of rings to her parents. Her mum repeated the lines that Uncle Stan said to her with tears falling down her face where she placed the ring on her mother's right hand before Uncle Stan did the same thing with her mother. After her mother placed the ring on her mum's right hand, Uncle Stan pronounced them married as they pulled each other into a long kiss where the children let out gasps in fake disgust at the adults kissing each other before Sebastian told everyone to go downstairs in the kitchen for drinks and dessert. Her mum wheeled her mother into the kitchen with everyone talking around them. She sat down on her own drinking a glass of wine until Daphne asked her if they could watch a movie where she nodded her head at her before Daphne ran over to the other children to tell them about it. Everyone except for her parents, Uncle Stan, and Thomas watched a movie in the living room on the couches where she was engrossed in the movie before her mum tapped her on her shoulder. As she looked up at her mum, she told her that her mother wanted to see her as she grabbed onto Sebastian's hand with him frowning at her where she followed her mother into her parent's bedroom before her mother laid down in her bed with Uncle Stan and Thomas. Once her mother signaled for them to leave the room, Uncle Stan and Thomas followed her mum out of the room with them squeezing her shoulder where she softly sat down next to her mother before she grabbed onto her hands. They sat in comfortable silence for a while until her mother broke the silence when she said to her daughter with a frown on her face, "I asked you here because I want to tell you something. I know the truth about your father. It's okay, baby girl. You don't need to protect me. I already know about it."

Her jaw dropped in shock as she tightened her grip on her mother's hands when she responded to her with confusion laced in her voice, "I don't understand, mom. How did you find out about it?"

Her mother blinked back tears that fell down on her face when she responded to her daughter with a sad smile on her face, "I knew it in my heart. No one needed to tell me. I didn't think that you knew about it until I found the poem that he sent us. My heart broke for you when I realized that you knew it too. It broke my heart even more when I read the poem that you wrote about him. It scared me to think that you knew what he talked about in his poem. The suicide note came in the mail, and it confirmed my suspicions about him. I knew that he was dead long before I read his suicide note."

She softly chuckled when she responded to her mother, "That's a relief. I thought that I was going to have to tell you about it in some grand gesture right before you died. If you knew all of this time, then why didn't you tell me about it? I felt like I was going insane keeping that secret from you."

Her mother cupped her hands around her face as she grabbed onto her mother's hands when she responded to her daughter with tears falling down her face, "Me too, baby girl. It was the hardest thing that I did. Keeping it from you. I thought that I was protecting you, but we see how far that got us. I didn't tell you because it didn't feel right to bring it up until the end. I'm not trying to be emotional here, but I can't help it. You're my baby girl. You will always be my baby girl. I thought that I was protecting you when I was hurting you. I didn't want to hurt you. I forgot that I was your mother, and you were my daughter. You felt like an extension of me. It was hard for me to accept that you were an independent piece of me. You could be anyone. It was hard to let go of you. It's a lot easier said than done to let go of someone that you love more than anything else in the world. I didn't want you to think that I didn't love you or I didn't care about you. I didn't know how to deal with the situation. I love you so much, baby girl. You are my heart. My heart breaks when your heart breaks. I cry when you cry. That's why it's so hard for me to say this to you. You made me feel like a person for the first time. I didn't know who I was until I had you. I was nothing without you."

As she let out soft sobs into her mother's hands, she pulled herself out of her grip as she laid down on the bed with her leaning her chest while her mother ran her hands up and down her back when she responded to her mother with tears falling down her face, "Thank you for saying that. I love you too, mom. It's hard to admit when you made mistakes because you have acknowledge that you aren't perfect. You have to work on being a better person. I know that you were trying to protect me, but you couldn't protect me from the truth. It was inevitable for me to find out. You couldn't protect me from everything. There are dangers so fierce that mothers can't protect their children from it. These dangers are so strong that nothing can stop it. The monster becomes you every way. Do you want to know what my biggest regret was?"

Her mother grabbed onto her hands when she asked her daughter with a smile on her face, "What's that, baby girl?"

She responded to her mother with tears falling down her face, "I wish that I spent more time in the light. I wish that I didn't spend my life in the darkness. What was your biggest regret?"

Her mother responded to her with tears falling down her face, "I wish that I didn't stop myself from enjoying my life. There were so many things that I wished that I did that I never got the chance to do. I regret not allowing myself to enjoy the beautiful parts of the world. My turn to ask you a question. What are you most proud of that you did?"

She responded to her mother with a face hidden in her chest, "I'm glad that I met Sebastian, and we had our family together. I'm glad that dad died. Not that I'm happy with him being dead. That's not what I mean. I'm happy that he died because I got close to him. I don't think that we would've been close to each other if he didn't die. He allowed me to be closer to him in death. I never would've known all of this about him if he was alive. He wouldn't have told me anything let alone let me into his life. This was the only way that we could be together. What about you, mom? What are you most proud of?"

Her mother ran her hands up and down her back when she responded to her daughter with tears falling down her face, "I'm glad that dad died too. He wouldn't allow me near him in life. I'm glad that I met your mum. I'm glad that I remained best friends with Stan. I'm glad that I had you. The thing that I'm most proud of was that I met Will. I'm glad that I let Will love me. I wouldn't be who I became without him. He made me into who I am. I wouldn't be successful without him. I wouldn't have found happiness without him breaking my heart first. One last question. What moment do you want to spend an eternity in after you die?"

She blinked back tears that fell down her face when she responded to her mother in a soft voice, "That's an easy question. I want to live in the moment that we got to the states, and we saw the Statue of Liberty.

You told me that this is a place where we can make a life for ourselves. A beautiful life that means something to the world. I would spend the rest of eternity happy if I was in that moment. What about you, mom?" Her mother wiped away the tears from her face as she tightened her grip on her arms when she responded to her daughter with a smile on her face, "I would live in the moment where I stared up at the stars with Will for the first time. I would spend eternity looking up at the stars. I have something for you. Grab the letter off of the nightstand. Go on, baby girl."

As she grabbed the letter off of the nightstand, she placed it in her mother's hands as she gently ran her fingers over it when she told her daughter with tears falling down her face, "This is yours. Read it tonight before you go to bed. I'll be gone by then. This is my farewell to you. Okay?"

Tears fell down her face as she grabbed the letter from her mother's hands when she responded to her with sadness laced in her voice, "I love you, mom. Thank you for everything that you did for me. I can't wait to see you and dad in the stars. Until we meet again, mom."

As her mother kissed her on the top of her head, she pulled her mother into a desperate hug with her sobbing into her chest where they didn't pull away from each other until her mum walked into the room with a shot of pain medicine that she knew what it was for before her mother grabbed onto her hands when she said to her with tears falling down her face, "I love you, baby girl. Thank you for making my life so beautiful. I'll see you in the stars. Until we meet again, baby girl."

After she cried in her mother's arms for a little bit longer, she squeezed her mother's hands one last time where her mum placed her hand on her shoulder before she said to her with a sad smile on her face, "I'll come to you when it's done."

She nodded her head at her mum as she wiped away tears from her face where she sprinted out of the room before she was alone on her balcony. Once she took a seat on the balcony chairs, she let out desperate sobs into her hands with her mother's letter in her lap where she didn't open the letter until she caught her breath again before she read her mother's letter aloud to herself. She looked up at the stars with tears falling down her face until her mum took a seat across from her where she grabbed onto her hands before she leaned her head on her shoulder. She perked up in her seat when she saw a shooting star falling down in the sky before her mum whispered to her, "Your mother is saying goodbye to us. Do you have anything that you want to say to her?"

She tightened her grip on her mum's hands when she responded to her, "Goodbye, mom. Thank you for the stars." There was nothing except darkness to comfort them where she looked up at the stars one last time before she followed her mum back into the house. She joined Sebastian in their bed as he wrapped his arms around her where she kissed him before she fell asleep in his arms for the night.

My baby girl,

This is the hardest thing that I wrote in my life. I didn't think that I would say goodbye to my baby girl. I didn't think that it was possible to do that. I still don't know that it's possible, but I'm going to pretend that I can for a moment. I am strong enough to do it even though I'm falling apart. This world brought me so much darkness. You were always my light, baby girl. I questioned myself at every turn if it was worth it. If all of that pain was worth something. You showed me that it was worth it. I'd do it all over again. I would do anything to have you in my life. You reminded me of everything that I deserved to have. You taught me how to love myself. You taught me how to believe in the world again. It's hard to admit that you want to believe in something greater than yourself. You believe that you can handle this life on your own. That delusion fades away over time. Soon enough you're left with an empty hole inside of you where your delusions used to live. The only way to live after the delusions are gone is to believe in something greater than the world. Your dad and I believed in the stars. It brought us comfort in times of destruction. It reminded us that we are not limited to this world. There's another life for us in the stars. We are waiting for it like a child waiting for Christmas. We can't wait to see it. What does the life in the stars have in store for us? Are we going to be a giant? Are we going to be a supernova? Are we going to be a galaxy? The possibilities are endless. There's no heartbreak in the stars. There's no pain or sorrow. There is only joy. A life of joy that is waiting for us. We aren't trying to figure out what life means because we already know what it means. We don't need to believe in delusions to get through life. We don't need to look for people who aren't with us. All that we need is that moment. I have this dream on the bridge in York with your dad and you. Dad and I are waiting for you to join us. We talk about everything while we are waiting for you. We talk about everything that we did to hurt each other. We talk about everything that we did to help each other. We talk about what it means for us to be together again. We talk about how there is someone always missing on the bridge. When you walk on the bridge with us, I pull you in my arms as you cry into my chest. I tell you how much I miss you in our time apart from each other. You tell me everything that happened in your life since I left you. You pull your dad into a tight hug where you guys' cry in each other's arms. You tell your dad how sorry you are about not coming to see him sooner. Your dad tells you how sorry he is for not being in your life when you were alive. You ask us where we are. We tell you that we are where everything started for us. Your dad tells you to look down at the view. You look down at the view. You see it for the first time. You see the stars.

I'll love you forever, Mom.

Chapter Eighty-One
(September 1st, 1988 – Long Beach, California)

It was ten years ago that her mother died from cancer. It was six years ago that Uncle Stan died from Aids. It was five years ago that Thomas died from Aids. It was three years ago that her mum died from old age. So much has changed since her mother died. Her children were grown adults. Daphne was eighteen years old, and she moved into her house with her fiancé Timothy McNalty. Daphne was an actress like her mother where she worked at the film studio that her parents ran. Timothy was an actor that she met through the studio where they fell in love when they were sixteen years old. Noah was fifteen years old, and he graduated high school a year early. Noah was a writer like his mother where he traveled from their homes in Sweden and York for his books. Noah published his first book when he was thirteen years old about the analogy of dreams and how they controlled our lives. Noah was working on publishing his second book about how astrology was able to predict our actions. Oliver and Juliet's children did well for themselves. Posey became a psychiatrist like her father was because she wanted to help people. She got married a few years ago and she had two children of her own where they lived in California. Eleanor became a writer because she was inspired by her aunt Isabella and her great aunt Ella. Eleanor lived with Noah wherever they traveled in the world. They were nomads more than anything else. They didn't stay in one place for too long. Oliver never talked to his sister Poppy or his brothers Tommy and Alfie again. Their relationship was broken beyond repair. Jack, Madeline, and Millie remained in York where they worked as farmers, and they had families of their own. Tommy and Lilly's children Emmeline, Annie, and Damon lived off of their parent's wealth for the rest of their lives. Charlie tried to make it on his own in the world, but he wasn't successful like his father was with his art. Alfie and Debby's children were a different story where some of them wanted to make something of themselves while others were content with their parent's money. Piper got married to her partner young.

Anastasia and Damien taught their children that hard work would make them successful where they took their advance to heart when they chose their paths in their lives. Alina took over the hair salon for her mother after she retired where she got married young and grew her family in New York. Viktor remained a bachelor for the rest of his life as he followed in his father's footsteps of becoming a banker. Angelina followed her own path where she became a photographer working for Gabriel's photography business in New York. Tolya was on his way to becoming an investment banker on Wall Street in New York. Charlotte moved to France to pursue her own career in modeling much like her mother. Nina and Joseph taught their children that anything was possible. Bridget worked at the hair salon with Alina where she got married and she grew her family in New York. Eilis was the top woman in her class in Medical School in New York where she was a practicing doctor like her father. Liam became a lawyer where he lived with his wife and growing family in Connecticut. Owen took his own path in life by becoming a businessman living in Massachusetts. Rose followed in her mother's footsteps in working in the hair salon in New York. Audrey and Teddy taught their children that their world didn't need to be big for them to enjoy it. Lena followed in her mother's footsteps by taking over the bakery after her mother retired where she raised her family in York. Leo followed in his father's footsteps by becoming a contractor where he moved to London. Mason forged his own path in life when he moved to New York to become an investment banker like his cousin Viktor who was his close business associate and best friend. Harper followed her mother's footsteps by working at the bakery with her sister where she had a growing family in York. Edward forged his own path in life by becoming a veterinarian. Amelia and

Troy raised their children in Hollywood. Katherine became an actress while Christian went into directing movies. Sean and Polly raised their children to understand the importance of family. Alyssa and Ashley got married right out of school where they raised their families in London. Arthur married young like his sisters where he became a pastor like his father in London. George and Annabell taught their children the importance of family too. Zoe and Sofie got married out of secondary school where they raised their growing families. Henri followed in his father's footsteps by becoming a pastor.

~

This was the day that she had waited for a very long time. For over ten years, she knew what was going to happen to her. She couldn't do anything except patiently wait for it to come for her. She spent so many sleepless nights thinking about it. The last moments of her life. The end of everything. She kept her promise to herself to not tell anyone about it. There were moments that she got close to saying something to Sebastian, Daphne, and Noah, but she kept her mouth shut about it. She couldn't explain to them how she knew about it. It was beyond anything that anyone would understand. There was a world where they knew the truth and there was a world where she kept the truth from them. She chose the latter. She was at peace with her death. It was a peace that she never felt before in her life. The calmness of the waves crashing on the shore. The calmness in the center of a tornado. She let that calmness take over her body. She let it win. Her daughter chose that same exact day to be her wedding day. She didn't know why Daphne chose this day to be her wedding day, but she wasn't going to talk her out of it. Daphne was always stubborn. Once she set her mind to something, she never backed down from it. She went into the wedding prep with Daphne and her bridesmaids Katherine, Charlotte, Eleanor, and Posey. Daphne tried on different wedding dresses until she found the one. She went to wedding venues with her daughter and Timothy until they found a place that they wanted to get married in California. She helped Daphne plan her wedding down to the little details on the tables. Daphne and Timothy were excited to get married to each other. She understood that excitement. She felt that way when she got married to Sebastian. Everything was so exciting for Daphne as she planned her perfect day. They begged Noah to give up his nomadic lifestyle for the weekend to stay for his only sister's wedding. It was a hard sell for him because he didn't like being in one place for too long. Noah said that he was antsy in California because he wanted to be anywhere else in the world. She didn't blame Noah for being like this because she was like that when she was his age. After Noah agreed to be in California for more than two days at a time, Daphne was confident that nothing was going to ruin her perfect day. She didn't want to ruin Daphne's delusions. She would find out for herself soon enough that they weren't real. Sebastian worked in overdrive to make sure that his daughter had a great wedding day. Timothy was less excited about the wedding, but she knew that it was the man's least favorite part of the ordeal. The honeymoon was what they waited for more than anything else. Daphne and Timothy were going to Sweden on their honeymoon. It became their favorite place to be in the world. She made plans with her lawyers to give Daphne the house in Sweden in her will. She gave Noah the farmhouse in York that he lived at with Eleanor off and on for the past year. That left with her giving Sebastian the studio. He would appreciate that much at least even though he would be upset about her not being there with him anymore.

In the weeks approaching Daphne's wedding day, she was nervous that Oliver was going to ask her about the letter. She asked for that letter to be sent to him on this day ten years ago and they didn't send it to him. She was beginning to think that they lost her letter in the decade of it sitting there. She considered another plan if that one didn't follow through like she wanted it to, but she proved to be wrong in her doubts. Oliver got the letter the day before Daphne's wedding. She didn't know that he got it because he didn't say anything until the next morning. She imagined a million ways that Oliver would approach her. In one of her fantasies, he yelled at her. In another one of her fantasies, he understood where she was coming from. In her favorite fantasy, he didn't say anything to her. They pretended that everything was fine until it wasn't. What actually did happen was nothing like her fantasies showed her. Oliver approached her outside by the beach where Daphne was getting married where he gave her a silent look that was urgent before she pulled him away from the crowd of people. Oliver didn't say anything to her as he handed her the letter that she knew was her letter where she handed it back to him before she walked away from him.

Oliver followed her down the rest of the beach until there was nowhere else for her to run away from him where he cornered her before he asked her what the hell was this. She didn't say anything for a long time because she didn't know how to describe it to him. She told him later that it was her time to go before Oliver scoffed at what she said to him. This wasn't going well. Oliver was very angry at her until she told him that she wasn't killing herself where Oliver scoffed at what she said again like he didn't believe her before she told him that she's been sick. This completely threw Oliver off because he didn't know about it. With more sympathy laced in his voice, he asked her what she was sick with where she fought back tears that fell down her face before she told him that she had the same thing that Jason had. Oliver was silent for a long time because he didn't know what to say to her. What did she expect him to say to that news? She knew that she had ALS for a decade, and it was getting harder for her to hide from her family. Oliver asked her when she knew that she had ALS when she told him that she knew for ten years where Oliver asked her what she was going to do. She told him that he didn't need to know where Oliver silently agreed with her before he asked her if she was going to tell anyone about it. This time she knew what she was going to say to him when she told him that she didn't want anyone knowing until tomorrow where he nodded his head before he pulled her into a desperate hug with her face hidden in his chest. They cried in each other's arms for a long time.

They went on with the wedding. She helped Daphne into her wedding dress. She cried with Sebastian how Daphne wasn't their little girl anymore. Daphne cried with them too. Noah even cried with them.

It was a beautiful moment. She told Daphne and Noah that she was so proud of them and that she loved them so much. She pulled Daphne and Noah into a tight hug until Juliet called out to her that it was time to start the wedding. After they pulled themselves together again, she grabbed onto one of Daphne's arms as Sebastian grabbed onto her other arm where they walked her daughter down the aisle before they left her with Timothy and George who was officiating the wedding. As soon as they kissed Daphne on her cheek, they took a seat in the front row as Sebastian grabbed onto her hands with them smiling to each other where Daphne and Timothy said their vows to each other before they kissed each other. She spent the afterparty dancing in Sebastian's arms where she danced with Noah when Sebastian danced with Daphne for the father-daughter dance. Oliver asked for a dance with her as she let go of Noah who had towered above her in height. She danced with Oliver's arms around her with them not saying anything to each other when he asked her why she never told him about it. She told him that she didn't want anyone knowing, but she needed someone to know now. It had to be him. Oliver asked her when she was going to do it where she told him that she was doing it when they got back to the hotel before Oliver told her that he wanted to do it. Since she didn't know what to say to him, she nodded her head at him where he told her that he would meet her at her hotel room before she walked away from Oliver who danced with Juliet again. They went through the rest of the afterparty without any mentions of what was going to happen to her tonight. After they sent off Daphne and Timothy for their honeymoon, she told Sebastian that she needed to go to Oliver's hotel room where he told her that he would see her when she got back before he disappeared into their hotel room down the hall. Even though she was going to pass out from being on her feet all day, she walked to Oliver's hotel room as she let herself inside of it where he waited on the bed for her before she laid down next to him. She would've passed out on the bed if Oliver wasn't talking to her where she looked over at him before he asked her where it was. As soon as she pulled the syringe out of her purse, he grabbed it from her as he placed it on the bed where he asked her if she had any last thoughts that she wanted to say to him before she shook her head at him. She said everything that she wanted to say in her letters and her poem. Oliver was very nervous as he wrapped the tourniquet around her arm where he positioned the syringe into one of veins before he didn't pull back on it to inject the poison into her body. She quickly realized that she needed to do that part herself. With Oliver holding onto her hand, she used her other hand to release the medicine in her veins as she closed her eyes in relief with tears falling down her face where she thanked him with a smile on her face before he told her that he loved her with tears falling down his face. She didn't get a chance to respond to him before her body gave up on her as she struggled to take deep breaths. She saw it all for the first time. She saw the doorway in front of her. As she moved away from her body, she walked towards the door as she looked at the chaos that was around her with Sebastian and

Noah running into the room where she said to them that she was sorry. They never heard her say that to them. She walked into the door. Once she walked through the door, she wasn't at a hotel room in California anymore. She was on the bridge in York. There were fallen leaves on the ground that she crunched with every step that she took towards it. She approached a figure where they turned around to face her before she let out a soft gasp in shock at what she was seeing in front of her. Her father walked towards her as he stopped in front of her where he pulled her into a desperate hug with her sobbing into his chest when he said to her with concern laced in his voice, "Butterfly. It's alright. You're home. Was it painful?"

She shook her head at him as she pulled her face out of his chest with his hands cupping her cheeks as tears rapidly fell down her face when she responded to him with a smile on her face, "It's not that, dad. It didn't hurt me. I'm shocked. I've waited my entire life for this moment. I can't believe that it's happening. I can't believe that I'm with you. I'm so happy."

Her father kissed her on the top of her head as she threw herself in his arms again with her sobbing in his chest where they didn't pull away from each other until she heard more footsteps coming towards them where she pulled her face out of his chest before her mother said to them with a smirk on her face, "Wow! What a reunion! How was the journey, baby girl? Hopefully it wasn't bad."

As soon as her father let go of her, her mother who pulled her into a desperate hug where she sobbed into her mother's chest when she responded to her in a soft voice, "I missed you, mom. Life hasn't been the same without you. I'm so happy to see you. I never thought that I would see you again."

Her mother tightened her grip on her arms when she responded to her daughter with a smile on her face, "I missed you too, baby girl. Of course, you were going to see me again. Tell me what happened when I was gone. I want to know everything that happened."

After she told her mother about everything that happened in her life, they pulled away from each other as she followed her mother over to her father who stared at the water rushing below them. She stood next to him with him wrapping his arm around her when he said to her looking away from the water, "Here we are. In the place where it all started. There's beauty in ending where you started, isn't there? It's so poetic of the universe. What do you think, butterfly? What did you think about all of it?"

She looked down at the water with her father doing the same thing when she responded to him with a wide grin on her face, "I thought that it was eye opening. It made me learn about the world. It made me learn about myself. I'm happy to tell you that I didn't let the monster become me. Things didn't end like that for me."

Her father flashed a quick smile at her when he responded to her with excitement laced in his voice, "Well, I'm happy to hear that. I'm proud of you, butterfly. You won. You did what I could never do. I think that's time to go. Isn't it, Ella?"

She looked at her parents with a confused look on her face when she asked him, "How do we go?" Her father grabbed onto her hands with her mother standing next to him when he told her with a smile on his face, "We look at the water. That's all." As she looked at her parents, she looked down at the water for the first time. She was finally dancing through the cosmos.